D0442116

Book Three of the

SECRET WORLD CHRONICLE

BAEN BOOKS by MERCEDES LACKEY

BARDIC VOICES

The Lark and the Wren
The Robin and the Kestrel
The Eagle and the Nightingales
The Free Bards
Four & Twenty Blackbirds
Bardic Choices: A Cast of Corbies (with Josepha Sherman)

The Fire Rose

The Wizard of Karres (with Eric Flint & Dave Freer)

Werehunter

Fiddler Fair

Brain Ships (with Anne McCaffrey & Margaret Ball)
The Sword of Knowledge (with C.J. Cherryh, Leslie Fish & Nancy Asire)

Bedlam's Bard (with Ellen Guon)
Beyond World's End (with Rosemary Edghill)
Spirits White as Lightning (with Rosemary Edghill)
Mad Maudlin (with Rosemary Edghill)
Music to My Sorrow (with Rosemary Edghill)
Bedlam's Edge (ed. with Rosemary Edghill)

THE SERRATED EDGE

Chrome Circle (with Larry Dixon)
The Chrome Borne (with Larry Dixon)
The Otherworld (with Larry Dixon & Mark Shepherd)

HISTORICAL FANTASIES WITH ROBERTA GELLIS

This Scepter'd Isle
Ill Met by Moonlight
By Slanderous Tongues
And Less Than Kind

HEIRS OF ALEXANDRIA SERIES

by Mercedes Lackey, Eric Flint & Dave Freer
The Shadow of the Lion
This Rough Magic
Much Fall of Blood

THE SECRET WORLD CHRONICLE

Invasion (with Steve Libbey, Cody Martin & Dennis Lee)
World Divided (with Cody Martin, Dennis Lee & Veronica Giguere)
Revolution (with Cody Martin, Dennis Lee & Veronica Giguere)

To purchase these and all other Baen Book titles in e-book format, please go to www.baen.com.

REVOLUTION

Book Three of the

SECRET WORLD CHRONICLE

Created by Mercedes Lackey & Steve Libbey

Written by

MERCEDES LACKEY

with **Cody Martin, Dennis Lee** *&* **Veronica Giguere**

Edited by Larry Dixon

Revolution: Book Three of the Secret World Chronicle

This is a work of fiction. All the characters and events portrayed in this book are fictional, and any resemblance to real people or incidents is purely coincidental.

Copyright © 2014 by Mercedes Lackey, Cody Martin, Dennis Lee, & Veronica Giguere

All rights reserved, including the right to reproduce this book or portions thereof in any form.

A Baen Books Original

Baen Publishing Enterprises
P.O. Box 1403
Riverdale, NY 10471
www.baen.com

ISBN: 978-1-4516-3932-2

Cover art by Larry Dixon

First Baen printing, January 2014

Distributed by Simon & Schuster
1230 Avenue of the Americas
New York, NY 10020

10 9 8 7 6 5 4 3 2

Pages by Joy Freeman (www.pagesbyjoy.com)
Printed in the United States of America

DEDICATION

Ascendant ("with an 'a'") of Virtue server, City of Heroes
aka
Donald "Tre" Chipman

We miss you dreadfully

ACKNOWLEDGEMENTS

"Hole Hearted" Extreme

"Dare to be Stupid" Weird Al Yankovic

"Firefight" Blackguard

"Nox Aurumque (Night and Gold)" lyrics: Charles Anthony Silvestri; music: Eric Whitacre

"Chasing Shadows" Deep Purple

"Run Through the Jungle" Creedance Clearwater Revival

"Obsessions" The Subways

"Leap of Faith" Bruce Springsteen

"The Seven Deadly Virtues" Lerner and Loewe

"In One Ear" Iron Chic

"Smoke and Mirrors" Gotye

"Bedlam Ballroom" Squirrel Nut Zippers

"Terminal" Static-X

"Resolution" VnV Nation

"Mother Knows Best" Beccy Cole

"You Have To Believe We Are Magic" Olivia Newton-John

"Enemy Mine" Beloved Enemy

"Heaven Beside You" Alice In Chains

"Heart Like A Wheel" Human League

"You're Only Human" Billy Joel

"Save Me" Remy Zero

"Descent" Fear Factory

"Testament" VnV Nation

"Here With Me" Dido

"Running Up That Hill" Kate Bush

"Fire On The Mountain" Grateful Dead

"Where There Is Light" VnV Nation

We would also like to thank Eben Waters and Gigi Troemel who made the winning bids in two charity auctions to have their characters Paperback Rider and Frankentrain respectively meet a horrible, but heroic death in this volume. Their characters were so engaging and so different, instead of a mere page or two, they integrated seamlessly into the chapter "Descent." Thank you both! You rock!

Book Three of the

SECRET WORLD CHRONICLE

INTRODUCTION

Vickie took a deep breath and another look at the clock. Speed-reading through this compilation wasn't taking as long as she'd feared. Looked like she was going to get it done before Zero Hour. She went back to adding notes.

So, whoever you are that's reading this... there we were. In shambles. Alex Tesla dead, Bulwark in a coma, and the vilest man on earth in charge of Echo. Thulians still free to do their pop-up attacks, the US Government making noises about taking Echo over, or at least the parts on American soil. Most people would just have lain right down there and given up.

But maybe we were too stupid. Or too stubborn. Or both.

And the stubbornest, maybe the stupidest, and maybe the most desperate, were Acrobat and Scope.

CHAPTER ONE

Killing Time

DENNIS LEE

There were many things they could train into you. They could drill you, make you practice until your body screamed in protest, and when all else failed, they could beat it into you. Pain was a great motivator, after all. But what they couldn't change, at the very heart of it, was who you were.

Bruno had been put through the steps from the moment he had joined Echo. Everything had to happen on a schedule, something he had not been prepared for. He had come to them as a simple kid with a meta talent for balance and coordination, but with nothing approaching the discipline needed to become a fighter. For him to achieve the proper maturity to be a valued member of Echo required time and patience, something his trainers had little of. It wasn't until reassignment, until Bulwark, who had picked him up, dusted him off, and with a brutal level of emotional detachment, had hurled him through the steps of his own personal boot camp, that Bruno had begun to show signs of improvement.

You went through the steps, and you did them again and again and again until you got them right. And you kept doing them, until the muscle memory stuck, and before you knew it, you were dashing across uneven terrain riddled with gunfire, you were anticipating your opponents' strikes and formulating blocks and counters, you were learning how to disarm bombs and provide basic CPR in the eventuality of your medic falling in the field. You learned all these things that could even become second nature to you, but they could never train you for everything. Even if they could, there were areas they wouldn't touch, they couldn't, not without stepping over certain lines. As much as Echo needed fighters, needed well-honed warriors in the field, they had always drawn the line at making cold-blooded soldiers of their metas. There was something in the initial charter that stressed the strength of individualism in the meta-powered backbone of Echo's security forces. They would show you how to hold a gun, how to clean and fire one, but they weren't about drilling you on how to *feel* about it. It was something they left to individual morals and experience.

As he kicked in the door to the safe house and raced in, pistol first, Bruno wished that perhaps he had spent at least a little time auditing a firearms training course with a more emotional slant. "You and Your Inner Gun 101" might have done wonders for him. The solid chunk of metal and reinforced polymers had never felt right in his hands. He had never actually had cause to shoot anyone, even in combat, preferring to stay with his strengths of evasion and basic hand-to-hand training. He had spent enough time on a firing range, and he was reasonably confident of his aim, though you'd never know it from the way his hands trembled around the grip. He had all the training in the world, but he wondered if anything would ever make squeezing the trigger on another life a part of him.

It was Scope who had insisted on it. "We're going to be barging in, and we have to move fast, Bruno! Use the surprise, get her on the immediate defensive. What would you feel more threatened by? The barrel of a magnum pointed at your head, or those little chew-toys you call your fists?"

She had a point. If only his hands would stop shaking.

"Clear!" Scope's voice, heavy with disgust, rang out from the next room. Bruno lowered his weapon in relief. No, he didn't think he would ever get used to a gun. What part of himself would he lose if he ever fired a slug into another person? He hoped he would never know.

The safe house was, as is typical, in the middle of nowhere. They had come here chasing yet another lead on Harmony, but from the dismay in Scope's voice it was clear that, once again, they were too late. With each lead, they found themselves just steps behind her, but the trail was always cold when they arrived. Except for the bodies. Each time, there was always a corpse left in her wake.

This time wasn't an exception. Bruno joined Scope in a small makeshift office at the back of the cabin, and found Harmony's mark sitting in his chair and slumped over his desk. Scope had fingers pressed to his neck. Bruno gave her a questioning look, and she simply nodded. This one was an inventor, an applied physicist, and like the others they had found him cold and lifeless, without a single mark on him, left as a rotting husk which would surely yield little more than probable signs of a stroke or heart attack.

He'd hoped with each new body they found, it would be easier. Like the thought of firing a bullet into a human being, each time hit him just as hard. So much for ease through experience. It was times like these that Bruno wondered if he was really cut out for this.

"This is getting stupid," Scope muttered and collapsed on a nearby couch. "We're never going to catch up to her at this rate."

"She's too fast," Bruno agreed. "Anytime we get wind of one of her jobs, she's already done it and gone. Same MO too. She leaves them without anything traceable, just drains them."

"Yeah," Scope said, covering her face with tired hands. "What the hell, do the sweep anyway. Maybe she left something behind this time."

Bruno shrugged and began searching through the cabin for something, anything, that might give them a clue to what and where Harmony was planning next. He didn't expect to find anything, they never did, and they would have to start at square one again, waiting to hear from questionable contacts about the latest assassination attempts with rumored links to Blacksnake.

As he searched, he found his thoughts sifting through old memories, back to a time when he had first met Scope and Harmony. As new recruits, they were a bit of a mess. Harmony had barely spoken, and when she did she quickly became agitated to a frenzied pitch of anxiety. She had shuffled about, her head down, her face hidden behind her long, golden hair. If you so much as touched her lightly on the shoulder, she would scream and run about while wringing her hands, like an unleashed banshee. Bruno remembered the first time Harm had lost it, how Scope had rolled her eyes, muttering that she was in hell. In those days, Scope walked around with a strut. Her attitude was simple: everything was under control, and everything was beneath her. She found fault in everything they did, and made a point to let them know the correct methods to fastening their gear, to assembling their firearms, even how to tie up their laces. At the time, she wasn't what one would call a team player. Her disdain for their basic training regime, their limited field tasks, and her teammates, ensured they all kept a safe distance from her. Bruno was the opposite. All he wanted was to fit in, to be part of a team. His eagerness to be useful might have been commendable, if he didn't fail at almost everything he did. He did everything wrong, and from a deep desire to make the grade, he was constantly second-guessing himself. It led to bad decisions, to fumbles and trips and falls over routine maneuvers he had done hundreds of times before. What he lacked was what Scope seemed to have in abundance—self-confidence. It took months to realize that Scope's facade of inhuman superiority was simply overcompensation. Scope demanded a lot of herself, and others. She wanted to be the perfect soldier, the quintessential Echo warrior, but at heart she wasn't so different from him. They both lacked any real sense of self-worth.

Bull had seen their value, as he did with most of his trainees. Bulwark was a towering figure, immensely strong in mind and body, and channeled a protective field that could withstand insane amounts of punishment. Yet Bruno suspected Bull's true power was his ability to size up an individual, to see through whatever mask a person chose to hide behind, and to nurture their true potential. Bull had done that for him, for Scope, and for countless others.

Which was what made this hunt so unbelievable. When they had received word of what had happened in Alex Tesla's quarters, of how their boss had been murdered, how Bull had been left in a comatose state, and by *Harmony* of all people, Bruno and Scope began a long chase beset with wrong turns and dead ends. They chased down any lead they could find on their former teammate, hoping to catch up with her, and to bring her down. With luck, they could even take her alive and bring her back to pay for her crimes. With each failed attempt, with every passing day, this seemed less and less likely. Forget bringing her in alive when they couldn't even find her.

After an hour, Bruno gave up. As expected, there was nothing. The cabin was unbearably normal. Nothing seemed out of place, with just enough mess to appear as if the mark had been there for a few days before meeting his untimely demise. A few dirty dishes in the washbasin, some opened and rinsed food cans in the trash, an opened bottle of Hennessy on the kitchen counter and a dirty tumbler, and nothing else. He returned to the office, where Scope was meticulously going through the dead man's laptop.

"Nothing," he reported.

"And nothing here," Scope snarled. "At least, nothing that isn't encrypted to hell. No idea what this guy was working on, no idea why they wanted him dead..."

In a burst of rage, Scope slammed a fist down on the corpse's back, and was rewarded with a dull thud. Bruno stiffled a chuckle, caught in the shame of such dark comedy. It took a moment, but he composed himself, and before he realized what he was saying, "If it's encrypted, then maybe we could ask—"

Scope silenced him with a sudden, rather unladylike gesture. "*No,* Bruno, do not suggest that again!"

"But you know she can help, she can get past..."

"Forget it, we are not contacting Victrix on this. We *decided* already, or do we really have to go over this *again*?"

Bruno sighed and nodded. They were on their own. That was the price of going AWOL. They couldn't risk contacting any of their former crew. Victrix could have worked her magic, literally, over any coordination efforts or computer hacking they needed. Djinni's expertise on guile, infiltration and disguise might have placed them within the very bowels of Blacksnake itself, placing them within the heart of Harmony's base of operations.

And Bull...

God knew if Bull was even awake, or alive. It was the one thought that kept them on task. They had to do this, for Bull.

So all their Echo contacts were off limits. It was too risky, too great a chance they would simply be hauled back and thrown in solitary for the duration. And there was no way Echo would approve of what they were doing. If they ever did manage to catch up with Harmony, they had decided that one way or another, she would answer for what she'd done. If she could be taken alive, great, but if not...

And there it was again. If they had to, they were going to...

Can I do that? Can I really?

It was a question that had plagued him since the day they had abandoned their posts in the Echo compound, the day they had begun this not-so-merry chase for their former teammate. Harmony, who had once seemed like a sister to him. The girl who had always offered solace in the face of overwhelming self-doubt and despair. The girl who was quick to encourage, and never judge, who by the end Bruno had felt safe enough with to bare his soul to. That was the girl he remembered. As far as he knew, Harmony was the only one in the world who knew his true feelings about Scope, that he was hopelessly, desperately, in love with her.

Could he do it? If he had to, could he kill Harmony?

He didn't know.

Scope, on the other hand, didn't seem to have any doubts on the matter. She grudgingly admitted that, *yes*, if possible they would take Harmony alive, but she made no effort to mask her desire to plug many bullets into Harmony's screaming body. For Bull, of course. Scope's love for Bull had always been palpable to anyone with even a passing acquaintance with them.

God, we're such a mess, Bruno thought. *Weird-ass love triangle, and oh look, some nifty revenge motifs, a coma victim and pacifist tendencies thrown in for good measure. New daytime series, coming this fall. These are the "Echoes of our Lives"...*

Bruno grunted, shook his head, and rubbed tiredly at his face. "Well, we're going to have to mix something up, 'cause this just isn't getting results."

"I'm open to suggestions," Scope said.

"There's just one option left to us, y'know."

"God!" Scope exploded. "Not that again! Blacksnake itself is off limits!"

"We've got nothing else!" Bruno protested. "You said it yourself, we're on our own, so forget getting backup. We need to get closer to the one place that we *know* Harmony checks in with. We have to get into Blacksnake!"

"And here we go again," Scope groaned. "How many times do I have to *explain* to you that infiltrating Blacksnake is even riskier than calling in Victrix, the Djinni or Bella? You think they won't have files on us? You think they won't make us within the hour that we show up at their door? There's still a recruiting war going on, both Echo and Blacksnake have files on *everybody.* Let's say we go with your idea, show up and apply as non-meta personnel, as simple mercs with some experience with firearms and combat, they'll still recognize us by our faces! Dammit, Bruno, we've got nothing. *Nothing!*"

Bruno stared at her. It pained him to see her so distraught. And she was right. They were out of options. There was really nothing left to do...

"Nothing left," he whispered. "Nothing left, but go home."

"Not necessarily," a new voice grunted.

With a shout, they were up and armed, pointing their guns at a shadowy figure crouched in the corner. Slowly, the figure stood up, stepped into the light and lit a cigar, his face masked beneath the brim of a weathered duster hat. He took a slow drag and raised his head, reaching up to address them with a brief touch of his hat brim.

It was Jack.

"You have got to be kidding me," Scope said. "And here I was, thinking I had no one to shoot today."

"Might want to let an old man say his piece," Jack said, "before you go firing that thing off."

"Where did you come from?" Bruno exclaimed.

"Been following you both for a while now," Jack answered. "Seems like we might have similar interests."

"Oh, this should be good," Scope spat. "Go on then, tell us what we would have in common with the man who helped put Bull in a coma and Tesla in the grave."

"Harmony," Jack said calmly. "From what I can tell, you both have the same itch that I do. See, that desire for revenge? It's awfully recognizable to those who share it."

"And what would you want revenge for?" Scope asked, her eyes narrowing.

"Well, for starters, for setting me up," Jack said with a shrug. "See, I came that day to your little corner of Atlanta with a genuine offer to make peace between Blacksnake and Echo. Pool our resources, maybe get some good done for once. And I have to say, the negotiations were going just fine until Harmony had to up and knock me out and take out everybody in that damn room."

"You really expect us to buy that?" Scope snorted. "Why would she turn on you, her boss?"

"I wasn't really her boss now, was I?" Jack chuckled. "Oh, they played me good, I gotta admit, her and Verdigris, they set me up and I just took the fall."

"Wait. Verdigris?" Bruno asked. "The billionaire?"

Jack shrugged. "He's more a trillionaire, I think, but yeah. You two really *have* been out of the loop, haven't you? Who do you think took control of Echo after Tesla got his neck snapped by Harmony? Who had the shares, and the motive, to have Tesla taken out of the picture? He did it old school, too. Big messy murder, a patsy to take the fall, and some market manipulation, leaving him the major shareholder in the company."

"How would we prove that . . . ?" Bruno started.

"Don't know, don't care," Jack interrupted. "I'll worry about Verd later, and it sure won't involve a simple case of exposing his crimes. It'll need to be a bit more . . . lingering, to satisfy my tastes. No, right now, I want Harmony. And you two seem like the best way to manage that."

"What do you need us for?" Scope asked. "You're still Blacksnake, right? I'm sure you can just . . ."

Jack shook his head in disgust. "Christ, I thought you two were smarter than this. Piece it together. After I came to, can you imagine that I might have taken some issue with the way I was played? Let's just say Harmony, Verdigris and I didn't end things too cordially. I get anywhere near them or the Blacksnake compounds, I'll be taken out, guaranteed. What I'm offering is knowledge and supplies, how to disguise yourselves, how to get in and stay undetected, to blend right in with the lower caste of merc forces. Get in close. Whether you snoop around for info and track her down, or can somehow manage to corner her in there, you'll be able to get close to that bitch and put her down. Or at least have a shot at it. If you mess it up, I suppose I'll have to find another way. But for now, this seems like the best way for me to deal with this pesky little itch of mine. And you two, you finally seem out of options, and desperate enough, to even consider trusting *me* enough to help you out."

Jack took another drag on his cigar and chuckled.

"Took you long enough too," he said.

CHAPTER TWO

Stone Cold

MERCEDES LACKEY AND CODY MARTIN

Dominic Verdigris III, the man in charge of Echo. I have called him the vilest man on the face of the earth. I'm not sure that's strong enough. A classic sociopath, and one with a level of genius so far off the scale I am not sure the scale could measure it. A man with more money than I have ever been able to ferret out. And as a classic sociopath, no one mattered to him but *him. The rest of the world was just tools—something to place between him and the fate that the Seraphym had revealed to him at the hands of the Thulians. He would do anything to keep that fate from coming true. The Seraphym had set him in motion, unable to tell for sure whether what he would do would help or hinder. In a way, we were* her *tools, too, but the difference was that she cared about us, about the world, and she would ruthlessly use whatever she had to save as many as she could. Verdigris would ruthlessly use whatever he had to save only one.*

Himself.

Ruthless enough to try to use someone else *who would use whatever he had to save the world—save the world* for *himself. And that was the spirit of what arguably might have been the greatest general in history, Shen Xue, who now lived inside the body of what had been Commissar Red Saviour's right hand—People's Blade. Shen Xue had arrived there via the sword Fei Li used with such skill, Jade Emperor's Whisper. For quite some time, he had been content to remain dormant.*

Not anymore.

So Dominic Verdigris III, the most evil man in the world, was about to meet General Shen Xue, who might be the most despotic…

✧ ✧ ✧

One would have thought, mused General Shen Xue, *that a street urchin would have been more resilient in the face of catastrophe.*

The General—who at this point was nothing more nor less than the spirit that had inhabited the supernatural blade Jade Emperor's Whisper—was now, in fact, inhabiting the body of one Fei Li, aka "People's Blade," member of the metahuman group CCCP. Fei Li was asleep, deeply asleep, in the sword, as the General himself had been for centuries. She had begun succumbing to despair as conditions with the Thulians worsened, as if the malaise that had infected Alex Tesla had been contagious. And the murder of Tesla had driven her into retreat and catatonia.

Which suited the General just fine; it meant that he had complete and unrestricted control of both body and blade. While they had been of a consensus in most things, there were times when Fei Li's gentler sensibilities conflicted with his stern judgment; it was something that needn't concern him any longer, now. In earlier centuries, he would have been disgruntled at being confined to an inferior female form, but he had always been pragmatic, and the body was young, superbly fit, and what these "moderns" called *metahuman.* All these things outweighed any trivial inconvenience of sex.

He had, he was certain, completely deceived Red Saviour, who had no idea that her old friend Fei Li was, for all intents and purposes, gone. He needed to be in on all the councils, privy to all the . . . what did they call it? Ah yes. *Intel.* There was no doubt in his mind whatsoever that the Thulians were more ruthless than the Golden Horde, and would not stop until every blade of grass and grain of sand was theirs. They had learned from the fascists; this time there would be no quarter, no mercy, only abject surrender followed by annihilation. They had to be stopped.

Shen Xue was just the man to stop them. Perhaps the only man left in this age with the resolve to do what was necessary, whatever the cost.

But first, he needed to pick his allies.

Initially, he was as repulsed by Dominic Verdigris III as Red Saviour was. After all, he had engineered, brilliantly engineered, Tesla's assassination. But unlike Red Saviour, he was not prey to emotions. He was as a perfect piece of jade, smooth and opaque. As brutal and merciless as the sword he had wielded and inhabited for centuries. And as he studied the man, he came to realize that the removal of Tesla had been necessary. Tesla had been paralyzed with fear and indecision. No matter what Natalya thought, there had only been one way to move forward, and that was through—or over—Tesla.

This was not to say that he trusted Verdigris, not in the least. Verdigris was utterly self-centered. But Shen Xue could use that; just as different weapons had different uses, so too did men. And when the Thulians were gone, well . . . then Dominic Verdigris III could be dealt with. First, remove the Thulians; one threat positioned to destroy a greater one was an effective use of resources, after all.

And perhaps when he had struck an accord with Verdigris, he could persuade Red Saviour that this was no worse than many another deal that had been forged in the old Soviet Union with monsters. Not unlike the deal her own father and Boryets had forged with Stalin, and those lesser creatures that followed.

Or the deal her father had forged with the Thulians themselves; the removal of Hitler, the escape of Ubermensch. Of course, he had not been aware of the Thulians; he had only facilitated Ubermensch getting to Hitler's bunker in order to effect the assassination. *He had probably assumed he'd be able to ambush Ubermensch himself afterwards,* the General mused. Natalya's reaction when she had learned that little tidbit had been . . . epic. He pitied the girl, sometimes. Fei Li—and even himself, to an extent—had forged a unique friendship with Natalya, based upon mutual respect and dedication. But, for all of her hardness, Natalya was still naive in certain ways; betrayal should never surprise one. It was a lesson the General had learned very young.

But all that was past. While it might have bearing on the future, it was irrelevant in the present. First, forge an alliance with Verdigris. Then persuade Red Saviour. Or not. Every plan needed to be broken down into small steps, with contingencies at each step.

Which was why he was lurking in the shrubbery outside the high-rise Verdigris had taken over for his headquarters. Not for Dominic Verdigris III the confines of a shabby "portable building." Oh no, the new Echo headquarters was a sleek five-story building that belonged to a bank. Well, supposedly. The General suspected it had actually belonged to one of Verdigris' holding companies. Not that it mattered, except that the security was superb. Even the plantings were placed well back from the building and no one who had not the General's skill and Fei Li's diminutive size would have been able to hide there. Roving patrols on foot as well as in SUVs, guard house and secure gate, IR surveillance cameras, and more than a few extremely well-armed guards. It all presented quite the formidable appearance. *Every castle has drafts of air that steal inside, no matter how tightly the stones are laid together.*

Shen Xue simply had to find his way in, like one of those drafts. Not trivial. But for one of his experience, and that shared with a street urchin-thief... not that difficult.

"I need to invent something that will give me more hours in the day to read this tripe." Dominic Verdigris was talking to himself, a habit he sometimes indulged in partly out of the belief that the only person really *worth* talking to was himself. He sighed. "It's so difficult to be me. Maybe I should clone me." Now *that* would be interesting, if only because whatever inevitable struggle for power ensued would be challenging. He pushed the glasses he was wearing down to the tip of his nose, leaning back in the chair. The glasses were linked to his smart-desk, enabling a holographic and tactile sensitive display of multiple screens in front of him. Images and short bullet-pointed blurbs of pertinent information on some persons of interest that he had made sure were tracked were displayed on one of the screens, which went inactive or transparent as soon as he was no longer actively looking at it.

Since taking control of Echo, Verdigris had been nearly inundated with minor problems and complaints coming from his new employees; it was his one miscalculation to assume that the transition would be slightly less painful. Tesla, for the stagnated buffoon that he was, had engendered a surprising amount of loyalty in his people. In an effort to buffer himself at least partially, he had moved to this building, and made sure that accommodations were made for two offices; a public "Echo CEO" office, and then his real, private office, where he was now sitting. The former was very professional and almost Spartan in furnishings, in order to help drive home to any visitors the trying times that Echo had been through. The latter, however, was nearly the size of a small loft, with all the comforts that Verdigris had become accustomed to. It also allowed him to ward off anyone he didn't want to see, having "left the office for the day," while still being able to work uninterrupted.

"I really ought to have Khanjar look into one of those white cats again." He had been alone here for several hours for that very purpose, since the administration of Echo took very little of his time and entirely too much altogether. Which is why he was utterly surprised when a young, lithe Asian woman stepped out of one of the shadows in the far corner of the room.

It wasn't so much the woman that caught his attention, as the extremely sharp sword she had. *Chinese jian,* he identified without having to call up anything from the computers. *Definitely steel, probably meteoric steel. Probably late 400s*... His eyes took in the details automatically.

She held the sword easily, almost negligently. "Good afternoon, Dominic Verdigris," she said, in English that was only slightly accented. The voice sounded... *wrong* for her, somehow; it was undoubtedly her vocal chords that were making the sounds, but otherwise nothing about the words seemed to belong to the young woman. "I attempted to make an appointment but your receptionist was not accommodating." She advanced as far as the middle of the room, looking perfectly at home, perfectly relaxed. "You and I have important business to discuss."

He subvocally called for security; two guards outside of the door, followed in three minutes by a quick reaction force, would burst in the room in order to extract him. Verdigris licked his lips, pausing for a moment before speaking. "How did you get in here, my dear?" He tried his best to keep his voice even; it wasn't very often that he was taken unawares by a threat like this. And the automatically tracking guns hadn't yet been set up in this room. His other more personal defenses should keep him alive if the worst came to pass and this woman actually attacked him. But she had come this far without any warning already... He mentally cursed himself for his negligence.

"The Gentle Wind through the Grasslands," she said. An eye twitch to one of the screens came up with... nothing, nothing, nothing of any use on the first page of a search. And he didn't have time to tell it to translate to Chinese and search on that term. Damn these enigmatic Orientals!

"You said that we have business to discuss. So, I hope I can safely assume you won't try to kill me out of hand any time soon? It would ruin my evening."

"I have seen to it that we will not be interrupted," she said with preternatural calm. "The two guards behind the door have been rendered incapable of interference for now. I *assumed* you did not want them permanently incapacitated, although in your place, I would order them shot for incompetence."

"I see." *Dammit! If they're down, she might have done something to bar the QRF from entering... hopefully Khanjar is within a reasonable distance; I don't think any power on this Earth could keep her out of a room she truly wants in to.* "Well, with that settled, I recall you saying that we have some business to discuss? I'm not usually in the habit of discussing anything with someone that I know nothing about, miss. Particularly what that person's name might be." *If this is another crazed OpFour like that* angel, *I'm going to be very put out.*

She bowed, ever so slightly. It was not a bow of respect. "I am known by the callsign of 'People's Blade.' I am *currently* a member of the group known as CCCP. You may address me as General Shen Xue. As for the business we have to discuss... we have interests in common. Possible alliance."

"Alliance, miss? That suggests a shared purpose, of which I can see very little with someone from the CCCP. What purpose for this alliance, might I ask?" This was beginning to intrigue him; he'd scanned through the limited personnel files he was able to obtain about the CCCP, and written most of them off as of little consequence. He had not, however, seen anything about this "People's Blade."

"We both have a vested interest in removing the threat of the Thulians from this world," she said. "I am sure you can see this. Why else would you have placed yourself at the head of Echo? Someone of your resources has no need of an organization such as this, otherwise."

"An apt observation, I suppose, for one with a suspicious mind. Supposing that you are right about this, why ever would I need someone as yourself, miss? What, precisely, do you have to offer? If it is to be alliance, as opposed to let's say... employment, then there needs to be something brought to the table in exchange, yes?"

She smiled a little. "To be as blunt as a white-eyed barbarian, the only things I need to 'bring to the table' are myself and Jade Emperor's Whisper." Verdigris inclined his head for her to explain. "But really, Dominic Verdigris, even a fool can tell you are stalling for time."

It was at that moment that Khanjar chose to make her own dramatic entrance, stepping out of the shadows behind Verdigris. The difference between her and the intruder was that Khanjar already had her pistol drawn and trained on General Shen Xue, who was easily thirty feet away. "Move and you die."

Verdigris almost didn't see the woman move. He was used to metahuman swiftness, but this was something special. One moment she was in front of his desk. The next—Khanjar was staring in disbelief, the barrel and half of the action of her pistol had hit the floor, and the woman was pulling her sword back into the "ready" position. "I have moved," the woman said in a conversational tone of voice. "And yet, I have not died. You, however, have been disarmed. Which would be less of a problem if you had four, like Shakti. Out of compassion I have not removed any of your limbs."

Verdigris' jaw dropped ever so slightly. He turned his head so that he could look at Khanjar; there was a thin rivulet of blood running down from her cheekbone, made by the single cut People's Blade had used to destroy the pistol. *Khanjar almost never misses... and yet, she didn't even get a shot off.* He faced the intruder again. *And how in hell did that sword manage to cut her?* "General Shen Xue? I think we just might have something more to discuss, after all."

Again, the woman bowed, slightly. "Please to dismiss your bodyguard, then. What I have to say is not for her ears." Verdigris waved his hand over his shoulder almost absent-mindedly; his eyes were completely transfixed on Shen Xue. Because of this, he completely missed seeing the storm of emotions that played over Khanjar's face in a split second; first shock, then disgust, and then she went completely stone-faced before turning abruptly and striding out of the room.

Shen Xue waited until Khanjar had left the room. Then she seated herself. "As you are a barbarian," she said, "tea will not be required. Now. Let us begin."

CHAPTER THREE

Hole Hearted

MERCEDES LACKEY AND DENNIS LEE

I don't know how Bella did it, but we all took our cues from her. She didn't give up and lie down when Metis refused us help. She didn't give up and lie down when Alex Tesla died. She only got tougher when Verdigris took over Echo.

Somehow she decided that if no one else would lead the revolution and save Echo, she would. And if she had to rebuild one person at a time, so be it.

Starting with Bulwark.

She stared at her own face on the "Sexiest Healers of Echo" calendar on the wall of the med team locker room. She was the only one in a white version of the spandex pseudo-Echo uniform, in no small part because while the skin-tight blue spandex gave everyone else the illusion of being clothed, unfortunately when the day came for the shoot, it so perfectly matched her skin that it made her look totally naked. So Spin Doctor had sent people to ransack the supply rooms for something else, and the photographer had put her front and center of the group shot.

Which ended up making her the fanboi's fave and looking like a brainless bimbo. She'd hated that at the time, but now that turned out to be a good thing. A very good thing.

Now Dominic Verdigris III, Echo's lord and master and the man behind the assassination of Alex Tesla, thought she was a brainless bimbo. He had no idea that among herself, Yankee Pride, and Detective Ramona Ferrari, with the collusion of CCCP

Commissar Red Saviour, there was a quiet revolution brewing in his ranks.

The actual head of Echo Medical was... ineffective. She'd become the first go-to, and on the basis of "it's easier to ask forgiveness than get permission," she was making a lot of the decisions that the actual MDs couldn't or shouldn't be bothered with. And she and the actual MDs had quietly agreed that paperwork would be turned in without permission being granted. It was working. The bean counter in the head office was just as happy to sign everything put in front of him without actually reading it.

Which was kind of making her... operating head of Echo Medical, at least so far as the metahuman teams were concerned. On top of being one of the "Gang of Three."

She was off-and-on uncomfortable in this position, but... Johnny Murdock had put it best. "Ain't necessarily 'bout bein' the 'right one' so much as it is bein' the one that's there an' willin'."

As she had said, there were four people who could do this. Yankee Pride, Ramona, Bulwark and herself. Yank was being watched day and night, Ramona wasn't a meta, and Bulwark...

She pounded her fist into the wall beside the calendar and swore. Bulwark. Bulwark was still in a coma, the coma that bitch Harmony had put him into. And then she had murdered Tesla. But it was what had happened to Gairdner that really hit Bella hard; of all the wretched things that had happened since the Invasion, this was the one that made her heart twist up into a tight knot and hurt as if she was the one that had been on the wrong side of a gun. She'd only been to see him once, and she'd left feeling furious and helpless and—

—and her comm went off. Swearing again under her breath, she thumbed it on. "Belladonna Blue."

It was Ramona. "Bell, we've got a crisis in sickbay. Einhorn's having a meltdown, and you seem to be the only one that can handle her."

Of course Einhorn was having a meltdown. What else was new? "On it," she replied. Fortunately, she was only a few yards from the source of the crisis du jour....

"I can't!" Einhorn wept, wringing her hands and tossing her head so that the little pearly unicorn horn that gave her that callsign cut through the air. "I just can't! I've tried and tried and he's not getting any better!" Her voice spiraled up into a wail, and Ramona waved her hands placatingly at her. The rest of the Echo DCOs had left the room; Einhorn was a projective empath and not even remotely under control at the moment. Stay too close to her in this mood and you'd be throwing yourself out a window in short order.

But Ramona was right. Bella knew how to handle her, in no small part because Bella was a much more powerful—and much more controlled—empath than she was. So the question was—comfort or confront? What Mary Ann Booker wanted was comfort, and she usually got it. And in this case, she might just be due a little comfort, because Einhorn was the one in charge of Bulwark and Bella could understand and absolutely sympathize with her despair.

She had been trying. For once, she'd put aside a lot of her selfishness and had been spending hours beside the comatose meta. Maybe that was out of guilt, because Bull had treated her with respect and care. Bella wasn't going to argue motives; all she wanted was results.

But if Bella was going to successfully run this revolution, she had to have respect. And she wasn't going to get that by acting like a greeting-card angel and going "There, there, sweetie, it'll be all right."

So she marched right into the ready room, stood just inside the doorway with arms folded over her chest, and barked into the first moment of silence. "Shut the *hell* up, Mary Ann!"

Einhorn froze and fixed Bella with a deer-in-the-headlights stare.

Now Bella moved into the room, one slow, deliberate step at a time. "That's enough, girl," she said, quietly now. "You aren't doing Gairdner any good by having a fit, and you're doing everyone around you a lot of damage. I've warned you about projecting. Shut it off, or I'll shut it off for you, and you won't like that."

Einhorn immediately throttled down on the despair rolling out from her in waves. Ramona sighed with relief, and eased out of the room. Bella nodded. "Good girl. That's more like it."

Einhorn blinked, and tears welled up out of her limpid blue eyes, coursing down her cheeks. She was the only person outside of Hollywood that Bella knew who could look beautiful when crying. This time, however, Bella could tell the tears were genuine, born of real frustration and real desperation. Einhorn liked Gairdner, a lot. She might even have been one of his protégés; she'd certainly been the DCO for him plenty of times. And despite being one of Echo's strongest psionic healers, she hadn't been able to do a thing for him. "I can't bring him out of it," she sobbed. "I can't even get him to heal! I've tried and I've tried and—"

All right. Now is the time to comfort. Bella let her expression soften, dialed up her own projective empathy into what she called the "Momma Fix" mode, and let it wash over the girl. "I know, kiddo," she said. "Hell, everyone knows. You've been a trooper, and it's not your fault you're getting no results. We need to try a different approach. Boss says you need off the case. I'll take over from here. You're back on street duty."

Einhorn's eyes widened and the tears stopped. "You are?" she said incredulously. "I am?"

Bella nodded. The girl burst into tears again, but this time of gratitude and relief. Bella had come prepared, since there was very little that Einhorn did that didn't involve tears at some stage or other. She handed over a packet of tissues. "Go on, blow your nose, wipe your eyes and suit up. Check your comm for assignment. Shoo."

And here I am . . . not the boss in name of Echo's DCOs, but the boss in fact. Ramona defers to me. Everyone defers to me, where the healers are concerned. Jesus Cluny Frog . . . I have the healers. If I can keep this up, if, if, if . . . can I get everyone?

The girl took the packet, stammered something and hurried out. Bella took a deep breath, steeled herself, and headed for the ICU where Gairdner—aka Echo OpThree Bulwark—was hooked up to far too many machines.

And she wondered what the hell she was going to do now.

"Dammit, Jarhead," she murmured to the unconscious man. "What is wrong with you? You're like some kind of black hole."

It was horrible to see this man she knew, she admired, she—*admit it!*—more than admired, lying there like some sort of special effects dummy hooked up to so many machines he had to have the room to himself. No wonder Einhorn was in despair. Bella had been sitting here trying to pour energy into him, to kick-start his metahuman body into healing itself, for the last hour. And everything she poured into him vanished, as if he was a bottomless pit, as if there was a hole where his heart should have been. She'd never seen anything like it before. And for the last ten minutes, she had debated trying to find the Seraphym and hope to persuade her to help—

But the Seraphym had her own priorities and her own agenda, and if fixing Gairdner was part of that, she'd have already been here. If it wasn't, Bella could hunt Atlanta until she was old and gray and never find her. Or... more likely... if this was something Bella could do on her own, the Seraphym would not appear until after Bella had figured out how.

She reached out and smoothed a strand of his white hair back in place. "This has to be something Harmony did," she said, thinking out loud, as her heart ached to see him this way, and she repressed the urge to cry like Einhorn. "But how in hell did she do it? If I knew that, I'd know where to start to fix it." Only four people had been there when Harmony had planted Bulwark; one was Bulwark himself, one was dead, and the other two weren't exactly going to come forward and make confessions. Tapes didn't show her anything useful.

All right. Tapes showed her nothing. Her own psi wasn't helping. The docs hadn't come up with anything. That left a miracle or—

Magic.

She pulled out her comm, and scrolled through until she got the right callsign and gave it a ping. After no more than a couple of seconds, a sleepy voice answered. "Victrix."

"Vix, are you on duty?" That was a loaded question; in a sense, Vickie was always on duty, but that wasn't evident on the Echo duty roster, because only a handful of people were aware that Vickie was also Overwatch, running a very clandestine operation out of her own apartment for both select Echo personnel and CCCP.

"Clear for the next few. Why?" came the reply.

"I'd like you to come over to the Echo ICU and run an eye over Gairdner. And round up Sovie and see if she's free to do the same." Sovie was callsign Soviette, Jadwiga, the CCCP's chief MD and psionic healer. "He's not improving, he should, and I don't know why. I don't know what Harmony did to him. It's exactly as if he has a—an energy drain somewhere, but I can't figure out how, and I can't figure out how to plug it. I need more experienced eyes over here. Different ones, anyway."

There was a pause. "But that wasn't magic—" Vickie said uncertainly. "At least, not that I know. Harm wasn't a magician."

"No. But magic might tell me something that science and psionics doesn't. And Sovie might have seen something like this before. Marx knows the Russkies have more than their share of weird metas." She described as well as she could Gairdner's situation while Vickie listened. There was another pause.

"All right, I'll come with a kit and give it a shot. Be there in half an hour."

"Thanks." Bella settled back on her chair, and resisted the urge to take one of Gairdner's hands in hers.

Vickie brought two people with her, both CCCP. One was Soviette, but the other was the black-clad, porcelain-white-faced meta called Upyr. Althea Vladislava, was her given name, but even she rarely used it or answered to it.

"Why—" Bella began, when Upyr waved a gloved hand at her to cut off the question.

"Am beink to look for wolunteers for donations," the young woman said. "Henergy donations, *da*? Ven donation is villink, is cleaner. Purer."

"Oh..." said Bella doubtfully. Then. "Oh!" with realization of what Upyr was talking about. Upyr's power was like nothing Bella had ever seen before, but it could be exactly what they needed to at least hold the line. "Lemme text Ramona." Well, that would solve one problem. Upyr was... well, her name meant "vampire" in Russian, but rather than blood, she both took and gave some form of—Bella wasn't sure what to call it. Vital energy? Whatever it was, it was the same thing she and Einhorn had been pouring into Bull to no real effect.

Ramona appeared in person in answer to Bella's text, and went off with Upyr. After that, the girl came and went several times, arriving looking pink and nearly vibrating with vitality, leaving looking like her usual composed, white-faced self.

Meanwhile Sovie and Vickie both huddled over Gairdner, while Bella did her best to restrain her impatience, perched on an examination-room stool. The two of them muttered in rapid Russian; Bella was conversant, but not fluent enough to follow much of it. "*Da*" and "*Nyet*" and "*Nechevo,*" she got, but they were getting deeply technical in rapid-fire medical Russian and she was not conversant in that. Vickie sketched signs in the air over Gairdner's chest and studied them intently as they changed, then faded. Then she'd go to her laptop and tap a while, then go back to muttering to Jadwiga.

Then, after this had gone on for almost an hour, they stopped Upyr and muttered at her. There was a lot of nodding and further muttering before Upyr went back out again in search of more victims. Finally Sovie gave a determined nod and the two of them turned their attention to Bella.

"You are beink to haf good instincts, *sestra,*" the Russian doctor said warmly. "Comrade Victoria made postulate, Upyr and I confirm and agree. Harmony—created somethink like ve haf all three seen, but this"—she waved her hand at Bullwark's prone body—"it goes beyond vat ve haf seen before."

Before Bella could blurt that she wanted them to get to the goddamn point, Vickie stepped in. "Harm was something like Thea—Upyr. Her overt power was to amplify energy, but now we know she could take it too. Yes, I know you know that. But this wasn't a standard meta ability, obviously, and she hid it well. Until now, Upyr is the only one of her kind that Sovie's ever seen . . . I've heard of something similar, but I'd never actually seen it until now. And she could do something Upyr can't; just like you thought, she set up some sort of permanent drain on him, in the part of him that actually gives him his powers. It's like she's put a shunt in there. I don't know where it's going, Upyr can't suss it out, and neither can Sovie. We only know it's there, and though we've put a governor on it to slow the drain, neither of them can figure out how to shut it off."

At this point Bella was about ready to explode with frustration, but again, Vickie held up a gloved hand. "Whoa, wait. Just because they can't, that doesn't mean that I can't. Remember the almost-disaster with the comm unit a few days ago?" Vickie waggled her eyebrows like a couple of semaphores, and briefly her fingers formed a shape like the Tesla device. "That was when I found out that magic works enough like psionics that I can probably cut the drain. For all intents and purposes, Harm was a vampire, and that's one of the things my family specialized in for generations. I won't lie to you, it's magic, which means it's risky. I can't give you the odds on whether it will work or not right this minute, I can only tell you that if we don't do this, he's never going to come out of the coma, he'll just keep draining down, and you can't keep pouring energy down a hole. And you know this."

Yes, dammit, she knew this. Her fist hit the concrete wall beside her in frustration, but she did know this.

"Is not just his best chance, *sestra*," Jadwiga said solemnly. "Am tellink you as physician and healer, is his only chance."

"All right," she said, after weighing the alternatives as best she could, and coming up with nothing better. "Let's do this."

Vickie was in a hurry, and lugging an extremely heavy bag—an old-fashioned portmanteau that had been in her family since the 1800s in fact—and wasn't watching where she was going. As a consequence, she nearly ran into a chest. A male chest, covered only by a very nonstandard excuse for a T-shirt. Which meant that the chest could only belong to Red Djinni....

He caught her by the shoulders before she bounced off him. "Whoa, shorty. What're you doing out of your cave? For that matter, what are you doing here in Medical lugging a suitcase?"

She looked up and saw him sporting a different face today, one of his new favorites. If she hadn't been in such a rush, she might have laughed. He was getting better at his "George Clooney" every day.

Four or five replies passed through her thoughts; she settled on the quickest. "Bull," she said. "And we're on the clock."

His eyes narrowed further. "Bella—"

"Knows and authorized. Brought in me and Sovie on it." She fidgeted. "Djinni, I really am on the clock."

"Brought in the big guns—" He took the case from her before she could tighten her grip on it. "Explain while we move, then."

The hell— She almost told him to take a hike, but partly because she still was on the border about him scaring the crap out of her, and partly because... well, because... she didn't argue. She just set off down the corridor at a trot, which for his longer legs was merely a fast walk, explaining in layman's terms as best she could. "So that's why. My family specializes in vamps. All kinds of vamps. So I'm the closest we've got to an expert."

"All kinds of vamps?" His brow wrinkled. "There's more than one kind?"

"You don't know the half of it." She couldn't resist adding, "Though none of them sparkle as far as I'm aware."

They reached the door to Bulwark's private room. He opened it for her, and gave the relatively barren cube a good raking gaze as he closed the door behind her. "Room swept?"

"To the best of *our* ability," she told him, with emphasis. She didn't tell him who the "our" was, but he was smart enough to intuit they'd had some Metis help.

He watched her as she unpacked her kit, a mix of high-tech and antique. "Risk?"

"High," she told him truthfully. "But the risk is all mine and... dammit, it's Bull we're talking about. Bella will be here shortly as my monitor, and this time she's got some folks on-call if things go too pear-shaped."

"Like?"

"Sovie and Mary Ann."

Djinni rolled his eyes at the mention of Einhorn. "That's a lot of help," he said sarcastically. "Well, hell, I'm here, you might as well use me as your anchor."

"Uh... what?" She turned to look at him in complete disbelief.

"I said, you might as well use me as your anchor." He snorted. "It's not as if you haven't already infected me with your magic cooties, so I'm not exactly pure anymore."

She was so shocked that she didn't reply with equal sarcasm. "That... would be... amazingly helpful," she said instead. Then, thankfully, her sarcasm returned. "Did your priest require you to do some penance or something? A hundred thousand rosaries would probably be easier."

He snorted. "Make with the magic, Vix."

Red stood aside and let Vickie begin her preparations. He assumed a relaxed posture, his arms lazily crossed as he leaned back against the wall. At first glance, one might have assumed he was bored. Laying down a square of heavy canvas, painted with a double circle and a few arcane symbols, Vickie paused and glanced up at him. His eyes betrayed him. They bore into her, watching her every move. She felt a painful flush in her cheeks as the intensity of his stare made her acutely self-conscious of everything she was doing.

"Uh, do you want me to explain this?" she asked.

"Just keep at it, Victrix. Time. Issue. Remember?"

Vickie shrugged and continued to work, adding things at the corners of the square. A very heavy pillar of stone, an equally heavy copper bowl, a glass bowl with walls an inch thick that she poured a tiny amount of water into, and a cast-iron incense burner. They all looked old. Very, very old. Probably because they were very, very old. She put an LED light into the copper bowl, and a little computerized gizmo of her own design into the incense burner. Immediately a faint scent of amber filled the room. She didn't want any real fire in here. Not with Bull on an oxygen feed.

The Djinni stiffened up, then let out a subtle exhalation as he composed himself. *That smell,* Vickie thought, groaning inwardly. She had forgotten what that smell meant to him, how it might affect him, and she cursed herself silently for that. She needed him steady, focused. Still, it couldn't be helped. The "incense" (nothing that would compromise the breathing of Bulwark or any other patient) was necessary, and they would have to put aside any misgivings if they were to succeed. If they were to save Bulwark.

Red had, in his usual Djinni fashion, surprised her. To say he was skittish around magic was an understatement. That he would volunteer so readily to participate in this endeavor spoke of . . . what? Whatever the reason, he was trying too hard, straining to look calm when he was obviously on edge. Was it worry? For Bull? Before everything went to hell, when Bull's team had been getting solid at last, Vickie had seen them together via her high-tech Overwatch protocols, whether at work or in the quiet times between jobs. By the end, the conflict and near insults had become banter, and the sniping had . . . almost seemed forced. They would argue, but like two old friends who thrived on getting almost on each other's nerves without actually going over the edge. It had become clear to most everyone as well as to her that Bulwark and the Djinni had become friends.

Again, she paused and looked up at him. Red shifted his stance and looked away. She could see through it, he could tell, his bad attempt at nonchalance. He almost shook his head in dismay, but merely grunted. Despite it all, here he was again, at the heart of a storm. *I'm such a putz,* he thought. *After everything, I promised myself never again, and here I am, voluntarily chaining myself in the eye of the tornado.*

He knew what she was doing, of course. The stone was to represent the element of Earth, the bowls for fire and water and so forth. He had seen similar things before, the last time he had participated in something like this, what he had promised to be the last time . . .

He steadied himself as Vickie began to explain her setup.

"This is mostly old-school. Older stuff in magic has more..." She paused to consider exactly the right world. "...gravity. The more times something is repeated successfully, the more you shove the odds in your favor. I prefer to shoot from the hip and use cybermancy, but I refuse to take any chances when it comes to Bull." She pointed at her Elemental Pillars. "Earth, Air, Fire, and Water. All four objects have been in my family for five hundred years, minimum. That rock for Earth, which is my prime element, dates back to the Etruscans, we think. Those are my power points, what I'll use as my fuel lines while I execute the setup. They'll also be my protections from anyone with magic trying to get at me while I'm working."

The door opened. "I'd prefer mystical Rottweilers for that," said Bella, looking...odd...in doctor's scrubs. "Djinni, what the hell are you doing here? The wall doesn't need holding up."

Red didn't look at her. He simply shrugged, and continued to watch Vickie.

Well, that's a first, Bella thought. *The jerk's usually got his eyes all over me when I enter a room.* Bella felt an odd pang, disquieted by Red's lack of attention.

"He volunteered as my anchor," Vickie said. "Since we, uh... worked magic together, and no one else around here has, that's a plus, but even more..." She managed a wry grin. "Well, for an anchor I need someone with a strong will, and I can't think of anyone more pigheaded than the Djinni."

"Got that right," Bella replied dryly. She flexed her fingers and cracked her knuckles, a bad habit from her paramedic days she still hadn't broken. Then she checked to make sure her two panic buttons were right where she could get to them quickly, gave Bulwark another once-over to make sure nothing had changed, and plopped down on a stool between him and Vickie. "So, we ready?"

"Did most of the prep at home." Vickie stood in the center of the circles painted on the canvas and looked straight into Djinni's eyes. "Speaking of which, that is what I need from you. I'm casting everything loose in order to get deep into what's sucking Bull dry. Best picture is, we have a whirlpool and I have to go down to the bottom to plug it. I can't concentrate on anything but that. You have to do my concentrating for me on my lifeline. It's easy. Just think of everything that means home to you. Doesn't have to mean home to me, just you. It's the home part, not whose home it is."

"I can do that," Red muttered, and took a deep breath.

She gave him a real smile, not strained, not faked. "I know you can. You may have one of the strongest wills outside of a magician I've ever seen."

Home, he thought. *Right, think of home, c'mon Red, old hat, just do it like before... NO... not like before. Vix has got this, she knows the score. Not like Justine. Just think of home, of home...*

Vickie took a deep breath. "Right. Here we go."

And now all that work on the parkour course showed. Her hands moved smoothly in the air as she moved in a slow, precise circle, like a tai chi practitioner crossed with a symphony conductor, sketching lines that glowed, and stayed, weaving a web of symbols all around her until it solidified into a wall. And at that moment, she stopped moving, completely, eyes open, seeing nothing, and the four objects at the corners of the canvas began to shine: deep gold, emerald, sapphire, crimson.

From her perspective, she was free of that imprisoning body... but not free, for she was already caught up in the "gravity well" that was what Harmony had done to Bulwark. It was slowed, but not stopped, a black hole in slow motion. She could have fought the pull, but that wasn't why she was "here." She had to let it take her; had to fall into it. That was the only way to reach the heart of the process and cut the damned thing out.

Because a spell is a process, and not a thing. People forgot that, or never knew it in the first place. They treated spells like concrete constructions and tried to break them. That was not how it worked. Spells were things that kept going, which is why they resisted breaking. You had to interrupt the process. Once that happened, the whole mess would tangle up and fall down, and... and if you were very, very lucky, some of it would snap back on the person who had started it, like the end of a long and deadly bungee cord stretched too tight.

You also had to be very careful that none of those bungee cords snapped back on you, or (if someone else was involved) the person you were trying to help. There was a lot of energy tied up in spells, and in magic, the laws of physics worked pretty well. All that energy had to go somewhere when the process stopped.

She was treating this like a spell, and it was reading to her mostly like a spell.

People always asked, "What does magic look like?" and she always had to shrug, because when you were in the Between place where real Mage-Sight took you, it looked different to everyone. She saw it as elegant fractals of symbols, numbers, and relations, all in colors that told her yet more information about what was going on. But her mother saw it as lacework. And Hosteen Stormdance, one of her mentors and her parents' partner at the Bureau, saw it as a Hopi dance pattern.

So this swirl of symbols whirlpooling around her told her, among other things, "This isn't actually a spell, but it acts just like a spell, so you can treat it as a spell."

The black hole was very dark, and very deep indeed. But the bit of process at the bottom of it was as straightforward and as simple as she had hoped. The older a spell was, the simpler it tended to be, and the easier to deal with. Things that were natural abilities, like Grey's ability to walk through walls, were also straightforward and simple. Primal. It made her wonder where Harmony had gotten this... and if it wasn't a metahuman ability, what in the heck was it?

Whatever... it was something she could handle. She dangled right on the verge of being swallowed up and looked it all over, twice and three times, just to be sure there was nothing hidden from her. She found one fiendish little trap, but it was something she had seen before—and Harmony must not have counted on someone taking this approach to saving Bulwark.

Actually she probably counted on no one being able to save him.

All right then. This was a running machine of sorts. She and Upyr had put a governor on it earlier, but that wasn't going to choke the feed off for much longer. The fractals told her that the whole process was putting such strain on the choke point that it was going to shatter soon.

It was her job to shatter something else. To make the machine kill itself.

Stop the machine. Just a sharp, hard, immovable spike—there. The proverbial spanner in the works.

The process jammed. The tension built for a nanosecond, but a nanosecond is an eternity in the Between. She watched the fractals go red, watched the process strain and strain and approach critical. But her spike jamming the whole thing up held firm. The part Vickie wanted to snap . . . snapped. The machine blew apart.

And, as she had figured, utter chaos broke loose all around her. From being surrounded by a relatively orderly swirl of symbols and numbers, she was at the heart of an avalanche of nonrelated bits that obscured everything else. A blizzard of possibility, causality, and insanity. And all the flying bits were attacking her. Not deliberately, this was all pure accident. But she had to get out of there before it cut her to ribbons.

Now would be good, Red. She groped for the lifeline.

Across the canvas, Red stood opposite from Vickie, oblivious to everything but the creeping darkness that began to envelope him as she wove her spell. He was trying his very best not to panic. He felt a deceptive sense of peace surround him, a paradoxical calm before the storm, because he knew what was coming. Sooner or later, there would come the jolt of sudden energy, a quick roar within the depths of his mind, and the very strength of his resolve would be tested. And every time, she had saved him.

Amethist. Victoria. Vic.

If there had ever been anything that he equated as home, it was her. The way their laughs fell in line, creating a smooth harmonic blend that quelled whatever damned thing they had just been arguing over. Her hair, how a slight change in lighting could make her seem like she was ablaze in soothing warmth. How she had felt in his arms, falling into him, they just seemed to fit together.

Each and every time he had focused on her, on what she meant to him, and it had carried him through. With Victoria as his foundation, he had proved himself more than just an anchor, but stable enough to allow others to mind-ride with him, even taking complete control over his body in relative safety. It had been a rush, and giddy with the thrill of it, his crew had attempted some terrifying acts of magic, constantly pushing themselves to greater heights. By the end, they thought they were invincible. Though Red himself had no magical aptitude, the strength of his will fooled his cohorts into the belief they could manage anything. They began to overexert themselves, until that last attempt . . .

✧ ✧ ✧

It was Justine, of course, who had lost her grip. Justine the Bold, Justine the Pyromancer, the Chosen, the Forever Ticklish in Bed or whatever the hell she was calling herself that week. She had been a timid young thing when they had found her, but even Tomb Stone had to admit that she had some pretty remarkable firepower, raw as it was. And as her power grew, so did her confidence, her daring, and unfortunately, her recklessness. They should have seen it coming. It wasn't the extent of her power that was the issue, it was her control—control, from someone who notoriously did not have a lot of self-control. What they were attempting would have taxed even an experienced mage. A frame-up, making it look as if the Echo meta Pyroclastic had gone rogue. The first step had been simple. Red had done his job well, and he was the spitting image of the Echo operative. It wasn't enough to create the illusion of fire though. Pyro's ability to ignite his body and hurl blasts of plasma had to be authentic. Within the confines of their circle, Justine had channeled the flames to erupt from Red's body, from miles away. That alone had taken quite a bit out of her, but when it came time to rein it in she had felt her grasp falter, then slip. And with that, the power, and the fire, turned on her. Red, safely tucked within the recesses of his own mind, watched in horror as Justine tried to sever the link. In a panic she tried to withdraw and let the flames roar, unleashed, to draw upon whatever source was handy. She cried out, her screams a constant echo reverberating through his mind, when he gave her a mental slap and tried to calm her down. Too late, the fires recoiled and raced back through the mystic tether to ravage her own body. They "watched," stunned, as Justine's body became her own funeral pyre.

But that had not been the end. Oh no.

There was a moment's pause, just a moment, as they sized each other up. They had grown close in the weeks leading up to this job. Once shy and unsure, she had gladly followed Red's lead. He was the man with experience, the one who strode with confidence from one job to another. She had known little outside of her own sad world where others, be they friends or family, simply took what they wanted of her and left her to rot. Red had been the first to care, and she willingly placed herself in his capable hands, learning whatever she could. She had finally found a mentor, a brother, someone to look out for her. He had taught her to take shit from nobody, to know what you wanted, and to go for it. The world was yours, you just had to take it.

And at that moment, she knew what it was she wanted. This time nothing, and no one, was going to stand in her way. Not even him. There was too much at stake.

"I'm sorry, Red."

"Justine, hold on, we can figure this out—"

Red reeled back as she struck. His body staggered and collapsed, like a puppet with its string cut, as a battle raged within. A contest of wills. Two souls, where there could be only one.

"Dammit, girl, we're not doing this! You can't just—"

Red stopped as he felt her desperation. There was nothing there, nothing to reason with, nothing to talk down. What could he have said, anyway? With her own body destroyed, she was trapped inside him. All that kept her alive was her will, and when she tired she would slip away to nothing, unless she took this body from him.

It was a matter of self-preservation for both of them, and friendship, trust... love?... nothing mattered except to live. Justine struck first, impulsive as always, using the mental version of her fires. She tried to cage him in flames, to incinerate him at best, drive him out at worst. He dodged back, her cage grasping at nothing, though he felt the scorch as if from a real blaze. He responded instinctively with cold, *and oh, he could be cold if he had to be. He took the fuel, denied the energy. Justine countered by trying to smother him but he eeled out of her grasp, slippery ice. Without her fire, she had nothing except pure will. He kept retreating; she kept coming. He realized that this could go on... if not forever, for far too long. He lunged, enveloping her as she had tried to envelope him, and without her fire to protect her, he overwhelmed her, and with a great and desperate squeeze he felt something snap. She shuddered and stiffened in his grasp. Loosening his hold, he cradled her ebbing consciousness within his.*

"I didn't... I couldn't... oh Red... this isn't really happening, is it?"

She was fading too fast. Red clung to her, but there was nothing he could do. She slipped out of his grasp, and away, forever into the dark.

"Good-bye..." he sobbed. "Oh God... good-bye..."

...when nothing, not even Amethist, could have prepared him for the price of reckless magic. *It's different this time,* he reminded himself, again. *Different, with someone who's actually trained for this crap. Someone who knows and understands, and accepts the cost. Someone who's careful. Just reach out, Red, reach out and bring her back.*

He fell into his routine, alarmed at how easy it was to bring up his cycle of memories. Each of Amethist, each one a powerful glimpse into the heart of someone he had actually cared for more than he cared about himself. Their first encounter, her flash of anger, his dismay as she chased him with jagged shards of ice, and through the fear he fought down a growing attraction to this enraged—and feisty—girl. Their first kiss, after a titanic battle when he had finally, finally, gotten the upper hand and she lay helpless before him. She was vulnerable, all it would have taken was a slash of his claws, but he couldn't bring himself to do it. Instead he cradled her to him and carried her home, and as he turned to leave she reached for him, and brought his head down to hers. It had all changed then. Their first battle, as partners, how they moved in sync, and the sweet taste of that victory. One by one, he ran through them all, his mind afire with memories of love and the promise of forever.

And then, it all went wrong. Something new and unexpected, and in a jarring flash Red watched the memory he had been fleeing from for the past year.

Amethist, leaping to save him, and vanishing in a burst of white light.

And as the Djinni screamed his loss, the line anchoring him to Vickie fell away, lost in the void.

The lifeline . . . wasn't there. Instinctively, she curled in on herself, to preserve as much as she could, for as long as she could. But this was like being in a sandstorm, with the whirling remains of Harmony's trap etching her, scouring away at her protections. Without an outside source of power, she would last only as long as her will did. Or . . . or until Red could punch through again. If he could. If he would. If he had second thoughts, wanted to eliminate the uncomfortable magician from his life . . . now was the time.

No, she wouldn't think that of him. If he could, then he would. And if he couldn't—

Then at least I go out saving someone else. And until she knew that for certain there was no getting out of here, she would believe he could do it, he could reach her. Her will had kept her going for a long, long time now. She hardened it, and herself, and held on.

✧ ✧ ✧

Bella knew immediately when something went wrong. She sensed the drain on Bulwark stop, and her heart leapt, but then she sensed Vickie... go missing. Her attention was ripped from Bull; Vickie was white as a piece of paper, rigid, eyes glassy, a statue caught in the glowing matrix of her own protections.

If this had been anything other than magic, Bella would have lunged off the stool and grabbed Vickie with both hands—but Vickie had warned her, the protections would guard her from anything, including the best of intended help. There was no way to reach her—

—except through Red.

So Bella lunged for the Djinni instead, clamped both hands around his head, and shoved energy into him. *Dammit, chowderhead!* she "yelled" at him. *FOCUS!*

But she couldn't reach him. And he couldn't reach Vickie. He was caught in some terrible memory of pain that she couldn't break past.

Screw that. YES I CAN.

"*Red!*" she shrieked. "Snap out of it!" She backed up her physical shouts with psychic ones. *Home, you rat bastard! Bring her home!*

But instead of anger, she surrounded him with something else entirely. The satisfaction and pride she felt when he finally started coming up to the mark. The odd affection when he started helping Vickie. The surety that, yes, he could do this.

And... what do you call the opposite of loneliness? Whatever it was, she shoved that at him too. *You're not alone anymore. We're in this together. I have your back; now you get hers...*

It came back to him, those long days spent in that cramped Echo prisoner cell, the torture of sleep, the faces that came to the surface, taunting him with his failures. And her face, most of all, that serene beauty that could in an instant radiate girlish charm, infectious laughter, unwavering determination or a righteous wrath. Amethist knew he loved her, but she could never have guessed how much power she had over him. From her, a simple look of gratitude gave him a desire to accomplish five impossible things before breakfast. A mildly scornful expression would plague him with doubts and self-loathing for days. But the worst, by far, were her fierce stares of blame, and he would simply want to shrivel up and die, right there.

For weeks now, that had been the expression that haunted him most. Even though that was not what he had seen in that last moment. His fault, his fault, and surely, surely she must have felt that in the nanosecond of her death. He couldn't bear it, the accusation, the—hate—

It spilled over to everything else. She surely hated him in that moment, and so he hated himself, and so everyone else, by extension, had to hate him, and the fact that no one alive knew of his guilt but him was irrelevant. There were plenty of other things he'd done. How many had paid for his greed and ambition over the years? How many had he knowingly manipulated for some paltry sum? How many had died, whether by his hand or indirectly from his actions, simply because they had gotten in his way? And just this past year, god...

He'd almost killed Vix. He'd opened the door for Jack... so he was responsible for Tesla, and for Bull...

Here he was again, looking for redemption, fooling himself into thinking it was even possible. It was a tired lesson he could never seem to learn. There was no redemption, not for the things he had done. Any time he tried, it only seemed to make things worse. Amethist's look, that look... that wasn't just blame. It was every failure he had ever endured, masked by the illusion of past victories, shielded by false pretenses of atonement. The truth was, he doubted he could ever outrun his past.

He was utterly alone because he deserved to be. There was no one, no one...

Dammit, chowderhead! Her voice rang inside his head. *FOCUS!*

Red cringed in annoyance. For all her beauty, Bella had the most piercing voice of anyone he had ever met. It was typical of her too. Here he was, trying to enjoy some much deserved self-loathing, and she had to intrude with—

"*Red!*" she shrieked. "Snap out of it!" She backed up her physical shouts with psychic ones. *Home, you rat bastard! Bring her home!*

He felt her then, her presence, and through the darkness she appeared. Her look was encouraging, her posture inviting, and she smiled at him.

You're not alone anymore. We're in this together. I have your back; now you get hers...

He felt her pushing through the guilt, through the absolute cloak of solitude to where he was. He felt her bombard his mind with pride and friendship. He shrank away from it. He didn't deserve feelings like that. He was who he was, a cynical bastard, and as much as part of him longed for such acceptance, the rest of him knew better.

She persisted, stubborn wench, refusing his rejection, drawing ever closer, until he could almost feel her breath upon him. She was radiant. He had desired her since the moment she had first marched up to him and coldcocked him across the jaw. Here, in the dark weft of Vickie's spell, it was so cold. And Bella was so close, and so warm...

He reached out, drew her close, and kissed her. Hard.

She fought for a moment, a sense of shock, surprise, indignation blanketing everything else. Then, unexpectedly, she melted into the kiss, for just a moment.

Home, Red. This is home now.

Home, he thought, and gasped as the tether blazed back into existence.

She felt it, the lifeline, and grabbed onto it with everything she had, with the desperate will to live that had kept her going for this long.

Then, she was out, taking in a huge, gasping breath, as her protections blazed up around her, then winked out. She staggered backwards and came up against the wall.

That wasn't just Red...

She shook her head to clear it, and saw them. Together. Bella and Red. Which...explained why the tether hadn't been "just" Red.

Of course...

Bella had her arms around him. While it looked like it was for support, and Red seemed very shaken, in her estimation there was a ninety-percent probability that a moment before she saw them it hadn't "just been for support." Hell, she wrote romances. The guy the girl hates and fights with was always the one she ended up with. Right?

And now she felt the bitter bile of...not jealousy, no, how could someone like her be jealous of someone like Bella? But. Envy. The way Red was looking at Bella. No one, not even someone as damaged as Red, would ever, ever look at her that way. No matter what she'd...hoped? Subconsciously, anyway...

Yeah, right. And pigs would fly in attack formation over Beirut before that happened. Be grateful for what crumbs you get.

She fought down tears, swallowed down the sharp-edged lump in her throat. *Be happy for your friends being happy. Try, anyway. Because that's the closest you'll ever get.*

Still, they had just saved her life. You would think they would turn to look at her or something.

The terrible armor of her scars closed in around her, a tangible barricade that would, forever, stand as a barrier to anything beyond friendship. *Forget it, move on. Concentrate on something besides yourself. You aren't the star of this story, and it isn't all about you. It's about the team. Don't forget why you were here in the first place.* She clamped down on her heart, hard. *You get half an hour to feel sorry for yourself and cry when you get home. That's it, that's all the self-indulgence you get. Then you concentrate on something productive.*

While they were still staring into each others' eyes, she dashed her glove across her own to clear the burning tears away, and turned her attention to Bulwark. And frowned.

There were some things even she could tell, from the machines, and from him, thanks to Sovie's briefing. He was breathing on his own at last. And that dreadful draining was shut down for good. But he wasn't coming out of the coma, and she wasn't medic enough to guess why.

"Bell," she said, without turning to look at the other two. "What the hell is going on with Bulwark?"

Bella and Red came apart with a start, as if awakening from a dream, and looked at Vickie blankly. Bella snapped fully into work mode first, and wobbled a little as she raced to Bull's side. Okay, breathing on his own. She disconnected the respirator; there was nothing good that came of keeping a meta on one of those if he or she didn't need it. She checked the EKG; looked like a coma, but not a vegetative one—there was something going on in his head, something very active. But he wasn't coming out of it. She glanced at Vickie, who shrugged.

"Metas," Vickie said, and shrugged again. "I mean, I'm no doctor, but Sovie says you can't always tell how they're going to recover. For some of them, at least from the conversations I've had with her, it's like they're doing a systems check constantly, and they stay out cold until everything's repaired, then they come to all at once."

Bella scowled, Djinni, for the moment, forgotten. "Well... at least now I've got brain activity and I don't need to keep anything but the IV drip on him. So nobody's going to have the excuse to pull the plug on him."

They both knew who that "nobody" would be, too. Nothing like eliminating the last witness to what had happened in Tesla's office.

"I'll put a magic cyber-snoop tag on him. If anything looks hinky, it'll alarm for me, and in this state we can move him to Sovie's bay," Vickie said firmly. "Won't hurt him to be off the drip for the hour or two that would take."

Bella let out a sigh of relief. "That'll work. Murdock can probably do the heavy lifting. Or Chug."

Red looked back and forth between the two of them. "We done here, then?" he asked, finally.

Vickie jumped as if she'd been stung. "Shit! Sorry, Djinni. You were..." Her voice caught for just a moment, then she swallowed. "You did great. Like I figured. Thanks."

He shook his head. "No, I really didn't. Almost got you killed. Lucky Bella was here." He favored Bella with a strained look. Bella averted her eyes and turned back to Bulwark's monitors. Red shrugged in defeat, and stepped next to her. He paused, as if unsure of what to say, and shrugged again. He laid a hand on Bull's shoulder, and gave it a rough squeeze.

"Hope this helped, big guy," Red murmured. As he turned to leave, he brushed by Bella and felt her flinch away.

But Vickie touched his arm with a flick of a gloved finger, as if she knew how sensitive his skin was. Of course she knew. She'd been in it....

"With or without Bella, you did good. The only way she could have reached me was through you." She smiled wanly. "Thanks."

He wouldn't look at her. He and Bella were seriously off... uncomfortable. With the kind of confusion you saw in high school kids who just had a Moment with someone they'd never considered romantically before. She watched him leave, closing the door behind himself quietly.

She wanted to feel good. Instead, she felt like hell.

And it's not all about you, she reminded herself. She glanced at Bell, who was busy with Bulwark. *Go home. Cry. Then work on those sensor-balls and get them integrated with the cybermancy. You're going to need them. The team is going to need them and the team is counting on you. There's just too much at stake for you to play at self-indulgence now.*

It was a garden. A garden with no paths, arranged with little geometric plantings of flowers, green turf between them. So far as Gairdner could tell, it went on forever. There was a great deal of light, but no sun, no way to tell time.

It was peaceful here, but it was also . . . isolated. He hadn't been really alone in a long time. Alone, as in "no people around," that is. "Alone" as in "without someone" . . . he'd been achingly alone since Victoria vanished, but that was different. But so far as he could tell, and he had walked for what seemed like miles through this garden, he was the only thing in it that wasn't a plant or a bug.

So he finally sat down, even though he wasn't tired, and waited. Eventually, something changed.

The "something" was a light in the distance, growing nearer. It seemed in no hurry to get to him, but then, he was in no hurry to see what it was. There just was no sense of urgency here. Eventually, he saw that the light had a human shape. When it grew near enough, he recognized it, or at least, he thought he did, because he had never actually seen this . . . person . . . with his own eyes, only had her described to him. If he was right, this was the one that had been tagged as "the Seraphym." She wasn't in Echo, she wasn't in any organization that he could tell. Opinion was divided on whether she was a metahuman or a real angel.

It appeared that he was about to find out for himself.

She stopped, a few feet away, and contemplated him. Her gaze was somewhat unnerving, since her golden eyes had no pupils. "Greetings, Gairdner," she said, quietly. Her voice had some odd overtones, as if more than one person was speaking with her mouth.

He nodded politely. "Ma'am," he said in way of greeting. Heaven wasn't exactly as he had pictured it. As inviting as his surroundings were, he felt wary and on his guard. Still, minding his manners seemed the thing to do.

"I assume you understand at this point that you are not . . . in the world you knew." There was no irony, no amusement in her tone; more like a grave serenity. "And no, this is not Heaven. Although there are as many of those as there are believers, and for some, this might be Heaven. For you, however, this is... call it a rest stop."

He glanced around. "So this is my Platform Nine and Three-Quarters?"

Now she smiled. It was a radiant smile, one that bathed him in approval. "Clever man. Yes, in a sense. And in that same sense, thanks to herculean work by your friends, you actually have a choice in destinations. I think, however, given your temperament, you would prefer to think about those destinations before choosing."

"Careful consideration of options and assessing the cost, risks and potential benefits of each." Bull bowed his head for a moment, then looked up at the Seraphym. "Yes, that sounds like me."

"It is permitted me to tell you a great deal. This is because if you should choose one particular one of those options, you will not retain the memory of what I tell you. That option is, of course, to go back." She blinked, slowly. "It is in my gift to See the futures. You are important to them. Not absolutely vital, but I See you in many of the ones that lead to... success. As opposed to failure, which for humanity, would be total." She paused as if thinking. "However, you are not absolutely vital. It will be difficult, but I can find ways and means to replace you. If I must."

"You mean my value in this world is nonessential," Bulwark said. "You're saying I have really nothing to sway my choice to either return or to go on."

She sighed. "You all really are caught up in hearing what you choose to hear, not what I actually say... No, I did not say that."

He held up his hand. "No, please, do not misunderstand. I am not assuming a tone of self-deprecation. I'm merely trying to understand the full extent of the ramifications of my choice here. If, as you say, I return, then I may be of use in the trials before us. If I choose not to return, my choice alone will not damn all of humanity. Correct?"

"Correct."

"Just checking," he said and held his hands behind him, standing at ease. "Please, continue."

"Should you choose other than return, your options widen. To... well, the universe is yours. To share with Victoria, with others, if you wish. To find incarnation in some other form—'return to the fight' as it were, elsewhere, elsewhen. The possibilities are infinite...." She tilted her head to the side, looking curiously alien.

"Wait..." he interrupted, and held up his hand. "Did you just say I could rejoin Victoria?"

She nodded. "If you wish. I can tell you it is her wish. But no individual's wish is forced on another. Free Will is the Law. She knows this, and accepts it. She also accepts that your choice will not be indicative of your love for her, or lack of it. She does not doubt that."

He glared at her for a long moment. "She is dead, then," he said finally.

"Yes. But in your heart, you have known this for a very long time."

"I am a soldier, ma'am. I needed confirmation."

"I understand. This is why I told you. In this moment of choosing, you must have all the information you need." She spread her hands a little. "It is not permitted that I recommend a choice—"

"How did she die?" he asked, interrupting.

The Seraphym sighed, and closed her eyes for a moment. "I cannot tell you," she said, finally. "That is not permitted either."

"Not permitted," he repeated. "Not permitted..."

"No, it is not," she said. "I am only an Instrument. I am constrained by the—"

And again, Bull cut her off, but this time not with words. She fell silent, genuinely surprised, as his face began to redden, his lips curl back in a snarl and his entire body began to quiver.

With rage.

"Not permitted?" he roared, and a force erupted from him... expanding outward like the force field of his metahuman power. Where it touched, the garden disintegrated, shattered, as if the flowers, the turf, the trees and bushes, were all made of glass. Where it had passed there was nothing left but dust. But it wasn't enough. Bulwark reared back and bellowed, releasing all his pent-up frustration over Victoria's sudden and inexplicable disappearance, over the months of fruitless searching that followed, of the careful dance he had performed around the Djinni. The Djinni, who could never be coerced into anything, who had to be handled just so, and what had that gained him? Nothing! The Djinni remained tight-lipped about the whole affair, never once surrendering even a passing thought of the events of that day. Bull continued to roar, his bubble of force and rage ever-expanding in undulating waves of light. He began to manifest fire, which tore from him to consume everything within that expanding space. The field

shuddered and bellowed out as he gave one final dreadful push, as if driven by the fires within him, creating a small sun, until there was nothing left of the garden from horizon to horizon.

And even that did not satisfy his anger. In the blink of an eye, the fires contracted to a pinpoint of searing light... then exploded, taking everything—light, fire, all—with them. And then, there was nothing but darkness.

And a voice, her voice. Dry, but a little surprised. "I would describe that as... excessive."

In the vastness of the void, his consciousness sounded both overwhelming and somehow terribly, insignificantly small. "I didn't just wreck a common staging area, did I?"

"Only your own." A light grew in the darkness. It became the Seraphym. Light spread outward from her until she hung in the center of the brightness, fiery wings spread, perfectly balanced in the heart of a sphere of soft, white light. "Would you like it back again? Or do you prefer the dark?"

"A good question," he answered as he resumed his customarily neutral tone. He figured the Seraphym realized what a rare thing it was for him to externalize any internal conflict. This one was a long time coming, and still he was no closer to the answers he sought, except for one. Vic was dead. The how and the why aside, it was the certainty of her death that had finally sparked what rage he had bottled up over it. And now, she was being offered back to him. His heart leapt at the idea of it. But was he done? With everything? Was it time to rejoin his love?

He considered his choices, and realized there really wasn't any choice, not for him. There was nothing like destroying an entire plane of existence, even a personal one, to put things in perspective.

I'm sorry, darling, he thought in prayer. *Perhaps in time. I hope you understand, but I'm just not done fighting. Not yet.*

Seraphym somehow took on an aura of command, that cool impression of certainty he had always received from his best COs. "You are a soldier, Gairdner. In a sense, so am I. I have my orders; there are reasons for them that I am sometimes privileged to know, and you are not. And sometimes, even I am not privileged to know reasons or even information. But I trust that this is for the greatest good. Do you understand?" She waited for his answer.

"Not entirely, no," he answered. "But it's my choice, and I choose to go back."

"That will be permitted," she said, gravely. "But..." She paused. "Curious. It will be permitted... but not just yet." The light expanded until it filled everything again. "Do not be concerned. It will be permitted."

She vanished, leaving him alone, drifting in light.

"And now what?" he asked aloud.

You might consider rebuilding what you broke, rang the words in his mind.

CHAPTER FOUR

Dare to Be Stupid

MERCEDES LACKEY AND CODY MARTIN

None of us were lying down. Some of us, however, were not content to wait. And some... let's just say that a restless Red Saviour is a lot like a quarter ton of feral kittens.

Then add Pavel to the mix.

On the other hand, John Murdock and I had managed to penetrate that Thulian Command and Control silo, and we had gotten some intel on another Thulian stronghold right there in Kansas City. Wait too long, and intel goes stale, really quickly. Their C and C had been destroyed; they might decide not to take the chance that their KC hub had been compromised too.

We had to move. And by "we," I mean CCCP... and yours very truly.

Strange bedfellows. But at least someone was moving.

It was hard not to gloat, just a little. There was so little to gloat over, after all, that finally having *something* go right felt like a victory. But here was little old Victoria Victrix, absolutely, utterly disregarded by Dominic Verdigris... gleefully piloting the tech that Dominic Verdigris, Super Geeeeeneeeus, had been unable to make work.

'Course, I have magic.... She floated the "magic eyeball" in through the door of the CCCP break room. None of the occupants noticed. Which was a good thing, since it was supposed to be invisible.

There were only three bodies there at the moment, but as they were three very different sorts of metas, that gave her the opportunity to see if some of the scanning equipment worked. She had to give Verd this much credit; he'd packed a lot into a very small space, and if he'd only been able to work out the antigrav problem...

Well, good thing he hadn't.

Subject one: the new gal, Mamona. Well, callsign Mamona. Which was a nasty little dig on Nat's part, giving her that callsign. Cici DuPre was a homegirl from John Murdock's adopted Atlanta neighborhood who had manifested confusion-psi powers; she interrupted central nervous system signals in her targets. Mamona was Russian for Mammon, the god of wealth. If there was anything *less* wealthy than Cici...just one of Nat's little moments of contempt for the US lifestyle.

Or maybe, just maybe, Nat was showing a rare moment of humor, however cutting it could sometimes be.

Mamona showed up as pretty normal in the scans, except for the eleventy-billion throwing knives she had hidden all over her person. The two big fighting knives, she didn't bother to hide.

Subject two: callsign Untermensch. Georgi did not show up "normal" on scan. Vic had to call up extra stuff to get through his near-impervious skin on his hands and forearms. And as she scanned, he suddenly looked fractionally more alert. She wondered if he didn't have marginal sensitivity to scans that even he wasn't aware of, maybe an aspect of his healing factor.

Subject three: *Sovietski Medved. The* Soviet Bear. *Oh lordy, lordy, Pavel.* There was nothing about Pavel that was normal. In fact, even for a metahuman...he just flat out should be dead. Nothing about him should be working. Not the kludged-together, WWII-era prosthetics—"Height of Soviet engineering," as he said. Not the gods-only-knew-what-it-was power source he had instead of a heart. Nothing. Pavel should flat out be dead—either from extreme age or his ramshackle mechanical body—and all her computer-assisted semi-AI was insisting that none of what it saw should be real, working, functional, or in this space-time continuum at all. And somehow, he wasn't dead.

Might as well drop some eaves while I'm here.

As usual, Pavel was eating and drinking—Chef Oh Boy canned ravioli, and rotgut vodka, which were the only two things he ever seemed to eat and drink. Although she'd heard rumors about a small scandal involving Pavel and the International Waffle House.

He had monopolized the TV remote, allegedly watching *Mayberry RFD* reruns. American television was utterly entrancing for him; particularly older cop dramas and soap operas.

"Ah dunno how y'all can watch that crap," Mamona said in disgust. She was busy sharpening all of her various blades in turn, inspecting each one carefully before moving on to the next. Whenever asked about it by one of the other comrades, she always replied, "They're never sharp enough," followed by a smile that seemed to reflect a joke only she knew the punch-line to.

"I am not knowink how he can *eat* that crap," Unter replied.

"Easy, *tovarischii*," said Pavel, holding up a spoon. "You are to use a utensil and eyes!" He shifted on the lumpy couch. "And to be sitting. Usually helps."

The intercom crackled to life. "Comrades Mamona, Untermensch and . . . Pavel to office, spasibo. *Davay*, am not wastink time with dally dilly."

"Commissar calls, comrades." Pavel hefted himself from the couch, metal joints squeaking and straining with the effort. "Georgi, you go first. You are sturdy enough to take statue to head, *da*?"

"And you are to be puttink toys away and reportink in person, comrade," came the unexpected addition on the CCCP Commissar channel in Vickie's ear. *"I am insistink on seeing eyes of my comrades in briefink."*

Crap. How did she know I had an eye out? Nat knew *about* the eyes, of course; some were going with this team out to JM. But how had she detected one active? "Coming, Commissar," she replied, and gave the AI the command to bring the eye back to a homing cradle. *Good thing I have an apport landing pad in their HQ.* Not that she actually wanted to be there . . . Djinni and Bella she was barely comfortable with. Bulwark, maybe. Anyone else ranged from nervous-making to terrifying, with the Commissar pegging the scale at *I am about to have a meltdown, right here, right now.* Oh well.

She paused long enough to gulp down her antianxiety meds, then shuffled with resignation to her magic room.

On a scale of one to meltdown, I think Untermensch is up there with Nat for who burns me out the most. Vickie did her level best to shrink into the corner of the room. The three comrades all stood in a very loose approximation of "at ease," especially Pavel.

The CCCP had discipline in plenty when it came to important matters and fighting, but in private they often tended to be at a sort of "relaxed tension" when dealing with each other. It was very strange, and far different from what was the norm in Echo.

"Comrades, I am now briefing three of you on operation in—" she glanced at Vickie, ever so marginally.

"Kansas City," Vickie queued the Commissar's channel and whispered into her own mic, taking the hint.

"—Kansas City," Red Saviour continued smoothly. "Intel provided us by decoded information placed Command and Control center for Thulians in decommissioned missile silo on outskirts."

"Is being... reliable, Commissar?" Untermensch subtly glanced at Victoria before locking his eyes on Natalya.

"Not only reliable, successful," the Commissar said with a smirk of satisfaction. "Comrade John Murdock infiltrated on solo recon." Unter cocked an eyebrow, the only hint of emotion he showed. "Center was being deactivated, but we reached it in time to retrieve more excellent intelligence. This intelligence places a probable Thulian dispersion unit within Kansas City. I am sending you as backup to comrade Murdock."

Pavel piped up, raising a hand. "Who shall to be the team leader, Commissar?" He puffed his chest out as much as he could. "I accept this honor—"

"Shto?" Red Saviour said, looking incredulous. "Comrade Murdock is team leader. Comrade Untermensch is second. You... are to be distraction. No one will suspect covert team of beink covert that has you on it."

Mamona smothered a giggle with both hands. Georgi and Pavel shared a look.

"To continue." Red Saviour gave Mamona a glare. "You will to beink use Overwatch. Georgi, Pavel, I know you are familiar. Comrade Mamona is not. Comrade Victrix will beink see to this. Plan must remain fluid. Ideally, you will discover if intel is correct, infil, collect intelligence, and exfil." She sighed gustily. "However, with Comrade Medved on team, plans seldom go according to... plan."

Georgi was the first to pipe up. "Transportation to site, Commissar?"

"Comrade Victrix?"

Vickie took a shaken breath as the eyes of all four focused on her like searchlights. "Already arranged, Commissar. Echo cargo plane, regularly scheduled. You are not listed as CCCP. You are Echo SupportOps in the commissary unit. When you arrive, your cover will be as a fencing team from Vladivostok University."

"Fencing, comrade?" Pavel leaned forward. "I am having many accomplishments in this field, from my time—"

"Your time sticking fork into *blinis*, Old Bear?" Unter elbowed Pavel in his metal ribs.

Mamona giggled again. "Ah dunno, he's pretty quick at gettin' the last ravioli outta the can. Gotta watch them suckers, they's slippery."

"*Da*, *da*, enough." The Commissar cut them short. "Comrade tells me fencing is strange enough no Amerikanski will be able to ask you questions or ask for demonstration, but Amerikanski Olympic team did well enough they know is sport. And they know Russians are best in world, naturally. Is good cover."

Unter straightened up. "When do we leave, Commissar?"

"As soon as you and I are finished speaking." She eyeballed Mamona and Pavel. "You and you, go, make preparations." She glared at Vickie. "You stay." Georgi stood his ground, unmentioned but understanding the Commissar's meaning. Pavel, completely oblivious to the snub, slapped Mamona's arm and merrily escorted her out. Perhaps he was under the impression that he was supposed to keep an eye on her for the Commissar. Vickie made her spine as one with the corner.

Georgi stepped forward. "Commissar, might I be speaking without reservation on this?" His eyes shifted to Victoria for a split second.

"Daughter of Rasputin has our confidence," the Commissar said firmly. "We will speak on this later. There is much you need to know."

He nodded. "*Da*. But is Murdock ready for this? He is still fresh comrade and—"

Now it was Red Saviour's turn to glance at Vickie, not with a glare, but a lifted eyebrow and a little nod at the stack of papers Vickie had given her earlier. Vickie didn't take long to think about it. If there were three people in all of CCCP that Natalya trusted above all others, they were Mojiotok, Soviette, and Untermensch. She nodded fractionally. Red Saviour handed over the stack to Georgi.

Oh... my god. She just asked me *for permission to hand over intel...*

Unter took several long minutes to read through the papers, flipping the pages and occasionally grunting or nodding. When he was finished, he set the stack upon the Commissar's desk. "*Da*. Will suffice." His face betrayed nothing, at that moment.

"Now, *davay*. Comrade Victrix, brief Mamona on Overwatch. Georgi . . ." She sighed, then made a shooing motion. "Be to herding cats."

The glory of the floating eye was that Vickie wasn't restricted to any one—potentially obscured—viewpoint. And she could double-check the stowage while Georgi wrestled his "cats" into their seats. She didn't miss any of the dialogue though.

"Just cause we're supposed to be commissary crew, that don't mean ya get t'inspect all the food crates, Pavel," Mamona scolded Soviet Bear. "I promise you, they ain't got any ravioli in there." And she added under her breath, "'Cause they actually got taste buds."

"Your logic does not follow, *tovarisch*. Comrade Chef Oh Boy is *bolshoi* cook, *nyet*?"

"*Nyet*, is being correct, Pavel," Untermensch growled. "But if will make you feel better . . ." He paused. Vickie blinked, as she realized he was waiting for *her* to give him a cue or a reason to get the Bear settled into his seat.

"All food on Echo campuses is sourced locally," she supplied smoothly on his channel. "It's too expensive to ship food."

"Echo is not to being waste money shipping food they can get at same price locally," Georgi growled. "You are too used to thinkink America is like Siberia. Food is everywhere, here."

The Bear stroked his chin, considering their words. "There is wisdom in this, I suppose." He gave one last sorrowful look at the commissary crates, and then clunked over to sit in his jump seat. "How long are we to fly?" He looked up in the air, perhaps expecting Vickie to materialize in front of him.

"Your flight time is two hours, seventeen minutes," she replied on the open channel. "You'll be landing at general aviation, cargo, not the passenger terminal. Transport will be ready and waiting offloaded from this plane, CCCP van with a GPS set run by me to guide you to where you will set up a temporary HQ." She paused. "I've already arranged for a grocery delivery, Bear. You won't starve."

"Good. This bear hates fighting on an empty stomach; had enough of tastings for it in Great Patriotic War." The Bear nodded solemnly.

"You've made up for it since, Old Bear. With how much we spend on food for you, we could feed a battalion. I've heard mention of the Commissar drawing up orders for you to go . . . on a *diet*." Untermensch grinned cruelly, and Mamona smothered giggles.

Pavel blanched. "*Shto*?" He shook his head, throwing his hands up in resignation. "I be doing as ordered, as always. Commissar knows a sturdy bear when she sees one." The wizened Russian leaned forward, planting his elbows on his knees with an audible clank. "Speaking of Commissars and the judgments they are to be having . . . what do you make of the American as a team leader?"

"He was a sergeant in the US Army," Vickie supplied. "Got buckets of experience at it."

"*Da*, *da*, but Amercanski way of war is different from ours, from Soviet perfection." Vickie figured at this point he was actually looking to Untermensch for his answers, so she kept her lip zipped. After all, Unter had been on the same teams as JM on more than a few incidents, including the one where they extracted Bella and her Echo squad from Rebs with rocket launchers. It had ended up being a trap, however; meant for Echo rather than CCCP, but the Thulian metahuman Ubermensch had taken full advantage of CCCP's appearance. Both CCCP and Echo had taken casualties and fatalities. One of them had almost been Red Saviour herself. Vickie still wasn't certain how Bella had managed to save the Commissar. You just didn't normally survive having a building dropped on you unless you were someone like Bulwark or Chug.

"He has fought well enough, to date. So we are to be seeing how he does in command." Untermensch leaned back in his seat, stretching as he did so. "Worst thing that can be happening is that we die."

"Oh. Well, when is put that way, is not so risky, *nyet*?" Amazingly, the Bear actually seemed to mean what he said. He was possessed of an odd sort of fatalism; so long as he did his job the way he was supposed to—which was a very subjective thing for him, admittedly—he was perfectly happy to accept anything that came his way. "One can't trust fire throwers too much, though. They are to being apt to burn themselves as they are to be being burning others."

"You're prejudiced. Besides, Supernaut was a fool and a blowhard. Murdock has not shown to be either. So far." Unter actually hadn't put any *criticism* in that statement... which for him, was praise. *Huh. Guess all that shite in my analysis and intel report didn't rattle his cage.* She'd kept it all cut-and-dried, just reporting what she'd decoded from the Project; his training, capabilities... actually pretty much verbatim what was in the Project reports.

"Hmph. Comrade Mamona, you are also being Amerikanski. What is your take on our soon-to-be team leader?" Bear was stroking his chin again. Unter strapped himself in as the jet engines ramped up, and raised an eyebrow at the American.

"I like 'im. If it hadn't been fer him an' that angel, my hood'd be in a world'a hurt right now." Mamona nodded decisively. "'E managed t'get everyone workin' t'gether, and kicked most of the assholes out. The assholes that stayed, well, they ain't operatin' on *our* turf no more."

"You're all big boys and girls," came the pilot over the intercom. "And I don't have a flight attendant to make sure you're strapped in. We're going to take off hot because this is a big, heavy bird and I don't have a lot of runway, so if you haven't already battened down the hatches, too bad, you can tend your own boo-boos. Captain out."

"He means it," Vickie warned them. And the plane began accelerating.

Pavel cleared his throat as everyone made their final preparations. "I am having one final question as to Comrade Murdock's sturdiness. Then I shall be satisfied."

Untermensch sighed. "What is it, Old Bear?"

"He can fight, and can be seeming to lead, both qualities I expect from any Russian... but can he be drinking like one of us?"

Georgi guffawed. "*No one* can drink like you, Old Bear. Not even alcoholic Cossack."

The ride to the motel had been... interesting. After much objection from the Bear, Unter had overridden his insistence that he drive, and installed Mamona in the driver's seat of the van. Vickie had seen to it that there were actual gym bags with actual fencing equipment in them, and athletic clothing in red and white that would pass for uniforms; Bear's was oversized to accommodate his frame. After exploring the contents of his bag and being forcibly restrained from waving the fencing saber around while Mamona was trying to drive, the Bear was mollified to discover—yes—a couple cans of ravioli and a fork tucked into a corner. After that, he was content to make comments about Mamona's driving with his mouth full.

Mamona wasn't the world's best driver, but she did respond fairly well to Vickie's directions, and they managed to arrive at the motel without incident, and without anyone's eye being poked out.

"You must be aggressive, comrade! Don't letting every car push you around!" Bear was gesticulating with his fork, speaking around another mouthful of ravioli. "If you let one dog push you around, others will be coming sniffing."

"That makes no sense, Old Bear. Quit stuffing your face and grab the bags."

"Suite 122, comrades," Vickie said. "Townhouse, one down, three up, Murdock is waiting at the door." *I am going to be glad to get these cats herded up and let JM take over. Bear is worse than ten two-year-olds on a sugar rush.*

Just as Vickie had said, John was waiting in the doorway; he had his arms crossed and was leaning lazily against the frame. "Right on time. Y'all got everything outta the van?"

"*Da.* All of our gear, including a case of ravioli and enough vodka to drown a moose. Hopefully, it'll be just enough to shut up a grousing bear." Unter shouldered his gym bags into the townhouse as Murdock stood aside.

"Ah. That'll explain the six cases of ravioli Overwatch had delivered. Privyet, Pavel. Ya ain't gonna starve." Vickie floated the eye in through the corner of the doorframe and made it visible.

"Hiya Johnny," she said, using the tiny speaker in the eye.

"Creepy. Welcome to the party." John stood aside and motioned for the others. "Get everything stacked in there and get settled in. Rest up; we go in tomorrow on our first pass at the target."

"Before you ask, I can't get these things too far from you guys before I lose signal," she told him. "So no insertion to your target. Working on improvements."

"S'alright, Vic. I like having actual eyes on an asset before committing, anyways." He frowned. "Erm, I mean real eyes. Not black magic thingies. No offense."

Okay, don't undermine the man. "Not black magic, just magic, and mostly tech," she said in his ear. "I don't do black magic; it's very much against the code."

"Got it. And thanks." John closed the door after all of the team and their gear had passed him. "Get fed and bedded down. Who's on first watch?"

"I will take the honor, *tovarisch*." Bear immediately plopped down into the single lounge chair, a can of ravioli and a jug of vodka in hand.

"All right. Unter, keep him sober for the watch; we'll drain the vodka after we get outta this alive, but not before. Got it?" John gave Unter an assessing look.

"Bear needs a fair amount to function, comrade," Unter cautioned, and shrugged. "A sober Bear is an ugly creature."

"Understood; but *you're* gonna keep him in hand. We've all worked together before, so let's make this easy on everyone. *Da*?"

Untermensch sketched a salute, but as near as Vickie could tell, he seemed pleased. "I am hearing you, comrades," Bear grumbled from his seat. "Ears are not being defective, you know."

"Excellent. That means y'can keep the volume down on the tube. Sack time for me, y'all. I just spent the better part'a the day securing this joint." He nodded at Vickie's eye. "Overwatch ain't exactly got hands." Murdock was asleep almost as soon as his head hit the pillow, leaving the others to finish getting food and settling in.

"I will to be sharing room with Comrade Mamona," Bear piped up during a commercial break in whatever soap opera he had tuned in to.

Mamona opened her mouth, glanced at Unter, and shut it.

"You will be taking room on the left upstairs," Unter said firmly. "Mamona will be in the right. I will be in the middle. Doors will be left open."

Bear actually turned around to look at Georgi. "Are you implying something, comrade?" he said in Russian.

Georgi replied in Russian. "Yes. I'm implying that I don't want you to *imply* Comrade Mamona, you rotten lecher." Unter glared at him. Mamona looked from one to the other, lost.

"Imply her, comrade?" Bear guffawed. "I hardly even know her!"

Georgi groaned. "*Borzhe moi*, it's going to be a long mission."

CHAPTER FIVE

Firefight

MERCEDES LACKEY AND CODY MARTIN

John had changed hotels after the last operation's debriefing; Vickie had pointed out that it wouldn't do to stick around long enough for folks to start to get to know his face. Besides, he needed a bigger room; he had some guests from Atlanta coming in to help him with the next job. One of those "extended stay" places seemed about right for the size of the group, and it came with a kitchen, which meant no obvious Russians in restaurants. He wanted everyone in the same place too; no running around between motel rooms to attract attention. After the Commissar and Bella had finished analyzing the intelligence that Vickie had downloaded from the Thulian base, they had quickly found that there was another site of tactical significance not very far from John's current location. So, it had now become his job to organize the team, prepare them, and then get on with another operation.

It had taken three days for everyone back at HQ to get their ducks in a row. Soviet Bear, Untermensch, and the American girl Mamona had come to Kansas the same way John had, unregistered passengers aboard an Echo transport plane. All three had come wired with Vickie's rig. And all three had brought more supplies, including, this time, another beat-up van that looked like it had barely survived an encounter with Chug, and had a V8 engine that purred like a contented cat. It was the old van he'd nursed back from that swamp in Georgia, with a much-beefed-up motor and suspension. Once they had found his hotel, John wasted no time in getting everyone bedded down; after the trip they had made, getting a night's rest would serve them better than jumping straight to work. The only one that didn't sleep was Old Man Bear, but he never slept; he volunteered to stand watch for the night, which was just as well.

John had become accustomed to waking up early without an alarm, and busied himself with making a light breakfast for everyone in the built-in kitchen for the room.

"Damn, it cooks too. You're gonna make someone a fine wife." Evidently Vickie got up early too. The voice in his ear sounded entirely too chipper.

"You're gettin' unplugged, next one of those."

"In fifteen minutes there's going to be a knock at the door. It'll be the grocery delivery that comes with the room. I took care of it and it's paid for. Now do you love me? He brings more coffee."

"It's a start." John finished cooking breakfast, woke everyone up, and received the grocery delivery while the rest of his comrades went about their morning routines. Once everyone was showered—except for Bear, who just needed a ten-thousand-mile checkup and a light dusting now and again—and fed, John started going over the particulars for their mission.

"Glad to see everyone survived the night."

"Could have done better with good bottle of cheap vodka," grumbled Bear, over a bowl of the canned ravioli that was all he ever seemed to eat.

"We make do, *tovarisch*." Unter was sitting next to Pavel on the bed, his arms folded in front of his chest.

"Beats the roach motels I've been in," Mamona said, then shrugged.

John retrieved a small dry-erase board from one of his duffel bags. "All right, listen up, folks. Based upon intel we received recently, we've got another Thulian target to go after." He coughed into his hand, clearing some of the cobwebs from his chest. "It's suspected that there's a shippin' depot in Kansas City that might be a Thulian interest. I say suspected because the information we have is partial, due to some . . . er, complications durin' the retrieval of this info."

Bear was the first to pipe up. "What are we supposed to do with this information then, comrade?"

"Simple. We scope out the depot, report back any Thulian presence, and then pendin' a go-order from the Commissar, raid it."

"Any support?" Unter had leaned forward, listening intently.

"Just Vickie on the comm," John said, looking at Unter, "an' each other, I'm afraid. She'll work on getting building plans for the area, as well as anything else pertinent to the operation. Anyways, we'll watch the warehouse for a few days, try an' feel out anything that's going on. We've got all sorts of techno-wizardry to help us, which you were briefed on 'fore y'left Atlanta. Once surveillance is complete, we figure out where to go from there. Questions?" There were none; the Commissar had seen to it that everyone knew as much as possible before they arrived, which wasn't very characteristic of her.

"Now for the boring part."

"And I am not gettink to show anyone my lunge," Old Bear complained, miming what he probably supposed was a sword attack. "Not even at United Hut of Pancakes."

"Is International House of Waffles, dotard." Unter and Bear were both on stake-out duty, and after seven hours in the cramped conditions of the van, Bear's manner was beginning to wear on his comrade.

"Same difference. My English is perfect; jealousy does not become you, friend."

"Bah. *Tikho, Staryj Medved.* Shut up, Old Bear." Unter slumped down in the seat with his arms crossed. But his attitude of apparent inattention was just that—apparent. "*Nasrat.*" He didn't so much as twitch, but Bear's attention was immediately transferred to the place Unter's eyes were glued.

"*Poihol.* What is Delex truck doing here? Is not Europe."

"*Damn good question,*" Vickie said into their ears as the foreign courier truck backed into the warehouse. "*According to everything I just pulled up, that truck should be making a delivery in the Czech Republic right now.*"

"Record and report it. This may be break we are lookink for."

Fifteen hours later, the team was briefed, prepped, and given the go-code by Natalya. Vickie had downloaded them the proper files regarding the building layout, as well as police patrol paths, radio frequencies, and a score of other bits of information.

There had been a slight hiccup in the planning, however; the warehouse was guarded by night security—plain old rent-a-cops. This complicated things, because it meant discretion needed to be used at the outset. The CCCP wasn't out to hurt regular folk, and

John certainly wasn't bloodthirsty enough to take out a couple of regular Joes pulling in a paycheck. After consulting with the team, John had a flash of inspiration.

The two guards were situated in a small gatehouse booth. They spent most of their time listening to sportscasts on the radio, playing cards, or sneaking the odd drink when the traffic to the warehouse was low. The company that had contracted their security firm kept odd hours, but mostly kept to themselves. Workers and trucks, loading and unloading whatever they stored at the building. It didn't really concern the guards, so they never really cared to ask.

They were both debating the merits of redheads versus blonds when they heard a terrible keening noise in the distance. A drunk came stumbling around the corner of the building to their right, belting out a truly horrible song that neither of them could recognize. As he came closer, the older guard stepped out of the booth to confront the man and send him on his way; he continued staggering forward, and the guard could smell cheap whiskey on the man's dirty poncho from a good distance away. "All right, buddy, take it home, or wherever you come from."

"But, mistah, y'sure y'don't got some change fer a vet'ran?" The man tripped over his own feet, lurching forward into the guard. The guard caught him, gasped, and then sank to the ground, unconscious. Just as the second security guard saw the glint of a needle in the drunk's hand, his entire body locked up. Suddenly, he couldn't move, couldn't speak, and was barely able to breathe. Every muscle had gone rigid, and he felt himself topple helplessly over sideways, stiff as a log, into the side of the little guard shack. There he lodged, like a mannequin. He watched with wide eyes as the stranger, obviously *not* drunk at all, strolled up with a needle in his hand.

"Sorry, fella," the man murmured as he bent down. There was a sting, and then there was sleep.

"They're down. Unter, bring the team up." The battered van across the road from the warehouse opened up, three figures dressed in nondescript coveralls exiting. John nodded to Mamona as she came to a stop in front of him; her powers did something weird to a person's nervous system. It's what they'd used to shut down the second guard long enough for John to stick him with the knockout drug they'd been supplied with. "Get 'em both set in the guard booth, and shut the door. We breach the service door in two."

The others did so, stripping out of their coveralls as John removed the poncho; it stank of alcohol, and he could see Bear looking forlorn at the hint of a drink. Each member of the team was outfitted identically, with much the same equipment that John had used on the previous mission. Bear was the exception, due to his mechanical body; he still had a load-bearing vest carrying everything he needed, strapped around his shoulders and waist. He also had rubber slip-on caps for his feet, so that he wouldn't make any noise while walking.

"You have five minutes till the next cop car, ten before the rent-a-cop on the next warehouse makes his rounds, there's nothing on the scanners and no alarms went out." That was Vickie, working her electronic wizardry.

"Roger. Let's move it."

"Remember, if you need magic, I have to have contact with something natural. Wood, dirt, anything but metal and plastic. That means your bare skin on it. Brick will do. Concrete is iffy."

"Gotcha, Sammy. We'll letcha know when to twitch yer nose."

"If you think you're a wit, you're half right."

Mamona was studying the door, casually, but professionally. "Ah think Ah can handle this, y'all." Mamona was an Atlanta street kid, and had a variety of useful skills besides her metahuman abilities.

"Can the chatter and do it, comrade." John was starting to like this new gal's spirit, but he had a job to focus on. Still, he recalled that even when he last did things like this professionally, the best of the best horsed around constantly. It reminded him of a story a friend had told him about two artillery teams. One was completely by the book and clean-cut, and the other was full of jackasses. The two teams decided to have a competition to square away in preparation for a fire mission. The clean-cut team did everything right, but the goofs did everything better, and faster. And had time to throw rocks, while half-naked, at what they described as a "lizard-thing."

Mamona bent down next to the lock, pulling a lock-pick kit from a pouch on her vest. It contained several dozen different picks, jimmies, and other assorted instruments that John couldn't immediately identify. Even with her apparent skill and impressive tools, it took her several minutes to crack the lock; Vickie had given John updated timetables for the police cruiser and security guard that were due on the scene as per their schedules.

"Dammit. Okay, JM. I'm gonna have to make a diversion. Everybody, get flat. I don't want any shadows in that doorway." She repeated it in Russian. *"Vse ujditeiz polia zrenia. Mne ne nuzhny teni v prohode."* John went prone after a moment's hesitation; he didn't like being given vague instructions, but he knew enough that complying was in his best interest.

"Okay. You look good on the camera. Count of five. Piat'... chetyre... tre... dva... e..." An alarm went off down the street, if John was any judge, about three city blocks down the street. *"That was me. Wait for the cops to get past you."* A police cruiser, as if on cue, came around the corner of the street at that moment, followed shortly by another. Both had their roof lights on, and completely bypassed the team as they sped towards Vickie's distraction.

"We clear, Vic?"

"One sec... okay. The guard's gone to see what's up, too."

John switched over to a private comm line to Vickie. "Just gimme a little more heads-up, if'n ya can." He didn't wait for a response, clicking back over to the team channel as they waited for the all-clear.

"Okay. The cops are inside making an eyeball check of the warehouse, and I fried a circuit in there to account for the false alarm. The guard's back on his rounds but he skipped your side of the building to make up for the time he spent rubbernecking. Go."

"Roger. Mamona, wrap it up. We're still on the clock." The team recovered from their prone positions, watching all the areas of approach while Mamona went back to her job.

"Good work takes time, y'all." As an Atlanta native, her accent was deeper and more pronounced than John's. Some of the Russians had trouble understanding her. Sooner than John expected, she gave a gasp of surprise, and the door gave an even quieter click. "We're in."

"All right, stack up, and let's do this." The team formed two separate lines on opposite sides outside of the door. Each member of the team was equipped with an AKSU-74, so they could share ammunition magazines if necessary; it was a favorite of Spetsnaz teams, especially with the affixed sound suppressors that John's team had the good fortune to be issued. Pavel was the odd man out, with his ever-trusty PPSh-41.

Mamona was the only one without a gun; not that she objected, but she hadn't been trained on the AKSU yet. It was something that bothered John, but he had his orders, and there wasn't anything to do about it now. She had knives that she clearly knew how to use, and use well, and she had her powers. John was reminded of a quote from *Star Wars*, as well as an old axiom about knives and gunfights. He shook his head to clear it and focus on the task. John was on point for himself and Mamona, while Unter was in front of Bear. John took what looked like a dentist's mirror to peer under the door, and quickly assessed that there were no immediate threats or traps of any sort. With a quick nod, he pulled the door open. Unter and Bear both button-hooked through the door, while John and Mamona did so simultaneously. John's job was to clear the rightmost corner of the room; it was a reception office, and was completely empty. Once the entire team was inside and had made sure there were no enemies, they closed the door behind them, and regrouped for the next door. This one would take them inside of the warehouse proper, if Vickie's building plans were correct.

"You sure you're right on the money for this, Vic?"

"No guarantees, but there was a fire inspection a month ago. Mandated after the invasion. No one wants people trapped in buildings under fire with chained exits and rooms you can't get out of."

"Roger. Stack up." The door here was smaller than the one to the street, so the entire team had to line up on one side. "Status?" Everyone on the team signaled, "Up," which indicated their weapons were loaded and their gear was checked. Unter took the lead this time, opening the door. The rest of the team flooded in, crouching to stay low while keeping their weapons trained in front of them for any potential targets. John was the last person through the door this time, and what he saw almost literally took his breath away. *We should've brought more guns.*

"Uh. I think you need a bigger boat," Vickie said quietly as her "eyes" on John took in what he was seeing. The warehouse couldn't have been bigger than the plans said, but what filled it made it look much more massive somehow. The armored suits. Hundreds, maybe a thousand of them, standing in ordered ranks, waiting for bodies to fill them. They gleamed with a soft sheen under the dim lights. There were terminals that John immediately recognized as being of Thulian origin. The screens were an eye-burning yellow, the lettering red, the keyboards had never been meant for human hands; they were too broad and had too many

keys, and they were kidney-shaped. *You'd think that an advanced alien race would have more ergonomic tech.* There were dozens of technicians and workers standing around; several resembled the Thulian soldiers John had fought in person recently, while others looked as human as could be. John noted that, filing it away in the back of his mind.

John triggered his throat mic. "We're here for a sneak and peak. Let's snatch some more intel, then scoot the hell outta this joint."

Unter's eyes burned with hatred. "We can take them."

"*Da,* but that ain't what we're here for tonight. We don't have enough personnel, and sure as shit not enough ammo. We figure out what's goin' on here, and then we'll burn the joint down tomorrow night." He looked to each team member in turn. "All right, stick together, and keep quiet."

"*No way they can empty all that shit out overnight, people.*" Vickie didn't have to whisper, but she was doing so anyway. It was a funny habit that John had noticed about tense situations. The team crept forward, using shipping crates, weird metal containers, and even armored suits for concealment. The Thulians continued going on about their business; it looked like they were preparing several of the Nazi suits for transport in the Delex truck that the CCCPers had spotted earlier.

"This looks to beink major catheter of transport for the *fashista,* comrades."

Mamona piped up. "Pavel, where'd y'all say you learned English again?"

"Watching Ricky Lake and *E.R.*, of course. Is not where all Americans learn?"

"*Could be worse,*" Vickie said on JM's private channel. "*Coulda been Springer.*"

John could almost feel Unter's mental face-palm.

A new voice came in on the channel. "*Comrade Murdock,*" Red Saviour said crisply. "*Please to be remembering your orders. Once intel is secure, I will to be organizing proper immolation party.*"

"We're on it." The team crept forward, keeping adequate spacing between each member. "Our goal is the foreman's office, in the southwest corner of the building. We get in there, snag anything of importance, and then get the hell out." John absorbed as much about his surroundings as he could in as little time as he could manage. The big thing was to make sure he had his area of responsibility covered; with Vickie looking through her set of "eyes" on him, there was an ongoing recording, and anything he missed, she should catch, or would get later when the home team looked through the record. The lighting was dim, orange sodium bulbs that always seemed to make the shadows look deeper. The Thulians moving through the warehouse looked almost androgynous and identical, lemmings following one another and going through the same mechanical routine.

Mamona was sweeping her eyes over her sector when she caught the guard; a roving sentry on an upper catwalk that was sneaking a cigarette in a corner, away from the prying eyes of his superiors, she guessed. He spotted the team of CCCPers in the middle of taking a drag on his smoke; the burning coal reflected from the lenses of the odd goggles he was wearing, lighting them up like a crazed devil's pupils. He was just about to exhale when Mamona flipped one of her blades over, paused for a moment to gauge the distance, and threw the knife.

Sailing end over end, the blade connected with the Thulian guard, catching him in the throat. John's altered hearing heard the man's dying gurgle, and he immediately centered his rifle at the source of the noise. Another few milliseconds to assess the threat, and John pulled the trigger twice; two suppressed rounds from his AKSU-74 hit the guard's head. As if in slow motion, John noticed that the guard already had a weapon drawn from a hip holster; the gun looked like something fresh from a *Commando Cody: Sky Marshal of the Universe* episode. A reflex action moments before John had fired, the gun was pointed towards the ceiling, and fired. It didn't have much of a sound signature; kind of like a bug zapper with the volume turned down. What was very obvious, however, was the bright blue-white glow it gave off, lighting up that entire corner of the warehouse. *All of their damned weapons fire that blue raygun crap.*

The muzzle blast and light from the weapon's beam perfectly and unfortunately outlined the team. The Thulians scattered throughout the warehouse all immediately turned to see what the disturbance was.

"Soldat! Was machen Sie?" came a barked query.

Untermensch was the first to orient himself and fire at the Thulian that had spoken. The alien crumpled as the bullets struck him. The team dispersed and took cover behind crates and boxes;

it seemed as if everyone was shooting almost immediately. The suppressed rifles cracked the air like some sort of maniacal sewing machine, while the Thulians' weapons fizzled and burned through the air. Wherever the blue beams impacted, the impact area melted, splattering gobs of concrete and metal in all directions. John barked into his comm, "Vic, we've got trouble! Any help?"

"I"m gonna send a big surge through their electrics." Saviour repeated what Vic said a second later in Russian, *"I sobirajus' poslat' moshnij impul's cherez ih elektroprovodku."*

"Get the snoopers on. Flash first. Watch out for falling glass. On three. Two. One..." Every light bulb in the warehouse exploded in a shower of sparks at that moment; more of Vickie's techno-wizardry at play, whether legitimate magic or just her awesome hacking abilities, John didn't know. The team already had their NVGs mounted, and it only took a few precious seconds to fix them over their eyes and turn the monocles on. The warehouse was lit up by the infrared lights that the NVGs used in total dark situations; the blue-white beams from the Nazi guns came out the characteristic night-vision green, scintillating across the team's vision. The sparks, raygun fire, and muzzle flashes from the rifles all played merry-hell with John's goggles, so he turned the light gain down with his off hand, still firing. Some of the Thulians were climbing into the armored suits, powering them up to help fight off the interlopers.

"Don't let them get in the suits! You guys don't have armor-piercing rounds!"

"Stay tight, and pick your shots! Get anyone going for a suit!" John gritted his teeth as he expended the last rounds in his weapon's magazine. "Mag change!" He hit the magazine release, his free hand already prying a fresh ammunition magazine from his LCH and slamming it home into the magazine well. He charged the rifle's bolt, and began firing again.

"Frag out!" It sounded like either Unter or Bear; the team hunkered down slightly, still firing, when a tremendous explosion went off several meters to John's right. It was still close enough to rattle his teeth in his skull. John could make out several Thulians screaming while the shrapnel and debris settled. *That's gonna get some attention.* The police officers were only a few blocks away; even if they hadn't heard the explosion, someone nearby might call it in.

The team was pinned down, facing far too many Thulians for his own taste. If any of them were able to get into their monstrous suits, the cover that John and his comrades were hiding behind would quickly turn into only so much easily destroyed concealment. Cops would be here soon, maybe even that one security guard; more people that would be caught in the crossfire and probably killed. Probably? He'd seen with his own eyes how cops with sidearms fared against those suits. They might as well be kids armed with water guns.

Mamona was keeping low behind cover, making herself as small as possible. Since she didn't have a firearm or training with one—a fact that John was seriously regretting at the moment—she was focusing her energies elsewhere. She was using her metahuman powers to disrupt the aim of as many Thulians as possible. It was working, but only barely; even with the team taking down the Thulians at a fair rate, there were just too many of them for her to keep tabs on. Eventually, she was going to lose it, and one of them would connect with a shot on someone in the team.

John was thinking at a mile a minute. He knew how this was going to end unless the team could withdraw; they wouldn't be able to fight their way out and concentrate on the Thulians going for suits, though. They were surrounded and outgunned.

At that moment, he felt something horrible well up inside of him, engulfing him in a maelstrom of pain and memory. Frozen solid, he stopped firing and—almost unthinkably, given that he was trained to the point of instinct and muscle memory—dropped his rifle. His entire body started to spasm. Visions of jungle canopy, muzzle flashes through night vision, friends and comrades gunned down and left bleeding flashed through his mind and took the place of the warehouse around him until that was all there was, all there ever had been, all there ever would be...

John screamed uncontrollably; it wasn't out of fear or anger, but a guilt so fierce it was eating him alive. The weapons' fire from both sides slackened momentarily at the almost inhuman sound coming from him.

Dimly he heard a voice that used to be familiar screaming in his ear. *"Lozshites' na zeml'u e ukroites'! Bistro! DROP AND COVER! NOW!"*

There was one, tiny, sane little bit of his mind left—just enough to register that the concrete floor suddenly erupted all around his friends, that shields of earth and broken cement mounded above every member of the CCCP team except for him with a roar like a Richter 8 earthquake, and the ground around him shook, knocking some of the nearest Thulians off their feet.

Half standing, John threw his arms out wide, his back arched. He was exposed to the Thulians, and still screaming when it happened. A low boom sounded throughout the warehouse as a giant pulse of plasma exploded outwards from where John stood. Everything near him was bathed in flame, waves of fire splashing over everything. Metal, even the Thulian alloys in the suits and equipment, turned red and white-hot in an instant, exploding from the sudden temperature change. Boxes were blown apart, and concrete split open. The Thulians were incinerated almost immediately, not even conscious long enough to feel pain; several had their silhouettes burned into the brick behind them at the first blast of the fire storm.

John shook, screaming and crying, as pulses of fire raced away from his body. Then, as suddenly as it had erupted, the fires ended, and with them, his strength, He dropped to the floor, panting, for a moment lost in confusion. Where was he? What—

Behind and around him, mounds of smoking, blackened—and in some places, vitrified—earth erupted up again, freeing his comrades from their improvised shelters. Unter was the first to leap out. "*Nasrat!*" he spat. It seemed like the entire warehouse was on fire; the entire place looked like something out of a Baptist minister's brimstone sermon with the few Thulian suits still standing passing for demons.

The world of the *real* flooded back to him. He was *here* again. "Finish the job," came John's shaky reply.

"*Take them,*" said Vickie, and Saviour at the same time barked something in Russian.

There were very few Thulians left alive, much less able to fight back. The CCCPers dispatched them easily; with Mamona concentrating her disruptive powers on such a small number of targets, the team was able to eliminate them with concerted rifle fire.

John coughed heavily, holding his headset close. "We need to clear out. We sure as hell are gonna get some attention, now. Everyone, pull out an' head to the van, an' do so on the bounce."

"Cops are holding; fire's on the way. I leaked it was Thulian; anonymous tip from someone at a pay phone who saw a couple of Nazi suits and was running away scared."

"Good. That means they'll let this joint burn a bit more, an' don't think it's a crime scene just yet."

Bear, bringing up the rear of the team's formation as they jogged through the burning wreckage, shouted, "Comrades! I know perfect song for occasion! 'Da roof, da roof, da roof is on fire! Let the mother—!'"

"Pavel!" Saviour growled. *"Enough!"*

"*Da*, Commissar. I will restrain my exuberance."

"Keep your heads down. Blacksnake is sticking its nose in."

The team exited the warehouse easily enough with the confusion outside, generated by the fire department, the police, and several other entities in official-looking flak vests that Vickie had managed to call to the scene; they were just another bunch of ash-smudged workers amongst the rest.

"There's carry-out steak coming to meet you at the suite. Firm is called 'Takeout Taxi,' branded car, driver is named Tony." Vickie allowed a hint of concern to creep into her voice. *"Be careful on the way back, gang.*

"Private channel, Johnny, You need anything special?" An ironic tone crept into her voice. *"I'm . . . kind of an expert on aftermaths. Name it, I can arrange for it to be delivered. Vodka with a Valium chaser, for instance."*

John sighed, swaying with the battered van as it bumped along the road. "The three B's wouldn't be all that bad."

"Beer, bath and—what, exactly?"

"Wouldn't be gentlemanly fer me to say."

"Broads. Beer is in the fridge, you're in the hot-tub suite if you check the bathroom. Broads, you're on your own."

John half-smiled. "What do we pay ya for, then?" Without waiting for a reply, he removed the earpiece, resting his head against the van's metal wall with a heavy sigh. *Perfect end to an utterly imperfect day. Quit your bellyaching, loser. You'll have plenty of time to mull this over on the trip home.* With that parting thought, John indulged in one of the oldest traditions of the infantry: catching a catnap.

CHAPTER SIX

Nox Aurumque
(Night and Gold)

MERCEDES LACKEY

While we were "housecleaning," so to speak, the Seraphym was doing some housecleaning of her own. It seems that we were not the only ones who were not inclined to sit down and wail.

Of all the burdens that the entity called the Seraphym carried, the heaviest was obedience. How many times she had longed to intervene, only to be told "It is not permitted," or "This and this only is permitted"! How many times had she wept to see the mortal lives snuffed out or ruined . . . yet known that the *reason* she was told "It is not permitted" was because she was *not* the Infinite, that however powerful, she *was* limited and that there would always be ones she could not help because she was stretched too far . . .

Already she did far more than anyone ever guessed. Mostly what was needed were such small things—a flash of light in the eyes, a breath of air to deflect, a flash of knowledge just *before* something happened, a whisper of warning in time to plan. But for all these things, she had to be there. They could not be done from afar. And sometimes, there *was* direct intervention.

It was what the mortals called "The Lifesaver's Dilemma"; if the lifesaver drowns trying to save too many, who will save the swimmers in the future?

Obedience saved her. Obedience saved those who would matter in the days to come.

But it did not help to know this.

Rebellion was also a burden. Not because rebellion was forbidden, but because of how it was permitted. It must not be because of pride, or wishing only to glorify one's own self. It must not be because of hate, or even dislike. It must not be—well there were many causes for which one must not rebel. That was the thing that those who had rebelled and Fallen did not understand. There was room even for rebellion in the Infinite. But it had to be the right sort of rebellion. It had to be less rebellion and more . . . creativity.

One could only rebel when the Infinite itself was silent. When neither she nor any other Siblings could See a way.

When it cost one's own self dearly. When rebellion became a sacrifice.

When it was, truly, for the greatest good, the greatest number.

Thus far, the Seraphym had not yet found the time and place to rebel. But this—this might be the time and place.

The Thulians were about to descend in force upon a little town in the red clay hills of Georgia. They were going to wipe it from the face of the earth, and every living thing, down to the insects, in it.

The Seraphym had not Seen this becoming a certainty until—well, until a mortal hour ago, when an earnest conclave had swayed a single mind, and that mind had given the order. And that had been set in motion by the contacting of an aging, bitter man in Hungary. And *that* had been set in motion by something the Doppelgaenger had learned. And—

Well . . . it was fruitless to speculate further. As always with the futures, nothing was certain, until just before it was.

And now . . . now 9,376 men, women and children, and countless creatures that were not human, would suffer from the arrogance of one creature.

By the time Echo or CCCP learned of this, it would be too late. Angusburo would be a plate of glass. There was no one to stand between the Thulians and their goal.

Except her.

She stood, invisible to mortal eyes, between the Thulians and the place they would destroy. She would not suffer this to happen.

The Infinite was silent, thus far. She had not been told "This is not permitted"—but she had not been told that it was.

The Death Spheres were not in sight, but black clouds boiled up with terrifying speed on the horizon, and she knew they were inside. This was new. The technology to make the clouds triggered fearful lightnings within them. This was also new.

She dropped that which made her invisible. She called her aura of fire, her spear, her shield, and her sword. She would give them warning. They had seen her at work. She would give them the chance to turn back.

The clouds surged towards her, alive with lightning. Behind her, the people of the town were running for cover, certain this was some freak storm that held a tornado, or worse. How much worse, they did not yet know. Most of them still either did not see her, their minds refusing to encompass her, or saw her and thought she was some Echo meta, here because—well they did not bother to wonder why, as they headed for their basements. Seeking shelter was paramount in their minds, and everyone knew there were no metas whose powers included controlling the weather.

And still the Infinite was silent.

They came at her in silence, and she saw them despite the cloaking clouds. Then the clouds engulfed her.

With a thought, she burned them away, spreading her flame-wings wide, wide, creating a sphere of clear air within the cloud bank. The lightning struck her, but she felt it only as a distant pain, one that meant nothing to her. It was not that she could not be hurt—it was that she did not *care* if she was hurt. It lashed her, and she made it her own, taking it away from them and surrounding herself with its dance.

Still, they came, so sure of their own mastery. They thought they had studied her; they thought they had an answer to her.

She let her voice thunder in their minds.

Stop.

The energy cannons whined defiance. She felt the same defiance in the crews of the ships. She was only one being; how could she presume to stop them? She saw the commander call up his library of information, find her, and swiftly review what little there was—and reject it. The other captains had been mistaken, or inferior, or caught unaware. She could not withstand them.

You shall not do this thing. I shall not allow it.

"It's a bluff!" she heard the commander of the fleet below communicate to the other ships. "She's never taken a stand like this before, and she won't win now!"

Oh, she said into their minds. *Be not so certain. Go. This place is not for your taking. Go and live, stay and die.*

And—

Defiance. The defiance of those who see no other path but their own will. The ships began to move on her.

And in the still, profound, and waiting silence of her heart, she heard, with great sadness, *So like the ones lost to us... Seraphym, it is permitted.*

"I bring you Fire and the Sword!" she cried—not with joy, oh no, never with joy for such a task, but with release. The words rang across the sky.

The Seraphym danced.

To oppose mortal, material force, she must be, if not mortal, certainly material. Oh, she *could* have waved a hand and obliterated them all in a wash of plasma, but that was not appropriate. Each creature in this fleet must be given his own opportunity to rebel, to turn back. And for that, she must take them one by one.

And they must all see it, and be aware of what she did.

This was the work of an Instrument; always, always, the wicked must be given that chance to repent, to redeem themselves, for forgiveness was always possible. So she danced, and the first ship that she danced with came at her with newly hardened tentacles reaching with inhuman speed, and energy cannon seeking to lock onto her. But a moment, a heartbeat later, the tentacles were raining down on a pasture, severed by her sword, and the ship reeled beneath the beams of its own cannon deflected back to it by her shield. Then with a leap, she was atop it; her spear piercing the heart of the control mechanism, her hand hitting the metal of the shell with a hollow, gonglike *boom.*

She leapt away; the ship canted sideways, half its flight controls gone. She ignored it; it was of no more moment to her. Undaunted—or perhaps unobservant—another was attacking.

Near-infinite power wielded by precise control; that was the work of an Instrument. No less than what was needed, but not one particle more. This time as she landed, a cascade of fire waterfalled from her down the sides of the ship—a white-hot waterfall that fused the portals for the weapons shut, and blinded the ship, a torrent of plasma that was *so* hot and fierce that it did so and dissipated without cooking the crew inside—though the climate controls nearly fused themselves trying to compensate. As the ship blundered off, blind and deaf, she leapt again.

Her fire-wings buffeted the next ship, destroying the sensors an instant after blinding the crew. She left the weapons live on this one; the tentacles flailed aimlessly, the cannon blasted, and it left three more of its kin mortally wounded in the half minute after she left it and moved on.

In his ship at the rear, the commander screamed at his captains, ordering them to destroy her, berating them for incompetence and worse. The black clouds boiled up again as she waited amid the dying ships of the front rank, giving the rest yet another opportunity to turn back.

Instead, heedless of their crippled fellows around her, they opened up on her, pouring an inferno down upon her.

Of *course* it hurt. She had a physical body—one that renewed itself as fast as it was injured, but a physical body nevertheless. The trick, as T.E. Lawrence famously said, was not minding that it hurt. Pain is information. The information is that the body is injured. Her body was already healed by the time the pain registered. The information was not relevant. She could ignore it.

Ignore it, even as her body was burned and renewed, burned and renewed, for as long as they poured their deadly energies into the spot where she hovered.

Even the Thulians could not keep up such a barrage forever. One by one, the exhausted guns flickered and went out. And she remained, burning, burning, within the fires of her own creation, the fires of the Infinite, wings of flame spreading wide once more.

In his craft, the commander screamed imprecations at his underlings. Briefly she bowed her head. There was doubt in them. But the habit of obedience was bred into them. There was only one way to end this.

And again, she moved.

From ship to ship she leapt or flew, a slash of sword or spear crippling each as she passed over it. Some of these creatures would die. Some already had. With each death, the spear and sword felt heavier in her hands, laden with death, tarnished with tears. And yet, they burned the brighter for that.

At last she came to the ship of the commander, who thought he was safe, in his one undistinguished ship among all the rest just like it, insulated, isolated, at the rear of the flotilla.

She hovered, wings barely beating, and gazed at him through the lenses of his cameras. She knew that her face, her eyes, filled the picture in his viewscreen. Her mind bored into his, as her sun-bright eyes bored into his.

It is as I told you. You shall not do this thing. Turn back.

But in him was only madness, and that madness frothed and ordered destruction.

So be it. So you have chosen.

She flung the spear.

It pieced the heart of the ship, burned through it as if it were paper, transfixing the commander to his chair and turning him to ash in the blink of an eye.

As she called back the spear to her hand, the crew of the ship utterly stunned, she spoke again into all their minds.

Go. Leave this place. Never return.

And now, without their leader to urge them on, they fled as best they could, trailing smoke and flames, and taking their unnatural storm with them.

And weary, weary with war and tears, she flew heavily away, back to Atlanta, back to one place, at least, where she could rest.

She drifted down out of the night sky onto a roof where a mortal man she still did not understand was resting too, after battle, his arms folded along a crude concrete parapet, a bottle of beer in one hand, untasted.

He did not turn around as she landed, but she knew he knew she was there.

"Well, Angel," he drawled, finally taking a sip of his drink. "Whatcha been up to?"

She considered many answers, and settled for one. "Much the same as ever," she replied. "And you, John Murdock?"

The furtive man delivered the memory card to the one who had offered so very much money for footage of the Seraphym "in action."

"I hope this is all you said it is," the man said, in a neutral voice.

"It's like all the other footage, you don't see anything of her but this . . . light thing. But you sure as hell see what she does," he replied. "I wasn't exaggerating."

The buyer held the little card up to the light and considered it. "In that case, it's worth every penny." He jerked his head at the videographer. "Pay the man."

A coldly beautiful woman who moved in a fashion that suggested she was as deadly as she was lovely handed over a thick stack of hundreds. The furtive man scuttled away.

"I hope this is what you want, Dom," said Khanjar. "It certainly cost enough."

Dominic Verdigris only smiled.

CHAPTER SEVEN

Chasing Shadows

MERCEDES LACKEY AND CODY MARTIN

Verd was ruthless, and no fool. You don't get where he is by being reckless, nor by taking anything at face value. If you are someone like Verdigris, you test first, and you test, if possible, to destruction.

Dominic Verdigris III did not like to be kept waiting. It had been over an hour since he had sent a message to People's Blade, summoning her to his office. Since she had come to him offering her services, Verdigris had gone to great lengths to keep her under a watchful eye. Satellite surveillance, tracking devices, plainclothes agents to follow her; he had even dispatched Khanjar to tail the General's movements. All of it was to no avail; somehow, Shen Xue was always able to slip away, seemingly at will. It annoyed Verdigris; it wasn't a feeling he was very accustomed to dealing with for a prolonged period of time. Most things that bothered him were taken care of, quickly or quietly or brutally, whatever the situation required.

And aside from the annoyance, there was another disquieting emotion associated with People's Blade; a feeling of powerlessness. He had not felt powerless in a very, very long time, and now he was confronted with being unable to control not one, but two creatures—that so-called "angel," and now People's Blade. He didn't like it. And he intended to change things.

He stabbed a finger at his desk's display, bringing up the intercom. "Khanjar, have someone bring in a stiff drink, or five. And keep looking for her. I don't want to spend all night on this."

He let a hint of his annoyance creep into his voice, but none of his apprehension; it wouldn't do to let anyone see him start to doubt. His mind was going in circles, like a mouse in a wheel, unable to come up with a way to get control of this situation. It had to begin with People's Blade. She was the only creature he'd found with a chance of capturing that "angel" for him, so far. And that meant he had to control People's Blade. Only he *hadn't* been able to control People's Blade...

"*Ni hao,* Dominic Verdigris."

One moment the office had been empty. Now, there she was. Relaxed. An arrogant calmness of purpose, denoting her presumptions of superiority. Damn her. *I'm not going to flinch in front of her. I'd rather piss glass.* "How nice of you to grace us with your presence, General. I had almost given up hope of seeing you tonight."

One elegant eyebrow rose. "I have many things that occupy my attention, barbarian. I attend to them in their order of importance." She shifted her weight slightly. "I assume this is about a matter of importance to you?"

"That it is; thus it's important to both of us, and our shared cause. Wouldn't you agree?" He didn't give her an opportunity to reply; he needed to take control of this conversation. "I have a task for you. Should you prove successful in what I have laid out for you, I will have more... pertinent things for you to attend to. Things vital to the war against the Thulians." The edge of his mouth quirked in a smile as he leaned forward. "Interested? Or is your schedule too cluttered, General?"

"So, despite what you already know, you have decided I must pass some childish little test to prove my worth?" The General didn't sneer. Somehow, the fact that she didn't curl those young lips made her contempt all the more apparent. "Really, Verdigris, this is a waste of both of our time."

Verdigris shrugged. "It is something I need done, and need to be certain will be handled appropriately. If you won't do it, I can pass it off to some lesser minion, but I'm all about the efficiency of effort with my plans. I'd much rather you took it, so I could rest easy." There was a slight hidden in there, and he knew that the General would see the implication. *Will she rise to the bait, though?* "Besides, you don't even know what I'm going to ask you to do, yet."

People's Blade half-lidded her eyes. "True. It might be worth my while, if it is challenging enough. All right, barbarian. What is your foolish test?"

"Challenging as you asked, so it's sure to not disappoint. This is a special case. In the war we're fighting, there are going to be losses. In an effort to keep that to a minimum, with regards to winning the battles more efficiently, we will need the right weapons. In this particular case, the weapon is a person." He tapped on the display in front of him, bringing up several very grisly pictures of crime scenes. "We need the man that was responsible for these... gruesome images."

People's Blade looked at the displayed pictures without even a hint of flinching or distaste. "Interesting, but I see only the savage hand of a common criminal. What is it that differentiates this creature from any other mass slayer?"

"One, he's never been caught. This individual was given the code name 'Shadow-Storm' by Echo. His or her list of exploits is long, but surprisingly mundane: racketeering, bank robbery, extortion, blackmail, and plainly some rather messy murders. He operated for over forty years, and never once was caught or even seemingly hurt, even when confronted with nigh insurmountable odds." Verdigris tapped on the screen again. "Two: This is what he did to an advanced reaction team from Echo." Another image came to life on the display; it was hard to tell where the room began and the bodies ended. "Those were three OpThrees and an OpTwo, all of some small fame. They were torn to shreds.

"During his career, this Shadow-Storm is estimated to have accumulated quite the fortune, but never seemed to do much besides run-of-the-mill savagery and crime, with a few grandiose capers thrown in. Then, suddenly, he dropped off the map. Echo's detectives had several sources that confirmed that the subject had died in a plane crash." Verdigris steepled his fingers in front of his chest. "However, I have quite a few more resources at my command than Echo does. I've found this Shadow-Storm. Given his past, I think he could be useful against our enemies." *And not just the Thulians; there are more enemies in this world for a man like me than you can imagine, General. You're probably one of them.*

"So, you ask me to recruit this creature for you, with no more information than this?" The eyebrow rose again. "I fail to see how he could be useful. I suspect your quaint little bodyguard could accomplish similar goals. Certainly she could serve the same function as I, if you insist on recruiting him."

"Khanjar has her uses, but every weapon is suited to one type of a task or another. This one does not suit her. Truth be told, we don't have much more information on this target. Which is precisely why I'm sending *you* to deal with him." With a quick twist of his hand, the screen cleared. "And that is the third reason. All that we know about his powers are that he somehow uses shadows, manipulates them in some way. Recordings from the victims' comm units are fragmentary, but there are shouts about 'the shadows' before the comm links ended—sometimes in screams, truth be told. From the results, we can presume he's extremely deadly; he's been given a probable classification of OpFour, due to the length of time he was active, the destructiveness of his abilities, and the fact that no one could even seem to hurt him." Verdigris leaned back in his chair, tilting his head to the side. "Will you take this on? If so, we have his location and a jet to fly you there, ready immediately."

There was a little glint in Shen Xue's eyes. "Well. You have intrigued me. I believe there is—how is it you barbarians put it?—room in my schedule."

"Excellent." *Touchdown.* He reached into his jacket, pulling forth a small envelope. "This has most of what you will require: pass for the jet, a card for expenses, access to our armories and equipment locker. Just make sure to sign out for anything; no, don't bother me with it, that's for whoever is in charge of those areas. Also, there's a cell phone. Keep me updated, if it pleases you, General."

People's Blade said nothing; took the pass, left the card and the phone. Did not so much bow as incline her head ever so slightly. Then she just sauntered out, with a very slight swagger in her step. A few moments later, Khanjar entered, carrying a tray with glasses of Scotch and a small bucket of ice.

Khanjar was frowning. "Why was that... *thing* here?" she asked. "I do not trust it. It is arrogant, and it distracts you."

And she puts you on edge; worried about our position on the food chain, dear?

"She *is* arrogant, and you certainly shouldn't trust her, dear. But sometimes even dangerous foes can be put to a very good use.

People's Blade is one such foe, and I have many uses in store for her." He fished one of the glasses off of the tray, sipping at the drink. "Never forget; just because someone is against you doesn't mean you can't still use them for your own ends."

"He who uses a crocodile as a stepping stone generally loses a foot," Khanjar replied crossly. "Don't come complaining when that thing betrays you. And it will."

He feigned a look of hurt. "Darling, you misjudge me. I'm not blind; she's using us, as much as we're using her. She simply thinks she's on the winning side of the equation. Everyone breaks faith, everyone betrays, *everyone* becomes a traitor; life has taught me that, if nothing else. It's a matter of when, and how it can be used to our benefit." He chuckled, taking another drink. "If I had half a mind, I could immortalize myself with a proverb book, or something equally egotistical."

"You already waste too much time adding to the Evil Overlord lists," she countered. "Why did you not give the 'useful' monster the files on Shadow-Storm?"

"You mean the complete files?" He laughed a little. "Simple. I didn't want her to have them. We'll see how well she can adapt. If she wins over the target to our side, we have another tool at our disposal. If she fails, then we still gain; we'll be left with one less enemy to keep a watch over... one less *distraction*, as you put it. I imagine that'd please you quite a bit."

"Well, you had better hope that Shadow-Storm never discovers it was you that sent her." Khanjar's frown deepened. "I do not wish to have to counter an assassin that uses magic. It is not my strong suit."

Magic. Pff. Khanji's superstitions win out again. No matter how hard he tried, he still couldn't seem to cure her of her insistence that some metas were actually magicians. Or worse, wholly supernatural. "My dear, in my experience there are very few things that can't be bought, reasoned with, or killed. In that order, preferably." He waved at a chair. "Don't trouble yourself with it. Drink your scotch before it becomes too watered down. We have to sit through another fundraiser for the opera house this evening."

SUNSET MANOR: HOME AT LAST. That was what the expensive, sandblasted, laser-cut redwood sign said in Victorian-style lettering. It was not what Shen Xue had been expecting. Volcanic lair? Unlikely, but possible. High-tech safe house? Certainly. High-tech safe house hiding beneath the facade of a warehouse or a tenement or a half-abandoned old farmhouse? Almost not worth mentioning the near certainty of it.

But an *entire* expensive, exclusive, gated community for wealthy, retired people, disinclined to put their trust in their former servants or current relatives? Definitely not.

Presumably by prowling on the network of computer connections that Shen Xue loathed, one could discover a certain amount about this place. It would almost certainly be all a front. Shen Xue preferred to do his investigations the old-fashioned way: with his feet on the ground and the wind in his hair. Nothing else gave a man proper grounding for a battlefield.

Walls were hardly even an afterthought to him; once inside with a uniform stolen from one of the grounds-keeping staff, his Chinese features and a pushcart laden with gardening tools ensured he would be ignored. He entered the community early in the morning, with the rest of the laborers; another female ethnic face as part of the "help" was nothing for anyone to pay attention to.

He learned that Sunset Manor was extensively patrolled by a well-trained security staff; that visitors were only permitted during daylight hours and required much the same identification procedures as anyone gaining admittance to, say, Echo HQ, complete with identification tags that broadcast their whereabouts. He learned that staff also had these tags, but as long as he stayed a respectable distance away from the rest, with his hands busy in the dirt, no one checked to see if he actually possessed such a tag, and there was no way to flag someone untagged out in the open.

The General also learned that Sunset Manor had three tiers of residents. The third tier were those who were bedridden; these were housed in luxurious "apartments" that were as unlike the standard "nursing home" room as an Italian villa was unlike Chinese government housing. The second tier were those who were infirm, but not bedridden; these were housed in true luxury "apartments" and looked after by staff assiduously. The first tier were those who qualified as "assisted living"—and could have been living in their old homes, presumably, except that they no longer trusted the honesty of their own staff or their heirs (who could bribe their staff). Here they had the assurance that the staff was hired by an impartial outside source, their belongings were inventoried on a daily basis, and similarly impartial accountants kept track of every penny. And all of those pennies went towards paying extravagant fees to ensure that everything was in place. Extravagant perhaps... but cheaper than being robbed by the maids, the heirs, the accountant using *their* funds on *his* speculations. And of course, there was the safety. Despite more than a few of the residents having lists of enemies that would rival those of third-world dictators, everyone here was absolutely safe. You could safely leave your doors unlocked and your windows open, when state-of-the-art security was monitoring your home with an exactitude presidents would envy. You need not concern yourself about thieves, Thulians, natural disasters, insurrections... in exchange for privacy and a none-too-modest amount of money, you need never worry again.

In this first tier, unlike the model-village look of most "retirement communities," individual expression in architecture was encouraged. So the handsome minimansions spread across acres and acres of property were of styles ranging from ultramodern to antique.

Among such a disparity, the original Victorian mansion that had stood on the original property did not even stand out, except for the old-growth trees and plantings on its grounds. You couldn't successfully transplant an oak or a beech with a girth that was several feet around, nor peony and rose bushes standing six feet tall.

The General was able to pick out the house from his first glance. Instinct counted for as much as intellect, in his experience. What "intelligence" he was able to gather from listening to the other workers, seeing who went where... it was clear where the "boss" lived, even if no one truly acknowledged it. The old home that the community was built around had taken on the air of a legend; it was maintained, but not *too* well. It never had anyone come out, but deliveries were regularly made and always by different people.

He is there. He does not want anyone to know it, but one cannot help some things. And besides intellect, besides intelligence, besides instinct, there were... the senses. The General was a creature of magic and legend. Like called to like, and he sensed the magic in that house, magic that appeared nowhere else on the grounds. Now he understood why Verdigris had wanted *him* to pursue this creature, and not Khanjar. He was uniquely suited to this task; the General was a scalpel, in this case, and she was an axe. *It would not do to send peasants after dragons, when a warrior is called for. For a barbarian, he seems to understand at least this truth.*

So, now the question: how to penetrate this edifice, which was surely better guarded than any other on the grounds, and approach the owner? Simple; walk through the front door. He had already proven himrself; he had penetrated the worst of the overt security, for the outer perimeter was the most heavily guarded. After that, it was assumed that there wouldn't be anyone dangerous enough to get close, no more than the occasional geriatric who had become lost on the golf course. Why take the chance of setting off alarms before one even had a chance to speak? Someone as obsessed over his own protection as this target was... it would be much better to take the direct approach. Dressed as a member of the staff, with the Jade Emperor's Whisper hidden in a golf club bag, it was easy enough to walk to the front door of the old Victorian house near the center of the property.

One hopes this Shadow-Storm has not degenerated into senility, the General thought, his hand on the door. *After all this... it would be a grave disappointment.* Taking a breath, the General twisted the handle and gently pushed the door inwards, placing his sword hand inside of the golf bag.

The sound of a chime marked his entry. Nothing more.

Inside, the antique house was decorated in a curiously Spartan style, almost Oriental in its simplicity—the so-called "Swedish Modern" look, executed in the finest of materials and workmanship. The tall, narrow windows were shrouded in wooden slat blinds and plain curtains, allowing very little light in from the fading sun.

There was no answer to that chime. Not by the appearance of a servant, nor a voice. There were cameras, however. Many, many cameras. They seemed to sprout from every corner, and all of them were tracking him automatically. Shen Xue was not familiar enough with the interiors of houses like this to tell if the layout was normal. He stood in a small entryway; to his left, a staircase led upwards. To his right, a hallway ended in a closed door, with two more closed doors along the right-hand wall. Up, or further in? Or wait for a response? *Action. Never look behind; dive forward with all of one's might.* Well, perhaps not "diving." The General paced deliberately forward. Most main rooms were on the ground floor, in his experience. But he was presented with the choice of three closed doors. Which?

He chose the middle; the second door along the wall. Tactics said to choose the center of the enemy's power; the logic was as ancient and as proven as the General.

The door opened with little effort.

It was a room full of electronics. Or rather, of electronic screens. It looked strangely like one of those decadent display rooms for expensive televisions, except that the screens were all the same sort, and each one showed a different view of some point—presumably in this house. The screens were the only light sources in the room; most of it was draped in heavy shadows. In the center of the room was a wheelchair, and in the wheelchair was a man.

"So, they've finally sent someone, have they? I was starting to wonder if I was important enough to kill anymore." He was wizened, decrepit; skin hanging off of bones, looking feeble. Was this what the barbarian had sent her for? A living corpse?

"The world has been somewhat preoccupied," Shen Xue said politely. This was, after all, an elder. "Also, perhaps you have been mistaken in my purpose."

"Oh, what's your purpose, eh? A little fanny to seduce me while you cut my throat? No one comes in here, missy. No one living."

"Negotiation," suggested the General. "The world has greater concerns at the moment than the sins of the past."

The man sneered. "The past? Lemme tell you about the past. Snubbed! That's what I was! Everything I have ever done, for nothing. Nothing but a graveyard, full of walking corpses and what's left of them that don't walk anymore. Everything I've done... for nothing!" He jabbed a crooked finger at her. "Negotiation? What negotiation? What can you offer me that I couldn't steal for myself still, hmm?"

Shen Xue considered this, with growing impatience. Verdigris had sent him on a fool's errand. Verdigris may well have known this. But if he did not... this impertinent creature was not worthy of Shen Xue's time, but the General also did not wish to permit anyone more to know of his own considerable abilities. This meant killing him, which would be a pleasure after the insulting way the creature had spoken to him, elder or not. But it would have to be killing him in a way that Verdigris could not put down to pique.

"I fail to see that you are able to steal anything more than my time, broken old man." The General looked down his nose at the man in the wheelchair. "Boast to the shadows and wind, I am done with you. If you are truly brave, you will end your own wretched existence yourself. Only a coward would continue a life so shrunken." Deliberately, he turned his back, expecting to hear the sound of a weapon.

"Fucking Chink," said the man in a growl. The General tensed. There was no sound other than that insult. But something...

Instinct warned and her senses were on fire, and Shen Xue acted on that instinct, pulling Jade Emperor's Whisper from the golf bag with one hand, and flinging the bag in the direction of the threat he sensed with the other.

The bag exploded in the air as a tendril of *shadow* whipped from a corner, ripping through the bag and scattering the bent clubs. The General was holding the jian in a low ready, eyes scanning the room. The shadows seemed to be roiling like black clouds, as if they were... restless and *alive. What sorcery is this?* "You use tricks when your opponent has their back turned. It is the mark of a dishonorable cur, old man."

The man cackled, and rose easily from his wheelchair; no longer looking nearly so feeble. "There's no honor among thieves, you stupid Chink. You came here to steal my life. I've been a thief longer, girl. I'm going to take yours from you." The shadows were starting to gather around him, tendrils draped around him like wisps of infernal smoke. "I'm going to make you scream first, bitch."

The man leapt towards the General, covering the space between them far too quickly for someone of his advanced age. The General, ready for such a charge, sliced the air in front of himself effortlessly; the Jade Emperor's Whisper hummed as it rose to meet the foe. But the old man wasn't there when the blade was supposed to slice through him from stem to stern. Instead, he was to the General's left; Shen Xue narrowly dodged a fist that was aimed at his temple. In the slow half second it took to pivot, the General noticed that both of the old man's hands were holding brass knuckles, studded with spikes and covered with ancient runes and hieroglyphs.

The General backed away with his sword pointed at the man's throat, being mindful not to tread too closely to the shadows at his back. They were all around, lurching forward whenever he came close.

"Noticed something, bitch? Not what you were expecting, huh?" He cackled again. "You're better'n I thought. I didn't expect you to block one of my friends there; he was going to take your pretty head off with that swipe. Might be you can give me a fight. I need one; it's been years since I killed anyone properly."

The General moved warily. It would be no bad thing to keep him talking. "So this is the source of your secret? You command shadows?"

The old man barked a harsh laugh. "Shadows? What are shadows, you silly bitch? Nothing. These aren't shadows. They're what you're going to become: one of the dead. These?" He raised his hands, looking around the room. "All of the dead I've killed, all of the dead I've found. They serve me, now; not in body anymore, heh, I took care of that. I took their fucking souls. Pretty soon I'll have yours, too." He moved in again, swinging the brass knuckles in crude arcs.

Normally, the General wouldn't be fazed by such a lack of finesse. Somehow the man was moving faster than any man should be able to, and his blows were strong. The General had to focus on keeping his jian between them and dodging blows to keep from being mutilated or worse. The General could sense the power in the man now that he was clothed in his shadows; the brass knuckles, the shadows, and even the chain he wore around his neck reeked of magic.

"Not fast enough. Don't think you can tire me out, either. My friends will see that I'm standing long after your petite ass has gone cold."

The shadows . . . they are empowering him. The General could see it now that he was looking; human forms, always shifting. The lines of shadow that were covering the old man looked like hands and arms, with fingers digging into his skin. He was on the General again as soon as Shen Xue finished the thought. *He's trying to drive me into a corner, into his captured souls.* There was a long tradition of captive, murderous ghosts in Chinese literature, and of the witches, male and female, who commanded them. The old man probably had caught Westerners unaware, but this was not a handicap the General suffered under.

"Do you want a good death, old man? I will not give you one. You are below me." The General tried to press the attack this time. The old man simply dodged each of her swings by a hair's breadth, laughing the entire time. It was effortless for him to avoid the attacks. When he was up against the wall, he kicked off of it and launched a flurry of his own; he seemed to be trying to strike the General from every direction all at once. The more he moved, the more the General became certain that he was, in fact, the very sort of witch that the legends described. No other creature, human or otherwise, could move like a spider, a monkey, and a snake combined. Underneath the spells and magic, the man was just a common thug; it showed in his fighting and in his speech. But with such terrible power to back up feckless brutality...

The General was forced to retreat again, cutting and slashing to keep the old man at bay, but never striking flesh. This dance could not be kept up forever; even with the General's prowess and the Jade Emperor's Whisper, a misstep could be made and the beast would be upon him. The shadow souls were starting to come free from the walls; one actually grazed the back of the General's coveralls with unearthly cold claws, ripping the fabric and barely missing flesh. The General countered with a backhanded cut, expecting nothing—but the jian met with resistance and a horrible wail as the shadow's hand fell away and melted into the ground. What was most interesting was the scream that the old man gave; he stumbled, his eyes growing wide as he looked past the General. *Oh. Aha. Now I have you, old man.* The sword itself, Jade Emperor's Whisper, was the secret to killing the shadows. It was divine, and could slay them, magic to magic. Nothing less would touch them.

"How in the hell?" the old man sputtered, shock evident in his tone. The General quickly turned his back to the old man. The Jade Emperor's Whisper knew the taste of these abominations, and wanted more. The sword blurred against the background as the General did an entirely different dance; pieces of shadow lay scattered on the floor as he cut through them. More sprang into place, trying to overwhelm the General, but this was trivial. The General knew Jade Emperor's Whisper could hurt them, and there was nothing more perfect than the General with his sword in hand.

"What are you doing? You—stop, goddammit!" He came at the General again, another lazy blow with those brass knuckles. But it was slower this time. The General scored the old man's arm at last, sending a thin stream of blood to splatter on the ground; it didn't melt away like the shadows.

"No. No. No no no!" He backed away from her like a wounded animal, cradling his arm. "You can't do this!" The shadows all surged forth again, and the General went through them, rending them asunder with the Jade Emperor's Whisper as easily as if they were grain and he was a sturdy peasant with a freshly sharpened sickle in hand. With each one that the General cut down, the old man seemed to shrink in on himself. He couldn't hold himself up as high, couldn't stand straight, and finally couldn't stand at all. As the General cut the last shadow soul in half, the old man crumpled to the floor. The room had brightened considerably; with the evil the old man had wreathed himself in gone, the light of the fading sun made itself known once again. With an effort, the man raised himself up off of the floor. The General casually walked towards him, spearing him through the chest with the tip of Jade Emperor's Whisper. His face contorted in surprised agony, and he slid off of the sword point before hitting the ground with a soft thud.

"They're—they're all gone now. My slaves, my—my power. Gone, gone again, just like everything. Everything... gets worse, everything becomes broken. Everything—it goes to hell."

"I believe Jade Emperor's Whisper shall send you to a very special hell," Shen Xue said thoughtfully. "The Chinese have a great many hells. Which one shall it be, I wonder? Dismemberment? Crushing? Boiling? There are many kinds involving fire or cold... oh, and blood. And the removal of body parts."

The old man's life was bleeding out through his chest. He had minutes, at best. "I'm going to be remembered, bitch. E-everything I've done, all the people I killed—they'll know me where I'm going." He coughed, producing more dark blood. He looked much as he had when the General first saw him: frail, small, broken. "They called me Shadow-Storm. B-but—my name... my name is—"

With a flick of Jade Emperor's Whisper, the General opened his throat, drowning his words in his lifeblood. "No one knows your name, old fool. No one will. And no one cares, except maybe the demons you will meet." The old man's eyes bulged, and a single wisp of shadow extended from his fingers before he collapsed, still wide-eyed and in agony but finally dead.

The General left the old Victorian house in the same way he had entered: boldly and through the front door.

Verdigris was surprised when People's Blade actually notified his receptionist that she—*he*, the General referred to himself as a male—was coming. Granted, she brushed aside any attempts to keep her out, and strolled straight in as if she'd had an appointment, but at least she stopped at the desk first.

She swaggered to stand in front of Verd's desk, and looked down her nose at him. "I have, as you barbarians say, 'good news and bad news.' Which would you prefer first?"

"In my experience there's not always that much of a difference between the two, depending on one's perspective. The good news." He gestured for the General to take a seat in one of the hand-crafted leather chairs.

People's Blade remained standing. "The good news: Shadow-Storm is no longer a threat to anyone. He was disinclined even to consider negotiation, so in the interest of removing a potential hazard, I eliminated him." She considered the nails on one hand. "That is the bad news; I was forced to eliminate him, even though I approached him peaceably and attempted to recruit." She was intentionally leaving something unsaid there; Verdigris knew better than to fall into such an obvious trap, though, deciding to use a different tack.

"How did you dispose of him? Anything that I have to worry about making the papers?" He kept his face and voice calm, as if this was merely a cleanup detail. *Never show your cards if you can help it.*

"Please. How do you think?" There was a distinct edge to her voice.

"You're a person of many . . . talents. Your cutting wit may have done him in, my dear." He allowed himself a smirk.

She glared at him. "You neglected to tell me much about this target. Your primary neglect was to tell me that his power derived from magic."

"Magic? Impossible, General. Surely it was something else;

sufficient technology appears magical at first glance. I should know, I've made some things that would qualify as magic to the uninitiat—"

The General cut him off with an abrupt gesture. "You are a barbarian. You do not know the power of magic. This is why none of those *technologists* were able to defeat him, and I *was.* You would be wise to listen to one who is an expert... fool. If you wish my alliance, there will be no more nonsense about how *impossible* magic is."

"I—"

"And nothing will be kept from me from now on. No more games. No more tests. If more nonsense follows this episode, our arrangement will be ended. With finality." The General's glare gave ample warning of just what she meant.

Verdigris cooled immediately, his face hardening into a rock. "Understood. General, I have something very important for you. This will be a long-term project and a vital target, and one I suspect only you have the ability to accomplish. I'll send for you when I have a proper file updated."

People's Blade raised an eyebrow. "Really. What, do you have a god in your sights as a possible *recruit?* Nothing less is worthy of my time."

"Not a recruit. That's been tried. You know the value of weapons. I mean to *steal* one. Whether or not she wants to be stolen."

Khanjar was listening, from the spy post, and her frown deepened. This... was *stupid.* There was no other word for it. Bad enough that Verdigris was dealing with the General—Khanjar had done some information-seeking on her own and knew what the creature called People's Blade was, or at least what she had said she was to the communists. That sword she carried—Jade Emperor's Whisper—was supposed to be divine, forged by the order of the Jade Emperor, the chief of all the Chinese deities. That was bad enough, but to make things worse, it contained the soul of Shen Xue, an ancient Chinese general, one of the most ruthless leaders ever to walk the earth, a man who would spend the lives of hundreds of thousands—enemies, noncombatants, or his own men—to accomplish his goals. Not that Khanjar objected to this level of bloodshed in principle, but in practice, in this day and age... it was injudicious and tended to get the attention of other people with armies.

Allegedly, the General had only served as the advisor to the blade's "owner," Fei Li, a peasant thief girl. But given the way that People's Blade had been acting . . . Khanjar was relatively certain now that Fei Li was no longer in possession of her own body. The General was in charge now, and given his nature, he was unlikely to hand the body back until he had accomplished whatever his current goal was. Perhaps not even then.

Verdigris had no idea what he was metaphorically climbing into bed with. This was . . . insane.

And if this was leading where she *thought* it was leading . . . to the capture of the Deva, the Seraphym, and presumably the coercion of said being . . . it was more than insane.

You did not capture and coerce a Deva. Not if you wanted your karma to remain neutral. Such an action would send your karma somewhere below that of "you will be reincarnated as a starving alley dog for the next twenty lifetimes." Even being associated with such a thing would send her karma plummeting to somewhere below "reincarnation as a nanny-goat."

Not acceptable.

Khanjar, she told herself, as she continued to keep her post at the spy hole, per Verdigris' orders, *it is time to look for an exit strategy.*

CHAPTER EIGHT

Run Through the Jungle

MERCEDES LACKEY AND CODY MARTIN

Seraphym felt a kind of comfort in perching on the roof of John Murdock's squat. It was a comfort she sorely needed. The futures had changed, and yet, none of them had lightened any. Except for the ones centered by that enormous blank into which she could not see. Only *there* was there any hope, at the moment, and she still could neither see a reason nor deduce her way to that hope.

She was so deeply immersed in her meditations that although the least hint of an inimical presence would have sent her hurtling back to awareness in a nanopulse, a friendly presence did not so much as make a feather touch of an impression on her mental state.

"Evenin', Angel. How's kicks?" John was wearing a pair of CCCP coveralls with the upper half tied around his waist, a muscle shirt covering his upper torso. He was carrying a very large brown paper bag in his right hand, and a pair of sitting cushions in his other.

Seraphym was catapulted out of her meditations so quickly that for one moment she could only blink at him. "Greetings, John Murdock. I was . . ."

"Becoming One with the All, or somethin'?" He flashed his characteristic lopsided grin. She found her own lips curving up in response without a single thought.

"Of a sort." She wondered how much or little she could tell him.

"Put the All on hold, for a bit. Got a special treat for tonight." He set the brown bag down, then threw a pillow each at their feet. Unceremoniously thumping down onto his, he started to pull Styrofoam cartons out of the bag. "Take a guess."

She felt herself smiling a little more. How . . . odd. "A true guess, or cheating?"

"Can ya pick one already? I'm starvin'."

She knew what they were of course. Carryout food. She could even trace back along the path they had been carried in a flash and see where they had come from. But, taken with his whimsy, she laid a forefinger on one that seemed to have a little red sauce at one corner of the lid. It was a lovely, deep color, and it pleased her. But she was puzzled as to why there were so many cartons of food. "This?" she said.

"Chinese. Good choice. We've got Chinese, Mexican, good ol' American burgers an' fries, pizza, an' somethin' from that Thea gal—you guessed it—borscht." He opened each box, then plopped two plastic sporks in front of each of them.

She looked at all the containers, and looked at him in mingled fascination and horror. "You are going to eat all of this? Will you not explode?"

"Could give it a shot, but I got just enough to tide me over till next meal. Meant to share this tonight, though." He dug his spork into a pile of greasy noodles and chicken, shoving it into his mouth. "Figured that 'tween do-gooding and bein' the Hand of some Fluffy God, that your sort didn't have much time to sample the finer things in life," he said, speaking around his food.

"I . . . have never eaten," she said. She *could,* of course. She could have her body do anything she chose for it to do. She picked up the container and opened it. Her vast memory identified it for her. *Sweet and sour shrimp.* Tentatively, she used the implement to convey a little to her mouth.

It is one thing to have the memory of millions of other peoples' eating experiences available to you. It is quite another to taste something for yourself, with your own mouth, for the very first time in corporeal or incorporeal existence.

"Whaddya tink?" he mumbled around a mouthful of pizza.

Her eyes widened as dozens of nuances and tastes hit her mind at once, and she stopped everything, dead, to analyze them.

"Don't miss the churros fer dessert. They reminded me of ya; cinnamony an' too light for their own good."

"I . . . am full of wonder," she managed at last. She told her body to take its cues from his; a new sensation came to it. Hunger.

With pure, unfettered delight, she began to eat, tasting, tasting, reveling in the taste. She ate carefully and daintily—but hugely.

He retreated for a few minutes as she dug in, returning from the roof access with a glass of water and a large case of beer. He set the water in front of her and immediately cracked open a bottle for himself. Gulping down the first beer, he paused before the second. "So, whatcha think?"

"No wonder mortals grow fat."

"It's one of my favorite sins, despite bein' a fan of all seven." He took a long pull from his beer before setting it down and taking one of the two hamburgers.

"That which gives joy is not a sin, John Murdock," she chided very gently, and gave herself up to a slice of pizza, as different from the Chinese as could be.

"No such thing as too much of a good thing?"

"Overindulgence at the cost of others or one's own self—that is selfishness, and that is a sin." She nibbled, craning her head around at an odd angle as the tip of the piece of pizza began to droop, until her head was almost upside down. "This is a very floppy food—"

"Just gotta hold it right; same principle as a gun. Proper support." Washing down the last of his burger with a swig of beer, he demonstrated the proper way to fold a pizza slice; he'd bought a half pie, pineapple and ham, his favorite. She gave his demonstration all the studious attention of a scientific lecture, and copied him.

"You lucked out tonight, Angel. I haven't properly eaten since the op in Kansas."

"I knew you were gone. I did not know where." The next words came from her mouth without thought. "I missed your presence."

He looked at her soberly, still chewing his way through the pizza. "Well, shucks, Angel." Then he broke into a smile again, looking away from her just as suddenly.

"Why did you go to Kansas?" she asked. "The CCCP is here."

"I suppose this is violatin' all sorts of OpSec, but I *don't* suppose that you're the sort to go spreadin' information 'round, either. We got word that the Thulians were kicking around in Kansas. I got sent in to find out 'bout it, and then take care of it." John got a slightly faraway look in his eyes, as if an old and ugly wound had begun to pain him.

She regarded him somberly. She *could* look into the past to find out what had happened in Kansas, but..."It was disturbing to you. Was it very horrible?"

"The sort that we're fightin' are the worst sort. They're horrible. In my line of work, it's not all that often that y'come across true evil, irredeemable bastards without a prayer. These Thulians, though... they're not just bad. They're *other.* Gives me the creeps whenever I get near 'em. Just no shades of gray with these guys." He mulled over that for a moment, then quickly changed the topic. "So, how's the CCCP been while I've been outta town?"

She hesitated. "John Murdock..." She waited for the echo in her mind. *It is permitted.* "John Murdock, I may tell you a thing."

"By all means." He waved his hand, leaning over to retrieve a fresh bottle of beer.

"You know now that the Thulians are *other.* Not from this world. They are... they do not regard humans as anything but insects to be amused by or swept away. You have no meaning for them, except as you irritate them by your persistence in failing to fall. They take their cues from their human allies in this. They will not rest until you do fall, and lie beneath their feet."

"Enough on those bastards. Again, they give me the heebie-jeebies. How've my people been in the neighborhood?"

"We have watched over them. Insofar as they can, they prosper." She took a deep breath. "Something troubles you. More than troubles you. This is why you try to take the conversation to inconsequentials. Will you tell me?"

"The CCCP and the folks 'ere are inconsequential?" Again that smile, trying to turn her own words back on her. This was important. She sensed it. And she was not going to let him distract her. This—this was driving deeply into that blank that *he* was, and if she could not get some insight into it, and soon...

"When you know, when you can see, have seen with your own eyes that all was well, yes. Will you tell me? I... I cannot lie. I will tell no one."

"Things got a little hairy on the last mission, t'say the least."

He was not going any further unless she prompted him, so she did. "Hairy?"

"I acted... unprofessionally."

Her brows furrowed. "I fail to understand."

"Long story short, the Thulians got wise to the fact that we were onto them in the middle of the operation. Part of it is my fault as team leader; I should've made sure everyone on the team was equipped right. Part of it was just bad luck. Anyways, we got bogged down, and things were looking bad." He sighed heavily, and again with that far-off look. He took another drink from his bottle.

"And something happened. Something that gives you great pain."

"Again, I acted unprofessionally. I . . . lost control of myself. I was the team leader for this mission; I'm supposed to keep track of everyone an' make sure that everyone comes home. Y'need to be really in the moment for that, an' have as complete tactical awareness as possible. An' I lost my shit, an' endangered everyone. If'n Vickie hadn't had her techno-wizardry up an' seen what was comin', I could've killed the entire team." He laid one of his hands on his knee; it seemed to Sera as if he was bracing himself under the weight of the memory.

She was . . . moved to not just compassion, which she always had, but pity. No mortal should labor under the sort of burden he seemed to be carrying. Impulsively, she reached forward to touch his fingers, perhaps to impart some sort of comfort.

For the first time in her acquaintance of him, his barriers were completely down, and there was the sense of *trust.* But that was followed in a flash by such a blow of shock and horror that she jerked a little, as a mortal would when jolted by an electric current. *His* shock and horror . . . it flooded her. And she knew what this was. It had impacted her once before. *The Program.*

Quickly she withdrew. He had not wanted her to see this before. She knew what the Program was, of course, but not what it had meant to him. That was shrouded from her.

Unless he chose to show her.

Then she felt his assent; in fact, felt him seize her as if she was a lifeline. And then they both fell into memory.

There was weapons' fire to their left and Randolph went down instantly, his head exploding into a red mist. There was shooting coming from all directions. It was a perfectly executed ambush. On *them.* John fired at muzzle flashes, wasting precious seconds to turn his NVGs on. There had to be thirty of the bastards, which was impossible; intelligence said that they had a clear approach to the encampment that they were supposed to destroy.

Gomez was next; he died screaming, still firing, bullets stitching across the jungle canopy as he went down. There was no time to react; John kept firing, trying to move and regroup with the rest of his troop. Whenever he came close to any of his men, they were cut down.

John knew that the situation was hopeless when Ross died; there were only four of his troop left, including himself. Ross had simply crumpled bonelessly to the ground, as if he was narcoleptic. John rolled him over, stopped to fire at someone charging towards him. He checked Ross; he had been shot through his right bicep, the round piercing both of his lungs. He'd died nearly instantly, and his lifeless eyes peered eerily at John through the green haze of his night vision. *No time! No time.*

John stood to run, to find cover and see how many of the enemy he could take before he was overcome. That's when the shot came, thudding and heavy and knocking him down. He wasn't dying, though, which wasn't right. He should be dead, dead with everyone else.

The firing slowed, became more sporadic, and finally stopped. John struggled to breathe, and couldn't find any blood that was his own; he wasn't bleeding where he had been hit. He started to lose consciousness, his vision going out. But he swore, *swore* that one of the bastards that had killed his troop was wearing NVGs. *The rebels aren't supposed to have those...*

"—very lucky that our CIA assets in the area were able to find you when they did. Otherwise, you would've probably been taken hostage by the revolutionaries. With what they've been doing to the foreign contractors they caught last month, it's safe to say that you would be in a bad way."

John simply nodded, still too hazy to offer a meaningful response. He had been given a stunning amount of painkillers since his arrival in the hospital, and hadn't been conscious all that often. The bruise on his chest, they explained to him, was from a grenade that misfired and failed to explode. If it weren't for his body armor, he'd have a baseball-sized hole in his chest instead of a cracked sternum.

"We're in a unique position here, though, Staff Sergeant. At the moment, you're officially listed as Killed in Action... so far as anyone is admitting that you exist at all. It'll officially be written up as a training accident, if you accept."

John's head lolled, and he replied groggily. "Accept what?"

The man smiled. "I'm glad you asked, soldier. You're a patriot, yes? We have a one-of-a-kind opportunity for you to serve your country. Something that'll help give America an edge, to keep us safe. It's Black Project, of course, since the Program itself could be considered . . . somewhat . . . controversial."

"What would I have to do?"

"We'll get to that later. Right now, you just heal up, soldier."

In order to be torn to pieces, it apparently took a lot of training to get in as good a physical shape as possible. They worked out daily; John was in superb shape, and he only got better over the weeks. Most of the others were good; he figured that there were two hundred-odd "trainees," all volunteers.

Most were "former" military, like him, from across the services; always a combat MOS, though. A few others were law enforcement, usually federal: FBI, US marshals, Treasury agents, and even a true-to-life Texas Ranger. The training was hard, but it had to be for what they were going to do.

They used morphine like saline solution here. They needed to. It took those that survived the surgeries roughly six months to fully recover. It was as close to *Six Million Dollar Man* stuff as John figured there would ever be. The technical terms for what exactly they had done were lost to him; he was well-read, but most of it was truly next-level, genius work. Enhanced senses, faster reflexes, stronger bones and muscles. He wasn't invincible; a bullet or bomb could still kill him just as dead as before. But he was a helluva lot *harder* to kill.

As for what they were trying to do? Make metahumans out of normal men. That simple, and that complex. Metahumans on demand. If the processes that they were using could be streamlined, they could be mass-produced. It would ensure America's military dominance, by giving them the "better, faster" soldier to match the rapidly advancing technology of war.

They were told that the science that was being pioneered with them would also have practical applications; helping the blind to see, the paralyzed to walk, and so on. That all of the ones that hadn't survived the surgeries—all forty-one percent of them—would not have died in vain.

Once they recovered, the training started again. To relearn how to do everything, but faster and better. And that's when John discovered, much to his surprise, that he could produce fire on command. The doctors were at first shocked, and then delighted. They spent a lot of time determining how it had happened; it certainly wasn't anything that was a result of the surgeries. The labcoats figured out that his mitochondria somehow processed energy differently, maybe even drawing on an extradimensional source; John was able to psionically use this energy to create flame, even create the fourth state of matter—plasma. It came to him naturally, and his only limit was his own concentration; not to expand his powers, but to keep them in check. Because the first time he'd manifested them, he'd taken out a hardened concrete bunker during a live-fire exercise, purely on reflex. Good thing there'd only been a robotically controlled machine gun in there.

He wasn't the only one who'd triggered metahuman after the surgeries.

They had a whole special unit for people like that.

She was gorgeous, and constantly amazed John when they were allowed to see each other. Her name was Jessica, and she was a psychometricist; she could read objects and places, their past and present, simply by touching them. They said she'd make the perfect spy. Get her in, let her touch something barehanded, get her out again full of intel.

Their contact was minimal, due to the nature of the special "Natural Meta-Soldiers" unit. Their training regimen was different from the other trainees, far more specialized and detailed.

And... he knew they had to be hard, had to push people to their limits but...

Her name was Jessica; she was tough and smart and liked a lot of the same things he did. She was beautiful, too, not like supermodel beautiful, but like *completely alive* beautiful. She knew poets, and poetry, and could quote them. She'd read Dylan Thomas and Barry Longyear. She liked zombie movies.

Her name was Jessica, and they were falling in love, and that wasn't allowed.

They called it a training accident, which, of course, was a lie. She was dead, and they—the Program chiefs—had killed her. John was certain of it.

It had happened shortly after lunch. The Natural Metas had their own time for the mess hall, separated from both the researchers and the other trainees, but she had bumped into a straggling doctor, one of the department heads, who had accidentally stayed late after his chow time. He was carrying a stack of papers and folders, and looked bored. When she bumped into him, the papers went everywhere. As soon as she knelt down to help him pick the scattered papers up, as soon as her hand touched the first folder, she froze.

John saw her face fall from across the room, the color draining out of it. She quietly helped the doctor finish picking up his papers, and then took a seat next to John. She was completely silent for their entire meal, until two armed guards approached from the commissary door. She looked him in the eyes and whispered one word: "Run." And it was over. They took her away.

Three days later, she was dead, and they had killed her. John became "uncooperative." That was their word for it. He didn't have a word for it; he wanted answers, didn't get them, and so he set out on a one-man mission to beat the answers out of every officer and labcoat he could get his hands on.

"—subject one-zero-six-four, beta series, has become uncooperative and disruptive, even violent towards Program staff. Dr. Chandresekhar, our lead therapist and behavioral psychologist, has determined that the subject is a total loss. No chance for meaningful rehabilitation and orientation for Program goals."

It was Dr. Jacob Garvey. John had only seen him once before, shortly after he went into surgery. Garvey was the Program head researcher—the entire thing was his idea, his brainchild. He was supposed to be unbelievably smart, ultra-genius level. John didn't care how smart he was. What mattered was that Garvey was as sadistic and inhumane as Mengele.

He was strapped down, and waiting to be euthanized. They had pumped him full of drugs to keep him compliant. They needed to; when they first tried to take him, he had killed five guards and hospitalized three others. But the Program leaders didn't leave anything to chance, and quickly had him subdued. John thought it might have been the same Valium gas that the Russians used in that one hostage situation, but he couldn't be sure.

Garvey continued to dispassionately drone on to someone John couldn't see. "It's almost a waste of resources, but necessary. After execution, autopsy is to be performed immediately upon the cadaver. If we can learn more about the natural processes that contributed to Subject one-zero-six-four's spontaneous metahuman ability, we might be able to figure out how to replicate it. While not the most practical 'superpower,' my maxim has always been 'waste not, want not.'" He nodded to the other technicians in the room. "Let's begin."

He moved in with the needles, handed to him by one of the nurses. There was no lethal injection machine in this exam room. Then again, Garvey was supposed to be a hands-on sort of man when it came to "interesting subjects."

John felt what was about to happen; the cold-eyed men and women around him seemed a thousand miles away. He saw Jessica's face, felt her warmth, and remembered that she was gone forever. The hatred, the fury welled up inside of him, burning through him like lava. He strained against his restraints, the metal and Kevlar straps creaking. Garvey stopped short. "He shouldn't even be conscious. Interesting." John saw red. Literally. Everything around him was washed in a hot red haze. He hated them all, hated the entire facility, hated Garvey, and finally hated himself. Because he had let them take her. Just sat there, and let them take her.

I'll drag every one of you down to hell with me.

The explosion came too quickly for any sort of fire suppression system to have a chance to save anyone. He hadn't ever used his powers in that way before. He didn't know he was capable of it. The worst part was . . . it was easy. John just . . . let go. The entire facility was blasted through with a plasma wave, intense pressure and heat destroying everything—and everyone. When it was done, John found himself lying outside of the smoldering ruins of the underground facility. He had blacked out, blanked his escape from memory. But he knew: everyone behind him, everyone in those bunkers was dead.

He had killed them all, but it wasn't enough. Because he had let them kill *her*.

She was supposed to be . . . detached. She was supposed to be able to sense and understand mortals, feel compassion for them, but she was not supposed to feel as they felt. She was supposed to take the longer view. After all, death was not an ending. Pain was not forever.

But she was, for a brief, and terrifying moment, furious. Furious with the anger of an Archangel, the kind of anger that destroyed worlds. Furious enough that, had she not been able to control herself, she would have razed the Program buildings across the world to ashes and strewn salt where they had been. She would have brought Fire and the Sword to those who had conceived of it, and let them experience the true wrath of a Seraphym in the instant before they died.

Instantly, she throttled her reaction down. She was an Instrument of the Infinite, here for a specific purpose, and revenge in this case was not a part of that purpose. But the anger . . . the rage . . .

She cooled herself. She was a Seraphym and this was not her purpose. But she wondered if he had felt her rage rise with his own.

And after the rage had cooled . . . came the grief. She mourned for him, for what he had lost. And mourned that he, himself, could not yet grieve. She wept, that he could not weep and begin to heal.

When John opened his eyes, the first thing he saw was the Seraphym's tears. He opened his mouth, and closed it just as quickly.

What can I say? What can I tell her after she's seen, been through that? Seen who I really am, and what I've done?

"Sera? Are you all right?" He had very carefully withdrawn his hand from hers, keeping it in his lap.

She looked up at him and made a little motion with her hand, as if to try and take his back, then stopped. "I . . . grieve," she said, after a long silence. She made no move to wipe her tears away; another moment of un-humanity.

John couldn't look at her anymore. "I'll understand if you don't wanna come around anymore. I wouldn't." He sighed, taking a noncommittal sip from his beer. "Knowin' what I've done."

"What?" She sounded startled. "But—I grieve for what was done *to* you. That you have not healed. That you have not found forgiveness." She actually took a deep breath. "John Murdock, forgiveness is always possible, but you must forgive yourself first. This changes nothing for the worse between us. You are my friend, my true friend. I only have one other. I would not lose either of you, for . . . for any cause."

And she was right, at least about them being friends. That bothered John, a little. He had been so caught up in everything, that making friends... it sort of just crept up on him. Unter and Old Man Bear weren't quite like his old drinking buddies, or his friends in the service... but that bond was still there. And Jonas, who was more like an uncle than anything. Then there was Sera, which still confused him to an extent. But it was happening, no denying it; he was making friends. He would've judged allowing something like that to happen to be too dangerous, before the Invasion; for himself and said friends. Things had changed in the world since the Thulians decided to try their hand at genocide and conquest. Things had changed in John. "The only other person that really knows, or at least knows part of it, is Bella. She knows I was in some black-budget deal, and turned out bad, which was why I was on the run. The Commissar has the general idea. But that's it." The fear was still there; the memories he had from the Program were carried with him, deep down, while still being ever-present in his mind. A background of regret. A barricade of guilt.

"This was very hard for you. Showing me." Her eyes were dry again, and again unreadable behind the blaze of gold. "Perhaps, for now, we should say goodnight."

He nodded, gathering up the take-out containers and cushions. He was uncomfortable, and tried to break the tension. "Sorry for bein' a buzz-kill tonight. Same time tomorrow? I cook a mean steak, if Jonas has any in the store. I don't even need a grill." He flashed a smile; it wasn't as confident as before.

She looked as if she might say more, then simply took the trash from him, and incinerated it, the residue falling in a snowfall of ash from her hands. "Neither do I. Goodnight, John Murdock. We will meet tomorrow."

"G'night, Angel."

But then, she stopped. She turned and reached out to him; the gesture compounded part of compassion, part of entreaty. "I do not wish to part like this. There is too much that is not right. *Koyaanisqatsi.*"

He cocked his head to the side, taking her arm. "I know that word. 'Life out of balance,' right?" *A fair descriptor of things, if there ever was.*

"Yes." There was a ghost of a smile. "The Hopi have many simple words for profound and complex things." She took another step back towards him. "I only have two friends, you and Bella.

Bella is my . . . protégé. I do not have a word for what you are, not even one in Hopi."

It was John's turn to take a step forward. "What would y'like me to be, Angel?"

Her brows furrowed again. This was the blank place, the heart of the blank in the futures. She couldn't see, nor anticipate anything. And that left her floundering, trying to sort things that did not want to sort into neat paths. "I . . ." she said, thinking out loud. "What would *I* like? No one asks me what *I* would—"

"Hmm." John waited half a beat, then leaned in to kiss Sera. He did it almost without thinking, and realized fully what he was doing only after he was already committed. *This is the part where I'm struck by a lightning bolt for my transgression.*

Sera froze. Not out of fear or anger, not even out of shock. She froze because in that moment, another new thing had occurred in a day of new things. She had never touched, nor been touched by, another physical being in this way before.

Of course she knew what a kiss was, and she knew all the possible nuances of the gesture, but again, they were all abstract. This was anything but abstract. He had *wanted* to do this; now he was a little afraid, perhaps, that she would not like it, but he still *wanted* this. He had let down barriers to her that he had never let down to anyone else. She hadn't regarded him as a monster.

She closed her eyes and concentrated on the experience. It was . . . warm. Exciting. Strangely comforting, and she had not thought herself in need of comfort. And pleasurable, more deeply pleasurable than she would have thought. *Why am I allowing this?* she wondered. *But . . . of course, I am allowing this, because . . . because I like this. I like him. Human emotions. Will this affect him? Affect his judgment? Affect my judgment about affecting him?* Her mind spun for a moment, then settled on one thing. One Law that was always true. *That which makes us care unselfishly for another is always permitted.*

Why the hell did I do that? I'm still alive, and I have not been transfigured into anything like a newt or a rock. God . . . have I ruined this? He decided that he not only needed to kiss her, but he *wanted* to. It had been a long, long time since he had allowed himself any desires, other than surviving. But, with the

Invasion . . . everything had changed. He had friends now, he had a purpose, heaven help him, a cause to fight for. And now he had . . . whatever this was becoming, with an Angel. With Sera.

John was the first to pull back, slowly. His hand didn't leave her arm, nor did he step away. His eyes studied her, waiting and expectant.

She opened her eyes, faintly disappointed that the sensation had ended, and smiled up at him. He was taller than she. How had she never noticed that before?

"I do not think there will be lightning to strike you, John Murdock," she said softly, and felt another new thing, a kind of impish amusement.

"Well, shucks. An' here I thought I was gonna be famous: 'First and Last Man to Kiss an Angel.'"

She laughed aloud. "Who would know but me?" She raised her hand and gently touched his cheek. "New things, John Murdock. So many new things tonight. For both of us, I think."

He let go of her arm, with a nod. Instead of flashing away as she usually did, she walked, slowly and deliberately, to the roof edge, then lifted off as softly as a moth into the night. *Huh.* John bent over to retrieve his forgotten drink. "I think I ought to try that more often."

CHAPTER NINE

Obsessions

MERCEDES LACKEY AND CODY MARTIN

"What do you mean, she's dead?" Dominic Verdigris looked up from his desk display, sweeping his hand to hide the windows. This was annoying, more than anything. He had completely lost his train of thought on a personnel selection; he hated to be interrupted when he was working, even on trivial things such as this. "Well?"

Khanjar pursed her lips. "She was alive, and now she's dead. I thought that that much would have been obvious, Dom."

Verdigris had first found her by chance, years ago, and had tagged the file on her in case he ever needed someone like her. Rachel Hiller was a Las Vegas native who had never held a real job in her life. It had occurred to Verd that one day he might need a precog, but genuine precogs were hard to find and generally flaky. It wasn't a talent that was at all reliable, and those who had it were prone to mental instability. Matthew March had just been the most extreme example of the type. Verd treasured efficiency, and precogs were inefficient in the amount of resources you needed to devote to them relative to payoff.

He needed reliability. The sort of reliability that allowed someone to live off their talent and never actually work. So he wrote a series of algorithms and statistics tests, looking for people who held no jobs, cross-correlated with people with a very comfortable income, those who were always in the right place and time during disasters, people who consistently won lotteries, won enough at casino-gambling to bring in substantial money without triggering the "cheating" safeguards, and people who never lost in the stock market.

Finally after a lot of number-crunching, one name fell out. Rachel Hiller. In her late twenties, she brought in about forty thousand a month in a combination of lottery wins, scratch-card wins, and casino wins. She had never had an accident, had a perfect driving record, on the day of the Invasion had been in Pahrump, Nevada, rather than Las Vegas (allegedly looking at a used car).

She was very careful. She made sure never to strike it rich in the same place twice, and never got too much; she wasn't too greedy. It helped her to stay off the radar of the nice men in tailored suits that were behind the management of the casinos. If there ever was attention drawn to her, she was always able to slip away at the last moment, knowing exactly what to do and where to go. There were some very close calls, however. Unexpected changes, wild cards thrown in, new variables at the last possible moment; they seemed to trip her up. And that's how Verdigris figured her out.

Failing being able to convince or coerce that "angel," he needed someone who could do what she could do. And it wouldn't hurt to have both. So his first job was to acquire Hiller, his second to figure out how to boost her abilities, and his third . . . the "angel project."

The acquisition part was easy. She'd skated close enough to the surface of getting caught that all he had to do was wait until she walked into a casino he owned. He only owned a few, bought on a lark a few years ago. Using some more number crunching, Verdigris figured out the three most likely casinos that Rachel was going to visit next . . . and bought all three of them, quietly. It was the easiest solution, considering everything, especially when you left the existing management structure intact.

She struck on a Friday at the second casino; it was called the Golden something-or-other. He had thought about renaming it something ironic, but that would have signaled a change in management and he didn't want that. He didn't want to scare her away. This should all be part of her comfort zone, places she knew, places she thought she knew well enough not to have to think twice about. Once he had his agents confirm that she was inside and following her usual routine, he waited. Verdigris had gone to lengths to make sure that everything inside of the casino was business as usual. The slightest change might throw a wrench into his plans, and send Rachel running. She went about the casino floor, seemingly stopping at random among the slot machines. There was no pattern to where she stopped, varying from quarter to dollar machines, and her payouts never went high enough to trigger the jackpot. She took her pay slips to a different cashier each time. He had to admire her cleverness. All it took was five coins; she'd get an instant payout, she'd cash out and move on, and by keeping her wins modest, never triggering the automatic visit from the IRS agent who was always waiting in the casino to claim the government share, within a couple hours she probably had five thousand dollars. Do that eight nights in a month and you had a very nice income.

Springing the trap he had set for her was no small task; all of the security staff had to be briefed at the very last moment, without giving away exactly who the target was. But as soon as she entered the casino, he made sure that everything was quietly locked down. Verdigris had kept all of the security personnel and pit bosses on their usual rotations on the floor; nothing could seem out of place. He waited until she had passed close to several of them. No one knew when they'd be looking for someone or who that someone would be. After the fifth one, he radioed the next person she would pass by; the radio message instructed him to grab the nearest person. That just so happened to be Rachel. No warning, no premeditation, no pattern to be followed. Verdigris watched through the security monitors with a quiet satisfaction.

"Miss," the security guard said, the standard speech when a cheater had been caught. "I am afraid you are going to have to come with me."

Rachel knew better than to object or argue. Casino security's word was law in Vegas. Making a fuss was guaranteed to get you thrown out and banned for life. If she went quietly, there was a chance she could wiggle out of it. Or at least, only end up getting banned from *this* casino, and not every casino in Vegas.

Now Verd spoke into the radio. "Take her to the special office."

The way this was supposed to go was that the suspected cheater would be taken to the security area, questioned, and perhaps if they denied everything, video footage would be shown to them. Most times, unless they made a big deal out of it, any money they had won would be confiscated and they would be told not to come back. If they raised a fuss, well... that was when the Vegas cops got called, unless there was no way of actually proving that cheating had taken place. Most casinos didn't care if a cheater went to another casino so long as it wasn't one in their franchise. But the penalty for denying everything if nothing could be proved was generally getting your face sent to every casino in town. Facial recognition software then ensured that you could never work your scheme again.

Of course, Rachel was going to get a very different sort of treatment.

They left her in a chair in the center of the office, completely alone for about thirty minutes. This was to allow her time to wonder in how deep a vat of shit she really was. When Verd saw her start to sweat, he sent the manager in.

"You've been really careful, Miss Hiller. But you finally waltzed onto the wrong dance floor."

"How do you know my—"

"We've had suspicions," he interrupted, "about your little scam. You've made quite a living for yourself these past few years, for hardly any effort. Isn't that right?" He paced in front of her, making a show of inspecting his fingernails. "But no one is lucky forever. The house *always* wins, one way or another."

"What do you—"

"You cheat, Miss Hiller. It took us quite a while and a lot of analysis, but the numbers don't lie. Your mistake was that you never, ever lost. You're a metahuman." He smirked. Rachel started to look alarmed. "You're using telekinesis to trip the relays. We can probably prove it, but we don't have to. First, we are going to teach you a little lesson. Then we are going to send your videos and pictures to every other casino in Las Vegas, and in Reno, just so you don't think you can move down the road in a couple of hours."

"You can't do this!" She was panicking now. "I-it's illegal!"

"Illegal? Everything was illegal at one point or another. That's never stopped the house from making money on it, Miss Hiller." He took off his jacket, setting it on a nearby table. "So, the question is; how many fingers do you want to walk out of here with? I'm an accommodating man." He took a step towards her, a grin creeping across his face.

When the manager was less than a stride away from her, his radio squelched. He plucked it from his belt in annoyance. "Yes? I'm in the middle of something." Something unintelligible to Rachel came through the speaker, but she could see that the manager's demeanor had changed drastically. He shifted uneasily, looking back to her. "Wait here." Replacing the radio on his belt, he scooped up his jacket and hurried out the door, slamming it behind him.

After what seemed like an eternity to Rachel, but was in fact only two minutes, the door opened again. She was terrified, shaking like a frightened rabbit, choking back pitiful sobs. She didn't dare look at who had walked in. A handkerchief suddenly dangled in front of her face; she was startled into silence for a few moments. Warily, she looked up. A man in a very expensive-looking suit stood in front of her, smiling; not the same shark smile that the manager had, but one with genuine warmth and compassion.

"Good afternoon, ma'am. My name is Dominic Verdigris III. I noticed you out on the floor; I have a keen eye for talent, you see. Once I saw your predicament, I decided to step in." He chuckled, mostly to himself. "You could say I have a certain... pull with the management here. Anyway, I think I might have a proposition for you that would be mutually beneficial for both of us; you get to keep all of your fingers, and both of us get rich. Does that sound good to you?"

At this point, anything that didn't involve a beating and being forced to move across the country sounded appealing. But as with all things—there would be strings attached, and she'd only get thrown to the wolves again if this man thought she was something she wasn't. "I'm not a telekineticist," she said, wiping her eyes.

He chuckled again. "Of course you aren't. Remember, I said I had an eye for talent. And I have a specific need of someone like you." He extended his hand to her. "So, are you in, Rachel? May I call you Rachel?"

Well, what choice did she have? She'd figured she was safe, and yet she'd been caught. She could move across the country and this might happen again, but without the White Knight showing up at the last minute. "All right," she said, shaking his hand. After all, how bad could it be?

✧ ✧ ✧

"Well, that certainly puts a kink in things, and not the fun kind." Verd scowled. "Was there any damage to the device? What was done with the body?"

"There was some damage," Khanjar said, reading from her PDA. "Evidently there was thrashing, a seizure of some sort. And screaming. One of the techs is apparently somewhat traumatized. The body has been removed to the lab for autopsy."

"Unfortunate about the equipment." His scowl deepened. "I put some of it together while—I don't know, sleep-working or something. I had fallen asleep in the workshop and when I woke up it was done; haven't been able to figure out how the hell I did it. See that the report on the autopsy comes to me directly, of course. Oh, and make sure the technician is taken care of; best care possible, with one of our doctors. If he can't be discreet or made to be discreet with treatment, make sure he's taken care of permanently. Whatever your fancy is on that part."

Khanjar nodded, tapped a few things on the PDA, and closed it. "Well. Do you wish to launch a search for a replacement subject?"

Verdigris looked up from his desk, his thoughts obviously having drifted already. "What? No, no time for that. The search I ran found her to be our most stable and reliable candidate; no one else that I've found was as strong, for what it's worth. We're moving on. After I check the equipment, I'll send it to storage."

Verd closed up the last panel, irritated and frustrated. There was nothing wrong with the equipment. Everything checked out. Had it been the protocol?

He had been attempting to use Rachel Hiller's predictive ability to feel out not just the immediate future as it related to her, but potential futures, further out than a few seconds or a minute; days, months, years. The computers he had set up were supposed to interface directly with her own brain, to augment her in a variation of the whole brain-in-a-box idea. Or maybe more like the wet dreams of the cyberpunks. Essentially, to focus her ability and make sense of the inevitable jumble that would follow. Her predictive ability relied upon stimuli; if you gave her no stimuli to form patterns off of, she wouldn't be able to see what was happening. The system he'd set up force-fed her stimuli. Part of it included an induced coma, a truly potent cocktail of nootropic drugs, and microelectric shocks.

Something had gone wrong, though. From all of the evidence, it wasn't the machine that killed her. It had been set to keep up with Rachel; the more information she could take, the more it would give her. Looked as if he would have to wait on the autopsy to tell him why she failed. Or . . . hmm. Didn't he have a psion somewhere in the building? A telepath? He always made sure he had one on hand; utterly loyal, of course, with safeguards in place to make sure that his mind was sacrosanct. Maybe something got picked up.

A quick check gave him the first bit of good news he'd had; the tech that was traumatized was his telepath, so chances were good the psion got something. No leaving this to random questioners; he'd go down to sickbay himself and find out.

But as soon as he cleared the door, the fellow literally shot off the exam table, flung himself across the room, and grabbed his arm. "You can do a wipe, right? I want a wipe! I'll debrief, but after that, I want a wipe! You've *got* to do a wipe!"

For a moment, Verdigris was stunned. Two security guards were right behind the tech, and pulled him off of their boss. Verdigris could see the pleading in the man's eyes; if he was offered a bullet right now, he'd probably take it. He nodded slowly, and the tech broke down into long sobs.

"She saw it all. She saw everything, everything at once! It burned her up, and it's going to make me explode . . . then, there, now, all of it. She got everything, all in a few seconds . . . and she *screamed*. God, it was horrible, it just cut through everything, I thought she would never stop screaming and then she did . . ." The tech couldn't manage coherent speech after that, just broken syllables mixed with sobs.

Verd nodded at the medics. "Get him sedated and give him Procedure three forty-two." One of his own, of course. It wiped out short-term memory. It wasn't a total brainwipe; that would have to wait. Verd wanted to see if merely wiping the short-term memory would solve the trauma without losing some of the data. There *might* be something he could salvage out of this.

As the tech continued to sob—though it seemed now it was with relief—Verd left. So. The machine hadn't broken Rachel, Rachel had broken the machine. It ran itself out trying to feed her new stimuli through the relays; *kaboom*, shortly after she expired. Evidently there was no way that the human mind could see all of the futures at once and still stay sane. He had the feeling that when the autopsy report came back, the cause of death would be an aneurysm or at least look suspiciously like one.

Maybe a metahuman psion . . . but . . . no. No, Matthew March had been a metahuman as well as a psion, and he'd set fire to himself rather than live with what was in his head. Probably the only thing that could survive that sort of barrage and make sense of it would be a precognitive with a relative-time-dilation talent. In other words, an OpFour. Even an OpFive, if there was such a thing.

Which left him only one option. The one creature he knew that could do everything he wanted, but was certainly not going to be as easy as Ms. Hiller to bring into the company. Back to Plan A.

"Angel-napping." Khanji would have a cow. Better not tell her. He cued up his PDA, this time using voice. Nothing for Khanji to "accidentally" run across that way. Good thing his PA knew when to keep her trap shut. "Miss Grancher? Would you please send a nicely worded invitation on the appropriately respectful stationary to People's Blade for a meeting at her earliest convenience? Khanjar does not need to be informed."

"Sir?" the PA said, before he could disconnect. "You need to supply a new head of Echo Medical."

"Oh, right, I had completely forgotten." That's what he had originally been working on before the unfortunate business with Rachel had cropped up. He opened a new window on his PDA, scanning through the files linked from his desk computer. "Let's see . . . this one. Bella Dawn Parker. Send the relevant paperwork to my desk; you know the drill, Miss Grancher." He had to grin at that a little. Parker wasn't an MD, she was a rebel against the rules, and on top of that, her chief claim to fame was as the fanboi's fave hottie from the "Sexiest Healers of Echo" calender. *He* could justify the promotion on the basis of Echo needing a fresh take and a friendly, well-known face. She would have *everyone* mad at her within twenty-four hours of taking the desk. In forty-eight, Echo Medical would be in chaos. And as soon as his plan to weed out the troublemakers moved into high gear, they would be losing metas almost as soon as they hit triage.

At least one thing had gone right today.

CHAPTER TEN

Leap of Faith

MERCEDES LACKEY AND CODY MARTIN

"What the hell have I done?" John stared out over the Atlanta skyline, beer forgotten in his hand. It was late. He hadn't been able to sleep. He'd been playing that interaction with the—well, *she* thought she was an angel—in his mind, over and over. *She* thought she was an angel, which didn't speak too well for her mental stability. And he'd gone and kissed her.

Why did I do that? Everything had been going so well. She was strange as hell, granted; she had her delusion, she knew things that no one else did, and seemed capable of anything. But she never really asked anything of him; she was just there with him, sharing moments without taking.

But this was a complication. He didn't need complications. Especially right now. Life was complicated enough. So far, he'd had Blacksnake come calling, twice, and neither time had been exactly a laugh riot. Echo had tried to recruit him, too, though with a damn sight less "prejudice." He was still settling in with the CCCP; they were a whole different kind of weird on their own. Between Bear's antics, Unter's grousing, and Natalya's penchant for throwing ceramics at people, it was a lot to take in and adjust to. He'd been his neighborhood's version of law enforcement and "physical conflict mediator" for a while, but being part of a uniformed and sanctioned force again was going to take a lot of getting used to.

Then there was what had pushed him into the arms of the CCCP in the first place; Echo, Blacksnake, and of course the ever present shadow of the Program. The first two had taken a keen interest in him once things had started to come back together after the Invasion. Echo was too busy to waste too many resources on him. Blacksnake was another matter; they had already sent two recruiters, with the caveat that refusing the offer included a ticket to the morgue. Whether they didn't want to draw any heat down on themselves from the CCCP, or if they were just tired of having teams go missing completely, John couldn't say. He hadn't run into any more of their goons since, but that could always change in an instant.

As bad as Blacksnake was, the Program was far worse. Just because he'd knocked out one facility, that didn't mean there weren't more. They didn't get tired of losing people. They didn't run out of money. They didn't worry about pissing anyone off. If they wanted something, they got it, or they killed it. Maybe both. Joining the CCCP was more about getting extra protection for the neighborhood from any fallout that might befall him than it was about saving his own hide. He just hoped that when—not if—they came for him, that not too many other people would get hurt. It was too late to run again; they'd tear up the entire neighborhood and everyone in it, if they had to; he didn't have any doubts about that. It wasn't about the money and time spent, or the effort; knowing the sort of people behind the Program, they'd keep coming after him simply on principle.

John, in typical boneheaded fashion, had just made things that much worse. With a kiss.

"It would've been better if she slapped ya, moron." But Sera had reciprocated. And what did *that* mean? "That's she's crazier than I am." *Dammit all.* He knew exactly why he'd done that; he wanted to, simple as that. But why did he want to kiss her? Why did he want *her*? It wasn't as if he couldn't get women. Even Bella had flirted with him—she hadn't meant anything really by it, but he could probably work on that. He wouldn't abuse his position to trawl around the neighborhood, but there were plenty of other neighborhoods in Atlanta. What the hell kept him around her, as opposed to anyone else?

This was another thing he couldn't run from. Things had changed for him; it was slowly draining from his constitution to be able to run from the big problems. The Program had done that to him, turning him into a fugitive. The Invasion and everything since... well, it had changed everyone. John couldn't deny his growing feelings for "Atlanta's Angel," and he sure as hell couldn't stop them. Right now he just wanted to understand the whole stinking mess. And maybe try and figure out if he had done something unbelievably stupid.

He could just tell her not to come around. He could just cut all of his contacts to the most impersonal level.

He could, but he already knew that he wouldn't. Besides, he doubted that very much in this world could keep her from seeing him if she wanted to.

He could try, though. If he really wanted to...

But just the thought of that... made his insides knot up a little. Made him feel hollow inside. And gave him an ache in the back of his throat.

You don't want her to stop coming around, bonehead. God, even his own self-deprecating thoughts were starting to sound like Vic's chiding. This was eating at him; he had to figure it out. Part of it was safety; he cared about her, and didn't want his past to catch up with the both of them. He just couldn't let this rest, or else he really wouldn't be able to sleep anymore. There was one thing that was digging at the back of his mind, the key to this. It seemed like it was just out of his reach, but if he could get it he'd know.

"Well, genius, let's go 'bout this logically. Somethin' is different. Yeah, yeah, besides the fact that ya like a gal." He took a swig of his beer absentmindedly. "Somethin' is there now where there wasn't anythin' before. Nothin' else has been doin' it all these years on the run. So what is it?"

Well, for the first time, he'd been concentrating on something other than pure survival. He had a squat, regular meals, and a sort of security in CCCP. He wasn't living hour to hour. So now he had time to think... and to feel again.

He brought the beer bottle up to his lips again, but stopped short. It had hit him. *I'm not lonely anymore when I'm around her. I feel accepted; like I'm a* part *of the damned world again, instead of a shadow up against the edges.* John set the beer bottle down on the ledge, unfinished. "I'll be a son of a bitch. That's it." He stared out at the city, mulling over this revelation. "Okay. Now what do I do with *that*?"

John had already made his mind up; he couldn't shut off his feelings anymore, even if he wanted to. It would've driven him over the edge if he still could. But he was still worried; what happened if the *worst* happened?

Well, Sera seemed able to take care of herself, but that fact didn't shake his fear. He'd already lost enough people; he wouldn't let hubris claim another one, especially someone that he'd finally come to genuinely care about after so long utterly alone.

He was fighting with shadows, though, and he knew it. There was really only one course open to him; keep going as best as he could, and hope that the worst didn't come to pass.

More than that, he hoped he got to see her again soon.

Sera had a new perch; the Suntrust Plaza was too exposed, too many people could see her there, even though it offered her an unparalleled view. She had found a most peculiar structure, a sort of Greco-Roman temple placed, for no apparent reason, atop one of the other high-rise buildings. It pleased her. It afforded her some measure of concealment; the best view of it came from an expensive restaurant and the sorts of people who frequented such a place were very unlikely to see her unless she intended them to. The same held for those who had offices in the surrounding buildings. Without all of those eyes on her, she felt more herself.

The place also had an excellent view of the CCCP headquarters and John's squat. Not a trivial consideration.

She never actually rested as such; her mind was always working, sifting through futures, on the alert for moments when she was needed. But tonight, for a few moments, all those things had been shunted aside, in favor of a single astonishing sensation.

A kiss.

It was one thing to have the memories of billions of human kisses and caresses of all sorts available to one. It was quite another to actually experience such a thing.

John could only have surprised her in this way because his future, his present, increasingly his past, and his thoughts were all so opaque to her. In fact, she was almost *certain* that she had known more about him before she came to know him better. It was as if the Infinite was removing her access to that information, so that she had to rely on what he revealed to her himself.

This was a little unnerving. She was not at all used to the

Infinite leaving her on her own, blind, relying only on a single, mortal, fallible source.

But John himself was unnerving. *Though . . . in a good way,* she thought, suddenly. *Certainly . . . that kiss . . .*

It was, most definitely, a sign, though not in the "sign from God" sense. His barriers were breaking down. He was willing to share things with her, things he had kept hidden from everyone. And he had finally made a firm emotional contact with someone.

With her.

Instinctively she put her hand to her lips. It had not been chaste, that kiss. Not the "kiss of peace." Not demanding either, nor aggressive. Playful? Perhaps . . .

Permitted?

He had asked her, "What do you want me to be?" And she had been astonished. For no one, ever, had asked her what *she* wanted. She had said as much aloud. And then he had kissed her, and for that short time, she had not thought of anything else.

She had *told* herself such a thing could surely be permitted. All things that brought creatures together were permitted . . . but had she known this, or merely told herself so because this was how she wanted it?

The fact that you can ask the question tells you the answer, Seraphym.

Well . . . there it was. Not the exact answer to her question, but certainly implied, by virtue of the fact that all good was in the realm of the Infinite, and that which was not good . . . was not.

So, there remained, what to make of this? She was flying blind here, with John, with these very mortal things, with *emotions.* And what to do about it? Should she pull back? No, that was unacceptable; it was needed that he should become more human, more connected, not less, and withdrawing from him would only put back all those walls he was pulling down. Should she foster only friendship, as Bella did?

Or should she just stop trying to calculate, and to steer, for once? Should she just . . . see what happens? Just let go?

Was that why the Infinite was withholding information from her? To force her into the position where there were no maps and guides? To make a leap of faith into the dark, and trust that she would find the way?

I think... that is exactly what I must do. And... strangely... the thought comforted.

She looked down upon John's roof, and saw the lonely figure there, gazing out over the city. But just at that moment, she felt it—the sudden need for her, and knew that she must not yet answer it, and John would be alone with his thoughts a bit longer.

Not tonight, friend John, but soon... soon.

CHAPTER ELEVEN

The Seven Deadly Virtues

MERCEDES LACKEY AND CODY MARTIN

The obliviousness of the ultrarich never ceased to amuse Verdigris. Out there, just inland from the Port of Savannah, there were entire stretches of major cities that still looked like the aftermath of a nuke strike. But here he was, with a thousand of his closest "friends," partying the night away on his own little "island"—one of his many company container ships, the deck mostly stripped of the containers—which had been transformed into a snapshot of any one of those destruction corridors. Only clean, sanitized, and with caviar and champagne.

The theme of the party was "Post Apocalypse," and like all of Dominic Verdigris' parties, it was epic in scale. Costume was required, but these people didn't have to worry about trivialities like coming up with costumes. Their personal assistants took care of that.

There were four bands, more refreshment tables than Verd cared to count, and a nice sprinkling of Echo metahumans dragooned into providing "glamor." And "entertainment." Verd stood on the bridge of the ship and looked down on his tiny kingdom. Directly below him was . . . what was his name? Aqua-marine? *Jeezus, what a stupid name.* The dweeb had some sort of telekinetic water control. It actually had some practical application, since he could become a metahuman water cannon, but right now he was making impossible shapes in midair, like some sort of magic fountain. Fractals made of water astounded the oohing and aahing crowd of socialites that had paused in front of the Echo Op. Verd tapped a command to his party staff on his comm, and almost instantly the onboard lighting crew had the water sculptures lit up with lasers and colored lights.

Khanji, as always, was at his side. Her costume was pretty amusing, really. It was actual Echo-tech body armor, carefully made up with little shreds of net, bits of leather, and splotches of paint. Not that she really needed body armor, but it was the only thing he could coax her into. She'd been very sullen of late, jealous of the attention he was paying to People's Blade, no doubt. Maybe tonight would sweeten her temper a little, with the Chinese girl nowhere in sight.

"These rich yuppies just can't seem to wait to rip their expensive suits and dresses up and cover them in dirt and charcoal. It's actually kind of funny."

"You're not in costume," Khanji observed.

Of course he wasn't. He was in a completely immaculate white silk suit. "I'm King of the Apocalypse, of course I'm clean; I own all the soap. Besides, it's rather appropriate, don't you think? All of these sots in rags?"

"And why would that be, Dom?" Khanji replied coolly. "If you are making some sort of ironic observation based on media memes, you forget I spent most of my childhood in a Pakistani slum, so I didn't get a lot of exposure to that sort of thing."

"Never mind, darling. How are things coming for our plans in Hong Kong?" He hoped that would distract her, sweeten that sour temper. After all, ordinarily *he* would have overseen everything, but this time he had put *her* in complete charge. "After turning the Bombay fiasco into a win, you deserve some more authority," he'd said. He'd meant it as a compliment to smooth over her increasingly prickly disposition, but in a rare miscalculation it'd only made her colder. *Women. Can't live with 'em, can't sell 'em for parts. Well, actually, there are those Triads that keep on bugging me...*

"On schedule and running smoothly." Her tone was completely dismissive. So much for that attempt.

"Well, good. Good work." He fidgeted with his drink, looking at his shoes; maybe feigning embarrassment at his earlier gaffs would bring her out of the rocky shell she was in. "I guess we'd better go mingle, huh? I mean, it's my party, the host has to put in an appearance."

She snorted. "Half of them are already so drunk or high they'll swear they've been talking to you half the night."

"Oh, that reminds me, the surveillance cameras are running on every corner of the ship, right?" Parties like this served multiple functions for a man like Dominic Verdigris. There were chances to take people aside to slip them a bribe, to have sequestered meetings that wouldn't be noticed, even to have people murdered. His absolute favorite thing about these sorts of parties was the opportunities for blackmail; when intoxicated with their favorite poison—and sometimes drugs that they never even knew they had taken—people would do the *darnedest* things. And sometimes, just for the hell of it, even if there was no advantage to it, really embarrassing stuff could mysteriously end up on an internet video site. He always loved it when one of his leaks went viral. Sometimes it took a little bit more help than others, but that was part of the fun, too. Like that congressman that had turned into a squealing little heart-eyed fangirl over one of his pet metas at the last gig. One of those skinny, freaky Winds. *Closeted, much?* "We'll wanna double-check the audio pickups; I'll have my computer run all the recordings through a few filters, see what delicious dirt we get."

Khanji didn't even bother to reply to that. She had very little to do with the electronic end of things; her expertise was at the physical side. She turned on her heel and left him alone on the balcony. It wasn't as if he *needed* a bodyguard tonight. He was on his own ship, triple-checked by his own security, and staffed by his own security. And under the silk suit was a nanoweave bodysuit. Why, the automatic deterrents alone would take out an assassin before he even finished aiming. There was truly innovative research going on in predictive threat algorithms as well, something he had taken a keen interest in lately.

Still, it felt pretty odd to head down to the party without her. It wasn't attachment, per se; Verdigris had never been terribly attached to much of anything, other than power; wealth was just a byproduct of that, and only an ancillary concern of his. He was simply *used* to always having Khanjar there with him. And this was their first real row. She'd voiced her disapproval of things before this, but she'd never taken his decisions so personally.

Verdigris knew where her real hostility was coming from, of course: the General. Ever since that first night, something had been off. At first he thought that it might simply be rivalry—one lioness sizing up the other. He hadn't favored one over the other, so far as he had seen. In fact, the General's "initiation test" was almost designed to fail; he had been pleasantly surprised when she had come back, whole and victorious. So, he had set her to tasks that suited her abilities, just as he had always done with Khanjar. All of this taken together suggested something deeper . . . but what?

Could Khanjar have sensed he was considering making the General his second-in-command? But why would she be jealous about that? It wasn't as if *she* had ever shown any interest in the position. Verdigris made his way down a set of metal stairs to the main floor, taking his time and contemplating the recent troubles he was having with Khanjar. It didn't take long for someone to spot him and come stumbling over.

"Senator! Lovely to see you and your darling wife able to make it tonight. I trust you're enjoying this quaint little gathering of mine?"

"Mr. Verdigris, you sell yourself short! I haven't had this much fun since my frat days at Texas Tech! Ain't that right, honey?"

The trophy wife smiled vacuously. She was number three, if Verd recalled correctly. Former Miss Texas. Literally a trophy wife. Though it looked like she'd gone from blue to red ribbon quality in recent years; having a senator for a husband could be quite trying. "Yes, dear."

The senator and his wife were both dressed in completely white western suits, complete with an expensive ten-gallon hat. What completed the picture, however, was that both of them were covered from head to toe in crude oil. Or at least, what looked like crude oil. It didn't smell like crude oil, it didn't have that sulfur stink, which could be eye-watering. It smelled like designer fragrance from Chanel.

His thoughts drifted back to People's Blade and Khanjar as he politely tore himself away from the Texas couple. People's Blade was a superb tactician; she was already making her presence felt on whatever tactical teams he paired her with. He'd originally had his doubts, though he was careful never to betray them; someone claiming to have the soul of a general, thousands of years dead, does tend to make for skepticism at best, and the conviction of outright lunacy at worst. Despite that, she tended to get the job done, whatever that job might be. She always seemed impatient, however; she wanted more and knew that Verdigris sensed it.

Another one of Verd's guests leapt out from behind the shelter of one of the cargo containers—this one hid a luxurious little lounge behind the layers of camo-net shrouding its open end. He pretended to hose down the whole area with the scrapyard chain gun he had slung at hip level. It was a pretty piece of FX work, it produced very realistic sound and a lot of spark and flash as it "fired." The man himself was dressed like an extra out of *Mad Max*, complete with assless chaps and football shoulder pads, all studded with spikes and spray painted. The one off detail was that the man's vanity prevented him from turning what had to have been a five-hundred-dollar haircut into anything but a faux-hawk.

"Whoa! Sorry there, your Royal Highness!" the man giggled. "Didn't realize the King of the Apocalypse was with us. Hope I didn't smudge the suit!" Verdigris peeked behind him; judging by the mini pharmacy that had been set out on the lounge table, the man was seeing everything in rainbow.

"Not to worry," Verd replied, making a little brushing-off motion, and going along with the fantasy. "Force field, don't you know. No blood, no foul." What he didn't say was that he'd had to switch off one of his security systems with a discreet hand gesture to keep it from turning the man into a red splotch against the wall behind him.

"Seriously, Dom, this is a kick-ass party. Haven't had this much fun since me and some of the boys from the office went out paintballing bums from the Beemer." Dom didn't actually recognize the man behind all the fake grunge and paint; it had taken that clue to ID him. Trent Perry, Wall Street investor. "And thanks for that tip-off on those water treatment hedge funds. I took out a derivative investment on them going bad. You made me a bundle." Verdigris smiled and nodded as he walked away. It would certainly come as a shock to ol' Trent when evidence was found that implicated him in a conspiracy to make sure that water treatment deal went bad. *You win some, you lose some more. Now, where was I?*

What was Khanjar to him? Bodyguard first, lover a distant second. *And growing more distant with each passing second, dammit.* In the beginning when he'd hired her, it was only for her efficient deadliness and mercenary attitude, two things he could appreciate. In time, it had become economical and appropriate for him to tell her more and more about his plans and operations. Not everything, of course; he would have rather eaten his own tie than reveal *everything* to even someone as trusted as Khanjar. Then their sleeping arrangements had become coterminous. It occurred to him that the General's rise was mirroring Khanjar's, though he knew that even the mere suggestion of bedding her would likely result in the loss of some of his more important body parts.

Right now, it was best to play the wait-and-see strategy; set up People's Blade with a full access pass, same as Khanjar's, and watch them both. In the end, it only mattered who was the more useful of the two, anyways. That, and who was least likely to plant a knife in his back or a bullet in his forehead.

He strolled along the deck, vaguely aware that he was . . . bored. Just then, movement off to one side caught his attention. It was a group of his guests, but the group was utterly atypical. Instead of taking advantage of one of the cozy lounges, they had pulled up bits of the "stage dressing" to sit on—boxes, burlap bags full of kapok, overturned buckets. They were clustered around one of his metahumans, who was also sitting on a bucket. Big black wings, black nanoweave uniform . . . Corbie, that was it. One of the minor talents. Verd remembered why he'd recruited the Brit—he could fly, and Verd had thought vaguely that he might do some sort of aerobatic nonsense.

But no, he was just sitting here, talking to these people. No, he was doing all the talking. They were listening, and only occasionally asking questions.

". . . so busy tracking the dogs and Johnny M and Motu they weren't payin' attention to me, plus it was dark, so I zipped in and planted those limpet bombs on top of them and zipped out again."

"But you don't wear armor do you?" gasped one socialite. "That was incredibly brave!"

Corbie made a *psh*ing sound. "Lot less brave than those National Guard blokes. No armor, no powers, and what they had was like carrying a popgun against a tank."

Verdigris stood there in the shadow of one of the containers, watching and listening. *They're eating right out of his hand. He's not* that *good of a storyteller, either. But right now, I'd bet donuts to dinars that he could sell them anything in the world, and they'd lap it up.*

But there was more to it than that. He watched the Brit's face. There was no trace of boredom, no guile, no sense that he had told this story a million times over—and he probably had. It wasn't macho-bravado glory-hounding either, relishing the awe of his audience, reveling in the sense of "I am so wonderful." The ego boost. No, it wasn't that. Verd, who was an astute observer of humanity, knew exactly what it was. Corbie was a hero. Whether he was born to be one, or circumstances had made him into one, that was what he was. He constitutionally would not be able to stand aside when something needed doing, and it wasn't that he was reckless or thought he was immortal, it was that at that moment, the risks were not relevant to him, because other people were far more important to him than his own survival.

They saw him as a hero, too. They *believed* in him as such. That was why he held them spellbound. He was, at one and the same time, Everyman and Larger Than Life. He was one of them, and their potential savior. And not one of them, picturing him or herself in danger, had the slightest doubt that if Corbie was there, he'd risk everything to get them out.

Was he doing something right? Was there something to really playing it for the team, not just pretending to?

"...and besides," Corbie was continuing, "that frickin' bastard owed me a beer!"

They all laughed. "Corbie, what about that business last week, with the Djinni?" asked someone else, and Corbie was off on another story.

"Ah, now, the Djinni...now there is one weird bloke..."

The waiter had to call his name three times before Verdigris knew he was there. "Sir? Mr. Verdigris?"

Dominic almost allowed his annoyance to show as he turned away from Corbie and his audience. "Yes? What is it?"

"Champagne, sir?" The waiter was new to the job, that much was plain; most of the staff that he hired knew that when Verdigris wanted something, he damned well asked for it instead of being pestered every five seconds.

"No, that's fine, thank you." He waved his free hand to make the dismissal that much more obvious. The waiter wandered away meekly as Verdigris turned his attention back to Corbie.

So, where was I? Verdigris hated losing his train of thought; his mind often took him to strange and unexpected places, and it was particularly vexing when that journey was interrupted. *Right. Him. He's happy. He's not rich, he's not really famous, and all he's got is a pair of wings, so he's kind of a flying target. And he's still happy. If he got a call right now to go throw himself after some Thulian or something, he'd leave this party without even thinking about it and do it.*

Verd frowned a little. *He's happy.* He did something he rarely did. He took his own emotional temperature. He had accomplished the impossible. He was incredibly rich. It was trivial to make more money. He commanded both Echo and Blacksnake, not to mention all of his different proxies throughout the world. He was in the position now to do something about the Thulians.

He wasn't *happy.* But what more could he possibly acquire? What could he control that would *make* him happy?

Well, not ending up as a brain in a box would be a damn good start. His frown deepened a little. That was the missing part of the equation; he still had that sword hanging above his head. Did anything else really matter while that possibility was still open?

No. That's what's standing between me and everything else. I mean, no point even in going for world domination if that's at the end of it. All of the doubt and anxiety melted away. Pleased that he had identified the cause of his lack of happiness, now he just had to go for the cure. And he knew the shortest cut to that cure.

So, full speed ahead with the Project. Get the Chinese chick up to speed; she's made for this sort of job. Appease Khanji somehow, since I still need her. Trap angel, interrogate angel, implement whatever I need to get myself off the list of "to be boxed." He pondered a little more. Would it be worth negotiating with the Thulians once he was in a better position to do so? Probably. Very probably. Always have to leave as many options and plays open as possible, of course.

And meanwhile, in the shortest of short terms, work the party. Verdigris was fairly confident that he'd have quite a bit of fun reviewing all of the surveillance tapes later.

I wonder if finding someone for Khanji to kill to work off her aggression might help. He lifted a finger and a waiter—one of the old ones, who knew his signals—was instantly at his side with champagne. *There's that... oh wait. I think I've got it. I get rid of dead weight, potential trouble, and Khanji's mad, all at the same time. Brilliant, as always, Dom. Heh.*

This party just might turn out to be fun after all.

CHAPTER TWELVE

In One Ear

MERCEDES LACKEY

Bella, if you are reading this, this is going to embarrass the hell out of you.

I don't know how Bella did this.

Of all of us, she never lost hope, never lost focus. When something went pear-shaped, she was always the first one to pick herself up off the ground. No matter what she might have thought herself, she was the only *one fit to lead the revolution. I'd be sitting there in the Overwatch suite, paralyzed, trying to make my brain work, and she'd be on the wire going "Vix? What about—" and kick start my brain again.*

Like this. None of us, none, saw this coming. It blindsided us all.

And she grabbed the ball and ran with it.

This has to be a joke.

Bella stared at the email. It didn't make any sense. True, she was *acting* as de facto head of Echo Med, but Verdigris didn't know that. She was being very, very careful to make sure he didn't know that. Almost everything was running through Doctor Luke Sanders, aka Doc Fluke (his strange little metahuman power was to be able to diagnose really weird stuff instantly, while missing the common things completely, which made him incredibly useful to Echo Med). What wasn't running through him was going through Ramona. Maybe by now Verdigris knew she was the only one able to calm Einhorn down, but surely that was *all* he knew....

It is permitted me to tell you. Verdigris believes you are an incompetent airhead.

Bella looked up so fast she nearly gave herself whiplash. The angel was sitting on the chair across from her tiny desk in the little storage closet Ramona had stolen her for an "office." The Seraphym looked like a Sulamith Wulfing painting; wings folded, hands laid one over the other on her lap, strange eyes staring through her.

"You know, things like 'incompetent airhead' sound really odd coming from you." She ran her hand through her bangs, fluffing them to cool herself. The room always seemed too small and too warm when the angel was in it. Even when the room was the size of a football stadium.

The lips curved a little. *I seem to be picking up odd phrases from John Murdock. But it is permitted me to tell you that your ruse still holds. Verdigris selected you* because *he believes you are a fool.*

Bella narrowed her eyes. "So . . . he wants Echo Med to be in chaos. The titular leader is a moron. And . . ." she sucked on her lower lip, and thought aloud. "If I were a vain little airhead, I would turn all bitchy boss on everyone. I'd insist on doing the running of things even though I don't know squat about it."

Yes.

Bella smiled grimly. "All righty then. We'll give him the show he expects. Overwatch: Command. Call Victrix." She heard the tiniest of clicks as her Overwatch wire came on. "Vix, you live?"

"I'm never not live. You check your email?"

"That's a Roger." The angel smiled at her, and vanished. She shook her head. She was never going to get used to that. "How many Overwatch wires have you got now?"

"How many you need?"

One by one, the staff of Echo Medical filed into the conference room. Most of them had been taken aside by Ramona Ferrari over the course of the last day, taken to a broom closet that emitted a curious hum, given a couple of sentences of briefing and given what looked like a perfectly ordinary Echo field op headset—the sort that was easy to hide. They were all wearing them now.

Vickie watched them from the cameras in each corner of the conference room—cameras Verdigris was either watching now, or would pull the footage from some time soon. As the doctors and nurses and techs and support staff shuffled around to find seats, she cued a discreet little bird chirp to their headsets to alert them.

And Verdigris would never, ever be able to detect this. Overwatch no longer used radio signals. Every one of those headsets was getting her voice via the magical equivalent of a radio frequency. It had taken her a lot of brain sweat and even more work to get it working right, but now they were *secure* in a way no encryption could ever manage.

"Good afternoon, ladies and gentlemen. Don't look startled. You are now listening to the Voice of Overwatch, a very clandestine little operation that started as a support net for a few chosen field teams and allies, but is now the coordination arm of the revolution to take down Dominic Verdigris III. Most of the people in the room have these headsets. The only ones who don't are those whose discretion is somewhat lacking, or who we suspect are Verdigris plants or sympathizers." Einhorn was one of the former. She couldn't keep a secret for thirty seconds. Fortunately, she was one of the few who didn't *care* who was in charge. "The voice in your ear will be giving you Bella's *real* speech. So pay no attention to what comes out of her mouth. This little show is all for Verdigris' benefit."

Bella came into the room at that point, looking flustered and smug and pleased all at once in a . . . somewhat radically tailored version of her Echo uniform. She looked like what Verdigris thought she was—a supermodel put in a position of power she in no way deserved or was suited for.

She had papers in her hand and arranged them on the podium, and cleared her throat. "Hi everybody!" she chirped. "I guess by now you all know who's head of Echo Med!"

Vickie cued what Bella had recorded previously. While Bella churned out a speech consisting entirely of clichés, this was what was playing into the ears and minds of the people who were the heart, hands, and backbone of Echo Medical.

"First of all, I know most of you, and most of you know me. Some of you like me, some probably don't, but regardless, I am pretty damn sure that all of you are in some stage of disbelief, anger, and resentment over this whacked-up promotion. I'd like you to try to continue to look that way, please, if you can."

Vickie could see that some of them were doing their best to do just that. Some were just looking bewildered. That would work too.

"No, I didn't sleep my way to this. This is our Lord and Master's way of turning Echo Med into a seething mass of unorganized chaos. Some of you are going 'wha—?' and some of you have suddenly had your suspicions confirmed. Yes, Verd wants us to fail, spectacularly. He wants all of Echo to fail, I suspect, so he can disband the entire organization, cherry-pick the pieces, and put together his own version of Echo without any messy nonsense of preexisting charters or legal considerations—or the safety and continued existence of the metas in it."

Vickie was very good at reading expressions. The flashes of anger she saw would be read by Verd as anger at Bella. But those expressions boded very well for Bella's ability to *be* what Verd had set her up for, and more.

"I'm not alone in this little conspiracy, although for a while it was just me, Ramona, Yank, and a couple more folks you'll be hearing about later."

Brief flashes of relief at the mention of Yankee Pride and Ramona. *Good move, Bell.*

"Yank and Ramona are obviously too high profile with Verd to be the chief rabble-rousers for this, so it kind of fell to me. We were going to bring you guys in slowly, but Verd forced our hand. Now, if you want out, turn in your headsets to Ramona later today. No one but you and Ramona will ever know who you are. No one is going to judge you either. If I was in your shoes, I'd be thinking twice and three times about this myself. Going up against Verd? We gotta be nucking futz."

Not a word about "don't rat us out." *Another good move.* With people who were nervous, but mostly trustworthy, implied trust tended to become real trust.

"If you're sticking, or even if you're not, I want you to act the way you would if an incompetent, power-hungry moron just got promoted over you. We need to make Verd think Echo Med is about to fall apart as soon as we get hit with a big emergency. This is going to have to be the most convincing acting job you've ever done in your life, and I hope to hell we are all up to the performance. The lives of our friends are going to depend on it. Overwatch will give you all a further briefing later today after those of you who are opting out have turned in your headsets. So, okay, everybody, thanks for listening. I'm about to wrap up the speech now. *Showtime.*"

Vickie cut the recorded speech, as Bella chirped into the mic at the front of the room. "And I just *know* we are all going to be the best team there ever was! Thanks for coming, everyone!"

There was tepid applause as Bella beamed fatuously. People began filing out quickly, even before she had a chance to step from behind the podium. The only person who came up to congratulate her—and sincerely no less—was Einhorn. Vickie found that oddly touching. Too bad she didn't have the sense God gave a goose.

Ramona was outside the conference room door with a bag open just enough that people could discretely drop their headsets in as they filed out. When they were all gone, Vickie cued up her freq and conferenced with Bella's.

"Okay, give us the bad news. How many bailed?" Vickie asked, before Ramona could say anything.

"Zero."

Vickie was sure she hadn't heard right. From the sound of Bella's voice, so was she. "Uh—what?"

"Zero," Ramona repeated gleefully. "Zilch. Nada. Everyone's in."

There was silence from Bella. Then, "Goddammit, I want to holler and dance and I don't dare with the cameras everywhere."

"I'll do it for you," Vickie replied gleefully. Even at her most optimistic she had figured for about a third to bail. Pessimistically, she had figured more like half.

"Okay. Phase two. Vic, I'm signing off the ranch right now, and heading for a very noisy, very trendy hotspot. Which is exactly what an airhead would do to congratulate herself. Let me know as folks come off-shift, and conference our headsets so I can do more detailed briefings." Bella let out her breath in a long, heartfelt sigh. "God, I hope I am up to this..."

"You are," Vickie and Ramona said simultaneously.

"I'd better be."

Bella took a long pull of a virgin Bloody Mary as inane chatter rang around her. She'd chosen the latest, hippest bar in Atlanta as being a place Verd was least likely to have ears, and as one that would have enough noise to cover her subvocalizations. *Her* headpiece and mic were no longer visible at all. Vickie had implanted them, somehow. She was the walking test subject for that particular piece of magic. If her body didn't have some sort of horrible reaction to the apparatus, they'd implant the rest of Echo Med and Sovie first. And if *they* didn't, everyone but Djinni would get the implants. He, obviously, didn't need his gear implanted to hide it. Then again . . . maybe Djinni would get them. Vix had hinted she had more planned than just the mics and pickups.

She was glad for the cool-down period before everyone else started coming off-shift. She needed to stare something right square in the face and decide if she had the . . . well, it wasn't bravery . . . she wasn't sure what it was. But working with the paranoid Vickie had convinced her that if Ramona and Yank's plan to use the Charter against Verd didn't work, they needed a backup.

Talking with JM had convinced her that there was only one thing that backup could be. Someone was going to have to take out Verdigris, permanently. Echo could not survive his leadership. And if Echo didn't survive . . .

This was not something she could confide in anyone else. This was a plan that had to stay in her head, and her head alone. Yank couldn't assassinate a fly. Ramona didn't have the skills or the means. CCCP? Could, and would, but the only one with a chance in hell was People's Blade, and Nat had confessed the little Chinese girl had gone off the reservation—and was probably working with either Verdigris or Blacksnake.

The angel could, but wouldn't.

At least, Bella didn't think she would. Assassination didn't seem to fit the parameter of "permitted."

That left Bella, who had the power, the skills, and the access, now that she was head of Echo Med; who could kill him in a way that would leave no sign that he'd suffered anything but a perfectly natural aneurysm or heart failure. All she had to do was touch him.

But could she?

I don't want to. . . . Murdering—there was no other word for it—that gang-banger still left her feeling sick and filthy and guilty as hell. And he'd been about to kill her and her friends. This would be murder in cold blood.

What would that make her?

What other choice would I have? It was like that old sci-fi cliché. If you could go back in time and murder Hitler—would you? Could you?

She thought about Tesla. About Bulwark, still unconscious. About all her other friends who would certainly be picked off one at a time or by wholesale groups if she didn't do this.

I can't let them die.

No matter what this does to me.

Then she felt her mouth quirk in a wry little smile. *Of course... if that creepy bodyguard of his figures out what I did, I might not have to worry about what it does to me.*

The chirp of Vickie's incoming signal put an end to any further thoughts on the matter for now. *"Okay, Bells, I have Doc Fluke, Panacea, Chiron, Gilead, Doctors Read, Morse, Sayers, Childreath, Kyne and Joyce, and Nurses Romanski, Charam, Fields, Liam, Lin, Wong, Sakamuti, and Jeanne on conference. Folks, the floor is Bella's."*

She took a deep breath and a last sip of her drink. "First of all... thanks, guys. You are the bravest, best people I know..."

CHAPTER THIRTEEN

Smoke and Mirrors

DENNIS LEE AND MERCEDES LACKEY

Even in the middle of everything falling apart, even in the middle of war, revolution, disaster, people stubbornly have the habit of falling in love. Part of it is the old survival instinct, by which I mean survival of your genes, not yourself. Fall in love, do the wild thing, make a baby or more and your genes go on, in theory at least. Part of it is that in horrible times we either break apart or come together.

But of course, when one person falls in love, it doesn't follow that the other person is going to do the same. Or at least, not with the person who loves him.

And if the person falling in love is me? Well, in that case... I already knew it was going to end in tears.

"... so there was this artifact that the Hungarian side of the family had, that went all the way back to the Romans. It hid the bearer from the fangs. Small problem: once every twenty-eight years it had to be renewed with the blood of an innocent child, by which I mean"—Vickie made a throat-slitting motion, barely visible in the gloom where they were waiting—"and once every ninety-nine, it had to be done with the blood of twenty-one innocent children. Charming, huh?"

The Djinni rolled his eyes. "I swear, you're making this up. It sounds like some god-awful drive-in flick from the sixties."

She managed a feeble smile, the merest flash of teeth in the dark. "Yeah, well the Dark Ages were evil and brutish. You could pretty much find dead or dying kids anywhere without having to kill any yourself. And my family line is pretty serious about fang-hunting. It started getting really problematic the closer we get to modern times. Nobody really wanted to start offing infants until Uncle Bela got his hands on it. That was when this guy I had the hots for in college turned up. Alistair Greenstall, and I swear, in college he was okay. I mean, I know all about good girls always falling for bad guys, but when I knew him he was fine. One thing led to another, and the pillow talk turned into 'how can you let him have this thing when you *know* he intends to repower it?' And that was where I let my hormones do the talking. And it turned out Alistair was a Renfield."

Red frowned. "Why does that name sound familiar?"

"It's out of Bram Stoker's book. Handy term for what the Hunters call people who are still normal who serve the fangs." She shrugged. "Some people will do anything for the promise of power. Magic wasn't enough for Alistair. Or maybe I should say, the magic he had wasn't enough for Alistair." Vickie paused as the memories flashed through her mind. She was actually pretty proud of herself. She'd gotten choked up a time or two, but she hadn't lost it. It just took some controlled breathing, a few choice, silent mantras, and a lot of willpower.

"Victrix, you don't have to go on..."

She waved him off and continued. "Let me cut right to the chase. I grabbed the dingus from Uncle Bela; as per the plan, Alistair and I were going to ambush him when he came after us. Alistair bailed when I wouldn't just hand it over to him for *safe-keeping.* So I broke the dingus just as Uncle caught up with me. Uncle was very mad at me. Mage battle ensued. Uncle Bela is a fire mage, and what he lacks in understanding of the modern world, he more than makes up for in experience. You know the saying, 'old age and treachery beat youth and idealism hands down.' I lost. So, that's how I ended up like this. It never was losing control of magic, it was being a hormonal overachieving kid out of college, falling for the wrong guy and pissing off someone bigger, stronger and nastier." She pondered that for a moment. "Not that I wouldn't have gone after Uncle Bela and taken that thing from him when I found out he was going to murder all those kids to repower it... but without Alistair in the picture, I would have gone to Hosteen Stormdance and got *him* to get me backup if my folks wouldn't agree to help. That was where I was *monumentally* stupid." She licked her lips. "Just goes to show that Mom was right. You just can't trust vampires." She cupped her hands and brought them to her eyes, cueing the little spell that let her use them like real binoculars. "No sign of life at the alleged rendezvous, by the way. Are you sure this was good intel? Did it sniff of something not on the level from Verd?"

"No," Djinni said. He crouched next to her, bobbing gently on the balls of his feet. "Verd's got a particular style. He either knows something's so concrete he doesn't even bother to hide what he's doing, or he goes for the extravagant to beat you over the head with how clever he is. This is pretty run of the mill, probably masterminded by one of his flunkies. Small stuff, by the smell of it. Simple munitions deal."

"Yeah, well the last 'simple munitions deal' we knew about netted the Rebs a freaking shoulder-held missile launcher. I can really do without them picking up a satchel nuke or something." She shifted her position, missing her zero-gee chair.

"Yeah, well, that's why we're here, isn't it? To keep an eye on things, to make sure they don't get out of hand."

"Yes," she agreed. "To *watch*. Which, I'll remind you, I would be doing with a cup of coffee and a Reuben from my chair right now if you hadn't persuaded me I needed 'fieldwork.'"

Red didn't answer. It wasn't the coffee, or the damned sandwich, that Vickie was missing. It was her fortress of an apartment she craved. It was the security, the safety of it. Overwatch was a good idea, but he knew, in his bones, that she needed to get out of that hole and start pushing her boundaries. Now. Or one day she'd never be able to cross the threshold. Even up here, in the relative safety of unlit rooftops and sheltered by a rough canopy of camouflage tarp, he could tell she felt exposed. Across the street, the warehouse was dark. Two in the morning in an unused section of the industrial district. It didn't seem to matter, he might as well have asked her to sprint across I-285 during rush hour. Still, baby steps. The girl needed to feel the night air, to get back to acting like a human being and not a troglodyte.

Sharing stories had been his idea. He could feel her bursting at the seams. It wasn't a particularly cool night, but she was shivering. It seemed best to get her talking, and what better topic than what had scarred her, both physically and emotionally, so totally, all those years ago? Finally get her over that hump. Desensitization. She had been reluctant, at first, but once the floodgates were open she went on a tear. Red sat and listened, trying not to interrupt. She needed this.

"So that's why I just don't think of magic as something that causes me problems, since... I've been practicing discipline since I started. Now, it's more like art. Magic is just... so elegant." She was peering through her hands again. "Am I boring you? I'm probably boring you. You always say I talk too much."

"Yes, you do," he said. "Keep going."

"Math. I love the math. When you finally get everything lined up, it just... I dunno, it *sings.* It's like Bach." She paused. "I wish you could see it the way I do, but everybody sees magic differently. My mom sees it as needlework, tatting or knitting or something. Dad doesn't see it at all, he's just a werewolf." She giggled nervously. "There's your drive-in flick. *I Was a Werewolf for the FBI.*" She paused again. "So... you can tell me to shove it and never ask again, but why is it you've got such a burr up your butt about magic? You obviously know a lot about it, and most people who've cracked past *magic doesn't exist* can't get enough of it."

He considered that, and shrugged. "Let's just say that the magicians I've known were not as fastidious in their approach as you are. They were junkies, of a sort, and I was along for the ride. How do these things always begin? We were young, cocky, and there just wasn't enough of a rush to feel sated. I was the one who brought us together. I think I was on a losing streak at the time. I needed a new gang. The one I found was different. Not your usual group of metas, these guys were based in weird powers of the arcane and occult. Individually, they were small time. When I brought us together, they found a way to tap into each others' potential, and as a group, they found a way to overcome each others' vulnerabilities. As for me, well, you've channeled through me, you know how easy it is. I have no talent whatsoever, but as a medium I was like a sponge. I could hold power like a battery and they could direct it to do just about anything they wanted to. Together, we got stupidly strong, stupidly fast."

"Oh... hell." She sounded stricken. "We'd postulated that could happen, that kind of spontaneous synergy, but we've never seen it in the wild. I'd bet your ability to be a medium is meta in origin. I'll let some people know. We need to keep an eye out from now on before things escalate." She shook her head. "We're kind of a chaotic bunch, but there are people who try and... cut that kind of trouble off at the pass. Not block it or burn it out! Not unless we are dealing with sociopaths. But... teach 'em before they get themselves in trouble, I guess."

Red shrugged again. "I don't think we would have listened to anyone outside. We were all caught up in our own cleverness. The closest we had to any kind of moral compass was Tomb, but even he was riding the wave of our successes..."

"Tomb?" Vickie interrupted. "Tomb Stone? That's where you know him from?"

"The one and only." Red grimaced behind his scarf. "Why do you think he only exploits part of his gift anymore? He could have kept going, but after what happened... he lost his taste for it. He leaves the heavy lifting to his brother now. Anyway, we got to a point where we rarely had to leave the safety of our den to pull jobs. Our typical nights were spent in our base. I'd be the focus, sitting dead center. The others would form a circle around me. Tomb could conjure spirits and wraiths. Martin was the geo. He could grant them substance and ground them to this plane for a while. Justine was the pyro, in case the summoned needed a little firepower. I was the medium, directing them with my will. Like I said, it was a rush. As far as we were concerned, we were perfectly safe. If things ever got hairy, Tomb would break the summoning and they would vanish in a flash of fire and exploding rock. No one ever traced anything back to us. We did a lot of smash and grabs that way."

Vickie gestured to him to slow down. "Whoa, let me make a couple notes. That's... wow, I've never heard of anyone working like that. I need to work on the math." She tapped a couple of things on her PDA.

"Talk to Tomb sometime," the Djinni said. "Just get him drunk first. He doesn't like talking about those days."

"Or I can ask his brother first." Her voice softened a little. "Jacob is a really good man, Red. But... what did you do before all that? Nobody wakes up one morning and says, 'Hey, think I'll start a metahuman gang.' Well... okay, nobody but Verd."

Red favored her with a pitying look. "Really, Victrix? You've read my file, you can piece it together."

She gave him back a skeptical one. "There's next to nothing *in* your file, Red Djinni. At least, nothing before you got hooked into Echo. You are the Great Enigma. Lots of conjecture, lots of rumors, damn little in the way of facts."

"But enough," he said. "I guess it's obvious I was careful, by the lack of evidence, but it's clear I ran with mercenary groups, your standard small-time gangs of thieves, even a meta group here and there. And solo, sure. What do people with those skills and abilities do, Victrix, if they're not off saving the world?"

"Well..." she shrugged. "Making a living. I mean, I can give you a long list. You—you could have made a good living being a body double or stand-in for just about any studio, you know. It wouldn't have been the same adrenaline rush, I guess."

"And the rush kept me going, most of the time," he admitted. "Still does, if I'm going to be honest."

She sucked on her lower lip. "Yeah... given the pain you're in all the time... yeah, there's no way you could keep going without a rush."

"Back then, it kept us experimenting. We were pushing the limits, things started to get dangerous. We started leaving the base, doing open rituals without safety nets. Tomb was conjuring some pretty wild constructs. Martin was doing reversals with his protections, getting downright aggressive with offensive spells. And Justine was out of her mind, openly channeling fire. At the end, we were about ready to take on Echo. We got hired to do a frame-up. It was trickier, since I needed to be out there doing the impersonation while the others were miles away in our base. Turns out it was our last job. We'd tried our luck one too many times, I suppose. It was the distance that did it. Justine just couldn't hold it together. Her fire backlashed, incinerated her body. And she was still mind-riding me..."

"...oh hell..." Her hands spasmed into fists. "...Red..." She shook her head wordlessly.

He paused to steady himself. "Yeah, I guess you know what happened next, since I'm still here and eyeballing the ladies and not the guys. It was over fast enough. Girl had power, just nothing approaching discipline. She tried, dammit, but I ended up smothering her. That's how it ended. My will, wrapped around hers, and I felt her die."

Tentatively, she put one gloved hand on his. But she didn't say anything. Not "I'm sorry," not "Shit happens," and not "It wasn't your fault." All platitudes he might have lashed out at. He could feel her shivering, however; trembling with barely-controlled reaction. The image of Justine's body burning away was probably pretty hard for her to take.

Wordlessly, he gripped her hand, and let it go as he came to his feet. There, in the warehouse, he had caught a flash of light.

"Showtime," he said, grimly. "Start it up, Victrix."

That instantly put some steel back in her. She did something on her PDA, drawing a diagram on the plate with her finger, and touching the center of it, then keying in a couple of numbers. They began to receive sounds of people walking inside a large, echoing building. Good. Her little arcane-powered bug was up and running, sending feed to her headset and his.

There was some grumbling, some cursing, and finally the footsteps came to a halt.

"Can you zero the bug on their position?" he asked.

She nodded. "Give me a sec to bring up the vid feed." This seemed to involve some more complicated number-punching, but the little screen finally lit up with the POV from a warehouse shelf. "I don't suppose you remember the raid on the Echo Vault?" she asked, as the view rotated, and slowly moved.

"Christ, how could I forget?"

"Well, after you and I swapped places, we did some snatches there, like you said to in the planning stage, in order to cover up what we were really taking. I got a box of these little spy-balls that were one of Verd's failures. He couldn't make them fly, and he couldn't come up with a compact enough power source to run them for long. I can power them, make them fly and make them invisible. This is my first live run. I've done . . . bunches . . . that weren't on mish."

"Oh," he said. "Right. *That* Echo Vault."

"And no, I won't send one into the ladies locker room at Echo Med." She looked up briefly, with a raised eyebrow. "But if you ask nicely, I *might* send one to Lady Godiva's Gentlemen's Club."

"Don't bother," he replied. "I've got backstage privileges."

They watched the vid feed as the spy cam took to flight. Vickie piloted with her tongue stuck in the corner of her mouth, which looked oddly childlike and endearing. The view rotated a lot as she checked her positioning so she didn't run into anything. Finally it settled on an overhead shot of two groups converging.

"Looks like we've got an arms deal," the Djinni said grimly. "Odd, I don't see any of them carrying any cases."

She boosted the volume; the voices came in clearer.

"...thought you said he was a meta?"

One man, clad in typical Blacksnake armor, had stepped forward, his hand resting gently on his sidearm. He watched as the opposing Rebs looked to their leader, a heavily tattooed thug in a mullet who flashed him a near-toothless grin.

"Wha' make you think he ain't?" The Reb leader scoffed, beckoning another to come forward. From the shadows a scrawny boy crept up. He was nervous, his eyes darting back and forth between the Blacksnake goons and the Rebs. He held himself with his arms, his breathing shallow and stuttering.

"Oh lord," the Blacksnake op said, dropping his guard as he rubbed at his eyes. "I think I understand your desire to trade. I take it this one isn't up to your standards?"

"Kid don't have what it takes to be one of us, do you, Pike?" The Reb leader leered at the boy, who shied away. "Still, we heerd y'all want metas, and y'all got good spendin' cash. We don' hear 'bout how picky y'all are about 'em."

The op ignored that, and began to size the boy up. "That your name, kid? Pike?"

The boy nodded, and stammered a "Yessir."

"Well, at least you can talk. Not like that last mute idiot we took off your friends' hands." The op sneered at the Reb in the mullet, who just shrugged as if he didn't care. He probably didn't. Why should he? Cash talked bigger than words. "So, *Pike*, what is it you do?"

Pike looked up at him. He was obviously confused.

"He mean what yer power, boy," the Reb leader laughed. "He wants ta see it."

Pike nodded, a bit foolishly, and closed his eyes. His skin began to darken, then swell, and with a noisy crunch, his now bulbous flesh collapsed on itself to form a scaly carapace. His face contorted in apparent agony and he fell to his knees from the effort of transformation. He took a few deep breaths, and stood up. He looked as nervous as ever.

The Op looked genuinely pleased. "Not bad, not bad at all. Looks like he's gained some muscle from it. That shell looks like it'll be tough to penetrate. I'm almost surprised. You Rebs could use someone like this. Why you letting him go?"

The Reb leader laughed again, and motioned to strike the boy. Pike shrieked, his hands flying up to guard against the incoming blow. When nothing happened he lowered his arms, though not completely.

"Oh," the op said. "You people really are morons. A few sessions with a good deprogramming shrink and we'll have him—never mind. Let's talk price then, shall we?"

From their perch across the street, Red and Vickie watched and listened. Red felt a tide of disgust rising in him. He rose to his feet with a grunt. "Okay," he said. "I've heard enough."

"Red," Vickie said, her voice rising with alarm. "What are you—"

"You were right, this isn't a standard arms deal. They're trafficking in people, Victrix. I don't think we can really let that go on, do you?"

"So I call for backup!" She held her hand up to her ear, shielding her implanted rig. "Echo Dispatch, this is One Dog Victor. We need backup yesterday. Double trouble and human trafficking, A and D."

The reply was prompt, but not what they needed. "*Roger that, One Dog Victor. Backup in fifteen.*"

She switched to rapid-fire Russian—Red figured she must have switched frequencies to her special Overwatch setup. He didn't understand all of it, but *nyet, tovarisch* in tones of sympathy were clear enough. He turned away, straining as he listened to the deal unfold. Finally, he shook his head. "Forget it, Victrix. Backup won't be here soon enough. They're about to wrap it up. We need to buy some time."

"How—?" she gulped, standing up and bracing herself against the wall, as if taking some scant comfort from having it at her back.

"We're going in," he said. "We're going to give this kid another option."

He expected her to protest. She didn't. Though she was visibly shaking, she didn't. Instead, with what looked like extraordinary effort, she pushed herself away from the wall, and managed the couple of steps to his side.

"I'm . . . not packing," she squeaked. "Just . . . armored." She was wearing standard Echo nanoweave; so armored, but not armed. Except for magic. Would that be enough? It would have to be. And the Djinni, sometimes it felt like he could read her mind.

"You're never unarmed," he said. "You can do this. C'mon."

He favored her with a long look of encouragement. Finally, she nodded. Drawing a short crossbow, Red took aim and fired a zip line across the street. He turned and fired the anchor at his feet.

"After you," he said, gesturing.

You picked a fine time to go all heroic on me, Red Djinni.

It had taken the better part of a month, but Christian was finally going to make his quota. Pickings were getting slim, what with Echo ramping up their efforts to recruit every last meta they could get their hands on. As far as he could tell, Blacksnake and Echo were neck and neck in the meta arms race. He almost grimaced as he haggled with the Reb over the price of this reptile boy, but managed to keep his poker face on. It was a formality, really. He would have paid ten times the going rate for this find, just to put this all to bed. This Pike boy would make his ten, and he could go back to doing his real job at Blacksnake—shadow ops, assassinations, all the good, meaty, wetwork stuff. Not crap that any two-bit pencil pusher could do. He would haul this boy back to the barracks, drop him off with personnel to mind-wipe and reprogram into something useful, and get back to work. He was very much looking forward to it. Hey, who knew? Maybe he and the kid would be working together someday. Once reprogrammed, the kid could be a great asset.

The Reb was grinning, enjoying the haggling a little too much. Christian fought down an urge to pop him with a solid right, or better yet, gut him where he stood. He restrained himself, although, personally, this was not to his taste. From his own perspective, that would throw them all into a bit of welcome violence. He could have used the exercise, and he suspected his boys felt the same.

But that was counter to his orders. Giving in to his own impulse would end any future dealings with the Rebs, and he really wasn't in the mood to deal with the higher-ups on that score. Best to play the game, come to fair terms and leave. He hated Atlanta anyway.

"So, fifty thou, ten cases of RPGs, thirty pounds of plastic explosive... I think y'all oughta throw in five'r six bikes too. Ain't like y'all cain't afford 'em." Christian really, really was beginning to hate Mullethead, with his beginnings of a beer gut, his sense of entitlement, and his foul breath. "Mistuh Christian, if y'all come t'negotiate, better bring some serious shit."

"Look, if you're not going to take this seriously, we can always walk," Christian said. "The deal was for twenty even. And don't even bring up the bikes again. They're too easily traced back to us."

"Hey Christian," Mullethead said, spreading his hands wide. "You came to us, remember? The fifty's negotiable, but you *gotta* throw in dem bikes! They're too cherry. We can paint 'em, grind off the numbers, no one'll ever know they're Blacksnake!"

Christian rolled his eyes. "*Paint them* . . . you think some cheap paint job is going to hide the fact that you have *hoverbikes*?"

"Hoverbikes aren't their speed, anyway," a new voice said. "Give 'em a short bus."

"Who the hell—" Christian began, and did a double take. "*George Clooney?*"

"Evening, boys," Red said amiably, looking rather at ease as he emerged from the shadows. "Tell me . . . can someone direct me to the nearest Waffle House? It's late, I know, but don't you ever get that hankering for a big plate of fat-soaked carbs and bacon by the pound?"

Christian was still staring at him. Evidently the sight of a bare-chested George Clooney ambling up out of the darkness had put him into some sort of fugue state. He managed to shake himself out of it. "Who the hell are you?" he demanded, realizing that, of course, it could not possibly be the world famous actor . . .

For one thing, the Cloon wasn't quite so tall.

For another, he might be shirtless, but those were Echo nanoweave pants. Something jostled in Christian's memory, something recent. Echo had managed to find themselves a shifter, none other than . . .

"The Djinni!" he shouted, unslinging the M4 from his back and pointing it at Red.

"Hey, hey," Red cautioned, holding up his hands. "No need for that, Chuckles. We're just talking here. Why don't we keep it that way?"

"Nobody invited y'all," growled the Reb, wrapping a bike chain around one fist.

Red raised an eyebrow. "I needed an invite? I'm sorry, I thought this was an open market. Or do you have a problem with money?"

The Reb just stared at him, confused.

It was Red's turn to roll his eyes. "Money," he repeated, slowly.

"Whatever Mr. Wonderful here is offering, I'm betting I could do you one better. Maybe you've heard, but Echo's in the market for metas too." He craned his neck, and looked at the boy. "I'd also bet the kid would rather come with us. Wouldn't you . . . ?"

"Pike," the boy stammered. "I don't really know what's . . ."

"All right, that's enough!" Christian barked. "I have had it with this shit!" He pointed at Pike. "You are coming with us!" He pointed at Mullethead. "You are taking this briefcase!" He pointed his gun at Red. "And *you* can piss right up a rope and bugger off!"

"Well that's damn rude," Red scoffed. "You tongue-tango your boyfriend with that mouth?"

Christian snarled, and answered by shooting.

Instead of hitting the shirtless meta, the bullets struck a wall of dirt and broken concrete that somehow erupted between them.

"God*dammit,*" Red yelped, as he took shelter behind the rampart Vickie had thrown up. "Shooting again! What the hell? I've gone almost a month without being shot at!"

"You were overdue!" Vickie shouted back, emerging from her hiding spot and flinging herself into the shelter.

"I was just trying to be friendly! Maybe this wasn't the best approach . . ." They both winced as rounds ricocheted off the concrete.

"You *think*?" Vickie covered her head with her hands. "Now what's your plan? Aside from catching bullets with your teeth?"

"I am planless," Red replied. "This is more or less diversion until the cavalry arrive. What we need here is less Butch and Sundance, and more *Reservoir Dogs*." He raised his voice to shout to the Rebs. "Yo! I'm serious about upping the offer! Tell you what, we'll throw in a little extra for helping us nab these Blacksnake goons!"

The gunfire came to a halt.

"Don't even think about it!" Red heard Christian snarl. "You think Echo's going to let you boys walk away from this? Double the twenty if you perforate this idiot and his girlfriend."

"I'm not his girlfriend!" Vickie yelped, her voice shrill and Chihuahua-like.

"From the diaphragm," Red said, dryly. "Your voice will carry more indignation that way."

On the other side of Vickie's shield, there came heated whispers and threats. Finally, there was a grunt of agreement, and the shooting recommenced.

"Well, so much for that idea," Red winced as the concentrated gunfire began to eat away at the barrier. The ground under them trembled, and another layer shoved up, thicker and higher. Red drew two pistols from his holsters, and fired blindly around the edge. The assault faltered as their would-be killers dove for cover. Red flipped one of his guns to Vickie, who caught it with deft, if shaking, hands.

"They're going to try to flank us in a moment," he whispered. "Ideas?"

"I—I—could bury us, maybe tunnel us out." The idea was exhausting just to think about, but they didn't seem to have much choice. Without the suite in the Overwatch room, she didn't know where the storm sewer lines were. She'd have to build everything herself. Then again, if they weren't ducking bullets, she could take her time.

"Can you grab the kid too?"

She groaned. "I'm a geomancer first, techno-mage second, and unless you've got a piece of him, I can't apport him to us."

"So I just need to get to him," he confirmed. "And you need a piece of me."

"Yes," she said automatically, then did a double take. "*Are you insane?*"

"I swear," he muttered. "That should be the Misfits' battle cry." He handed her his remaining gun, took a breath and grunted as claws sprang from his hands. To his surprise, Vickie took that moment to pop over the top of the barrier and return fire before ducking back down.

"I don't suppose you brought extra magazines?" she asked, her voice shaking and high-pitched.

"In my belt," he said through clenched teeth. He had wrapped his hand around one of his claws, and with a groan he brought it down and snapped it off. Vickie paused briefly before tucking one gun in her armpit. She snatched the broken claw, stuck it between her teeth and dipped into his belt pouch for ammo magazines. Her hands still shaking, she dropped the partial mags from the pistols and performed an admin reload, saving the partial mags for later.

He nodded in encouragement. "On your count, I go, you cover."

She shoved the broken claw down her shirt, checked the chambers on the pistols, and got ready. Turning to him, she mouthed it silently.

One . . . two . . . GO!

She flew up and onto the top of the barrier, flinging herself flat on the dirt and broken concrete, and began to lay down cover fire. Red sprang from the safety of her stone wall and sprinted for the shadows. Both her volley and his appearance were met with shouts of alarm.

She laid down general fire for effect until she ran out of ammo, then dropped back down. With the same gut-wrenching effort it would take to bench-press her current maximum weight, she reached into the earth around her and heaved up more into a cone-shaped protection, not unlike an anthill with her safe in the middle.

With shaking hands, she ejected the empty mags and slammed in fresh ones, just in case. Outside, muffled by the earthen barrier, she heard Rebs and Blacksnake shouting at each other.

"Where'd he go?"

"How'n *hell* do I know?"

"Well, *get the goddamn girl!*"

"How?"

Any more of this interesting dialogue was suddenly cut off by the eruption of gunfire. A few shots pinged off the top of the cone, but so few that it was obvious they weren't actually shooting at her.

She turned her attention to the ground at her feet, which, fortunately, was already broken up by her early efforts. Like a kid compacting wet sand, she shoved magic force into the churned-up dirt, pushing it to either side, making a hole, and kept repeating the action, driving downwards.

Outside, there was more gunfire, and now, screaming. She continued to work; she was about six feet down when there was sudden silence.

That brought her head up like an alarmed deer. She turned, and started to scramble up to the top of her cone, when the screaming started again. Fueled by adrenaline she returned her attention to the hole, and at ten feet, suddenly punched through cement.

A storm sewer! *Oh, thank you, Mother . . .*

And just in time, it seemed.

"Now, Victrix!"

She clapped both hands, guns and all, over the claw in her shirt, ran through the equations in her head at light-speed, found the mass, and *pulled.*

She had them, she *felt* them. Red had managed to grab the boy, by a fistful of hair from the feel of it. She willed her power to engulf them, through the earth, to her. And just when she was sure of her grip, she hit a snag. There was something wrong... the mass separated, and the Red part was engulfed by a much greater mass. Too much she couldn't ID... too much to pull without an ID... she didn't have a choice, she dropped Red and hauled on the other piece, which still bore his faint trace, just enough to use the Law of Contagion. She pulled.

The boy dropped into a shivering heap at her feet, and she sagged back against the dirt, panting.

"You!" she snapped at him, voice more of a squeak than a bark. "Down! Go!"

Somehow he understood, and dropped down into the storm sewer. No longer her problem.

She scrambled back up over the top of the cone and out. The sense of "Red-ness" still told her where he was. Firing to give herself cover, she scrambled down the slope of the cone, into the shadows, following that tug of direction.

There! Shouts and a mass of bodies, chaotic in light from a night lamp swinging wildly overhead. She made a quick estimate of where he was in there, and shot high. Shouts turned to screams. The screaming multiplied, and Red erupted from the crowd, claws slashing. Vickie gasped. Only minutes had passed, but the Djinni was in tatters. His bare torso was riddled with bullets, embedded in new layers of thick and now broken skin. His face and arms bore fresh cuts, and slabs of epidermis even hung in torn places. His victims were screaming, but Red didn't make a sound. His face was cold, his lips a thin slit as he lay into them, his hands moving with surgical precision. It was doing a number on the Blacksnake agents and the Rebs, but it had left him open. While the Rebs pressed the attack, the remaining Blacksnake ops had fallen back to regroup.

Her shots drew their attention, and they turned to focus on her.

That was when she saw it.

The Blacksnake with the flamethrower, the little ignition flame flickering ominously at the mouth of the muzzle.

Pointed at her.

Fire...

Her mind went blank with black terror. The guns drooped in

her nerveless hands, as she froze, unable to think, move, or even breathe. No, not true, there was one single thought overwhelming her mind.

Fire... as she saw herself blazing, felt the flames even though they hadn't reached her yet, felt every nerve screaming with agony.

Again.

...feint... there, exposed armpit, drive in, opponent down... next target... disarm Mullethead, he's watching the claws, do a sweep, he's open, spin, get his throat...

Red was fighting for his life. He didn't have the luxury to feel anything resembling remorse for his victims; he didn't have the luxury to do anything but survive. They were out to kill him, they were many, and they were armed to the teeth. The years spent as the underdog, the thief in the shadows, had taught him many things. One of the most important was just how dangerous these sorts of fights were. You avoided them whenever possible. Even a complete amateur could get in a lucky strike. It helped to have fingers with razor-sharp edges, just as it helped to have the ability to grow an instant bulletproof vest. To have meta-strength, speed and endurability were all assets, but he wasn't invulnerable. He had faced odds like this before, and he had managed to survive, even if sometimes survival meant he had been the last one to crawl away. Still, all it took was one well-placed bullet in the brainpan, just one blade to find his jugular.

His skin was screaming. Not just from the pain of being shredded pretty badly in places, but with other, more useful, information. Even around corners, he could "see" them, sense their number and movement. He had gone for the gun-toters first. His hit-and-run attacks had kept him from getting shot up *too* badly, but a fair number of rounds had found their mark in him. They had swarmed him in the end, just as he had managed to work his way to the kid, and had resorted to pummeling him with their bare hands. He had felt the boy slip away, his odd musky aroma, akin to a ferret, wild and pungent, fading away into the very floor. That's when the insults began, and the Rebs began reveling in taking turns delivering deadly kicks and darting in to hold him down while others landed on top of him with pointed elbows and harsh laughter. In the seconds that Victrix was away they had almost knocked him out, when he sensed her return.

Through the crowd of bodies that stank of sweat, grime and god knows what other filth, her amber scent blazed into the room like a beacon, like a ray of hope. He heard the shots ring out, and sensed a sudden opening. Delirious, he managed to get to one knee and with a jolt fueled by desperation, he lashed out. The ones on top of him were thrown off, colliding into others, and back on his feet he returned to his task. The boy, presumably, was safe. There was still the matter of battle-hardened thugs who were bent on killing him. He had only one focus now. Get rid of them. The icy clarity of it would have shocked his newly found sensibilities, an old voice trumping more recent revelations of morality. Any such inclinations were drowned under a tidal wave of cold detachment.

As he came out of his spin, neatly slashing through Mullethead's throat, he saw the remaining Blacksnake ops, their backs to him, trained on...

"Vickie, move!" he cried, but she stood in shock, her guns sagging in her hands. She was frozen in fear. What was it? *She was up to this!* He had been so sure of it.

Then he saw the flicker of flame, smelled the acrid gas, felt the heat of the igniter and tasted the metallic propellant, cutting through the murk of filth and sweat and blood like a honed razor as the Blacksnake merc charged his flamethrower. Her eyes were fixed on the weapon, like a bird's fixed on the snake about to strike. She could no more move than that bird could.

Red charged. He couldn't see much choice in the matter. The mercs heard him thundering towards them. They turned as one, and opened fire. Some shots found their mark in his chest, but a few struck his unprotected legs. Red faltered a bit, but kept coming. His eyes were fixed on the flamethrower. The merc, who had been so intent on dousing Vickie with fire, leveled the muzzle at Red and a gout of flame and propellant belched out, washing over him. It was surprisingly quiet. It was also hot. A lot hotter than he'd expected. The ragged, dry tatters of bloodless epidermis that had been shredded in the fight caught fire.

And hell. It *hurt*. Worse than the bullets.

Before, he had been able to mute the pain somewhat. It was something he had picked up over the years. The level of control he had over his skin used to frighten him. The first trick he developed was directed growth, which later led to a complete reversal of directed necrosis, allowing him to shed away what he grew. In the early years, the acute sensitivity of the nerve endings in his skin yielded not only heightened senses but extreme pain. He had to learn some control over that, if just to keep from going into shock. Cuts from blades and bullet punctures were sharp stabs that could be muffled, and he could muffle the continued throbbing of wounds, but this . . . this was a perpetual torment, and it seemed to be *everywhere.*

Red stumbled and collapsed, screaming.

Vickie's scream pierced his. He hadn't known a human could hit that high a note.

She couldn't have moved, wouldn't have moved, until *he* flung himself between her and death.

Then it wasn't she who was the target, and she shrieked in fear and pure fury as he went down, burning. Equations exploded in her mind; power rushed into her, and she found a completely new level of force and concentration inside her. Time slowed. She pulverized concrete with a thought, flung it without even that, smothered the flames engulfing the Djinni, blinded the rest of the mercs. In the next moment, she had found the right support, caved in the floor beneath it and brought part of the roof and some of the loaded industrial shelves down on them. One of them got off a shot that burned across her bicep before she smashed him with an avalanche of broken concrete.

Then she was stumbling across the broken floor, sobbing, praying he wasn't—he wouldn't—

His body was still smoking as she scrambled next to him. "Djinni! *Djinni! Vse zayebalo! Pizdets na khui blyad! DJINNI!*"

"I cannot believe—" he coughed. "You actually—eat with—that mouth."

Vickie exhaled in relief, hugging him instinctively.

"Ow," he said, though he did nothing to stop her.

She cradled him gently, and just as she did, she heard a buzz over her embedded earpiece. "Five minutes, inbound," followed the buzz. She recognized the voice as Panacea, one of the Echo Med team; she'd be the DCO, then. The cavalry was almost here. The Djinni looked terrible, however. He had a habit these days of getting pretty beat up, though he seemed to heal remarkably fast each time, and if he wasn't invulnerable, he was frighteningly resilient. Stabbings, multiple GSWs, even disembowelment, but with the help of Bella and Einhorn, he would manage to pull through. They never had to worry about anything on the surface, at least. Left on his own, he could knit his own skin together. Still, she had to wonder how bad it would be this time. Bella could fix a lot of it, but the damage covered so much of his body, and it was hardly skin deep. She fought down a wave of panic as she took in the blackened areas, already cracking open to show oozing red beneath, already starting to flake away leaving what looked like half-cooked meat, leaking juice. It was all too familiar, and at the same time almost foreign. She dressed in the dark, these days. She hadn't looked down at herself in years. Still, the memory of that day burned so very brightly, so terrifying it could catch her unawares at almost any time. She could be caught up in the most delicate of operations, running missions in the safety of her own home, and yet something could jar those horrific moments from the cobwebs of her mind, and she would freeze, or shiver, or even cry out in fright, caught in the memory of pain and terror. They said you couldn't remember pain properly. They were wrong.

"Tell me what to do," she told him, tearfully. "I'm not a healer. Tell me what to do!"

He opened his eyes, painfully, from the look of it. "Tell me," he croaked. "Tell me . . ."

"What? What is it?"

". . . tell me about the rabbits, George."

The incongruity jarred her out of panic. "Red Djinni, you are such an ass," she said, though with a startled laugh. It never changed with him, he would always be an asshat. She continued to chuckle, but it was mixed with a terrible sadness. He was in such agony, but he persisted in playing the clown. For her benefit, she supposed. He must have known what the charred sight of him must be doing to her. Or perhaps it was more than that.

"Your file," she said. "I told you there's nothing in your file."

He looked up at her, and for once held his tongue.

"You said I could piece it together," she continued. "You were right, in a sense. You've been at this game a long, long time. Still, Echo has next to nothing on you. What it tells me is that you've always been careful, and methodical, probably even paranoid. Rightly, of course, given what you were doing and who you were up against. You're not paranoid when they really *are* out to get you. So what does it tell me when I've watched you be reckless and living on the edge for the last year? What does it mean when you let yourself get so hurt, even close to death so often?"

Red didn't answer.

"I don't know if you want to hear it. I make my living—or I did—dissecting characters and putting them back together. That makes me pretty good at analyzing... but not so good at dealing with real live people."

"You're the most social, outgoing hermit I know," he assured her, and paused. She didn't laugh, and held him with her eyes. He coughed, and nodded. "Maybe I don't have to be so careful anymore. Maybe I was never meant to be. Maybe I'm finally living."

"And maybe monkeys will fly out of my butt." She shook her head. "Color me skeptical. You're acting like your life doesn't mean that much anymore, like you're trying to pay back for something and you think there's no way you ever can."

"Maybe, but that's my choice."

"Yeah?" She huffed out a breath she had been holding in. "Well, that would have been true right up until you started getting people actually caring about your miserable carcass. Not your choice anymore. Or not so much, anyway."

He drew in a breath, ready to deliver a heated reply, then stopped.

"Be still, my heart. I've rendered the Djinni speechless." She gave him back as best she could; a smart-ass answer to lighten the air a little, and now she could think. She fished one of those Echo standard high-energy shots (trace elements and glucose so concentrated it made her teeth ache to have to choke one down) out of her own belt pouch. "Open your mouth, dork," she said, and dripped it in when he did. That was what he needed most; the raw material, the energy to rebuild himself. Before he could come up with some other smart-ass comment, she dripped another one in. She was about to administer a third, when everything went white, then black, as something too abrupt even to register as pain smacked her in the back of the head. She didn't quite pass out, but she fell limply back, stunned.

The energy shots she shoved down his throat were enough to jolt Red back to some semblance of life, but it was the sight of her falling back, of feeling her hands falling away from him, that drove him to his feet. He was struck by a rush of blood to the head, and he gasped from the sudden vertigo as he fell back a few steps. Before him, a bloodied figure stumbled back into a spotlight, a broken two-by-four in his hands. It was the Blacksnake commander, Christian. He was favoring one leg, the other looking fairly mangled. Red imagined it had taken quite a bit to have wrenched that leg free from the fallen ceiling, and silently at that. Red's eyes had begun to swell over, but through his obscured vision he saw the mound of debris that had once been an intact ceiling, industrial shelves, and the body parts that had belonged to at least three previously healthy Blacksnake operatives. Christian had lost his weapons somewhere in the wreckage. Red stared down at his hands. All his claws had been not-so-neatly broken off, leaving hard and ragged stubs, charred and dull and useless. He looked down at Vickie, who lay sprawled and helpless on the ground, her guns lost somewhere in the fight.

"I know what you're thinking," he said. "The Djinni's next to dead, I've taken out his only backup and all I have to do is swing this thing enough times into his head and it'll be done."

"Pretty much," Christian said through clenched teeth. He didn't advance, though. Why should he? Red looked like he could barely move, much less fight. Let the Djinni try and come to him. "Of course, while you're lurching at me like a zombie, I'll have plenty of time to finish off the bitch."

He raised the two-by-four and hopped a half step forward. Red lurched forward in response, and the two began a slow and grotesque race towards the fallen Victrix. It *was* like a hideous zombie race. Time slowed to a crawl for the Djinni, making it even worse; it felt like one of those awful nightmares where he moved as if every limb was laden with chains. Each step was an exercise in torture. It took everything he had to keep moving forward, to not fall over, and through it all his body screamed at him to stop. Christian matched him, step for step, but it was clear who would win this race. As Christian took a final lunge forward and raised his makeshift club, Red dipped into his ravaged belt, drew out a small blade and smoothly hurled it at him. He saw Christian's eyes widen and his swing falter as he dodged to avoid the incoming blade. The blade missed its target, narrowly, and instead of catching Christian full in the gut it bounced off his sturdy gun belt and clattered off to the side. Red took the opening, drawing upon whatever strength he had left and dove forward over Vickie, catching Christian in a desperate bull rush. The momentum drove Christian back and they both tumbled together into a disorganized heap on the rubble. Christian shrieked in pain as his leg folded under him. Red was in his own hell of burnt and smoking flesh, and screamed his own rage as he lashed out wildly, driving a solid hit into Christian's ribs. He was screaming as much at himself as he was at his enemy, egging himself on to do the impossible. He had to keep the pressure on, to keep moving, to keep driving blows and try his luck on a feeble offense. But he was losing steam fast. He felt his arms failing him, he could barely raise them up. He settled for the pitiful expedient of wrapping himself around Christian like a spastic octopus, with limited success. Christian fought the grapple, freeing an arm which he used to lash out at Red in short, ugly jabs. Finally, he reared back and delivered a devastating elbow to Red's midsection. Red coughed blood, spewing the frothy mess into Christian's face, but managed to hold on.

Christian howled. "Why . . . won't . . . you . . . *fall?*" he demanded, hammering Red again with his elbow.

Red coughed up more blood, and didn't bother to answer. Instead, he held fast and waited for Christian to try for another elbow strike. The Blacksnake op didn't disappoint, and when he reared back Red released him, rolled left and snatched up his throwing knife. Christian, taken completely by surprise and unbalanced, rolled with the momentum of his desperate swing, and howled again as Red dove back in, double-pumping the blade into Christian's side. Christian doubled over to clutch at the wound but stopped as his neck met the edge of the blade.

Red held it there, almost gently, as the two broken men simply stared at each other.

"Why don't I fall?" Red asked, his voice ragged and hoarse. "'Cause that's not really an option for me. Better men than you have tried to take me down. I'm still here and I'll be damned if I finally get taken out by some two-bit Blacksnake thug. I broke a lot of my own rules tonight, all because you and yours can't see your way to do some good when the rest of the world has gone to hell. We should be past this kinda shit, we should be working together. Instead we're just wasting our time in some stupid, pointless arms race. You, and your greed, and your . . .

yeah, I can see it. It's there, it's plain, right on your face. Your bloodlust. You're addicted to the hunt, the kill. Well, I've certainly sent enough of your men to hell tonight, what's one more? I'm willing to bet if anyone ever had it coming, it's you . . ."

He tightened his grip on the knife. Christian's eyes began to bulge, as if daring Red to do it. Slowly, Red began to push the blade against Christian's neck.

"D-Djinni. Stop. He's down, out. You broke him."

Though groggy, Vickie had managed to get to her hands and knees, and painfully pushed herself up.

"It's enough. It's more than enough. You saved that kid from these monsters." She shuffled a step closer. "You saved *me.* Please. You can stop now."

Red didn't look at her. He was fixed on Christian, and the knife he held. His torn and bloodied lips curled back over his teeth as he hissed. The blade was shaking in his hand, a testament to the internal struggle that raged inside of him.

"For *godssake,* Red!" she croaked. "Listen to me! You don't have to—have to go back to what you used to be! We'll put him away, he won't hurt anyone ever again! You *have* a choice here! Take it!" She held out a shaking hand, as if that hand held his options. "If you won't take it for yourself, take it for your friends, the people who believe in you! Me! Bella! The Misfits! *For Bull!*" Her voice cracked and broke, and when she resumed speaking, it was softer, a mere whisper. "You have a choice, Red. Rise up to it."

The knife continued to quiver in his hand and the hiss that escaped his teeth crescendoed to a roar as Red erupted. He threw the knife aside and struck Christian with a clenched fist instead, knocking him out.

Before either Red or Vickie could say or do anything else, the faint sound of a trickle of cascading pebbles made them both glance to the anthill of rubble Vickie had made. Poking his head and hands cautiously over the edge was the boy, Pike, eyes bulging with disbelief mingled with fear.

"It's okay, kid," Vickie croaked. "Come on down."

At that moment, Red collapsed, and she hobbled to his side. "And I could use a hand here," she added.

When Red's head was cradled on her knees, and with Pike's help, the Djinni was as comfortable as could be under the circumstances, and with three more of those energy shots in him, she sighed. In the distance, she heard the distinct howl of Echo sirens *finally* coming. Late. *Quelle surprise.* Verdigris had probably found some way to delay them. Her suspicion hardened to certainty; their erstwhile overlord was doing his best to cull the ranks.

"Help's on the way," she said to the Djinni. "Within shouting distance, in fact."

Red looked down at himself and grimaced. "Bella's gonna have a hell of time fixing me up this time."

Vickie opened her mouth to answer, but there was really nothing she could say to that. She felt crushed with guilt. If she hadn't frozen—

Instead, she simply smiled tremulously at him, when Pike cleared his throat and timidly waved his hand to get their attention.

"Uh, sorry . . . but . . . what are you going to do to me?" the boy asked.

Red looked up at him, his eyes swollen, his lips cracked and peeling. He managed a grotesque grin. "Nothing, kid. We're just going to give you something those guys wouldn't."

"Wh . . . what's that?"

Red exchanged a look with Vickie.

"A choice."

CHAPTER FOURTEEN

Permitted

DENNIS LEE AND MERCEDES LACKEY

Bella had been avoiding Red ever since the unexpected kiss. It had sparked something she wasn't quite prepared to admit to herself, and she didn't have a clue where to begin with him. There was no avoiding Red this time, though, considering he had been brought in studded with bullets and looking like a quarter cow cooked by a Neanderthal.

"Jeebus, I need angel juice," she muttered, as she hooked herself up to her rig and prepared to pour everything she had into the Djinni. *Good thing I'm in sickbay.* There were a lot of things she could do to herself here that would keep her on her feet that she couldn't do in the field. She had a rig repurposed from one of the ancient hemapheresis machines that literally took blood, scrubbed it of fatigue toxins, and pumped it back into her supercharged with glucose and additives. And she had a pair of permanent ports installed so she could just plug it in. A good dose of energy from the Seraphym, however, was about a million times better, and more effective.

"Wha—?" Red asked.

"Nothing. You want drugs or not?" It would be a challenge to find a vein for a morphine drip, but hey, that's what powers were for.

"Christ," Red muttered. "You kiss a girl, and she loses any semblance of bedside manner."

"The bedside manner you're interested in doesn't have anything to do with a morphine drip. And no, you cannot play 'doctor' with me." She grimaced. "Unless, of course, the doctor I get to play is Dr. House." She raised an eyebrow. "You don't have lupus. Or sarcoidosis. Or—"

"How's the kid?" Red asked, interrupting.

Bella shrugged as she looked him over, gauging which wounds needed her immediate attention. "He seems a bit shell-shocked. Considering you've been tenderized, perforated and fried crispy within an inch of your life, you should worry more about yourself. I'm amazed you're still conscious, and not screaming in pain. This another meta ability we should know about?"

"Trust me," Red grunted. "I'm doing plenty of screaming, it's just on the inside."

"Well, don't keep me in suspense," Bella said, grimly. "It's the inside I'm worried about, if you're suffering from any internal bleeding. Vickie said you took a good beating, even before the flamethrower came into play. Your mental functions seem intact, as obtuse and as irritating as they are. Any abdominal pain? Can you pick up on anything past the damage on the surface?"

Red exhaled, and motioned for her to step back. He closed his eyes in concentration, then doubled over, clenching his teeth in agony. Bella rushed forward, but he waved her off. His breaths were shallow, but after a moment they evened out.

"What did you do?" she asked.

"I turned the pain back on," he gasped. "Just for a moment. And no, doesn't feel like anything major's going down in there."

"You're sure," Bella asked, doubtful.

"I'm sure," he replied. "Believe me, I know when something's really wrong."

"Well, do you want drugs, or not?" she asked. "Because based on what we've done in the past, I'm going to be accelerating your natural ability to regenerate once I start on the burns and bullets. If I recall the last time . . ."

"No, no drugs. They wouldn't do much good, I've already numbed myself to most of it." He gave her an odd look. "How is she?"

"Who?" Bella asked.

"Victrix."

"Concussed, bullet crease across the right bicep, multiple deep contusions, bone bruises . . ."

"I meant how *is* she?"

Bella sucked on her lower lip.

". . . PTSD and currently vomiting," she finished. "Expressing gratitude to you for saving her life, y'know, between hurls. Nothing near as bad as you."

"Damn," he said. "I shouldn't have taken her out there. I was so sure she was ready."

"Don't beat yourself up about it," she told him, cleaning up what she could. Or rather, what mattered; when she started healing him, a lot of this wouldn't matter anymore. Anyone else, she'd be debriding the burns; but for the Djinni, it would all just flake off. "Look, she was ready. How were you going to know someone was going to pull out a flamethrower? I mean, shit, who the hell packs a flamethrower to a warehouse?" Sucking her lower lip turned to nibbling on it, nervously.

"You can't prepare for that kind of thing," he scoffed. "You have to be willing to roll with it. She froze up; it's as simple as that."

She took a deep, deep breath. "I think she's ready for the same head stuff I did with Mel. I would have broached it today if you hadn't kidnapped her for the job. It's not a cure, but at least she won't freeze up again." She paused. "I figured she was ready for a field job too. Or I would have overruled you. I *am* head of Echo Med, remember? Now shut up and hold on for the ride."

What used to take her ten to fifteen minutes to prep for, in silence, now took less than five with bedside chatter. Knowing the Djinni had "turned the pain off"—and boy, would she ever like to learn how he did *that* trick—she just put her hands where she wanted to. One on his forehead, one on the charred and bullet-ridden gut. Then she closed her eyes—she still needed to close her eyes—and dropped into the healing gestalt.

The skin damage was a nightmare, and for that, she would need him to do the work while she powered him. He could do that. They'd worked it before. It was going to hurt, though. His skin seemed to be the one place he couldn't actually control pain. If anything, it seemed amplified there.

So work from the inside out; *she* didn't actually do the healing. For Djinni, as for most metahumans, all she did was supply energy and somehow accelerate peoples' natural healing. Hours became seconds; days, even weeks, became minutes. That was why she needed the pheresis rig, or she would pass out, working on someone as damaged as the Djinni was now.

The few bullets that had gotten as far as the muscle got pushed back out as she healed, falling to the table with dull metallic sounds.

Bones knitted, torn nerves regenerated. Muscle tears mended. A bruised spleen became a pristine organ, a kidney tear vanished. In ten minutes, there was nothing left to do but the skin.

"Okay, Red." She didn't open her eyes. "Turbo-charge on, powering up. Do your thing."

She poured in the energy. He started screaming.

She kept her emotions out of it, her mind detached—one of the surgeons said in this mode she worked exactly the same way he did, which she considered a compliment. Later, she'd cry for putting him through so much agony. Right now, it was fascinating to "watch," and each time he did this, she learned a little more about how to heal. Some people didn't respond as well to mere acceleration; some she had to "tell" the cells what to do. Watching him at work taught her more than she would ever admit to him. At least for now. More bullets dropped to the table; some rolled off and fell to the floor. Should she tell him there was a betting pool on how many he'd dump every time he was brought in? It might make him laugh.

She sensed Vix flinching, sensed the guilt in the next room, when he started screaming. As if the poor thing could possibly feel any worse. *Dammit all, why do my friends all have to be emotional basket cases?* If she hadn't had Sera to talk to, *she* would probably be an emotional basket case. The angel was a wonderful listener, and entirely without judgment. It was the greatest relief in the world to be able to say the horrible things she wanted to do to some people, confess her nastiest secrets, and know that there was nothing but acceptance behind those strange eyes. Acceptance, and forgiveness. No one had any idea how much she needed forgiveness. Nor how much she *might* need it if things went pear-shaped.

"Better now?" Einhorn asked anxiously. She had come in just after Bella left, since Vickie was in nothing nearly like the shape Red was in. Mary Ann was no Bella, but she was competent enough to take care of the brain-bruising of the concussion, and the bone bruises of her ribs, so she could breathe again.

"Much, thanks," Vickie croaked. At least the skull-splitting headache was gone.

Einhorn beamed, and her little pearly horn sparkled. Vickie had to hand it to Bella, her handling of the healer was turning her from a self-centered little diva into a real asset. "Okay!" she said brightly. "Now just stay there and be quiet while it all catches up to you. I'll send someone to check on you in a little bit."

The recovery room was quiet. Too quiet. Quiet enough that Vickie could hear both the Djinni and Bella talking all too clearly.

"Christ," Red muttered in the other room. "You kiss a girl, and she loses any semblance of bedside manner."

She winced. So . . . she had caught them in a clinch. And dammit, it shouldn't *hurt* so much. She knew she had about as much chance with the Djinni as Herb did. *Of course* he'd be all over Bella, most guys were.

And now they were talking about her. It made her cringe. It made her want to run back to her apartment. Not that she was in any shape to run.

"She froze up; it's as simple as that."

She hadn't wanted to freeze . . . she'd been doing okay up until . . . it's not as if she'd planned this. She had thought the Djinni got that. Maybe not.

Dammit. Don't cry. Don't cry.

"Sweet Baby Jesus." Bella took a deep breath. She'd tried another trick this time, something she'd picked up from Soviette: empathic pain resonance, otherwise known as "pain absorption." Wow, that sucked. But it had halved what the Djinni had been going through, which was just as well, considering—from what she could tell—he'd been on the ragged edge of sanity the entire time. "Okay, I take back every nasty thing I have ever said about you. That took guts." There was no immediate answer. She poked his now-healed and baby-pink shoulder. "Djinni? You in there?"

"I honestly don't know," he whispered. There were no quips, no stupid jokes, nothing. Bella laid a compassionate hand on his shoulder. Without a word, he reached up and grasped her fingers. He was just a fragile pile of flesh, and Bella felt his relief and near euphoria now that the pain had stopped.

"Wait a sec." She unhooked herself and moved the couple steps to the minifridge she kept in here. "Cherry, grape, or banana? Or—wait, there's one orange left, yours if you want it."

"Orange," he replied, pushing himself up to sit lightly on the exam table. "One part orange, ten parts vodka."

"I can do that." That weird gal Upyr at CCCP made the most

amazing, restorative popsicles. She pulled out the orange one and stuck it in a glass she poured full of vodka (which she also kept in the fridge), and handed it to him, then grabbed a banana one for herself. "Want me to suck on this provocatively while you drink yours?"

"Oh good, a show. And here I was thinking I'd miss the main stage at Lady Godiva's tonight."

"Moron," she said, good-naturedly, and bit off the end of the frozen treat.

He reached up and felt about his face. "Is the Cloon still there?"

"A little," she said. "Mostly around the eyes and mouth, but you lost a lot of it."

He nodded and reached for his scarf. He belted his drink and wrapped the scarf around his head before reaching for a fresh shirt someone had laid out for him. Pulling it on, he felt Bella's eyes on him.

She flushed. "Uhm . . . I thought you might want to know . . . Bulwark. I was able to take him off all the life support except feeding. And . . . I got something from him." She flushed even deeper. "So, he's in there anyway, and as near as I can tell, he's all there. He's just not ready to wake up, and I don't know why."

There was something about Bull she wasn't telling him, that much was clear. Bull couldn't be getting worse, she wouldn't have kept *that* from him. Whatever it was, she was acting different. For one thing, she wasn't hitting him. Granted, she had just spent a good deal of herself healing him up, but she knew he could take a hit. It was almost endearing, in an odd way, how she would sometimes accentuate her points by delivering a swift right to his chin. But that was mostly when she was mad at him, and generally she only got mad at him when it had something to do with Vix. He wondered what she was thinking.

Bella wondered what he was thinking. Before all the crap hit the fan, it looked as if he and Bulwark were getting kind of tight, in that manly-man sort of way. Afterwards, he picked up the slack with what was left of the Misfits, which was mostly Vickie. Well, and herself, she supposed. He'd actually had her along as a DCO on a couple jobs that weren't covert, mostly to help her look as if she was utterly incompetent as the chief medical officer. I mean, come on, only on *Star Trek* did the CMO go on away teams; the previous, non-"Acting" CMO had been Doc Bootstrap, who'd almost never left the Echo campus. Djinni was turning himself around; so . . . how much could she actually rely on him for the Big Picture stuff?

For that matter, how much could she rely on him for other stuff? He didn't make any secret of the fact that he found her hot and hit up on her at every available opportunity, but how much of that was her, and how much was because he was a horndog?

"You frustrate the hell out of me," she said, without realizing she'd said it out loud until the words were out of her mouth.

"Well . . . yeah," he said. "Sorry, I thought we were talking about Bull. You just feel the need to pepper our conversations with derogatory statements towards me or something?"

She felt heat rush to her cheeks. "I can't read you," she admitted. "I mean, I'm a fricking empath and I can't read you. I don't know when you're joking, when you're just being a . . . *man* . . . or when you're serious. It's frustrating. Especially when I want to know if you're serious."

"I'm always serious," Red said with a shrug. "Just 'cause I throw in the occasional dick and fart joke doesn't mean I'm not being serious. Really, give me one example when I haven't been serious."

She thought of their last assignment together.

"What about the way you let me sock you in the jaw all the time?" she demanded. "I've seen you take sledgehammer hits and not go down, and a little tap from me puts you on the floor? Ha! And what about the way you strolled up to that contact on our last job and said 'Hi sailor, new in town'? Christ, you almost blew his cover *and* his mind!"

"He was about to blow his *own* cover, the way he was staring at you. Or more specifically, at your legs. He was supposed to be playing the role of a priest. Kind of a tough sell when his robes are sporting a tent, don't you think? He needed something to jar him back to the job."

"He wasn't staring at my legs," she muttered. "And neither are you. Horndog."

"Hey, what do you want from me? Yes, I think you're the hottest girl this side of Toronto, and I don't hide that. I'm pretty up-front about it, you have to admit." His eyes narrowed a little. "And yeah, I take your hits. You seem to enjoy them. I know I do."

She stared at him.

"Are... are you suggesting you *let* me hit you as a form of *foreplay*?"

"Yes," he replied. "And I'm very, very serious about it."

Before she could stop herself, her hand was flying at his face. Her fist met his outstretched palm before she'd gotten more than a couple of inches. *Crap! And I thought his chin was hard!* He was scary-fast. And she still couldn't read him.

"I... don't think..." She gulped. "No matter what you think, I'm not the sort who gets into slapping each other to sleep at night."

"C'mon," he said. "That's not what this is about. It's about two people who just get each other."

What was he talking about? She didn't get him at all! She couldn't read a single thing from him.

"You're delusional," she said flatly. "I can't get a single read off of you. You have to be the most exasperating, aloof, secretive..."

"Of course I am," he interrupted. "You seriously want to get involved with a guy you can read like an open book? Where's the fun in that?"

That got her. He was right, of course. How many of her relationships had petered out, simply because she could predict exactly what was coming next? Because she could sense at any time almost exactly how a man felt about her. How much had that cost her? She had never felt that wonder at the beginning of where something might lead. She always figured this was a good thing. No mystery, no unpleasant surprises, no stupid games that could ultimately break her heart. She never thought she was missing much, and if anything, had been dealt a strong hand. But now, looking into Red's piercing eyes, she felt something unsettling—uncertainty, and a strange attraction to it. Here was a man she couldn't read. All she could trust were her instincts. They told her he was the classic bad boy, the sort that good girls always fell for, then got their hearts and sometimes more broken. Yes, but that only went when the good girls were going into the relationship thinking they could change the bad boy... not when the bad boy was changing himself. And Red was changing. Look how he'd overcome his negativity about magic... how he was helping Vickie over every single one of her neuroses. He'd done more for Vickie than she had.

And that kiss that they had shared, she finally admitted to herself why she had surrendered to it. The Djinni was completely unknown to her but in that place, in Vickie's spell, she had finally seen into him, just enough, to feel what for him must be *home.* And it felt right, it felt like something she could be a part of...

She looked at him blankly, and felt herself moving closer.

Come to think of it, I couldn't ever read Bull all that well either... talk about Captain Control...

And completely unbidden, without any warning, that little bit of memory that had leaked over from Bulwark flashed into her mind. It had surfaced earlier that day, finally something that could give her some clue as to what Harm had done to him. But instead of answers, it plagued Bella with more questions, and hurt and jealousy. Harmony, leaning over Bull, as seen through his eyes. Harmony's last, poisonous kiss, the kiss that stole his life-force and planted that draining, life-stealing hole in him. And her last words...

"I think I loved you."

She had loved him. Had they been together, all this time? How could Bella not have seen that? You couldn't be a human being and not want to know about love, want to be in love, want to be loved. A time always came when the love of your parents, of your friends, just wasn't enough. It wasn't enough for Bella, but nothing had ever been *right,* not the right person, not the right time. And dammit... dammit... Harmony and Bulwark... It wasn't fair! That *Harmony,* that treacherous, lying bitch, had gotten to have all that and a guy like Gairdner and had *killed* it.

And now, after having never really had a teenage crush, never had a first love, never had anything stick past "Mister Right Now," here it was. Hope crushed by pain, longing by jealousy, everything hit with a freight train of despair and confusion. She'd been avoiding even thinking about that fugitive memory all day, maybe with the vague idea that if she ignored it long enough it wouldn't hurt, or it would fade. Only it didn't; it lurked and ambushed her, right in the middle of—whatever was going on with Djinni.

She couldn't take it. She had to get away from both of them. Lose herself in work or go for a long exhausting workout, or maybe just drink herself cross-eyed. But she had to get away, now, before she said or did something irrevocable.

She wrenched herself away from Red. She wasn't sure what she babbled, only that she said something to him. She couldn't stay in the same room with him, not when she was being torn up by a million conflicting emotions. She couldn't afford emotions like that. Not now.

Maybe not ever.

She fled, without even a backward glance.

Vickie didn't want to listen. Didn't want to hear it. But there was nothing in this room she could use to drown the voices out, not even a pillow to put over her head, just the flat paper-covered thing on the exam table.

But at the same time, like poking the wound to see how bad it is, she had to listen, had to know what was going to happen. Had to know the worst. She was a pessimist after all; she always wanted to know the worst. Even though, along with everything else, there was a heaping helping of guilt sitting right alongside the anguish.

Then there was a moment of terrible silence. Then Bella blurted something unintelligible, there was the sound of running feet, and Bella wrenched open the side door, careened through the room without noticing Vickie, and fled out the hall-side door, leaving it wide open.

Red followed her as Vickie sat bolt-upright, movement and emotions making her nauseous all over again. Unlike Bella, he noticed her and stopped short, surprised.

"Oh, hey..." he began, lamely. He stared at Vickie for a second, then at the door Bella had gone through, then back at Vickie. He seemed caught in an infinite loop of indecision.

Her cup of bitterness overflowed. She clasped the ice bag Einhorn had brought her to the side of her head, lurched to her feet, and stumbled out into the hall. Doing a slow-motion imitation of a ball in a pinball machine, she careened down the hall, heading for the brightly lit door at the end, fell against the bar, and stumbled out into the bug-filled night.

Before she could even manage to marshal her thoughts enough to *wonder* how she was going to get home, the sound of a motor approaching made her turn and squint into headlights bright enough to send twin daggers into her skull.

What might have been the strangest contraption she had ever seen pulled up at the Med building door. A canopy slid back revealing half a man, a man with a neat, short afro and skin the color of dark coffee. The rest of the man was buried in machinery. She blinked. Between one blink and the next, he looked up at her.

"Mutual friend said you were gonna need a ride home," drawled the... driver? "Echo OpTwo, 'Speed Freak' at your service Ms.

Victrix. Oh, and same friend said to ask you to get me wired in." He winked. "If y'all know what I mean."

The hell? It had to be Ramona. Though how Ramona had known... never mind. She was just feeling too battered and too anguished to think about it, and fell into the passenger's side seat, which embraced her like a comforting hand. The canopy slid closed, leaving her in darkness, with machinery between her and... Speed Freak.

She felt something hard and lumpy stuck in her bra. She fished it out. It was the Djinni's broken claw.

She stuck it back in, as the last of her control shattered. The motor howled, and the vehicle accelerated off, allowing her to lean back and cry for loss and loneliness without anyone knowing.

But how can you lose something you never had?

Red stood in awkward confusion, staring at the door through which the two most important women in his life had just fled. From him.

Ah, Red ol' boy, you still got that magic touch.

Bella... Vix... what was it about him that made them both turn into neurotics—or in Vix's case *more* neurotic—around him? *Women. So. Messed. Up.* And what was it about women that the better they were, the more messed up they got around him?

Who to go after? Bella or Vix? One way or another he knew, absolutely knew, that he was going to have to put some sort of conclusion to this running away shit. And he knew there was one woman he had to deal with now, right this minute.

He started for the door, to follow—determined to have this dealt with one way or another, when the door shut in his face.

The hell?

Suddenly, and with no warning whatsoever, the room got very warm. There was a scent of sandalwood, cinnamon and vanilla. And simultaneously as he sensed a presence behind him, the room seemed to get claustrophobically smaller, as if something far too big for it had crowded inside.

"I greet you, Timothy Torres," said a voice that was inside his ears and his head at the same time, a voice that had so many over- and undertones it sounded like a chorus.

He yelped and stumbled back. *Great, let's add* another *woman to the equation. Bring on the crazy!*

"I am neither mortal woman, nor crazy, Timothy Torres," the voice said, sounding faintly amused.

He turned. And there she was. It was her, the one talked about in hushed whispers and furtive glances, as if they were all afraid she could overhear them. He understood. She seemed like the real deal, had that whole aura thing going and everything, and pupilless golden eyes that seemed to peer into his very soul.

Ugh, that can't be a pretty sight.

It was hard to tell what she was looking at, exactly. Without pupils to follow he had no reference, no way to read her. He checked for body language instinctively, and got another disconcerting jolt, because she didn't have any. She was *still* in a way no one he had ever met—at least no one who wasn't in a coma, dead, or "almost dead" like Tomb Stone—could be. In fact, everything about her threw off everything he knew about reading people, and he might as well have been blind and deaf. He closed his eyes, ignored the scents that assaulted his skin, and there it was. What he couldn't see, or hear, or smell, he *felt*. It was judgment, her judgment, and it was harsh.

"She is not for you, Timothy Torres." Now it wasn't amusement in her voice, but admonishment. *"It may be that she is not for anyone. But she is not for you. The path you take pursuing her is not a good one. Not for her, and not for the futures."* Then she sighed. *"I determine, I do not judge. I . . . may sometimes inform. You may ignore me. You would not be the first. But this path is not a good one—"*

"Yeeeeahhhh . . ." Red interrupted, his hand held high and timid like a schoolchild, his eyes still shut, his expression pained. "Why don't we start with something simple. Hi, I'm Red. Not Timothy Torres, and I'd *really* appreciate it if you never said that name again."

"There are but three that know that Torres and Djinni are the same, two are dead, and one is myself. I shall not speak the name again." A pause. *"Does that please you?"*

"It's a start," he answered, and stopped. Red opened his eyes, and started counting on his fingers. He waggled two fingers speculatively, but looked confused at the third.

"It is not permitted for you to know," she told him. *"Not yet."*

"The hell with that, lady!" He would have continued but she interrupted him.

"Enough. You have a choice before you," she said. *"There are those who matter to the futures, and there are those who do not. I do not See you in the present, Red Djinni. And I do not See you on the path you intend to pursue. But there are other paths, and they branch from this moment. I do not order, I do not advise, I only give information. And in this, I am permitted to only tell you so much. Unless you choose to be UnSeen, and matter not, not even so much as a cipher on the pages of the futures, she is not for you."*

Red found it hard to look right at her. He had never believed in God. Of course, there was a time he hadn't believed in magic either. He had since accepted that much of this world, this reality, was a mystery for a reason. The blatant transparency of having a bona fide *angel* telling him what to do, or rather what *not* to do, sort of flew in the face of that. And in typical Red fashion, he stiffened in anger when he should have fallen to his face in abject terror of being held in judgment by a higher power.

"Lady, despite what you've heard, I'm really not all that egotistical. Not enough to care about being *seen*. If you haven't noticed, I'm more about not being seen."

"You are deliberately misunderstanding. Or feigning that you are." There might have been a tiny shading of irritation there. *"I know you, Red Djinni. I can read you. When I say that you are not Seen it means that you are not important to the lives, not only of those you have connected with, but those so far outside that web that you have only taken brief thoughts for them. And that they still will not know your name, nor who you are, when this chapter ends, but* you will have mattered to them. *You will be part of the reason they still live. That the world still lives. Even if no one ever knows it was you.* That *is what it means to be Seen. And that is your choice. Do you matter? Or do you not?"* Again, she lost even the slightest shading of expression, and went utterly and completely still. Even when his eyes were closed, he read nothing but waiting.

"Man, and I thought Vix was long-winded," he said finally. "You're telling me it's about choice, that through a simple matter of choice, I have to become someone important, someone who can change or even save the world."

"Yes," she said, simply.

"Who do you think I am, Jesus?"

"No," she replied. *"For one thing, Jesus had more hair."* Her eyes blinked slowly, as if startled by her own joke. Red watched her intently. She was so alien, so unreadable, and yet there it was, finally, something to catalog for future reference. A touch of... humanity? She wasn't completely indecipherable after all.

"It is always about choice," she continued. *"Free Will and Choice are the ruling Laws of the universe."* A very long pause. *"To save the world, Red Djinni, you first must save yourself."*

"Lady, I don't want to save the world! You think I asked for any of this? I'm just trying to get by here!" The words sounded anything but convincing, especially to him. It was clear he wasn't fooling her either, as if he could.

"Like so many, you seek redemption. You fear you will not find it, that you may not even deserve it. I am here to tell you, Red Djinni, that redemption is within the grasp of all who seek it, of all who would sacrifice what is needed to earn it. Forgiveness is always possible." Those strange eyes felt like lasers, burning away every bit of bullshit he had buried himself in. *"Always. The question is if you yourself are ready to pay for forgiveness. Forgiveness itself is there, waiting for you to accept it."*

Those that had witnessed her arrival during the Invasion would have said her power lay in her fire, in her sword, and the merciless way she cut down her enemies. They were wrong. Her power lay in her words, in revealing simple truths that stripped away all manner of concealment. Red had shielded himself behind not only his signature scarf and any number of disguises, but with lies and half-truths that he had persistently piled upon himself over the years. He had been relentless, unable to deal with even simple insecurities with anything even remotely resembling reality, that in time he had accepted his own illusions as fact. The Seraphym, with her burning clarity, had neatly cut a swath through them all, and he felt his innermost demons laid bare for her to discover. At his core, he was an opportunist. That might have been bad enough, but there was always that voice in his head, Amethist's voice, as a constant reminder that he could be more. Every once in a while her voice won, and he would try to make amends, usually with disastrous consequences. It didn't matter what he did, he would always hurt people, especially those he loved. He was nothing, no, worse than nothing. He was a curse to all around him—

"Stop."

Visions flooded in on him. The most recent, just charging in to help that kid, Pike. Hours spent coaxing Vix out of her apartment, over the obstacles, real and in her mind. The gut wrenching moment when he just convinced himself to *accept* her and her magic as inseparable, even though he loathed the thought of it. And further back . . . moments when he had done exactly the right thing, even when it cost him. The visions engulfed him like a tidal wave, but thank *god* they stopped just short of his life with Amethist.

"Enough. Use the past to change the future." Another set of rapid blinks. *"You must cease beating that dead horse."*

He could barely look at her, she was so radiant. He felt the tears in his eyes and wondered how she had broken him so quickly, so completely.

"So tell me what to do," he said, surrendering.

One single, perfect tear formed at the corner of her left eye and traced a path down her cheek. *"I cannot. It is not permitted. I can only tell you there is a choice, and not dictate what that choice may be."*

"Please," he begged. "I'm so lost."

"It is before you. I cannot tell you what to do. It is not—" Abruptly her head came up, like a hound scenting danger. *"I must go."*

"What?"

"There is a need. It is imperative. I must go." She started to fade.

And with that, Red felt all sense of awe and vulnerability fall away, leaving only his anger.

"Hey! You can't just leave me with this crap! We're not done here; I'm coming too!"

She solidified again, looking at him with astonishment. *"You cannot follow where I must go."*

"Like hell I can't!" In desperation, he leapt for her and grabbed her arm, pulling her back.

"It is not—" Abruptly, her words cut off, and a look of utter astonishment came over her face, as if he had somehow managed to shock God Himself. Something had changed, profoundly.

"It is permitted," the Seraphym said, and the world went blank.

In the beginning, there was darkness.

The Seraphym had suggested to Bulwark that he should begin by reconstructing his little "waiting space" after having so efficiently destroyed it—rather in the manner of, "You broke your toys. Here are glue and wire and tools. If you want something to play with, you will have to fix them yourself." Given his will, energy, and creativity, she expected to find *something* "liveable" when she returned.

Instead, she found one, shadowed, claustrophobic cube, with Bulwark in it. This . . . was not good. Finding his image sitting cross-legged and hunched over on the "floor" of the cube was even worse.

"Gairdner Ward," she said, in mingled alarm and admonition. *"Why are you . . . what are you doing?"*

"Waiting," he replied, dully. "For you."

"You are doing rather less than waiting," she replied. Because with every moment that passed, he was fading a little, as were his surroundings. In human parlance . . . "circling the drain," she believed it was called. *"What is wrong?"* She stepped into his space and flung her wings wide, blowing open the walls, and with a thought, reestablishing some of the ambience that had been here before he destroyed it. Light, grass, flowers. Mostly light. He appeared not to notice.

"Wrong?" he looked confused. "Nothing is wrong. I'm not sure that anything is approaching right, either. Is it time to go back now?"

She could fix this. She could fill him with hope. She could show him things he would not remember when he awoke but which would awaken his desire to join the world again—

It is not permitted. He is not ready.

She shook her head. *"You were tasked with restoring this place,"* she said. *"Why have you not done so?"*

Bulwark stood up, came to attention, and looked around. He gave her a slight shrug. "What would be the point?"

He was, as ever, a soldier. He stood at ease, though some spark, something vital, was missing. She saw his willingness to return, to carry on, though it stemmed from a sense of obligation and responsibility. There was nothing but a stubborn code of duty that fueled him, and that would not do, not at all. No one ever returned from these crossroads with anything less than a strong will to fight, driven by something that simply could not let them pass onward. While he was prepared to face life again, he was not willing to embrace it. In fact, he would dutifully perform until something killed him, a mere animated shell.

She could fix this. . . .

It is not permitted. He is not ready.

This was not the Gairdner Ward that *mattered.* A robot would do better. *Red Djinni* would do better... though not by much, nor in the needed direction. Briefly, she considered allowing him to fade anyway—but nothing in the futures gave her the clue of how to make Red Djinni into what was needed.

"You know," a familiar voice said, "I can kind of hear snippets of your thoughts here." She turned and saw the Djinni grimacing. "And thanks for the vote of confidence."

"If you deserved confidence, I would have it in you," she said sharply, perhaps more sharply than was warranted. She felt... rattled. Unworthy of being trusted as an Instrument. She should be able to see more solutions; instead, her paths just became more muddled.

"The point would be to be willing to live, and not just exist, Gairdner Ward," she said equally sharply, ignoring Red's snort at hearing Bull's real name. Bulwark didn't seem to hear Red, or even realize he was there. *"The world does not need another short-timer, going through the motions. The world needs those who are fully engaged in it, who have a stake in seeing it survive."*

"Call me Bull," Bulwark said.

"Appropriate, since that is what you are feeding me." Again, she heard the Djinni snort. *"Be willing to tell me the truth. What is holding you back?"*

"Nothing," Bull answered. "I am prepared to go back. You have my promise that I will do everything in my power, use everything in my arsenal, to fight whatever is thrown at me."

Desperately, she began to sort through futures, narrowing her focus to Bulwark, trying to find a thread, any thread, where she could reengage his will for life. Dimly she became aware of someone peering over her shoulder, as it were. The Djinni. The Infinite was allowing him to See what she could, even as it had allowed her to bring him here. She didn't know why... but she was a seraphim, one of the Siblings, and the seraphim trusted the Infinite at all times, and in all things. The Infinite wished for this, and so it would be.

Perhaps there was something there that it wished him to know, something it would take too long for her to tell him, or to convince him of. Sometimes Seeing was Believing.

So she sorted and allowed him to watch.

✧ ✧ ✧

Red felt as if his mind were expanding. It had to, to accommodate the near infinite stream of realities that seemed to run through it. It was the perspective that made it both manageable and utterly chaotic at the same time. From a single point in time, the possibilities streamed out as countless rays, each leading to countless more, a forever tree with crystalline branch points, beautiful and horrible to behold.

"Yes," said the voice, dryly. *"This is what I do. Perhaps now you understand why those who are Seen are important."*

Red didn't answer, he was locked in place, unable to tear his eyes away from it. He couldn't make out much in the way of specifics, but he was able to ascertain various patterns and general outcomes. There were some branches that ended abruptly with something... he understood it to mean *"This is not permitted."* Those branches were ones that began with an action on *her* part. There were a lot of those, and more sprang up as she frantically sped through her task. "Frantic" was the correct word. He was somehow able to sense more stress, more anxiety with every moment. And he understood, though he could not have said how, that such emotions—emotions in general—were utterly foreign to her. Oddly enough, love (a sort of generic, all-encompassing, "brotherly" love), compassion, grief... those she knew. Fear though—that was new. And she was afraid.

...those who are Seen are important...

He understood, and slowly he found his perspective hurtling *into* the infinite futures, to pick out key moments, key players, and the impact they made on this universe. Bella seemed to be pivotal in many of them, and she was either alone, taking strength and support from her closest friends, or with either Bull or, in a very, very few, Yankee Pride. Mostly she was alone or beside Bull, the very embodiment of his callsign, a true Bulwark. The Seraphym concentrated on those, and whether he liked it or not, Red was along for the ride.

Bull wasn't perfect, neither was Bella, but at the most key moments, he did the right thing. Protecting when she was at her weakest. Standing at her back when she needed support. Waiting when she was strong. Never holding her back even though he wanted to for her own sake, but mostly never urging the selfish over the selfless. Together they *meant* something, and although Red was not allowed to see the ends of those branches, it seemed that they were making a difference in—well—"saving the world" all out of proportion to what two people could reasonably be expected to do. But—it wasn't perfect. They fought. Some of those branches ended with Bella alone again. Some, a lot fewer, ended with her with Pride. Some . . . just ended. It was the ones with Bull that the Seraphym just kept coming back to. Red felt his stubbornness hardening, like cement setting.

Big deal, I could have that! I can do that!

He pursued the branches where *he* was the one who had Bella. Where Bull came back and, with dull and lifeless fortitude, pursued duty until duty *killed* him, or where he didn't come back at all. And he and Bella were fine together, more than fine! They were happy. Of course they were, he knew how to make her happy, and she was looking for someone she could make happy, someone who could surprise her, someone she could surprise—

But something was wrong. Something was terribly, horribly wrong. *They* might have been happy, but no matter what he did, no matter how good they were for each other—

Well, the branches that the Seraphym was chasing all dove into this huge, blank area. And on the other side of that blank, a blank he understood instinctively—partly from her frustration—that the Seraphym could not see through either, the world had gone to hell. *All* parties were losing, no matter what they did. Whether they all fought separately, or somehow united and fought together, it all went down into flaming hell.

"This is what Matthew March saw. This is what Alex Tesla called 'The Ides of March.' This is why Matthew begged me for death."

And no wonder. *You die, he dies, she dies, everybody dies.* He and Bella were just *fine* right up until they died horribly along with everyone else. And whether they died early in the massacre or late, what happened after that was the world going under the grinding bootheel of the Thulians, and . . .

. . . and then the Thulians turned their attention outward. And he knew it wasn't going to stop with the Earth.

He felt the Seraphym's frustration, anxiety, even terror. She wanted to intervene, but every single branch where she did was slammed with that big fat "no entry" sign. She had to intervene. But she couldn't. And she couldn't make out what it was that would turn them all away from those paths into hell.

Shit, woman, just make something up!

But it seemed that she couldn't.

So, frustrated, he felt her turn her attention away from the futures and into the past. And now the past—one, solid, unbroken braid made up of a multitude of threads—stretched out before them both. He sensed she hoped to find an answer there, as she began tracing back the path of Gairdner Ward's life, working from this moment backwards.

Which meant they were both looking right into the man's past thoughts, at the moment when he destroyed everything in his "holding pen" in his surge of grief, pain, and rage. Rage at...

Being told his wife was dead, and the Seraphym refusing to divulge the information of how, when, and why. His wife.

Victoria Summers.

Amethist.

The Seraphym found herself somehow abruptly shoved aside. It made no sense; a mortal was not supposed to have that sort of power over a Sibling, but she felt the reins of this particular horse seized from her hands, and the Djinni took over. He didn't have control of more than a fraction of her abilities, of course—he couldn't. The sheer strength of the torrent of information should have made him go madder than Matthew March had, instantaneously, but he used what little that he could control to sift ruthlessly through Bulwark's past.

Mostly, the reason he had been able to take over was because he had taken her utterly by surprise. Mortals could do that. Mortals were unpredictable, and even she could be surprised by them. Mortals had the most precious Gifts of the Infinite, Free Will and Creativity. But he could not keep control for long, and she moved to take it back.

No, Sibling. This is permitted.

Astonished for a second time in as many nanoseconds, she held her hand and her power, and watched over him, ready to move in at any time if *her* powers endangered *his* mind. The Infinite had spoken. He was now... potentially... Important, and had earned that much protection. So she lent him stability, trickled power to him, and subtly guided his hand when she knew what he wanted, so that he became a laser scalpel, rather than a case of dynamite. She struggled as he floundered, overpowered by so much disbelief and rage that it was all she could do to keep him contained. This was the past, and he could not change it, no matter how much he might want to. And . . . it was not memory, which could be mistaken. It was *what had happened,* unvarnished, and unshaded. Amethist and Bulwark. Victoria and Gairdner Ward. He witnessed all of it, from their first meeting, their first mission, their growing attraction to each other and when it had finally blossomed into love. Their wedding, long conversations concerning children, their future, their loved ones. It seemed as if Amethist had indeed moved on. The Seraphym felt the Djinni's pain, his denial, and finally, his anguish, as Amethist never once mentioned him to Bulwark, had never seemed anything but complete and fulfilled with this man. She watched as Red brought up Bulwark and Amethist's first date, and with longing reached up to cup Amethist's blushing face in his hand, finding nothing to grasp but a faded image from the Heart of All Time. And then, with his other trembling hand, he brought up an image of Bella, the first time she had spoken to Bulwark, just seconds after she had driven the Djinni to his knees with a well-placed punch. She was blushing, and the Seraphym was struck by the similarities shared between these two women. Djinni saw it too. Both strong. Both determined to do what was right, regardless of what it cost them. Both beautiful, both unconcerned with their own beauty. Both not just ready, but eager, to give everything to help another.

Both, if he was to be honest, attracted by the same qualities in Bulwark. Qualities he was noticeably lacking in.

"I am sorry for your loss." These were more than words. They were backed by what the Seraphym was. She *did* understand. How could she not? She felt what he felt, and shook with the power of it. His heart wailed with the injustice of it, of losing not just one, but two women to this man, and she wept with him.

"Show me," the Djinni said.

"What do you wish to see?"

"Show *me,*" Red snarled. "What happens to *me,* without her?" He didn't have to specify who he meant.

"Much of that future is hidden from me," she said, and uncharacteristically knelt to him for a moment in humility. *"I am truly sorry. This is the source of my own uncertainty. I . . . think . . . it is not so much hidden, but so in flux that even I would go mad trying to sort through it all. I will show you what I can, and I*

beg you, believe that I would show you more, if I could. I will show you all I am permitted—in fact, all that I *am permitted to know. Will that... be enough?"*

"I'll let you know," he replied. "Do it."

And so, she did. Fragments, mostly, as much as she could snatch from the branches that were changing so quickly that they were blurring even to her. Mostly, he was in pain. Mostly, he was achingly alone. But too much was unknown, too much was obscured, and within such a short period of time. Past a year, at most, the Seraphym's vision revealed nothing for this man.

But around him, the world was slowly improving. They won victories, small ones at first, then greater—then the Great Blank. But on the other side of that... on the other side of that, instead of virtually every branch of the future ending in hellfire and Thulian conquest, something else flared into existence. A few tenuous strands of fate began to burn with hope, began to pulse with renewed vigor, with the promise that all was not lost. And there were glimpses in those futures of the people he had come to care about despite himself, battered, worn, almost broken, but triumphant.

"It's what needs to happen," he said, finally. "It starts here, doesn't it? With a choice."

The Seraphym nodded, reached out for him, and gave him what compassion she could.

"With a sacrifice," she said. *"But the choice is yours. It always has been."*

"No, it's not much of a choice at all." Red replied. "But you're going to make me say it, aren't you?"

She nodded, and Red turned to meet her unearthly gaze.

"She is not for me," he said.

The little pocket of unreality rang like a bell.

It is permitted, Seraphym. The Red Djinni is ready.

Of course! It had not been *Bulwark* who was not ready! It had been the Djinni!

With pure joy, the Seraphym leapt from the "gate" like a racehorse released, and poured herself into Bulwark. She gave him glimpses of his future; she gave him glimpses of his past, the things that would galvanize him rather than sink him. She showed him how very much he meant to those around him.

But most of all, she gave him hope. That, too, was another

thing she knew, and knew well. The bits of the future, she knew he would forget as soon as he awoke. But he would remember the hope. She was like a radiant torrent refilling a dry, parched lake. No matter how profound his grief, it could not prevail against her. And she found, and ruthlessly slew, the little worm of despair the evil thing called "Harmony" had left to gnaw at his soul, a thing that Vickie and Bella had both missed. This, too, was permitted.

She filled him with her fire, and pulled him back from the abyss. And then, she used words to trigger that fire.

"I had not thought that Bulwark was a coward," she said, scathingly, lashing him with contempt.

That got his attention. Gairdner Ward may have been called many things in his lifetime, but "coward" wasn't one of them.

"Nor did I believe that he was lazy," she continued. *"Yet, there you stand, taking the coward's, the lazy man's way out.* 'I will do my duty,' *you say, knowing very well that merely doing your duty is not enough, is* never *enough. Knowing that everyone who steps back into life must be invested in life, and determined to fight through whatever life flings in his path. But no, you will walk in, and walk out, not even so much as an extra on the stage because you are too much a coward and too lazy to step up and actually live."*

She sensed his anger slowly igniting. But that was not what she wanted. Anger alone would not bring him through this.

"Yes, coward, I say again. You knew *Victoria was no longer living long before I told you. And yet, you fought. You lived. You even loved. You connected with and cared for those around you. But now, you use this fact of her death as the excuse to give up. Death is* nothing. *Even if you had not the evidence of your own experience, of my presence, to prove that, you know that death is* nothing. *But no. Now you will give up, let loose of those connections you have made, deny the ones you might make in the future if you were not such a coward, if you dared to have the courage to care, to have the hunger to feed mankind, if you dared to reach out. You are angry? Prove that I am wrong!"*

Again he would have said something, but she cut him off. *"Yes, you are in pain. So is everyone around you. And you* know *that! And you are lonely. All mortals are lonely! That is the condition of mortality, that you can only, briefly, touch one another, and only if you have the great courage to reach out, to risk more pain, to risk rejection, to bet all against the chance of that connection! You* had *that, Bulwark! You could have it again! But no, you are afraid.*" Terrible contempt colored her words. "*And you think you are all alone in that. Fear. You know nothing of fear.*" And she showed him. Vickie, fighting back panic from the moment she woke to the moment she slept, wrestling with more fear in her very dreams. Acrobat, battling constantly with his own insecurity. Scope, certain that she was never, ever going to come up to the mark she had set herself, no matter how well she did. She even gave him brief glimpses of Red's pain—though not the cause, never the cause, and not his thoughts.

And Bella, struggling every moment of every day beneath the burden of being the de facto leader of a rebellion with few resources and no assurances whatsoever, a role in which she felt crushingly inadequate, and a role which she knew was one that could (and probably would) kill her friends. Friends who trusted her and her decisions, that she would knowingly send straight into the jaws of death.

"Are you finished?" Bull asked.

"*Are you?*" she countered.

"No," he said, and she felt his resolve, the fires she had lit within him die down to bright, self-sustaining coals. And that was all, he was Bulwark after all. She had restored his connection—his willingness to connect—with those he held dear. Before, he felt a duty to return, now there was impatience. There was work to do, and he was Bulwark. He was ready.

She softened, and surrounded him with compassion. "*No, you are not finished. You have not yet begun. Let us go home.*" She held out her hand to him. "Now *it is time.*"

He didn't hesitate, and took her hand in his.

This time, the world didn't fade to black. Red felt his hand fly to his eyes as a crescendo of light flared up around them. When it subsided, he found himself standing next to the Seraphym at Bull's bedside. Bella was there, sitting next to Bull and sprawled across his chest. She wiped the tears from her face and looked up at them, astonished. And then, without fanfare, Bull opened his eyes and sat up. He gave Bella a soft pat on her arm, and turned to the Seraphym. He nodded.

She smiled. There was still compassion in that smile, and sadness, even grief. There was understanding, and shared pain. She knew this was no "happy ending," that the odds were terribly against them, and that she had asked them all to step forward, unflinching, to accept that world of anguish. She said nothing. Her look said it all.

Bella gave a low cry and threw herself around Bulwark. He patted her back gently. "I've been told you might need my help in the next little while," he said. Red chuckled and shook his head. Bull was back, definitely back.

"Did you take a graduate course in 'Understatement'?" Bella asked, around what sounded like a few tears. "Don't you ever, *ever* do this to me again, you hear me?"

"Yes, ma'am," Bull said. "I apologize for the delay in returning. You'll have a full report on the matter on your desk in the morning."

"Moron," she replied.

Red chuckled again, but the laugh died in his throat. Bella's joy and Bull's palpable if somewhat veiled relief at being back felt like a dagger twisting in his gut. He tried not to think about what had just happened here, what his choice had cost him. He made another choice then, one to leave, when he felt the Seraphym stop him with a touch. He turned back, and met her gaze with his own.

"Red Djinni," she said, touching his face with shaking hands.

"Yeah?"

"I can See you." Her eyes held him, full of grief and remorse, compassion—and maybe, just maybe, a touch of pride, pride in him.

"That's great, darlin'," he said. He turned away, walked purposefully to the door, and left.

CHAPTER FIFTEEN

Bedlam Ballroom

MERCEDES LACKEY AND CODY MARTIN

Of course, while some of us were fighting the internal Echo revolution, others were concentrating on the real enemy: the Thulians. After KC, they'd been quiet. Consolidating the forces, we figured. Trying to work out how we had found their staging depot. More than that, maybe, trying to figure out what impossible weapon we had that took out their entire staging depot in a few minutes.

Some people were not content with waiting for the Thulians to make the first move. Some people wanted to take the fight to them.

If you guess those people were Red Saviour and the CCCP... well, you win the Kewpie doll.

Red Saviour drummed her fingers impatiently on the desk, staring at the mountains of paperwork. Moscow always wanted paperwork. Which made no sense, since this was no longer the old days of the USSR where paperwork provided the jobs for thousands of low-level clerks. She privately suspected her father of demanding it just to keep her off the street and out of the headlines.

"Bah!" she said aloud. "Am *nyet* being out to pasture put." Truly, there was no reason for the Commissar to be doing the daily street patrols, but surely there was something she could do. Some action! That was what she needed.

Untermensch poked his head in through the open door. "What was that, Commissar? Did you call for me?" He had been on desk duty right outside of her office, organizing a file cabinet.

"Are there no current targets that we can be making hits on?"

she asked. "My behind is growing fat with chair sitting. Soon I will look like Desperate Housewife."

Georgi thought for a moment. "*Nyet.* We have assets assigned to all known targets, at the moment. Until we have better intel, we are currently doing all that can be done, Commissar."

She snorted with disgust, then thought a moment more. "*Nechevo.* I will find target." Georgi cocked an eyebrow at that, then went back to working on the file cabinet.

She stalked out of the office, goal firmly in mind. Unter scrambled to follow her a moment later... perhaps a bit desperately, she thought. He was a soldier at heart, and craved action as much as she did; Natalya imagined that he was going as insane as she was after being cooped up in the HQ doing busywork.

She didn't head for the armory, nor the garage, as she suspected Unter thought she would. Instead she went deep into the bowels of HQ, into what might have been an interrogation room if the Americans in general and the blue girl in particular hadn't been so squeamish. But, ah well, at the moment it held something a lot more valuable.

The techno-witch had set up all the locks to answer to the Commissar, of course, who wasn't going to be locked out of her own base, in any fashion. A small price for their cabal of conspirators to pay in order to house their "secret weapon." She opened the door and faced the curious mechanism that its owners referred to as a "quantator." Untermensch respectfully stood behind her and off to the side, waiting to see what his Commissar had in mind.

"*Dos vedanya!*" she called to the odd contraption, which sat quietly on top of one of the ancient industrial desks that had been left behind when this building had been abandoned. "I am needink to speak to Tesla!"

For a moment, nothing happened. She tapped her foot impatiently. Finally parts of the thing began to unfold; a couple of spindly antennalike things deployed, and a bluish field sprang up between them. After a moment longer, the wire-frame image of a genial man's face appeared in the field. "*Bon giorno,* Commissar. Tesla is occupied, will Marconi do?"

"Tesla, Marconi, ghost of Marx, I do not care," she replied. "Am needing target."

"A target?" The lines moved in a way that suggested an expression of puzzlement.

"*Da!* You have havink all manner of uploadings from Kansas City after-action!" she exclaimed. "And I am needink to break heads!" Her fists glowed a little in reaction to her pent-up frustration.

The expression of puzzlement turned to one of mild alarm. "Ah . . . I see. Let me see if we've managed to decode anything useful for you yet . . ." The wire-frame head went very still. Natalya folded her arms over her chest and tapped her foot. It took longer than she liked . . . though really, less time than it took one of her people to look something up on a computer . . . and the head was moving again. "Well, as it happens, since you indicate you are looking for something for a little personal attention, there *does* seem to be a very small Thulian intelligence-collecting cell located right in Atlanta. It's probably no more than three or four technical personnel, perhaps a few armed troops to guard them, since it's in the Hayes Street destruction corridor." Helpfully, the face winked out and was replaced with a map. "If our translation is correct, they seem to be working with a local collaborator."

Natalya's eyes lit up. *"Shto?"*

"It's not within your allotted area of operation as CCCP . . ." Marconi said, voice trailing off a little

"It's an area nominally controlled by Echo, Commissar, though their presence is light." Georgi leaned back, looking from the Commissar to the image of the map.

"Technically, I suppose you ought to inform them and let them handle it, but . . ." Marconi's face replaced the map.

Normally, Saviour would have ignored all that—something told her to wait. "But?" she prompted.

"Then you would have to inform them where the intelligence came from or they would not believe you. And that would . . . well . . ." Was there a look of mischief in those wire-frame eyes? "Given that we are supposed to be a secret, I can imagine that *Signorina* Parker, *Signorina* Vickie, and *Signore* Pride would have, how is it? A litter of cats?" There was an exaggerated electronic sigh. "In fact, all things considered, given the—how is it?—need to know, I fear you will be forced to deal with this yourself, with as few others involved as possible."

Nat managed to suppress a whoop of triumph as Georgi rolled his eyes. "I'll be getting a van out of the motorpool, Commissar." Georgi turned to leave.

"Wait." He turned back to face Natalya and she continued,

"Rouse Chug as well. I am not wanting him to be eating HQ while we are gone." With a nod, he left to do as ordered. Briefly, Saviour considered involving Overwatch, but then (a little to her relief) she realized that with everyone but Gamayun and Soviette out on patrols, there were no headsets left in HQ. Good! Executive decision. She sketched a salute to Marconi, who nodded and faded out and the apparatus folded back up again. She followed Untermensch out, and locked the door behind her. "Ha. We do this old school!"

"I am not sure that city's already strained insurance will cover the damages if we do it 'old school,' Commissar. Whatever that means."

"It means, is a good thing this cell is already in destruction corridor, comrade," Nat said with poorly repressed glee. "Cannot destroy what is already ruined, *da*?"

"How much ammunition should I bring? Grenades?" Georgi gauged the look in her eyes for a moment before giving a sigh. "Many of both. I'll suit up and prepare everything, Commissar."

Saviour allowed herself a full-on wolfish grin. "What is Trek Star captain say? Ah, *da*. 'Make it so.'"

Ten minutes later, Untermensch was suited up and had the van started in the garage. Chug was with him; he was sitting on the rear bumper, the suspension sagging under his compact weight. If there was one thing both Saviour and Georgi fully and unreservedly approved of, it was the nanoweave combat suits that Vickie had "lost" out of Echo inventory via her hacking skills, and Ramona Ferrari and Belladonna had brought over to CCCP two and three at a time. Of course they had to be retailored with CCCP colors, but they were a vast improvement over the old Kevlar vests that had been used for years; less bulky with better protection, they granted improved mobility and speed.

Chug looked up from the ground as Natalya approached. "We go out for a ride, now?" His stony eyebrows lifted in anticipation; it was always a highlight for him whenever he was able to leave the HQ, but it happened rarely due to the fact that he always needed supervision. It wasn't that he wrecked things on purpose, or even by accident; it was mostly that he got hungry a lot, and when he got hungry, he just took whatever looked good to him—which was virtually anything and everything, from garbage to motorcycles—and ate it. He could actually eat things larger than a motorcycle, but it usually took him a few moments to break it down into small enough pieces. No one knew how he actually metabolized it all; his rock hide was virtually impenetrable, to scalpels and medical scans alike. The tragedy was that before his metahuman abilities triggered, he had been a brilliant research physicist. Nat tried to never remind him of his past . . . the few times dim, dim memories had been briefly triggered had been the only times—outside of the massacre in Moscow at the start of the Invasion—that she had seen him cry. He still had glimmers of his former intelligence, but they were as few and far between as his memories of the past. All that was important to him now were pleasing his comrades, feeding squirrels in the park, and his pet hamster; for a creature with such immense strength, he could be exceedingly gentle when he wanted to.

"*Da*, Chug. We are going for a ride. We have *fashista* to meet." Chug's lips curled into a craggy smile as he hopped off of the bumper. Natalya opened the back door of the van for him, allowing him to clamber in; the rest of the van's rear seating area was covered in ammo cans and grenade boxes. Natalya called up to the front. "What is all of this being here for?"

Unter looked over his shoulder from the driver's seat. "You said we did not need to worry about damage. As Murdock says, it is better to have more than less. Or something like that." The Commissar couldn't help but to agree with that, so she shut the doors and walked around the front to climb into the passenger seat.

"Move out. We don't want to keep our hosts waiting for the party."

The ride was uneventful; the sun had set maybe an hour before, so the city was still sticky with trapped heat. Natalya had not been to this part of the city since her first visit with Bella; the CCCP's area of responsibility had grown, but not this far out. Incredibly, a rectangular yellow sign shone in the dusk, still in operation. "Oh, look. Is Waffle House. *Horosho.*"

"Waffles?" Chug perked up. "Like waffles."

Nat tried not to groan, but Unter had come prepared. "Here, comrade lump," he said, tapping a box between the front seats. "Be lookink in there. Comrade Upyr will make you waffles for reward if you are good when we return."

Chug looked. "Oh boy!" he said happily as he opened the ammo box and dug into the contents.

Nat did a double take. "Are those—" she began incredulously.

"Depleted uranium bullets, no casing or propellant, *da,*" Unter shrugged. "Moscow sent them with other useless garbage. They are being dense enough to keep Chug happy for hours. He eats them like hard candy."

Saviour rolled her eyes. *"Borzhe moi."* At least they weren't going to cause any problems with disposal. With all the nonsensical American laws, they probably would have been unable to send them back to Moscow, or get rid of them here. It was a wonder that they had even made it through customs, truth be told, though perhaps being Echo allies, the CCCP shipments had gotten the "hands off, we'd rather not know" treatment. They certainly couldn't *use* the bullets here.

The van lurched to a stop, then turned off. "Commissar, we have arrived. I have parked us a block away, just in case they have lookouts." Georgi turned around in his seat to face her. "What is our plan?"

Saviour sucked on her lower lip. "Much as I would like to go in smashink, I suppose we had better scout first to have an idea of how *many* heads we must break, *da*?" She winked at Untermensch, to let him know she *really* didn't want to just send Chug in ahead of them and follow shooting... much, at least.

"*Da*, Commissar. I will be taking point, if it suits."

She nodded, then turned to Chug. She had to give credit to the Blue Girl; the meta did have some very good ideas most of the time, even if she was too soft with criminals for the Commissar's liking. "Chuggie," she said, coaxingly.

Chug looked up with his mouth full of bullets, and swallowed. "*Da*?" he replied.

"You know Comrade Blue Girl's whistle?" She held up an ultrasonic dog whistle; somehow Belladonna had discovered Chug could hear the damned thing for the better part of a mile.

Chug smiled beatifically. "Yes, Comrade Commissar," he said happily. "When you blow the whistle, Chug comes. Right?"

"*Horosho.* Exactly right. Stay in van until you hear the whistle. Then you come. Then you smash what I say, and we go home and have waffles."

"Can Chug have Mikhail Mouse waffle?" he begged.

She sighed. Too much *Amerikanski* television. "Yes, but only if Chug also has proper Comrade *Mischa Medved* waffle." She didn't envy Thea; with Chug's appetite, she'd likely be spending all day cooking waffles to sate him. She hoped he'd fill up on bullets before then.

The stony creature clapped his hands. "Yay!" he cried. "Chug will be *very* good!"

Untermensch opened the driver's side door and hopped out of the van; he was completely silent as he slunk away into the shadows. It seemed to take forever before Saviour heard her encrypted radio squawk. "Approach is being clear, Commissar. Move up on the alley; I'll be waiting. Untermensch out."

"Remember, Chug, wait for the whistle," she warned, pulled on her NVGs and slipped into the ruins without waiting for his reply. *Hmph. "Move up on the alley"... am not sure there is any alley left!* The destruction corridors were always bad, but this one was—well, she could certainly see why no one had bothered trying to clear it yet. Something had come through here and toppled three- and four-story-tall buildings like a bad Japanese monster movie. Nevertheless, she could tell where the alley *should* have been, and managed to worm her way in, noting as she did so that there was a disabled trap; something that looked like a grenade that had been attached to a standard trip wire. With the Thulian tech it was sometimes hard to tell the purpose of their artifacts. Untermensch stuck his head out of the doorway; she hadn't even known he was there. He motioned for her to come forward while pressing a gloved finger to his lips.

She followed him into the building; from the surroundings, it looked like an old hotel, and he had taken them in through a service entrance. They were both wearing NVGs now, lightweight Echo models courtesy of Vickie. Saviour did her best to keep track of all of the corridors, but after a while she was completely lost. Finally, Georgi gave her a hand signal to come to a halt. He crouched low outside of a double door; she reflexively took up position on the side opposite from him on the door frame.

"Intel was good," he whispered. "Four *fashista*; one officer and three technicians. The collaborator appears to be inside as well. You may recognize him as Councilman Richard Saint. He appears to be feeding them information concerning the police, clean up efforts, and some other things I could not make out. They are in a meeting, currently; their security is nonexistent outside of traps and early warning devices at the entrances, so far. The *fashistas* seem to be fairly confident." Georgi allowed himself a thin smile.

"Then I think we should shake that confidence, *da*?" Saviour shook her hands down at her side, feeling her power gathering. Her own inherent energy blasts would be safer in here than bullets; with all the masonry and crazy angles, ricochets were a concern. Untermensch, having only his healing and his invulnerable hands for metahuman abilities, unslung his KS-23 in order to give himself a way to "communicate party doctrine... at range" as he liked to say.

"On your command, Commissar." Georgi checked the shotgun's chamber, making sure a round was ready.

Saviour took the fiber optic camera from Unter and slipped it under the door. Unter was right; their opponents were entirely preoccupied, with one of the creatures talking to the alderman, two more dithering about on some sort of computer equipment that had been set up on round wooden tables that clearly belonged to this old hotel. She straightened, and grinned wolfishly. *"Davay,"* she said, and blew the whistle for Chug.

Untermensch stood up and kicked the door open, leveling the shotgun on their targets. Saviour allowed the power to charge her fists until they glowed crimson, holding them in front of her in a fighters' stance. The room was scattered with Krieger computer terminals and desks piled high with documents. The room itself had once been a very posh ballroom; the Invasion had seen it ruined, all of its former majesty now making it seem all that more tragic. *"Privyet,* scum," she said, her voice oozing glee. The Thulians and Mr. Saint were all motionless from shock; none appeared to be holding weapons. "We will be allowing you one second to surrender. Oh. Too late!"

At that exact moment, the main entrance to the ballroom opened. A small contingent of Thulians, two of them in power armor carrying large metal crates, emerged from the portal. Suddenly finding themselves confronted with Unter and Nat, they froze.

"Comrade, your surveillance was not accurate," Nat growled. "There will be excoriation."

"They weren't here before. Excoriate them for not being on duty. Must have been out getting decadent Caffeebucks."

There were a few heartbeats of silence before the high windows near the ceiling—no doubt to allow natural light and stunning views of the night sky—exploded inward, causing everyone but the armored troopers to duck and cover their heads. Over a dozen figures clad in black rappelled in through the broken windows, landing on the ground in unison with assault rifles leveled at both the Thulians and the CCCP.

"Everyone on the ground, now! We will open fire if you do not comply!"

Natalya quickly surveyed the newcomers; the lack of insignia, the weapons, and the way they carried themselves all pointed to Blacksnake. Everyone was frozen, weapons pointed at one another.

"Borzhe moi," Nat muttered. "Is Canadian standoff. How could it get worse?"

The wall near the entrance that the Thulians came through exploded into chunks of brick and plaster as Chug bashed through it. As the dust settled, the rocky creature looked confused.

"Oh. Chug didn't see the door over there."

Gunfire erupted then; the Thulians were firing at the Blacksnake operatives, Blacksnake was firing at the CCCP, and the CCCP was firing at everyone. Chug waded into the fray, bludgeoning and knocking over the two armored troopers with his fists.

Untermensch unloaded his shotgun in a flurry of shots, taking out two of the Blacksnake mercenaries. Grabbing one of the heavy oak tables, he effortlessly flipped it, providing some cover. Natalya discharged the energy from her fists into the floor under a huddled group of Thulian technicians, sending their bodies flying. She ducked back down behind the cover as a volley of return fire from Thulian energy guns and Blacksnake rifles riddled the table and the wall behind her.

Georgi shook his head as he reloaded his shotgun. "Oh, how could it become worse, *nyet?*" He finished loading the shotgun, racking the pump to chamber a round and load a final shell. He then retrieved a grenade from a pouch on his belt, pulling the pin and chucking it hard over the edge of the table. A few seconds later it detonated with a cacophonous roar followed by screams.

Nat was not about to try and fish out the camera to see around the edge of the table, but she didn't need to see when she could hear the sound of something heavy crunching its way toward them across the ballroom. Either the armored troopers had decided that she and Unter were a greater threat than the Blacksnake operatives or—

"Hullo, Commissar," said Chug. "Chug found crying man.

Chug brung him." Over the edge of the table tumbled the much-the-worse-for-wear councilman. Richard Saint was gutshot and weeping between screams of pain.

"Who are you people? Get me out of here!" The councilman was clutching his belly; from the look of the wound, he had been shot in the liver. With that much bleeding, he didn't have a lot of time to live. Well, at least it wasn't a shotgun wound; nothing to point to CCCP as the ones on the other end of the trigger.

"Get you out, *svinya?*" Nat barked, hauling him to her. "You are beink make many demands for a traitor." She thought about smacking him, but he was already in such pain he wouldn't feel it. *"Maybe* we will think about this, if you begin tellink us what you know."

"Anything! Anything!" Saint babbled.

"It might be worth the trouble, Commissar," Georgi observed, directing Chug to position himself between them and the firefight, which seemed to have turned two-sided instead of three. Chug watched the battle dispassionately; as long as no one was shooting at his friends, he didn't much care what was going on. "Best to do this somewhere else; gunshots and explosions make for hard hearing." With that, Untermensch unloaded his shotgun again in a rapid series of shots as Saint shook and wept on the floor.

"Oh, did you think being informant to *fashista* was all sunshine and *nekulturny* champagne?" Saviour mocked. She peeked over Chug's shoulder. The Thulians and Blacksnake were fully involved with each other; all of the technicians were dead and their equipment was a wreck, but the soldiers and the armored troopers were still going strong. She thought she saw what looked like a meta using his powers among the Blacksnakes, but it was hard to tell in the confusion. "Well, it looks to me that no one has any interest in a couple of Russian tourists. I think we go." She heaved Saint over her shoulder. "Might as well take you."

Saint screamed in protest, but Natalya was already charging through the door with him. She could hear Chug bellowing and Untermensch firing his shotgun behind her. She ran down the hallways, but quickly lost her way. *"Chyort voz'mi!* Where the hell are we?"

Untermensch shouldered past her while leading Chug by the hand, casting a glance behind them as he loaded the last of his shells into his shotgun. "Allow me to lead the way, Commissar. The exit isn't far, thankfully. We will have to run for the van, however."

"*Da, da.* Get moving on!"

They ran through a dizzying series of hallways; she wasn't sure how Georgi had kept track of where they were until she saw surreptitious marks made with what looked like a grease pencil on the baseboards of the walls; they barely stood out against the other scuffs and scrapes, but apparently it was enough for him to navigate by. Georgi shouldered through a final door, and they were out into the humid air of Atlanta again. Both he and Natalya stripped off their NVGs, replacing them on their belts.

"Van is this way! *Davay,* comrades!" Untermensch charged ahead, keeping his shotgun at a low ready position. They were all breathing hard, save for Chug, when they reached the van. Saint had given up his screams for pitiful moans, and he had bled stickily all over Saviour's shoulder. They all piled into the van; Georgi took the driver's seat, while Saviour shoved Saint into the back and herded Chug in before jumping in herself and slamming the doors. With a screech of rubber on torn asphalt, they sped away.

"So, *suka,*" Nat said, grabbing the man by his collar and shaking him. "Be talking, or I will to be opening door and dumping you out for your friends."

"You can't—" he gasped.

"Oh no?" She kicked the door open; it wasn't that hard in this van. "Who will tell anyone?" She dragged him to the edge, hanging his head and shoulder out over the road speeding away under them. "I am thinkink you will not last past first bounce."

"Oh shit! You crazy bitch! This—this is illegal! I'm a city council— Aah!" She pushed her fist against his gunshot wound, grinding her middle knuckle in particularly viciously.

"And I am to be havink diplomatic immunity," she said sweetly. "You will be tellink me everything you—"

Behind them in the direction of the hotel, a gigantic fireball loomed bright against the Atlanta sky. The sound caught up with them a moment later with the accompanying shock wave; windows shattered and dust fell from every building around them. Saviour swore under her breath as the rear axle of the van kicked up. Chug was shifting uneasily, causing the van to rock slightly from side to side.

"What in Lenin's name was that?" Saviour reeled Saint back into the van as Untermensch did his best to keep it on the treacherous road. He checked the rearview mirror, then looked ahead again.

"Hotel. Either *fashista* scum or Blacksnake running dogs did not want anyone to be leaving it alive." He hazarded a quick glance over his shoulder. "Since he still is, and we were to be seen leaving with him, I think we should expect traveling partners soon."

"You think Blacksnake is to care about traitorous running dog working with Kriegers?" Saviour asked doubtfully.

"He was our target. He seemed to be only valuable thing in room, besides destroyed *fashista* equipment. Blacksnake is not in habit of doing things without capitalist profits attached." He pointed at Saint over his shoulder. "Is profits."

"Bah." Saviour turned her attention back to Saint. "You. Councilman Profits. What else do you know?"

"No-nothin—" the man began.

Natalya pressed her fist into his wound again, slowly, causing him to squirm and scream. "Nothing? I am not needing nothing from you; would have left you there for nothing. You get to live for something. This is exchange, *da*?"

"I don't know—" Saint screamed. "All right! Stop, god stop it!" His shouts trailed away into one long unintelligible shriek before he started blubbering again. "I'll tell you! I'll tell you what I was giving the Kriegers!" Spittle flecked his lips as he gasped, catching his breath. "In my coat's pocket, there's a little black book. It—it's got everyone in it, all of the people that supply the Kriegers with intel from Atlanta; cops, Echo, politicians, officials. They've got a lot of—god, it hurts!—a lot of people on the take. Just get me to a frickin' hospital, goddammit! I don't care!"

Natalya fished the booklet from his pocket after a quick search; scanning through it, she saw names, vital information, job titles, and in what capacity they worked for the Thulians. It was everything that Saint said and more; he was an intermediary, funneling all of the information from the traitors to the Thulians, able to go anywhere because of his position with the city council, keeping them insulated from exposure. "You are lucky piglet, *svinya; fashista* would kill you themselves if they knew you wrote vital contacts down. Stupid and sloppy, like all bureaucrats."

"Commissar!" Georgi was calling from the front of the van.

"*Shto?* What is it?" she snapped. "Am busy here!"

Chug was peering out the back window, so she couldn't see what was behind them. "Are we in race? We are winning! *Yay!*" Nat looked around Chug to see out the window; a matte black

SUV was on the road behind them, and closing fast. From the lack of insignia or any other sort of identifying marks on it, she concluded that it had to be Blacksnake.

"Sookan syn. Prosrat!" She somehow managed to get Chug to move aside, picked up Unter's KS-23 and took aim for the windshield of the SUV. She discharged a shell into the driver's side, but the buckshot only slightly spider-webbed the glass; it was bullet resistant. She aimed and fired at the front grill, hoping to damage the engine and kill the vehicle that way, but the damage was cosmetic at best. The SUV continued to gain on them until it was keeping pace with the CCCP van; two mercenaries leaned out of the side windows and began to fire in short bursts at the Russians. "Armored vehicle! *Vse zayebalo! Pizdets na khui blyad!*" Saviour tossed the gun aside. "Chug, move in over here!" She positioned him on the left side of the van, so that his body covered Untermensch's seat and the prone form of Saint; it wouldn't do any of them good to have their driver incapacitated, or their captured asset killed. Chug would protect them from the Blacksnake's rifles, and give her cover to lean out and return fire.

Georgi leaned out of the driver's side window after weaving to the right to avoid a burst of rifle fire; he had drawn his GSh-18, aiming for the SUV's tires. After expending the pistol's magazine in a fast but measured pace of shooting, he ducked back into the van. "Airless tires. Language, Commissar. Remember troop morale." He dropped the magazine from the pistol, slamming another that was resting between his leg and the seat with one hand. "This may be difficult."

Natalya charged her left fist before ducking around Chug to fire; the scarlet energy lashed out and met the front bumper of the vehicle. Amazingly, the entire front end of the vehicle shimmered with the energy for a split second before it reflected back towards the point of origin: Natalya and the van. *"Khuinya!"* she cursed again from reflex, falling backwards as the energy blast ricocheted over the roof of the van, scorching it and screaming off into the night sky.

"Are you all right, Commissar?" Georgi called back. Between swerving around piles of debris from the destroyed buildings and dodging the Blacksnake guns, he seemed to have his hands full as well.

"Vsyo zayebis!" She got back onto her knees. "The vehicle is

reflective too. *Svinya.* How am I supposed to have big surprise victory if they anticipate me?"

"I am having idea. Come up and take wheel." Georgi swapped places with Natalya, which was an exercise in acrobatic maneuvers that should probably have been an Olympic event, and began stacking boxes together.

"What in Stalin's tomb are you doing?" Natalya wondered how Georgi had managed to keep the van moving; the rubble made this road all but impassible, never mind having to deal with the Blacksnake mercs hot on their tail.

"Fixing problem. Thing learned from *fashista* in Great War." He started wrapping duct tape around the stack of crates; there was something stuck in the middle of them that was leaving an open space, but the Commissar couldn't see what it was from the quick look she was able to steal. "You should drive very fast, then keep steady pace, Commissar."

"Well, if I can be finding a piece of road that does not resemble Stalingrad after siege—*ha!*" She spotted a relatively clear stretch and made a tire-screaming right-hand turn to get onto it. "Whatever you are going to do, *davay!*"

"Keep straight! Need to gauge timing, Commissar!"

The road, thankfully, looked as if it would cooperate with that idea. Actually it looked as if someone had come through here with a bulldozer shortly after the Invasion and just cleared off a good long stretch. Debris and wrecked vehicles were piled on either side of the cratered asphalt.

The gunshots continued to echo like a hellish typewriter, clacking and echoing back loudly among the gutted buildings. Georgi watched the road between the van and the SUV intently, bobbing his hand in time. Then, suddenly, he pulled something from the middle of his duct-taped crates and shoved the entire bundle out of the van. The SUV continued after them; both of the mercs that had been firing at them had reloaded after a brief pause, and leaned out to take aim at the exposed Russian. At that moment the bundle went under the SUV . . . and the vehicle did a violent front flip after a thunderous explosion; it landed on its roof, crumpling it violently down to the frame like it was nothing more than cheap construction paper.

Nat shook her head violently, her ears ringing from the blast. Glancing back, she saw Georgi pounding the side of his head with the heel of his hand to clear his hearing. Only Chug seemed unaffected; he was clapping his hands. "Do again!" he demanded. "Again! Fireworks!"

"*Borzhe moi*, must cut off access to *nekulturny* Tubbytellys," she muttered, then raised her voice as she slowed the van to a sane speed. "Georgi! What in name of the Manifesto did you do?"

"*Fashista* used to make grenade bundles as expedient antitank weapon in Great War. To use *Amercanski* thinking, I 'super-sized'; added many more grenades." He shook his head, sitting down in the van. "Also, added thermite grenade along with regular grenade to detonate. I did not know if normal offensive grenade would have enough generated heat or blast potential to detonate others; stable explosive compounds, you see." He looked up. "Oh, look. Mercenaries are now being on fire."

"*Horosho.*"

"Also, profits man is being dead. Or good job of faking." He turned around to face Natalya. "Apologies, Commissar. Did not kill our enemies fast enough to keep the traitor from expiring before he could be interrogated further."

Natalya chuckled. "Good, now is no need of making explanations. Profits man now becomes helpless kidnap victim, rescued by CCCP, but tragically, thanks to pursuing Blacksnake, we could not get to hospital fast enough."

Georgi thought for a moment. "Might help if we first are to wipe blood off of gloves. And rest of uniforms." He shrugged. "Plausibility."

"*Nyet*, is blood of hero we get trying to carry him to safety. Merely smear it around more. Looks more plausible than trying to remove."

"And the intelligence documents gained, Commissar? Do we... share this with Echo along with corpse of traitor?"

"What intelligence documents?" she dead-panned. "Eh, we share with Daughter of Rasputin. She will know what to do with them. Tragic death of civilian hero will not be spoiled."

"*Da*, Commissar. Very, very tragic. Flowers and such sentiment."

"Aha! Look. Hospital sign."

There was indeed a much battered and bent-over "H" sign by the cleared road, which explained why it had been cleared in the first place. Saviour followed the signs, eventually coming out onto regular city streets. There she accelerated, as if her cargo was still alive, and pulled, tires screaming, into the Emergency entrance. She and Georgi did a lot of shouting in Russian. Initially, there was a frantic scrambling of emergency personnel, and she made her predetermined explanation to the inevitable police and an Echo SupportOp that turned up (while Georgi pretended he only spoke Russian). She even managed to feign sorrow and disappointment when someone came out to report that Saint was dead.

"Terrible! Terrible! We have much sorrow for his family," she said, as (how did they *learn* about these things?) a television crew materialized. "If it had not been for Blacksnake, perhaps we would have come in time. CCCP will send flowers to funeral of this civilian hero. No, no more interviews, *spasibo.* We must back to headquarters. Chug is hungry."

Just then Chug poked his head out of the back door of the van. "Commissar?" he rumbled in Russian. "Was Chug good? Can Chug have waffles?"

No one but Nat and Georgi understood him, of course, but the television crew hastily agreed that it would be a good thing for Chug to be fed. Saviour and Untermensch piled back into the van, and pointed it back in the direction of CCCP HQ.

Unter glanced over at her. "Commissar, you are reminding me of wolf with calf in her mouth."

Nat realized she was grinning. "Eh, is just good to be back in action, *da,* comrade?"

Unter snorted. "Is very good, Commissar. So long as there is no paperwork, is very good."

CHAPTER SIXTEEN

Brothers in Blood

DENNIS LEE AND MERCEDES LACKEY

I had to get out. I had to. I could see where my path was going otherwise, locked in a small room with nothing but a coffee IV and computers. Because, frankly, the idea was incredibly seductive. Maybe it doesn't sound that way to you, but look at it from my point of view. It was now possible for me to be incredibly effective without ever unlocking my door. Djinni was even letting me channel magic through him. Why would I ever need to leave?

Except that... what if I had to? What if the Thulians figured out who I was and what I was doing and came to blow down the building? Would I die because I couldn't bear to cross my own threshold?

Or what if someone was in trouble out there, one of my friends, *and I was the only one who knew or could get to them in time? Would I let them die because I was housebound?*

Of course I couldn't. And Djinni was right. So. I started working on getting out. Little did I know how soon I would need *to.*

Vickie's eyes felt like someone had poured a pint of sand in each. Her nerves were fried, and her stomach sour from all the coffee she'd been drinking. She hadn't had anything close to a decent night's sleep in... longer than she could remember right now with her brain all fogged up.

And her bed did not beckon at all. In fact, she was doing everything she could to hold off sleep with both hands. Not that she didn't *need* it—she knew all too well that if she didn't get some soon, she was going to start making major mistakes. But sleep was going to bring anything but rest.

Bella had warned her that the "desensitization" they were doing was going to make things worse before they got better, and Bella had no idea how much worse it had gotten. Sleep had become an ordeal. She'd soundproofed her bedroom to keep from terrifying the neighbors, because if she didn't wake up literally screaming, she woke up crying. Either crying because she and Red were an item in the dream (like that would ever happen), or crying because as soon as she woke up, she realized she'd been dreaming herself back into that eighteen-year-old body she used to have, about how things used to be, and when she woke up, she woke up to the reality that they never would be that way again.

I am too damn old to be waking up in tears because I can't have a guy in love with me. Why can't I get my brain wrapped around being grateful to have Djinni as a friend? Crying about being a half cripple, though... that was probably reasonable.

If this kept up, she'd have to feed herself through a tube, because she'd either rot out her stomach with coffee, or her stomach would decide it was never going to hold anything solid again.

Just as she was trying to figure out if coffee or green tea or a nicotine lozenge would be the best option to gain herself one more precious nightmare-free hour—

All her magic-senses exploded with overload. Though her Overwatch room was always dark, it flooded with golden light. And she suddenly felt—crushed. Not emotionally crushed, but as if the room had suddenly acquired a second occupant that was much too large for it.

The normally cold Overwatch room also turned warm, and the air filled with the scents of sandalwood, vanilla, and cinnamon.

And all of her arcane senses shrieked *Kneel! Bow down in the Presence!* as her gut knotted with awe and terror.

She didn't even bother to look; she knew what this was, she'd encountered it once already, and she followed her instincts. She slipped from her chair to her knees, eyes squeezed shut, head abjectly bowed.

"*Oh. Bother,*" said the voice in her head and her ears. "*I am sorry. It is much easier to get your attention than certain other blockheads.*" The Presence and the awe and terror faded, replaced with an aura of kindness and compassion. Cautiously, Vickie raised her head a little, and cracked her eyes open.

It was the Seraphym, all right—the first time Vickie had seen her, except at a distance, since the Invasion. Fire-wings folded neatly, body clothed in flame, hair like a bonfire and eyes like embers, she was *not* the sort of thing to inspire welcome or pleasure in a pyrophobic.

And yet that all-enveloping blanket of compassion managed to keep Vickie where she was, and not running for the door. She squeaked, cleared her throat, and finally managed to croak, "Wh-what—how can I—h-help you? Eldest?" All the while thinking, *Either I have lost my mind completely and I'm hallucinating, or she's really here, and any second now the last nerve I have left is going to fry, or she's going to give me some quest or other, or...*

"You have earned a boon, magician." Those ember eyes regarded her with sympathy. *"And you are at the end of your strength. What is it you need? Ask."*

Oh, she knew this story. It began with "Be careful what you ask for..." Every magician knew this story. The greedy and the thoughtless got exactly what they deserved, and she could ask for just about anything, but if it was selfish...

Tears of exhaustion trickled down her face. This was a bad, bad time to be given such a decision, because she was sure to make the wrong choice. Words were power... words were spells... *oh, don't ask for Red to love you, that will only end in tears. And don't ask for your old self back. Uncle Bela will really come after you and everyone around you then.*

Finally... "Rest?" she whispered. "Please? If that's... all right? Just a little rest? But not if I'm needed, not—not if someone is going to be in trouble if I'm not available—"

"Enough. Your need is great, and your wish pure." The Seraphym smiled. *"And your understanding is sound. From this moment, you shall sleep peacefully, and rise rested, little magician. No more nightmares. Those dreams of the past that cause you grief, and those of longing, though you may have them, you shall not recall them on waking. You shall have rest. Go."*

She waved an arm and a wing at the door, and Vickie rose and stumbled past her, pausing only with her hand on the doorknob. "If I'm needed—" she said, turning.

But the Seraphym was gone, and it was all she could do to

make it to her bed before blessed, empty sleep, sleep flooded with gratitude, claimed her. And she never noticed that, as usual, her hand closed around the fragment of Djinni's claw she kept under her pillow.

With Bulwark back, Red had taken a back seat on training the new recruits. Bull had been to limbo and back, and the docs couldn't find one good medical reason to keep him off active duty, which the huge man had immediately seized upon. The way Red heard it, Bull had snapped off the monitoring tabs they had stuck to his body, climbed into his uniform and simply walked out. Bella had tried to talk him down, of course, scolding him about needing emotional, if not physical, rest. Bull would have none of it, and had simply marched into the barracks, selected a team of new recruits not yet assigned a trainer, and had gone to work.

For some reason, Bull had avoided Red who, with the exception of the occasional recruiting run, had found himself with little to do. He was still working with Victrix, making sure she kept to her training schedule on the parkour course and overseeing her marksmanship on the range. At least Vix was improving, though she still didn't seem able to acknowledge it...

Vix. When had he started calling her Vix? It seemed important for some reason, like it crossed a vague but certain line between colleague and friend. He found he was calling on her more and more these days. She was really the only person there he could call a friend. Most of the people at Echo still avoided him. He was a bit of a jerk, he supposed.

Of those left, well...

Scope and Acrobat were still AWOL, and things just got weird around Bella. The Rebel Alliance, or whatever they were calling themselves this week, had kept her pretty busy. Right now the best hope lay with Ramona and Yankee Pride and their administrative coup, or hostile takeover, depending how it went. If it worked, it would be mostly bloodless. Not that anything involving Verdigris was going to be completely bloodless. The man was vicious. Bella had the unenviable task of keeping on top of him, all the while keeping up the appearance that she was a blundering idiot, completely over her head and lost in the details of running Echo Medical. The few times they had run into each other, the awkward pauses were brief as she was rescued by yet another emergency. They seemed to follow her around these days.

She was also spending a lot of time with Bull. Red understood. Bull would be vital to that plan; no one knew and understood strategy, tactics, administration and bureaucracy like he did. He could sure see where Bull would be more useful to Bella and Pride than he was. Bull had been skating his way around petty bureaucrats to keep doing things his own way for . . . probably as long as he'd been in the military, much less Echo. There were other reasons, of course. When he had tagged a ride with the Seraphym, Red had become privy to a lot of things he probably shouldn't have been, including how Bull and Bella privately felt about each other.

He came to the sudden realization that he was feeling sorry for himself. They worked, anyone could see it. Still, that could have been him—and if they weren't facing the meltdown of the universe, by god, it *would* have been him.

Face the truth, you're holding a one-man pity party. You need to get your mind off the girl, and him, and keep your mind on—

Red gave a shrill yelp as he missed his footing and tumbled off the high beam. His arms flailed as he tried to get a hold of something, anything, to keep him from plummeting down from the highest point of the parkour course. He missed a handhold by mere inches, and let his body go limp as he rolled and bumped his way down the steep slope, shouting curses, to land in a heap on the dirt.

I just fell, and of course there's no way *no one saw me do that . . .*

"Nice dismount," Bull said. The big man was leaning up against a wall, where he would have been just out of Djinni's line of sight, his arms crossed over his chest. "I particularly enjoyed the alliterative f-bombs."

"Well, you know me," Red groaned as he forced himself to a sitting position. "Tell you what, next time I'll do my rendition of 'The Aristocrats' on the way down."

Bull strolled over and helped Red to his feet.

"Thanks," Red said.

"Need a word," Bull replied. frowning slightly. "I know you've been taking over the training of the new recruits while I was . . . gone. But I'm certified as back, and I'll handle it from now on."

"Well, duh. If you haven't noticed, I haven't lifted a finger with the recruits since you got back. And I've been busy..." Red hesitated.

"Falling off obstacle courses?" Bulwark suggested.

No, Red thought. *Avoiding you and Bella.*

Bull shook his head. "I was talking about our Miss Victrix. She wired me up yesterday, which allowed me to get a good look at her. She looks like hell. You're pushing her too hard, she's going to break, and she's the one component we can't do without."

Red clenched his jaw. What, was she whining now? "She hasn't complained to me. What's her beef? If she has one, she should be talking to me."

"She didn't say anything, but she looks like she hasn't slept in a week." Bulwark frowned. "And I looked over the schedule. Two-hour runs on the course, twice a day, and an hour on the range?"

"She's the one that wanted the second parkour session!" Red objected. "Dammit, Bull, don't put it on me that the woman drives herself harder than I could!" Vix had turned into a self-motivated machine. Red might have even admitted he was proud of her. True, she *did* look like hell lately, but he didn't think it had anything to do with the training sessions. In fact, he got the feeling the sessions gave her relief from—something.

"As a trainer, you should know her limits better than she does."

Now he was just being difficult. Bull didn't reveal much, he never did, but time spent with the man in missions and on the training field had taught Red a few of Bulwark's tells. He was never unreasonable, nor did his voice get any louder than it needed to, unless he was bothered about something. This was quite the opposite. Bull was *too* quiet, too controlled, and it screamed *overcompensation.* Red considered Bull's posture, the exaggerated stiffness in his stance, the careful, even tones of his voice. He was trying too hard. He cared about Vix, sure, they all did, but this was more than that. It was as if a new tension had risen between them...

Bella.

She must have told him, about their kiss, about those few shared moments when something seemed to click between them. Red could read it in the way Bull was *not* threatening him in his usual passive aggressive way, was not issuing commands, was not being his general, overbearing self. Instead, he was picking a fight in a very un-Bull-like way. He was telling Red straight out, that he was unfit to do his job. Red didn't bother with the jests, or with any innuendo. If the Jarhead wanted to have it out, that was fine. Red had some pent-up anger over the whole mess to vent out too.

Red made a dismissive gesture. "Fine. *You* tell her. You're the team lead. It's not my fault you pick women that are more mule-stubborn than you are. And don't be surprised if she tells you to go to hell."

Red hesitated again, confused. Amethist, Bella . . . and now Vix. Bull didn't see it, but suddenly, Red did. Three women, and Red could've made that statement about any of them. Three women, far more alike than he had realized until this moment. All three of them could be worse than a hog on ice when they got the bit stuck in their teeth—to truly mix metaphors. Red had lost two of them to Bull, and now the big man was out to take his friend as well? To hell with that. He might think of himself—maybe subconsciously—as the head stallion of the herd, but there was no way Red was going to play omega dog to his alpha. Hell. More scrambled metaphors.

"I'll tell her," Bull promised. "And given your history with her, I think you would agree she may be better off with my support rather than your abuse."

Now Red was starting to fume. "My history . . . about which, you know absolutely *nothing*. You were playing stand-in for a store mannequin while *I* was working with her. Did you even bother to ask someone about that? *I've* been the one that's been her main support while you've been gone. *I've* been the go-to guy, *not* you."

"Yes, while I've been gone. And now I'm back."

"How about if you act like it and get yourself properly briefed first, then." Red seethed. "Actually find out what's going on instead of *assuming* you know what's best for the girl. If I know her, she just might give you a slap upside the head for that kind of attitude." Was Vix listening in on this? He couldn't imagine her *not* giving both of them a piece of her mind if she had been. She never held back when she was the disembodied voice, yet there was nothing but dead air on his earpiece, and Red had to admit he was a bit relieved. The last thing he wanted right now was someone to hold him back, not when he was enjoying some much needed release.

"Unlike you, Djinni, I do not take pleasure from being beaten up by women," Bulwark said, with just the faintest twitch of his lip. "But I think you overestimate her anger. She has never been anything less than cordial to me. Perhaps she values the respect I have for her, or perhaps she has none for you."

"Oh, that's your take on it, Miss Cleo? I dunno, Bull, seems to me your powers of observation have taken a hit of late. Maybe you aren't as good at figuring people out as you think you are. I mean, you really missed all the signals with Harmony, didn't you?" Red applied another turn of the knife. "Didn't see what was behind the big lovelorn eyes, did you? Or maybe you just didn't want to?"

Bull didn't answer; his lip twitched some more. That was a warning sign, but the Djinni was relentless. "Or maybe you just didn't notice, you were distracted, while you were giving it to her..."

Red saw it coming, but even then he could hardly believe it. Bull reared back, his lips beginning to curl over clenched teeth, and drove a heavy fist up into Red's exposed jaw. It was a spectacular hit, and Red flew up and backwards, knocked skyward as Bull's kinetic shield flared to life with the blow.

I'm falling again, Red thought. *Twice in one day. Of course, this time I'm falling* up...

He spun around and caught himself on an exposed girder, twenty feet above the ground. He hung there for a moment, then looked down to see Bulwark standing below him, his hands clenched, his shield pulsating in fury.

"Foreplay, I love it..." Despite his aching jaw, Red reveled in his soiled triumph.

Bulwark stared up at him, face going flush—then abruptly turned on his heel and stalked off.

Red hoisted himself up on his perch, and watched Bull walk away. He had to admit, he felt better now. That punch was a long time coming, he knew, just as he knew that Bull was feeling anything *but* good about himself. Still, there was nothing like a solid strike to the head to get a little perspective, and through the regret and sadness of this whole fiasco, Red was experiencing one of those moments of absolute clarity.

"God, I really am a jerk," he said.

Pike ran up the slope towards the parkour course, excited to finally have a reason to talk to the Djinni. Ever since his rescue he'd secretly hoped to be assigned to Red Djinni and his team of trainees, but for some reason the Djinni had stopped his training exercises abruptly, except for his daily sessions with that Victrix woman. Pike couldn't say he liked her very much. He still remembered the way she had dropped him into a sewer. There was something in the way she had done it, something that he took for disdain. He would remember it. He had a way of holding grudges.

He stopped a moment to adjust the Echo trainee suit they had given him. It didn't fit right, being a bit too snug across the chest and shoulders and far too loose in the undercarriage. He wondered about its previous owner and what sort of out-of-shape loser it had to have been to stretch it out in such odd dimensions. He could have fixed it, he supposed, and willed his body to fill it out in the right places, but the thought disgusted him. Things would change, soon enough. And if they didn't, he would adapt. He was very adaptable, and he had a way of being patient when the need arose. The universe would provide, after all. It always did.

As he crested the hill, he came to a stop and smiled. Good. He didn't have to search for the Djinni, or run him down on the course. His quarry seemed to be taking a breather, resting on an exposed girder just a few levels up. He waved up at him, but the Djinni didn't seem to notice. He was, in fact, slumped over with his head bowed. He looked troubled. How curious.

"Mister Djinni, sir?" Pike called up.

Red's head snapped up at this unwelcome intruder.

"Do me a favor, kid. Don't ever call me that again."

Pike hunched a little. "I'm sorry, what should I call you then?"

The Djinni shook his head. "Red. Just call me Red. And you're . . . ?"

"Pike. You saved me from Blacksnake, remember?" Of course he would remember. The event, if not the person he had saved.

The Djinni peered down at him. "Pike. Yeah, sure. What can I do for you, Pike?"

"I've got something for you, Red." Pike grinned. That felt good, to be on a first name basis with this man. It felt like an accomplishment, a milestone. "Uh . . . think you might want to come down from up there?"

"Not especially," Red answered. He leaned back, stretched, and settled down on the beam in a lazy sprawl. "Tell you what, Pike. If you're able to get your ass up here, I'm all yours."

Pike glanced from the Djinni, to the girder, to the chaotic skeleton of metal bars and jagged concrete that made up this leg of the course, and nodded. He took a running start at a sharp incline and used his momentum to power a backflip away from the stone base, towards a small handhold at the foot of a rusty ladder. He swung there for a moment, his feet dangling a good eight feet off the ground, when he hefted his legs up and locked them in place through the rungs of the ladder. He righted himself, climbed a bit, and with a short leap he landed next to Red in a crouch.

"Well, that backfired," the Djinni muttered. "All right, kid. Not bad. Now what's so important you had to run all the way from HQ to give it to me?"

Pike shrugged. "Not important, really. They haven't placed me with a trainer yet, so for now they've mostly got me running packages across campus."

Red winced. "You're a freakin' gofer? Don't you think that's a little beneath you?"

Pike shook his head. "Oh, I don't mind. I've got plenty of energy, and it's either this or running laps on the field to keep in shape. I get to be useful this way. Besides, I've gotten to see a lot of the campus while I'm doing it. I've only ever been here once, and I didn't get to see nearly enough."

"One of those Echo guided tours or something?"

"Yeah, something like that." Pike grinned. "I was really rushed through it too. Guess a lot was happening that day. Anyway, here, I'm supposed to bring you this." He reached into his courier satchel, and brought out a small box. He handed it to Red.

"New comm unit," Red grunted, as he opened the package and held up his new earpiece.

"Yeah," Pike nodded. "They said you broke your last one."

"Yup," Red said. "Parting gift from that tussle with Christian."

"Who?"

Red gave Pike a look. "The guy who was trying to buy you."

"Oh," Pike said, embarrassed. "I, uh, wanted to thank you for that. For helping me out, that day. I really didn't want to go with those guys, but my friends—"

The Djinni's eyebrows furrowed. "Look, Pike, I'm going to guess here that you haven't had a lot of close buds in your life, but do I really need to spell out for you what shitty friends they were if they were trying to *sell* you?"

"Yeah, I guess," Pike nodded, if a little foolishly. "So, yeah, I guess I just wanted to say, uh, thanks."

Red gave him a pitying look, and nodded. "Don't worry about it."

There was an awkward pause. Pike looked around. "You're pretty good on the parker stuff, right?"

"Parkour."

"Uh . . . right. I don't suppose . . . could you, I mean . . . if I got someone to train me . . . maybe I could get on a team instead of running errands." Pike tried to look hopeful without looking like a puppy. "They said they don't have enough trainers, but *you* can train people, right? And you can shoot too; I remember you were shooting that night. I can prob'ly figure out making my armor work by myself okay, but until I can get a trainer . . ." He let his voice trail off.

Red looked pained. "Look, kid, I'll be straight with you. I'm not exactly in my right mind today. Normally, I would have sent you back to HQ with a swift kick in the ass. The only reason you've lasted this long is that I'm going through some severely retarded drama right now, of epically high school proportions, and it's got me a little preoccupied. *Severely* retarded. We're talking Betty-loves-Archie-level drama, sparkly vampires versus topless werewolves; hell, I'll bet I could draw parallels to the first season of *Gossip Girl* if I tried hard enough."

Pike increased the hopefulness in his gaze a notch, and debated which tack to take next. The "my parents kicked me out because I was a freak" angle? The "everybody just says 'go away kid' and won't let me try" ploy? The Djinni would probably respect that.

"Look," he said, looking as determined as he could. "I want to do stuff. I know there's ways I can help. But they won't even let me *try*. Maybe I'm just a kid, but am I gonna be worse at this stuff than some of the ex-alkies and druggies they've dragged in?"

"Wish it were that simple, Pike. I'm on a bit of a short leash right now, and if you don't mind, I'm not really up to ruffling feathers with the higher-ups just so you can stretch your legs."

Pike gave him a discouraged look, then grinned slyly.

"What if it wasn't on the record? I just wanna run, man! Stretch my legs and get out there! There's nothing in the rules about you runnin' with me, is there?"

Red considered that. "What did you have in mind?"

Pike gestured around him. "How many times you've been over

this course? You must know it cold. Don't you want to try tackling something different? Something that'll get your blood pumping?"

Red looked around, and nodded with a sigh. "Might be nice. Been feeling a bit caged up lately, probably why I've been volunteering for so many recruitment runs. You know a good spot?"

Pike's grin grew wider. "Boy, do I ever!"

Red blinked as he took in his surroundings. This destruction corridor still looked like something out of a post-apocalyptic movie. There were even fires burning here and there—no flames, but thin threads of smoke rising from the rubble. Unlike other parts of the city, no one had even tried to reclaim this area. It must have been pretty much toast after the Invasion, stripped by scavengers, so there was nothing really worth even squatters trying to take. Things had to be pretty grim when even homeless squatters didn't live here. Eventually the bulldozers would move in, but right now the area wasn't close enough to downtown for anyone to put a priority on cleaning it out. With higher-value real estate waiting to be cleared, it would be a while before anything lived here but rats, cats and roaches.

And the occasional roving band of Rebs.

Would they count as roaches?

"This isn't quite what I had in mind," Red said.

"Oh come on!" Pike spread his arms wide, obviously enamored with the view. "How does this not fit the bill? Treacherous terrain, multileveled, and yeah, just a hint of danger from my old pals!"

Red chuckled. The kid had a point. The buildings here hadn't been taller than four stories and a lot of them had been warehouse or old industrial buildings, but that meant they were all the better in their wrecked state for parkour. Add in the crushed and abandoned cars and trucks...

Come to think of it, coming out here was a better idea than working a course he already knew well enough to run in his sleep. He'd have to be sharp here. He couldn't afford to let his attention lapse if he was going to do it at any speed. Why hadn't he thought of this before? His estimation of the kid rose by a hair.

Already he felt more energized by the challenge. "So, kid, you have a start and finish line? Or you just want to follow me and see if you can keep up?"

Pike shrugged. "A start and finish, I guess. Start at that burnt-out bread truck, waypoints being at the Piggly-Wiggly sign, the bent-over cell tower, the old Winston factory, and the semitrailer up there that's on end, see it? That'll be the end. You lead; I'll try and keep up."

From where they stood, the landmarks were clear. The Piggly-Wiggly sign was only a PIGGL IG Y but if you knew the store, which everyone in this part of the country did, it was clear. The factory had been a four-story brick structure, and still had part of the old painted signage across the top, red WINSTON—presumably the cigarettes, before they had become "Winston-Salem"—on blistered, peeling white. The upended semitrailer must have been hurled there by an explosion; it stood up, leaning only slightly to the right, embedded in a pile of rubble, a strange sort of monolith.

Red eyeballed the run. It looked to be just about a quarter of a mile in total. A good warm-up for him, and he'd be able to see how good the kid was without killing him.

"Okay, kid," he said. "Quick trot to the bread van, stretch out and warm up on the way. Ready?"

The kid grinned, and Red took off at a gentle jog.

As he hurtled over a collapsed brick wall, Red risked a look back at Pike. The kid certainly had some natural talent for this sort of thing. He obviously had no formal training, simply adapting to the jagged landscape as he followed Red's lead, but he was naturally lithe and seemed to glide over the rougher patches of terrain. In that respect, he reminded Red of himself. That could be taken as either good or bad, Red supposed.

Pike was certainly matching Red's pace, he had to give him that much. Even after upping the difficulty, Pike had met each challenge without hesitation. Whatever holes Red dove through, whatever heights he had to spring to, walls to climb, or the occasional balanced sprints across uneven footing, Pike was right behind him, sporting a mad grin that seemed to split his face in two. He was obviously having a marvelous time, and was beginning to close in.

Red dropped any pretense of flashy acrobatics, and opted for speed. He somersaulted over broken flooring and landed at full sprint, darting around upended machinery on the factory floor and made a dash for the collapsed side of the building. All that separated him and the last leg of the makeshift course were slippery floors and piles of rubble. He slid through the puddles, barreled over the debris, uncomfortable with the immediate sounds of splashing water and shifting rock behind him. Pike was right behind him.

As he broke through the hole where a window had once been, Red went all out. The upended trailer, their impromptu finish line, was just ahead. What had begun as a simple training exercise had somehow turned into a serious race. Someone had dropped the ball on this kid; they clearly hadn't even tested him. He was good. Between the parkour talent and the self-armoring power, he should be out on the street with a team. Even if he couldn't do squat offensively, he could still protect the DCOs who (unlike Bella) really *were* uncomfortable with fighting. Pike had been at Echo HQ for two weeks, plenty of time to give even a simple assessment of what he could do. For the rest of it, Red supposed the shrinks were taking care of his apparent mental issues. With Bella's new interventionist therapy, recoveries from simple stuff were going really fast....

Was that where Pike's sudden attitude and confidence had come from? The last time Red had seen him, he had seemed shy, very unsure of himself. Still, that didn't explain how he had fallen through some very obvious cracks in the recruitment drive. No way this kid would have been overlooked by the trainers. Something didn't add up...

"Right behind you, old man!" From just over Red's shoulder, Pike's laughter rang out strong and unfettered. Great, the kid wasn't even winded. Red, on the other hand, was feeling a strong burn in his chest, legs and arms.

Hell with it, Red thought and pushed himself further. He heard Pike fall behind as he drove his legs harder, and as he closed the distance to the trailer he was keenly aware of how fast his heart was racing...

There was no warning. No hint that something was off. Just an enormous *whump,* a tumbling vortex of black smoke and red flame ascending from what had been the trailer, and a scorching pressure wave hitting Red in mid jump like a blast of wind straight out of hell. He was hurled back and landed unceremoniously on his side. He felt something tear in his back. That couldn't be good.

Looks like I'll be seeing Bella again real soon...

He propped himself up on his arm, and pondered that. He was thinking about how awkward it was going to be, forced into the same room with Bella, probably alone, and what he could possibly say to her that would sound even remotely sane. Sane? He had just run into an *explosion*! The blast had left him staggered, deaf, and even his skin-based senses seemed dulled in the wake of the explosion. Why was he concerned with Bella? The absurdity of the situation began to crystallize in his thoughts, of a semi blowing up for no apparent reason just seconds before he was about to slap its side in victory, when he caught a glimpse of an entire squad of armored Krieger powersuits climb out of the smoking crater that remained.

Christ, and we were worried about running into Rebs.

"Pike!" Red shouted. "We've got hostiles!"

Red felt Pike's hands on him, helping him up. The boy was shouting something, but Red couldn't make it out over the persistent ringing in his ears.

"I can't hear you!" Red shouted, pointing at his ears. "Big truck go kablooey! Red deaf now, not just dumb!"

Pike rolled his eyes, and slowly shaped the words with his mouth.

Brother . . . I . . . am . . . so . . . very . . . disappointed . . . in . . . you . . .

Red stared at him, dumbfounded. He didn't even have time to begin to parse what seemed to be an utter non sequitur when Pike pressed something into his side.

It felt like he'd been hit by lightning. His body convulsed, his mind blanked and he felt himself falling.

Vickie's hand was burning.

The pain jolted her out of a blissfully dreamless sleep, and for a moment she could not imagine what the *hell* was going on. She sat bolt upright, and looked dumbfounded at her hand. She unclenched it from around what felt like a red-hot coal and stared down . . .

At the bit of Red's claw that was lying in her open hand . . .

Jeezus . . . She recognized the magical tether. Emotional links did that, whether you liked it or not. Magic worked that way. Anything bad that happened to him was going to trigger some sort of alert to her, like this extremely primitive, extremely old sort of magic that caused direct pain to *her* if she was touching anything of *his* when he was in danger. Hell, she would probably just *know* he was in trouble from now on.

No point denying it now, I've got it bad for this jerk and it's not going to go away by willing it to.

"Computer: Command: open Overwatch voice command," she said aloud, shaking her head to clear it. She heard the little double *beep* on her embedded headset, then lurched out of bed. "Command: open Overwatch comm. Command: open comm Red Djinni."

She barreled through the door into the living room, and bumbled through the one that led into the Overwatch room.

"*Red!* Djinni! Acknowledge!" No answer. She fell into her chair and brought up the screens, typing in the command to Overwatch to locate Red on the map. Destruction corridor . . . the hell? What was he doing in that old factory in East Atlanta? *Okay, time to do something he kinda gave me permission for.* She used her pad to sketch in a glyph and punched *enter.* That brought up the external mic on his side, overriding the fact that he had turned it off. Now she could hear what was going on. She brought up his vitals.

Crap, vitals not good, heart racing, breathing labored . . . no way can I fly a spy-ball across town in any kind of time. And this was way outside of where she had a preprepared magical "landing pad." Absolutely zero chance of there being ATMs or security cams she could hijack.

Was he wearing his eye? She drew a different glyph and punched *enter.* Nada. Whatever he'd been doing, he'd left the eye at home. *Crap. Okay.* "Red. Red. Please, Red. Make any kind of sound if you can hear me." *Should I try boosting the sound at the other end? The earpiece is buried under his skin . . . Okay, breathe, wait, boost the mic gain first.* She keyed up a sound recognition/voice recognition program. She might get some clues out of that, even if the Djinni was unconscious.

Dammit, Red Djinni. Why can't anything ever be easy around you?

". . . you will tell them this, and they will come. Now. Tell them their lives depend on it, because they do."

Red shook himself out of the fog, and as his eyes opened a crack he saw he was back inside the crumbling remains of the abandoned factory. He stared, puzzled, as one of the Kriegers saluted smartly to Pike and backed away. The boy shook his head and strolled over to Red.

"You're awake," Pike said, grinning. "Very good, Red Djinni,

I am so pleased. For a moment I was worried my little toy had seared you with a touch too much current. I thought I would have to entertain myself while these *dummkopfs* strive to stay on schedule. Our transport, it seems, is running late. But no matter! This will give us a chance to chat, you and I. You notice I say 'chat,' and not 'get better acquainted,' since I must say I feel I know you quite well already."

Red gave Pike a wary look as he motioned to rise, but stopped as he heard the shackles clink from his hands and feet. He looked down at them. They lacked any obvious locking mechanism, but he could feel a subtle electrical hum emanating from them.

"Yes," Pike nodded. "I am aware of your skills. *Sehr flink.* You will not find these locks so susceptible to picking." He bent down and switched off the Echo communicator around Red's ear. "There, and now we are free to speak, without any unwanted interruptions."

"Right," Red nodded. "I'm your Huckleberry. You know me, so I can skip my life story and you can get right to telling me what you want."

"Is it not obvious?" Pike asked, chuckling in an incongruously deep tone. "I have been waiting such a long time to meet you, *mein Bruder.* You cannot know what a thrill it is for me that we have finally come together, face to face. I simply have . . . *chills* . . . thinking of what our futures hold."

"Oho, a fanboy," Red said, shifting uncomfortably. "You know, there are easier ways to get an autograph." He grimaced as he tested the shackles, and hissed as they delivered small, measured shocks to his wrists and ankles. "Nice bling. You didn't have to give me presents, you know."

"Careful!" Pike said. "Those were a warning. The current ramps up the more you struggle, and really, I have waited far too long to speak with you for you to simply . . . *die.* It would be an . . . *enttäuschung.* An anticlimax."

"I know what the word means, *onanist.* I have to wonder though, where a redneck street punk from the south picked up so much German."

"Come now, Red," Pike said, looking very disappointed. "You must have figured it out by now."

Red shrugged. "You hit me with an exploding semi and knocked me out with a taser. Forgive me if my brain is a bit scrambled, I feel like a brain-dead badger right now. And spare me the *schadenfreude*, okay? You're holding all the cards here. Hell, right now, you're even holding *my* hand. You obviously went to a lot of trouble to meet me, to get me out here alone. You even got Blacksnake to show." He shook his head. "You got some connections there, kid."

"That was a case of misfortune, I'll admit," Pike said. "I didn't anticipate Blacksnake's interest when I enlisted myself with those *unwissend* Rebs. I speculated it was only a matter of time until an Echo recruiting party would make their way to this corner of Atlanta, right in their own backyard."

"No shit, Sherlock," Red muttered.

"Imagine my annoyance when Blacksnake arrived first. Imagine my delight when it was you, of all people, leading the charge to my rescue."

"You had no intention of letting Blacksnake take you, did ya?"

Pike's smile vanished. "If not for your fortuitous intervention, I would have slaughtered them all. What a waste of time *that* would have been. I would have had to start all over." The depraved and hungry smile returned. "Ah, but the good universe in its wisdom stepped in. It does that, you know. It provides for those in need."

"Tell me what you want, Pike," Red repeated, making it clear that he was getting fed up with the runaround.

"Really, Red Djinni! You have not figured it out? We are brothers, you and I."

"So you keep saying," Red replied. It was getting hard to hold still; he wasn't well-balanced, and there were sharp edges sticking into him. But every time he moved even a little, he got warning shocks from the shackles. And the crap ton of dust in here was threatening to make him sneeze, which was going to make life uncomfortable as the shackles reacted. "I'm really going to have to go through the trouble of tracking down my dad one of these days, get a fix on what other mongrel blood I'm sharing."

"Oh, not by blood!" Pike exclaimed in disgust. "Truly you must see our bond transcends that!" He sighed. "Perhaps you are not as intelligent as I have observed you to be. And I was so sure. A shame. No matter. You will still give me what I desire."

"Something tells me it's not the autograph." Red wondered how long he could keep this maniac talking.

"Given the realization of your stupidity, your curiosity will not, I fear, be sated. I have much to do, and you will simply have to live without the knowledge of why, exactly, you must die screaming."

"Well, that's just not going to cut it," Red snarled. "I'm going to need a lot more if you're going to get anything from me."

"Have I not made it clear? *Unglaubliche schweinhund, verdammten arschloch*, you really are an imbecile. I do not need for you to be willing, Djinni, I simply need for you to be breathing. On your feet, *mein freund idiot*, let us not tempt the fates any more than we have to."

Pike motioned for Red to stand, and was rewarded with a scornful look.

"Well, like my old Uncle Sparky used to say, 'pot, kettle, black, asshole.'" Red looked meaningfully down at his hands and feet. "I try and stand up and you're going to have to carry me, Hoss. I do any more, and you might as well leave my carcass here as fertilizer."

"Oh, of course!" Pike laughed. "You will excuse my carelessness, I'm sure. I am simply impatient, you see! Impatient to begin what promises to be a glorious future! I can decrease the output, if you wish, just enough for you to move . . . slowly. Or I can, if you prefer, simply knock you out. My men can lay you on a litter and carry you out on their shoulders. Like the funeral of Siegfried! Fitting, don't you think?"

"Just do it," Red said, slowly lifting his arms and presenting his wrist shackles to Pike. "This place looks depressingly like Detroit on a bad day. If I'm going to have to listen to you, I want better scenery."

Pike played with his chin for a moment, like a villain in a B-movie. "Hmm. Make you walk, and watch you dance while you do so, yet suffer delays while you thrash, or watch my subhuman flunkies struggle to carry you? Decisions, decisions . . ."

Red could feel Pike's glee, his hunger, fueling his need to taunt his prey. It wasn't enough that he had won. He reveled in his dominance, and his eyes bore into Red's, excavating madly for as much misery as he could find. Red returned the maniac's look with disdain.

"Oh yeah," Red nodded. "Look at you, big man. You got me all tied up, helpless, probably hoping I'll do a little begging right now, huh?"

"Oh, would you?" Pike asked, his grin spreading even wider. "That would be so thoughtful!"

"Please, please," Red obliged, rolling his eyes. "I've got so much to live for. I've got kids... probably. I never learned to knit, and winter's coming. My DVR is full of *Community*s I haven't watched yet, and I'll be damned if I miss another Inspector Spacetime clip. And I still haven't..."

"Stop," Pike interrupted, his eyes narrowing, his smile fading away. "You're stalling. Why are you stalling?"

"PUNCH IT, VIX!" Red shouted, and with a brilliant flash of light the shackles fell from his wrists and ankles.

She heard voices, but not close enough to make out what they were saying. *Okay, screaming is going to get me nowhere, and someone might have meta-hearing and pick up on me screaming into his ear.* She settled for a jittery, "Red. Red. Red. Say something. Red. Say something," repeated ad infinitum, but with pauses for him to, well, actually respond.

She froze when she finally heard a clear voice. It wasn't Red's, but a young man. Pike. Only... it had a faint accent that sure as hell wasn't Southern. It wasn't just the accent. Pike spoke with confidence, a smarmy drawl that drifted back and forth between disdain and respect. And German. She definitely heard German in there.

She watched as one of Red's communicators went offline, the standard issue one from Echo. Pike, it seemed, did not want anyone listening in or pinpointing Red's location. He obviously didn't know about the secret Overwatch communicator or the throat mic, both buried under Red's skin, since his arrogant voice was still coming in loud and clear.

When Red did speak, it wasn't to her. "Right, I'm your Huckleberry. You know me, so I can skip my life story and you can get right to telling me what you want." They'd worked out a code a couple runs ago, half in jest, half in earnest. *"You know, I'm a writer... and if I was writing this, it'd be about time for a kidnapping scene."* He laughed, but they both agreed that there was some justifiable paranoia here. "Huckleberry" meant he was starting code-speak and "life story" told her he was captured, a hostage or both.

"Roger capture," she breathed. "Running VR program to see if I can ID anyone." She had a great voice recognition program, it worked on accents and speech patterns too. "I ID Kriegers obviously. What's your status?"

She listened carefully for the next code words while her programs ran, and was rewarded with the heavy crackle of feedback. She winced as the crackling subsided, and held her breath as Red spoke again.

"Nice bling. You didn't have to give me presents, you know."

Restraints, and given they knew it was the Djinni, probably shackles and cuffs. But what kind? If he could pick them, all she needed to do was make a distraction.

It was his captor, not Red, who gave her the answer. His taunting told her, after a few moments of racing thought, that they were some fancy high-tech, and they could kill him, possibly with shocks. That would explain the feedback. English was not sufficient for her response to that. *"Kutyafasza,"* she swore. She was reasonably certain Red did not know Hungarian. "Okay. Okay. Give me a minute, I'll figure out if I can do something about your bracelets."

"...I feel like a brain-dead badger right now. And spare me the *schadenfreude,* okay? You're holding all the cards here."

The badger reference. Code red, in Djinni-speak. At least five Thulians; they'd agreed to use poker talk for counting things. Then, when he said that his captor had both hands—that was ten. And—

Vickie felt a shock of panic. *Schadenfreude?* But that was Echo's code name for...

The answer came to her, a mere second before her voice recognition program flashed the name up on her monitor.

"Good God!" Vickie screamed. "It's Doppelgaenger!"

"No shit, Sherlock," Red muttered.

Not good. *So* not good.

"Bazd szájba a jó kurva anyád..." Vickie swore, and slammed Bull's panic button. Hopefully he was wearing *his* Overwatch ear. Not a good time to get Bella on this, and Vickie needed a tactical brain. Bull would get a steady alarm on his Overwatch freq until he answered her. And in the meantime...what? Red was being held by Doppelgaenger! He was helpless against a man that, by all accounts, was the most sadistic Krieger they had come up against to date. What could she do? What could she...

"Red!" she shouted. "Keep him talking! I've called for backup!"

"Well that's just not going to cut it," Red answered. Vickie frowned. Was he talking to her or to Doppelgaenger? Her mind raced with possibilities. She didn't have time for anything fancy—time *or* accuracy. No cam, no good way to read what was on him or around him, only the crude location and what he was feeding to her via the headset. Damn him and his refusal to go fully wired! It wasn't as if he couldn't just hide a button cam and grow some skin over it! All she'd need would be a pinhole—

Concentrate, bitch! "There's not a lot I can do at this range and shooting blind, Red," she said, trying to keep the panic out of her voice. "I can't do the tech-magic, it'll all have to be witchery and geomancy. That's not exactly needle surgery we're talking about." Nevertheless, she sketched in diagrams over his spot on the map, laying in prep work she hoped she wouldn't have to use. "It's like hitting bugs with the Oxford Unabridged, and I don't want you to be the bug." Her heart raced and her mouth was dry.

Her heart sank as she heard Doppelgaenger mention transports. They were running out of time.

"Well, like my old Uncle Sparky used to say..."

Sparky? He can't be serious... She was a techno-mage yes, but for the gods' sake, that required finesse and a *lot* of data, this situation was absolutely blind and...

"Have you lost your mind?" she demanded, leaping to her feet. "What's electrocuting you going to do other than leave you helpless *and* fried?"

"Just do it," she heard Red say defiantly. "This place looks depressingly like Detroit on a bad day. If I'm going to have to listen to you, I want better scenery."

Detroit. He wanted her to fry his cuffs... she'd read about how he had goaded that electric-powered meta into an uncontrolled surge to fry off his monitoring bracelet. Great. Just great. *Who does he think I am? David Copperfield?* It would be one thing if she could at least see what the damn things were, but she was operating completely in the dark and under time pressure. And there was only one way to do it. The nasty, dirty, primitive, and ugly way. Which was inherently the dangerous way.

She began to draw the crudest, clumsiest diagrams and equations she'd done since her high school days... no, earlier... and berated the Djinni while she did it.

"Right, shit-for-brains, have it your way. I am going to try to spring the cuffs but I don't know what they are so I have to do this the old-fashioned way, which means fry the tech. All I have is that piece of your claw so I have to use you as a channel, but I can't risk hurting you, so... *szar napom van,* this is going to have to be *kibaszott* medieval. I *hate* medieval magic, hate, hate, hate..."

This was horrid stuff, worse than hitting bugs with books, this was going after a gnat with a sledgehammer, and Red had to be just outside of where the sledgehammer came down. Reverse Law of Unity, with the piece of claw as the target. *Magic to be confined to what once belonged to this. Fry if you are not part of what* this *was part of.* Like nested Venn diagrams. So many ways to go wrong. So little time to set it up. So much at stake. Was Bull going to answer? Who to call next if he didn't? Call Echo and risk exposing the Overwatch program to Verd? Maybe call Corbie, or the Samoans?

Medieval was as good as it was going to get. "Okay, Red, we are a go. I don't like this. I'm having to sacrifice your Overwatch gear along with the cuffs. I kind of have you protected but I still could fry *you;* my odds are"—she glanced at her Prognosticator and blanched—"about fifty-fifty. I can trip this if I have to, but there has to be a better..."

"PUNCH IT, VIX!"

She punched it, unleashing Mother Earth's own electricity into him in a terrible surge. The spell, massive and unwieldy, fed off her own energy. Vickie gasped as everything literally drained out of her, and the world went black.

She woke up. A frantic glimpse at the time on one of the monitors told her she'd passed out for *maybe* thirty seconds. Another check showed her, as she expected, that all of the Djinni's reads were as dead as last year's leaves. Whatever was going on now...

I just hope the Kriegers near him got a dose of that too...

Feeling as if someone had been beating her with bags of sand, she punched back into Bull's Overwatch freq, interrupting the alarm. "Bulwark. Bulwark, this is an emergency." *If I can't raise him, it'll have to be Bella; she's the only one I can think of that knows who I should try for next.* Then what? Go out on her own? Bad idea, she couldn't call anyone from out there. "Operative Bulwark, this is a Code Screaming Freaking Red emergency!"

"Bulwark here," Bull's voiced rumbled in her headset. "Apologies, Miss Victrix, I was in the shower."

"Bull, the Djinni's in trouble. As in 'ass-deep in aligators and pteradactyls descending' trouble. He's at grid 32-101-12 in that East Atlanta des—"

"Roger that, Overwatch. I will dispatch a squad to his location immediately."

She felt her mouth falling open with astonishment. "Are you even *listening* to me? Your freaking *squad* is gonna get squashed like bugs on a semi! Assuming Verd even lets them go without intercepting them! It's Doppelgaenger and at least ten Kriegers, and they're trying to take him alive! I've lost signal on him on Echo and Overwatch both, I had to—"

"Doppelgaenger?" Bull sounded confused. "What would Doppelgaenger want with Red Djinni?"

"Will you *stop* asking questions and *move* already?" she shrilled, unable to keep her voice from spiraling up. "I'm calling Bella. If you won't move your bloody broad ass, maybe Pride will!" Her hands were flying over the keyboard. She knew she could use text-to-speak to Bella, Ramona, and Yankee Pride. "Then I—"

"Victrix, cease and desist," Bulwark said. "You're about to cause an enormous uproar, and you know certain parties would have to be deaf and dumb not to overhear it."

"You're not the boss of me!" she shouted back. "Bella and Pride are!"

"Stop and think, woman. If you start blaring an emergency on all your frequencies, you run the risk of compromising our network."

"Goddammit, Jarhead, it's *Red!"* She choked on the last word.

"Breathe, Victrix. Don't go rushing into this; you know it's a mistake, you're too good not to. Get your head back in the game, keep your heart out of it, at least until the crisis is over."

"While you're blathering they're *taking him." Keep your heart out of it,* he had said. He knew. He knew how she felt about Red, but she didn't care. "Fuck this. If you won't let me call anyone, I'm going in." Somehow. How the hell was she—

Apport. I can apport to the closest pad and—something. All she knew was she couldn't let Doppelgaenger take him. Not after what she'd been listening to. "I'm going after him. Nobody gives a shit about me," she said bitterly, without even thinking about it. "I'm expendable."

And then, Bulwark was shouting at her. She had never heard

him raise his voice any more than he needed to, and certainly with nothing even approaching anger. It was like a verbal slap in the face, and though he was miles away she felt herself flinch away from her keyboard, as if he could somehow reach right through her monitor and shake some sense into her.

"WILL YOU STOP ACTING LIKE A SCARED, LOVE-SICK TEENAGER AND THINK BEFORE YOU LEAP!"

Whatever he *intended*, the effect was to make her freeze, scarcely even able to breathe with the hammer blow of panic and fear that hit her. All that came out of her mouth was a strangled sob as tears leaked down her face.

"Now listen," he said, resuming his usual rumble. "You will not fix the situation by performing some ridiculous kamikaze charge. You need a plan—a plan that does not compromise Overwatch, that does not compromise *you*. We do not have the time to assemble our covert operatives. You will have to come up with something, right now, that will work with the limited resources you have. And when this is over, you and I are going to have a long talk about your incredibly pointless lack of self-worth. It's shameful and counterproductive."

"Please," she whispered. "We have to *go. Now.* He knows all about Overwatch and . . . and . . . if they . . ." Why was he stalling on this? Hell, give him a more urgent asset to safeguard, if he thought she was worth so much. "If you won't save *him*, then save *me*. They'll red-light me as soon as they know I exist and it'll be game over."

"Go and do what?" Bull asked. "What is your *plan*?"

Vickie cringed. What did they have? She took a breath and fought to control her fear. They didn't have access to Echo personnel, not without endangering all they had worked for. They didn't have firepower, not unless the Seraphym suddenly decided to show up . . . not likely. The big thing was those ten armored Kriegers; Doppelgaenger by himself wasn't so bad. Only fire made the outside of those things brittle, but where would she find a force large enough to break—

"Plan. Got one," she said, and briefly filled him in. ". . . but unless you're there, nobody's getting out alive."

"That's a risky bit of business," Bull said. "I can think of a hundred things that can go wrong with . . ."

"Bull!" Vickie shouted. What was *wrong* with him? This was

Red, a member of his own team! What was possibly going through this man's head to make him hesitate? *"I! Am! Going!* Are you coming or not?"

He didn't answer, not right away. She strained to listen, gritting her teeth, the beads of sweat falling down her face, while his rhythmic breathing betrayed his indecision.

Red cringed as sparks flew from the shackles, and he winced as mild shocks erupted from his throat and right ear. The shackles fell away as he clutched at his head. Vix had done it, she had freed him, but the surge had also overloaded his Overwatch communications tech. He was quite alone now, alone with—

Pike gripped Red by the neck, but he wasn't Pike anymore. He had discarded his disguise, and Red flailed helplessly as the man known only as Doppelgaenger lifted him high above the ground. Red gagged as he fought to release himself from Doppelgaenger's choke hold. He groped at the huge fingers, which held him like a vice, to no avail.

Christ, this guy's strong...

"Very clever, *schweinhund,*" Doppelgaenger growled. "Who was your coconspirator? This 'Vix'? Of course, that would be Victoria Victrix, the witch. I shall have to see she is rewarded for her diligence. Perhaps I shall send her one of your fingers. Is she nearby, Djinni? Are you still in contact with her, through her accursed magic perhaps? I can only assume so. So much for the pleasantries, we will have to move quickly then..."

Doppelgaenger tightened his grip with one hand, freeing the other to swat away Red's desperate swings. Red's eyes widened in panic as he took in the Krieger's massive build. He had read Doppelgaenger's file, and nowhere did it mention him being a giant. In fact, he was reported to be of average weight, average height, with slim if toned muscle mass. And he *had* been, just moments before, beneath the meek and naive facade of "Pike." Now, he was easily eight feet tall with a powerful build, and each of his hands looked big enough to encase Red's entire head. Of course. Red's own file was fairly scant. He had kept much of himself secret. Doppelgaenger was much the same, surviving by stealth, by hoarding secrets. He was a shapeshifter, a chameleon, and it made perfect sense that someone who could alter his appearance at will could bulk up to a muscle-bound powerhouse when needed. Except for Red, of course. At that moment, the ability to morph one's skin seemed like a very insignificant thing. He considered just how much power Doppelgaenger must possess, how much he had kept under wraps, just for moments like these when necessity called for more than just guile. Red would have done the same, and he still hadn't seen it coming. Maybe he needed a touch more of Vix's paranoia. She seemed to plan for everything to go wrong, where he pretty much made it up as he went along.

Still, he had always considered his ability to improvise as one of his strengths.

"Say goodnight, Brother," Doppelgaenger said, and reared back to deliver a knockout blow. "When you wake, we will have much to discuss, you might even say—"

The giant stopped, cried out in surprise, and released the Djinni with a start, his hand flying back in pain. Red collapsed to the ground and quickly rolled away. As Red came to his feet, his tattered scarf fell away to reveal his face of the day, a dapper rendition of Daniel Day Lewis, and beneath that, a forest of needle-sharp spikes protruding from his neck.

Doppelgaenger glanced at his hand, which was starting to ooze blood from a multitude of tiny pinpricks.

"Yes, *very* clever," Doppelgaenger sighed. "It seems we will have more to discuss than I previously thought. You play the fool so well. Another act, it would seem; another layer to peel back and discover what delights you hide beneath."

"What, you think I'm an onion?" Red said, stalling. "Careful, I might make you cry like the little bitch you are."

"Ah, the name-calling portion of the entertainment," Doppelgaenger said. "Really, Djinni, there will be time enough for that later. As I said, we have to move quickly."

It didn't take Red long to size up the situation. He was hopelessly outmatched here. Even if he could somehow outmaneuver and outrun Doppelgaenger, he had an entire squad of Death Troops to get past. It didn't look good. He had grossly underestimated what Doppelgaenger was capable of. Having Vix free him of his restraints had been his Hail Mary pass, and it had backfired. On his feet, able to fight, he was now a threat, one that Doppelgaenger and his group of armored goons were forced to deal with violently. If he had only waited, Vix would at least have been able to track them. Instead, he had opted to force their hand, and worse, Vickie's surge had destroyed any simple means she had of locating him. His only hope now was to fight, to last long enough for Vickie to come to his rescue.

She's never going to let me forget this one, is she?

One of the metal-clad Kriegers raised his energy cannon and aimed it at Red's heart.

"*Nein!*" Doppelgaenger barked. "*Hirnlose Trottel! Idioten! Denkst du, wir brauchen ihn am Leben zu bleiben! Stehen im Kreis um ihn herum, ihn zu beschränken. Ich werde ihn kontrollieren.*"

At Doppelgaenger's command, the Kriegers backed away, their cannons at the ready. Red considered his options as his adversary advanced on him. There weren't many. He had his back to a wall in an otherwise open area of the old factory floor. No cover to speak of, no handholds on the wall, nothing to get him to higher ground. All that marked his immediate surroundings were dirt, a few structural supports holding up a high ceiling and the smug bastard that was casually strolling towards him.

Maybe his newfound bulk will slow him down.

Red waited until Doppelgaenger crossed an invisible threshold, close enough to distract with a quick feint to his left. He followed with a sudden reversal and dove right, rolling with a nimble tuck and tumble to weave past his foe.

He felt Doppelgaenger's knee slam into his stomach, and he was driven back against the wall. Red saw stars as he lurched to his feet.

Nope, he's as quick as ever.

Red yelped as he ducked Doppelgaenger's punch, a solid blow which pounded into the concrete, raining dust and rubble down onto the Djinni's head.

And still strong as an ox.

Desperate, Red landed a palm strike against Doppelgaenger's midsection and was rewarded with a grunt of pain. He attempted another tumble, but was caught by the scruff of his neck and slammed face-first into the wall.

"I would advise you stop resisting," Doppelgaenger said, as he brought Red's limp form back and slammed him against the wall again for good measure. Red remained still, but groaned, still conscious. Doppelgaenger shook his head in impatience, and turned back to his troops. "What is our ETA?"

One of the Death Troops answered in German, an eerie and low, metallic-sounding noise accompanied by heavy breathing.

"Ten minutes?" Doppelgaenger barked. "Did the transport get caught in *traffic*? *Unglaublich*, it would seem I have much to attend to on our return." He turned back to Red. "Yours will not be the only blood spilt this day, it would seem."

"Yer damned skippy!" Red shouted, his head snapping up, and drove a newly clawed hand into Doppelgaenger's stomach. He felt his own stomach threaten to heave, as his hand tasted the cesspool of Doppelgaenger's guts.

Oh, Christ, is that headcheese?

With a roar, Doppelgaenger brought a fist down, shattering Red's claws, and hurled Red to the side. Red tumbled away and collided with a nearby support column. He heard the concrete support, already weathered and crumbling, crack from the impact. He was showered with more debris as the ceiling groaned and shifted under the strain. Short of breath, eyes tearing from the pain, he got his arms under him and managed to push himself up on his elbows. He glanced up at Doppelgaenger, and witnessed a truly terrifying sight.

The giant stood at attention, his face contorted in a grimace of pain, his belly now bleeding profusely from the five jagged claws embedded in his gut. His breathing slowed to a measured beat, and Red watched in horror as the claws were slowly engulfed by the big man. They simply slid into him. The wounds began to... *eat* the claws, making wet, slurping noises as they sucked the razor-sharp shards in. After a moment, the wounds healed, the bleeding stopped. Doppelgaenger looked down at his hand, concentrated, and in moments the pinpricks from Red's neck spikes were gone. Relief spread over Doppelgaenger's face and he smiled down at Red.

"Rapid healing," he sighed. "That is a most useful talent you possess, Herr Djinni."

Red shuddered, and collapsed. He was beaten.

As he waited for his tardy carrier to arrive, Doppelgaenger amused himself by snapping the thorns off of Red Djinni's neck, one by one, as one might do with flower petals. The Djinni, it seemed, was *still* conscious, and Doppelgaenger was rewarded with muffled gasps of pain with each fracture. He was pleased, he was beyond pleased. His quarry was remarkably resilient. It would be such a pleasure to break him, to delve into him, and retrieve the answers he had sought after for so long.

"She loves me, she loves me not..." he sang, happily.

Suddenly he was thrown up and back by a spike of dirt and broken concrete erupting right at his feet.

"She loves you not, *widernatürlich Scheisskerl,*" snarled the tiny woman peering from behind a concrete pillar. She had an automatic pistol pointed at his head. "Take your brown-shirted thugs and go home while you still can. And be grateful that my concern for my partner trumps my wish to splatter your brains on the wall behind you."

"Scheisse!" Doppelgaenger swore as he rose to his feet. "Of course, the rescue attempt. Is it not the way of things, *Fräulein*? To truly enjoy something, you must earn it first." He looked around. "Or not. I hardly see how this is much more than a minor inconvenience, like a bug to an eagle. Surely, there are more than just you, *kleine Kaefer*?"

"I'm armed," she pointed out. "You aren't. David killed Goliath with a bullet. I expect I can do the same."

Doppelgaenger laughed, and spread his arms wide. "By all means, *Fräulein* Victrix, fulfill all your biblical fantasies..."

She didn't hesitate, not for a second, and she didn't take just *one* shot. She unloaded three rapid and well-spaced slugs into his chest. Then she paused, waiting to see the effect. Doppelgaenger clutched at his heart, grunted, and drew his hand away with her bullets. She watched as the wounds healed before her eyes.

"And what now, *Herr* David?" he asked.

She dropped the mag and reloaded, muttering. "Dammit, I *knew* I should have led with incendiary rounds." She aimed again.

"Perhaps you need a bigger gun?" Doppelgaenger offered, sweetly.

An energy blast slammed into the wall between him and the Djinni, knocking them further apart. Doppelgaenger spun around, his eyes darting about to spot the source of the blast.

"Bigger gun, as you wish. Get your filthy hands off him, *fashista svinya,*" spat Red Saviour, swaggering into a patch of light coming from an overhead light fixture. "That wasn't a miss. The next one will flatten your *nekulturny* head. I will be extremely pleased to kill you."

"Chyort voz'mi!" Vickie swore, whirling to stare aghast at the

Commissar. "What do you think you're doing, jumping the gun like this?"

Saviour examined her nails. "Too much talking, time for smashinks," she said casually. Her fists began to glow as she turned her attention back to Doppelgaenger. "Inferior heir to Ubermensch could not kill me, *dolboeb*. You will not be givink me sweating."

Doppelgaenger sneered. "So, Mother Worker's Champion sends the supermodel instead of the real Red Saviour. Is the dog too old to bite?"

"The old wolf sees no reason to waste his teeth on inferior, mongrel meat, *huiplet*. The young wolf needs a chew-toy. You'll do." She bared her teeth.

Doppelgaenger signaled his armored troops to move in. "I think the young wolf is about to break all her teeth and be whipped. I could use a pet to tie to the foot of my bed."

"And I could use a new dummy at the target range. I wonder how many slugs you can absorb before you look like a lace shawl?" Saviour snickered.

"Enough of this," Doppelgaenger said in disgust. He motioned to his troops, who began to ramp up their cannons. *"Tötet sie jetzt! Schlagt sie auf—"*

He faltered as he heard the pounding of very heavy feet behind him. He turned, too late, and was struck by an enormous fist, encased by a small shimmering force field. Doppelgaenger flew back and collided with two of his troopers, bowling them over.

"Was?!" Doppelgaenger cried, struggling to come to his feet.

"Big Gun, reporting for duty," Bulwark said. He placed himself directly between Red Djinni and Doppelgaenger, and raised his glowing fist in defiance.

"It took you long enough," Saviour grumbled, as she and Vickie raced to Bulwark's side. "What did you do, take the route with scenery and be smelling flowers?"

"Bubble is a go!" Bulwark barked, ignoring her. "Execute!"

Doppelgaenger watched as they spun to face him. Under different circumstances, he might have admired their subterfuge. But today, so close to his goal, he suppressed an urge to scream. He had let them cut him off from the Djinni.

Idiot! You let them play you for a rank amateur!

They moved as one. Red Saviour brought her hands up and away, her fists glowing with a hellish blue light. She took aim and fired off two blue and brilliant bolts, shattering two opposing, weight-bearing columns. The ceiling groaned ominously. Vickie thrust both her hands into the air, palms upward, and Doppelgaenger heard an awful bubbling sound as the earth opened up in front of him, in front of all his troopers, as individual payloads erupted out of the very soil at their feet. His eyes widened as the rocket-shaped devices split open, contents mixing with each other and the air. Then there was nothing but white-hot fury, flames licking upwards as if from hell itself, engulfing his men with liquid fire. His troops began to scream, and he found he was screaming as well, when he witnessed Bulwark's force bubble blaze into existence around the heroes, just as the ceiling came down on all of them.

The CCCP van sounded as rough as it looked, but it seemed to have plenty of power, and someone had done a righteous job on the shocks and springs to allow it to get over the churned-up streets in this destruction corridor. Red Saviour had wanted to blast the siren, but Vickie shouted her down. It was bad enough they had to do this in broad daylight, and there was no sense in drawing even more attention to themselves. Besides, it was the destruction corridor. It wasn't like traffic was an issue here.

Vickie's heart was racing. They had done it! Bull had gotten out mostly on his own two feet, though even his trademark stoicism seemed to falter as he gingerly gripped his chest and sides. Cracked ribs and internal bleeding again, she figured. Even with the meta-powered Echo Med staff patching him up, it seemed a miracle this man had any intact organs left at all. Saviour had picked up and carried Djinni over his weak protests. They had made their way out of the demolished warehouse, piled into the van and been just enough ahead of Doppelgaenger's incoming transport that either the Kriegers didn't spot them speeding away, or they'd been too busy thinking about digging their boss out to care.

The van had been modified to serve as a makeshift ambulance, with two gurneys in the back and a fully equipped emergency unit "liberated" from Echo. Bulwark and Red lay on the gurneys. Red Saviour was behind the wheel (Vickie was too short to reach the pedals), and was perhaps enjoying her rare chance to drive a vehicle a little *too* much. She rocketed over potholes and only occasionally swerved to avoid the larger pieces of debris in what was left of the road. The van swayed dangerously, but whatever modifications had been done to it meant at least it wasn't bottoming out or breaking its spine. Gamayun remonstrated in Russian over the radio, while Vickie strapped the two broken men in. To save *everyone* the explosion that would occur if the two were presented to Bella, they were heading for the CCCP medbay and the tenderer mercies of Soviette. Anyway, it was closer, and any verbal flogging these two deserved, Vickie was going to deliver herself. She felt it was more than owed to her at this point; she had earned it, and by all the gods, she was going to have the pleasure of flaying them within an inch of their lives. She suddenly understood why Saviour always grinned wolfishly when about to unload an "excoriation."

"I don't know what the hell you two bucks were butting heads over that got both your panties in a wad," Vickie said, glaring at both of them as she belted herself into the passenger seat. "But *you—*" she pointed an accusing finger at Bull. "*You* are *kibaszott disgrace* as a Marine! I've got half a notion to call Retired Master Sergeant Hosteen Stormdance down here from DC and have him break your goddamn saber over his knee. *You* should know better. *No man left behind.* That's right up there with *Semper Fi,* you moron! I don't care *what* the man on your team did to you, said to you, *you don't leave him behind.* You don't even *think* about leaving him behind. You don't *hesitate.* And you *know* that." She turned to glare at Red. "And as for *you,* you *oslayob,* you are *polnyi pizdets*, and I have just one thing to say. Stop being a *kutyafasza.* We get it. You're a free bird, a maverick, a smartass, a loose cannon—all that and a bag of stale chips. And we are *tired* of it. Keep it up, and I swear to Herne, I am going to magic your mouth shut and have Bella feed you through a tube. *Labagiule!*"

Vickie slammed the divider closed, though she continued to shout curses from the passenger's seat. Thankfully, her voice was greatly muted by the thick steel divide. Red counted profanity in at least two more languages, not including the three she had used on him—Hungarian, Russian, and Romany. Romany? Where did she learn that one? Last he saw they didn't give lessons in the gypsy tongue in college...

"She's right," Bull said, finally. "What you said before...disturbed me, gave me pause."

"She was right?" Red croaked. "Do me a favor, don't ever tell her that."

They lay in silence, entertained by the muffled sounds of Vickie's ongoing rant and Saviour's persistent chortling. From the sound of things, Vickie had been keeping a lot bottled up for a long time, and she was letting it all out with the fluency of a dockside whore.

"You really thought about ditching me?" Red asked.

"For a moment, yes," Bull admitted. "But I didn't."

"No," Red said. "No, you didn't. Y'know, she did pretty good back there. Was that plan hers?"

Bull nodded, wincing as the pain flared up in his ribs. "She was the only one who could come up with it on the fly. She had the intel, the connections at her fingertips, and no time to explain it all. All she needed was a bit of a push."

"She did?"

Bull nodded again. "Just a little one. I'd say she pulled through just fine."

"So I wasn't pushing her too hard, was I?"

"No," Bull said. "You did a good job with her, Red."

Vickie opened the slide again. "And stop talking about me like you think I can't hear you!" she shouted. "*Bagami-as pula in mortii matii!*" She slammed the slide shut again. Saviour was howling. Romany was a great language for swearing.

"Chicks," Red said, shaking his head.

"Truly," Bull agreed.

"Hey Bull . . ." Red began, and paused.

"Just say it, Djinni."

"Thanks," Red finished, lamely. "And I'm sorry, man."

Bulwark nodded, closed his eyes, and let himself pass out.

His breaths came in short bursts. He seemed otherwise paralyzed, his body refusing to respond to the simplest of commands. They had dug him out from the rubble, the only survivor, and were carrying him gingerly to the transport when he finally fought past his rage and managed to order them to a halt. He lay on the litter and concentrated, willing his body to heal. His rescuers gasped, a strange, muffled sound that reverberated from their mechanical mouthpieces, as his burns reverted to pinkish flesh while his bones and joints set and righted themselves.

Gingerly, Doppelgaenger swung his legs over the sides of his litter and stood up. He thought about obliterating them all for their tardiness, thought better of it, and told them to retrieve the remains of their fallen comrades instead. It wouldn't do to simply leave that sort of technology lying about. Bad enough that Echo and Dominic Verdigris had retrieved as much as they had. His former elite squadron had been fitted with the next generation of energy cannons. It would be a mistake to let those fall into enemy hands. And he had failed enough for one day.

He strode lightly to the transport, a smaller and faster version of the gigantic Death Spheres, and pondered what had gone wrong. He had been arrogant, he supposed, overconfident in his own abilities, but he had earned that. It had been so very long since anyone had truly challenged him. No, that was unfair. Alone, the Djinni had proven no match for him. He should have taken him easily, if not for the inevitable interference by his allies. Little bugs, all of them, but together they had bested him.

He should have anticipated that, however. It had been the same in the War. These people never worked alone; no matter how much they cultivated the "lone wolf" image, the pack always came to the rescue. And the pack would never allow one of their own to fall without a fight.

To best the Djinni, he would need to best all of Echo, it seemed. No. Not all of Echo, only those closest and dearest to him. He needed...

Doppelgaenger grimaced. It would seem that game time was over. So much for fun.

"The pack will always come to the rescue," he mused.

It was time to go to work.

CHAPTER SEVENTEEN

Terminal

MERCEDES LACKEY AND CODY MARTIN

Verd had a plan. That plan did not include taking most of Echo with him. But being Verd, he liked having test runs.

It had been a good day for Dominic Verdigris, so far.

He had finished up an early lunch with Khanjar at one of the premier restaurants in Atlanta. She had found it strange initially, since Dominic usually took long lunches later in the afternoon, but quickly dismissed it. Working for Dominic Verdigris always involved putting up with personal quirks and ideas coming out of left field. If it wasn't that he could, and demonstrably *did,* keep his attention on one thing for hours, days, and weeks at a time, she would have said he had ADD.

There was a sort of manic air around Verdigris today, as well; he was in an *exceptionally* good mood, and rushed to get back to his office at Echo HQ. Once he was at his desk, he was back to work almost instantly, typing through the interface at a nigh feverish pace.

Khanjar was lounging on a leather-covered chaise identical to her favorite in his office back on the island. Identical, except for color that is; Dom had done this office all in creams and golds and browns. He had gone into one of those trances of activity that had been all too rare since the Invasion.

"Dom, what are you doing? It's been a while since I've seen you this..." She thought for a moment, as if rolling around the word she was going to use in her mouth. "Well, this happy."

He looked up for a mere moment, still typing away. "Oh, just my daily stock market manipulations, putting distortions here and there where I want them. I'm also keeping up with the ponies; something about the racetrack always draws me back, I don't know why. Getting a few different accounts taken care of offshore, more of the same ol' same ol', really. Setting up a deal with some of those chaps down in the Democratic People's Republic of whatever in Africa; seems they need some new guns to start up another coup. Oh! Almost forgot—" All of it had been spilling out in rapid fire before Khanjar cut him off.

"That's all nothing unusual for you. Something else is going on." She cocked her head to the side coyly. "Won't you tell me?"

Verdigris stopped, exhaling once. "Yes, yes, my dear. Come over and check this out."

One of the many windows in the monitor that was the entire surface of his desk showed a sandwich shop just outside of Underground Atlanta. Strangely, all of the tables seemed to be occupied by black-uniformed Echo SupportOps—and Khanjar recognized a few of those who were not wearing the uniforms to be Echo plainclothes. "Where is that?" she asked, leaning over the desk. "Oh, I recognize it, that's NomKitteh, the *banh mi* shop. I think half the Echo SupportOps eat there since you closed the campus to food trucks. Why are you watching it?"

"Wait for it. Best part is coming up." He checked his watch, a Patek Philippe that he had personally commissioned. "It should be . . . right about . . . now!"

A beat-up van rounded the corner and came to a screeching halt in front of the eatery. All of the patrons looked up in time to see the doors open and what appeared to be a half-dozen Rebs all brandishing shotguns and automatic rifles. Before any of the Echo personnel could react, the Rebs opened fire; most were cut down where they sat, while others were shot in the back as they tried to run or shoot back. After the rifles and shotguns were empty, one Reb lit a Molotov cocktail and threw it, setting the shop front and several of the bodies—some still moving—on fire. The doors slammed shut on the van as it sped away leaving a cloud of tire smoke.

Even Khanjar had to blink at the speed and brutality of the attack. "Dom . . . did you do that?"

He put on a look of mock innocence mixed with mock horror.

"My dear girl, how could you imagine that *I* would do anything to endanger the lives of my own Echo personnel? Didn't you see, right there? It was Rebs! Probably in retaliation for what happened to Rebel Yell and the sentencing of Bad Bowie."

Then he dropped the act, smirking. "You know my motto; it's better to bury trouble if you can't buy it off. And if anything is worth doing, it's worth doing with extreme prejudice. I just got rid of some specific people who were fomenting dissent down in the SupportOps cadre, and I distracted everyone else. And I did it in a way that will create a wave of sympathy for Echo. Oh, by the way, put a press conference together in say . . . five hours for my reaction to this despicable attack, won't you?"

"I should think your PA could do that," she sniffed, more than a little annoyed that he was treating her like a secretary. Again.

"Oh, stick around for right now. Part two is coming up. As they say, 'But wait! There's more!' This is where we get our money's worth, so to speak." He grinned, and tapped on his glass keyboard, closing the cam view of the sandwich shop and bringing up one of Atlanta Underground.

If there was one thing that Vickie was perpetually grateful for, it was that Dominic Verdigris didn't believe in magic. He was ridiculously careless about things like fingernail clippings and haircuts. She had enough of Verd squirreled away in various safe caches—including a packet filed with her mom—to clone him a million times over. Of course, cloning him was scarcely the point.

No, the point was that with such a tight-band connection to Verd, she didn't even *need* the Overwatch suite to keep tabs on him.

Although the suite was very useful in keeping a record of what he was doing. In sort of a magical version of keystroke-logging, she had a monitor and standalone computer setup devoted to tracking everything he did on his computers, whether they were Echo or not. She also had an alert wired up to tell her when he was looking at or tinkering with something out of the ordinary.

Tapping into a security cam just outside of Atlanta Underground was definitely out of the ordinary. Directing it to point at NomKitteh was wildly out of the ordinary.

Watching live feed of a van full of Rebs mowing down thirty to forty Echo SupportOps was off the scale.

"Shit!" She thought she had gotten inured to scenes of massacre by now. Evidently not; it took her a moment to swallow her revulsion before she simultaneously hot-keyed Bella's freq, put the Overwatch suite into full-boat recording of *everything* Verd was doing, and tried not to throw up.

Verdigris put an ordinary-looking Bluetooth earpiece on, holding up one finger to Khanjar. "Excuse me for a few moments, my dear. Personal finishing touches."

"I am going to assume that, appearances to the contrary, those were not Rebs." Khanjar examined the burning restaurant-front with an analytical eye.

"Of course not. Scum like that has its uses, but they're highly unreliable. This needed to be a precision job, especially with what's coming next." The earpiece flashed, indicating an incoming call. He tapped a button before answering. "Yes, still a 'go.' They'll be on their way shortly. Keep up appearances." He tapped the button again. "Dispatch? This is Verdigris; check the roster and find out who is nearest to the incident. Yes, yes, I heard everything on the comm channels. We need to deal with this, now; full response mode, our people have been hurt." With that he took the earpiece off and deposited it in a drawer from his desk. As soon as he closed it, there was a slight *whumpf* sound as the built-in incinerator kicked in. Another of the things that should have been on the Evil Overlord lists: never leave evidence.

Khanjar raised an eyebrow. "Obviously there is more to this than just removing a few SupportOps."

"Much more." Verdigris keyed up the desk display again, narrowing his eyes. "Things will be much easier for us with Echo after today, my dear. Then we can really get down to business."

". . . sending to your monitor," Vickie said. "I'm only getting his side of the conversation—Khanjar is a lot more diligent about her magic-protection, I still haven't got a piece of her yet—but this is only part one. Don't scramble yet, because there's more coming, and when you do, haul in protection with you."

"Jesus Cluny Frog," Bella replied. "Right, I just got the alert. I've tagged Ramona, she'll issue the scramble, since I'm supposed to look incompetent. Who's wired outside of Bull's Misfits, CCCP, and my med teams?"

Vickie was already calling up the roster. "Motu and Matai are your best bet. I think between them and me we can keep your guys protected. I'll tag them. I'll go ahead and liase with Gamayun in case we need more backup. Saviour may elect to send some anyway. You get your team together."

"Yeah. Armed. No Einhorn. Out."

Had Verd still been watching the feed from that security camera, he would have seen a curious thing happening. Or rather, things. Where there were no people, waves of earth erupted from the cracks between the cement paving blocks and smothered the flames immediately. Where there were people, dust gathered in purposeful swirls and did the same. Dust, after all, is powdered earth. Fire is a triangle: oxygen, heat, fuel. Remove one of the three and the triangle collapses. Dust smothers quickly enough to kill flames before it kills people.

And when that was done, more earth rose up into ramparts protecting the victims from any possible follow-up attack, with narrow passages that would allow the Echo Med teams in.

Vickie unclenched her fists and grabbed a fistful of energy shots, then sucked one down while pulling out one of the "talismans" she used to store magical energy in. This was going to be a test of her endurance. Because she had the sinking feeling that not only was this not over, but was only just beginning.

Corbie got the scramble order for his default "team"—although he wasn't officially a team leader, he seemed to be the one in charge for the loose group of himself, Silent Knight, and Leader of the Pack. Sometimes Motu and Matai came along as well, on loan from Bulwark.

But a split second after he got the go-order, the special tone came over his headset that signaled incoming from that magic bird, Victrix.

Oh crumbs. That can't be good... He switched freqs. "Corbie; go."

"Corbie, stop; I mean it, halt in place," came the grim response. *"PDA on, briefing incoming, you're being set up. Three guesses who, and the first two aren't 'Daleks' or 'Cybermen.'"*

Corbie clenched his jaw so hard his teeth almost cracked. "Right you are, love. Powered up, gimme the brief while I get the boys rounded up. We're in a destruction corridor, it'll take a minute to gather 'em up anyway."

During that minute, he watched the massacre at the sandwich shop, watched the "Rebs"—and if those were Rebs, with *those* weapons and short haircuts, well, he was the Prince of Wales—hole up in Atlanta Underground, and noted the location. Very nice. Lovely kill-chute. *What d'ye call... a channeling trap. Everyone files in nice and tidy in order to be chopped to mince.*

"Okay, now you can go. This is the first time for me being eyes-above for you, so let's hope my practice shows. I can see anything a security cam can see, and Underground is lousy with them. If you need anything let me know, otherwise I'll fly by the seat of my pants."

"Wot's the sitch with our ops at the shop?" He still felt vaguely sick after watching fellow Echo personnel being gunned down so casually, but tamped the feeling down. He needed to focus, and right now.

"We've got med scrambled with everything they need and most of 'em are packing heat. We have CCCP incoming for locking down the perimeter and cover fire. And since Motu and Matai are wired, if we need cover before then, they'll peel off to provide it."

"Roger, love. The boys're here, keep me updated." The rest of his team had formed a rough semicircle around him, with Leader's dogs occasionally poking their heads in between people. He left the mic on; he figured she was like every other intel officer he'd ever worked with. There was no such thing as too much data for those sorts. "Listen up. We got a hit on NomKitteh." He didn't have to say anything else; everyone knew how popular the shop was with the SupportOps. Leader cursed under his breath. Motu and Matai nodded; from their expressions, Corbie figured the witchy tech had already briefed them. "Med is scrambled, the bad boys are holed up in the Underground. They're *dressed* like Rebs." Corbie let the words hang in the air.

Silent Knight rumbled. "Clearly from your statement they are not."

Corbie shrugged. "Short hair, really good combat boots, and weapons I've never seen in the hands of scruffy rednecks that weren't stolen, yeah? And never that many of them." He shook his head. "My bottom pound is on it being a group of pros."

Leader's face darkened as his dogs all started to growl in unison. He quieted them with a quick look. "Blacksnake?" Ever since the confrontation at the shopping mall, he'd wanted a chance to mash some merc heads.

"No telling. They're not the only dirty merc outfit in town, but they are one of the best." He frowned in disgust. "It was an *efficient* and *professional* hit."

"Then let's stick their *efficient* weapons up their *professional* asses," growled Leader.

"Update. Med's on the scene, no sign of interference. CCCP is about four minutes out."

Corbie scrolled back to his shots of the mercs holing up, then pulled up his map of the Underground. "They'll be expectin' us to come in this entrance," he said, holding his PDA where everyone could see and pointing. "They're here."

"Funneling us into a kill zone," Knight noted.

"Update. SWAT just went in the CaffeeBucks entrance and got waxed."

"And SWAT just found out how much of a kill zone."

Leader winced. "What—"

Corbie cut him off. "Motu, Matai, CCCP ain't more than two minutes away, Med won't need you. You boys give SWAT the cover to get their men out, and that'll give us a distraction to come in from"—he studied the map—"here." They both nodded; Matai checked his paintball gun to make sure that it was loaded. Knight leaned over and peered at the map.

"Service entrance? Won't it be locked? Breaking it down would be noisy."

"Sorted. Electronic lock. Already tripped and waiting for you."

He couldn't help it. The words came out before he could stop them. "I love you," he said fervently to his little guardian angel.

Knight looked at him with that expressionless helmet tilted quizzically. "You know I do not swing that way. Nor do you."

He blushed. Knight, of course, couldn't hear her—yet. He was a good sort, but Corbie would have to consult the others about bringing him into the fold. "Right, then. Lock's been unlocked for us. We have Motu and Matai cover 'em from there. We come in from the other way, and sort these bastards out from both ends. Ought to put a kink in things for 'em."

Knight tilted his huge helmet to the other side. "There is an incoming transmission on your headset that is not Echo."

Before he could say anything, Motu made a shushing motion. "Not now, mon. Just say it's a friend that is helpin'."

Knight and Leader looked at each other, and Leader shrugged. "Commies," he opined. Knight nodded.

Corbie decided to leave them with that assumption. It was as good as anything else, and until Victrix brought them into the conspiracy, better than speculation. "Righto. That's about as much plan as we're going to get; we need to get these sods out of the Underground 'fore they kill anyone else." He unholstered his issued PDW, checking to make sure a round was chambered. "Let's move!"

Underground Atlanta was only ten blocks away; fast for him and Knight, who had built-in flying capabilities. Not so good for the Samoans, or for Leader, who could only go as fast as the dogs could run. "Vix," he said, once he was in the air.

"Go."

"If you got to split your attention, stay with the brothers until we all join up."

"Shouldn't have to, but that's a Roger. CCCP is on-site. I have one of their snipers on the roof of NomKitteh. If the goons have eyes in the sky, he'll pick them off."

He heaved a huge sigh of relief while pumping his wings as hard and fast as he could, feeling his back and chest muscles straining. He still didn't know *how* he could fly; his wings weren't nearly big enough to lift his mass, much less allow him to carry another whole human. Echo eggheads and plenty of professors had wondered over that for years to no avail. Well, time enough to worry about that some other day. Echo Med had the protection they needed, now it was just up to him and his team to show that bastard Verdigris that he wasn't going to get a second shot at anyone else. *The day we take him down and make him pay for Tesla, I'm breaking open that bottle of granddad's brandy.* It was supposed to be for his wedding... but that didn't look like a day that'd be coming along anytime soon, at this rate.

"Corbie."

"Go," he said.

"Come in hot. CCCP's taken out a sniper that was overlooking your entry point; only a matter of time before they get another one on the roof."

"Gents, we need to go in fast," he radioed to Silent Knight and the rest. "Door's probably hot. These guys are mercs, only a matter of time before they get a sniper up." A little editorial revision would not go amiss in keeping Vix's involvement a secret, here. Leader of the Pack's dogs rounded a corner half a block away, with himself in hot pursuit.

"I have Motu and Matai on your freq, they're getting what you get. Guinness is on me when this is over."

"Not that Limey crap," rumbled Motu over the same freq.

"All right, let's get the thing done." He could see the remnants of smoke where the NomKitteh was; the wind was carrying the din from all of the police and EMS sirens up to meet him. Below, he spotted his landing zone. Corbie did what a falcon does; he pumped upwards, then arced over into a dive, wings folded tightly against his body, the better to present a small target to anything unfriendly, and trading height for speed. His build wasn't the best suited for such a maneuver, but at least it was better than Knight's. The entrance was one of several in the otherwise blank walls fronting on an alley; at the last moment, he fanned his wings wide as an air brake and touched down hard, taking immediate shelter behind a dumpster, then unholstering the PDW from his leg. He bent to the side, reaching out to shove at the door with his free hand. It opened at his touch. "I really *do* love you," he told Vix fervently.

"Get a room," said Matai.

"You boys just get your arses over here. Clock is ticking." At that moment, Knight touched down beside him. Not long after that, the pack showed up, with Leader bringing up the rear, weapons drawn. He didn't go unarmed anymore.

"In, and stack up," Corbie ordered. "Knight first." Knight nodded his helmet, then rushed through the open portal. Corbie followed, with Leader and his mutts bringing up the rear. They were a dozen paces inside of what looked like a service tunnel when he started to get a gnawing sensation in the pit of his guts. "Halt. Wait a moment." *Why would they have a sniper guarding* this *specific entrance? That spot the bloke was at wasn't a good spot for much else than that.* "Knight," he whispered, "you made that mod to your suit that allows you to put out an echolocational ping, right?"

"That's correct."

"Do it. I've got a bad feeling about this hallway. Call it instinct." One thing that Corbie had learned early in his career with Echo was that one always trusted their gut feelings when it came to dangerous situations. Knight nodded again, then looked forward intently. After several seconds, he tilted his head to the side and turned back to face Corbie.

"There appears to be a trap of some sort ahead, near the door." He pointed to it; for the rest of the team it was barely visible against the wall from this distance, but Corbie's eyesight was better than the average chap's. He was able to see it clearly enough to make out specific details.

Corbie sighed. "Early warning device," he said into his mic. "We've found their escape route. Guess they liked this way as much as we did. Can you disable it from here?"

"I cannot. There's not enough ambient noise for me to generate a proper resonate frequency—"

"It's not wified into anything, so I'm out." Well so much for witchy-poo.

"Right, right." Corbie cut him off. "It looks like a simple laser trip wire; no explosives that I can see. We can get right up to it, but I don't wanna risk—"

He stopped short as one of Leader's dogs—the one that looked like it was mostly mastiff—trotted ahead of the group, right up to the device.

"Normandy!" Leader called out in a harsh whisper. "Back here, dammit!" Leader had named all of his dogs after famous battles; one of his quirks, it seemed. The mastiff looked back, snorted, and then lifted a leg over the device. And peed on it. There must have been a quart of yellow liquid arcing through the air to land accurately on the device. A few seconds later the device let out a shower of sparks and a small cloud of smoke. Normandy trotted back, just as nonchalant, and planted himself next to Leader, dopey eyes looking up for approval.

"I'm firin' you and keepin' the dogs, Leader," Corbie said, shaking his head. "The mutts are smarter than you." Everyone ducked as a cacophony of gunfire erupted on the other side of the door; dozens of automatic rifles and shotguns were all going off at the same time in measured bursts. The firing slackened, then stopped, and then there was muffled yelling: civilians and what Corbie assumed were the mercs.

Their radios cracked simultaneously. "*This is Matai. We were able to get the downed SWAT out, but their captain is pissed. He's trying to keep us from going back in. This might take a minute.*" He could hear the SWAT commander arguing with Motu; Corbie could swear that he heard one comment about Motu using the SWAT van for material for his armor, and couldn't help but smirk.

"Make it a fast minute. There's still civvies in there." He turned to face the rest. "We're going to hold here until they're in position. We need to do this at the same time to make it work—"

Corbie was interrupted when the door to the main concourse slammed open behind him. He whirled around to find one of the "Rebs" staring at him, slack-jawed. There was a tense moment where everyone was too shocked to react; the Echo Ops and the probable merc just stood looking at each other for several heartbeats.

Both had the same reaction.

"Shit!" Two voices rang out as one. Both grabbed for their weapons.

"Perimeter breach!" the merc managed to squawk—presumably into *his* headset—before Corbie could bring his PDW to bear on the man. The merc, even fighting against his rifle's sling, was faster on the draw; his gun was leveled at Corbie's chest. Before either of them could fire, a barking mass of fur and teeth sped around Corbie; Leader's dogs swarmed the merc, knocking him to the floor. Corbie heard the merc's head impact with a dull thud; he ran forward with his gun trained on the downed man, but he already knew by the sound that he was out cold.

"Dammit!" He slung his PDW to the side, relieved the merc of his weapons and radio, and then zip-tied his hands and feet together. "We've lost the element of surprise. They know we're comin'; we gotta move now! Matai! You get all of that?"

"*That's a big ten-four. Sorry, Chief, put in a complaint with the boss, we gotta move.*" Corbie could hear more shouting over the radio, followed by the shriek of crumpling metal. "*Ready here.*"

Corbie looked over his shoulder at Leader and Knight. "All right. Here we go!" He kicked open the door to the main concourse with his PDW shouldered, followed by the rest of his team. He took in the scene in front of them instantly; much of it was what he had expected; a lot of the stalls and storefronts were trashed from the gunfight between the mercs and the cops. There were several dozen civilians scattered like terrified rabbits wherever there was even a modicum of cover; some of them were clearly hurt. What he hadn't expected, however, was for the mercs to be ready for them; they all had their guns trained on his team. Some of the bastards were even smiling.

"Cover!"

Without a word, the mercenaries started to fire. Corbie dove behind the nearest pillar; he felt his nanoweave jacket stiffen with impact from two hits. It took him a moment to get his breath back and sit up; after switching the rifle to his left shoulder he leaned out from the left-hand side of the pillar, firing a burst from his PDW at the mercs. Their return fire forced him back behind his cover. Frantic, he looked around for the others. Knight was sending out blasts, but they weren't having nearly the effect they should have; the mercs must've had some sort of active hearing protection on. Leader was writhing on the ground, screaming and holding his ears; his dogs were all in similar condition, wild-eyed and frothing at the mouth as they pawed at their ears frantically.

"What the hell's wrong? What've they done to you?" Corbie leaned out, firing another burst from his weapon.

"Ultrasonics!" Leader gasped out, clenching his teeth against the pain. "They're hurting them!"

He looked for the brothers; surely they had to be faring better. If they could get to Corbie and the rest of the team, they'd have a chance to get to better cover, not pinned down against the wall. With Leader and his pack down and Knight's powers ineffective, they'd have to form an alternate strategy, and fast; some of those wounded civilians wouldn't make it unless they got to a hospital, and soon. It took him a few moments, but he was finally able to locate the brothers; his heart sank immediately. They were enveloped in a cloud of gas; tear gas or something like it, from the way they were coughing and choking. Both of them were blinded by it, especially Motu; with his amalgamation armor his vision was already limited enough. Heavy caliber rifles were pounding away at the armor; it was everything that Motu could do to shield his brother and try to renew the armor as fast as it was being stripped away.

Knight wasn't in any better shape; his armor, while sturdy, couldn't stand up forever to the barrage it was getting. Eventually they'd take him down. He knew it, too. But he wasn't moving; he stood there, continually blasting at the mercs and trying to protect his team. While they were focusing on Knight, they weren't shooting at Leader or his dogs.

They were ready for us. Not just ready—but for us, *specifically. They had to be. They've got our bloody number. We need to turn this around right now, or we're all dead. Think, man, think!*

"Vix!" he shouted into his mic. "Can you do somethin' to shield Knight?"

The answer came as the floor suddenly heaved up around where Knight had taken shelter. *"It's reinforced concrete, sorry; it takes me a little longer to work through that shite."* Earth ramparts, studded with bits of concrete laced with reinforcing rods formed around Silent Knight. A moment later, the ground shuddered and more heaved up to give Corbie and Leader and the dogs lifesaving shelter.

"This won't last. We need to go on the offensive!" *Think!*

Wait... Knight's suit didn't just collect and project sound, he could absorb it, maybe cancel it out in an area. Couldn't he? "Knight!" The armored engineer canted his head to the side, still firing sonic blasts. "Take all of the noise! Even the ultrasonic stuff!" Knight didn't make any move for a moment, then finally nodded. It was dangerous for his suit to absorb too much energy like that; it could become catastrophically damaged, maybe even kill Knight.

Corbie went around the right side of the pillar this time, switching his grip back to his strong hand. He fired two bursts, but something was wrong. He saw the muzzle flash, felt the PDW shake with recoil, and felt the hot brass of the casings as the odd few bounced off the back of his hand. But he heard nothing.

The effect on Leader and the dogs was immediate. The dogs stood up and scrambled to join their pack leader under the cover of Vickie's ramparts. Leader stopped writhing and gathered them in around him.

Evidently what Knight was doing didn't much affect the headset. *"I can't heave up the floor under those guys and knock them off balance. Those are load-bearing pillars they're under. I'll bring the whole thing down on you."* A pause. *"But I can screw with their comms."*

He didn't hesitate. "Do it, Vix." He turned to Leader, shouting. Back this far, they were out of the field that Knight was absorbing sound in. "We've gotta help Knight, right now! His suit can't take much more, bullets *or* sound." Leader nodded; a second later all of the dogs ran along the wall to the right until they were out of sight. Corbie noticed that very few shots were directed at them. Peeking around the edge of the pillar and over the top of the earthen barrier, he noticed that some of the mercs seemed to be confused. Their attention was split and they were distracted; a few were yelling at the others, trying to direct them, but it was clear that their ordered ranks were in chaos. It looked as if Vix was doing something a little more elaborate than just jamming the mercs' comm system. "Form up on Knight! Let's give 'em hell!"

Corbie vaulted over the barrier, bringing his PDW up. He started firing measured bursts, forcing some of the mercs to keep their heads down; he even caught one that wasn't as fast as his friends, shooting him in the chest. Leader was covering Corbie from the barrier; as soon as Corbie reached Knight, it was Leader's turn to advance. "Cavalry is here!" Just when it looked like the mercs were about to regroup and focus their fire again, a snarling blur of teeth and fur streaked in behind the mercs from the right. Leader's dogs tore into them, knocking mercs off of their feet and mauling the odd one here and there. Their speed and the nanoweave overcoats they had been fitted with protected them from any retaliation; whenever it looked like a merc was getting his bearings and was about to fire on an individual dog, the rest of the pack mobbed him.

Corbie, Knight, and Leader all started to advance towards the mercs' position; Corbie and Leader kept crouched behind Knight for limited cover, firing whenever a target of opportunity popped up. Knight was still firing sonic blasts, but was now keeping them narrow beam and focused for individual targets since the dogs were in the middle of things. Corbie's PDW ran dry when they were about fifteen paces away from the mercs. "Mag!" he shouted. Leader poked around Knight, firing his pistol to cover Corbie; by the time he was empty himself, Corbie had already changed mags and was firing again. Leader tapped Corbie on the shoulder twice.

"They're all down, mate! The dogs just informed me." As one, Corbie and Leader ran up to the mercs' barricade and aimed over it; all of the mercs were either dead or incapacitated. Several of them were being sat on by Leader's dogs. Leader moved quickly to those who looked as if they could still get up, securing their weapons and zip-tying their hands behind their backs. Some looked as if they were bleeding from the ears; the dogs must've removed whatever hearing protection they had been wearing, opening them up for Knight's blasts. *Not bad for a pack of mutts.*

There was still gunfire coming from the direction of the main entrance. "We've gotta get to the brothers." The team moved as fast as they dared; no telling what other traps the mercs might have set up to cover their backs. Corbie took the lead this time; when he rounded the corner he saw why there was still shooting going on. Motu and Matai both seemed to be blinded still; the gas had mostly dispersed, but the effects would take hours or some decontamination wipes before they went away. Matai was in better shape than his brother, though; he was actually behind Motu, steering him like a wrecking ball with legs. "Left, brother! No, your other left!" Pushing and cajoling Motu, Matai was wrestling him into position to beat the remaining mercs. There were already a half dozen of their still forms on the ground.

"It's Corbie, we're comin' in behind them to help you lot out. Try not to squish us." He motioned with his free hand to the rest of the team; as one, they sprang from cover. It was easy work, since the mercs all had their backs turned. The first one that Corbie spotted, he ran up to; the merc turned just in time to receive a kick on the point of his chin, knocking him cold. His friends on either side went down just as quickly; the ones on the left were convulsing, while the ones on the right were trounced by a combined weight of about one thousand pounds of dog.

"Boss," Matai was on his knees, his arms wrapped around one of Motu's legs. "I think I need a hand." Corbie left the others to secure whatever mercs remained alive, opting to run over to the brothers. Motu's armor sloughed off, clattering on the floor; his eyes and nose were streaming in between hacking coughs. Matai looked the same, save for a hole on the left side of his nanoweave jacket. Blood was coming out in frothy bubbles.

"I see you, Med is alerted. Bella's on the way; she's not more than a hundred yards from you guys."

Corbie sighed with relief. Vix was on the job again. He really wanted to meet this bird.

"I got a blowout kit." Leader was right next to him now.

"Tell Leader to get a chest seal out." New voice. Belladonna's? Sounded like her. *"That's a pneumothorax wound. Sucking chest wound to you. Swab it down, follow the instructions on the packaging and slap the chest seal on it. I'm almost there."*

Leader handed him what looked like a piece of plastic and a big pad of gauze; he followed the Echo Med leader's orders.

"Corbie, we have a problem." Knight was standing over him, looking down.

"I know, mate, I'm on top of it."

"No, a bigger problem." He canted his head to the side. "I can hear it."

Leader's head bobbed up, then his eyes grew wide. "He's right. The dogs smell it, too." Corbie stood up and scanned; one of the mutts, a bloodhound mix, was barking frantically at a large duffel bag. He ran over, shooing the mutt away as he unzipped it.

"Oh. Shit."

The duffel was filled with explosives. All of them were wired with blasting caps or some sort of electrical trigger; bombs weren't Corbie's area of expertise. He didn't have to be an expert, however, to recognize the little red LED countdown timer, with barely thirty seconds left on it. "It's a bomb! Bastards must've triggered it when they saw they were screwed. We've got less than thirty before it goes!"

"There's not sufficient time to get the civilians out of here, much less Matai." Knight examined the duffel. "With that quantity of explosive compounds, a significant section of the Underground will be destroyed, with attendant damage to the aboveground sections."

"We've gotta get as many people clear as we can!" Leader was marshaling the dogs, sending them to start picking up civilians.

"No time!" Without another thought, Corbie zipped the bag up and grabbed the carrying handle. He started running for the entrance, then kicked off with a leap into flight. He pumped his wings as hard as he could, sailing up through the ruined entrance to the Underground, his teammates cursing and calling after him. In an instant, he was awash in daylight and police sirens. For a split second he saw the remains of the SWAT van, the SWAT commander's car, the ambulances and emergency personnel, even Bella running as fast as she could with Echo Med right behind her. *No time, no time!* He flew straight up, straining against the weight of the duffel bag. He had to get high, as high as he could. How much time was left? He'd been mentally counting down, but had lost the count somewhere near the entrance. He was close to six hundred feet in the air when he judged that everyone else was safe. He did a pivot in the air, swinging around to his left with the duffel in his outstretched hands. With a final grunt of effort, he flung the bag as hard and high into the air as he could, using the momentum to send it further. Then he folded his wings, dropping like a stone. *Was I fast enough?*

Three seconds later, the bomb went off, and Corbie was swatted with the pressure wave. He went tumbling in the air, completely dazed. *I'm going to die. At least I got the bomb clear.* He mentally chuckled to himself, loopy from the blast. *What a way to go; asphalt pancake. Road pizza. New coat of red paint on some guy's car.*

There was a string of curses in his ear. At least, he thought they were curses; he didn't recognize any of the words. But as he somersaulted end over end, heading down towards a construction site, he was pretty sure he was hallucinating as well, because—well, because what looked like a sandworm out of *Dune* seemed to be reaching for him, coming up to swallow him.

Then he hit it. And instead of dying, he yelped with pain. Not the worst pain he'd ever felt though, just one of his wings getting twisted the wrong way, and his plummet turned into a kind of end-over-end roll down a long, steep slope, an angle that deepened and smoothed the closer he got to the ground until he came to rest in a pile of sand as fine and powdery as talcum.

Groggily, he tried to lift his head up before letting it fall back in a puff of dust. "Am I dead? It'd be a downer if I am."

"You're not dead. Bella might kill you for that stunt, but you're not dead yet. Don't move. Panacea and Gilead are hopping the fence to get to you."

His head cleared some, and he painfully tried to sit up. "What about the others? The people on the ground? Matai? Is everyone all right? What about the civilians?" The questions poured out of him as fast as he could say them. His heart was racing again.

"They're fine. Or they will be. Lots of shattered windows, a pissed-off SWAT commander, half of downtown has ringing ears, and we've scrambled CCCP Med as well as Echo. Shut up."

"Average day at work then, right, love?"

"Pretty much. Now shut up."

"I recall someone saying a little something about beer being on her, after this gig. Make it a case, love."

"You got it."

He fell backwards, another cloud of dust going up. "Now I'll shut up."

Verdigris watched in utter disbelief as his beautifully constructed plan fell completely apart. None of the important targets were dead, only some of the minor players, and not nearly enough of those! That damned blue medic had been dispatched with a competent team and somehow CCCP had gotten wind of the situation and showed up with a team of their own; all but a few of the SupportOps at the cafe would live. Worse yet, the contracted mercenaries had failed to die themselves; a handful had been taken into custody by Corbie and his team.

This was an utter disaster. And not the sort that Verdigris had wanted to see.

Khanjar folded her arms across her chest, grinning. "Is there a third act? That one was rather one-sided and boring, if you ask me, Dom."

He turned abruptly to glare at her, and what she must have seen in his eyes made the grin vanish. She had never seen him this way, that much he was quite sure of. How could she? In all the time she had known him, she had never seen him fail. Not once. Not *ever.* There had been speed bumps and unexpected events with some of his plans, but he had always had another pawn to bring into play. But this was an outright failure. It wasn't something that Dominic Verdigris III could abide.

He turned back to the monitors, cold hatred in his heart. This wasn't the doing of that incompetent blue bimbo; she didn't have the smarts to send in, not just a whole team, but exactly the *right* team. She wouldn't have been able to call CCCP. And she wouldn't have gotten the intel on the Underground that had allowed Corbie and his crew to move in smoothly, avoiding the traps his trained mercs had set up.

"Who could have done that magic with the earth?" Khanjar wondered aloud. "Echo doesn't have anyone like that onsite."

Verdigris spared her a single look of disdain at the mention of magic before turning back to the monitors. His fingers were already flying over his keyboard, punching in commands. "Insignificant. Probably some random meta triggering. What's more important is, *who coordinated that operation?* There. *Her.*" He tapped the display twice, bringing a log up in full screen. "She's the one that called in Belladonna and the med team, and also had some discreet calls, probably to Corbie's team. Ramona Ferrari. Look at all of those comm calls, hmm? Very busy for a nosy little detective." He tapped on the keyboard a few more times, bringing up dozens of records; case logs, phone conversations, times when she had entered and left the Echo campus, and countless other details all centered on Ramona. He smiled grimly. "Well, this isn't a complete disaster, after all. At least now I know who's playing the other side of the chess board. It seems I underestimated her."

"So do you want me to do something about her?" Khanjar asked. "It would not be difficult to arrange an accident. Although it might be difficult to keep her from calling for help if she is as clever as you say. She might even have some sort of bio-sign monitor in her person just in case of such a thing."

He turned to face Khanjar again, this time smiling broadly. "Not just yet. Killing a spy is never as useful as insulating them and having them work against their own purpose. This was... a bad day. But... there's always a silver lining to every cloud, my dear." There must have been something off about his smile, however; cracks beneath the surface of the mask that he was wearing. It obviously disquieted Khanjar even more than his brief flare of fury had. Well, good. It was time his little bodyguard saw the iron under the harlequin glove. "When the time comes, however, I'll want to put a personal touch on removing Ms. Ferrari from this world."

CHAPTER EIGHTEEN

Resolution

MERCEDES LACKEY

Something that came into play later... after Red almost ended up as Doppelgaenger's chew-toy, I decided I was never *going to be without fast transport again. Ever. A little more hack-liberation and there was an Echo-jet backpack in my closet. I may not be bright sometimes, but at least I learn from my mistakes.*

Overwatch was good, but it was a kludge. I knew it, even if no one else did. Hot news flash to you, dear reader, in case you have not been paying attention. Yes, I really am that paranoid. Yes, I really do second-guess myself that much.

Even if my parents and Hosteen were all over making a copy of it for Department 39. In the back of my mind, I'd been letting the math simmer ever since Mark One was up and running.

And eventually, as these things go, it was soup.

In Vickie's experience, although work might not be a cure for heartsickness, if it was technical enough, it was at least a distraction. It had been a very long time since Vickie had undertaken any truly major techno-magical projects. Overwatch as it existed wasn't one; it was a kludge, a lot of things she knew how to do fudged together. They all worked, but they did not compose the seamless integration she would have been proud to show off.

Overwatch also had two big problems. It wasn't nearly as secure as she wanted, and it couldn't self-repair.

A couple of mornings after the rescue of Djinni, her alarm had woken her with something a lot different from her usual musical selection; at the time she hadn't thought much of it since it seemed to be out of the Djinni's playlist, a song by VnV Nation. And the first verse had just seemed to play into her general depression... but then the lyrics, and especially the chorus, had taken an abrupt shift, and she couldn't get it out of her head. It had been like a shot of double espresso, and by the time she sat down at the keyboard and ran the usual trouble-shooting and coordination of the day, she was no longer content with what she had—and she had her much-needed distraction.

She set to work that night, when the action cooled down a little. The Thulians were into their predictable cooldown after a defeat, the Rebs were back to pettier crime, and Verdigris... was Verdigris. If there would ever be a good time to work on a revamp, it would be now. And if she ever needed a distraction, it was now.

As always, the math came first. The computer end of Overwatch was all right; some new programming and some tweaking would probably be needed, but the computer hardware was solid and most of the software just as good. So, begin at the beginning, the human end. What *could* she have... and what did she need? What would give them something that was bulletproof, or at least as close to ninety-nine point nine percent as Murphy and Schrödinger would ever allow?

She worked at it in a red-hot fever until she ran out of brain juice, went to sleep with diagrams and equations dancing in her head, got up, and in between jobs as the eye in the sky, kept at it. It took three days. And on the afternoon of the third day, with all of the glyphs and equations, the diagrams and signs, the interface parameters and her probability calculator, all floating in the air, in a full circle around her, she put the final variable into place.

As she sketched it in, everything snapped together in probability space, a full globe of flows and math and magic, coming together seamlessly with the sound of an ethereal chime, not unlike the pure note struck from a perfect bell of crystal.

Every mage knew that could happen, when you created something that was, well, *perfect.* She'd even been a witness to it three times in her life. But it had never happened to her, until now.

The air in her workroom reverberated with it, and she held her breath, awestruck at the wonder of the thing she had just made—in theory, at least, and in mathemagic, theory was most of the way to reality. She might have stood there forever if she hadn't been snapped out of her trance by the sound of tiny stone hands clapping together and tiny stone feet jumping up and down. She looked to the door to see Grey and Herb standing there. Herb was jumping up and down in glee, still clapping. Grey's eyes were as big as plates.

<*My gods . . .*> Grey said, all his usual sarcasm vanished, <*Victrix, that is a Masterpiece.*>

She felt a smile of sheer joy spreading over her face. "Yes," she said, simply. "Yes it is." Then she gathered up the design with a sweep of her hand, balled it up, and tucked it into Storage Space. "And now we make it happen in realspace instead of just theory."

When the design was complete, Vickie invoked the spirit of Nikola Tesla via the quantator with a request for the design of some very specific items. As it happened, these items were so small they required their own manufacturing process. Fortunately, it was a process that Echo already used in the medical department for nanosurgery bots (and probably was the same military process that had created John Murdock's implants, although no one was talking about that) and with one tiny adaptation, the nanotech churned out a hundred and fifty each of three devices. They were each about the size of a micromemory chip, and to keep from mixing them up, Vickie'd had them made in red, blue and green, respectively. Tesla had been very curious, and very puzzled, by what the empty socket was for. "Crystals" was all she would tell him. "Just add that to the design for the bot-maker. I'll supply the crystals."

"But what are they for?" Tesla wondered.

"If I tell you, I'll have to kill you," she replied, only half facetiously.

Bella had been just as puzzled by the bowl of silvery "sand" that had come with the meticulous manufacturing protocol, but she trusted that Vickie knew what she was doing—and asking for.

Bella had just surreptitiously delivered the results—not hard since all of them would have fit in a cereal bowl with room to spare. Now the real work was going to begin.

When she was done, she would have her Masterpiece. An Overwatch net that couldn't be spied on, couldn't be hacked, and wouldn't be bothered by a couple miles, or a couple *million* miles of earth and stone between Vickie and her teams. An Overwatch net that would fix itself. One she could replicate anywhere, anytime. One in which the components could never be taken and used by anyone else. One which . . . eventually . . . she might even be able to interface with a counterpart for the computer end that was pure magical energy. But that was down the road. This was now.

After the initial three castings to separate out the defective units, then the units that, for one reason or another, wouldn't interface with magic properly, she had a hundred full sets of three components each. More than enough for now, which would give her the window to make more later without running short now, as she brought people into the net that were not yet part of their pocket rebellion.

Initially she picked out three sets, one each for her, Bella, and Sovie. Herself, because she damn well wasn't going to subject anyone else to something *she* wouldn't use, and Bella and Sovie because, as healers, if something was going to trigger rejection in the user, they'd pick up on it, and they'd be able to save themselves from any ill effects.

With the first test run a complete success (and Sovie full of enhancement ideas specifically for the medical corps she wanted Vickie to add), she brought in Red Saviour and introduced her to the New and Improved Overwatch. Within an hour, the Commissar was ready to declare her a Hero of the People . . . which was kind of a nice change from being called a "Daughter of Rasputin." Of course, the fact that Vickie fudged a little and pretended that it was all tech and very little magic might have had something to do with that.

So . . . now the hardest sell of all. And . . . the biggest risk.

"Overwatch: Command: open private Red Djinni," she said, as she brought out the tiny box that contained the set of three devices that had been tuned to Red, and Red only, just as the other sets had been tuned to their respective recipients. Overwatch obligingly opened up Red's private freq. "Red, you busy?"

"Nothing I can't break off." There was a grunt, and a yelp of pain. Not Red's. "There. Broken. Damn, I hate dealers. Lemme deliver him to the cops, darlin'. You need me for something?"

"Yep. At my apartment."

A long pause. Most probably since this was the first time she had actually invited him here. The last time... well, he'd come in the window, and it hadn't been by invitation. *I wonder whatever happened to my letter...* She'd never found it after she woke up, alone, in her bed. Grey had probably gotten rid of it. He was good at things like that.

"Roger," he answered. "On the way over."

"Take the roof. I'll leave the window open." She didn't want Bella coming in on this, so while she waited, she went to the door and turned all ten locks. Doing the implants took a lot of concentration, and if that concentration was broken, she might have to retune and recast them all over again. Then she went and got Red's chosen tipple, Redbreast whiskey, out of the liquor box. She wasn't quite sure how he was going to react to this. She left the bottle on the coffee table and poured a double shot into a sour glass, and waited.

He did come in the window... cautiously, this time; eased himself to the floor, and stood there, looking oddly uncertain. She walked over to him and handed him the drink. He took it. Looked at it. Sniffed it.

"Are you seducing me, or bribing me, Vix?" he asked, finally.

She tried not to wince, and succeeded. "Bribing you," she replied. "Come sit. I have a lot of 'splainin' to do."

Gingerly, he took a seat in the chair across from the sofa. She sat on the sofa, and held the little box in her hand. The plastic warmed to her touch.

"Overwatch isn't perfect," she said, finally. "It's rather far from perfect. It's not the rig here, it's the interface with you folks. I'm using a kludge to keep track of you, another to futz the radio freqs so they're less likely to be read or hacked, the headsets are subject to being lost, broken, taken away... the list goes on."

"Yeah, well, it's a helluva lot better tha—" He stopped, and his eyes narrowed above his scarf. "You've improved it?"

"I've replaced it," she said, simply. "With what's in here." She held up the box. "Tested it on me, then Bella and Sovie, then the Commissar. There's just a few catches, so far as you are concerned, and the big one is... I have to implant the pieces. They're permanent." She grimaced. "I know how you are about your privacy and—"

He held up a hand. "Hold it. Vix... I trust you. Let's do

this. Then you can give me the sales pitch, or the test drive, or whatever it is."

She thought her jaw was going to hit the floor. She could hardly believe it. He . . . trusted her. Trusted her *with his privacy.* It was so stunning that she actually forgot to breathe until Grey swatted her ankle with a pinpick of a claw to remind her.

"Uh. Okay then." She swallowed. "Thank you. Thank you for that." She shook her head a little. "All the magic's been done except the implantation process; we can do that here rather than my workroom. Ready?"

He finished his drink. "Sure." Without being asked he took off the scarf. He was Brad Pitt today. She chuckled a little, despite still feeling breathless. Part scared, part wanting to . . . well, that was never happening. Part nerves. Maybe it was a good thing the welter of emotions was so complicated; he'd likely never be able to pick out the lovelorn part.

"Ear first. This is both a microphone and a speaker, and it goes in your middle ear. I'll be able to hear everything you do, you'll hear me normally . . . and I've got a gain rider on both input and output so even if I get hysterical and start screaming, I won't deafen you, and even if you get 'sploded, I won't get deafened at my end." She leaned forward with the tiny green lozenge, about the size of a large bead, on the end of her finger. "This is made by the same setup that makes the Echo nanosurgery bots." She was extremely pleased with herself that her hand didn't shake as she touched the device to just behind his ear and "told" it where to apport itself. She double-checked the placement with Overwatch. It was seated. Good, now part two.

"Now the voice pickup mic. This replaces your throat mic. Open wide." She extended her finger towards his mouth, which he obediently opened. The red one, the size and shape of a grain of rice, went up into his soft palate.

"Now the hard one. This replaces the camera. And it adds something more. You're getting a heads-up display." She grinned as his eyes widened a little, despite the churning of her guts. It was nice to surprise him. "It gets better. This is where techno-magic becomes magic-tech. There's no camera. There will be nothing for anyone to see if they look in your eyeball, or to interfere with a retina scan. It won't be *in* your eye. It wraps itself around the back of the eyeball between it and the socket and plugs into the optic nerves. No camera needed. It reads what the nerves send to the brain, and projects the HUD info directly to the brain from Overwatch. Unless someone gouges your eye out—may that never happen—they will never know it's there. It'll work with a gunsight, or anything else you use too. So, right or left?"

"Works with a sight—right, then, I guess." He licked his lips. "Can I have another drink first?"

She poured for him. "Now . . . this one has to migrate, so I need you to hold still while it does its thing. It'll feel creepy, until you stop feeling it. When you stop feeling it moving, it'll have settled in place."

He finished the drink, and she leaned forward and put the blue ovoid in the corner of his right eye and told it to start on its journey. "Don't touch your eye," she warned him, as his hand twitched. "Here, have another drink."

About the time he finished it, the HUD in her own eye reported *Red Djinni: Camera: Placed.*

"Feel anything?" she asked.

"Not now," he replied cautiously.

"Okay, the next step is for me to activate it, but not bring it up live yet." She sketched the activation diagram in the air between them, and said, *"Fiat: Red Djinni Overwatch Interface: Activate.* Let's go to the Overwatch room. I want you to see the whole boat. Bella and Sovie didn't care, and Saviour was so enamored with the new toy she just wanted to go out and do some smashings. I think you'll appreciate it."

It took about a minute for the whole array to get itself seated, verify that it was in the person it was intended for, and get ready for coming up live. She relaxed a bit more; only one hurdle to go. It took about the same amount of time for things to settle in as it took them to get to her Overwatch room. She motioned to him to take her chair. When he'd done so, she gave the final command. *"Overwatch: Command: Red Djinni: Live, go. Command: Red Djinni: Feed: Monitor Four."*

Monitor four opened up a window, showing—her, of course, with the HUD graphics coming on in Red's vision, and then as Red swiveled the chair, the view of all of the monitors, the HUD identifying all of them for him, obligingly.

"Overwatch: Override, override, override. Transfer control: Red Djinni: Red Djinni," she said with satisfaction. "There. Red, you

are completely in the driver's seat for your implants. It's got voice recognition. No one can override your implants but me now. If you want to go completely dark, just say the word 'privacy' and however long you want to go dark for." She raised an eyebrow as he swiveled back to look at her again. *Huh. Didn't know I was that good at the eyebrow*... "Mind you, if you go longer than eight hours, it *will* give you an alarm and you'll have to reinstate it. And I'll get the alarm as well. And if you go over the amount you specified... again, we'll both get alarms. The last thing I need is for another Detroit situation to come up."

"Yeah, well, I still cannot believe the mouth on you. I've heard five-dollar hookers who didn't swear like that. In—what? Three languages, so far? And the idea of finding myself in the middle of another lightning strike is..." He looked back at her, and the Overwatch system ID'd what she expected it to ID. She saw, on the monitor, what his HUD was telling him. "... Vix... why are you packing heat?"

But his reply had allowed her to release tension—and a nagging fear—that she'd had even though the devices had responded perfectly to him. "Because," she said, taking the Glock out of her waistband, and laying it down on top of a cabinet, "if you hadn't given me the right answer to the 'Detroit' cue, I was going to unload the full mag into you, reload, empty the second, and run like hell."

He considered that, and nodded.

"I was ninety percent certain it was you, because the devices are tuned to the recipient and *only* the recipient," she told him. "Even if someone was to dig them out of you, he couldn't use them, unless he was identical to you on the DNA level *and* the magical level. Still... better safe, and this was my last test. I don't know how good a mimic DG is... Anyway, you're you, so let's get on with the tour. The comm works by using Quantum Twinning and the Laws of Unity, Contagion *and* Similarity. I have crystals twinned and tuned with the ones in the implants in sockets in an array back there, and we actually do not use anything like a frequency. Quantum Twinning says that twinned particles always react the same, no matter how far apart they are. So when your crystal picks up or sends information, so does mine."

"No matter how far apart they are?" he said. It was his turn to pull the eyebrow trick.

"Quantum physics says so. In theory, you could be at the other end of the galaxy and it would be simultaneous." She shrugged. "In practice, we have an untraceable, unreadable, unhijackable comm link and it won't matter if you are at the top of Everest or the bottom of the Marianas Trench, you'll read me and vice versa."

He whistled.

"Having the mic in your mouth means you can whisper and I'll read you. Even if you're gagged, you can click Morse code to me, or just 'one for yes, two for no.' You can adjust how much info your HUD gives you. If you want to talk privately with anyone else on Overwatch, you can; you just say 'Command: open private' and their name. It's powered by body heat, kinetic energy, and the ambient magic energy that's pretty much all around." She handed him the little command sheet she had printed up. "Overwatch is a pseudo-AI, so if you don't like how I made the command structure, make up your own. All the instructions are in that printout; feel free to explore possibilities, and if you want it to do more things, let me know. Just—I *can* override anything you have set up if I have to—"

"Vix," he interrupted her, gently. "I told you. I trust you."

She flushed. "Thanks," she said, trying not to show how simultaneously happy and heartsick that made her feel. "Well . . . just one more thing. It fixes itself. It's magic, not nanotech; basically if it's broken, there's an autotrigger that tells it 'you know what you used to look like, fix it.' I think that's the grand tour."

He looked down at the command sheet briefly. "Overwatch," he said. "Command: HUD off." Then he looked up. "It's brilliant," he said, simply.

She let out a sigh of relief. "I wish you could—" And then it struck her. "Wait! You can!"

"Overwatch: Command: Activate: self-cam." She turned to him for a moment. "I'm going to overlay your visual with what I see. *Overwatch: Override, override, override. Command: Overlay: self-cam feed: Red Djinni visual input."*

She pulled the handful of the Overwatch redesign out of Storage Space and let it unfold around her, surrounding her again with the exquisite play of numbers and flows, patterns and matrices, and let him see it as she saw it. "There," she said, feeling again the flood of rare happiness as the design sang and danced around her. "Now you can see magic the way I see it."

She basked in it a little, then folded it back up and put it away. *"Overwatch: Command: reset all Red Djinni plus cancel override Red Djinni."* She sighed, and leaned against the cabinet. "There you are, back in the saddle. Saviour's teaching hers Russian. Bella and Sovie are experimenting with integrating the medical stuff to the HUD." She shook her head. "Not my thing, and I wouldn't know where to start, you know? Just remember that the main job of Overwatch is keeping you guys safer, and if it's something the computer system doesn't know how to do yet, it'll be low priority to what *I* need it to do for you." Her lips twitched in a small, wistful smile. "I know it's brilliant. It's the most amazing thing I've ever done. But the question is, do *you* like it? Because I know damn good and well that if you don't like it so much that it bypasses your need to be a wild card, you won't use it more than you have to." Something occurred to her and she held up a hand before he answered her. "Wait a minute. I want to do something."

She leaned over his shoulder and modified the Override protocol.

"Gonna test something here. *Overwatch: Command: Override override override Red Djinni.*" She waited expectantly.

"Just got three beeps in my ear," he said immediately.

"Good." She canceled the override.

"And three more, so now if you override me, I'll know. You didn't have to do that. I told you, I trust you." He looked at her quizzically.

"And I just confirmed that trust." She shrugged. "Trust has to be earned, and you have to *keep* earning it, Red. You know that."

He nodded, and almost absently, wrapped his scarf around his face again.

"And you haven't answered my question yet," she added.

But instead of answering her directly, he stared into her eyes with a sudden, fierce intensity, and a cold fear stabbed her. *Had* he figured out—

"Vix," he said. "I want you to promise me something." He didn't wait for her reply. "Promise me that you're going to fight this fight all the way through, as far as you can take it, no matter what. And promise me you won't let the fight, or anything else, break you."

For the second time today he had completely shocked her. With a slack jaw and a stunned mind, she found herself nodding in agreement.

"This thing we're in—it's too big," he continued, as if he hadn't seen her nod. "I know you, I know how strong you can be, and I *believe* in how strong you can be. You're the real wild card in this fight, with everything you can do, that you know, that you are. If you don't break, we can do this. But you *have* to be that strong. So I'm asking you—and I remember, you promised me I could ask anything of you, so this is what I'm asking, for real now—I'm asking you to bind yourself to this. Promise me you won't let your spirit be broken, no matter what happens. Promise me that, and that you'll fight this thing with everything you have to the end. Don't let *anything* break you. And make sure everyone *knows* they can't break you. People are taking their cues from you and Bella. If you two stand, everyone else will. I know Bella won't break. I need to know you won't; and you won't, if you put your will to it."

For a moment she wondered if he had been listening to that same song that had been driving her... but whether he had or not...

There was still that promise she'd made him, when she'd swapped bodies with him. It was still outstanding. He'd taken his choice back, but it was still outstanding, and now he was making his wish deliberately, with full knowledge of what he was asking her for. She didn't have any choice—

—and anyway, whether he was right or wrong about her being the wild card, he was right about her will, and he was right about the fight being too big to let any one person's desires or needs take precedence.

Strange words, unbelievable out of the old Djinni, maybe. But if nothing else, today proved just how little of the old Djinni was left.

"I promise," she said, mouth dry, and a lump in her throat. She felt the bindings settle around her again, but not like chains this time. Not like something that was going to weigh her down and sink her. Maybe more like something that was going to help hold her up, no matter how bad it got.

He relaxed, and the little smile lines showed around his eyes again. "Good. Thanks. And in that case... I like it fine, this new Overwatch. I like where it's going. And hey, maybe Bella'll forget and leave her cam on in the Echo Med shower room. Now, how about another drink?"

CHAPTER NINETEEN

Mother Knows Best

VERONICA GIGUERE

Now I need to backtrack. Not long after we started the Rebellion, Ramona and Yank decided they were going to look into a . . . more bureaucratic solution to having Verd in charge of Echo. They knew Echo had a founding charter, and they were hoping they'd discover he'd violated some nitpicky little clause in it so they could put Yankee Pride in charge the way he was supposed to be.

But there was no copy of the charter at Echo. And the road to finding it turned out to be a lot longer and a lot stranger than any of us ever dreamed.

"We can't keep meeting like this. People are going to start talking." Yankee Pride pulled the brim of his baseball cap down and folded his arms across his chest. "That is, if they haven't started talking already. This looks highly suspicious, Detective."

"Which part, sir?" She pushed up the sleeves of her gray sweatshirt, her back to Pride while she shoved a piece of gum into her mouth. "Our apparent lack of fashion sense, the fact that you and I have been working together after-hours an awful lot, or our continued patronage of what the press has cheerfully designated the 'Socialist Safehouse' in its most recent story?"

He snorted as he leaned against the worn brick of the converted warehouse. "Three for three, Detective, although the first doesn't cause me too much worry." He ducked his head to feign exhaustion, his voice low enough such that only Overwatch could detect the next few words. "They do know that we're coming, Miss Victrix?"

"Knowing is only half the battle." Vickie herself sounded beat on the channel. *"Getting to the door is something else entirely. Chug should be there soon."* As she said the words, the door creaked open and a squat, muscular green form lurched onto the step.

"Hey there, Chug." Ramona smiled warmly and lifted her badge just enough to show him the brass. He looked to Pride, who sighed and pushed one sleeve up to show a gauntlet. It pulsed a bright gold, which was good enough for the CCCP's impromptu doorman. Chug stepped aside and motioned them both in, then shut the door behind him with a loud thud. The locks whirled and clicked into place while Pride and Ramona followed him to the Commissar's office.

As usual, Red Saviour sat behind mountains of paperwork, scowling over a dossier with red pen in hand. She did not look up, but simply waved a hand back to the door. "Is not necessary, Chug. Disruptive detective and fellow legacy hero can speak with desk as they choose. Unless they bring someone of importance." She raised her eyes and arched a dark eyebrow at them. "I am not seeing anything important."

Chug nodded and copied the same shooing gesture that the Commissar had used with them as they got to the storage room that held Alex Tesla's desk. Ramona thanked him, smiled, and went through the fingerprint and retinal scans to enter the oversized closet. Pride followed, shrugging out of his windbreaker and setting it to the side, along with his hat. As before, the voice authorization allowed them to open the connection to Metis, and it wasn't long before the severe image of Nicola Tesla appeared in the center of the desk.

"Good evening, Mr. Tesla," Yankee Pride began. "I apologize for the late hour, but Ms. Ferrari and I need to speak with you about several matters concerning Echo. I'm afraid . . ." He cleared his throat and clasped his hands behind his back. "I'm afraid that we've suffered a setback of sorts courtesy of the new leadership at Echo."

Tesla's face shifted, the blue wireframe adjusting to show sadness. "I see. What sort of setback, specifically? While I appreciate your concessions to your southern heritage in discourse of delicate matters, I assure you that being direct is preferable." He smiled a bit, the outlines of his teeth luminous. "I was assured once, by my late nephew in fact, that you both have the ability to be quite direct when the situation warrants such behavior."

Ramona felt her face grow warm as embarrassment crept over

her. The noisy confrontation with Alex followed by their hours in the freezer were not a shining example of her professional demeanor. "Quite, sir. We just..."

"It's difficult, Mr. Tesla," Pride offered, the apology in his warm tone and genuine smile. No wonder Spin Doctor held him up as a constant example of the face of Echo while Verdigris tried to turn the campus into his personal playground. Ramona watched him incline his head to Tesla and slip effortlessly into one of the two chairs in the room. "You're something of a legend, and for my part, I certainly would not want to disappoint a legend."

The words made Ramona smile, yet the blue wireframe *tsk*ed in an oddly paternal manner. "You of all people should be able to communicate with legends, Yankee Pride. In fact, speaking with you is an honor, as you are the living legacy of Echo."

Pride didn't have an answer to that; in fact, Ramona realized, the words made him somewhat uncomfortable. His smile lessened and his chin lifted a bit higher, but he maintained his congenial rolling drawl. "Thank you, Mr. Tesla. The matter at hand concerns Dominic Verdigris and his takeover of Echo."

The blue bust of Nicola Tesla gave a snort that reeked of disdain. "As I have said before, I do not care for this man."

"That makes three of us." Ramona pulled up the other chair and shifted against the unforgiving wood seat. "He's weeding out people in Echo and doing systematic searches of the campus. I'm pretty sure we'll hear about a full-out merger with Blacksnake any day now, and I'll tell you right now, it wouldn't surprise me to go in tomorrow morning and have a pink slip taped to my door."

Pride nodded in agreement as Tesla's blue brow furrowed in front of them. "The buyout is particularly troubling. I was unaware that so much had changed, especially considering the charter. You have Alex's records of that meeting, I presume?"

Ramona and Pride shared a look of confusion, and Pride spoke first. "Which meeting would that be, sir?"

The blue wireframe gave a faint scowl, lips thin as he glanced away. "It would have been sizeable. Every member of the organization, as individual shareholders of Echo, would have had to turn over their shares. Signatures, notaries, all of the red tape and bureaucracy that allowed for such a provision in the first place. If none of this took place, then it would stand to reason that with enough shareholders..."

"We could kick him out." Ramona breathed the words, fingertips against her lower lip as she stared at Tesla. "With enough people, we could kick him out."

"Theoretically, yes."

Yankee Pride frowned. "Theoretically? How did this go from being a sure way to remove a slimy waste of skin and bones to just a possibility? Surely there are enough people in Echo, especially if you look at the retired members of the organization."

The corner of Tesla's mouth turned down in an expression of disgust. "There are, but such a meeting would require a copy of the original charter. As you may have guessed, I do not have one. My current state of being is quite lacking in pockets."

Ramona gave a weak laugh at the joke, but Yankee Pride leaned forward to study Tesla more closely. "This charter. Who would have had an original copy?"

"Hmm?" The blue wireframe tilted its head to the side. "Well, the original board members. The founding metahumans of the organization. Certainly, your parents have copies of the charter?"

Yankee Pride shook his head slowly and leaned back, passing a hand over his forehead. Ramona hadn't noticed it until now, but Pride had at least ten years on her. In uniform and on the field, he covered it with a cheerful smile and professional demeanor. In this dingy back closet in the CCCP headquarters, he looked like just another guy who needed a beer after a long day's work. He let out a long sigh, not looking at Tesla while he spoke.

"When Dad passed on, most of his things went to the museums. The paperwork that he had, anything that wasn't classified, it all went to Eastham Foundation of Metahuman History. What they didn't use went to the National Archives." He slid forward, elbows on his knees. "If I'd thought about it more carefully, I'd have kept more of it here."

"That is unfortunate." Tesla began to say something else, but he glanced back quickly as a small shuffling came from somewhere beneath him. "We shall discuss this more. Perhaps Enrico will have some ideas. A pleasure, as always." He gave a final terse nod and faded into nothing above the desk.

Ramona let out a long breath, suddenly exhausted. "Well, that's something," she offered hopefully. "At least we know where to start, right?"

Pride didn't answer; instead, he stood and pushed his chair

to the wall. "If you'll excuse me, Detective, I should be getting home. Searching through the records of the Eastham Foundation may take several days, and it's not something I want to attempt without sleep."

Something had touched a nerve during the conversation with Tesla. Ramona moved her chair next to the wall and leaned against the door. She studied the floor as she spoke, trying to be as delicate as possible. "Sir, with all due respect, did I miss something back there? You seemed upset."

He ignored her question with a polite smile, ball cap back on his head as he tipped the brim down ever so slightly. "Have a good evening, Detective. We'll discuss this tomorrow."

The Eastham Foundation's main building at 435 West Avenue had suffered a moderate amount of damage during the early waves of the invasion. Memorials for recently fallen heroes filled that part of the campus, with the broken concrete wall bearing a tidy engraving of names, Echo-issue and civilian, along with dates of service to the organization. Inside, the exhibits devoted to specific heroes as well as innovations attributed to Echo had a steady stream of visitors. Yankee Pride stood back from the crowd as the teenager next to him snapped a few pictures with an elaborate camera phone.

"Quite the exhibit, hmm?" The assistant director for the museum came up to Pride, a kind smile on his face. "We're in the early planning for Mr. Tesla's memorial. Considering everything that he did for Echo as well as the city of Atlanta, it only seems fitting."

Pride nodded quietly, his hands in his pockets. He had purposely worn civilian attire, khaki pants and a neat blue oxford buttoned at the sleeves. "A unique man, certainly. I enjoyed working for him."

The man frowned, not recognizing Yankee Pride out of uniform. "You work at Echo? Security?"

The lack of recognition brought a broad smile to Pride's face. "Something like that. I'm here doing a bit of research."

"Ah, wonderful! How can I be of assistance?" He motioned to the wall where a large touchscreen showed the Echo insignia over a silhouette of the Atlanta skyline. "Perhaps you'd like to start with our database?"

Pride followed him to the flat panel display and watched as the young man pulled up several images he remembered seeing in one of his mother's albums. "That's not necessary. You wouldn't happen to have a scan of the original Echo charter, would you?"

The assistant director shook his head sadly and motioned to the open area of crumbling concrete visible through the picture window. "Sadly, our original was destroyed in the first wave. We didn't consider scanning the documents until afterward, but we do train volunteers to assist with the backlog. At our current pace, I expect that we'll be caught up by the end of the year."

"Of course." Pride did his best to hide his disappointment by taking a renewed interest in the images on the touchscreen. "How does this work? Do you have them sorted alphabetically, by year, or..."

"You can search for any Echo metahuman by name, civilian name, ability, year of entry, year of retirement, or year of death." He tapped the screen twice; the chiseled image of Yankee Doodle appeared on the screen in telltale red, white, and blue. The press had likened him to the late Spencer Tracy, with an easy smile that could carry sympathy as well as triumph. Next to Tesla, Yankee Doodle had provided the image of the Echo Everyman, a public-relations dream that carried the organization from its early years through the turbulence of the post-war world. At every turn, he exuded charm and confidence. When he had finally retired from Echo, he and Dixie Belle had moved to a sleepy suburb of Atlanta to live out their days in peaceful philanthropy.

There were images of the funeral, ten years ago. Pride stood next to his mother, stoic as nearly all of Atlanta came to pay their respects to the man who bore the moniker of the North but grew to love the South as much as they embraced him. He had been larger than life, the figurehead of Echo as well as the entire metahuman movement during World War II.

"Amazing, isn't it?" The words brought Pride back to the present with a snap. "Would you like to see another one?" Without waiting for a reply, the young man flipped to a picture of a willowy blonde wearing a modified one-piece outfit reminiscent of a sailor's pinup girl. She stood in the classic pose of Rosie the Riveter, the glow around one hand as bright as the neat white smile she wore. Underneath the picture, the words "Dixie Belle" appeared in jaunty red script. "This is another one of my favorites."

Pride glowered at the image. "It's historically incorrect," he growled. "That is not Dixie Belle."

The man chuckled delightedly. "True, but it's a great picture. Amazing how people could accept mutations and fantastical abilities, but at the end of the day, all of Echo's darlings had to be..." He stopped himself and coughed. "Sorry."

"Where's the real picture?" Pride folded his arms across his chest. "The historically accurate one."

It took a few fumbles through the database, but a grainy image appeared on the screen. The real Dixie Belle was escorted from a small plane, flanked by two pilots attributed as members of the Tuskegee Airmen. Off to one side, Yankee Doodle stood tall, the military salute crisp and directed toward Dixie Belle. Pride allowed himself a small smile. "You got any more like that?"

The assistant director lingered over the picture, still flustered. "Not as many as we should. Prior to the establishment of the Eastham Foundation, Mrs. Davis had the largest private collection of metahuman memorabilia. She donated some things following the death of Yankee Doodle, but..."

Pride paused, glancing over his shoulder at the pile of concrete that had held the Echo charter. "Was that charter hers?"

"Oh, no. That belonged to Gordon Weddell. Did you know he donated his entire Echo pension to the foundation of the Weddell Endowment for Metahuman Education in..." The young man continued his short history lesson, but Pride's mind was already racing. If the place only had one charter, then it was entirely likely that a copy of the original Echo charter wasn't more than an afternoon away.

Pride grinned and patted the young man on the shoulder a little more enthusiastically than he'd planned. "That's excellent news. What's your name, young man?"

He recovered from the wallop to his back with an uncertain smile. "Michaels, sir."

"Well, it's been a pleasure, Mr. Michaels. Thank you again for the tour, and thank you for your service to Echo."

Ramona accompanied Pride and Jamaican Blaze on their trip to the outskirts of Atlanta to pay a visit to Mrs. Louisa Mae Davis, better known to the rest of Echo as Dixie Belle. While the other two acted as if it was any other trip to visit family, Ramona was acutely aware that this was a singularly rare opportunity to meet a piece of Echo's history. This wasn't talking to a consciousness via some advanced desktop device, she realized, as they pulled into the parking lot. This was real.

Jamaican Blaze wore a simple white sundress and kept a small lighter in her hand. Pride walked next to her, neat and pressed in a simple dress shirt and khaki pants. Ramona had kept to her standard Echo uniform and kept a few steps behind them. The conversation was one-sided, mostly due to Blaze being mute and her particular brand of telepathy. Every so often, Pride would pause and the flame would flicker in Blaze's hand, presumably to continue the conversation.

"All I'm saying is that you don't need to be concerned about working with any members of the CCCP. Especially the older ones." Pride stopped while the lighter opened and shut, a smirk on Blaze's face. "Well, okay," he conceded. "Perhaps everyone but Pavel."

The three stopped at the front desk and gave their names, but the nurse simply smiled and waved Blaze through along with the other two. She led them through a common area and outside through a tree-covered walkway, then stopped in front of one of the ground floor condominiums. She knocked once, waited a few seconds, then knocked again. A cheerful "One moment!" came from inside, followed by footsteps and the clicking of a few locks. Ramona couldn't help but hold her breath as the door opened and she came face to face with the living legacy of Echo.

"Well, well. Look who's here to pay a visit." Bright eyes crinkled at the corners as she opened her arms and waved Blaze toward her. "You come and give your Gram a hug."

The woman who had worn the moniker of Dixie Belle for over seventy years still stood tall as she gathered her granddaughter close and pressed her cheek against Blaze's forehead. "I am so proud of you, Willa Jean. I saw that footage . . . what did I tell you? Don't question what's been given to you, you just work what you have and it'll all work out in the end." She kissed the top of her head before letting her go and turning to Yankee Pride.

"And you. It's not a Sunday, Benjamin. It's not my birthday, and it's not a holiday." The words were warm and without judgment, but she spoke them with a hint of sadness. "But I've seen the news, and I've heard the gossip. You're here on business."

To Ramona's surprise, Yankee Pride ducked his head and mumbled a "Yes, ma'am," every inch of him waiting for some type of backlash. "It's not a bad sort of business, Mom. I mean, it's not urgent."

Dixie Belle didn't appear convinced of this. She looked past her son to focus on Ramona, who responded with a nervous smile and a proffered hand. "Detective Ferrari, ma'am. It's an honor."

The older woman waved it off like a compliment on a well-worn pair of shoes. "If it's not business, then I don't want to hear any bit of 'detective' around here, Miss Ramona Ferrari." She followed with a wink. "I know who you are, young lady. Now, let's get out of this doorway before someone gets suspicious."

In a few minutes' time, they sat around a small table in the apartment's modest kitchen. Pride bustled about, making coffee and boiling water for tea. His mother patted Blaze's hand as she talked. "You really shouldn't be so surprised, Ramona. Just because we leave Echo doesn't mean that we stop paying attention to what goes on. In fact," she leaned forward, the whisper loud enough for Pride to hear, "without all of that promotional nonsense, we have the time to really watch what's going on."

Ramona nodded in thanks as Pride slid a blue ceramic mug in front of her. "And? What do you think about what's going on so far?"

Dixie Belle snorted, taking her own cup of tea in one hand. "In the kindest terms, dear? Bullshit."

Ramona choked on her coffee. Vickie, ever present as Overwatch, chuckled in her ear. Pride let out a soft groan. "Momma, please."

"I said that it was the kindest term," she reminded him, then looked to Blaze. "I did say that, baby girl, didn't I?" Blaze nodded in agreement, grinning silently at Pride. "Well, then. To be more specific, that slimy egomaniac with a receding hairline has his designs on more than just Echo. Mark my words, I'm certain of it. I know that Alex Tesla didn't die the way that the papers said that he did, and I know that it's not just coincidence that those rats over at Blacksnake are now trying to be all friendly."

"You know about Blacksnake?" Ramona frowned over at Pride. While she hadn't considered it before, the number of retired metahumans around Atlanta made the assisted living complexes and retirement communities a prime target. She made a mental note to speak with Vickie about comprehensive background checks for the support staff. "What do you think of them?"

To Ramona's surprise, Dixie Belle didn't respond with the same immediate harshness as she did to Echo and Verdigris. “Now that there, that’s a little more complicated. I know plenty of folk who came out of retirement to go and work with them, because they didn’t like the way that Echo limited them. They wanted the money or the risk, or both. It’s not a choice I’d make, but that’s it.”

“They didn’t come after you, did they?” Pride slid into the chair next to Ramona, his brow furrowed. “They haven’t been back here to bother you, after—”

Dixie Belle shook her head and laughed, squeezing Blaze’s hand. “No, no. They tried to talk to Willa Jean, but she’s too smart for that nonsense. Burned the eyebrows off of a fool smoking menthols on my front step. That’s why she’s my favorite grandbaby.”

“Your only grandbaby,” Pride corrected, smiling over the edge of his coffee cup.

His mother conceded. “Well, you and your sister had different priorities. As long as you’re happy, that’s all that mattered.”

Ramona smiled at the conversation, sipping her coffee. Three generations of heroes, and the talk was as warm and simple as any other family. Dixie Belle caught her grin and the corner of her own mouth twisted up. “Something funny, Miss Ramona? Good to see you happy... you keeping up with that handsome beau of yours?”

“Wow, she’s good,” Vickie murmured.

Again, she choked on a mouthful of coffee. Ramona shot an accusing look to Pride, who put a hand up in the air. “I didn’t say anything. I didn’t know she knew half the people in the organization.”

Dixie Belle waggled a finger in their direction. “I didn’t. I did my research. Just because I look like a relic doesn’t mean I don’t know about all of those newfangled technologies. Body might be old, but the mind’s still going strong.”

Pride nodded again slowly. “So, then. What would you do in our situation, Momma? I mean, we have a plan, but...”

“But you’re concerned,” she finished. “You’re just like your father, rest his soul. So, I’ll tell you what I told him. You trust what’s in here.” Dixie Belle pointed at her chest, fingers resting against the soft blue fabric of her blouse. “Don’t ignore what’s in your head, but you trust how you feel. You surround yourself with the right people, you stick to your decisions, and you own those decisions, good and bad.”

"And how'd that turn out?" Ramona already knew the answer, but Dixie Belle smiled at the question.

"Handsome, if not a little thick in the head." She sipped her tea and winked at Pride, who ducked his head over his mug. "He still hasn't said what he needs, you see? Comes over, makes me tea, but he can't be direct. Too much of a gentleman, but it's so damn frustrating."

"Momma." He passed a hand over his eyes. "Please."

"I'll do worse, Benjamin."

"I know." He took a breath. "We need a copy of the original Echo charter. The one at the Eastham Foundation was destroyed, but we think—"

"They were careless. Nice folk, but careless. No planning for the future." She *tsk*ed and stood, leaving her tea on the table. "And what makes you think I still have a copy?"

This time, Ramona piped up. "Well, I don't know about them, but if I don't trust my employer, I save every scrap of paper. That way, when the time comes, I've got the upper hand."

Dixie Belle's smile widened. "That," she declared, "is one smart woman. I *like* you, Miss Ramona. You and me, we should talk more often. You listen to her, Willa Jean. Echo needs more smart heroes like that."

"But I'm not a . . ." Ramona stopped as Dixie Belle pulled a tattered Bible from a bookshelf. It was worn at the edges, the gold lettering on the front faded. The binding creaked as she opened the book, turned to the middle, and extracted a slender envelope. She offered it to Ramona with a wink.

"Don't scan it yet," she warned. "Making a copy will just give you a blurry page. Find a magician. A good one, and one you can trust. They'll know what to do with it."

Pride frowned as Ramona tucked the envelope inside her jacket. "And after that?"

She didn't answer immediately, but sat down at the table and sipped her tea. "After that, you'll have to work to bring everyone together somehow. Keep in mind that 'together' has different meanings for you and whatever mage-worker you can find. I don't know much about what could happen after that. Magic was never my strength."

"Somehow, I don't think that magic will be a problem," Vickie remarked dryly in Ramona's ear. *"Call it a hunch."*

Ramona placed a protective hand on the outside of the jacket. "Will they stay safe, ma'am? You've heard what Dominic Verdigris has done to his better business partners." She had images of aging metahumans caught off guard by Blacksnake operatives as they traveled to doctors' appointments and grandkids' parties. The possibility for what she thought of as civilian casualties made her nauseous.

Dixie Belle smiled. She reached across the table and took Ramona's free hand in hers. "Ramona, darling, you're going to have to trust an old woman when it comes to these sorts of things. The people you're going to find, they've faced worse things than that oily little weasel on the best of their days. Dominic Verdigris doesn't scare me, and he doesn't scare a lot of the others." She squeezed Ramona's hand and waited. When Ramona finally nodded, her smile broadened. "Good. You'll have to start this rolling. Leave the smiling and shaking to Benjamin."

Yankee Pride let out a long breath. "To make this happen, we'll have to work with the CCCP. Is that going to make any of the older generation nervous?"

At the mention of the CCCP, Dixie Belle got a devilish twinkle in her eye. "That depends upon what you would call 'nervous.' Is that handsome wolf still in charge of things?"

"Momma!"

CHAPTER TWENTY

Leap into the Wind

MERCEDES LACKEY AND DENNIS LEE

There was something odd going on with the later generations of metas, and this one in particular. We had combined powers. We had powers that improved with time and practice and honing them. And we had powers no one could categorize. None of this had ever happened with the first generation, and nothing like this had happened with the speed and chaos of this one.

Bella was about to find out just how strange things were getting.

The knock at her door was expected, but Bella double-checked the little video monitor Vickie had installed for her to be sure of who it was out there. It hadn't taken much persuasion to get the camera installed after the first time she'd looked out of the regular peephole into the muzzle of one of Vickie's Glocks—and that had been *before* Verdigris had murdered Tesla. Having an extremely paranoid neighbor/patient was not such a bad thing.

It was, as anticipated, Bulwark. But she used the intercom anyway. "Sushi's here."

"You promised me spaghetti," the big man rumbled with amusement. That was the right answer. Relieved that it was him and not Doppelgaenger, she let him in and locked the door behind him.

"Clean?" he asked in an undertone. She nodded.

"And Vickie's glass thingy is running," she added. Vickie had demonstrated how one of the most common bugs didn't rely on having a physical bug present at all; it was tech that picked up voices from the vibration of the glass in your windows, from as far away as a mile. Vickie solved that with tiny speakers attached to each pane, playing whatever you had on your stereo directly into the glass. That pretty effectively scrambled what people were saying inside a room without raising suspicion. If anyone was listening tonight, they'd be treated to the full Ring cycle. "Oh, Vix wants to see you after this. She wants you wired with the improved Overwatch. That way we won't have to play question and answer anymore." She wrinkled her nose. "Some magic hoodoo about how because she tuned it with a sample of you that she got before DG infilled, if it takes, she knows it's you for sure. She'll tell you all about it."

Gairdner lowered himself down to the couch with a sigh. He was actually skirting the edge of visible emotion . . . which was close to being out of character for him. Then again, he'd just come back from the brink of death, so perhaps a few lapses in his iron control could be forgiven. "No scolding, please, Bella," he said. "Trust me, Victrix has already delivered everything you could want, and more. In . . . I think Djinni counted three Eastern European languages. Maybe four."

Bella raised an eyebrow. "You must have really popped her cork. She only swears in the Slavics when she's so mad only cussing like a dockside whore will relieve the pressure. Lie down, please."

Gairdner did so. The oversized microsuede couch was just barely long enough for him. She knelt down beside him and held her hands just above his torso, brows creased with concentration as she checked on how his insides were healing.

"Why?" he asked. "Why Slavic?"

"Because her mother only speaks English and Irish, and as a teenager she didn't want her mouth washed out with soap for language. Her father thinks it's hilarious, so she tells me." Her expression eased a little, when she found nothing wrong. "Sovie did a great job. Not that I didn't expect it, I mean, she *is* a medical doctor and I'm not, but it makes me feel better to be sure. Go ahead and sit up for now."

When he had made room, she joined him on the couch, with just enough distance between them to make it . . . nonpersonal. Like two people in a waiting room. Good thing she *had* an oversized couch; even when he was sitting up, Gairdner took up a lot of real estate. She reached for a mint from the bowl on the coffee table and shoved the bowl towards him. "I think it's time to bring in Silent Knight and Shakti. Ramona's felt them both out, and they're definitely disaffected. Vickie's new Overwatch rig means we won't be running the same risks wiring people that we were before."

His brows creased ever so slightly. "Will the rig work within Knight's armor and without being disrupted by his sonic power? He can't keep running to her to replace it. And I'm not certain Shakti is . . . stable. Losing Handsome Devil like that . . ."

"Vix assures me the answer is yes to Knight, and that's why I am asking *you* about Shakti. She's definitely skittish about seeing me or anyone else for head work. I can barely get her to come in to see Mary Ann when she gets injured. You know her better than I do." It was *such* a relief to be able to bounce things off of Bulwark. She didn't feel as if she had to keep second-guessing herself all the time anymore. "But wouldn't giving her something else to think about and work towards actually do her good? I mean, yes, we have our covert goal, but in the long run, this is all about making Echo as solid as it ever was in the best days, and it's all about making sure our people are given what they need."

He thought about that. "Perhaps," he said finally. "Work has certainly proved beneficial for me."

Hooboy. There it was, the opportunity to talk about the Elephant in the Room. She grabbed it. "After Harmony?" she asked, and quickly snatched the imp of jealousy that scratched and clawed its way out of her id and stuffed it back inside the mental box she'd been keeping it in. "Bull . . . I haven't had a chance to say this, but I am . . . I'm horribly sorry for your loss. I'd murder her in a New York minute if I ever see her again, but I am sorry for . . . hell, I can't even begin to think what it feels like to be in a relationship with someone and have her turn on you like that. And if there's anything I can do to help—"

Like rip off your shirt and drag you off for a good therapeutic . . . DOWN, GIRL! Business face, business manners. Just get the Elephant out of the way and move on. *On*. Not in. He wasn't a slab of beefcake, after all. This was just like all the other times he'd been here; this was to take advantage of his deep knowledge of Echo, his much broader experience, and his superb sense for tactics and planning. One of the smartest things she had ever heard a military man say was that a really good leader didn't try to know or be everything; a really good leader made sure he had people around him that he could trust, people who knew their stuff and were going to be blunt and honest. And he kept those people around to advise him, and never got angry when they said something he didn't like.

That was Bull. Smart. He thought in terms of the long and short goals. Patient, more patient than she was. Experienced in ways she never would be. Indomitable. Never ran out on an impulse. Okay, *sometimes* you had to do that, when your back was to the wall and you had no plans and no choice, and that was her strength, to leap into the wind when the chips were all down and trust that something would turn up, that at the last minute she'd spot something that would pull everything out of the fire. But most of the time you needed plans, you needed strategies, and when you were running a rebellion, you needed a military turn of mind. Which she most assuredly did not have.

He was staring at her as if she was speaking Urdu. "What?" he said.

She found her cheeks turning hot. "Uh . . . you. Harmony. Relationship. When you were . . . out . . . I got a flash of when she kissed you, what she said. I didn't mean to, but the telempathy is something I don't have a lot of control over. I'm . . . really sorry your . . . uh . . . girl . . . turned out to be so toxic." *God, did that come out as clumsy as it sounds to me? Probably. Great, now I sound like an idiot.*

"There was nothing of that nature between myself and Harmony," he said, looking slightly perplexed. "At least, not from my end. She may have been 'playing for the cameras,' or who knows? Perhaps in the dim recesses of her demented mind she truly has such feelings for me. Not that it matters. I grossly misjudged her."

Great, now I feel *like an idiot,* she thought, her cheeks getting hotter. *And . . . great, so the "I've benefitted from work" thing is about Amethist, not Harmony. My competition is the dead wife. Yeah, that'll be easier.* "Well . . . that's . . . good, I guess. If I ever see her again I can clean her clock without worrying about making you feel bad."

Bull looked into her eyes, and favored her with a rare smile. "No, I think I would enjoy seeing that."

The flush of embarrassment changed to a blush of mingled confusion and pleasure. But she played it for comedy. "And here I thought you only got off on watching me put the Djinni on his keister."

He nodded. "That's good too, but you know as well as I do that of all of us, he gets the most pleasure out of it."

"Perv. Him, not you." But she said it without rancor. "Uhm... speaking of the perv, I've been studying how he heals, and that gave me an idea, so I looked up a couple of other metas and studied their innards. In between, you know, running Echo Med and a rebellion." She gave him a wry grin. "I know you're going to keep right on trying to hold up the world, and I figured I'd see if I could improve your odds of doing so. So... uhm... I was wondering if you'd let me try tinkering with you a little. It won't be anything drastic, but I *know,* provided you have the healing factor in you, that I can make you heal faster. And I think I can fix things so you don't stand the risk of losing your spleen every time you try and hold up a building. As long as it's only two stories. I make no promises for three or more."

Bulwark considered that. "Near-death experiences from being crushed by countless tons of falling concrete, steel and glass. Yes, that is indeed getting old. What are you suggesting?"

"Red's skin heals almost instantaneously, but the rest of him can as well, when properly amped up. I can't deliver that, but I think I can teach your cells to speed up a bit, from what I've learned from him. It *seems* to be a pretty common metahuman ability, just not everyone gets it triggered. I think I can trigger it in you, provided you have it. For the rest..." she pursed her lips. "Navy Seal—he's over in the retirement community with Dixie—his organs are conditioned to take compression and decompression like a marine mammal's, and here's the weird thing, my research says there's records showing regular non-metas can do that too, so I bet I can do the same for you. The last thing is Untermensch. He's got some extra reinforcement, like the 'silverskin' you find around beef primals on all his muscle groups, around each of his more fragile organs. I know I can get that to grow. It's just a matter of convincing a few cells to differentiate. So, that's the untested part. You game to try?" She sighed wistfully. "I'd love to do this for everyone, but... I mean, this is a gamble. An experiment. I'm totally confident it will work, but I can't try it on *me;* that's the thing, I'd do it on myself first but it's not possible. You're the best and most needful candidate, but it's never been done before and not everybody wants to be Number One."

Bull thought it over, and finally nodded. "It seems we have

an opportunity here. If you truly think you can speed up my natural healing, reinforce my body against harm and do so safely, I think we owe it to the others to try."

"Lie back down then, I need to do the whole 'laying on of hands' gig." He obeyed her, and she placed her palms flat on his torso, shoving her concentration strictly into business mode. She moved her focus down to the level of the very, very small, looking for that elusive whatever it was that meant a meta could heal faster than normal. "Sovie thinks the healing factors are in the mitochondria," she said conversationally, her eyes half-closed as she "looked" with that inner eye. "She doesn't know why it gets triggered in some metas that have it and not others. And she doesn't know why some metas have it and some don't. I've got a theory, though. The first of the metas—they could ever only do one or two things at most. And they *always* triggered in pairs, almost like gladiators. The way La Faucon Blanche got triggered by Valkyria—the powers weren't duplicates of each other, but they were matches in strength. Around the sixties, though, metas started triggering in isolation, in a vaster spread of relative strengths, and there were metas with several powers. Things have just gotten even more chaotic since then. The only one consistent thing is that for those few metas that had children, the children are *always* meta. So . . . it's like whatever was at work started going into a cosmic blender, and you never knew what was going to come out. And . . ." She felt a grin coming on, as she identified what she was looking for. "Bingo. You are one of the lucky ones of the lottery. You have the healing factor. And there was much rejoicing."

"I'll admit I find that surprising," Bull said. "I always thought any secondary abilities would be based in raw power, like my shield. Now, you're sure you know what you're doing?"

"Healing factor, absolutely. I've triggered this before. I did Corbie and Knight. It's kind of neat, it's definitely a catalysis reaction, it spreads like a firework exploding. And here . . . we . . . go."

She "talked" to the cells under her palms, and felt them respond, wake up, and then—it was like a *whoosh*, as the trigger spread outwards, like one of those elaborate domino setups, as each cell triggered the ones next to it, and so on. Corbie had said it felt like tossing down a shot of high-powered Scotch. Knight had said it was like the buildup before he emitted a sonic pulse. She wondered what it felt like to Bull.

"You should be feeling *something,*" she told him. "It shouldn't be unpleasant..." She closed her eyes for a moment, tracking on the wave as it moved through his body. "To go by Corbie, on your own you'll recover from—say—a gunshot wound in days instead of weeks. If one of us healer types is boosting you, it'll be hours instead of days. And if it's me and I'm hooked up to the pheresis rig, it'll be under an hour."

"Excellent," Bull said. "Though you will forgive me if I am in no hurry to test this out."

She took a deep breath and sat back on her heels, opening her eyes completely and flexing her fingers. "Now comes the tricky part. We see if I can make you as tough on the inside as you are on the outside." She leaned forward again, and put her hands back on his abs. Such gorgeous abs...

Focus!

Find the spleen... that was the one that threatened to rupture first every time he deflected enormous weight with his power. *There you are...* Now go and explain to the thin membrane around it that she wanted some of the cells to look, not like *this,* but like *that...* Yes, and start to multiply, please. And form a nice, tough sheath... flexible, but hard to rupture...

It was fine with the spleen, fine with the kidneys, fine with the lungs and the heart—everything was moving along just as she had pictured, and then she moved on to the stomach and that was when suddenly, everything went pear-shaped. One moment, everything was proceeding exactly as she expected it to. Nice, steady, predictable growth.

The next, there was a runaway process that was exploding in all directions, the way the triggering of the healing factor had. And it wasn't doing *anything* she had expected.

Somewhere in the back of her mind, in the part that wasn't screaming with hysteria, she realized she must have triggered something else, something new, some factor she had never seen before. And it triggered *explosively,* an entirely different sort of cell rocketing out from her first point of contact, enveloping and changing the "silverskin," making it tougher, which would have been fine, but making it *thicker,* picking up some sort of fibrous texture that *seemed* to have metal or something in it, and threatening to choke off the organs from their own blood supply! Frantically she sent her mind and her talent racing after it, diverting it *just* in the nick of time, over and over again, but it kept getting away from her and racing off in a different direction.

Omigodomigodomigod I just killed him!

When it hit the heart she completely panicked and sent a raw *jolt* of energy at it, throwing it into the rib cage—

It *liked* the ribs... it dove after the calcified tissue like a hummingbird on nectar, and she panicked all over again until in the next instant she realized that all of the cellular "cats" she'd been chasing seemed to have picked up on that, and were also leaping for the nearest bone.

And it wasn't hurting him. In fact... in fact, as the stuff made its replicating race over his skeletal mass, it was strengthening that, toughening it, actually penetrating into the surface, making his bones as strong as Untermensch's were, with a sort of nanotube reinforcing structure of something that definitely *was* metal, maybe silica. Had she inadvertently triggered *that* in him? Untermensch's power?

Where's he getting the extra mass—

She dared to open her eyes, just as the coffee table fell over, half of its steel-and-glass expanse eaten away. Of course. He'd been resting one hand on it...

Omigod, this is... this has to be the factor that La Faucon Blanc had, the one that made her meld with her plane. The World War II French meta had long since vanished with the others of the Ghost Squadron, in that last fight over the Bermuda Triangle. The same fight that Eisenfaust had vanished in... only to turn up in Atlanta just before the Invasion, trying to warn them.

And then... it was over. At least, she thought it was. She came in closer and laid her head on his chest. She had to be sure. Yes, she felt the last remnants of the multiplying silverskin begin to revert into a quiescent state. It was remarkable, as if the ravenous tissue had instantly been sated. She probed deeper, and realized with some alarm that Bull's bones were almost completely interlaced with metal, and were now as much metal as calcium. They were lined and meshed with something else, an organic alloy of iron and carbon... steel? If so, it was severely modified steel. With a kind of cellular sigh, everything settled happily into place and began humming healthily along. Terrified of what she would find anyway—afraid to see that his organs were half siliconized—she began a layer by layer check.

He was fine. He was more than fine.

It was the calcified bone, she decided. It had somehow served as both a catalyst and fuel for the silverskin, and when it was depleted, the silverskin had simply reverted to a basal state bent on simple maintenance. The osseous tissue was partly replaced by the organic metal stuff, whatever it was, while still somehow being able to store calcium and keep the bone marrow. It was a little like the titanium matrices injected as a foam that were being used as bone grafts. He certainly wasn't going to have to worry about buildings falling on him now. At least, not unless they were bigger than four stories. Maybe not even then. And God help anyone who threw a punch at him; the fool would end up with broken fist *and* arm.

Note to self; no right crosses to his *chin. Oh my God, that was lucky, so very lucky...*

She opened her eyes and burst into exhausted tears, throwing herself at his neck impulsively. "Gairdner! Gairdner, oh God, I almost killed you! I'm sorry, I'm so sorry—I was stupid, I should *never* have tried that—" She couldn't say anything more; she just choked on sobs.

She pulled back and watched as waves of intense pain began to subside from his features. He drew in a long breath and finally his head fell back on the cushions. She hadn't even realized the agony she had just put him through, having been so focused on fighting back the sudden attack. He never made a sound, there was nothing to reveal the hell he had just gone through. Now, he just lay back, his chest rising and falling in a rhythmic pattern of relief.

"Did it work?" he said, finally. His eyes were still closed, his body limp and vulnerable.

"It did... but I kicked off something else. I had *no fricking clue* I could trigger anything besides the healing factor. I didn't when I set off the healing factor in Corbie and Knight." She choked on another sob. "I am *never* doing that again. It's too dangerous."

"Well, at least we know now," he grunted, pulling himself up and sitting gingerly with his head in his hands. The couch creaked ominously.

"You... ate half my coffee table," she said tentatively, still trying to stop the tears of remorse and guilt.

He nodded. "So, guess I don't have to worry about eating more fiber today."

He startled her into a nervous laugh. "It's—whatever I triggered off started a runaway reaction in the silverskin I was creating, then jumped to your bones. So . . . you kind of have steel and silica bones now. And very tough guts. No thanks to me." She started crying again. "Gairdner, I almost *killed* you!"

He patted her gently. "It was a risk; no matter how sure you were it was safe, these things often are. We got lucky, it seems, but I can live with that." He tested himself, flexing his arms and lifting his legs with tentative gestures. The couch creaked some more. "Feels a little strange, a little stiff. I suppose I have a lot to get used to now."

I'm going to have to keep a close watch on him, Bella thought. *Make sure there aren't any bad side effects out of this.* At least his smile was normal. She'd stopped it before it got to his teeth. She looked down, and realized her hands were still pressed to his chest. She covered for it and ran them up to his head and back down his arms, probing what she had done to him in a calmer state of mind. It seemed complete. All the old bone had been completely altered, and the tendons and ligaments strengthened so he wouldn't tear himself apart trying to move. She wondered how it would heal when broken—how it was going to keep growing back and replenishing. And what about the marrow? *Closer watch. Daily checkups at least. Oh god, what* have *I done?*

Finally she grabbed a tissue from the wreckage of the coffee table and wiped her eyes, and *looked* into his face, into those intelligent, kind eyes, eyes she desperately wanted to see warming with something other than friendship. And that was when it hit her. Competing with a dead woman or not, stupid or not, he'd almost ended up dead, and she'd never—

She thought about every stupid rom-dram she'd ever seen, every television show that had this sort of situation, and how she had always cursed the stupid writers for doing the same damn cliché over and over. One or both of the leads were in love, never said anything, and then they ended up wasting time until the last reel, time that they could have been spending together. Or at least, wasted time in *not knowing*, dithering around, never just saying something and getting rejected—or not. They were always saying "they were afraid of losing what they had," which was just moronic. She could handle rejection, and Gairdner wasn't the kind of guy to panic and run away if she bared her soul to him, given everything else that absolutely *required* his partnership with her.

"Gairdner . . . I don't know what you're going to think when I say this, but don't interrupt me till I get done blurting all this out, okay?" she said, leaping into the wind again. "I'm crazy nuts about you. I don't know for sure if it's love, I've never been in love—it's the telempathy thing, when you know exactly what a guy is thinking once he touches you, it kind of kills romance. Now, I can't read you, and *maybe* that's all this is, but I don't think so. All I do know is I'd give an arm and a leg to be with you, and that I can't just bottle this up anymore, and I sure as hell don't want to find myself staring into that Khanjar bitch's gun tomorrow and find the last thing I'm thinking is regret that I never said anything. And I sure as hell don't want to find out something happened to *you* and end up with the same regret for the rest of my life, though the way things are going that might not be all that long." She let it all out in a rush, and almost ran out of breath at the end of it. "There. I'm done now. Now you get to be Captain Perfect Control and pat me on the head and tell me that a leader can't afford to feel that way and we pretend I never said this and move on."

Except, of course, I did, so now there's a whole new Elephant in the Room. Still, there was some relief in finally getting the Elephant out of her heart and into the open.

"Bella, I . . ." he paused, as if unsure of what to say.

Oh god, she thought. *I knew it.* She steeled herself for the inevitable "Let's just be friends and colleagues" speech.

Instead, she let out a shrill cry as the couch collapsed under Bull's augmented weight. Well, that would be where the *rest* of the metal had come from . . . the reinforcements on the wooden couch frame. They crashed to the floor, thrown together, and Bella found herself staring into Bull's blue eyes in shock.

"Overwatch to Bull and Bella. You two all right? Do I need to get paramedics or the fire department, or were you just breaking furniture for the fun of it?"

Bella was mortified, and looked at Bull helplessly. Bull's face cracked, his lips twitched, and he broke into helpless gales of deep, rumbling laughter. She felt her expression melt, from horrified embarrassment to mirth, and she joined Bull, hooting wildly until her sides ached. She became very aware of his arms, which had slipped around her.

"We're fine, Vickie!" she managed, finally. "Just fine!"

"If you say so," Vickie answered. *"And I'll let the office pool know I won. You* do *break things when you're doing it. What were you doing, swinging from the chandelier?"* There was a pause. *"You guys do realize everyone in Echo Med is sure you're boffing like bunnies, right?"*

CHAPTER TWENTY-ONE

You Have to Believe We Are Magic

MERCEDES LACKEY AND VERONICA GIGUERE

It took some serious research on the charter, pretty much all of which I did under such tight security a nanobot couldn't have gotten into my place, but I finally got all the ducks in a row.

There was just one, teensy, tiny little problem...

But hey, for that, I had Ramona.

The streets of downtown Atlanta buzzed with the usual sights and sounds of a Sunday afternoon. People still dressed in their finer clothes to go to worship services, while others lounged at tables outside coffee shops with newspapers and casual conversation. With less than a year having passed since the day of the Invasion, many of the smaller establishments had managed to return to some semblance of normal. Orange construction netting provided a reminder of the damage to some of the larger buildings, and the boarded-up windows of other restaurants and businesses offered proof that not everyone would make it through these hard times.

Ramona Ferrari folded back a page of the *Atlanta Journal Constitution* and took another sip of coffee. The editorial section burned with the wrath of angry readers who demanded that the city do more about the Kriegers and that Echo step in and solve the problem, and that the inability of either to solve the problem meant that there were issues with the leadership in both. One particularly amusing article blamed the recurring wrath on the apparent heathenism of metahumans, while a rebuttal from a prominent Atlanta minister attributed the remaining Echo personnel as proof that greater powers had not forsaken the God-fearing people of Georgia in these dark times. Ramona shook her head and scanned the page, decided that nothing important remained in the newspaper but sports scores and coupons, and set it neatly on the table. As she did, the familiar Echo insignia caught her eye. She scowled, picked up the page, and scanned the small ad.

"To remember those who sacrificed their lives in duty to the citizens of Atlanta, Echo plans to dedicate a memorial on the one-year anniversary of the Invasion. Chief Executive Officer Dominic Verdigris will present the plaque and statue at the event, which will be open to the public."

Ramona reached for her phone and snapped a picture of the ad, tagging it for later viewing with the hope that Victrix had already seen it in one of her many data-mining passes through the Atlanta media. A sick feeling lurched in her stomach as she reread the paragraph. A public event with Verdigris in charge of metahumans, cementing his image in the minds and hearts of everyone attending, everyone watching. He would own controlling shares of Echo alongside the gratitude of the people of Atlanta, and there would be little that anyone could do about it.

She shifted in her seat, fingertip brushing the side of the earpiece as she hummed. "Overwatch? I know you read more than I do, but what I'm seeing doesn't look right."

"I'm not a mind reader, I only live next door to one. What page of the paper are you looking at? The cam in the coffee shop only shows you from the front." There was a pause. *"Scratch that, bring the paper and come by my apartment. I'm getting you rewired, you're too important for the old rig."*

"Okay." Being a civilian with Echo meant not asking questions about tech when confronted by those who breathed it, and Ramona knew she could trust Vickie. "You want anything? This place is really good, it's a shame they don't do delivery."

"Pick me up one of those gigantor things that's all espresso with a double shot of cream and sweet, and yeah, a couple something or others from the case. Use that as your excuse to come visit the poor phobic shut-in. I like their coffee, I just don't like going out for it."

As instructed, Ramona appeared at the apartment with not one but two coffee disasters and a box of cinnamon coffee cake. She shifted a bit as if to knock, but realized that Vickie likely heard her breathing, let alone knew she was there.

To prove the point, she heard the sound of five locks being thrown, and Vickie opened the door for her. The young woman looked... surprisingly well. Better than Ramona had ever seen her look, in fact. No more dark circles under her eyes. She actually smiled a little as she waved Ramona inside. "Now, what did I ask you to bring me, exactly? I forget."

"This." She thrust one of the coffees at Vickie. "Gigantor, which they call 'venti' over there, all espresso with a double shot of cream and sweet. The 'couple something or others' from the case are cinnamon. Oh, ye poor phobic shut-in," Ramona finished.

Vickie sighed with relief, and unburdened her. "Once I get you wired I won't have to make with the passwords, thank god, but now that we know Doppelgaenger was inside Echo and we presume has had access to all sorts of people, I'm not letting anyone in without a check." She shut and locked the door.

"Makes sense to me." She deposited the rest of her wares on the counter. "So, wired? I get to be the FerrariBot 9000?"

Vickie put the cup down on the coffee table and picked up three tiny plastic boxes. "Okay, first things first, off with the old, and before we stuff ourselves, on with the new. I've got these running on Bella, me, Red, Saviour, Untermensch, Sovie, I'm about to grab Bull after I get you, and Pride after I get Bull. These"—she held up the boxes, which each contained a tiny beadlike capsule—"are the new, improved, techno-magic Overwatch. You could be on the other side of the galaxy, and I'll pick you up; no one can use it but you, no one will know you have it but you, and no one can pick up the signals but me unless they happen to be as good a techno-mage as I am and break in here to twin my rig." She grinned. "Impressed yet?"

Ramona grinned back. "I haven't stopped being impressed with what you can do since I met you. This is amazing. They work on every variation of metahuman? Even Red Djinni?"

"Like a charm. Better on him, actually. I didn't really need to worry about rejection with him. Okay, first we do what we replace the earpiece with. Just hold still." Vickie picked up one of the "beads" on the end of her finger, touched it to the back of Ramona's ear, and muttered something that sounded like "*Apport.*" As far as Ramona could tell, nothing happened, but Vickie seemed content.

"Now the pickup mic." She picked up another "bead." "Open wide."

So far as Ramona could tell, Vickie just touched the top of her soft palate.

"And now my pride and joy, and this is going to be a little creepy. *Don't move* till I say so, and don't touch your eye." This time the "bead" went in the corner of her eye, and Vickie actually grabbed both her wrists.

Staying still was a challenge, and Ramona could sense something smaller than an eyelash but larger than a grain of sand shifting around and *behind* her field of vision. The gritty sensation went away, but the barest touch of pressure someplace behind her eye resembled the beginning of a migraine and she tensed. "How long does this last?"

"Not long. Maybe another minute, just hang in there. It'll flatten out once it's seated."

True to her word, the pressure subsided and Ramona could feel herself relax. "Better, I think. Now what?"

"Overwatch: Command: activate Ferrari," Vickie said. Her grin spread like a kid with a Christmas present. "Overwatch: Command: activate Ferrari HUD live. Now, check *that* little goodie out. Just scan me for starters."

Obediently, Ramona looked over the wisp of a woman in front of her, toes to head and back again. Not a lick of skin showing below her jawline, but the all-black ensemble didn't make her look sickly. As she scanned a second time, other information appeared to the side of Vickie. Time, location, general address as well as latitude and longitude. She allowed her gaze to linger for a second longer, and Ramona's eyebrows went up as a red icon flashed over the small of the woman's back. The bulky sweater hid what the HUD determined as a Glock, fully loaded, and even went so far as to correlate that information to Vickie's full profile from Echo. Ramona was less surprised when it recommended "no engagement."

"Only packing one? I guess I did get your coffee order right."

Vickie chortled. "Oh, I have plenty of mags within reach. If you want to play Easter Egg Hunt, be my guest. Overwatch:

Command: Transfer control: Ferrari: Ferrari. Now you're in the driver's seat. Anything you can hear, I can hear. Anything you can see, I can see. I can talk to you without anyone overhearing because there is a pickup and a speaker smack in your middle ear, and you can whisper because there is a second pickup in your soft palate. Here—" She handed Ramona a little printed folder. "That's your basic commands, but if you don't like how I set it up, and I admit it's kind of geeky, then teach it yourself, the instructions are right there. Now, *I* can override at any time and take control and turn things on. You can turn it all off for as much as eight hours at a time for privacy, any more and it'll alarm and force you to do it again. If you go over your designated time, it'll alarm for me, too. So yes, you are now the Ferrari 9000, congratulations." She paused then added, "Oh. Lower left-hand corner of your HUD, little camera icon, tells you the feed is live, and there are two dots next to it, one is the mic, the other is the speaker. Same thing. Turn them off, the icon and dots go away. Now, have some cake and tell me what brought you here in the first place."

"Well..." Ramona tucked the folder into her purse, trading it for the newspaper. She unfolded the first page, then pressed it back along the crease so that Verdigris' ad would be perfectly centered. "This. This isn't something that was publicized in-house, and only a one-week lead makes me suspicious. Plus, he's using 'Chief Executive Officer' in reference to himself, which isn't quite accurate. Something's rotten, Vickie."

Vickie frowned. "You think he's copped to us? Or at least that we're up to something?" Her frown deepened.

"I don't know." Ramona flicked the edge of the page with her finger. "What this does, or could do, is make him the benevolent darling of the media, earning the adoration of the public by commemorating that day. No one will want to touch him after that kind of gesture."

"Overwatch: Command: open Bella private. Bells, we have a possible sitch." Vickie explained, then listened. "Roger, that's a go. Overwatch: Command: close Bella private." She turned her gaze back to Ramona. "We're on accelerated program, Detective. Double-time if we can manage it."

"How close are you to unlocking the charter?" She had made sure the document had arrived safely at Vickie's apartment less than a day after her meeting with Yankee Pride and Dixie Belle, but the legendary metahuman hadn't been joking about the need for a good mage.

"Close. I know exactly what we need now. The obvious stuff was keyed as tarot code, which is why you kept seeing cards on the edges of the charter parchment. Major Arcana represent actual people. The Emperor—that's Pride. The High Priest—that's a tricky one, that's Nicola himself. The Tower—that's the other tricky one, Marconi. Minor Arcana represent objects. King of Staves, Queen of Pentacles, King of Swords—physical bits of the three original signatories, that'd be Dixie Belle, Yank, and Alex's father. And I worked out the unlocking ritual, which is a very pretty and neat piece of mathemagic, and I would love to know who did it for them." Vickie pursed her lips. "So, can you get me all those things?"

"We can get Pride, sure. Bits and pieces might be a little harder, but since Dixie is still alive, she can help." Ramona let out a quick sigh, part thought and part frustration. "Mr. Tesla's going to be the hard one, since I'm guessing that you can't up and transport your 'rig' into the CCCP closet."

"Actually I have carte blanche from Nat ever since I wired her up. I have gone from 'Daughter of Rasputin' to 'Hero of the People.' I think she's decided I'm close enough to science to get a free pass."

"But is it safe for you to take all of that out? I mean, the man is an electronic ghost... and how do we have both Marconi and Tesla there at the same time? Only one can use the box at a time."

"Tch." Vickie waggled a finger at her. "O ye of little faith. I have a portable version of my workroom. The magician isn't the workroom, the workroom is the magician. And I am a techno-mage; you didn't see me unlock the MacGuffin in the first place, but trust me, tech is safe around me. Have I never *shown* you the Overwatch suite? But about Tesla... hmmm. The logical solution is to let Marconi use the box and make you Tesla's proxy. I hope you don't mind being possessed."

Ramona searched for the right word that would give her some shred of magic street-cred. "You mean, to serve as a, uh, conduit?"

"Pretty much," Vickie said, cheerfully.

"If it keeps the slimeball from taking over, I'll spit pea soup on the ceiling. I think, if you're not busy, we could probably get

Pride on his way back from his weekly visit to his mom." She tried not to think about Tesla's voice coming out of her mouth.

"Let's get him. The sooner I wire him, the better, anyway." Vickie sighed. "Right, this is going to take some prep. And it's going to take some convincing. Tesla isn't going to like riding a body, he might not believe I can do this, and he is probably going to be afraid he won't be able to go back to his box when we're done. So now, Detective, you get to do what you do best. While I prep, you go talk to the Great and Powerful Oz."

"Me?" Ramona goggled at her. "Why me—?"

Vickie gave her a look that clearly said *don't play coy with me.* "Because you are Ramona Ferrari, who has a better chance of talking Eskimos into buying bikinis than anyone I ever met in my life. Now go. Shoo. I'll meet you at CCCP HQ."

She gathered up her things and slung her oversized purse over a shoulder. In the spring, the overwhelming heat had not settled over the city, so she managed the six blocks to the CCCP headquarters without melting. She banged on the door twice, readying for a third knock when the door swung open and a severe man in military fatigues appeared. He did not smile as she produced her Echo badge and cleared her throat.

"Detective Ferrari, sir. I'm here to speak to the Commissar about the item you have in, uh, storage." He didn't show any signs of understanding, so she held up her badge a little higher. "Echo? I'm a Detective, with Echo—"

"The Commissar is familiar with the operatives of Echo. Where is Yankee Pride?"

"I'm here on my own. Pride will be here soon. Listen, I'd like to speak with the Commissar. It's important," she added with a frown. "Is she here?"

The man began to shake his head, but Ramona heard Vickie's voice pipe through her ears, presumably also on the CCCP channels. *"You have clearance to go through HQ, Detective. Unter's just following procedure."* The man gave a crisp nod, stepping to the side just enough for Ramona to slip through. "Turn left at the first entry and head down the stairs. You know the way from there."

Ramona knew her way to the small room that held Alex Tesla's desk. As the door clicked shut behind her, she realized that she didn't know much more when it came to the communication device. Pride was the one who was able to authorize it and open the dialogue with the Metisians. Ramona didn't have any sort of card or key that would open the desk, and she was fairly sure that Vickie couldn't override the communicator to give another person access. She passed a hand over the smooth wood surface and sighed. The charter was still locked, Verdigris was tearing Echo apart piece by piece, and she couldn't do much without the assistance of an actual metahuman with some measure of authority.

"Well, what do I do now?" she muttered aloud. "Wait for Metis to call me?"

The surface of the desk shifted, the two antennae rising and the blue lattice connecting rapidly. Ramona pulled her hand back from the desk and held her breath. As before, the semblance of a severe man with a starched collar and impeccable hair emerged from the field between the wires. It shifted and blinked, features relaxing in recognition at Ramona.

"Detective Ferrari. You have need of assistance?" Nicola Tesla's voice held a crisp yet congenial tone, as if he had expected her call and had been waiting for her. "Is Yankee Pride with you?"

She shook her head, still amazed that the desk had responded to her voice. Ramona hadn't thought that Victrix had overridden the box to allow more than just Pride to call Metis, but she had worked with the woman long enough to know that there was plenty she didn't understand about magic. "No, sir. I came on my own. We found the charter and we spoke to Dixie Belle, but she said something about unlocking the charter and finding a good magician."

"And do you not have a mage with sufficient talent?" The blue mesh eyebrows came together in a show of concern. "I confess, the arcane is not my area of expertise."

Ramona shook her head. "No, we've got the best that anyone could ever want. The issue is that it requires authentication from both you and Mr. Marconi in order to begin the process, and our only direct connection is here." She gestured to the desk and the walls of the small room. "Our resident magician is equally good with technology, but circumstances being what they are..."

"You are serving as the operator for this call." Tesla nodded crisply. "Very well. We will assist in this matter, provided that the charter is at the secondary location. You will need to maintain the connection here."

"Listen, there's something I need to ask—"

But Tesla wasn't listening. He turned, fading slightly as if to call someone from another side of the room. Ramona watched as the more jovial face of Marconi appeared, blue wire-frame eyes dancing. "Signorina Ferrari, a pleasure to see you once again. Yankee Pride is not with you?"

"No, sir. I'm here on my own." She waved to the walls before patting the back of the chair. "Playing the intermediary, as it were."

"Alone?" Marconi's voice carried a hint of mischief as he feigned disbelief. "Truly a terrible thing to befall such a lovely lady as yourself. A moment, please? Nicola, he forgets the most important things sometimes..."

"Sir? I don't—" The wireframe disappeared from view and the image flickered once, as if someone had changed the channel on a television set. What had been blue on gray-black was now full color on white, and a shirtless, upside-down Mercurye stared back at her. He blinked, eyes widening as he recognized Ramona's face, and scrambled to right himself.

"Rick? Rick, is that you? Can you hear me?" Excitement got the better of her and she leaned closer to the quantator. "Is that really you?"

"Ramona? How did you hack into this? Is it over? Did we win?" He tapped once, a tinny sound that made the image shake. "What's going on?"

"It's a long story."

He motioned to the white walls and carpet. "Well, as you can see, I've got a break in my oh-so-busy schedule. I haven't heard much from Mr. Tesla or Mr. Marconi since Yankee Pride made contact. Is it true that Verdigris is in control of Echo?"

"For now. We might have an out, but Victrix is working on it." Ramona sat back as she realized that she was inches from the quantator. "How much do you know?"

Mercurye shrugged, sitting on the floor and folding his legs beneath him. "Some. I heard that our Mr. Tesla was killed, and that Verdigris had a hand in it. I heard that the Metis groupthink doesn't want to help, but would rather wait and watch us like bad television. Other than that?" He shook his head ruefully. "I don't hear a lot from the few who are allowed to talk to me."

"Well, what do you want to know?" She checked her watch, hoping that it would take Tesla and Marconi more than a few minutes to discuss whatever they were going to discuss. "I know it's been a while, so ask away."

He frowned, shaking his head as he drummed his fingers lightly on his knees. "I don't know where to start. What day is it, anyway?"

She suppressed a chuckle. "Sunday."

"Felt like one. Guess my internal clock is still working. Is Pride still around at Echo?"

"Yeah, he's still the face of things. We've been working with the Russians. They're good guys, once you get used to the protocol and procedure." Ramona lowered her voice and leaned closer. "Really, if you watched enough *Rocky and Bullwinkle* as a kid, they're not hard to understand."

Mercurye laughed. "What about classic *Star Trek*? I always understood Chekov."

"Natalya would have made Chekov curl up in his chair and cry for his mother before they went to warp." She giggled as his eyes widened at her attempt at *Star Trek* humor. She thought she caught a snort from Overwatch, but she didn't want to disturb Vickie. "So, what else? These are pretty easy questions."

The image shifted and blurred as Mercurye moved in and out of the frame. He settled cross-legged on the floor, bare feet tucked underneath and looking like a New Age surfer-shaman. He pushed a hand through his hair and let out a long breath of air. "Well, I guess the most important one is, are we still winning?"

Ramona considered how to answer. She didn't want to lie to him, but she didn't want the man to lose all hope, either. "We're still fighting," she finally decided. "I don't think any of us are ready to give up, especially with Verdigris waiting in the shadows. I have to tell you, it does get pretty difficult sometimes."

He nodded and rocked forward. "Yeah. Yeah, I bet it does. I don't hear anything in here, other than these Metisians still don't want to interfere in human business. If you ask me, they're not all that evolved and intelligent as they're supposed to be." Mercurye gave a bitter laugh and glanced to his left. "Then again, what do I know? I'm just the dumb jock."

"Don't say that." Ramona heard the words shoot out of her mouth before she could stop herself. She cleared her throat. Blush crept into her face as he grinned through the quantator at her. "I mean, you're not dumb. You're a metahuman whose abilities are mostly physical in nature, rather than being mental, but that hardly makes you a dumb jock."

Mercurye seemed content with that answer as he rested his elbows against his knees. "Nice to not have to live up to a label, I guess. So, just how did you come up with an Echo charter? Some top-secret clearance?" He leaned forward, eager as a kid watching Saturday morning cartoons.

"Talked with Dixie Belle, actually. She's a sweetheart, full of fire and loads of ideas. Can you believe she actually . . ." Ramona trailed off, realizing that Mercurye stared at her with eyes as wide as saucers, his mouth hung open. "Rick?"

"You actually got to meet Dixie Belle? *The* Dixie Belle? Dixie Belle, who helped to begin what we now know as Echo?" He shook his head slowly. "Wow. She never comes out to the bigger events unless it's some anniversary thing or commemoration, and she's always surrounded by a full security detail. And you, you got to meet her? Face to face?"

The awe in Mercurye's voice made her smile. "Got to have tea with her, too. She and Pride together are something special, that's for sure. Oh, and she knows about you, too."

"Dixie Belle knows who I am?"

Before Ramona could feed the eager fanboy with even more about her visit, the image of Nicola Tesla replaced the view of Mercurye. The thin blue lines that composed his face made his cheeks and jawline seem especially sharp, and Ramona leaned back from the screen.

"Where is the charter, Ms. Ferrari? We will need to establish a link with the system prior to beginning the necessary exercise." The quantator lit up as Tesla spoke. "Your mage is aware of the technological considerations, yes?"

Ramona took a deep breath. *Bikinis to Eskimos,* she thought briefly. "She is, yes. In fact, that is why she will be here momentarily, with Yankee Pride and the charter. For this to work, she needs to be as close to the quantator as possible, with as few . . ." She worked to come up with the right terminology that would make sense for both Tesla and the necessary ritual. "Barriers."

He nodded. "Excellent. As both myself and Mr. Marconi will be present, this should be relatively uncomplicated."

"Relatively, yes. At the same time, the rules of the charter's unlocking require that there be one entity per conduit. Even though the quantator is here, we still need you present in a more tangible fashion." Ramona leaned forward, her words firm and earnest. "We're going to need to channel you through a separate host, rather than via the quantator in order to properly complete this ritual."

The blue wireframe stared at her, something like static causing the image to fuzz at the sharp edges of Tesla's cheekbones and the end of his nose. The eyes flicked down, to the left, and then back to face her with an expression of annoyance and faint anger. "Channel."

"Yes, sir."

"And by 'channel,' I am to understand that my very nature, my consciousness, will require projection through a living being in the room as the ritual takes place?" He bit off the words crisply, his tone cool. "Is this correct, Ms. Ferrari?"

"Yes, sir."

His mouth drew tight; if Nicola Tesla had stood in front of her, Ramona thought she would have seen the thin arms cross over the front of an impeccably clean suit and the chin lift in a show of scientific arrogance. "Then you and your mage will need to investigate a second means of completing this ritual. Such an arrangement is not possible for myself."

Ramona froze. "With all due respect, sir? That's not an option. We need you here to unlock the charter, and this is the only way that we can do it safely."

"Safely?" The quantator popped and crackled as the blue wireframe glared back. "Ms. Ferrari, you do not have any idea what 'safely' would constitute, considering my current form of existence. I am 'safe' because I am contained here, within Metis."

"But, Mr. Tesla. This is the charter that you yourself agreed upon! This is the foundation of Echo!" Ramona's voice rose in the small space. "Without this charter, the organization that you helped to create is going to fall into the hands of a madman!"

Tesla glanced away, blue lines wavering. "I cannot participate in such a fashion, Detective. To leave such containment would invite the possibility of erosion and possibly death."

Ramona drew a deep breath and stood, eyes closing briefly as she lay a hand flat against the surface of the quantator. "With all due respect, Mr. Tesla, that is a risk that the entire organization has taken in your absence. The minute that I walk out the door of this safe house with the badge that bears the Echo insignia, I take that risk on the walk back to the train, on the ride home, even while I'm sleeping in my barely slept-in apartment." Her eyes narrowed, but she willed her voice steady in the role of the proverbial "good cop" with a side of guilt trip. "I can promise you, your own nephew took that risk when he met with government agents who wanted to take hold of the organization, and I was with him when a half-dozen Echo operatives defended him from a wave of Death Spheres and Kriegers."

Now she turned, and Ramona jabbed a finger at the floating head. "Every single day, there are dozens of Echo operatives and civilians who are still clinging to those ideals that make up the institution—your institution—and you've got the nerve to sit back in your perfect little jar back in Metis and tell me that you can't risk death?" She snorted and leaned down, her face so uncomfortably close that the wireframe of Nicola Tesla shrank back a bit. "Your nephew died protecting Echo. My friends died protecting Echo. I'm ready, if I need to, to die to protect Echo. If you're trying to invoke some bit about how you can't risk death because you're afraid to die or that you're too important to risk it to save Echo, then I may as well just hand Verdigris the keys and we all sit back with popcorn to watch the Thulians swarm the planet."

"Ms. Ferrari, you don't—"

"*Coward.*"

The floating head twitched; the thin lines connecting the myriad of nodes became fuzzy for a split second. Ramona's lip curled. "How do you think it makes me feel, knowing that I have to be the channel for some entity who knows how far away, who only exists as a connect-the-dots hologram? Do you think I jumped at the chance to participate? Don't you think I'm a little concerned that if this goes south, I have to deal with your consciousness behind mine for all eternity?" She jabbed a finger at the wavering blue head. "In case you've forgotten, Mr. Tesla, I'm the last so-called normal you have in this organization who has a clue as to what's really going on and who wants to help."

The wireframe blinked, grew fuzzy, and slowly faded out.

Ramona sagged against the quantator, hanging her head. This wasn't what Vickie had asked her to do, and desperation had turned the negotiation into an argument. She expected the chirp of Overwatch through her inner ear at any time, chastising her for screwing up their one chance of getting Nicola Tesla to help them unlock the charter. Ramona halfheartedly scrolled through a list of possible outcomes, each one more hopeless than the last, so caught up in her own thoughts that she almost missed the hiss and crackle that preceded Tesla's voice.

"You are correct, Ms. Ferrari." The blue mouth moved slowly, the words deliberate. "This venture is not without risk for the both of us. And yes, I had forgotten that you are the last remaining non-metahuman within the upper tier of the organization who understands the gravity of the situation."

"It's not a badge I wanted to wear," she offered softly.

Nicola Tesla inclined his head, mouth drawn tight. "Nevertheless, I concede that your concerns are no less than my own. These processes that involve the arcane carry with them a certain risk, for all involved."

Ramona held her breath and nodded once, hope glimmering inside.

"If you, in your current state, are willing to endure this risk, then I will do so as well. Given our respective circumstances, you have far more to lose than do I."

"Thank you, sir." Ramona nodded politely, smile held in check. She kept her words short and gracious. "We will call you when ready."

The blue wireframe winked out, with Marconi's faint laughter coming through before the quantator antennae sank back into the desk. She lifted her voice, a smile on her face. "Overwatch?"

"Here, Detective. Whatcha got?"

Ramona sank into the chair, relieved. "Bring it on. The Eskimos have their bikinis."

Yankee Pride had obliged without any question or comment when Vickie hooked him up at the CCCP headquarters, although Ramona had seen him squirm a little when the optical piece found purchase behind his eyeball. Thanks to his weekly visits with Dixie Belle, he had the personal items that Vickie required. He offered them to her with a smile.

Vickie stood just in front of the quantator like a priestess at an altar, head down, arms out at her sides, palms down. Then she dropped her arms about halfway, inverted her hands to palms up, and slowly raised them to shoulder height again. The hair on the back of Ramona's neck stood up as the cement floor *crumbled* in a very precise set of patterns to about an inch deep in lines about half an inch wide. It looked for all the world as if an invisible force was stamping a double circle, around Vickie and the quantator, with four smaller circles at equal intervals between the inner and outer circle. The quantator itself sat precisely in the middle of one of those four circles.

"Okay, YP. You stand here, and hold your mama's hair." She pointed at the one of the small circles immediately to her right, and Pride stepped gingerly into it, taking the lock from Vickie.

"Now we get to play 'ghost in the machine.' Ramona, come over here, please." Vickie crooked a finger at her. Ramona marveled at the change in the woman, when she was doing something she was the expert at. This was an entirely different Vickie, scarcely recognizable as the nervous creature that hunched her shoulders and tried to be invisible when more than three or four people were in the same room. Ramona stood in front of the quantator, and placed her hands on it where Vickie directed, trying not to shiver. "All right, Mr. Tesla," Vickie continued as Tesla's solemn wire-frame visage appeared between the antennae. "Are you ready?"

"Are you certain this will work?" There was real fear in Tesla's voice, and Ramona didn't blame him. If this didn't work... he'd die. Forever.

"As certain as Heisenberg will let me be," Vickie told him. "Remember, this is largely governed by will. You really have to *want* this. Truly, and without reservation. Can you do that?" She patted the quantator reassuringly. "Remember also, once this works, I've got you set up to transfer to any other chosen vessel and back. That might turn out useful, or just entertaining."

Tesla paused for a very long moment, then his expression firmed. "You have all risked your lives over and over in this endeavor, Miss Nagy. I can do no less. Yes. I want this."

"All right then." Vickie stepped out of the quantator circle. "Then here we go."

Her hands moved in tai-chi-like patterns, sketching things in the air, things that sometimes looked like arcane symbols and sometimes like equations. They made Ramona feel a little dizzy, so she shut her eyes and concentrated on feeling—like a hostess, waiting for a welcome guest. But she could also feel the hair on the back of her neck rising involuntarily, and something like a charge building in the air, just before a lightning strike. The tension began to ratchet up, and just when she wanted to scream at Vickie to get it *over* with already, the mage finally barked the word *"Fiat!"* and—

And suddenly there was someone else in her head.

This wasn't like being with a telempath like Bella, or a telepath like Jamaican Blaze. This was . . . it felt as if there was someone *behind* her, except when she turned, there wasn't.

It is very disconcerting for me, too, Miss Ferrari, said an apologetic voice that came from everywhere and nowhere. *At least it seems to have worked.*

Vickie peered at them, and seemed to intuit that Tesla had made it in, since she nodded in satisfaction. "Okay, let's try the control thing for just a second. Ramona, relax, and think about anything pleasant. Especially relax your jaw. Mr. Tesla, please try saying something."

Ramona's thoughts immediately went to Rick, and she was so busy blushing she didn't even notice when Tesla started to speak. He pitched her voice oddly, and it had his own distinct accent. "Testing. Well, it appears we have a success." *Disconcerting* did not begin to describe how she felt when her mouth produced words that she had no control over.

"Good." Vickie nodded. "Let her have control back for a moment, you haven't piloted a body in a long time, and you probably won't remember how. Ramona, here—" Vickie handed her the sample of Alex Tesla Senior's blood that Bella had found in cold storage. "Take the circle opposite Pride, please." She placed the second lock of hair, this time from Yankee Doodle, on top of the quantator, put the charter on the floor in the center of the main circle, and stepped back to the last empty small circle as Ramona took her place. "Now the real show begins. From now on, *nobody move.* I don't care if there's a fire, a flood, an earthquake or an Echo full scramble. Until I tell you, *no moving.* I'm playing with space-time here, and bad things happen when you cross space-time boundaries."

Once again, she bowed her head and held her arms out to her sides. Again, her hands were palms-up. This time, however, her hands made identical, rotating, gathering gestures, before she opened her palms and suddenly brought them up, like a conductor calling for the opening chord from an orchestra.

Ramona nearly leapt out of her skin as she was *answered,* both by a sound, like the ringing of an enormous bell, and by an uprush of blazing green light that abruptly filled all the channels that had been cut in the floor. The light in the outermost circle streamed upwards in a curve and met to form a half-dome over them. Vickie made a second gesture like the first; more light blazed up and another booming note answered her—this time the light was gold. She did this twice more, with red and blue light answering, all the colors finally mingling to form a steady white blaze that reminded Ramona, somehow, of starlight.

Vickie raised her head, dropped her left arm, and made a lifting gesture with her right hand, and the charter levitated upward to about waist height on a pillar of white light.

"We stand in the place outside of space, and the time outside of time, where only truth can be spoken, and only truth can be revealed," Vickie said, her voice having a curious, echoing tone to it. "Yankee Pride, for that is the name that is truer than the one you were born with—do you speak as the heir to Alexander Tesla?"

"I do," Yank said, steadily, though he was looking a little pale.

"And do you bear the token, freely given, of your mother, Dixie Belle?"

"I do."

"And is it your will that this charter be unlocked, laid bare, and revealed for any to read?" There was something oddly ominous about the way Vickie said those words.

"It is."

"And will you lend your strength to this task?"

"I wi—" Yank said, and then he could say nothing more as the blue light erupted from *him,* and a beam as thick as his arm streamed out of him and into the pillar in the center. It was hard for Ramona to tell for sure, but he looked like someone who had grabbed a pair of hot wires and was frozen in place. She licked her lips nervously, and sensed Tesla inside her, shivering.

I do not care for magic. When Jeremiah Stone performed this the first time, I did not like it, and I like it even less now.

Wait—who? *Jeremiah* Stone?

But Vickie was asking the same questions of the quantator, and Marconi was answering them, steadily, the same way. This time the beam of light was red. Then it was Ramona's turn. Or rather—Tesla's...

If you don't do this, she thought fiercely at him, *we might as well all take out big life insurance policies, because our heirs are going to need them.*

She waited apprehensively as Vickie asked the questions, and...

Her mouth opened, and Tesla answered them. And the beam of green light erupted out of her, and it was *exactly* like grabbing a couple of hot wires. She was barely conscious of the fact that Vickie was speaking again, barely registered the words.

"The words have been spoken. Consent has been given. Strength has been lent. Now I, Officiant, give consent and lend my strength to the support of all. Let the charter be unlocked, the words laid bare for any man to see. *Fiat!*"

The word ended in a high-pitched keening of pain as the final beam of yellow light erupted from Vickie's chest and hit the pillar. The light in the center of the room went from brilliant to blinding. Ramona closed her eyes, and she could still see it burning through her lids as her body was held rigid in the magic's thrall.

Then, abruptly and with no warning, the light blinked out, and whatever held her in its grip let her go. She slumped, but mindful of Vickie's warning, she teetered and held herself as still as she could as she opened her eyes.

Still in there, Mr. Tesla? she thought.

Yes, Miss Ferrari, came the weary-feeling answer. *That... was no easier the second time.*

"Stay put a little longer, folks," Vickie said. She sounded as if she had just done three rounds of the parkour course. With a hundred-pound backpack. Backwards.

The light still shone around them but depleted and dull, and the charter was lying on the floor again. Vickie made the reverse of the gestures she had before, and the dome of light faded, the colors shining up from the channels in the floor faded, and finally, there was nothing but the room with its single electric bulb, the quantator, and the paper on the floor.

"Now you can move," Vickie said, and flexed her fingers. "And now, Mr. Tesla, we can send you back home again."

"Now the sixty-four-thousand-dollar question," Ramona said, when Tesla was safely back in cyberspace, or whatever electronic afterlife it was he inhabited. "What *is* it that is in this charter that is going to..."

All three of them were scanning it, but Vickie was evidently the speed-reader among them, because she let out a whistle and planted her finger on a paragraph in the middle of the last page. "This," she said. "Holy Cauldron, this changes *everything.*"

Quickly Ramona skipped to that paragraph.

This clause is to establish the leadership and fundamental rule, in perpetuity, of the organization to be known as Echo. As with all organizations, shareholders and stockholders will be established. All metahuman members of Echo, from this day forward, are shareholders of one and only one share each. Only shareholders may vote on matters pertaining to the leadership and their own welfare. For the purposes of establishing and continuing the leadership of Echo, and ensuring the welfare of the metahumans of Echo, stockholders in Echo are not voting shareholders. The Chief Executive Officer of Echo will be, in perpetuity, absent the failure of the bloodline, the direct heir in the bloodline of Nicola Tesla. The Chief Executive Officer cannot be replaced, neither by vote, nor by dismissal. He can only step down of his own will. In the event that there is to be no direct heir in the bloodline of Nicola Tesla, only the previous CEO can designate an heir, that heir must be a metahuman of Echo, and only the shareholders of full voting shares can ratify that heir. In the event no heir is ratified, a new Chief Executive can only be elected by the shareholders of full voting shares. Only metahumans of Echo, past and present, will hold full voting shares. Voting shares may not pass to heirs, in order to ensure the welfare of the metahumans of Echo. In wartime, should the CEO not feel capable of fully directing Echo, the CEO may designate an additional, temporary position, Acting Executive Director, with whom he, or she, may share leadership and executive decisions. The Acting Executive Director must also be a metahuman of Echo, and the position is not heritable nor transferable. This clause cannot be changed, nullified, nor revoked, either by the stockholders or the shareholders. Should this clause be changed, nullified, or revoked, the Charter will be deemed null and void, Echo will be dissolved as an organization, and the resources therein will be divided among the voting shareholders. Stockholders will derive no benefit from the dissolution of Echo.

"You guys realize what this means, don't you?" Vickie said. "Verd's toast. If he tries to get a stockholder vote to kill the charter leadership clause, he loses Echo. If you think the rumblings of revolt are bad here, you should catch the scuttlebutt from some of the other Echo chapters. He made a big mistake in exiling folks he didn't like elsewhere—all he did was spread dissent around. The second we get all the metas together to vote, he's out, and Pride's in. And"—she added gleefully—"he just set that meeting up himself."

"The memorial—" Pride said, stunned.

"For which Verd is providing all-expenses-paid tickets to all the retirees, and any other metas who want to come, yeah." Vickie's head bobbed. "I can make sure the lines are clear for phone-in votes too, once we start the meeting."

"What about the charter itself? Where do we keep it now?" Ramona looked to Pride apologetically. "I know this is your mother's only copy, but I can't say that I feel good about it leaving here now that it's unlocked."

Pride shrugged. "Then it doesn't leave here. I don't know of any place in Atlanta that's more secure than this building, save for Ms. Vickie's apartment. Do you think that the Commissar would mind keeping this for a while?"

"I wasn't about to let it leave, actually." Vickie made another gesture toward the desk. The top drawer opened obediently, and she slid the pages inside. She etched a small inscription against the lock, effectively sealing it beneath the quantator. "Now, all we need to do is pretend that we don't know anything about this."

CHAPTER TWENTY-TWO

Enemy Mine

MERCEDES LACKEY AND CODY MARTIN

Sometimes it felt as if for every single thing we learned, we uncovered three more mysteries.

One of those mysteries was why the Thulians never seemed to fully commit to anything. Another was why some of their people seemed to have agendas of their own... agendas that came at us out of nowhere.

Commercial airline travel sucked. It had all the discomfort of those jump seats on the Echo cargo jobs, with none of the legroom. At least on Echo standby flights, you got something to eat. And you didn't have a kid kicking the back of your seat the whole time. And a screaming baby three rows up.

But John Murdock wasn't with Echo, so although CCCP was technically "allied" with them, anything that wasn't a screaming emergency or a stealth mission meant... commercial air. Currently, he was flying back to Atlanta after checking on a weapons shipment that had gone over its allotted timetable. It wasn't too much to worry about, and he'd set everything to rights; the people involved with the container ship were all Russian, and having the CCCP badge did wonders for making sure everything went smoothly. The thing that bugged him the most was that he felt that being sent on this errand was, for starters, boring, but more importantly a waste of his time and skill sets. But, perhaps fortunately, it was up to his betters to decide where his time working ought to be spent.

He was doing his best to sleep fitfully through as much of the flight as possible, despite the cramped conditions and droning noises of screaming babies and overtalkative businesspersons. Right when he was finally about to nod off, a voice chirped in his ear.

"Got bad and good news for you, comrade."

"Is the good news that you're a dream, and I can keep on sleeping?" He scrunched up his face, readjusting himself in the seat and sitting up straight. "Lay it out for me. What's up?"

"The good news is that you get to jump off the cattle car at the next stop, the better news is that I have a car with a meal in it picking you up. The bad news is that you have a job."

"I thought that developing an exquisite contempt for commercial travel *was* my new job."

"Naw, that's for standup comedians."

"Bella said I oughta pick up a hobby."

"Here's the skinny. Seems the Rebs have been doing out-of-town recruiting since you ran them out of Atlanta. We think there's a base. I've already sent Zhar-ptica out with a vehicle. He'll meet you at the airport and he's got all the briefing materials with him." There was a dry laugh. *"If you turn on your comm to double-check me with Gamayun, the stewardess will have a coronary, and you'll end up getting arrested by the Sky Marshal, so it'll have to wait."*

"Okay. So, remind me, where am I getting off again? An' who's this Zhar person?"

"Brand new with the advantage of having a genuine USA education. Minor firepower, too minor to interest the home team. Speaks good English, as opposed to Pavel English and knows how to read a US road map. By the time he gets there with the miserable excuse for a vehicle that Nat authorized, you'll be at the curb."

He mulled over the information for a moment. "So, the new guy is my sidekick and support. I do a snoop and scoot on this base, report back, and wait for more instructions. Right?"

"Pretty much. It's halfway between Savannah and Atlanta."

"Anythin' more of import 'bout this mission that y'need to tell me?"

"The important stuff is in the briefing you can download when you hit dirt."

"Good. Then quit yer yappin'. I'm gonna pass out. Y'might want to call the cops, though; I'm gonna kill the rug rat that's kicking my seat. Slowly."

✧ ✧ ✧

If John hated the actual process of commercial flying, he utterly despised what it took to get out of an airline terminal. Jostling and bumping through thousands of other tired, cranky, and overcaffeinated travelers did nothing to improve his mood. When he had finished collecting his single bag, he wanted nothing more than a hot shower, some strong liquor, and a bed. A soft rock would've sufficed, but a bed would be better. It was while he was waiting at the curb for his comrade to meet him when he noticed something from the corner of his eye.

It was a woman approaching him; everything about her posture said that she was nervous. She looked like someone's secretary, dishwater blonde, a little dumpy, getting wide in the hips from sitting at a desk all day. What was out of place about her was that she had a bodyguard with her. *He* was easy to spot for what he was when you knew what to look for; part of it was the fact that although you couldn't see his eyes behind the dark glasses, there were tiny telltale motions of his head as he scanned the crowd like a preprogrammed machine.

Shades at night? What a putz. John turned to face them, setting down his bag and shrugging off his backpack. "Somethin' I can help you with, ma'am?"

The woman, despite looking like she was about to come apart at the seams, managed to sound very bored. "Look at this, Mr. Murdock." She handed him a PDA. On it was a picture of a young man, probably in his early twenties. He was bound and gagged, tied to a chair, and looked like he had been beaten up pretty thoroughly. That day's newspaper was being held under his chin. "If you don't come with us, we will kill this individual. Make your decision." John groaned internally. These goons weren't Blacksnake; Blacksnake, thankfully, wasn't this cheesy. And while this woman could conceivably be connected with someone or some organization that he knew nothing about, he got the sense immediately that this was Thulian.

"Firming up the visual." The familiar voice was very quiet in his ear. He was awfully glad there was nothing for these bastards to see that would let them know he was wired.

"Whaddya think I'm gonna do?" *Let's see how this plays out.*

"Positive on the hostage; Reb bagboy, minor police record. Negative ID on the contacts." A car pulled into the curb with a screech of brakes. *"Nat says your call, go or no-go."*

They could've killed me with a car bomb or a drive-by or any other number of methods; if they wanna risk talking to me like this, there's a reason.

John stooped as he bent down to get into the car, looking at the bodyguard. "Get my bags, Fritz."

The car ride took close to an hour and a half. John was fairly good at keeping time internally, but the bag they had put over his head had made it difficult. The entire ride was silent, without so much as a sniffle or throat clearing from the other three in the car. This was all very cliché, but he didn't allow that to lull him into any false sense of security. These people were all enemies, and he could end up very dead very quickly; it didn't matter if it was by the hand of an amateur or someone with experience and brains.

It was a good thing his lifeline to Vickie was an implant now. Nothing for them to see. Nothing for them to hear either; Vickie was being as silent as he was. That was probably smart. If either of them had meta-powers they might hear something if she spoke.

Then they stopped, although the car was still running. He heard the bells of a railway crossing, then the approaching train. When it was near enough that the sound actually rattled the frame of the car, the voice was in his ear again.

"Zhar's behind you by a good bit, and I have your loc. Looks like you're heading for the same place we wanted you to go. Got more backup on the way now, but they're at least two hours at top speed."

Which means I'll either be clear or dead by the time they arrive. At least someone might be able to clean up whatever's left, in the case of the latter. The thought of the angel flashed across his mind. Strangely... being dead had an entirely different slant to it now. The fear wasn't so much that he would have *lost,* as it was that he would have lost seeing *her* again. He'd been doing nothing but surviving for so long, that these past few months of... well, really *living,* had sort of crept up on him. What would she do if he was killed?

And if... if she really, really was an angel... would it matter?

He got a brief flash of her, hands on her hips, scolding him for getting killed the way his ma used to for getting into something, and nearly choked on a laugh.

The train passed; the car was in motion again, bumping over the tracks, then taking a right onto what felt like a dirt road. "Are we there yet? I'm getting hungry." He uncrossed his arms, fidgeting intentionally in the seat. Distracting them had its own perks, one of which was that annoyed people sometimes let things slip. And this bunch didn't exactly look like the cream of the crop.

"Shut up." Male voice, directly to his right. The bodyguard.

John decided that it would be all right to gamble. "Make me." The guard clamped his left hand on John's shoulder, which was what he had counted on. The guy was big, bigger than John, and was used to intimidating people that way. In a blink, John had locked his left hand onto the guard's wrist and pulled him forward. After twisting the wrist just a few inches, he applied his elbow to the guard's outstretched arm, hyperextending it until he heard a loud *pop* and a strangled cry. The bag was very suddenly snatched from his head; the woman was pointing a small pistol at him, the driver was turned around in his seat, and the guard was nursing his broken appendage. After a second of studying it, John realized that the pistol was Thulian; one of their weird rayguns. It further confirmed his suspicion about who these goons were. "What?" He shrugged nonchalantly, as if the violence that had just taken place had nothing to do with him at all.

"Get out of the car, Holz. And you. Do not move quickly. I can choose to make you hurt very, very much." The woman didn't look frightened now.

The bodyguard fumbled open the door, hissing his pain as he did so, and got out, leaving John with a clear view of his surroundings.

It looked to be what was left of a farm; John wasn't at all familiar with farming equipment to identify what sort of farm by the old, rusted-out hulks of machinery parked beside what remained of a wooden barn, but the blowing bits of white fluff everywhere did that for him. Cotton, and it must have been abandoned for a long time, to have built up the little drifts of dead, grayish fiber against the weed-infested fence line and the base of the barn timbers. The driveway they were parked on was mostly crabgrass with only a hint of the original gravel.

There was a second barn next to the wooden one, in somewhat better shape; sheet metal over steel, it looked like. And big. Probably where the cotton bales had been stored. John got out, taking his time. The whine of what sounded like a million cicadas filled the air.

The group—minus the bodyguard, who was leaning against the car—strolled through an open door in the second barn, guarded by an equally serious-looking and for-show-big tough guy. Cotton lint was everywhere; cotton fibers and dust were so thick in the air it looked like a Ridley Scott film. The guard nodded to the group, stepping aside to let them inside. The barn looked a lot bigger from the inside than from without; big enclosed spaces had that effect. The place was almost completely empty, except for several scattered stacks of crates, some more bodyguards and the "hostage" sitting in the center, still tied to a chair. The hostage was dressed plainly enough; he almost looked like a college kid instead of a no-account piece of Reb scum. The question was, why hold one of their own guys as a hostage? Unless, of course, they were counting on him to think the kid was a civvie.

"So, what's the play here, folks? I haven't got all night, and I'm still hungry." He crossed his arms and rolled back on his heels. "Your hostage isn't much of one; should've told the Reb to bathe before y'tried to set this gig up."

"And what makes you think he is a Reb, *schweinhund?*" Something very like a Teutonic god leapt down out of the upper story and landed in a cloud of dust and cotton lint. John knew that particular Teutonic god though. Ubermensch.

Oh. So that's *why they went to the trouble of dragging me out here.* John was immediately uneasy. Ubermensch, while probably not the smartest man John had ever met, was definitely one of the strongest. John shrugged, again trying his best to appear unconcerned. "Couldn't have been plainer than if you'd stuck jackboots on him, Fritz. Beer, sauerkraut an' back bacon on his breath." John wasn't about to give away the fact that his "eye in the sky," Vickie, was the source of the information. He uncrossed his arms, taking a step forward towards the Thulian and the bound Reb. "What do you want?"

The Thulian stuck a thumb at him. "You shamed me. You shall not shame me again. This time we fight—"

"Not to interrupt what sounded like a towerin' righteous rant, but y'ought to have your barber here fer shamin' ya. That haircut went out in the seventies. Nobody wears mullets anymore." *Piss him off. Couldn't really make things much worse.* John tensed, readying himself to see how the big—the only really appropriate word to describe Ubermensch—meta would react.

He was disappointed. Ubermensch's brows knitted. "*Was ist ein* 'mullet'?" he muttered to the woman. She shrugged.

"I wouldn't be too quick to talk about fighting, Adolf. You're talking to a real man here, and you couldn't even take out one little slip of a Russian girl."

The Thulian's face screwed up in rage. "You insolent pig—" John snapped his right arm out almost instantly, fire cascading down it in a thick stream. The flames jumped and impacted directly in front of Ubermensch and the Reb "captive." John had paid close attention to the cotton lint and dust that permeated this warehouse; such things were really, really flammable. The space around Ubermensch erupted into a mini fireball, causing him to throw his hands in front of his face; the Reb, still tied to the chair and gagged, had no such recourse. John didn't waste any time; he darted immediately to his right, taking the half second to burn the nearest bodyguard with a spurt of flame large enough to swallow a Buick. Skidding to a halt behind a stack of crates, he waited and listened.

Everyone else scrambled; the aide went straight for the door, and the remaining bodyguards followed suit, sliding and slipping in the accumulated cotton lint. The Reb was the only one that remained still; he had begun to scream around his gag. Ubermensch brushed the ashes and soot from his armor. Although he did not have his sword, the rest of his armor was the same as the last time John had seen him. His golden helmet had been made in the shape of an eagle's head, an extremely stylized, art deco sort of eagle's head, with two equally stylized wings sweeping back from either side. The eagle theme was carried out on the breastplate, where another eagle was incised into the metal, a double lightning-bolt "SS" in one claw, a stylized skull in the other. In the way inconsequential thoughts had a way of intruding when you were under heavy fire, John wondered if this was the same armor that the first Ubermensch had worn—or if the new version had had a new look designed to match the power suits.

He lifted one gauntleted hand to the helmet, and raised the beak-visor, revealing a head that looked like it had been taken straight off of an old Third Reich statue, scanning the warehouse. His eyes settled on the stack of crates that John was hiding behind. "You'll suffer for your tricks, pathetic worm!" In five great strides, Ubermensch was at the crates, smashing through them with his shoulder. John barely escaped from behind the bursting wooden boards, sending a jet of flame over his shoulder. The pile of broken crates began to burn around Ubermensch; the light cast reflected off of his gleaming armor, making him look even more like a raging devil.

John took a deep breath, still running, and his enhancements keyed. He moved at a blur, kicking up clouds of cotton dust. He stopped very suddenly, whirled, and braced his right arm. Concentrating and relaxing, he let the flame on his arm build and coalesce; the blast lashed out to strike Ubermensch directly in the chest, splashing flames across his upper body. *I've gotta keep him outta reach until I can get some good distance between us; then I'll have time to really unload on the son of a bitch.* The Thulian stomped after John, swatting away the fire from his face. "You cannot keep this game up forever!" He bumped into a metal support beam, one of dozens in the warehouse; stopping, he ripped out a meter-long section with one hand. Putting up his free hand to shield himself from the flames, Ubermensch side-armed the hunk of metal at John.

John dropped prone to the floor, shutting off his flames; the beam sailed overhead fast enough to create a violent vortex in the air above his head. It would've bisected him if he'd still been standing upright. John was back up on his feet just as quickly, but Ubermensch had seized the opportunity to close the distance. John feinted to his left, then juked to his right towards the center of the room. Ubermensch followed, unfazed by John's feint. They met right next to the Reb, whose eyes had gone wide in abject terror. Ubermensch caught John in a viselike grip with a meaty hand inside his metal gauntlet; John wrenched his shoulder, barely slipping out of the hold. *This is bad.* He jabbed twice, connecting with his opponent's jaw; it didn't budge, but something in John's hand almost cracked. He wouldn't be able to hurt Ubermensch, not close-up like this.

The problem was that the bastard was so damned *strong.* John's mind, flooded with adrenaline and moving faster than his enhanced body could keep up with, jumped back to training with Bella at Echo, teaching how to handle superior strength when you were just a weak human. All the CDOs had to take this training. The highlight had been when a small, unassuming man with a huge bushy mustache and coke-bottle glasses had instructed John to try to strike him with all of his enhanced might; the next thing John had known, he was on his back and halfway across the room. John was a fast learner; he'd picked up quite a bit in that one session.

Flashing back to the present, John watched in not-quite-slow motion as Uber snapped a fist toward his face; it was a haymaker, and more than powerful enough to kill him. John pivoted, his right and left hand coming up to loosely hold the Thulian's arm; moving off the line of attack, he guided Ubermensch's fist in the direction that the strike was already heading. Unable to stop himself, Ubermensch found all of the strength he had planned to use turning John into mush redirected forward. His fist must have seemed to pull him like a rocket as John dropped to one knee and he found himself soaring over John's head in a parody of flight. His landing sounded as if someone had just flung a '57 Chevy at a junkpile.

John kept the dance up, redirecting the Thulian's enormously powerful strikes to work against him. The superstrong meta clearly did not "get" what was happening to him, and his face reddened with fury. *I can't do this forever; I'm not that good, and he'll get lucky.* As if fated, John saw the blow coming; his feet were planted wrong, and he wouldn't be able to avoid it this time. Without a single thought, he snatched the tied-up Reb, who was in the middle of the raging fight, and placed him squarely in front of his chest. The Reb gave a single strangled squeal right before Ubermensch's fist impacted with him.

Stars exploded in his vision, and John went sailing end over end through the air. He'd been through rough fights, crashes of various sorts, and explosions; none of them seemed to compare with how hard he'd been hit. His back impacting with the metal siding of the warehouse seemed significantly gentler, as did his landing. It took what seemed like ages for his vision to clear and for the black to fade from the edges. Looking down at himself to make sure he was still whole, he noticed that he was covered in the pulpy remains of the unfortunate Reb fake hostage. Brushing himself off and coughing violently as he stood up, John glanced at the new hole he'd helped make in the warehouse. Ubermensch was marching out through the missing piece of sheet metal, infernally haloed by the small fires inside the building. Part of the roof began to cant and collapse inwards as he exited.

"Johnny, heads up. He's ramping up something in his armor. It's not energy beams . . . grav manipulation or something? I can't tell, just that there's something going on, and that can't be good for you. Wish to hell I had some more complicated sensors."

"Now . . ." Ubermench's face was scarlet with rage. "Now I become serious." He stepped next to what looked like a thresher of some sort, setting his hand upon one of the massive blades in its exposed internals. Without any apparent effort, he yanked out the gigantic piece of metal, taking it into both of his hands like an oversized axe.

Two green bolts split the air around John, coming from the far corner of the collapsing warehouse. The bodyguard whose arm he'd broken earlier was firing.

Ubermensch whirled on the underling, spitting out something in German. It sounded like obscenities. From the look on the flunky's face, it probably was. *"Das is* mein, *scheisskopf!"* Ubermensch finished, flinging a hand towards John. *"Mein! Gehst du! Schnell!"*

Apparently the flunky didn't react quickly enough to suit Ubermensch. Dropping the combine blade, Ubermensch touched something on his left gauntlet. Immediately, he sank up to his ankles into the dirt. *That's his grav stuff kicking in, then.* Twisting to his right, the Thulian grabbed the edge of the combine, and *dragged* it single-handedly towards him. In one smooth motion, he had hefted the entire contraption above his head, rusted metal whining and creaking pitifully. He hurled it at the barn with impossible, inhuman force; it was mind-blanking for John to witness. The combine tumbled through the air towards the bodyguard; his shriek was cut short as the farm machine impacted with him and the entire end of the warehouse, completing the fiery collapse.

John took advantage of the moment. Uber's back was turned and he seemed to be literally planted. John focused again, thrusting both arms out to help direct his flames. He was sloppy in his aim this time; his beam gouged into the ground, cutting a burning trough as it tracked up to connect with his adversary. Ubermensch whirled around, but he seemed to be going much slower. He had to make an effort against the grav manipulator in order to move around. This was very good for John; he'd be able to leverage his mobility over the Thulian even more. *I'd kill for an airstrike or some artillery. I wonder if they could shoot Chug outta cannon?*

Ubermensch made his way to another large machine, this one the size of a dump truck; with his freakish strength, he lifted it. John's enhancements were still going, so he was able to move out of the way of the thrown equipment easily. So long as he had to keep dodging all of this farm crap, though, he couldn't set up for a powerful shot. This was a stalemate, and that just wouldn't do.

Ubermensch hefted another machine: some monstrous Deere contraption, maybe a cotton picker. It still had cotton fluff in its rear catch, floating lazily around. John made a split-second decision, and held his ground. He'd need to be spot-on with this shot. Focusing again, he fired—not at Ubermensch, but at the machine.

There must have been some fuel still sloshing around in the bottom of the tank, and plenty of fumes to go with it, not to mention all that flammable cotton lint. Gas fumes too, not diesel. The explosion swatted John flat into the ground, sending a massive cloud of smoke and fire into the air. Shrapnel rained down around John, and his entire front felt like it had been sunburned. His ears were ringing; the violent noise certainly didn't do anything good for his sensitive hearing. He scanned the area; the secondary fires that the explosion had created were giving off a lot of smoke. John was barely able to make out the outline of Ubermensch, struggling to stand up.

Using the smoke for concealment, John dashed through the smoke, closing to Ubermensch's side. Moving with a practiced economy of motion, he grabbed for the Thulian's left arm trying to deactivate the gravity manipulator. Ubermensch was still stunned, flailing about blindly while John scrabbled at the device.

"Johnny, if you can get anywhere near his controls, they'll be heat-shielded on top, but not underneath. If you can find a seam—"

John took her advice instantly; instead of trying to switch anything on, he simply allowed his fires to spring from his hands. A half second later, the fires transmuted and became plasma. The housing for the forearm device glowed, crumpled, and then shorted before melting. Some sort of strange pulse of force blasted out of the device before it died; it flung him backwards as John's senses all failed and his stomach lurched and spasmed.

He skidded along the ground, his back plowing through some of the spot fires and getting cut up by protruding rocks.

Still conscious somehow, he tried to stand, but the entire world had gone completely sideways. *Must've done somethin' to my equilibrium.* The thoughts came sluggishly, and he finally dragged himself to his feet. The barn, the wooden one, was right there. He stumbled towards it drunkenly, falling twice before locking himself inside.

Gutteral howls—more like animal sounds than German—echoed outside.

There was a burst of static inside his ear that made him wince. Then: "*—think you got his attention.*"

John tried to keep walking, but his legs refused to carry him anymore. The world spun again, and he slumped to the floor hard.

"*You really gonna let him talk about your mother like that? I'm pretty sure she didn't service Croatian troops . . . at least not in that capacity.*" Her tone changed. "*JM. Johnny! Talk to me! Come on, snap out of it! Get moving! He's still up, and he's still coming! If you don't get back in the game, he's gonna squash you like a cockroach!*"

John didn't have any strength left to bother answering Vickie; he barely had enough to roll onto his back. The door that he'd locked on the barn exploded inwards; Ubermensch stepped through, looking as furious as ever. He was also bleeding from the ears and nose; a side effect from his gizmo going berserk, probably.

"*Dammit, Johnny, talk to me! Zhar-ptica is about five minutes out!*"

Ubermensch looked down at him, and smiled. "*Amerikan schweinhund.* You have no stamina. Now you are a dead man." The Thulian lifted one of his armored boots, savoring the moment before he crushed the life out of John.

Despite feeling like he'd dug his way out of hell with a spork—a plastic spork at that—the adrenaline running through his system and his enhancements allowed him to see things happening in "stretched time."

This gave him enough time to remember Perun, and that battle in Atlanta. The old man shouting as he used his powers to save his teammates, his comrades. It was the first time that John had met the man, and the first time he had fought Ubermensch. At this exact moment, the two incidences seemed identical for some reason. John's mental barriers fell, and his fire welled up inside of him until it shot forth, his arms reaching out almost of their own accord, as if to embrace a loved one. The beam was gigantic, encompassing Ubermensch's huge body. It blasted through the roof of the barn, shining through the darkening sky like a demonic spotlight. John's mind, still operating somehow, idly worried about whether some unlucky flock of birds or an airliner might be in the way.

The beam shut off unexpectedly, leaving John gasping. The barn was completely ablaze now; the neat hole cut into the roof had quickly caught, and with the cotton lint and dust everywhere, and the aged, dry wood, the building was basically tinder waiting for a spark.

John summoned more strength, willing more than commanding his limbs to do his bidding. Slowly, he rolled onto his belly. His arms came up in front of his face, and he pushed himself off the ground and onto his knees. Gasping for breath, he came up into a kneel, turning painfully to look where Ubermensch had been.

The Thulian was lying on his back, groaning weakly. The elaborate set of armor had been mostly blasted off; what was left had melted unevenly to his hide. A glob had cooled over his eyes, blinding him at least temporarily.

Finish it.

John stood over Ubermensch, their positions from seconds before reversed. He hated Ubermensch, hated everything that the man and his fellows stood for. The Thulians were malignant, an infectious sort of evil and alien. The hate rose like lava inside him, flowing through him and powering him just as much as his blood did for his enhancements. It felt as hot as the fires raging around them, seemed to take life and strength from the blaze. John felt the sweat mixing with his blood, the ashes, and the dirt. When he'd killed before, it'd often been impersonal, necessary—and that meant different things depending on the situation.

This was something he wanted. He wanted to destroy this man, this travesty of a human, this monster, utterly. To wipe him clean from the world and leave no mark of his passing. The fires came back to John; his restraint was not there, because he didn't want it to be. No familiar twinge of pain. The fires boiled through him, ready to be loosed and to do their work—

—and then they died. John felt as if he was suddenly plunged into darkness, into the depths of an Arctic ocean, as if he was sinking into it forever. With a strangled gasp, he fell backwards, helpless and powerless. Vaguely, he saw Ubermensch's aide, the woman from the car, running to help carry the Thulian away. He felt arms encircling him soon after, hooking under his own and dragging him. Everything was burning; the barn, the ground, the stars were even blazing. The world was wreathed in fire for John.

Someone . . . a voice he knew . . . was yelling in Russian in his ear. Vickie responded in the same language. He heard his name, but couldn't seem to make his mouth work. He was just . . . tired. So tired. It seemed a good time to sleep.

"We are havink problem."

Red Saviour sat on the edge of her desk, arms folded, looking down at John. Untermensch leaned against the wall behind her, arms similarly folded.

John had been through some dress-downs in the past, and this debriefing was sure feeling like it would shape up to be an epic one.

"Problem is being, Comrade Murdock, that you were to be landing at different airport altogether from your destination, and were rerouted."

It was Untermensch's turn. "So how is it that the *fashista* swine are meeting you when you land?"

"Permission to speak?" John kept his tone neutral and respectful.

Saviour nodded. "Do not be thinking is little recluse magician. She is never leaving apartment except for physical training and did not know any sooner than you."

"Naw, Vic's straight. But still, somebody somewhere fu—er, messed this one up. They had that joint set up proper, with Ubermensch running the show."

"As in trap?" Untermensch's eyes narrowed.

"Sure felt like one. Reb stooge for a hostage, cars an' guards waiting. The fact that the location was one that we were already gonna check out due to new intel, an' the fact that the entire site was scrubbed of anythin' useful 'cept for bodies before I got there . . . it all seems to point towards a trap."

"Hrrrmm." Saviour considered this. "So . . . not so much that you were intercepted, but that we were lured there from beginning?"

"Y'all tell me. Where'd the intel come from? The warehouse my team hit, but it got passed through Marconi an' Tesla. I'd start from there, see what they've gotta say 'bout this. See if it was properly vetted." He shifted uncomfortably. He was still extremely sore from the fight; Jadwiga had initially patched him up when he came into HQ, and given him enough stims and painkillers to allow him to get through the debriefing and remain clear-headed.

Saviour nodded again. "That is being our job. Yours is to be telling us everything, from beginning. You land at airport. *Da*?"

"Roger that, Commissar." John went through all of the details, from landing, the Thulian flunky contacting him, the ride and the fun that entailed, all the way through to the fight and his collapse. The last part troubled him; he was definitely not in fighting trim. Despite that uneasiness, he didn't hold back any pertinent information.

Saviour and Unter, for all their faults, were good strategists. And once they had made up their minds that the "fault," if fault there was, lay elsewhere, the debriefing evolved into only that. But it was intense. And detailed. They questioned his reasoning behind every move he had made. Why had he not kept Vickie more informed? Why had he broken the guard's arm? Why had he not fled?

It wasn't any worse than he had expected; and that was good. They needed this information to figure out where things could be improved in the future. The Thulians were definitely playing the game in a new way, and everyone had to try to stay a step ahead of them. The world couldn't afford to react to another Invasion.

Unter tapped his finger on his chin when John was done. "One thing I fail to see. This . . . does not fit the pattern. It is not Blitzkrieg. It is also not infiltration. It is not selective assassination. Why is it like . . . a personal challenge? Armies do not send challengers."

"Permission to speak freely?"

"*Da, da.*" Unter waved at him,

"Y'got it nailed already, Georgi. This 'Ubermensch' has a hard-on for me." John shrugged. "He was pissed off from when we first saw him here in Atlanta. Got angrier the more I taunted him. An' he finally snapped when I mentioned the Commissar."

"*Borzhe moi.* This is making no sense—" Saviour began. But Georgi interrupted her.

"Is making *old* sense, Natalya. Is like first days of Great War, when metas dueled while armies fought below or around them, like idiot knights. Is exactly like old days. You think in logic. This has no logic." Georgi rubbed his temples. "Be asking your father, or Boryets. Ask them what it felt like." He turned his attention back to John. "Would you say, *obsessed,* Comrade Murdock?"

"I would, comrade. I wouldn't go s'far as to say it was like a couple of gladiators; I'm not that grandiose. But he certainly wanted to make a moment of separatin' my head from my shoulders."

"Could to be weakness we can exploit."

John nodded. Live bait was always the best sort of bait. If they could take advantage of Ubermensch's seeming incomprehensible desire to defeat John—because the Commissar was too important, in the scheme of things—then they might be able to take him down for good. Ubermensch was a big name for the Thulians, back in the "Great Patriotic War." Good things could only come from his heir-apparent no longer being around to bolster their forces and their morale.

"We will be discussing this. You may go. I need not warn you not to be making gossip?" Saviour raised an eyebrow at him. John nodded, saluted, and turned on his heel to leave. The Commissar spoke just as he was in the doorway. "Oh, and you are to be going to Jadwiga directly. This business of power going with no warning . . . not good. You may still be suffering from injury."

"Will do, Commissar."

It seemed that the past year's theme was scars; John had been collecting new and interesting ones at a prodigious rate since the Kriegers had decided to try to burn down the world. Amazingly, things were holding together, if barely.

Still, despite the demonstrated resilience of the human spirit, the attack from the Thulians had left marks on everyone. Scars of the soul, the heart, the body.

Scars. That's what my life has boiled down to. John held up his left hand to examine it as he took another swig of beer from the perspiring bottle in his hand. The asymmetric lines covering his entire body save for his face were the only outward evidence—save for his tattoo—that he had been part of the Program. But even without the scars from the surgeries, he still bore its marks. Just like the people he was now helping to watch over.

"*You are melancholy.*" He should be used to the way Sera just *appeared* by now, but maybe the last twenty-four hours had made him jumpy. It's not every day that you almost get stomped into a puddle by a Nazi giant. She had alighted on the roof just in his blind spot. When he pivoted so fast he almost lost his balance, she was right there in his shadow, probably as close as she'd ever gotten to him. Well, except for that stolen kiss.

"Just thinkin' 'bout things a little too hard, Sera. Ain't nothin' that some rest won't cure."

"Rest, which you never allow yourself." She looked very alien tonight. There was nothing soft about her; she was all hard edges and fire. He got the peculiar feeling that something had happened. He didn't like it, but figured he'd let the issue lay for the moment.

"Ne'er any for the wicked, right?"

"There are many more wicked than you, who sleep well of a night." Definitely, she was angry. Not at him, but . . . angry.

"Yeah, well, there's more of them than there are of us, so I'm forced to pull the occasional double." He took another sip of his beer, thought for a moment, and decided to chance the question. "Y'already know my problems. What's on yer mind, Angel?"

"Frustration. It is a common human feeling, I am told." Abruptly, the fire dimmed, the hard edges softened. Her voice lost the otherworldly quality. "Therefore I should do better at controlling it. This half-and-half life, spirit and material . . . confuses me, at times. And you *should* rest. What happened?"

"I'll rest when I'm dead; ought to be plenty of time for it, then." He gazed off towards the city. "As for what happened, well, I got in a fight with a—"

John was interrupted when the door to the HQ's roof opened; it was Untermensch with a pack of cigarettes in his hand.

"Apologies, comrade. I did not mean to interrupt." He picked a quiet corner opposite from John and lit up. When John turned back to where Sera had been, he found the space empty.

"Catch y'later, Sera," he muttered under his breath.

CHAPTER TWENTY-THREE

Heaven Beside You

CODY MARTIN AND MERCEDES LACKEY

Only the Commissar and a few choice people—of whom I was one—knew that Fei Li had gone off the reservation.

None of us knew quite how far...

The General arrived at Verdigris' office at the appointed time, dressed in conservative business attire. The snake had recommended it after Shen Xue had started to turn heads and become the topic of gossip in reception. The General did not care for the opinions of lesser men; there was only one purpose that tied him to Dominic Verdigris, and that was the destruction of the Thulians at all cost. Still, if Verdigris believed that he would arouse less suspicion and garner less attention by dressing in such a deplorable fashion, he would suffer it. Though it did itch terribly compared to the silks from his homeland that he normally wore. Was there such a thing as a silk suit?

The General pushed through the double doors to Verdigris' office, striding toward his desk confidently. Khanjar was by his side, as always, and looking less than pleased to see him, as always.

"Thank you for gracing us with your presence, General. You're ever a vision for these poor eyes, especially in that lovely suit! Would you care for some tea, perhaps something stronger?" He gestured towards an amply stocked bar to the left of the desk, all of the libations in tasteful crystal decanters. Perception and what it accomplished meant a lot to this fiend.

"What do you require of me now, brute?" The General was in

no mood for pleasantries. Normally, he encouraged formality and passing time with honored persons before getting to the heart of whatever matter was at hand. But Verdigris was no honored person to him.

Verdigris sighed theatrically. "Straight to business as usual, I see. If nothing else, you are admirably consistent, General. Which is precisely why I need you for this next task. In fact, it's safe to say that it is the reason why I brought you into our little cabal." He gestured to a chair in front of the desk. "Please, take a seat while I brief you on your latest target." The General did as asked, crossing his legs demurely and waiting with restrained impatience. He always felt as if he needed a bath after dealing with this man. A screen rose from the edge of the desk, oriented towards him and began following his sight line.

"We've identified a particular metahuman that we believe is of vital importance to the war effort. At first it was thought that there were a group of metahumans with similar powers operating in concert during the Invasion, thwarting some of the Krieger forces. Since that time we've revised that hypothesis in favor of one singularly powerful metahuman. In addition to the obvious abilities demonstrated in these videos," he paused momentarily as scenes of a single fiery entity in different locales was shown decimating entire groups of Thulians single-handedly, with swords and spears of fire along with its bare hands, "we also have a strong reason to suspect that this metahuman is precognitive, in a way that is unmatched by those metahumans so far known to have that sort of power." He spread his hands wide. "It's obvious how that last bit there could be of tremendous use to us; anticipating the Kriegers with one hundred percent accuracy, knowing where and when to strike at them . . . it could help finish the war in a week. Overnight, even."

The General's interest was honestly piqued, now. To know the outcomes of battles before they happened, to see the moves and countermoves of an enemy perfectly . . . it was every battle commander's dream. He turned his eyes to look into Verdigris'. "If this being is able to see the future, will it not be able to see me coming and destroy me?"

"Aren't you supposed to have some sort of 'celestial' abilities yourself?" he countered, and sat back with folded arms. "This would be the time for you to prove that." The General knew that he didn't believe in magic; he always saw it as "science through unknown means," whatever that meant. The General knew better. There were eldritch forces that moved the world, for good or for ill, with a power that few understood. The General's being and blade were proof of that.

"I will find this being, and bring it into my service."

"Surely you mean *our* service, my dear?" The snake kept the same bemused smile on his face, but his eyes had changed ever so subtly. Shen Xue could almost hear the cogs and wheels working behind those cold green eyes of his.

"Of course. I misspoke."

Verdigris bored into Shen Xue with a stare for half of a heartbeat before he rocked back in his chair, the cold look in his eyes gone once more. "Good. You'll have all of the resources you need at your disposal for this task. It means that much to all of us, to the war effort, General. Once we have this 'Seraphym' in our custody, we can find out what it can really do, and force it to operate in our favor instead of at its own whim." He retrieved a large manila folder from a drawer in his desk, pushing it towards the General. "Everything else you need to know is in there."

The General stood from his seat after grabbing the folder. "Understood." *The Seraphym? Hmm.* There had been one appearance of the creature by that name at the door of the CCCP HQ; Shen Xue's entire being had rung like a bell in the proximity of its presence. Verdigris was a fool. The creature was far more powerful than he guessed.

But perhaps a wise fool. No matter how powerful this creature was, no matter what magic formed the foundation of its powers, Shen Xue carried Jade Emperor's Whisper, the sword formed for the Jade Emperor Himself, and even the most powerful magician in the world trembled before the might of the Supreme Ruler of Heaven's power.

Perhaps it is time to channel some of that power to a purpose. Shen Xue paused in an empty corridor and "pulled" Jade Emperor's Whisper from the place in reality where it rested in the times he had no need of it. He directed his will at it. *We must have this creature, the continuation of the world may require it,* he told it sternly. *You will hide me from it.* He felt the sword's assent. The sword was more than a simple tool to beat things into submission; it was an entity almost on its own, with moods and wishes that needed to be appeased. Satisfied, he put it "back" and continued on his way. Time to find a quiet place to study the information Verdigris had provided; after all, there was the off chance that it might prove to be worth something.

And more than time to get out of this damned *suit* and all the hellish feminine contraptions that went with it. It was days like these that Shen Xue wished fervently for a return to ancient China. *Perhaps we can make what was ancient new again... one day.*

The moment was too important for the Seraphym to chance interruption. So, no going to her perch among the arches and pillars of her rooftop lookout, nor the top of John Murdock's building. The best place to sit and sift through the threads of the futures was the old, mostly deserted cemetery. It was a weekday, the caretaker was taking his nap, there were never any visitors during the week, and this was a spot where there were no living left to visit the dead. In fact, if she chose—and she did—she could create the illusion that she was just one more angel statue among the many, one kneeling with downcast eyes and folded hands. It was one of the least involved illusions she could invoke in the minds of those around her. She simply willed it, and it was so.

As she concentrated, the threads of the future played out in front of her, flooding her mind with possibility.

The Djinni had accepted responsibility. He had sacrificed his own self-interest for the sake of the greater good. He had accepted that his future would be subject to pain, loneliness... but that this would all mean something profoundly important to the outcome of the war. This had taken him out of the realm of those who did not matter against the Thulians, and put him in the ranks of those who did. He was a new, brighter thread added to the tapestry, and he must be sorted into it.

Bella had found her rock in the form of the aptly named Bulwark. She would cease to need Sera and could continue her growth on her own. Bulwark would keep her steady, and become part of her moral and ethical compass. That must be sorted. And if she had to make a terrible and morally ambiguous decision, she had someone to steer her back from it. That greatly changed the patterns.

And... John Murdock. That... situation... both excited her and made her uneasy. It grew more personal with every encounter.

And she was supposed, or so she thought, to remain impersonal. But the Infinite had registered no disapproval of this. In fact, the Infinite appeared to register tacit approval. And certainly, as the bond between them grew more familiar, Murdock pulled back from his former distance from the rest of humanity and joined more fully into life around him, became more committed, made more connections. Each time he did, it changed the futures, ever so slightly, for the better.

And yet... this was so dangerous. It opened her in ways she didn't understand, to emotions... the Siblings did not experience emotion directly, only indirectly, through the memories and experiences of mortals. This was new, and a new thing such as this, after her long, long life... was unprecedented.

But she shook her head to clear it of the thought of John Murdock. This was not the time for such thoughts, for there was another subject of more urgency than that. Ramona Ferrari was on a collision course with Verdigris, and there were many ways that this could end. This, at the moment, was one of the sections of the futures that most concerned the Seraphym, for the threads here were terribly, terribly tangled. The Seraphym bent her mind to them, concentrating on these things to the exclusion of all else. Even *looking* at them changed them, or had the potential to change them. This was a critical juncture.

Her concentration was interrupted by a lithe figure dressed in red and black silk sliding over the outer wall of the cemetery, silent and graceful as a cat. The figure regarded her coolly, her face serene and her eyes calculating. Sera recognized the figure, of course. The shell was Red Saviour's oldest friend, Fei Li, otherwise known as People's Blade. But there were two inside the shell. Fei Li herself was sleeping, encysted, refusing to come out into a world that had turned so unrecognizable, and kept enclosed by the dominant entity—the one now in total control of the shell. That was the great General Shen Xue, a most ancient soul, who had, until the reversal, resided in the equally ancient sword Jade Emperor's Whisper, to which his immortal soul had been confined for crimes of monumental cruelty and hubris. He had, until Fei Li's moment of crisis, been content to expiate those crimes by serving as Fei Li's mentor in all things martial.

Not anymore, it seemed. Fei Li's fall had become Shen Xue's window into the modern world, with a new body.

"*You are not as hard to find as I would have thought, sorceress.*" Shen Xue spoke quietly, but never took her eyes off of Sera.

"*Seek, and ye shall find,*" the Seraphym replied dryly, speaking in perfectly accented, and quite ancient, Qin. But it was strange that until this moment, she had not been aware of the General's presence . . .

Hmm. Now this was odd. Shen Xue was "absent" from the futures—like John Murdock, he was a blankness, but it was not the same *sort* of blankness. This was not caused by the Infinite. John Murdock was a blank, but his life intersected with virtually all of those who were important to the futures—Bella, Victrix, Red Saviour, even the Djinni, Bulwark, Ramona, and those with whom he had no obvious direct connection. Even Verdigris. Shen Xue intersected only with those who were important, but . . . dangerous. Unethical. Even sociopathic.

What could that mean?

Shen Xue paused mid-stride for a moment before she continued, weaving through the gravestones and circling Sera. "You have something I need," she continued in slightly accented English. "Something that the world needs. Will you give this thing to me? Or will I have to take it?" She stopped in front of Sera, her hands folded behind her back. Shen Xue cocked her head to the side, waiting for a response.

"It depends entirely on what you believe that I 'have,'" the Seraphym replied. "Considering that I own no possessions."

Shen Xue moved her left hand in front of her face, waggling a finger back and forth. "No. We own many things, beyond the material. Our minds, our thoughts, and our . . . abilities. No one can lay claim to a swordmaker's skill, though they can bend it to their will. No one can own an athlete's prowess, but they can persuade him to compete for the glory of a nation." She leaned forward slightly, canting her head towards Sera. "No one can own the future . . . but you."

"I do not own the future. That is in the hands of mortals." The Seraphym shook her head. "You labor beneath a misapprehension. It is not permitted that I direct the futures as a general directs his armies."

"I do not need you to steer the course of history, sorceress. I can do that perfectly well, for I *am* a general. I simply need you to tell me where and when to best swing my sword to defeat the Thulians and . . . other threats." Shen Xue regarded a gravestone in front of her, running a finger softly over it before looking back to Sera.

The Seraphym smiled sadly. "You do not require me for that. Find the source of the Thulians' power, and remove it."

"You mistake me. I am not asking for your permission. A good general marshals all of his assets and strengths before battle. You will come into my service. This is the nature of things."

So that was the way the wind blew. "It is not permitted," the Seraphym said steadily. "I already serve another."

Shen Xue sighed heavily, looking down at the grave dirt beneath her feet. "We all serve many masters, sorceress. Of our choosing, and others through necessity."

"Not I," the Seraphym replied. "I serve only the Infinite. You are not the first to want me as a servant. You must go on wanting."

Shen Xue looked up sharply from the ground. "So." Without another word, she charged Sera, sprinting as fast as a top Olympic athlete. The General, seemingly from nowhere, pulled Jade Emperor's Whisper from behind her back, leveling it at Sera.

But the Seraphym, old in battle, was not taken by surprise. Her own fiery blade sprang to life in her hand as her fires blazed up around her. She moved as lithe as flame, stepping lightly aside and parrying Jade Emperor's Whisper in a way that left the General unbalanced for a moment. The General quickly spun around, bringing her sword up in a one-handed grip, circling with Sera.

"The wise man does not shout defiance into the tempest," said the Seraphym, "but accepts the inevitable with grace." She followed the General's movements without seeming to. Shen Xue now discovered that facing a creature who had no pupils to her eyes was disconcerting. It was not possible to read such blankness; an opponent's eyes were usually telling of many things. Not so with this one. Shen Xue continued with her flurry, launching attacks high and low, each of which was countered with what seemed thoughtless grace. "Does the butterfly spar with the dragon? Does the wren seek to drive the eagle from her nest to claim it? What is it that you can possibly expect to get from me?"

Shen Xue lunged with her sword, aiming for Sera's throat. "One must persevere to accomplish impossible tasks." She followed with another barrage of strikes, ducking and weaving and even leaping off of gravestones in almost impossible but perfect acrobatic moves, only to be perfectly countered each time.

"Why not put the same effort into pursuing the Thulians?" the Seraphym asked. "Others are doing the same. You could accomplish far more. As I told you: find the head of this serpent and strike it off."

"Half measures," Shen Xue grunted as she readied her sword again, "will never win wars. Others are not willing to do what needs to be done. Few are. With you at my side, I will be able to do what is necessary to defeat the Thulians, and all other threats." She renewed her assault, with cuts coming from as many angles as she could manage, faster than probably any mortal swordsman alive.

And for the first time in her unnumbered millennia, Seraphym's sword of flame had not instantly destroyed a mortal weapon. She Looked at the sword that Shen Xue wielded, and instantly knew why. Because it was *not* a mortal weapon. Improbably enough, Jade Emperor's Whisper was not forged by mortal hands, but by the hands of those who were, if not Siblings, certainly not subject to the same limitations as mortals.

"And how would you know I was telling you the truth and not something designed to send you to your death?" she replied, serenely, although . . . beneath, she was anything but serene. She was afraid. Something was going on, far from here. She sensed that in this same moment as her battle with the General, John Murdock faced an equal enemy for, perhaps, the first time in his life. He was hurt. He was in danger. She had not foreseen this, and she could not be *there* and *here.* Yet she could not leave *here* to come to his aid while the situation with Shen Xue was so uncertain.

And suddenly, out of nowhere, as if her momentary thought of him had pulled all her intention towards John Murdock, she felt his powers falter, and the earth became unsteady beneath *her* feet. Her thoughts went blank for a fraction of a second.

Shen Xue seized upon the moment. The flow of her attack abruptly changed, and she sliced downwards viciously, scoring Sera's left wing, as Sera belatedly reacted and pulled it partly out of reach.

As with the attacks by the Thulians that had touched her, the key was that she did not allow the pain to matter. But it was agony, and whiter, blinding flame followed the line of Jade Emperor's Whisper down the inner face of her wing. Even Shen

Xue shaded his eyes and flinched from the light for a moment, as the Seraphym's true nature showed through the cut.

She healed it without a thought. But it took more time to heal than the wounds caused by the titanic mortal weapons of the Thulians, things that disintegrated mere matter in a nanosecond. Jade Emperor's Whisper could *hurt* her.

Time to finish this.

She went on the offensive for the first time, her sword engaging with Jade Emperor's Whisper and binding it. "*Enough*," she said, allowing a touch of anger into her voice. "This has gone far enough, and I have wasted enough time here." She sensed the celestial blade recoiling from her own, and from her anger. With a flick of the wrist, she wrested Shen Xue's sword from the General's grip and sent it flying into the shaggy, unkempt bushes. "Trouble me no more with your concerns. I have told you I serve only the Infinite. You are a tactician. Find another solution to your problems."

And with that, she turned her back contemptuously, and flew off.

Shen Xue could only stare for a few moments, breathless. It had been the hardest battle he had ever fought, and one of the few without clear victory. Pausing for a few moments to reflect on the fight, he collected his sword, replacing it in the "nowhere" place between space and time, and left the cemetery.

This task would require quite a different approach.

Verdigris was trying desperately to clear his head. Things could have been going better as far as his plans went, but a day at the track always seemed to set him to rights. Through a few minor called-in favors and discreet words, he had gained the opportunity to test-drive the new prototype Bugatti Veyron Super Sport, earlier than most. It wasn't even a full production car yet, just a camera-ready test mule, primped and prettied for the reviewers later this month. That didn't stop him from putting it through its paces; Dominic was an expert driver, and loved nothing more than to take one of the supercars from his garage or an experimental design that he'd come up with out on the track.

Usually that was good for clearing out the cobwebs. These beasts, with their twitchy handling and crazy speeds, required an enormous amount of his own attention. After he finished thoroughly wringing the car out at close to its maximum performance for an hour and a half, he pulled into the pit station near the starting line. A crew of mechanics and technicians ran over immediately, wasting only a few moments to shower him with praises for his performance before they began to inspect and do a teardown on critical components for the Bugatti. Behind the barrier for the entrance to the track Shen Xue was standing, arms crossed. Verdigris smiled broadly as he walked towards her, peeling off his racing suit. "Fascinating machine, isn't it?"

"A diversion for those that should be spending their time on more pertinent pursuits, brute."

"Too much work and no play isn't good for the mind or the body, General." He picked up a water bottle emblazoned with the Echo logo off of a nearby table, taking a swig from it. "So, what news do you have? Made any progress with our recaltricant friend with the wings?"

"It depends on what you would refer to as progress." Shen Xue steepled her fingers. "I am certain of what she is now, regardless of your stubborn disbelief. It will require an extraordinary effort and some extraordinary equipment to capture her, but I believe it can be done."

Verdigris frowned. "Tell me that you don't honestly believe that she's an angel." He toweled his face off with a terry cloth hand towel that had Blacksnake's crest sewn onto it. He sighed heavily. "I took you for a more rational individual, General."

"What you take for rationality, I take for stubborn refusal to accept what is fact," Shen told him with undisguised contempt. "She is celestial in origin. As is my..." She shook her head. "Never mind. The point is, your insistence on referring to a spade as a hammer does not make it suited to drive nails."

"What a quaint little saying. Whatever. I care about results, General, the same as you; it's why you're in my employ, after all." He set down the towel before leveling her with a stare. "Can you deliver, or should I find someone else that can?"

"That will depend on your ability to acquire the tools I will need." The General narrowed her eyes. "They are precise, they are absolutely required, and they must be exactly what I ask for. No substitutes will do."

He waved his hand, smiling again. "Of course. Money is no object where this project is concerned, General. That just leaves one final question."

"Which is?" Shen Xue looked suddenly wary for a moment.

"Do you take cash, or will a check do?"

John was on the roof of the building that held his private space. He called it a "squat," presumably because he was squatting there without permission. Their conversation had been interrupted on the roof of the CCCP headquarters, and Sera was anxious to resume it.

"Anxious." That was new for her. Like so many other emotions. She had never suffered anxiety before. It was as if mortal emotions were infectious, a virus she could somehow contract. Anxiety . . . fear . . .

There had been a moment of fear when Shen Xue had hurt her. Pain, she was used to, at least in the form of the all-obliterating weapons that the Thulians used. She was fully prepared for pain, secure in the knowledge that she could renew herself as fast as they could tear at her.

But what Jade Emperor's Whisper had done had not been so easy to remedy. The sword had the potential to cripple her in a way not even the Thulian weapons did. Of course, all she needed to do was be *aware* of that, and take steps accordingly, but . . . she had not known such a thing was even possible until now, and that made her afraid, if only momentarily.

John saw her coming, as she intended. He waved; she took that as invitation and touched down.

"Welcome back, Sera. Thought my sturdy Russian comrades might've scared you off for good last time."

She smiled a little at that. "I am not sure that Untermensch would even be able to see me. Best he not see you speaking to the empty air." She spoke aloud, carefully confining her "voice" to ears alone. She knew that John preferred that as opposed to mental communication.

"He'd probably just think that I'd been hanging around Ol' Man Bear too much; finally driven me nuts." He took a drink from a bottle of beer that he had been holding. By the way he moved, she could tell that he had been injured recently; but it was not those injuries that had caused her to falter. Something more had happened to him, and somehow, she had *felt* it, and that had taken her attention from her own battle, making it possible for Jade Emperor's Whisper to strike her.

"You are hurt," she said with concern.

He waved his hand dismissively. "I'll heal up; been hurt a lot worse than this before." He turned to face her, resting his elbows against the edge of the roof's wall. "Somethin' was buggin' you the last time we spoke." John gauged her for a moment. "It still is, isn't it?"

"What happened, when you fought?" she asked. She didn't ask who it was, that was irrelevant. She hesitated, then confessed, "Something happened. I think what happened to you was the cause."

He looked puzzled. "I don't understand. Me getting hurt? That affected you somehow?"

"It was more than your injuries. Something else happened." Her eyes flared with light. "Please, what was it? I—we are connected somehow, John. I do not know why . . ." But her voice trailed off, because she suspected, even if she did not know for certain.

John sighed, obviously reluctant. "I didn't wanna worry you. Back on the last op, I ran into someone. Well, more like I bumbled my way into a trap. It was set up by Ubermensch, one of the Kriegers' heavy hitters. He apparently doesn't like the cut of my jib, or something; he's keen to see me turned into a smear on the ground." He took another pull of beer before he continued. "Despite it being a decently laid-out trap, I was able to get the better of 'im. I had the murderin' bastard on the ground, and I was gonna finish him . . . but I couldn't. It was like all the energy ran out of me in an instant." He looked into her eyes, plainly concerned. "The fires died instantly; it was like I had run outta steam."

"I felt that," she said, slowly. "I do not know what it means. But I felt that. And People's Blade saw me falter and cut me—"

She had not meant to say that aloud but it was too late to call it back.

John set down his beer. "Wait, hold up. Fei Li *attacked* you?"

She nodded. "I think . . . wait, let me sort." She sifted through immediate future and past. "It seems," she said bleakly, "that Fei Li has thrown in with Verdigris. And although he *is* head of Echo . . . I do not understand why she would attack me."

"Go on." She could almost feel the cold anger emanating off of John. His friends, his comrades, and he himself had been betrayed. But that was only a small part of it, she thought.

"Why... why are you so angry?" she asked.

His demeanor changed instantly, as if he had been snapped out of a trance. "I'm sorry. Fei Li's gone back on every promise she's made to the CCCP. Nat's gonna be pissed—though I'm a little fuzzy on the details of how I'm gonna break this news to her." He looked down at his feet for a moment. "If y'wanna know the truth of it, though, I'm furious that she hurt you. I didn't even think that such a thing was possible, given how powerful y'are." He let the implied question hang there.

"It is the sword," she told him. "It was created by a celestial being. It would not matter if I did not take physical manifestation, but... such things can hurt me." She felt vexed all over that she had *allowed it.* "But only if I am careless. I will not be again."

John shook his head. "You won't have to worry 'bout her anymore. I'll make sure it gets handled; she's one of ours. We'll bring her in." He was adamant in his conviction about this; Sera knew that he wouldn't stop until People's Blade was stopped. But did he realize how much of an adversary she would prove to be?

"She is very powerful," Sera began to warn him, with a little reluctance. How *much* to warn him about? Should she tell him that Fei Li was no longer the controlling entity, that Shen Xue had taken over completely?

"I'm no pushover, darlin'. If I can take the likes of that windbag Ubermensch, I think I'll be all right with Fei Li."

She was distracted by his phrasing. "The Red Djinni called me darlin'... and now you. Why is that? Does it have a meaning I do not know?" Her brows furrowed. "I hope it does not mean 'do not worry your pretty little head'... I do not care for that."

"That crook called you that, too, huh?" John seemed to bristle slightly. "I know you can take care of yourself; you're too smart for me t'say 'do not worry your pretty little head,' nevermind the fact that it is pretty. I'm just sayin' that you've got help." He grinned lopsidedly.

"It... seems strange... to have help that is not one of the Siblings," she said, blinking. "I should beware of pride. It does go before a fall. I am not the Infinite," she added, reminding herself. Then she smiled shyly. "Thank you."

He shrugged casually. "Ain't nothin', Sera. You'd do it for me just the same, right?"

She nodded, seriously, adamantly. "I would. I have." Again,

something that just slipped out before she realized it. This speaking aloud was treacherous!

John cocked his head to the side, his grin turning mischievous. "I was just teasin' a little. But, now that we're talkin' 'bout it—what did you mean by 'I have'?"

"The night when you came to CCCP," she replied, hesitantly, compelled to speech because she was, by her nature, compelled to the truth. "There was a sniper. He... was startled by what I said to him, and fell. There have been other times..." Perhaps best to leave it at that.

"Huh. So I really do have a guardian angel." He smiled genuinely, not one of his guarded smiles—she had been learning the difference as of late. "Good to know."

"Well... you must take more care," she admonished. "So that I do not have to. No more permitting yourself to be lured into traps, please." She was trying to make a joke, as she had with the Djinni.

John chuckled, then offered a mock salute. "Affirmative, Commissar."

She laughed with delight, made him a little bow, and fanned her wings to take her upwards. She chose her favorite perch, the faux-Roman temple atop the high roof. She felt herself smiling. And wondering. All these emotions, these... feelings. She had not experienced them when she first became an Instrument. In fact, it had been some time before she had noticed them.

It seemed... she sorted through the past, dispassionately. "Yes," she said aloud. The pattern was there. The more she connected to John Murdock, the more she *felt*.

This was good in a mortal; connections were important. But was it good for *her?* She made herself still, and listened, but the Infinite did not answer. Neither *This is not permitted,* nor *This is permitted.*

Finally, she shrugged. Best to take a leaf from John Murdock's own book. "It is easier to beg forgiveness than ask permission."

After all, forgiveness was always possible.

CHAPTER TWENTY-FOUR

"Heart Like a Wheel"

CODY MARTIN AND MERCEDES LACKEY

Life was getting to be one uncontrolled tumble after another. Oh, I could put a good face on it, we all could, but...

Let's just say things had gotten so unpredictable that Mom called to tell me all of Department 39's seers had gone offline.

I sure as hell couldn't blame them.

After the throw-down in that abandoned farm, the CCCP HQ felt like a haven of peace and quiet. There was Bear yelling at the television, the familiar machinery noises out of the garage, even Unter marching through random rooms swearing under his breath seemed sane compared to the world outside. John had the feeling that even if the Kriegers descended again with five times the force they'd had before, Nat would just throw a commemorative ashtray at the door and mount up the troops as if it was nothing more than an annoyance. Things just seemed to be falling apart faster and faster, and sometimes it all made him wonder if, after all, he was babbling in a corner of an asylum somewhere and *all* of this was an hallucination.

In the day since the debrief, he'd been doing a lot of thinking. About the trap, Ubermensch, the Kriegers and the war, and more and more about Sera. The one thing that was troubling him the most was the information about Fei Li; how was he going to tell the Commissar? She would never believe the intel if he told her where it had come from; Sera wasn't exactly the sort of "person" that Natalya would consider reliable. The allegation that Fei Li had defected and thrown her lot in with Verdigris was chilling, to say the least; she knew everything there was to know about the CCCP's operation in Atlanta. If she wanted to, she could make things interesting for everyone at HQ, and not in a good way. He'd been doing his best to avoid the Commissar while he puzzled it out, but that plan shattered when she had Thea sent down to summon John to her office. *No avoidin' it now, I suppose.*

Still, he was a soldier at heart, and when he got an order, he obeyed it. Even though he really wanted to take a long stint at guarding a cot, or even go back to his squat for a piece, when Red Saviour called, he answered. He mustered to the Commissar's office when ordered to, in a "new" pair of worker's overalls. John knocked at the door, awaiting permission to enter.

"In." Saviour was nothing if not direct. "In" when you were allowed in the office, and crockery to the door when you weren't. Often it was an ashtray filled with cigarette butts; it was a good thing that the Russians were all metahuman, since about half of them smoked like chimneys and a normal human might very well be dead of cancer or emphysema by now if they had tried to keep up.

John walked in, stopped before reaching the desk, and came to attention. "Comrade Murdock, reporting as per instructions, Commissar."

For a moment, when she looked up and John saw the look in her eyes, he wondered if the crockery was going to get thrown at his head after all. "Have you noted the absence of People's Blade?" she asked darkly. This was not the direction he had anticipated the conversation going. His mind flashed for a moment to Sera.

"Fei Li? I have, Commissar. But it's not unusual for several of the comrades to be gone on different operations at any given time, so I hadn't given it much thought." The hairs stood up on the back of John's neck. Statements like that weren't simply given out unless there was something unpleasant attached to them. What should he tell her? Spill everything now, about Fei Li, Sera, and Verdigris?

"Fei Li is defected." The reply was so flat that only immense rage could be behind it. "To *svinya* Blacksnake."

John was silent for a few moments. *Well, that solves that problem. How to play this and toe the line?* "I was . . . unaware, Commissar." It wasn't *technically* a lie; he only knew that Fei Li had gone over to Verdigris. Nevermind that that slick bastard controlled Blacksnake. He decided that now was a good time to shut up; it wasn't his place to pry for more information, even though this meeting seemed to be somewhat more informal than he was used to with Natalya. She was disregarding some protocol, and her tone was... different. Something beyond the anger she was clearly feeling.

"To be exact," Natalya said between clenched teeth, "General Shen Xue believes we are not doing enough to ferret out the location and weaknesses of the Thulians. He is of the opinion that all means necessary should be used to track the *fashistas* to their center of power and eliminate them. When I suggested that laying waste to entire cities of workers, or engaging in total war, might be counterproductive, Fei Li vanished, leaving only a letter saying that Verdigris understood the concept of acceptable losses. I believe she does not know that *I* know Verdigris and Blacksnake are one. I am relieved we did not include her in Overwatch. Small favors."

John merely nodded. He had a feeling that this was going to get worse before it got better. Best to wait and see, and roll with the punches.

"I am assignink you to retrieve her. You are powerful enough to defeat, and if necessary, eliminate her." A spasm of grief and pain flashed across Saviour's features; John almost flinched, witnessing it. *So, that's what's behind the iron mask.* "I cannot think of anyone in CCCP, even Chug for all of his strength and resilience, who would be able to best her hand to hand. Not so long as she holds Jade Emperor's Whisper. But you can keep her at a distance. You are also a skilled tactician, when you are actually thinkink, and not actink like *nekulturny* John Wayne. You are excellent at covert operations. With sorceress, you are more than excellent. And you are not so attached to the comrades as any of my countrymen or long-term CCCP members. You should be able to remain... detached, and not let past relations get in way of what needs to be done."

John felt his stomach twisting tighter with each word that she spoke. He thought that he had been somewhat prepared for this, but it didn't make the situation any more palatable. "What're your conditions for conducting the operation? What're the parameters, Commissar?"

"You will persuade her back if you can, and neutralize her if you cannot." Saviour's eyes were now nearly black with barely restrained emotion. This was probably the most unsettled that John had ever seen her. "Absolutely neutralize her. Blue Girl is not being trust Verdigris so far as he can be thrown by infant. Neither do I. Maybe he wishes to end Krieger menace, but I am thinkink he is quite ready to throw us all under tractor to do so, as long as *he* is still drinkink champagne in bunker at the end. When Shen Xue was alive, he did not blink at ordering what would cause the deaths of hundreds of thousands. He will not hesitate now at actions that would kill billions."

He bit his tongue so hard that he could taste blood; it didn't show on his face aside from his jaw tightening almost imperceptibly. "Understood, Commissar. And what about Blacksnake personnel on-site, if there are any?"

"Your best judgment." She shrugged. "Lackeys are of no concern. It is Fei Li and Shen Xue that are dangerous."

"To review, my orders are to retrieve or . . . neutralize Comrade Fei Li, contain any Blacksnake personnel on-site, and procure any intelligence on-site once the primary objective is completed. Correct, Commissar?"

"*Da.*" The word was bitten off.

John was very uncomfortable with this entire damned mess. Fei Li was dangerous; to the CCCP, his comrades, and the war effort against the Thulians. With her on their side, she was a tremendous asset. With her gone over to Verdigris . . . she could very well sabotage everything they've worked towards while trying to accomplish her own goals. He'd wondered at the time why Saviour hadn't included her in the merry gang of conspirators; now he was just glad it hadn't happened. If Fei Li had known about them—about Overwatch—

He didn't relish the idea of having to fight one of their own, though, no matter how misguided she might have become; being able to rely on your team was something he had learned early when he was a soldier, and it had been reinforced through the years. Being ordered to reign in—and potentially kill—a one-time ally . . . it all tasted of the Program in a way that he absolutely hated.

Some of his doubts vanished when he began to think about Sera, and the danger that Fei Li posed to her. He had promised that he would keep Fei Li from hurting Sera again; this was official sanction to do so. It didn't mean he had to like it, however.

John must have allowed some of what he was thinking slip

out onto his face. "Murdock. Fei Li was my mentor. My *sestra.* There . . ." He could hear her teeth grind. "There is no one dearer to me. But Shen Xue . . . go to your Wikimedia. Look him up. He was—is—brilliant, a genius, and a monster. If he has decided that CCCP is of no more use to him and may be an obstacle to him, he will not hesitate, not even for a moment, at eliminating us. And Fei Li is party to all of our weaknesses and strengths. She is only not knowing of Overwatch, and of the—device."

And the CCCP, and the people associated with it, are important to the cause, from what Sera has hinted. "I understand, Commissar. Permission to speak freely?"

"It is not just CCCP, Murdock. He has decided that the Thulians must be destroyed, and he will allow nothing to interfere with that. If someone, or something, holds what he believes to be a key, he will *have* that key, by whatever means it requires." She smoldered a moment, then waved at him. "Permission."

"I don't like this. Y'know my background, and this is an aspect that I'm uncomfortable with. But I realize the necessity, the dire urgency . . . and I'll carry out your orders." He believed what he was saying, fully; it all made sense. But that didn't stop his words from tasting like ash in his mouth.

"I would do it myself. I had rather do it myself." Her shoulders sagged. "I have not a chance of a butterfly against an eagle against Shen Xue and that sword. You are not only the best hope, you are the only unhandicapped hope. Shen Xue has not seen you fight as much, or worked beside you for years. You are unknown to him." She shook her head. "Further questions?"

"Only one, Commissar. When do I ship out?"

Her lips thinned into a hard line. "Now. Verdigris is here. So probably is Fei Li. Be going to sorceress. Likely she can find both."

Victoria Victrix lived in a five-story brick apartment building in a blue collar area of Atlanta. There wasn't much of anything here that was newer than the fifties. The elevator was so old it had a brass grille you pulled back after the door closed, and it creaked and wheezed its way up to the top floor. The hall carpet was so worn you could see the warp threads, the lighting had to be twenty-watt bulbs at best, and at intervals along the wall were things John guessed had to be old gaslight fixtures. But it was clean, and in fairly good repair.

He knocked on her door, checking the hallway again as he did so.

There was a long pause. Then the sound of one lock after another being unlatched. Finally, after the fifth one, the door opened.

"Afternoon, Harvey. How's kicks?" John hooked his thumbs in his belt, trying to look casual. Truth be told, he was still on edge from his meeting with the Commissar.

Vickie didn't look as if she felt any easier than he did. "Saviour said she was sending you over. I said I don't see people. She said I was seeing you."

He held up a manila folder. "I've got an op; this is all of the particulars. It's something she didn't want sent through the usual channels, and I figured it'd be best to review it with ya in person, anyways. I've already read it." He cocked his head to the side, offering her a lopsided grin. "Mind if I come in? Unless you're cool with the whole building knowin' 'bout super-secret spy shit."

She scuttled out of the way so he could come inside, then threw five of the locks. John noticed out of the corner of his eye that there were ten on the door. The apartment was—cozy was the only appropriate word for it. There was the faint smell of cinnamon and vanilla in the air, the lighting was dim but not uncomfortably so, it was wall-to-wall books and music, the furniture was all . . . soft.

There was a cat. The biggest cat that John had ever seen, outside of zoos, but not because it was fat. A huge gray thing. It was looking him up and down as if he was being sized up for an interview. Or just possibly a meal. He hadn't known that she had a cat.

Vickie sidled past him and saw where he was looking. "Oh. That's Grey. He owns me. He allows me to buy him cat food and provide him with an apartment. And Internet. And cable." She said this as if the cat really was actually using the latter two. Then again, maybe it was.

"Huh. I'm more of a dog person, to be honest." When John spoke, she seemed to shrink into herself. She was definitely a different person from the one that John had spent hours with over a radio connection; the confidence wasn't there, in person. "So, y'wanna get started?" He held out the envelope for her.

She took it, gingerly, in gloved hands, then took a seat as far away from him as was physically possible, while still allowing them both to review the operational material. He noticed then that she was completely covered from the neck down, with almost less skin showing than a devout Muslim woman in a burka. *There's a lot more to this witch than meets the eye.* He instinctively wanted to poke and pry for more information, but his gut also told him that he'd be overstepping some serious boundaries in doing so. And he couldn't have his Overwatch operator seizing up and not trusting him, so he let it rest for the moment.

She went through the papers, quickly developing a fierce frown. "This isn't good," she muttered several times. And when she finished, she looked up at him with the expression of a stone. "This is seriously FUBAR."

He leaned against a wall, his arms crossed in front of him. "I know. And I told Nat as much, personally. But it just might be necessary, too. Got any other morons lining up that can pull it off? Better question: any that can do it without getting a lot of people killed?"

She clutched the papers, which trembled in her hands. "That sword... you know what that thing is? I mean... okay, magically speaking, most of the rest of the world is Steam Age and that's like a Jedi Lightsaber."

"So, are you saying I'm dead and I don't know it yet?" She was the expert here. The number of magicians available to Echo was still low; having one as strong and knowledgeable as Vickie was a major plus.

"No... no, the Commissar is right. Since you're a distance kinda guy, you have the best chance against her of anyone that *can* get pulled in. Can't call in any of our crew that's in Echo; Verd'll find out in a heartbeat. Especially since Fei Li is an OpThree, and there aren't a lot of those floating around. Wouldn't surprise me if he had the OpTwos and Threes tagged and watched twenty-four, seven. So anyone we rope in to deal with her is going to show up on the radar on the instant." She ran her hand nervously through her short hair.

"Concerning the particulars, I think it's doable. I drew up a basic operations order, that I'll need your help reviewing and tweaking. We can get to that in a minute. What's more... do you think that this is a justifiable mission?" John had mostly reconciled the necessity of this task with himself. He needed her to be okay with this. If she wasn't, he couldn't do his job. Or at least not nearly as well.

Vickie licked her lips. "I hate this. 'Cause she hasn't actually done anything yet. It's like Mind Police. But . . . look . . . I've worked with you and . . ." She seemed to decide on something. "Murdock . . . I'm a certified paranoid. 'Kay? So . . . don't freak on me. Gonna show you something."

She led the way to a locked door, and unlocked it. Inside . . .

Inside it looked like a movie set for what movie directors fondly imagined the computer room of, say, the FBI looked like. Six, no, eight flatscreen monitors, enough equipment to make him blink because it filled virtually every inch of space.

"This is where the magic happens," she said, sounding not proud, as he would have expected, but . . . sad. She sat down and began typing. Windows popped up, with encrypted passwords. Lots of them. She typed too fast even for him to figure out what they were. Finally she opened a folder marked "CCCP" and there were . . . lots of little folders, all with names on them.

"All right, I'm lookin'. So, what am I lookin' at?"

"You remember when I showed you your file, right? I go that deep with everyone, even the paperboy. I'm . . . paranoid, John. I'm not kidding about that. I . . . have a lot of reasons to be. Like you saw, I can go very, very deep indeed. But when it comes to people who are magical? I can go a lot deeper." She closed his file and clicked on Fei Li's.

Fei Li's was actually two. The file on the pretty little Chinese woman was actually fairly slender. But the one on General Shen Xue . . .

And when Saviour had said that the General was a monster . . . she had not been exaggerating. Collateral damage seemed to be a completely acceptable option for him; if something prevented the General from completing an objective, it was swept aside. Entire cities, tribes, even the damned livestock in an area. The General was single-minded in his pursuit of a goal; it was this tremendous drive and determination that allowed supremely heroic acts right along with some of the most deplorable crimes against humanity that John had ever heard of.

And as for the sword . . . it seemed to be a major magical artifact, on the order of the Holy Grail or the Horn of Roland, or Excalibur. Vickie's own note, written in a cramped text on the margin: "I'm not sure what it *can't* do."

"So. We're in the right, then. Even if it sucks, it's something that might have to be done if it can't be avoided."

Vickie sighed. "I hate it. But... I'm with Bell. Verd is almost as bad as the Thulians, and if Fei Li has just thrown her weight in on his side... I don't think we have a choice. Oh. If you're wondering how to find her, that's no problem. That sword casts a big honking magical shadow. I have more trouble shielding out its influence than in trying to locate it. I don't think she realizes I'm working with CCCP, and she knows Nat loathes magic, so the last person she would expect Nat to allow on an op against her is me. As long as she doesn't know I'm looking for her, she's on my radar."

Some of the tension left John. Vickie was with him on this; now that he had that settled, the rest would be routine. "Let's get down to brass tacks, then."

The location that Vickie had used her hocus pocus to track Fei Li to wasn't the only old, apparently abandoned motel in Atlanta that was surrounded by chain link fence with razor wire on top of it. Too many old motels became the home to squatters and druggies, especially now, with all the folks made homeless in the destruction corridors. This one would have made a good target for that, since it was about ninety-five percent intact.

This had been a big motel too, on old Highway 20 before the Beltway and the freeways came in. It had three big units, each four stories tall, in a U-shape around a swimming pool long since filled in to prevent the skaters from using it as a free ramp. It still looked abandoned... except just out of sight, there were a couple of vehicles that were way too armored to be civilian trucks.

John had inserted into the motel through the roof; through Vickie and Bella, he was able to procure one of the Echo jetpacks that their front runners sometimes used. He had picked it up from a dead drop in one of the destruction corridors, and lugged the package on foot until he was about three miles from the target area. Then it was time to play Rocketeer. Vickie had given him a crash course in its operation over the headset; there were a few abortive false starts, but he eventually was able to get it off the ground and heading in the right direction. After getting to a safe altitude, well above any visual searches or passive scans that Blacksnake might have been running, he had cut the jetpack, fallen, and then trigged his parachute. *Airborne trained are cocky for a reason, suckers.* As he descended, he scanned through his NVGs for any lookouts while Vickie gave him some help through the use of one of her seemingly innumerable gizmos; the coast was clear as far as the two of them could tell. He'd made a perfect landing on the roof, dragging his chute in quickly. After stuffing it under an inoperative air conditioning unit, he made his entry into the building's roof access. Inside, what had been separate units and rooms had been made into a single, large room, at least on the top floor. On the first floor down from that, there were several rooms, and it was pretty clear that the utilities were all live. *They're confident, I'll give them that.* All of the floors leading down were abandoned as he swept through the building.

It was when he got as far as the basement... and the brand-new subbasements... that things got interesting.

There were surprisingly few traps in the motel: a couple of Claymore mines, a few trip-wire flashbangs, and a single laser sensor near the basement access. John chalked this up to the large number of personnel they had patrolling; there were over ten Blacksnake troopers going through the hallways or waiting in rooms, almost always in pairs, throughout the entire building. They reported in regularly, too. With the entire working building situated almost completely underground, however, Vickie's witchcraft came in handy. She was able to hack quickly into their systems using magic, replicate their voices and call in for multiple troopers at once, in order to answer their designated sentry calls. She'd gotten a lot better at that since the Kansas op. That, combined with the knockout drugs that John had been equipped with, made getting to the subbasement easy.

All of the Blacksnake troopers were alive; most of them never saw John coming, before they felt the sting of a syringe in the side of their neck. He figured that, while the Commissar wouldn't quite approve of leaving them breathing and relatively unharmed, it was within his discretion to do so, and what the Commissar didn't know, she couldn't excoriate him over. They were all low-level flunkies, anyways; veterans, most likely, guys just in it for the pay. They didn't know shit, and probably figured they were the good guys.

The final door wasn't any more of a challenge. No password, no biometrics scan, not even a guard. *Sloppy. Must've figured that no one could get this far.* Either the General was cocky, or working with Blacksnake had kept her from running a tight ship.

Blacksnake was good at what it did mostly for its brutality and the precise application of it; other areas were naturally more lax on standards than professional military units. That showed up in ways that could come back and bite them in the ass. Like now.

"Big honking magical signature on the other side of that, Johnny."

John growled low, keeping his voice down. "Roger, Vic. Any idea on the opposition?"

"Fei Li for certain, three other probables. I'm mostly reading the probables by reflection and interference from what Fei Li is putting out."

"All right. I'm breaching the entrance. Stand by." John stood against the door jam, then tested the doorknob. It didn't squeak, which he was thankful for. In one smooth motion, he opened the door and brought his M4 up, moving silently and quickly. There were crates stacked all over the place; he took cover behind the closest to the door. John peered around the side; peering—or shooting—over the top of cover exposed more of a person's head to enemy fire. The entire room was filled with crates, and several cages.

"*—Xie xie.*" Whoever was thanking someone in Chinese was female and didn't sound all that . . . grateful. It was more like automatic politeness. Not that many female Chinese speakers in this building, John figured. "I want the full sensor suites in place and capture teams knowing their areas of responsibility well enough to react in their sleep before we even begin this operation."

"Of course, *General.* We've been given orders to that effect." A male voice, and one that was notably agitated.

"Eye out, Johnny?"

"Hit it, Vic, and go quietly. Gimme their disposition and that of the rest of the room. I wanna know where I can move."

There wasn't as much as a whisper to show that Vickie's "eye"—a magically cloaked and levitated button cam—was moving. John only knew it because he felt it brush against his hair as it rose from its pocket on the back of his vest. This was Vickie's techno-hoodoo; she'd stolen nonworking cams from the Vault—stuff Verd had not been able to get to work—and instead of using tech to make them float and hide, she used magic. Brilliant, despite the shivers that stuff gave him. One more thing they had that Verd didn't.

"Most of the room is clear. On your three o'clock, two guards, one manning a monitor bank, one live, two dead. Dead ahead, another that looks like he has officer pips. Crates at your ten o'clock, he looks like he's talking to someone on the other side of them. Lemme get a better angle on the speakers." A pause. *"It's Fei Li all right... she's... OH SHIT!"*

There was the sound of metal hitting metal.

"Go red. She spotted the cam."

That should've been goddamned impossible. John didn't like to lose the element of surprise.

John came out from behind his cover, suppressed rifle aimed towards where Vic had told him Fei Li was. As if on cue, the General himself—herself?—strode out from behind some crates, illuminated in the green glow of computer screens and harsh fluorescents. She—he—well, it was the General in command; the figure, though that of a diminutive Chinese woman, walked with a slight swagger, like a man. Hair in fancy braids, dressed in the same "black pajamas" as the Viet Cong had favored, she pinned him with her gaze.

The two Blacksnake guards and their officer all immediately drew weapons; submachine gun PDWs of some sort; John was too focused on the General to try to figure it out.

"So. CCCP sends you, comrade?" She sneered. "They chose to send their American? How sad. Perhaps Natalya did not want to risk my powers of persuasion with those that know me."

"You can come in voluntarily, *comrade.* We can do this easy like that, or we can do it *really* easy. Your choice." John kept his rifle trained on Fei Li; even though he had three other firearms pointed at him, she was without a doubt the most dangerous person in the entire room.

"Really easy? An interesting choice of words, considering that you are outnumbered even without my presence here." She shook her head. "Terrible tactics, comrade. Your John Wayne maneuvers are and have always been ineffective."

"Wonder why you didn't know I was here till just now? Because the rest of your numbers are down an' out. Now quit stalling, an' make yer decision."

The General sighed. "Very well. Men, take him, without killing him if possible."

Without preamble, John turned his rifle slightly to aim at the closest Blacksnake operative and shot him in the face three times. The other two were fast, and closed with him quickly; at this distance, they were inside the length of his rifle before he could reorient and fire again. Shrugging off his sling, John swung the rifle at the other grunt; it caught him on the edge of his chin perfectly, causing his teeth to click. He went down like a puppet with the strings cut, crumpling into a pile on the floor. The officer was competent, and wasn't so quick to rush in. John, frowning at the merc, threw his rifle at him; the man caught it, instinctively. *Bad move, pal.* John kicked him, hard, in the groin, and then dribbled him around the floor with kicks and punches until he was rendered unconscious.

"So," John said, "are you ready to come in quietly? Or do I have to beat the hell out of more goons?"

"I must definitely speak to Verdigris regarding the lack of competent help he has provided me," Shen Xue said, and launched into a flying kick at John.

He twisted in place, swatting her leg out of the way. She landed perfectly right beside him, looking serene. What happened next was a complete blur. John struck at her as hard and as fast as he could; Fei Li flawlessly countered every blow he launched. She did it effortlessly, as if she knew every move he was going to make. And she was *fast,* just as fast as John. With his enhancements, that was a feat that probably only a few metahumans in the entire world could claim.

Then, her assault came. It was everything John could do to keep from being hit; he felt his stealth suit literally tear when she grazed him with an open-palmed strike.

The effect was exactly like being in the middle of a martial arts movie with a combat between two evenly matched masters. In his experience, most fights were over in seconds, usually with whoever messed up first being the loser.

Her technique was impossibly precise, almost exquisite in its flow. John was good, and had spent a long time becoming that way; but he knew he couldn't keep up with this. She spun, swinging an elbow at his temple; ducking under it, he was immediately pounded with two open-handed strikes, a sweep, and a series of jabs. He blocked and dodged most of them, but she could see that he was giving up ground.

Fei Li unsheathed her sword without any sort of flourish, and nearly bisected John. An unearthly whir filled the air where her sword cut through the air.

"DISTANCE!" Vickie yelled in his ear. *"That thing is celestial!"*

John dropped to the ground, kicking at Fei Li's knee. She jumped back out of reach, swinging her sword through where his ankle had been a moment before.

"You need more distance than that! Like the next county! She can slice through an I beam without losing speed!"

John sprinted towards the door, stopping abruptly and turning to face her. She stood poised and ready, sword tip resting on the ground. "Are you running, comrade? You should."

"Last chance to see reason an' come in to talk this over. 'Fore this gets lethal for you, comrade." John stood up, motioning plaintively towards her. "Y'can still come back, rejoin the CCCP. It isn't too late for that."

"Natalya-chan is insufficiently committed. She will not do what must be done to end the Thulian menace." Fei Li brought the sword up into guard position.

John shook his head. "You're wrong. I think you know it, deep down. But I can't change your mind." She charged, sword in a high guard. When she was within spitting distance, John released his carefully maintained control slightly, and loosed his fires. A wall of flame shot up in between the two fighters. Fei Li skidded to a halt, pirouetting, and then actually *vaulted* over the flames. John ran to his right, snapping his wrist out; a gout of fire smashed into the ground in front of Fei Li, kicking up smoke and half-melted rock.

"If'n ya think I won't kill ya," John shouted over his shoulder, "better think again. I'd just rather avoid it!" Two more blasts of flame; Fei Li deflected one with her blade, which began to glow red-hot.

"She's moving too fast for me to bounce her with geomancy," Vickie said grimly. "And way too fast to bury her. Assuming she doesn't cut herself out if I did."

John, taking the initiative, stopped dead in his run, and turned toward Fei Li. He focused for a moment, then shot a concentrated stream of fire at the roof of the basement. Rubble poured out of the hole he gouged, directly in front of Fei Li. Her path was completely blocked, obstructed by the debris and crates.

"We seem to be at an impasse, comrade," Fei Li called. "What you call the Mexican standoff."

"Only because I want you to live, comrade. Come in, an' this'll all be forgotten." It might've been a half-lie, but even that was better than having to resort to killing someone who was supposed to have been an ally once. Normally, he would have burned her the moment it was apparent that she was trying to kill him. He'd killed plenty of other people that way, and with a lot less screwing around. But this wasn't nearly that simple.

"I believe that is not a possibility, American. Natalya is my pupil; she knows she cannot allow me to live if she has the means of making an end of me. I believe I will take advantage of the exit that you provided me." Without another word, the General gracefully leapt, no running start, through the hole in the ceiling of the basement. An impossible jump.

John stood dumbfounded for a moment, gathering his wits before he keyed his comm. "Lemme guess, Vic. She's already gotten the hell outta Dodge, and the cavalry is just now arriving. Right?"

"Ten-four." Vickie sighed. *"And now I think she's figured out how I can track her, 'cause she's gone blank on me."*

"Hellfire an' damnation. Guess we'll have to salvage this somehow. Get one of your other cams on scene. We're gonna need documentation for all of the intel on-site."

"Roger."

John scratched his head. This was a hell of a mess, and part of it was his doing, again. The clean-up team would be in here soon. *Time to face the music.*

The fifteen minutes it took for the cavalry to show up didn't help to ease John's tension. He had completed his mission, with regards to locating Fei Li, disabling the Blacksnake personnel, and securing the site. But People's Blade had slipped away. He didn't want to chase her, anyway; if he had, one of them would probably be dead, and John wasn't so sure that he'd be the victor.

Vickie alerted John when the backup team arrived; he keyed his comm unit. "Way's clear, Commissar. Twelve unconscious Blacksnake goons, one dead. All of their countermeasures and traps are deactivated; everything is ready to get swept up. Come on down."

"Remember, Commissar. Technically these rats weren't violating any laws..." That was Vickie. Saviour's reply was a grunt. It was Untermensch that replied.

"This is why Soviette is giving them sleepy shot and we are dumping them... elsewhere." The way he chuckled made John think that the "elsewhere" was likely to be very unpleasant for the Blacksnake operatives when they woke up.

The team worked their way down methodically, and finally Soviet Bear poked his nose around the door frame. "You are having tourists for us, Comrade Murdock?"

"Two breathing, ayup. Come on in, Pavel." John stood up, brushing dust off of his torn stealth suit. *She got way too close with that sword. Hell, she was lethal enough barehanded.* Bear whistled, and Jadwiga followed him in with her medical bag, examining them carefully.

"Why is this one beink dead?" Oddly enough, that was Red Saviour; she was poking the dead merc with her foot. He hadn't expected her to be concerned about collateral damage.

"I was in a hurry, and they weren't being friendly." John automatically straightened up as the Commissar approached. "This little command center they have here has plenty of intel; they never had a chance to destroy any of the hard-copy or computer drives."

Saviour turned towards him as the two unconscious Blacksnake ops were carried out, leaving no one there but herself and Untermensch. "Report, comrade." She scowled. "I can be seeing you encountered Shen Xue."

"After liaising with my Overwatch, I breached the building following the approved plan, utilizing an Echo jetpack, followed by parachuting to the roof. Upon entry into the building, I wasn't confronted by any opposition until I reached the lower levels. I incapacitated ten roving and static guards, and neutralized several traps; standard fare, mostly early warning devices or trip-wired explosives." John paused, shifting his weight. "When I reached the command post, I encountered the target and three more Blacksnake operators. A sensor deployed by Overwatch was unexpectedly detected, and I was engaged by the target and her guards. Once the guards were taken outta the picture, I tried to bring down Fei Li."

"But you failed." Saviour's scowl deepened.

"Couldn't be done without killin' her outright, which I gauged wouldn't have been acceptable." John looked straight at the Commissar. "Attempting to pursue Fei Li would have resulted in either her death, or mine. It was a stalemate."

Saviour's face darkened. "Is there something about 'by any means neccessary' that you did not understand, *tovarisch?*"

He hesitated. "No, Commissar. I used my judgment on the scene, to the best of my ability."

Saviour's eyes flashed dangerously, and her hands clenched at her side. And then she gave him the worst tongue-lashing he had ever had in his entire career. Never mind that at least half of it was in Russian; the venom in her tone more than made up for the fact that he couldn't understand her.

Finally even she ran out of words. "You are dismissed, Comrade Murdock," she said in disgust. "I will be wanting report in triple on my desk within the hour. *Dos vedanya.*"

Without a word, John saluted, turned on his heel, and left. *Coulda been worse. She could've shot me. Or called me by my full name.*

"He could be right in not killing People's Blade, Commissar," Untermensch said softly. "If it was truly a stalemate... Shen Xue is hardly a fool, and he would escape rather than continue to fight. Once outside this building, he would have not hesitated to use bystanders as shields."

Saviour waved off the comment, but as John glanced back at her, he thought perhaps she looked torn, as if having second thoughts.

The collection team began boxing up and carting away all of the potential intelligence it could. Reams of paper in binders, computer hard drives, maps and communications gear. As Bear was clomping towards the doorway to the stairs, a glimmer caught his eye. It was one of the several cages that lined the far wall; it was covered in very strange symbols, none of which were familiar to him. "What strange sort of zoo is People's Blade being to make?" He sniffled, then turned back to leave. "A decadent fetish, maybe."

John Murdock completely vanished from the Seraphym's awareness.

It was not the "died" sort of vanishing. That wouldn't actually be vanishing at all, more like "moved to another state of being." No, this was... vanishing. As if something had made him disappear. Just as—

A completely unaccustomed feeling overwhelmed her, because of the only other creature she knew that could vanish from her awareness in that manner.

Shen Xue. If John was near Shen Xue, and Shen Xue had for *any* reason extended his powers to make John disappear, then John was in deadly peril.

She panicked.

She did not react as a mortal would, of course; she neither flew off wildly, nor froze. But a great wave of primal panic fear engulfed her, and although she did not cease the task she was on—the elimination of a Thulian cell and the rescue of another person who would become important—she was shaking to her very bones in reaction.

And when John finally "reappeared" to her, it was all she could do to keep herself from racing to him. This was a delicate task, one that required tiny interventions in a long sequence, both to keep the prisoner alive and to aid Echo personnel in finding him, and it was only when it was completed that she gave herself leave to fly to John.

In fact, she did more than fly. She apported herself to just above the roof of his squat, and once she was sure he was alone there, she folded her wings and plunged down to him, relief at seeing him not only alive, but whole, making tears stream from her eyes.

He saw her at the very last minute out of the corner of his eye and turned to her, face full of shock and astonishment. Impelled by instinct and impulse, she did not think. She flung herself at him and embraced him with everything she had; then, as he started to speak, again without thinking, she kissed him.

To say this kiss was nothing like the embrace of Siblings was to say that the ocean was, perhaps, a bit damp. And yet... strangely... it was *exactly* like the embrace of Siblings. It was utterly, completely *right* in ways she could not codify, and at the moment, had no interest in thinking about. It was intimate in ways the Siblings never experienced for themselves.

She did not want it to end. Ever.

After filling out his after-action report in triplicate as requested, John had stripped out of his kit, then washed up and toweled off before he made his way back to his squat. Everything was fairly quiet in the neighborhood, and he hadn't received any messages that required his urgent attention.

It was only after he was back in his squat with all of the security reactivated that he felt safe enough to relax again. "What a helluva day." Not wasting any time, he tied the top half of his issued coveralls around his waist, grabbed what was left of a six-pack, and made his way to the roof. A light breeze was blowing, taking some of the edge off of the oppressive Atlanta heat as it radiated off of all of the concrete and asphalt. He hadn't even had a chance to bring the first beer to his lips when he noticed a blur of motion out of the corner of his right eye. Reflexively, he dropped the beer and turned to face whatever it was. It was too fast, but some instinct inside of him told John that it wasn't a threat. His mind processed everything in a flash; it was Sera, and she was clearly distressed. Her arms flew around him, gripping him tightly and desperately. He returned the embrace, again on automatic, before his words found him.

"Sera? What's—" Before John could utter another word, he found himself occupied with the most passionate kiss he'd ever received. After another moment of being startled, John returned the kiss with just as much feeling. He wrapped his arms around her, bringing her in close. He was confused, excited, dumbstruck, and about a dozen other emotions all coming almost too fast for him to process. The kiss lingered on . . . and it was good. He didn't want it to stop, not the kiss, and not at *just* the kiss. Hell, it had literally been *years* . . . but good judgment and caution won out against desire. Finally, but without a sense of urgency, he slowly pulled away, looking down into Sera's eyes as they slowly opened; two molten orbs of amber awash in tears and light.

"You were gone," she said. "You were there, then you were gone. And I know it was Shen Xue."

John stared for a moment, then chuckled while he ran his hand through his hair. "You're right. You were right 'bout her, too. She's gone over to that rotten bastard Verd, completely." He looked down at his feet before meeting her eyes again. "I was sent after her, to bring her in—or kill her. It almost came to that, but she escaped. She's a helluva fighter, Sera; too dangerous for her own good."

"You don't understand. It isn't *she*. Fei Li is not there. It is Shen Xue. And the sword . . . it is celestial, John. It is like me. It can even hurt *me*. You, it would obliterate, if the full scope of its power were unleashed. You were in terrible, deadly danger!" Her arms tightened around him again.

John grinned lopsidedly: a real grin, as opposed to the affected ones he sometimes wore. "Darlin', we're all in terrible, deadly danger, all the time. In peace an' in war; doesn't make much of a difference. I had a job that needed doin'." He sobered then. "Had to protect all of the people that trust me; my comrades, my neighborhood . . . and you."

And then, suddenly, she went still. She blinked, and looked down, as if realizing only now what she was doing. Her arms loosened, and she took a single, small step away. The distance between them was only inches now, closer than he had ever allowed anyone. But could it be closed again?

She looked up. "I have . . . enormous . . . feelings . . . for you, John Murdock," she said. "This is a new thing. The Siblings do not themselves have such feelings. And yet, the Infinite is not saying it is not permitted . . ."

John took a small step towards her, closing the distance between the two of them again. *This is the part where I'm struck by a lightning bolt, or burst into flame, or explode or something . . . yeah, worth it.* "I won't pretend to know or believe in that . . . but I do know this." He slowly—very slowly—allowed his hands to hold Sera by her shoulders. "Anyone that would say that this is wrong, well, they just couldn't be right. So . . . is this all right? With you?"

She blinked again, slowly, and a little smile creased those perfect lips. "Yes," she said simply, and lifted her chin a little, plainly waiting for him to kiss her.

John pulled her close, still grinning while he leaned in for the kiss. She started to change subtly, as he did so. Her hair started to dim, from fire to a shining fall of *hair;* the wings began to fade. He stopped short, holding up a hand to her face. "No. You're perfect the way y'are, darlin'." As he caressed her face, it changed back to her true form where he touched, spreading until the changes had completely reverted.

"I am not perfect, John," she said, seriously. "Perfection is stagnation, and stagnation is death. I would not wish to be perfect. Even the Infinite does not seek perfection."

"Eye of the beholder, darlin'. Now, shaddup an' kiss me." He finished the sentence with a kiss deep enough to match her first one. In that moment, the world could have ended for John Murdock, and he would have not been more content.

CHAPTER TWENTY-FIVE

Kingdom

MERCEDES LACKEY AND CODY MARTIN

Dominic Verdigris had gotten to where he was because he was always one step ahead of the opposition.

And now that he knew there was an *opposition... that hadn't changed.*

"I think I need a moonbase, next," Verdigris said.

"A moonbase, Dom?" Khanjar didn't turn to face him; she was too busy taking in the sight through the viewport. A typhoon was fast approaching from the west, causing massive waves to crash against the rocks at the base of the mountain cliffs. This particular retreat of Verdigris' was located on Isla de Serpiente, a volcanic island off the coast of Peru. It was so named for the shape of the island, which resembled a coiled snake; the active but stable volcano was located inside of the highest mountain at the "head" of the snake right about where its "eye" would be if seen in profile. It made for a very impressive view from the air.

"Well, what else do I have left? The Russian submarine was just recently refurbished, but I don't feel like taking a trip underwater anytime soon. And this place doubles as an airship; at least this section, anyways. A moonbase is the next big step; wouldn't hurt just in case something cataclysmic happens to this wonderful blue marble of a world, besides." He frowned a little. "And if I *have* to, it would be a good place to skip out in case the Kriegers..." He didn't finish the sentence.

Khanjar didn't finish the sentence either. Just at the moment she didn't want to ruffle any feathers by pointing out that if the Kriegers were as powerful as the Deva had shown Verd, the moon wouldn't be far enough to escape their clutches. When you were living on the edge of a volcano, it wasn't a good idea to upset the master of the house. The prospect of Verdigris being out of moves wasn't exactly a comfortable one for Khanjar, either. She didn't think the Kriegers would have any use for her.

"Would you care to see Harmony now?" she asked instead. "The shuttle from the mainland docked just ahead of the storm."

Dominic looked up from his desk, taken out of his moment of brooding. "Yes, yes. Have her come up immediately. You know what to do, my dear; keep on your toes."

Khanjar spoke briefly into the microphone pinned to her collar. Harmony would be escorted from her guest room to the office by no less than four guards, all of whom would be completely armored and helmeted. No nice bare skin for her to get so much as a finger on. Certainly, she was their ally. Certainly, so far as they were aware, when she was bought, she stayed bought. But it was Khanjar's job to take no chances. She, by nature, suspected everyone and everything. It was one of the reasons that she had stayed alive this long and had become as rich as she had in Verdigris' employ.

Harmony bothered her. It was not only that the woman's metahuman power was . . . unsettling. It was that she had come out of nowhere, and risen to this current position, bypassing most of the normal rungs on the ladder. What was worse insofar as Khanjar's feelings of *stability* were concerned, she wasn't the only one who had done so lately. Khanjar preferred things to proceed in an orderly, predictable fashion. Lately, Dom had been making moves she considered risky—first in hiring Harmony, then, more alarmingly, allying with the Chinese woman. *That* one was dangerous . . . and Dom refused to listen to her about the General.

Still . . . this woman was nothing like Shen Xue. She was not arrogant, she did not presume, and she didn't hold herself as if she thought she was Verd's equal—or superior. She knew her place; below Dom, and more importantly, below Khanjar herself. Harmony was a hireling: useful, but not valued beyond what she was paid to do.

There was nothing about Harmony that seemed to inspire

Dom to take the risks he was taking with the General. Thank the gods. What was it about the General that so fascinated him, and made him reckless? There were moments when Khanjar even wondered if Dom was toying with the notion of... surely not. Surely he knew better than to try and replace *her*. Still... the idea was chilling. Someone who knew as much as Khanjar did could only be "replaced," never "retired." Dom's usual generosity with his employees would not, could not, extend to a professional assassin who knew every detail of his security arrangements. But then... everything had changed since the Deva had visited him. Would it come to that, where he would have to sacrifice her to save himself? Of course it would. She harbored no illusions where Dominic Verdigris was concerned. He feigned "caring" very well, but when it came down to it, there was only one person of importance in Verd's life, and that was himself. Everyone and everything else was just an accessory or a tool. She resolved to redouble her efforts at making herself indispensable.

The office door slid open, and Harmony entered with her escort; it was plain to see that the security guards were nervous around her, though they did their best to hide it. Strange. She had looked very, very American when she had been with Echo, as if she could have been sitting behind the desk of a receptionist in any corporation, or been going to classes in any university. Now, however, there was something exotic about her. Her hair had been arranged in a loose fashion faintly reminiscent of an ancient Grecian statue, and the draped dress she wore only emphasized the resemblance. She appeared quite relaxed, even a little amused, and when Khanjar looked briefly into her eyes, she got the unsettling impression of great age.

"You sent for me, and here I am, Verdigris," Harmony said, with an artful little gesture, with the merest hint of a bow in it. "What can I do for you?"

"Thank you for joining us, my dear. We have a great deal to discuss, but first let me compliment you on your handling of the last few affairs, and a bit of a surprise following the necessarily gruesome spectacle we had to make of Tesla. Very tidy, natural-looking deaths, I commend you." Verdigris flashed his best smile, but Khanjar had learned to read his moods. He was anything but happy at the moment. The failure with the trap in Atlanta Underground was still haunting him. "Please, take a seat."

Harmony did so, gracefully. Khanjar admired her dispassionately. There was nothing of the "old" Harmony about her, now; how had she managed to feign naïveté, inexperience, the callowness of youth? She must be a superb actress. Still, she noticed a bit of steel in Harmony's look as she gazed at Verdigris, betraying a slight irritation with the billionaire.

"Thank you," Harmony said. "I do take pride in my work, after all. I gather this meeting is in regard to our arrangement? One final task?"

"Yes, of course," Verdigris said with a smile.

"One final task, and the prize will be mine?" Harmony leaned forward, her eyes locked on Verdigris.

"Absolutely, my dear," he smiled, though he spared a look up to Khanjar before continuing. "It appears we have some malcontents brewing revolution within our own ranks."

"By which you mean Echo, of course," Harmony said smoothly. "And Dominic, please don't tell me this surprised you, I know you are much too intelligent to think that you could simply walk in and take over an organization like Echo without problems from malcontents."

"Yes, well." He sniffed, mock hurt playing over his face. "You would have thought that, as ineffective as Tesla had been since the Invasion, they'd at least have given me a *chance* before fomenting revolt. *I* would never have let the Mountain suicide so spectacularly, for one thing. Waste of resources. Well. They have been commendably cagey about it. Look here." He pointed to one of the pop-up monitors that rose silently from the edge of the desk nearest to Harmony.

Her brows creased as she watched the data stream scroll by. "Dominic, I'm not... particularly technically ept. What on earth am I looking at?"

"To sum it up, I've been keeping tabs on nigh everyone in my employ, particularly everyone in Echo. As you said, these sorts of takeovers can be... tricky. From what I've been able to gather tapping into a series of phones, computers, and physical surveillance, I think it's safe to say that there's a small group of personnel that wish to oust me. And they might have found the means to do so." Verdigris tapped on the desk twice, and all of the screens now displayed the same image: a scan of a paper document.

Well, it was a scan of *something* on paper. Whatever it was, it was completely unreadable. It was as if the scan had been taken while the letters were moving from one bizarre, alien language to another.

Harmony blinked. "How... intriguing. What is that supposed to be, do you know?"

Khanjar felt herself grow a little more alert. Harmony *recognized* that... or at least, recognized something like it.

"It's supposed to be one of the original copies of the Echo charter—the one that belonged to Yankee Doodle," Verdigris replied. "If legend is true, all the original signers of the charter got a copy." He laughed a little, a laugh with no humor in it. "And if legend is true, they all had some sort of spell cast on them so the copies were—like that. You couldn't read them, and you couldn't use code-breaking techniques on them because the letters moved and changed all the time." He frowned. "I'm still determined to fix that little problem with this image. An original would be much more useful... but that's something for me to worry about. The point is, the conspirators are going after a copy of the charter, and I think they might actually have one. I'm pretty certain who two of them are. Yankee Pride and Ramona Ferrari. Yankee Pride, well, he's obvious. I ousted him when we took Tesla out."

"Ramona Ferrari?" Harmony's brows arched. "The *detective?* Why in heaven's name do you suspect her? She's nothing, not meta, not... attractive... oh, she has a certain rudimentary cleverness, but..."

Verdigris spread his hands wide. "One and the same. She's just far enough below the usual radar, since she's not an op, and as a detective, she has a lot of latitude to work within the rest of Echo. That, and she's annoyingly dogged in her pursuit of her goals. Normally a trait that I'd love in an employee, but this one isn't the sort to be bought out by me."

"Well, you seem to have figured out who your enemies are, and you know what they intend... why don't you just eliminate them both and have done with it?" Harmony tapped a long, graceful finger on the side of her face. "I really don't see what I can help you with here."

Verdigris shook his head, smiling, as if he was correcting a mistaken child. "No, no, Harmony. I'm all about not wasting effort, and to kill them outright wouldn't only be wasted effort, it'd also make martyrs of them. Not to the masses, or even most of Echo initially, but martyrs have a habit of growing followings. What I have in mind is a bit more . . . artful. When we're done—and I do mean *we*—their deaths will have served more than the singular purpose of securing my position as the head of Echo. Are you beginning to understand?"

Harmony sighed. "Since Jack made himself scarce, you want me to take over Blacksnake and engineer something suitably appalling for them. That way, once again, Blacksnake is reinforced as the villain, and you get to play the astonished and grieving Father of Echo's Children."

"Not in so many words. I'll certainly help you to make sure that it all turns out poetic and beneficial enough. But yes. Your reward hinges upon it, shall we say?" That shark look, eyes shiny and black, that Verd's eyes sometimes had, came back right then. Khanjar didn't like that look, but she had come to expect it over the years.

"You hold all the cards. But Blacksnake is notoriously misogynistic, Dominic. Will your operatives take orders from me?" Harmony's eyes were just as cold in that moment. "Or will you let me show them why they should?"

"You forget. The world runs on one thing; it isn't strength, or fear, or power. It's money. Money can buy and control all of those things. And *no one* has more money than I do. They'll listen to you, Harmony," Verdigris let the words hang in the air for a moment, "because I'll *tell* them to. Agreed?"

She nodded. "Agreed. You might have to make some examples."

The cold look vanished from Verdigris' eyes, and he waved a hand dismissively. "Cost of doing business. I'll attend to it if and when the issue crops up. I expect regular reports and will need to approve of any plans before they're put into effect. Any other questions?"

Harmony laughed. It had a disconcertingly *young* sound. "Oh, Dominic, how soon you forget. I am she of the *hourly* reports, remember? You had to ask me to make them less frequent on the last op."

"Yes, well. Call me a stickler for the details when they're important." He gestured towards the doorway. "Be sure to help yourself to any refreshments in the anteroom on your way out. We'll be in touch, Harmony."

"I think I'll leave via sub, considering the storm," she replied, and rose. "And considering the storm . . . I'll refrain from eating until we're clear. Unless you count that charming receptionist as *refreshments.*"

He waved a finger reprovingly. "Good help is hard to find. It's why you're still here. Leave her be."

She laughed. "Then I'll just have to get some dockside take-away when we hit port. Ta-ta, Dominic. First report will be in your mail when we have 'net." She rose as gracefully as she had sat down, and winked. "I'll just see myself out. I know the way to the submarine docks."

She made good on her word, and the door slid shut behind her. Verdigris waited for several long moments after the door closed before he turned to Khanjar, fingers steepled in front of his chest. "So, my dear. What're your thoughts on how things are going to proceed?"

Khanjar pondered. "I can see why you did not place me in charge; you need me here with you. I can see why you did not place any of the current Blacksnake officers in charge; after the debacle at the Underground, it is clear they are not competent to devise a good plan or follow it through. And the General . . . ?" She left the words hanging.

"The General's goals only coincide with our goals to a point. Beyond that, she is not *with* us. I'm glad you see this, Khanji." She could tell that Dominic was expecting something from her now.

"Well . . . Harmony devised her own op, went underground within Blacksnake, then got herself placed in Echo as a double agent, and remained completely undetected for . . . really, right up until the moment she *had* to reveal herself." Khanjar pursed her lips. "I would have said that I doubted her ability as a leader until just now, but it is evident that she has many more layers than I had assumed, *and* she is intelligent, clever, and a superlative actress. Certainly she doesn't doubt her own ability to lead. And I don't think she is inclined to hubris. So I would have to say that of your limited choices, she is probably heads above the rest."

"But?" There was still something that he was waiting for. He wanted her to reach the conclusion herself; it was important to him that she do so.

"She does not serve out of loyalty." *And neither do I, not any-more, but you don't know that, do you, Dom, dear.*

"It's one of the most expensive commodities, and requires to be constantly purchased for potentially higher and higher prices. But it's valuable for that very reason." He smiled again, self-assured. "Thank you, my dear. Are you hungry? I'm famished."

"Chef Hudson probably has something special for you. You know how he loves storms." She nodded to the door. "As ever, after you, Dom."

Yes indeed, after you. And one of these days, if it comes to that, when you turn around and look, I'll be gone.

CHAPTER TWENTY-SIX

You're Only Human

VERONICA GIGUERE AND MERCEDES LACKEY

Ramona Ferrari couldn't remember the last time she had been at her apartment to do more than sleep and exchange one Echo uniform for another. She fumbled her keys in her hand and managed to unlock the door to her apartment. As she stepped inside, a faint blue overlay courtesy of the Overwatch system allowed her to do a brief sweep of the rooms. Icons blinked to show her the pile of mail on the counter, with the most important bills flagged as "due" or "overdue." In the kitchen, icons popped up to remind her of what was and wasn't in her refrigerator, what had likely spoiled, what she needed to have delivered from the grocery service that Vickie had recommended, and a list of vetted restaurants that could have dinner at her door in thirty minutes or less.

The amount of information overwhelmed the detective. The beginning of a headache throbbed at the base of her skull, and another panel of information came up with a list of her vital signs, potential triggers, and no less than four solutions. Ramona gritted her teeth and screwed her eyes shut. This was not a way to relax for the few hours she didn't have to be on duty. With a curse, she turned off the HUD and kicked off her shoes, only to decide that she didn't have the patience to put up with delivery food. She summoned enough energy to make it to the kitchen, pour a bowl of cinnamon frosted Ech-Ohs—she smiled at Mercurye's cheesy grin on the front of the box—and slump at the kitchen table.

She didn't bother with milk. According to the readouts, what was left in the fridge had spoiled days ago.

Ramona thumbed the TV remote and scanned to a small local station not affiliated with the bigger networks. Reality was ninety percent perception, and she wanted to see just how the lesser media saw Verdigris and his gesture of goodwill. As skeptic after skeptic voiced concerns about cost, aesthetics, proximity, and even the continuing failures of Echo to address the greater rebuilding processes in the city, Ramona felt reassured that she wasn't the only non-meta who saw the man for what he was. People on the street questioned the benevolence of a man so tied to his money, who relied upon an attractive female bodyguard, and who seemed to do things oblivious to the resources of a city so diverse as Atlanta. Even the news pundits wrinkled their noses when they spoke about the dedication and promised complete coverage.

With some satisfaction, Ramona realized that Spin Doctor had not appeared on this smaller station. She felt certain that Victrix would keep him out of Overwatch until the very last moment necessary, and she agreed wholeheartedly with that decision. The less people knew about the entire operation, the better.

"Ferrari, are you there?"

Ramona paused, her mouth full of cereal as Pride's voice came through the Overwatch channel. Even in the confines of her own home, she couldn't escape responsibility. "Yeah, Pride." She swallowed and muted the television as the weather folks started to talk about the perfect day for the dedication. "What's going on?"

"Logistics for the event." His voice came in a whisper. *"Verdigris called a meeting ten minutes ago, to start in an hour. Were you invited?"*

She set her spoon down with a hard thwack and took a deep breath. Her phone on the counter flashed a small green light to show unread messages. She reached over and scanned through the list of emails, but nothing corresponded to a meeting with Verdigris and his bodyguard Barbie. "Negative, sir. Should I invite myself?" Even as she asked the question, she stood and began gathering her things, putting the half-eaten bowl of cereal on the counter.

"He's talking about other memorials to follow this one, including a plaque near Stone Mountain. I think it's mostly just talk, but I know how you felt about Bill's situation." Pride sounded as if he was trying to keep his own temper in check. *"How soon can you get here?"*

It took a great deal of control for Ramona to not fling the bowl to the ground in frustration. She had left her car at the CCCP headquarters, trusting the Russians under Vickie's direction to outfit it per the Overwatch specifications. That left the detective at the mercy of MARTA and the rest of the public transportation system to commute to the Echo campus. "About forty minutes if I leave right now. If you can, tell Spin to flip to the local channels and figure out a contingency plan postdedication. We're losing face fast among the hometown crowd, and I don't think we can afford it."

A pause, then Yankee Pride's voice rumbled in her ear. *"Will do, Detective. And thank you."*

The mandatory meeting of those Echo personnel that Verdigris decided as necessary to his brilliant public relations demonstration sat in the small press briefing room. In the surveillance video, Dominic Verdigris gripped the sides of the podium and smiled at those assembled. The newer faces, handpicked from the faithful of Blacksnake and appropriately threatened by Khanjar, watched him with varying expressions of interest and curiosity. The others, Echo faithful still mourning the loss of Alex Tesla, showed everything from fear to open hostility. Verdigris noted that Yankee Pride sat in the front row, gauntlets dim and his mouth set in a firm line. He chuckled with satisfaction as the man fought back a scowl.

"Ladies and gentlemen, I appreciate your being here on such short notice. As many of you are aware, the remembrance ceremony for what we have termed the Invasion will take place in less than a week, and it is imperative that you—" The speech stopped as the door on his left snapped open and an Echo detective rushed in. Without any form of apology, she took a seat on the aisle and flipped open a small notebook.

Verdigris paused the footage and zoomed in on the image of Detective Ferrari. He snaked out an arm to pull Khanjar into his lap, motioning to the screen. "You're losing your touch, my dear. I think we have a 'no fat nosy detective rule' in place, don't we?"

Khanjar waited for Dominic's hand to rest securely on her hip before speaking. "Keeping her out was not advised. As a non-meta, she presents a lower threat, and she was not armed. Consider this a means to test a hypothesis."

"Oh, I love it when you talk scientific method." He sped up the footage, playing through the speech and watching the detective's reaction. At one point, she extracted a small tablet from her pocket and began typing furiously. After a few minutes, Verdigris watched in slight shock as she pulled up an invitation list for the event and began checking off those metas who had accepted and would be arriving at the airport. He straightened up, pushed Khanjar from his lap, and increased the resolution.

"That's my database! That's my one-thousand-twenty-four-bit encryption algorithm, and that woman is *in my database!* Reading *my* invitation list! During *my* press conference!" With the grace of a spoiled child, Verdigris pounded the keyboard and pointed an accusing finger at Khanjar. "This is your fault! How could you let this happen?"

The meta smoothed her pristine white jumpsuit and tucked a strand of dark hair behind her ear. She had endured many of Dominic's tantrums, and this would pass like all the others. "As you claim, I 'let' this happen to prove a hypothesis. Regardless of what you wish to think, that fat nosy detective is your mole."

Verdigris snorted. "Impossible. She's a civilian detective, no abilities, certainly average intelligence. I don't believe you." He crossed his arms and slumped in his chair, pouting.

Khanjar offered a small sigh of exasperation as she leaned over Dominic to bring up another series of protocols and video feeds. The images did not have the crispness of the Echo camera, but she could still easily point out the figures of Ramona Ferrari and Yankee Pride leaving the building that was occupied by members of the CCCP. Another series of photographs showed the detective and Yankee Pride in civilian clothing, standing closer than one might have thought appropriate for just coworkers. Finally, a classified report from the investigator he had bribed, with a footnote that Khanjar highlighted to show the suspected ties between Ferrari and Pride, as well as...

"Ferrari and Tesla? Alex Tesla?" Verdigris' forehead creased, the thought so absurd yet so utterly plausible that he nearly fell out of his chair. Khanjar continued to show photographs, including one showing them sharing breakfast in a diner away from the Echo campus. "That... that is..."

"Your problem," she finished in a crisp tone. She straightened up, noting that his eyes followed the scoop neckline of her jumpsuit.

"Not everyone has the same motivations as you do, Dominic. The little people are not always insignificant."

"Just easier to squash. Like an annoying mosquito," he quipped. He drummed his fingers against his desk, biting his tongue as he considered his options. Verdigris flipped through the photos a second time, lingering on the one that showed Ferrari and Tesla outside the trailer that had served as the director's office. His scowl deepened, but quickly turned into a hard grin as he spun in his chair.

"Call the boys downtown, Khanjar. I think it's time to retire the detective, before she can do any more damage to our memorial ceremony." Fingers danced over the keyboard as he pulled up schematics, maps, and several video feeds from the transportation surveillance. "I didn't want to invite her, anyway."

Ramona made it to the MARTA station with less than a minute to spare, the last train of the night giving the alert for the closing doors. She shifted against her seat and tucked up her leg, resting her cheek against the cool metal wall. The thrum of the train made for a steady and soothing vibration as the announcements began and the doors closed. As she was one of the last to leave the Echo campus for the night, Ramona had no company save Vickie's equally tired voice in her ear. The dim car clicked through the outer areas of the city faster than rush hour traffic, but the winking lights let Ramona know that there weren't many people out on the streets past midnight in the middle of the week.

"I'm checking on the intel regarding a memorial at Stone Mountain, but I'm not getting anything. He might have been bluffing, Detective." The words were calm and hopeful, yet Vickie sounded as tired as Ramona felt. *"He likes to talk, and he likes to see what people do while he talks. I think you can stop worrying about him doing anything for Bill."*

"Thanks, Overwatch." Ramona stifled a yawn, her eyes closed as they continued north into the city. There was some bit of comfort in knowing that Verdigris wasn't trying to use the memory of the Mountain for his personal gain. "And thanks for the link to the database. Were you able to contact most of the retired metas to tell them about the charter?"

"Affirmative. Pride went to talk to the locals face to face, but it looks like everyone's on board."

"He's a good man," she murmured. Exhausted, she fought to stay awake against the gentle rocking of the train. "Pride's one of the good guys, yeah. Shame he's married to the job, though. Maybe if he was younger . . . nah, too serious. But he's good-looking in a suit."

A tired laugh came through. *"Don't tell me you're going to give up on Mercurye, Detective. You know when he gets back, you'll be the first person he'll want to see."*

In the dark of the car, a sleepy smile spread across the detective's face. She thought of the grinning speedster, the awkward science-fiction fanboy transformed into a living hero, still stuck in Metis with a few blue wireframes to keep him company. "Yeah, I know. He's pretty cute, huh?"

"If you go for shirtless and blond."

"I was thinking more along the lines of blue eyes and Trek-obsessed." Ramona gave a soft sigh of contentment as she let her mind wander back to the image of Rick Poitier sitting in front of her, eagerly discussing the news from Echo, smiling at her with that beautiful . . .

"FERRARI, GET DOWN!" The voice screeched in her ear, jolting her up from the light sleep. In the light of the coming station, Ramona could see the first set of charges detonate against the concrete supports. The metal supports groaned and snapped, sliding forward to push the train sideways off of the track. *"ACTIVATE THE DISPLAY!"*

Ramona blinked, the display from the implant coming into view. Her vision blurred briefly, too much information about the car, the charges, and the crumbling concrete that pressed against the windows. More information flashed to the right and left, telling her that the first set of charges had triggered a rush of neurotoxins into the forward area of the car. "Overwatch, I've got chemical contamination! You're going to need to prep an evac, this isn't going to be—"

A second set of charges exploded ahead, tearing through the metal train like tissue paper. The force of the blast threw Ramona to the floor, the momentum of the car sending her sliding to the side of the car. Her head hit the side of the bench with a loud crack, and the detective flopped like a rag doll as blood poured from her face. Glass shattered, concrete and rebar coming through the window. Ramona tried to throw an arm over her face, but her shoulder hung limply and she couldn't feel her fingers on her left hand. She struggled to lift her head, blinking to refresh the view. A small oblong icon showed at the rear of the car, a few feet from where she had been sitting. The tiny timer displayed a very brief countdown to ignition. "Overwatch? Can-cancel evac. There's no—"

The final charge under the back of the last car peeled the metal forward and forced it from the track. Ramona felt the shock wave push her away from the car, the bottom giving way as the car bowed out and tumbled to its side. A rush of heat burned over her, her face raw and wet for an excruciatingly long moment. The heavy night air replaced the heat, and Ramona found herself faceup in the twisted metal, unable to comprehend the flurry of voices in her ear. Something like sleep pulled her away from Vickie's frantic voice, and Ramona slipped beneath the rush to a place absent of noise and pain.

The Seraphym alerted, like a dog catching a scent. *Ramona Ferrari.* Not once, but now twice she had Seen this woman in the futures. She paused in her conversation with John Murdock, her eyes far away and distant as she felt the ripple in the fabric of the futures. She bowed her head and left the rooftop in a surge of light and fire, with the barest of apologies on her lips.

In the end, they would all need this woman. She had to bring her to them, in the dead of night, in order for the futures to take hold. The Seraphym touched the broken earth, scorched and torn around the broken body. The briefest bit of life remained; she held onto that life and cradled the woman in her arms. Another step, and she stood once again on the rooftop, eyes full of tears as she gave the woman to John. He held back as many questions as he could, the now-frantic voices of Vickie and Bella filling the Overwatch channels.

The Seraphym nodded her thanks and waited, John's sure steps down the stairwell soon echoed by the frantic footfalls of the CCCP medical team. A high-pitched voice gave orders and demanded answers, and the Seraphym knew she would be needed again to assist the young medic.

Thankfully, this was permitted.

Soviette hooked the Echo detective up to life support, and began her own frantic efforts to keep the woman alive psychically. In the end, she was quickly exhausted and barely holding Ramona Ferrari in a precarious state of stasis when Bella shoved in the door of the medbay.

The blue medic swore steadily under her breath as, with practiced motions, she plugged herself into a repurposed hemapheresis machine, and placed her hands on the blackened flesh. And then paused with shock.

"Sovie. Vic. We have . . . shit . . ."

"What?" Vickie all but shouted, as Soviette blinked and echoed *"Shto?"*

"She's meta."

"Say what?" Vickie blurted. *"She can't be! She's never triggered, not even during the Invasion; she's a norm!"*

"I'm telling you, I read it. Whatever she was before this, she's meta now. She's got the healing factor, it's partly triggered and it's the only reason she's still alive now, and . . . something else, tied to the healing factor." Bella kept both hands on the unconscious woman, but she was fighting a losing battle and she knew it. There was only one way she could save Ramona Ferrari.

Trigger her completely.

And she knew very well what had happened the last time she'd done that, to Bulwark. She'd almost killed him . . .

Sovie knew, too, and showed it with a swift intake of breath. *"Sestra*—leave alone the ethics of doing a trigger without consent—"

"If I don't, she dies," Bella said harshly. "If I do, maybe she lives, but if I don't, she *dies.* We can't hold her much longer."

There was a moment of silence among the three of them, Soviette, Bella, and Vickie still listening on Overwatch. It was Vickie who finally spoke.

"In the absence of patient preference, what is the primary duty of a physician? Screw that you aren't a doctor, Bells, you might as well be. So what's your duty?"

Sovie's eyes cleared, and she nodded. "*Vedma* is givink correct thinking, *sestra.* I *am* physician, and I say that."

"Make every effort to preserve life," Bella said, through gritted teeth and anxiety so high it made her voice go up half an octave. "All right then, stand by, Sovie. God and Marx only know what's going to happen."

She plunged deeply into the healing gestalt, and "spoke" to Ramona's cells, fully triggering the metahuman healing factor, and "watching" in a state of near panic as the unknown "other" triggered after it in a cascade.

Then she was too busy trying to keep control of the situation as Ramona began *pulling* energy out of her, rather than passively receiving it. Somewhere in the back of her awareness, she heard Soviette call urgently for Upyr, and felt a pair of cool hands going to her temple, infusing her with somewhat musty "flavored" power.

Nat must have some thugs in the CCCP brig... who are going to wake up with a helluva hangover...

Three times more this happened, and then—

I am here, little sister.

And the flow of slightly tainted power was replaced by that impossible geyser of pure, sweet energy that she could only, barely, sip at without being overwhelmed. Once again, Sera had come to the rescue.

And finally, the *demand* on her shut off. With a feeling of relief—at least Ramona hadn't died from whatever she'd triggered—she opened her eyes, and took away her hands.

"Well," she observed wearily. "At least I didn't kill her. And she only looks half-cooked now."

The blackened skin was flaking away as Soviette cut off what was left of the detective's clothing, leaving behind something that looked like second-degree burns, rather than third- and fourth-degree. But Soviette was frowning.

"What?" Bella asked.

The physician pointed with her chin. "There was being a cart with tray with surgical instruments there," she said. Bella blinked, and craned her neck a little. There was nothing there now next to the surgical table but four rubber wheels. "Am thinkink it was good thing table is beink plastic."

But—there hadn't been any of the cellular changes there had been to Bulwark! In fact, Bella hadn't noticed *anything* other than the incredible draw on her own powers and energy. "Where'd it go?" she asked, feeling stupid. "I mean, what'd she *do* with it?"

"I do not know," Jadwiga replied, with a touch of irritation. "But scissors are all I was beink to save, and I am *nyet* pleased about losink equipment!"

"Fret not, Echo Med will provide," Vickie's voice answered, before Bella could. *"Or better still, I'm diverting a nice package*

on its way back from autoclaving and sterilization that's coming from Greenboy's private Blacksnake clinic."

"*Horosho,*" Jadwiga said, mollified. "*Spasibo,* Overwatch."

"*Think nothing of it. I got visual feed from Sovie if you want to see what happened, Bella, but basically near as I can describe, it was like some sort of movie SFX, the stuff just started sucking into her, with no obvious changes in* her *other than the healing.*"

Bella pulled the feeds to the pheresis machine out of the plugs in her arms. "Sweet mother-of-pearl," she said, suddenly *feeling* every bit of what she'd just gone through. "Did you do that pain-sharing thing? Because that's the only part I don't think I did."

Soviette nodded. "Was not beink pleasant, let me tell you. Would not have wished to be you when doing similar healink on Djinni." She hung an IV bag on a stand, and prepared to insert the needle in Ramona's arm. Thankfully, the detective had not woken up yet. She was still going to be in a fair amount of pain when she did, until they got some painkillers into her. "If it were not for—*borzhe moi!*"

"*What?*" Vickie and Bella said, simultaneously. But Bella had already spotted what had made Soviette exclaim and drop the IV needle.

The back of Ramona's hand—where Soviette had been trying to insert the IV needle—now sported a shiny metal shell.

Ramona blinked open one eye, the effort Herculean as her eyelids felt like lead weights. She immediately regretted the motion, light streaming from the overhead igniting a headache. Soft whirring preceded a trio of gentle beeps from the corner of the room. A soft voice spoke in Russian, followed by a higher-pitched response that started in Russian and ended in English. Both sounded exhausted.

"Is good to see you awake, Detective." The gentle face of the CCCP's lead medic came into Ramona's field of vision. She laid a hand against her forearm and studied Ramona's face, as if the simple gesture could tell her more than the nearby machines. "Do you know where you are?"

Ramona worked to open her mouth, but her jaw felt incredibly heavy. She struggled to move her tongue and her words slurred, the taste of copper and aluminum foil filling her mouth. Her face screwed up and she tried to form the words again. "CCCP HQ," she managed. "I was on my way home, it was the last train of the night, and the explosion..."

"The explosion ripped four cars from the track and rendered the southwest routes completely useless. Due to the time of the explosion, no civilians were present. As far as the public knows..." Bella moved next to Soviette, her face twisted in a half-smile. "Detective Ramona Ferrari is dead. Congratulations, you're a ghost. Feel free to pull the bedsheets over your head and make scary noises."

"But I'm not dead."

"Nyet." Soviette and Bella exchanged nervous frowns as Ramona shifted and struggled to sit up. "You are beink very much alive, and remarkably so. Would not have expected you to survive."

Even her fingers felt heavy. Ramona gripped at the sheets and tried to sit up. She expected wires and tubes to stop her movement, but as she pushed herself up against the pillows, she found nothing. An unfamiliar queasiness rumbled in her stomach. Given what they had said, Ramona expected a spiderweb of medical connections. "How... how long have I been asleep?"

"Nine hours. Is quarter past eleven." Soviette pulled up a stool, Bella following suit and resting her hands against the bedsheets. Ramona thought the blue girl looked too pale and exhausted to be awake.

"The... next day?"

"Yeah, the next day." Bella exhaled slowly, gathering the little strength that she had. "Like Sovie said, we didn't expect you to survive. We worked on you, but we had to take some extreme measures."

"Extreme measures?" She could still taste tinfoil on her tongue. Ramona quickly checked to make sure that she still had both legs, both arms, and the ability to wiggle fingers and toes. Her entire body ached and her lower abdomen felt as if someone had wrapped her in flaming barbed wire from the inside out, but she seemed to be whole. Memories of her leaving the Echo campus progressed to boarding the train, a quick debrief with Victrix via Overwatch, and then...

Ramona felt her entire body shudder. Anxiety welled up and she couldn't control the trembling, her heels knocking hard against the end of the bed. As if she had been waiting for the shakes to come, Bella reached for Ramona's hands. Weak waves of calm moved over them both. "Our priority was to keep you alive. During the first fifteen minutes, it took everything to keep you from fading out. If it hadn't been for... for the evac, you'd be a smear underneath metal and concrete. When JM brought you in, we did everything we could, but..."

"Am I still me?" Ramona gripped Bella's hand tightly. The blue woman gasped in pain and Ramona quickly let go, apology on her lips and fear in her eyes. Instinctively, the detective searched for a mirror, any kind of reflective surface. Fingers flew to her face as she tried to reassure herself that "extreme measures" didn't mean some self-contained suit or some full-body transplant.

Bella flexed her fingers. "Yes, you're you. But I had to trigger something in your cells to help you to repair the damage. You came in burned, and flooded with toxin from the inside out and broken all over. Anyone normal wouldn't have survived to make it here." She took a deep breath, steeling herself to meet Ramona's eyes. "You had a latent meta factor. I don't know if it's always been there, but I saw it and used it. After that, you..."

"You healed yourself." Jadwiga laid a gentle hand on Ramona's shoulder. "With help from others, but you healed yourself."

"A latent meta factor? As in metahuman meta?" The queasiness increased, although the trembling and anxiety didn't return. "So I'm like you? I can regenerate and heal other people?"

The two women shared a worried glance. "No," Bella finally admitted. "You're a metahuman, by all definitions, but healing isn't what we'd call the origin power. From what we saw, you're one of those who's able to manipulate inorganic material and incorporate it into your cellular structure. It's not uncommon, but it's one of the harder ones to manage."

"Inorganic... cellular... what?" Ramona pulled her hand away and threw back the sheets. She started to move her legs, but she screamed when she saw the mottled metal around her ankles and calves. With no concern for modesty, she pulled away the top of the hospital gown. Where she had felt burning wire around her torso, swaths of surgical steel covered her skin, the edges pink and tender. She pushed back against the pillows, futilely trying to distance herself from the injury. Instead, the bed groaned with the stress and weight. The two women grabbed her arms, keeping her from getting up as Ramona thrashed and cried.

"Ramona! Stop! You're not... please, we can't give you anything!"

Bella grimaced as she fought with the detective. "Calm down, or I'll have to—"

Ramona struggled for half a minute more, fear and anger giving way to despair and loss as she didn't wake up from some horrible dream on her way home from Echo. She felt Bella's attempt at consolation, but she finally gave in as the Russian woman put both arms around her shoulders and drew the blankets up around her chest. With nothing left to do, Ramona gave in to her grief and sobbed, exhausted and full of questions that neither of them were able to answer.

"Well?" Red Saviour stood outside the room, arms folded across her chest. Bella slipped out the door, rubbing at her face. "Is *nyet* accident that caused this, I am certain."

"As am I. Miss Victrix confirmed that from the cameras around the station. This was planned." Yankee Pride's gauntlets glowed with energy, his mouth drawn tight. "And for us to succeed, Verdigris has to think he won this round."

Bella nodded once. "Then we tell him nothing. Let him draw his own conclusions. Keep her here to recover in the meantime. Everything surrounding the ceremony goes as planned. And Pride . . ."

"I know, Miss Parker. Miss Victrix says she can supply some convincing remains. Officially, Detective Ramona Ferrari is dead."

CHAPTER TWENTY-SEVEN

Save Me

MERCEDES LACKEY AND CODY MARTIN

All I can say is that in the middle of all the hell we were going through... there was still time to be human.

Even for those of us who weren't.

It had been another long day for John Murdock. So much of what he did on a day-to-day basis was what a neighborhood cop would have been doing, if there had actually been any neighborhood cops left; police forces all over the world had been decimated, and they were scrambling for recruits. Hard to get them when merc organizations like the cheaper versions of Blacksnake were offering more money than any police department could offer. The rich in their gated communities were getting protection from gangs, thieves and Thulians alike; as ever, the poor were left hanging in the wind. Until the cops could get their numbers up, most beat cops were kept to high priority areas; John's neighborhood didn't qualify, so they rarely saw so much as a patrol car.

So John and CCCP were taking up the slack. Lots of walking, talking to the neighbors, showing the colors. Sometimes rousting out a dealer, or a thief, or a bully. Domestic disputes. Sometimes a genuine bad guy. Not a lot of action today. After his patrol with Georgi and Bear he had made sure to stop in at Jonas' shop to see how the neighborhood was doing socially, get the lowdown on how things were shaking out that didn't involve busting a head or three; there were a few minor chores that he had to take care of, all of them adding time to his already long shift. Tired as he was—and damn if it seemed like he could never get enough sleep these days—he was happy to take care of the tasks. The last was to check up on the community garden; it was a sight different from when he'd first helped the neighborhood start it up. Vegetables, some dwarf fruit trees, and raspberry and blackberry bushes donated by the Hog Farmers, herbs and flowers all sprouted and grew where there had once been a lot strewn with rubble and broken glass. Kids were encouraged to play carefully between the rows of plants and pull up weeds while they played. There were a lot of "weed houses" and "rock forts" in the shade of the taller plants. Action figures and dolls salvaged from the destruction corridors acted out high drama under the tomatoes. People in this neighborhood were still "shopping" in the rubble, and who could blame them? Anything that had belonged to someone still living had been claimed.

John was inspecting a short row of cornstalks when he heard someone working on the far side of the garden. Quietly he made his way around the side until he saw Upyr diligently cultivating around the roots of some bean bushes. Well, they *looked* like bushes, anyway; they were certainly waist-high and didn't look as if they were going to stop growing any time soon. At the same time she was instructing a little girl who was squatting next to her with a completely absorbed expression on her tiny face. John leaned against a post and watched the exchange.

"So, plants are beink like little girls with growink feets. You must to give them room for toes to wiggle in dirt, *da*?" The little girl giggled, and nodded. "But you do *nyet* want to tear up shoe or scratch feets at same time, so you must to beink careful." She looked up and spotted Murdock. "*Privyet,* Chonny."

"Evenin', Thea. Burnin' the midnight oil?"

She shrugged, and tossed her snow-white hair out of her eyes. "Is only sunset. And is beink too hot for pale *devushka* to vork garden in afternoon." She stood up and handed the little girl a kind of basket or bucket carefully folded out of newspaper. It was full of beans. "Now, beink take home to mama. Tellink her kale be ready for pickink tomorrow." The little girl dashed off, both arms wrapped around her bundle. Upyr picked up her gardening tools. "Are you hungry for beans, Chonny?" she said, with her Mona Lisa smile.

He held up his hands, smiling. "Naw, but thanks, comrade.

Not feeling too hungry at the moment; just a bit under the weather, lately."

"Too much Amerikanski fasting food, not enough wegetables," she scolded. "You are to beink look pale, like me! People vill to be sayink you are my twin *brat.*"

"I ought to be so lucky as to be so pretty." He grinned at her. "Now, git. I know for a fact that there's gonna be a long line at the soup kitchen. I'm gonna take a shift tomorrow morning."

"And you vill to be eatink my good borscht," she said, with a *look.* She was very proud of her borscht. She'd even gotten some of the die-hard Southerners who wouldn't eat anything that wasn't deep-fried or covered in bacon grease to slurp it down.

John just winked at her. *Nothing wrong with her borscht that a little ol' tabasco can't fix.*

She put the tools in the common storage box at the side of the garden. They were safe enough there; it wasn't as if people were likely to be stealing the garden tools they *all* needed when a two-by-four was a better weapon anyway, and the more dangerous implements, like the big shears, were kept locked in the lower half with one of those school-locker combination padlocks. Anyone who would properly need one of those had the combination.

John watched her leave, but remained. It was rare to get quiet moments like these where he could just be still and not have to think. Everyone would be at dinner now, some trying to get some sort of picture out of their jury-rigged TV antennas. Cable wasn't even *pretending* to make an effort to restore service out here; they knew damn well that no more than a third of the households had money to spare for even basic service. That was all right with John, it meant that things were quieter; how much time had people wasted in front of televisions? He felt it was better all around that they now had to actually get out in the sun and *do* something. There were benches cobbled up out of debris placed all around the garden; he walked over to one and sat down heavily, watching the sunset turn into twilight.

He felt, more than heard, the sound of wings, and a warm breath of air scented with vanilla and sandalwood wafted over him. Sera alighted on the back of the bench, and stepped from there lightly down to the ground. "I brought you food," she said, her hands cupped around a bag.

"Not borscht?" he asked.

She laughed musically. "Not borscht. Peaches." She handed him the bag, which held fragrant peaches still warm with sunshine. "The farmer told me to take them."

"Did y'scare him half to death by showing up looking like that?" He chuckled, removing a peach from the bag and taking a bite out of it.

"No-oo. He thought I should have a reward," she replied, although she didn't specify *why* the farmer had thought that. Just another one of her mysterious, ambiguous statements that implied a story she never got around to telling. She took a peach herself and nibbled it. "Oh!" she said in surprise. "They are just as good as they smell! So many things are not."

John took another bite, then chewed and swallowed. "You're an angel, Sera." He tilted his head to the side. "I only now realize how ridiculous and redundant that is for me t'say."

"Well . . . yes. But I take your meaning." She smiled at him, peach held in both hands. "Perhaps you might come to actually believe it, if you say it often enough."

He pointed a finger at her, peach still in hand. "Don't get any ideas about convertin' me just yet." He sighed, putting his elbows on his knees. "Still too much to do, an' not enough time or energy for it."

As if on cue, his CCCP-issue comm device beeped. John held up a finger for silence apologetically, then keyed the comm device. "Murdock, here. Go."

It was Jadwiga on duty, this time. *"Comrade Murdock. We are needing you to be reporting for another shift; cannot be helped, as we are short-handed. Report to HQ in all haste. HQ, out."*

John sighed again. "No rest for the wicked, nor any for the bone-tired."

"You are weary," she said, sympathetically. And there it was, another evidence of how *alien* she was. A human woman, meeting at last with her—what was he to her? Not a lover . . .

Not yet, but . . .

Well, a *human* woman would have been unhappy at the least, angry or annoyed or petulant at the worst, at having the meeting cut so short, and would have voiced a complaint, or a demand for him to tell HQ to find someone else. But Sera—Sera just looked at him with sympathy and understanding, and spoke of his weariness.

"That could be said of the whole world, darlin'." He shrugged, but... that attitude, that understanding, was unbelievably liberating. Her regard lifted him, rather than putting him in chains.

His neighborhood was a standout from many areas; here the people actively tried to help each other. In a lot of other places, especially in countries without an Echo presence or an organization like the CCCP to bolster security forces, everyone was forced to look over their shoulders. Things were downright medieval in some areas. Still, Sera's attitude and presence did more for him than he could adequately express to her.

"Oh, you are *all* weary, but you are particularly weary. I believe I can help. Remember?" She tilted her head charmingly to one side.

"Tryin' to fish for another kiss, Sera? First you bribe me with peaches..." He flashed her a lopsided grin, nudging her shoulder with his own.

"I like kisses," she said thoughtfully. "Very much. But I do not *need* to kiss you to help you, only touch your hand."

"Heh. I almost forgot that you can do that." In truth, he had *not* forgotten. But it just wasn't John's way to ask for help any more than absolutely needed. He did want Sera to help him... and more than just help him. But he'd never ask for it.

"You are a very stubborn man, John Murdock," she said severely. "If you do not learn to *ask*, very often you will not *get*."

"Others with more of a need than mine, Sera. Just the way it is; anyways, I'm tough." He smiled again, leaning closer to her. "I'll manage."

"You are stubborn *and* foolish," she replied.

"Funny, Ma said the same thing 'bout me all the time."

"Your ma was right. Be quiet and be kissed." She put her peach pit aside, and put her arms around his neck, and suited her actions to her words.

John leaned in closer, wrapping his arms around her, and reciprocated with equal fervor. Instantly, he felt better: more alert, stronger, and nowhere near as tired as he had been. His emotions lifted as well; the edge of depression that had been on everything faded. After what seemed like a long time, not long enough, and no time at all, he pulled away, the smile still on his face, the scent of peaches mingling with her sandalwood and cinnamon and vanilla, wreathing them both. "Like I said before, if'n you could bottle that, we'd make a fortune."

She wrinkled her nose at him. "Bella says the same. And no, I do not *kiss* her."

"Well, shucks, there goes all my adolescent fantasies." He touched the tip of her nose with his finger. "Don't worry, Angel; you'll suit me fine all on yer own."

She chuckled. "I hope so. I do not intend to indulge your *adolescent fantasies.* Bella would be horrified. And then she would hit you. You should ask the Djinni about her right hook."

"Don't need to ask him; she's hit me before, for entirely different reasons." He checked his comm device, which was blinking still. "A story for another time, I'm afraid. Duty calls. Again. It's kinda like a bad ex-girlfriend that way. Always showin' up at the wrong times."

"I will meet you on the roof. I shall bring beer. You must bring some of that lovely floppy pizza stuff. I too have duties, and I should be about them."

"Sounds like a deal to me, darlin'." He stood up, kissing her on her brow. "I'll see ya in a few hours." With that, John started jogging towards the CCCP HQ, feeling and looking much better than he had just a few minutes before. *Turnin' out to be a fine evening, if I do say so myself.*

The Seraphym stared after him, with longing, and with a little unease. It had taken more energy to heal and fill him than she had thought it should. She wondered if there was something wrong; he had been getting sick and even injured often these past few months, but the work he did often had him becoming injured and stressed. Even a metahuman physiology could only contend against such a rigorous routine for so long.

She *listened,* but the Infinite offered no hints. She shrugged and touched her lips, smiling again, thinking of the kiss. There was much to be said for being material. Mortal memories of such things were no match for experiencing them firsthand. She sat there for a little longer, before the sound of a soft footstep made her look up.

There was a little girl standing there, looking at her expectantly. It was one of the ones she had told stories to. She smiled, and beckoned the child to her, and put the rest of the bag of peaches in her hands. "Take those to your mama, love," she said. The child peeked inside, gave a squeal of glee, and ran off.

Then she picked up the two peach seeds, hers and Johns, and

took them to an empty spot in the garden where a rose bush had failed to thrive and been taken up. She put them gently into the earth, and patted the soil over the top.

"*Grow,*" she whispered, and felt them respond.

But then she felt the calling. It was time for her to return to the work, as well. And with a flash of flame, she was gone, another life to save.

CHAPTER TWENTY-EIGHT

Descent

MERCEDES LACKEY, DENNIS LEE, CODY MARTIN

"The best-laid plans of mice and men aft gang a-glay. . . ." Robert Burns said that. Truer words were never spoken. For both sides.

The Echo locker room was packed. Bulwark's full team of trainees was suiting up for duty for a fairly routine and very dull escort mission for the retirees of Echo. There weren't a lot of them, enough to take up about two cars of the MARTA red line train from the airport. About two or three retirees per escort.

One of those escorts was . . . very loud. Loud out of all proportion to his size. "I am telling you, Bulwark and the blue chick, the CMO, are *totally* getting it on. I heard it all over in Echo Med. He's over there practically every night, and what *else* would you be doing with a gal that's that smokin' hot?"

Frank—who had taken the callsign of "Frankentrain"—had been a member of Echo two years before the Invasion in, of all places, Providence, Rhode Island. His power was that his skin was nearly granite-tough, and he was, as he put it "pretty hard to kill." He and the only other OpTwo in Providence had both been steam locomotive hobbyists, and had been at an antique rail museum working on one of their "babies" when the Invasion began. His friend who, unfortunately, had been stronger but not nearly as hard to kill, had squeezed boiler plate into makeshift armor for both of them before they answered the red alert. Frank had kept the armor, now worn over a nanoweave suit, and kept the nickname he'd picked up that day as his callsign.

"I don't know, Frank," drawled Paperback Rider, from the corner where he was (as always) half-immersed in a book, print scrolling over his paper-white face as he read. "Bulwark just doesn't seem like the type. Really doesn't seem like the type. If I were making bets, it would be on . . . chess matches, maybe."

Frankentrain guffawed. "You have *got* to be kidding me. Her? I'd say more like *chest* matches, if ya know what I mean. I bet her chest size just about matches her IQ. But ya don't date a chick like that for intellectual talk. More like the other four-letter word, right?"

Frank had not noticed that the rest of the room had gone oddly quiet.

"Man, I envy him. What's he got that's so special anyway? He's got about the same amount of expression as a brick. If he's not all over her, *he'd* have to have the same IQ as a block of linoleum, and hell, we all know he's not that dumb. No, he is *totally* doing her. Absolutely. I am so sure I would bet on it. I . . ." Frank felt a chill as an enormous shadow fell over him. ". . . he's right behind me, isn't he?"

"Yes, Frankentrain, I am," Bulwark rumbled. "Don't you think you should be armored up by now?"

Bella smiled for the cameras. There were hundreds of them, and that didn't count the cell phones and so on in the hands of the audience. She smiled and stayed one careful step behind Verdigris, but kept the artful, hip-shot, swimsuit-model poses that the cameras wanted. Verdigris had ordered a special uniform for her just for this occasion; in her personal opinion, it looked like something a very high-class, role-playing hooker would wear for a client, but based on a doctor's smock rather than a nurse's uniform. It was just that *tiny* bit too form-fitting, showed just a *little* too much cleavage, for anyone to take her seriously. Which was the point, probably. It had the Echo logo superimposed on the standard red medical cross just over her right breast.

I hate this, she thought resentfully. She wasn't even sure why she was here. *She* hadn't been on the Echo campus on the day of the Invasion. It would make more sense to have someone who had been there standing here now.

On the other hand . . . this might be her one, best shot to get at Verd and give him that stroke . . . she'd been completely unable to get anywhere near him until now. Her requests to make reports in person had been sloughed off, and anywhere he went in public, Khanjar was right at his elbow. Now... she wasn't. She was directly behind him, but standing behind Bella, and her attention was directed more at the audience than at the people on the podium.

I bet at some point he's gonna grab me around the waist for some sort of photo op. That would be the time to do it. Ramona and the others were confident that the charter plot was going to work, but she wasn't so sure. After all, this was Verdigris they were dealing with. He had a history of being one step ahead of his enemies. So what should it be? Should it be something minor, in the cerebral cortex, something that would just hamper him? While that was the option that gave her the fewest ethical heebie-jeebies, and it was the safest for *her* since it was unlikely Khanjar would even notice she had done anything, it wasn't one she particularly favored. Because... this was Verdigris. For all *she* knew, his brain could rewire itself in a situation like that. So the only other options were a psionic lobotomy, something massive to turn him into a vegetable, or something fatal.

Which might very well turn fatal for her if Khanjar decided correctly that Bella was the cause when Verd collapsed. Bella reckoned the odds were about fifty-fifty that Khanjar would do just that. Higher than that if Khanjar remembered how Bella had taken out that gang-banger back when she was just a DCO.

She glanced over to Verdigris' other side, where Yankee Pride stood, looking entirely comfortable with the attention, yet appropriately solemn. Would Pride notice in time to intervene, if Khanjar attacked? Could he hold the assassin off if he did? Did she want him to try?

Well... no. Because tough as he was, he wasn't ready to take on an assassin in hand-to-hand combat.

Which of us is more important to Echo, him or me? Him, of course.

Behind them was the monument. It was elevated on a Carrera marble pedestal that had bronze plaques with the names of all the Echo metas that had died in the Invasion. It was a very tall pedestal; they were on a platform in front of it, and the pedestal top ended about six feet from the top of the platform. There would be no climbing up on it to view parades and tag the extremely expensive sculpture itself with graffiti. Bella had no idea what the sculpture looked like. No one did. Right now it was swathed in a huge blanket of canvas, banked by two Jumbotrons so that *everyone* could see Verdigris as if they were in their own living room. She was pretty sure it cost enough to keep every school in Atlanta funded for the next ten years. It had been created by a computer rather than an artist, and it would be devoid of meaning. Well, except as a monument to *just how rich* Verdigris was, since he'd been making the point he'd funded this out of his own personal fortune.

Everyone had begun to line up just right. The news vans had already disgorged their news teams, who had all set up their cameras and lights, jockeying for position to get the best shot of the unveiling of the "Echo Memorial for the Invasion." Verdigris was busy making small talk with all of the luminaries that he had invited or who had invited themselves; no one wanted to be left out of this event. There was still a lot of unrest, especially among the journalists, about Echo: why weren't they doing more, why were there still Thulian attacks, when would everyone be safe and how it was all Echo's fault. He'd been carefully manipulating opinions for the last month to be more favorable toward Echo; nothing too overt, but just enough so that today's events would serve as a catalyst for a wave of overwhelming support. That support would help him get done what needed to be done, what *had* to be done. Sometimes Verdigris wanted to just sit down in front of the cameras and outline for the whole world how if they just did what he said, then everything would make sense and go *so* much smoother and more efficiently. All they had to do was follow his directions completely and without question. After all, wasn't he arguably the smartest man in the world? Shouldn't they just quit jockeying with each other and listen to him for a change?

Verdigris flashed another perfect and perfectly fake smile as he shook hands with the mayor. The world didn't work that way, unfortunately; nothing would be so simple that he could just lay everything out for everyone and have it happen. Today, however, would work: another thing that needed to happen, for the good of everyone. Even if they didn't know it or agree with it.

He was aware of Bella Dawn Parker behind him, and Khanjar

behind her. Bella was performing exactly as expected; eye candy for the cameras, with an outfit he had strategically picked out. She posed as if she had been born to model. Sex sells, no matter what anyone will tell you; he needed to sell her right now not only as the brainless bimbo but also as the calendar fodder. Both images served his purposes. After today, she would become irrelevant, anyway; all of Echo Medical would be replaced by his own people, people he was completely in control of. Without Ramona Ferrari around to issue orders, they'd flounder in the crisis he was about to manufacture, and he'd have all the excuse he could ask for to shut them down and replace them with medics who would be sure to follow his orders. Just a little longer, that's all he needed...

There's that word, again. Need. Verdigris wasn't used to it; he'd never had needs, outside of the basic ones. He'd had desires, all of which he was able to fulfill with relative ease, either through his immense wealth or his intellect, or both. But today, he *needed* everything to go right. His life, his future depended upon it. It was an uncomfortable feeling, at best; he did his best to push it away as he moved on to the next city politician that had come to make an appearance and use the valuable photo opportunity; for all of the ire that Echo and metahumans had received for not doing enough during and since the Invasion, no one could afford to be seen as being anything but supportive of the metahumans that were really all that stood between them and the Kriegers.

Verdigris noticed Khanjar out of the corner of his eye; she caught his attention, subtly motioning that it was time to begin. *Good. The sooner this is over with, the sooner I can move forward with far more enjoyable things.* He checked his PDA—excellent. All the flights had been delayed *just* enough that the Echo retirees were all still waiting for the baggage, or slowly tottering up to the waiting point for the special Echo MARTA express downtown. They'd be delayed just enough to miss the ceremony, and as he had planned, they'd be sitting on the shuttle when he was about halfway through his planned address.

He graciously disengaged from the crowd of VIPs on the stage, waiting for everyone to take their positions before he approached the podium. Once he saw that everyone was ready, he turned to the news cameras and the gathered crowd, smiling, before composing his face in an appropriately solemn expression. The cameras got their cue from Khanji, who was supposed to be his executive assistant; they all focused on him. The Jumbotrons above his head filled with his face, and the speakers up and down the streets went live. Flawlessly, of course. No squeals of feedback for Verdigris Electronics.

"Ladies and gentleman. I'd like to thank all of you for joining us here today, on the anniversary of the Invasion..."

Bulwark looked over the specially modified MARTA trains for the Echo veterans and winced inwardly. As part of the festivities, the mayor had seized upon the opportunity to showcase the next generation of transit cars that had been sped up through production to replace those that had been destroyed during the Invasion. Only three of the seven train cars were actually new, having just been finished that week, the first car at the front and the two luxury passenger cars at the rear reserved for the veterans. In theory, every car could be the engine; they all had control booths and were automatically slaved to the car in the lead, but the lead today didn't even necessarily need a driver, though it had one. They certainly looked sleeker, he had to admit, but certain features had been lost in the rush for development. For one thing, the old models had allowed for easy access between cars. These new cars were sealed, each car separated from the rest. He didn't like it. Too many holes in their security, too many ways for their defenses to be compromised. Not that he really expected anything to go awry, but still, he had been tasked with escorting their honored guests, and he always took his tasks seriously.

And while he thought of himself as a patriotic sort, the wild and erratic red, white and blue markings that enveloped each car seemed rather gauche. Even worse, the insertion of the four older-model train cars in the middle gave the whole ensemble a sloppy, patchwork effect.

"Overwatch to Bulwark."

"Go ahead," Bull said.

"All your charges are suffering delays. Either in the baggage handling system or ground traffic control. Does that seem odd to you?"

Bulwark *hmph*ed. "Atlanta International's on-time record isn't exactly sterling."

"Roger that. Advise that you're not going to make it for the ceremony. Out."

"Well, we'll just see about that," Bulwark rumbled. He glanced around the platform, spotted one of the on-site organizers, and made his way over to her. She was a young girl, early twenties he would have guessed, if not just by her appearance but her overwhelming sense of purpose and enthusiasm. She clutched her tablet-sized PDA with aplomb and flashed a dazzling smile as she directed her crew to ready the train for departure. She gave particular instructions regarding the special passenger cars at the rear, peppering her underlings with enthusiastic reminders concerning the comfort of the guests of honor.

". . . and let's not forget those special cushions those darling children at the hospital made for today! I want one on each and every seat! Let's make sure these heroes have a safe and comfortable ride into the city! Now move, people, shoo!"

"Excuse me, miss," Bull said, and nodded politely to her. "It would seem we're running the risk of being late for the ceremonies. Is there anything we might do to speed things along?"

"Oh wow! You're one of the Echo people!" the girl gushed. "I'm sorry sir, you know how these things go, scheduling *never* takes flight delays and such into account. I'm sure our guests will be right along and we'll have them down to the celebration lickity-split!"

"Please, Miss . . ."

"Tammy," she provided, helpfully.

"Please, Miss Tammy," Bulwark said, with exaggerated patience. "I would appreciate your help in this matter. It would be a very poor showing if we arrived late."

"Oh bother," she scoffed with a flamboyant wave of her hand. "I'm sure they'll wait! These are *very* special guests, after all!"

"Please," Bull repeated.

"Oh fine, fine," Tammy said, and tapped on her earpiece. "Sheila? Can you give me an update on our guests? Are they through the . . . uh huh. Uh huh. Oh, that's simply darling, really? Well, please ask him to wrap it up. Nicely, of course. I'm sure security is simply en*thralled* by his D-Day stories, but he's got a ceremony to make and we're running late. Thanks, Sheila, you're a peach! Love to Sammy, talk to you soon, sweetie!" She turned back to Bulwark and grinned. "They're just coming out of security. We'll have them on the train before you know it!"

Tammy glanced back at the train and rolled her eyes. "That is, if my people could just follow a few simple in*structions!*"

Bull sighed. "I appreciate your . . . attention to detail, Miss Tammy, but I have to question if all that frivolity is really necessary. I would rather the train be ready to leave as soon as the passengers are on board."

"Frivolity?" she gasped in dismay. "Mister Hero, I would think *you* of all people would want these brave souls to have every bitty bit of respect we can show them! Don't you think we owe them that, hmmm? Didn't they serve this country and risk their lives, day in and day out, all in the name of peace and justice and all that good stuff, hmmm? I was told to get them downtown in *style* and that's *just* what I'm going to do! And I'll have you know that I *personally* worked on those lace curtains!" She sniffed. "If you want to speed things along, perhaps you and your people could lend a hand."

Bull looked at her, helplessly, and returned to his trainees.

"We're running behind," he told them. "Get in there and help them . . . set up the doilies."

He was met with incredulous looks and smirks, which disappeared once they saw he wasn't kidding. With Bull, it was sometimes hard to tell. A few of them muttered a few choice oaths about menial tasks, but proceeded into the train to assist the prep crew all the same. Most had learned the hard way not to disobey Bull's orders.

"You too, Rider," Bull said.

Paperback Rider looked up from his book. "Huh? What?"

Rider was never without a book in his hands; like so many of the newest crop of metahumans, his power had triggered on the day of the Invasion, and it was an . . . odd one. Whatever he read vanished from the page as he read it, and became briefly a part of him. If there was a character with a skill or a power in what he read, he *had* that skill or power until he used it. But as he used it, the print of the book scrolled rapidly across his paper-white face and hands—his whole body, Bulwark presumed, though he'd never asked—and once it was gone, so was that skill. And he could never use the same book twice.

When he wasn't in action, print still scrolled over him, but Bulwark assumed it was from one or another of the random books he had read, things that would give a man social skills, because he thought he could detect minor changes in Rider's personality from time to time. Echo simply made sure he had a steady supply of volumes of men's action-adventure, science fiction, fantasy, and metahuman fiction—and the occasional instructional manual for variety. They'd never given him metahuman *non*fiction, however, unless the meta in question was long dead. No one wanted to find out what would happen if he absorbed a book about... say... Yankee Pride...

"Get in there and help them out," Bull said, and frowned when he realized Rider was reading the operator's manual for the new line of MARTA trains. "Where did you get that?"

"It was lying on the conductor's seat," Rider said with a shrug. "Thought I'd absorb something while we were just sitting around. Never know when it might come in handy."

"Well you're not sitting around, not anymore." Bulwark pointed at the train. "Go, help."

Rider sighed, but got to his feet and shuffled off with his comrades.

Dusty "Troubadour" Markelhay wasn't your typical meta. He wasn't gifted with highly destructive powers or a chiseled jaw or washboard abs that so many Echo Ops seemed to have. He was rather homely, actually. The standard-issue Echo nanoweave clung to his disproportionate frame and bulged in all the wrong places. He had a noticeable limp, and years of persistent skin problems had left his face pock-marked and unsightly.

Dusty did, however, possess a rather remarkable smile.

It was an odd power, but when he flashed those pearly whites he found he could talk people into doing just about anything. A wry grin could smooth over a small argument. An open smile would get him into a complete stranger's confidence in an instant. A chuckle could bring an entire room to hysterical laughter, even without the benefit of a joke. He supposed his was an ability that could be easily abused, but the thought never crossed his mind. Fortunately, Dusty was one of those rare individuals whose entire purpose was to help his fellow man. Someone once described it as "the hunger to feed mankind," and he had to admit that was a nice way of putting it. He enjoyed life, he enjoyed people, and when Echo had come knocking on his door, he had jumped at the chance to join and serve. The problem was, no one had really wanted him on their team. Not even Spin Doctor. His powers didn't seem to work over video capture.

It had been Bulwark, of course, who had agreed to take him on. Bull had seen something in him that no one else had, that no one else seemed to value in a time of crisis. Dusty was an eternal optimist. He was an earnest young man who tried his best at everything he did, and did it with such cheer and warmth that those around him were often caught up in his infectious desire to do a good job. At that moment, Dusty was doing his absolute best to roll out a soft, red velvet carpet from the passenger cars to the escalators leading down from the main landing. He whistled a happy tune while he worked, doing his utmost to keep the carpet straight and tidy.

"Ooooh," a shrill voice squealed. "That's just perfect!"

Dusty turned, and smiled at the giddy and attractive girl.

"Thanks, Tammy!" he said. "There you go, just like you asked for. Anything else I can do for you?"

Tammy favored him with an appreciative look. "You're such a dear! Yes, my good little soldier, you can help me set up the champagne bar in the veterans' car! I've got a few boxes of the bubbly stashed in the storage room and I'm sure a strong fellow like you can help me cart them out."

Dusty chuckled. "It would be a pleasure, my lady."

Tammy linked her arm in his and led him away, chuckling and flattering him outrageously as they made their way to storage. As they entered the dimly lit corridor, Dusty was immediately struck by how dirty these maintenance halls were. Harsh fluorescent tubes glared nakedly from the cheapest of overhead fixtures, flickering and sputtering as they passed underneath. The clicks from Tammy's high heels echoed around them, and Dusty felt a momentary chill.

"Kinda spooky," he said with a nervous laugh. "Like in a scary movie."

Tammy giggled and patted his arm. "I'm not worried. I have you here to protect me!"

He grinned at her, then flinched. He pulled away and stared at her, just as the overhead light flickered off.

"Why, Dusty," Tammy said, puzzled. "Whatever is the matter?"

"I... I thought..." Dusty started, then laughed. "I thought I saw something. Must have been the light, but you looked like..."

The tube flashed back on, and Dusty's eyes went wide in fright.

"I knew I shouldn't have skipped breakfast this morning," Tammy sighed.

She lunged for him, grabbing him by the throat and hoisting him off the ground. Dusty tried to scream but she clamped down on his windpipe and hissed. Her skin had turned scaly. Dusty felt her claws dig into him, and he stared helplessly into her black, snakelike eyes.

"I guess I'll just have to settle for brunch," she said. She slammed him against the wall, covered his face with her free hand, and stole his life-force in great, ravenous draughts, her eyes narrowed in bliss. At last, she let out a sigh of contentment. She continued down the hall, carrying Dusty's lifeless husk by the throat, until she came to a trash bin. She raised the lid, appraised the frozen look of terror on his face with a smirk, and dropped him in.

"Thank you, my good little soldier," she purred, and slammed the lid closed. She drew a small compact from her pocket, opened it, and shook her head in dismay at the reflection.

"Well that just won't do."

Harmony squinted at herself as she rubbed the skin around her eyes and played with the tip of her nose. The scales were gone, at least, but the disguise had fallen away, reverting to her original bone and muscle structure. She took a breath, concentrated, and watched herself in the mirror as she willed Tammy to return. Her cheekbones dropped, her nose flattened, and the fullness of her lips blossomed to exaggerated proportions.

"There!" she said, her voice resuming a high-pitched, chipper tone. "Much better! Now then, let's go kidnap us some veterans before the strain of keeping this face on forces me to have an early dinner as well!"

Humming a happy tune, she proceeded to the supply room for the champagne.

As the train pulled out of the station, Bulwark grunted in relief. They would be late, of that there was no question, but at their current speed they could probably arrive before the ceremony finished. Provided, of course, that there were no further delays.

When the veterans finally arrived at the terminal, there were a few moments of happy reunions and some oohing and aahing over the new MARTA car models, before Bulwark and his team firmly but politely ushered them on. That, at least, had gone smoothly. They seemed eager to see the stylish interior of the rear guests-of-honor passenger cars. Bull left them with a handful of attendants and Echo metas and led the remainder of his crew into the older, middle compartments. Unlike the opulent rear cars these were strictly utilitarian, fitted with simple seating and compartments for baggage and cameras and the "Welcome to Echo Atlanta, Heroes" props.

It was actually a funny thought, amusing to Bulwark in a day so far filled with frustration, thinking about how the roadies must have run to set the props up a little ahead of the procession, then run behind them to gather them up again so no one in the terminal would suffer any inconvenience.

As his squads arranged themselves amongst the bustling group of organizers, trying not to get in their way as they continued in the preparations for their arrival, Bull opted to stand off to one side and take in the organized chaos. His lips curled slightly, his muted version of a frown, as he noted a few discrepancies. Some of the organizers were chatting loudly about body count, gear tally and checklists while others seemed engrossed in what he could only guess as busywork. They moved about, checking straps and harnesses to ensure their gear was lashed in tight, but otherwise didn't seem to be doing much of anything. It was almost as if they were pretending to be doing something, to be doing anything.

A shrill voice caught his attention. The main organizer, Tammy, was berating one poor girl. Something about frayed cushion seats. He supposed that explained a lot. You didn't want to appear idle under Tammy's watch, not unless you wished to suffer her wrath. He wondered how much of Tammy's brittle perkiness was due to her personality, and how much to heavy medication, because running that sort of job was probably a nightmare. Still, something didn't seem quite right.

He jerked to attention as screams sounded from the rear. The access door leading to the fifth car flew open and people streamed out amidst heavy clouds of smoke.

"Fire!" someone yelled. *"We've got a fire back here!"*

"Teams two through four!" Bulwark shouted. "Converge on car five! Investigate and put that fire out; we are not going to suffer any more holdups today!"

He joined his forces as they fought the stream of people fleeing from the smoke and joined what Echo personnel were already there. Visibility was nil, though there were plenty of confused shouts of alarm as his squads milled about the car for the source of the smoke. There didn't seem to be anything ablaze, no source of heat, as if...

"There's no fire here, Bull!" he heard Frankentrain shout. "There's just a lot of smoke!"

"Who's got eyes on the source?" Bull shouted back. "Where's it coming from?"

No one answered, and no one needed to, as the smoke dissipated. In an instant, the haze cleared and all the Echo metas looked about in confusion.

"That would be me," a voice giggled behind them.

They turned to see a girl smiling at them from car four. Faint wisps of smoke hung about her hands, and evaporated with a snap of her fingers. She laughed, and slammed the door shut.

"We've been had!" Bull snarled and leapt for the door, but stopped as a voice boomed over the in-train PA system.

"I wouldn't do that, Mister Echo Man!" Tammy shrieked, her shrill cry deafening over the crackling static of the PA. "There's an awful lot of boom rigged to blow on the last two cars, and guess who's got her finger right over the boom button?"

Explosives... which meant hostages... which meant whoever this was, they wanted something. Bulwark wasn't an *expert* in hostage negotiation, but by necessity, as an Echo op, he'd done his share over the years. Still... he *had* an expert negotiator on the team—

"Dusty," he growled quietly into his comm unit. "You're up. Get up here so she can see your face."

There was no answer. Bull turned to look back at his crew. Troubadour wasn't there.

Vickie didn't like it. There was nothing she could absolutely pin down—and Bull was right; Atlanta Hartsfield didn't exactly have the best on-time record. But was it reasonable that the baggage conveyers for the retirees—and *only* the retirees whose planes had come in on time—would suddenly malfunction? Was it reasonable that some kerfuffle in ground traffic control would keep planes on the tarmac when she could *see* there were open gates?

Was it possible that Verd had gotten wind of trouble?

It's Verdigris. Of course it's possible.

But what possible advantage could there be for him to delay the retirees' arrival until after the memorial ceremony? Delay was going to make no difference to the charter plans. The retirees were all going to go to a party CCCP was ostensibly throwing; the old barn of a building had several rooms that used to hold manufacturing equipment that were all linked together and more than big enough to hold everyone. Once there, Vickie would activate the conference screens for every Echo HQ on the planet. Dixie and Ramona would tell them the real reason for their assembly, Vickie would throw open the lines to Atlanta and the other Echo HQs for remote voting and that would be that. No one at the other HQs knew the reason for the remote link; they all thought it was going to be a chance to see and maybe talk with legendary heroes of the past, and virtually everyone had signed up for the conference. The only people who knew the truth here were all those wired into Overwatch. There was no way Verd could know.

The ceremony was well under way. By now it was obvious that the guests weren't going to make it in time. Verd improvised something . . . wait . . .

Vickie used a camera just behind Verdigris to zoom in on Verd's PDA. It was meticulously outlining a second-by-second set of notes.

That wasn't improvising! It was right there in his notes. *Regret that delays hit honored guests. Promise access later.*

The *hell?* He *was* behind it! But why?

Before she could signal Bulwark, Bella, or Ramona, the situation blew up in her face.

One of her monitors showed all the security camera feeds from every car in the train. It had been pathetically easy to tap into. The bulk of Bull's team appeared clustered in the fifth car, the rest were milling about confused with the guests of honor on cars six and seven. Bull himself was rushing for the door to the fourth car. The PA system on the train came to tinny life. "*I wouldn't do that, Mister Echo Man! There's an awful lot of boom rigged to blow on the last two cars, and guess who's got her finger right over the boom button? We're the Rebs, and we'll be your hosts during this hostage crisis. Don't try to leave your cars, don't try to use your powers or . . . poof. End of hostage crisis, and we wouldn't want to end the fun early, would we? So . . . yeah . . . we got us some demands . . .*"

"Rebs my ass," Vickie muttered, and paid no attention to the list of "demands" that were being read off, because at that moment her standalone "Magic 8 Ball" computer began flashing the full alert screen and sounding an alarm.

MARTA Hijacking: Current. Primal Cause: Dominic Verdigris. Probability: 100%.

Vickie swore in Russian, but her hands were already moving. "Overwatch: Command: open Red Saviour, Gamayun, Bella, Pride private. People, we have a hostage situation on the MARTA. Repeat, a hostage situation on the MARTA. Verd's taken the old-timers hostage. His people, probably Blacksnake, posing as Rebs. Armed and dangerous. Commissar, the train is still in motion and is not slowing down." She repeated the demands that the phony Reb leader had made. "Those are probably code or trigger IDs for something else; maybe to tell Verd what stage they're at. CCCP, you guys are the wild card; Verd won't be planning on you doing anything. So . . . whatever you do, it'll screw him over. Patching you all in full Overwatch group mode now. Those of you with the new rig, use it!"

John was in the break room with Pavel when the call came. Bear was expounding on the merits of *Roseanne* as a teaching tool for family dynamics; John had been doing his best for the past hour and a half to just nod and sip his beer without really listening. Unfortunately, he was just about out of beer; since he was technically on call, he couldn't leave the HQ for at least another four hours. *The sacrifices I make for my comrades . . . to protect them from my comrades.*

Just as John had finished the last of his beer, an alarm came to life briefly, followed by a burst of static on the intercom.

"Attention, attention; all hands. Situation on the MARTA line; Echo hostages have been taken. All on-duty personnel are to report to the briefing room immediately in full gear." That was Gamayun; she repeated the instructions in rapid-fire Russian. Then the alarm came back on. At the same time, his Overwatch rig came to life. "People, we have a hostage situation on the MARTA. Repeat, a hostage situation on the MARTA . . ." Vickie repeated the list of phony "demands"—weapons, money, about half of Georgia to be ceded to them and renamed "State of Rebellion." "Patching you all in full Overwatch group mode now. Those of you with the new rig, use it!"

John set the empty beer bottle down, slapping one of Pavel's metal knees with his free hand. "Time to go to work, old timer. An' not a moment too soon."

He was already up and jogging away when Bear stood up, shouting, "But I was about to be getting to my treatise on John Goodman's approach to fatherhood!"

Five minutes later, John was running towards the briefing room while still zipping up his vest. Some of the CCCP had nanoweave gear, mixed and matched with what was already on hand; it was lucky that CCCP uniform colors were predominantly black, since nanoweave didn't take dyes. John rounded the last corner and trotted into the briefing room, followed seconds later by the rest of the on-duty comrades. The usual suspects—Georgi, Pavel, and Mamona—all shared shifts more often than not, with the duty roster rotating so that they all switched patrol partners some of the time. Georgi was John's usual motorcycle patrol partner; they worked well together. The Commissar was already suited up and waiting for them. *I wonder if she sleeps in the damned patrol uniform; she's always first one here, even with no warning, an' always suited up.* She was grinning, her face down and eyes examining each of them as the team fell in.

When everyone was settled, she leaned forward, placing her hands on the worn table in front of her. That same smile, which would have seemed conspiratorial on anyone else but was disquieting when worn by the Commissar, was still there.

"Today, comrades," she said, drawing out the words as if to savor them, "it is, how they say here, 'open season' on mercenaries. And there will be *nyet* anything 'sublethal' about it."

"Overwatch: Command: Mark Two Overwatch. Open Corbie, Knight, Leader, Sammies, Ramona, Bella, Pride, Bulwark, Djinni, Shakti, public, public group link. Add Saviour, Soviette, Unter, JM, public, public group link." Vickie's hands flew over the keyboard. "Heads up, this is Overwatch. CCCP dispatched. Saviour is ground command CCCP, since she's free to move and Pride's not. Camera feeds on your HUD from the train. All of you with the new rig are linked up now. You can access folks with the old rig with the command Open Overwatch Mark One and their name, or let me handle it." People with the old rig were getting a recorded repeat of her original alert now, and responses were coming in as she linked them in group mode. At the ceremony, things were proceeding as if the hostage situation wasn't occurring at all. Of course they were. This was all being orchestrated by Verd, and he'd pull the reveal only when he was good and ready. She listened with half an ear while the others began coordinating with each other. After a few—surprisingly few—moments of confusion, that was exactly what they did. The past few weeks of working out the internal rebellion had done... wonders.

"Nat, Bull, I'm ceding strat as well as command to you," Yankee Pride muttered, unbearable tension and frustration clear in his voice. "Verd's actin' like nothing's happening. If I break away, he'll know we've copped onto it and we're reactin'—wait, somethin's goin' on."

Well that was clear enough. Verdigris had put one hand to an ear, frowning, then muttered something into a lapel mic. The "something" was fully audible to Vickie, using Pride and Bella's enhanced pickups. "Right. Dispatch Response Teams Gamma, Victor and Sigma. It's only Rebs; how hard can it be to put them down? No, don't bother scrambling Echo Medical, these *are* metas, after all, even if they are retired. They won't get hurt. This is no more than a publicity stunt and an annoyance." Then he returned his attention to the audience, continuing his speech as though nothing had happened.

"Patch me through to Echo Med," Bella ordered, turning her face away from Verd and Khanjar, her voice a thread of a whisper. Vickie complied, putting Bella not only on the Med comms, but the Med PA system. Bella's voice might be inaudible to anyone next to her, but Vickie made sure it was at a good volume going out. "Echo Med: this is Belladonna Blue. Red alert, full scramble. The MARTA with the retirees has been hijacked. I need the full response team up and moving. Ignore all other orders but mine. Dispatch to MARTA Five Points terminal and set up, but be prepared to move on the instant. Suit up in nanoweave. And go armed, if you don't have offensive powers. If you have the new comms, use them. Do you copy?"

Even if they weren't wired with Overwatch rigs, the past several weeks of Bella as their CMO had instilled a firm confidence in her in every member of Echo Med. And by this point, most of Echo Med *was* on Overwatch Mark One. Including the DCO with Bull's teams on the train—Gilead, who Vickie could see looking up at the camera from car seven and nodding slightly. Good.

The response was immediate. "Panacea here, lead DCO. We copy, CMO. Pacifist protocol off. Moving now. Out."

"I take it we scramble as ordered?" That was Corbie coming in. His team was one of the three Verd had ordered out. *Probably to be cannon fodder.*

"Yes," said Bulwark, very quietly. Clearly he too was avoiding being overheard. "Then ignore anything that doesn't come from me or Red Saviour."

"They could be to ignorink you, too, Comrade Bulwark," Saviour sniped. "I see you beink pinned down, I believe I am beink true free agent."

"Bull, how do you want me to handle the ones that aren't on Overwatch?" Vickie asked.

"Can you patch into the Echo freqs without Verdigris finding out about it?" he asked.

She ran through some mathemagical calculations in her mind. "Maybe. Fifty-fifty."

"Who's Echo Dispatch today?" he wanted to know.

"Dean Colt." She knew him by voice; he had been on the list of those they wanted to approach, but she hadn't gotten around to her usual grueling background check yet.

"Good man. I'll take the chance he's not on Verdigris' payroll. Contact him directly and do it through him."

Vickie's hands were flying again, while she issued more commands. "Overwatch: Command: open direct line Echo Dispatch op." Meanwhile she directed her rig to scan for Blacksnake comm. They were using one, of course, how could they not be? You couldn't pull something like this off without comm. Probably scrambled, but Blacksnake was a big organization, and the thing about big organizations was that they got lazy. There was a high probability that they were reusing an old code or an old protocol to scramble, and Overwatch had every old one that Vickie had ever been able to find.

"Operative Colt," she said as soon as the link was established.

"Ma'am, whoever you are, this is Echo Dispatch and—"

"This is Operative Nagy, callsign VickieVee, Echo Project Overwatch," she said, interrupting him. The Colt brothers, Sam and Dean, shared split shifts on dispatch duty, and they were polite Southern boys. It was almost painfully easy to run right over the top of them if you were female.

"Overwatch? But—"

"No, Overwatch is not the DNA storage project." She patched in Yankee Pride. "I have Echo Dispatch. Authorize me, Pride."

In the monitor she watched Pride turn his head away as if scanning the crowd. "This is Yankee Pride, Colt. You are authorized to give Overwatch any damn thing she wants."

Vickie blinked, It was odd to hear Pride say anything stronger than "darn," a testament to how much frustration he must be enduring.

"Y-yes sir!" Colt stammered. Vickie began explaining the situation to him in crisp, concise detail, pausing only when the search program reported it had found a presumed Blacksnake freq, and again when it reported that, as she had expected, it was using an old scrambling protocol and began relaying the little chatter there was through one of the auxiliary speakers.

"Patching you through to Operative Bulwark, who has on-site command at the train," she said when she was done, and turned her attention to the Blacksnake chatter.

"Colt," Bulwark said, sounding ridiculously calm. "I assume you've been briefed."

"Sir, yes sir!" Colt responded, and added heatedly. "When we round up Verdigris—"

"We'll deal with him later," Bulwark said sternly. "We do *not* tip our hand. The only way we'll get him is if he is unaware that we know what the true situation is. Now, this is what I want you to do..."

Natalya clearly hated every moment of the ride in the van. She kept threatening Mamona with excoriation if she didn't go faster; given the state of the van and the Atlanta streets between the HQ and the terminal, it was amazing that they hadn't crashed a dozen times over. More testament to Mamona's reflexes and knowledge of the city than anything else, but it still wasn't enough for the Commissar. Untermensch knew what she was thinking. *Is proper tactics to seal off the terminal, seal off the Blacksnake dogs' route of escape...* But he knew there was still the not-so-little voice clawing at the back of her mind, urging her forward to take the fight to the enemy.

Untermensch had been watching the Commissar from his seat on the left side of the van as he and the rest of the squad were doing final checks on their gear and weapons; merely habit and redundancy, since everything had been checked over rapidly right before they left. After having worked with Natalya Nikolaevna Shostakovich over the years, he had become a very good judge of her moods. Since before the van had screeched out of the CCCP garage, the Commissar had been chain smoking—far more heavily than was usual for her. She had just thrown her last cigarette out of the window and crumpled the empty pack with disgust, her knee bouncing frantic energy, when he decided to speak up.

"Commissar?" She waved a hand over her shoulder, indicating that she was listening. "Are you . . . all right?"

She whirled around in her seat so fast and viciously that for a moment Untermensch thought that the Commissar was going to strike him for daring to ask such an impertinent question. For half a second her face was cast with a crazed, manic mask. Just as quickly, however, she regained her composure; she looked like Natalya again, and not some crazed animal. *Well, perhaps not* as *crazed.*

"No," she blurted out. "I am *nyet* fine." The Commissar clumsily scrambled out of her seat and into the back of her van, her feet kicking towards the windshield and in front of Mamona's face as she climbed over the seat, causing the car to swerve several times on the road.

"Hey!—I mean, uh, Commissar. Almost lost a bit've control there." Mamona fixed her eyes front and grip tight enough to turn her knuckles white on the steering wheel, weaving in and out of traffic and down side roads in order to beat the MARTA train.

"Georgi, we are to be leaving the van *now.*" The Commissar turned in her seat to face John. "Murdock, you are in charge of evacuating and securing the station until I rejoin you there; no mistakes, understood? None of these *svinya* are getting away from us, not today."

John shrugged. "Roger that, Commissar; it'll get done." He racked the charging handle on his M4, chambering a round to punctuate his sentence.

"*Horosho.*" She turned back to Untermensch. "Come. Will explain plan on the way." The Commissar opened the side door of the van, the wind and humidity rushing in. "Time for us to get a horse in this fight."

"Dog," Mamona corrected automatically. "Dog in this fight."

"*Nyet*," Bear piped up, "is being correct Americanski saying about pig—"

"*Da, da,* what it ever is being! *Davay!*" Natalya threw an arm under Georgi's arms, and kicked out of the van on a plume of energy, causing the van to rock perilously from side to side as Mamona swore and tried to correct. The van quickly dwindled away below the pair as the rush of the wind in his ears grew louder. He saw that the Commissar was making a beeline for the MARTA line.

"Commissar!" Unter had to shout several times to get her attention; he'd hardly ever seen her fly this fast before. Finally he was able to gain her attention; she looked down at him, annoyed. "What are we doing?"

"Getting you to be on train! Echo is needing all the help it can get!" She outlined the rest of the plan to him by the time they had the train in sight; with perfect timing and more luck than Unter thought existed in the world, the plan just might work.

Good. I was needing a workout.

"Overwatch to Bulwark. Sitrep update. Teams that Verd scrambled diverted to clear Five Points station of civilians. Echo Med staging at Five Points. MARTA authorities contacted and all trains being halted or cleared out of the station. CCCP moving to rendezvous with Echo at Five Points. Red Saviour and Untermensch are leaving main force and heading your way by air. Your DCO in car seven is briefed."

"Understood, Overwatch," Bull said. "Dean, am I patched through?"

"Sir, yes sir."

"This is Operative Bulwark, coming across multiple Overwatch, Echo and CCCP channels. If you're hearing this, you're either already aware of our underground movement opposing Verdigris or we're sure we can trust you to join us. For the latter, we had planned to approach you in time but Verdigris has forced our hand early. He has staged a force of what we believe to be Blacksnake operatives posing as Rebs on the MARTA train escorting the Echo veterans and has taken the train hostage. We will advise on his motives when we have determined them. For now, if you are not already en route to the Five Points station, please proceed there ASAP. The train has been rigged with explosives, so our goal is to commandeer the train before it proceeds into the downtown core. This will likely be messy; expect casualties and well-trained foes. Bulwark out."

"Yankee Pride, verifying Operative Bulwark."

"Belladonna Blue, verifying Operative Bulwark. Echo Med, rendezvous with Panacea on the plaza level outside the MARTA police station."

Bull turned to his crew. "All right, give me the lay of the land."

"They've got us by the balls, Bull," Frankentrain said, jerking his thumb towards the front of the train. "That Tammy girl is now in the next car. Her thumb's not moving from what looks like a remote detonator."

"You're sure?" Bull asked.

Frankentrain nodded. "She's making a point of letting us see it."

"She's got about twenty with her in that car, sir," Rider added. "From what I remember, she's got another thirty in the other cars, not counting the lead car which is closed off. We're going to need a distraction, and somehow get out and over to it without them knowing."

Bull nodded. "We've got a couple of reinforcements from CCCP coming in. They'll head for the lead car. Rider, when I give the signal, you take Team two outside and join them. How are our captors for weaponry?"

"If they're Blacksnake, no idea on powers except for that girl who makes smoke," Rider reported. "I see a lot of pistols though, and some rifles."

"Rifles on a moving train?" Bull said, shaking his head. "That's a little careless for Blacksnake, isn't it?"

Rider shook his head. "Not conventional, sir. By the looks of them, I'd say they were packing electrical discharge cannons and projectile tasers."

"How do you know that?" Frankentrain asked.

"Read about 'em," Rider said simply.

"All right then," Bull said. "First things first. Before we move out to stop this train and take out those Blacksnake mercs, we need to get the veterans out of danger. We need to disable that detonator, and failing that, disarm those bombs. I need options here, and I need . . ."

"Mister Echo Man!" Tammy's voice chimed over the PA. "You know I can hear you, right? And hel*lo*, you should really get your story straight and know who your captors are. As a rule, us Rebs don't like to be confused with Blacksnake..."

"Save it!" Bull snapped. He approached the door leading to the next car. Tammy stood on the other side, smirking at him through the glass. In one hand she held a small comm unit to her mouth, in the other she kept her thumb gently pressed against an illuminated red detonator button. "We know damn well who you are, and who you work for. You also know we can't meet your demands before we get this train under the city, so why don't we cut the crap and get to it. What do you want?"

Tammy chuckled, her voice dropping an octave. "Oh good, that voice was beginning to grate on my nerves. So you know, Operative Bulwark. It changes little." She glanced down at the elevated track and the ground far below. "Tell me, Bulwark, have you ever wondered what would happen if you and your kinetic shield hit the ground from this height, and at this speed? Would you bounce like a shimmering ball? Or would the impact knock you out and dash your brains out on that cold concrete? Me? I'm kind of curious to find out."

"What do you want?" Bull repeated.

"Oh, don't you worry your giant, disproportionate head over that," she said with a smile. "You just worry about keeping calm, keeping your people still, and hey, maybe I'll even let you try to negotiate with us." She craned her neck to look around his crew. "Strange, I thought you even had a negotiator with you, the dumpy one with the nice smile. Oh well, the offer still stands."

"What did you do with Dusty?" Bull said, and slammed his hand against the protective glass.

"Careful!" Tammy hissed, and raised the detonator in a menacing gesture. "My thumbs feeling a bit... twitchy. Don't test me, Bulwark, I won't warn you again. We see any of you trying to leave that car, any motion to break down the glass or those doors, or any funny business from the vet cars, then I press this nifty little button to separate your cars off and blow you sky high."

Bull bared his teeth in frustration, and was about to retort when a new voice came across the PA system. A very familiar voice.

"Hey, Harmony!" the voice crackled against sounds of high winds. "Can you define 'funny business' for us?"

Bull turned around and stared through the glass at the other end of the car. Riding the outside of the veterans' car, a female figure hung by one hand between the compartments. Her face was masked by goggles and a scarf, though it was clearly her shouting through a handheld walkie-talkie.

"Unit Five!" Tammy shouted. "What are you doing out there?"

"Harmony?" Bulwark said, his head whipping back to stare incredulously at Tammy.

Tammy sighed and closed her eyes. Bulwark watched as her features shifted in place. When she opened her eyes again, it was Harmony staring back at him.

"That's a bit of relief, actually," she muttered. "Unit Five, I believe spankings will be in order when we get back."

"I'm looking forward to it!" the masked girl shouted. "But you didn't answer my question!" She jerked her head back to the interior of the passenger car. "Would *that* satisfy your definition of 'funny business'?"

Bull turned again. Inside the next car, the Echo metas stationed with the veterans, and it appeared, some of the veterans themselves, had overtaken and bound their Blacksnake captors. He looked back at Harmony, who was now seething in anger.

"Who is this?" Harmony demanded. "You seem familiar!"

"I should!" the girl shouted. "You almost spotted me a couple of times, but what can I say? I was well trained!"

"Can't have been that well," Harmony snarled. "Guess I get to see if Bull can bounce after all." She raised the detonator.

"No!" Bull shouted, and slammed his hands against the glass.

Harmony pressed the button.

Verd had paused again, frowning, with one hand on his earpiece. Bella knew why; Vickie was updating her practically by the second, and he must have gotten word from his goons that his plan had gone seriously pear-shaped. His frown deepened. "Go to Plan B, then," he growled, and wrapped up his speech.

But it sounded rushed, and nothing like in keeping with the rest of the speech. People in the audience were reacting with vague unease, detecting the change and not understanding what they were uneasy about.

His hand is being pushed. He's distracted. His timing is off...

"And now, Yankee Pride will unveil the monument to our honored fallen," Verdigris said, waving at Pride.

This was not in the script either. It was Bella who was supposed to pull the rope, which was on her side, and they had to swap places so Pride could reach it. That was when she suddenly realized that Verd's split concentration, the distraction of the fabric falling away from the monument, and increasingly negative reports coming in on his earpiece just might give her that opportunity.

She edged closer to him. Yankee Pride pulled the gilded rope, and the canvas dropped, revealing a bland and tasteful—and utterly soulless—abstract of a curving arc of stone rising out of what were probably supposed to be equally abstract ruins. The sharp tip of the arc glinted crystal. Polite applause began. Bella edged even closer.

Then—

"Bella, whatever you're planning, don't do it," Red Djinni's voice said harshly in her inner ear. *"Khanji's gone into full bodyguard mode, and I can't get to her before she gets to you."*

The hell? It took everything she had not to start in surprise. *"Where are you?"* she hissed.

"Close. Bull put me on bodyguard for you. Stay focused."

Oh, that was—frustration and anger welled up in her. What was he *doing* here? He should be with the rest of the team, not wasted on babysitting her! She was perfectly capable of taking care of herself!

"Dammit, Red, you should be on that train right now! And since you aren't, you should be at Five Points! We—"

"Don't be stupid," he interjected, cutting her off. *"You're too important. Now stop making my job harder and keep your damn head down. Verd's pretty pit bull is on full alert, and if you make any moves towards him, she's going to drop you."*

With the hope of refuting him, she let her empathic sense drift towards Khanjar...

Only to be slammed with a wall of adrenaline-charged *purpose.* Khanjar's attention was, impossibly, *everywhere.*

Red was right. All that would happen if she tried her planned move would be that she would—if she was very lucky—be dropped unconscious before she got close enough to touch him. It was unlikely Khanjar would give her the benefit of the doubt, so probably she'd be dead, and for nothing.

All right. Plan B. "What if I think of a way to distract Verd so Pride can get out of here without risking myself?"

"Only if you run it by me first."

"I just knew you would say that."

Harmony thumbed the detonator in fury, anticipating the rear cars to break off, the glorious explosions and flames to follow, and perhaps the sight of Bulwark attempting in vain to save as many as he could.

Nothing.

Incredulously, she thumbed it again, harder, then whacked it against the side of the car. Nothing.

"Whassa matter, Harm?" the girl shouted back. "Toy not work? I wonder why?"

"What did you do?" Harmony screamed back in a white-hot rage.

"Found all the bombs and defused them! Oh, and disabled the device to separate the cars! Told you we were trained well!"

The girl reached up to pull down her scarf and raise her goggles. She was grinning. With a feeling as if she had been drenched in ice-water, Harmony recognized Scope.

"Scope . . ." Harmony snarled. "And I'm guessing Bruno's with you?"

Acrobat rose up from between the cars. His face was also hidden behind a ventilator, mask and goggles, but his boyish salute and wave gave him away. Harmony realized something else. He was getting smaller.

No, they, and the vet cars, were getting smaller . . . because they were separating from the train. Acrobat waved again, and in his hand Harmony saw the manual locks that connected the cars together.

"Don't worry about us, Harm," said Scope over the Blacksnake comm. "We have someone in here who knows how to drive. Oh, and about your toy, you *did* realize there were bombs planted in *every* car, didn't you? We didn't want you to miss our show, so we disabled all of them for you. Wasn't that nice of us?"

If Harmony had felt drenched in ice water before, she now felt as if she had been frozen solid. Verdigris had sold her out and set her up, just as Verd had set Jack up. He had never intended to pay up. And he had figured on making sure he wouldn't have to by killing them all. She seethed with anger, but fought it down. She had other problems right now, loose ends to take care of before she paid Verdigris one last call. One of those loose ends was staring down at her, his jaw set, his face a stone mask to his fury.

"Just you and me now, Harmony," Bruno said. "I told you I'd see you again. Let's see how much *you* break this time."

"Fall back!" Harmony cried, and backed away from the door. "Defensive positions! If they breach, take them down!"

Bull turned away, and motioned one of his men to the door. The meta grinned and raised his arm. His hand seemed to disappear, replaced by a hot, incandescent flame that blew out like a torch. Bull let him pass to work on the steel door, and motioned to Paperback Rider. "Rider! Move your team out!"

Rider nodded. He motioned his team around him. They did a quick check of their gear, including their magnetized gloves and boots, and gave him the go sign. He knelt and raised one fist high in the air. As one, they reached out and took hold of his arm, and then they vanished.

Frankentrain whistled. "That's a new one!"

Bull grunted. "You know how he works, his powers are all one-shots. He's been saving that one for a while now, for when we needed it. Too bad it's short range, or he could've taken them all to the front compartment..."

They heard heavy footsteps on the roof as Rider's team leapt to the next car.

"...but that'll do. C-Torch, we through yet?"

"Just about!" C-Torch yelled, his hand burning a slow circle through the barrier.

"Frank, you've got point. You're on anything energy-based they throw at us. I'll pick up the slack behind you for any stray projectiles with the shield." Bull stared intently through the glass. Harmony's forces had set up a barricade halfway up the next car. "Standard melee assault maneuvers, ladies and gentlemen. We take territory and hold it. If you see Harmony, chance the artillery. She's blinding fast, and you don't want her touching you, is that understood?"

"Yes, Sir!" the Echo Ops answered.

C-Torch hooted as he finished cutting through.

"Then let's go to work," Bull snarled, and kicked the door down.

✧ ✧ ✧

"Overwatch: Command: full in slash out relay Gamayun, Echo Dispatch," Vickie ordered, giving Gamayun of the CCCP and Colt of Echo Dispatch full access to the chatter on all channels. That took some of the coordination off her hands. Which was a good thing, since a few seconds later, Bulwark came on her private freq. It was fairly noisy with shouts and sounds of combat.

"Overwatch, can you switch Scope and Acrobat's Blacksnake comm over to us?" he asked.

Hooboy. Don't ask much, do you? "Maybe," she replied, and quickly told her Heisenberg probability calculator to give her numbers. *"Uhm, probability, forty percent. With a seventy-five-percent modifier that we'll lose Blacksnake chatter altogether."*

"Anything we can do at this end to better those odds?" he replied. "I don't want to lose the Blacksnake chatter, but we need our ops back online."

"Will it to happen," she told him, honestly. He hesitated a moment, probably not sure if she was being serious or not. She was.

"Do it," he said. "Out."

Oh crap. She dove for her box of personal packets and got out Scope's and Bruno's, plugging them into the first available spots. "Overwatch: Command," she said as she worked. "My personal freq. Open Echo Dispatch. Open CCCP Dispatch. Colt? Gamayun?"

"Go, Overwatch."

"Da, tovarisch."

"I might lose the Blacksnake chatter in a minute; something I have to do might drop it. If you've got a free hand, try and pick them up. They're using Blacksnake Protocol Baker-Niner-One-Alpha, and they're on Harry Dog Six Seven Oh point One Baker. Colt, this'll mean you'll have to tap into Echo's comp capability and—"

"No worries, Overwatch. I woke up Sam and sent him down to the computer room. It's ours, and Greenboy won't get a whiff."

"I think I love you and will have your children," she said fervently, getting back into her chair. "Gamayun, CCCP's rig isn't as sophisticated—"

"*Da* but is more robust. Sturdy socialist construction. *Nechevo,* sometimes brute force wins day."

"Roger that. Okay, I need to do my thing. Pick up the slack for me for about a minute. Try and catch if the Blacksnake ball drops." She took her hands off the keyboard for a moment, closed her eyes, and calculated. Law of Contagion: Scope and Acrobat had their comms in their hands or on their belts. Law of Identity: Vickie could *see* those comms via the security cameras on the cars. Law of Similarity: make *their* freqs look like Overwatch freqs. *And in . . . three . . . two . . . one . . . go.* She blazed through the equations like a rocket, because there was no time. No time.

And in the monitor showing Scope and Acrobat's cams . . . the Blacksnake comms at their belts failed. Spectacularly. In a shower of sparks.

Oh, bloody . . . Vickie's thoughts dissolved into a cascade of Romany cursing, when two freqs that hadn't been live in *far* too long suddenly lit up. "Scope to Overwatch. Overwatch, did you hex our Snake comms?"

"Scope?" she yelped.

"And Bruno," Acrobat said gleefully. "Hiya, VeeVee. We kept our Overwatch rigs; we figured we might need them."

She thanked all the gods of communication as she typed commands into the keyboard. *"Overwatch to Misfits. Big Man wants you on comm instanter. Or in person. Can you make it to him?"*

"Sorry, Overwatch," Scope answered. "We're slowing down, the big guy's pulling away and we haven't learned to fly yet."

Vickie swore. *"Well that's just . . . wait. Did you say fly?"*

It only took a few minutes of flashing over the rooftops of the city before they neared the MARTA line. The train was easily visible, even from a distance. As they swooped in, Natalya glanced at the group of Echo metas on top, moving hand over hand towards the front car. She hissed as she saw another group of Blacksnake emerge between the second and third cars. A train-top battle! Unter knew that she had always wanted to take part in one of those. But there was other work to do first, then she could play. They had to take control of the train, and her cargo was just the sort to do it. The Commissar banked left to intercept the lead car, staying as high as possible until they were almost directly above it. At the last moment she dived, plunging them towards the unforgiving metal roof of the lead car; Georgi was afraid that she was going to smash both of them into it until she braked with another plume of energy. He gave her a thumbs-up, and she set him down. It was difficult, but he was able to land on the roof of the car without a loud impact; something like that would have surely alerted the occupants inside, which would ruin the entire plan. Natalya nodded to him once before rocketing off again, eager to return to the rooftop fighting.

Untermensch hunkered down, crouching on the train car's roof; the wind from the train's speed was enough to stagger him if he stood at his full height. Lowering himself so that his belly was flat against the roof, he slowly crawled until he was at the left edge. Gripping the edge of the car, he used his free hand to retrieve a tactical mirror from a pouch; it had an extendable neck, but he only pulled it out to about half a foot. He had to keep a firm hold on it; the wind kept threatening to tear it from his grasp. Carefully, he placed the end of it over the edge, and angled it inward. Squinting, he could make out the interior of the cabin.

There were eight "Rebs" in the car, including one that was at the controls. They were wearing a mixture of denim and leather, with typical biker patches and the Rebs' club patch on their cuts. He scanned each one carefully. *There.* Many of them had tattoos, but Unter noticed that they weren't biker tattoos; most of them were military-themed. Under their cuts were low-profile plate carriers and load-bearing vests. *True Rebs are never so well outfitted. Sloppy work, scum.* Replacing the tactical mirror in its pouch, Unter decided that the time to act was now.

Coming up into a crouch, Unter gripped the edge of the car, and then oriented himself to face inwards. He reversed his grip, and then kicked his feet off the edge of the car, swinging toward the center of the car feetfirst. The glass window in front of him exploded inwards, the sudden rush of wind in the car sending the shards flying. There was a Blacksnake merc directly in front of him; bracing his legs, Unter pushed against him as he fully entered the car. Taken completely by surprise, the merc was launched off of his feet and through the opposite window, sent screaming and bleeding to the ground below the tracks. Landing in a crouch, Unter unholstered his battered Makarov pistol; one of the Blacksnakes to his right was starting to recover and draw a weapon. Unter fired rapidly three times, striking the merc in the chest and arm. He went down, but Unter could tell he was only wounded. *Body armor! I must aim for their faces.*

Before Unter could line up another target his pistol was kicked from his hand. The Blacksnakes were circling around him as they regained their bearings. The one that had attacked him lunged with a knife; Unter caught it in his nearly invulnerable hand and snapped the blade off at the hilt, throwing it to the ground. The stunned merc still had enough sense to keep his guard up. Unter began pummeling him with blows, aiming at joints and weak spots not covered by the body armor under the merc's clothing. He had driven the man against the control booth for the car, and was about to deliver a crippling blow to the bleeding merc's neck.

Then he felt the muzzle of a pistol pressed against the back of his head. Less than a second later everything went dark, and Untermensch didn't feel anything more.

Natalya shot up into the sky, hung for a moment, then began a glorious swan dive and hurtled towards the Blacksnake operatives climbing up onto the roof of the train. She had never before had the opportunity to knock mercenary *svinya* off of a moving train, and she planned to enjoy herself.

"We can't be leaving Georgi to be having *all* of the fun." She was accelerating to ramming speed when the call came over her comm. She slowed her descent, and grumbled at the interruption.

"Red Saviour, this is Overwatch."

"*Da*, go ahead Rasputin's Daughter, I am listening."

"I thought you'd promoted me to Hero of the People, Commissar. I read you as being right over the train."

"Correct. Am going to be smashing mercenaries soon. Out with it, Hero of the People."

"You should see that the last two cars have separated from the rest—that's the ones with the WWII vets in them."

The young witch was right; the last two cars had detached from the main section and were slowing down. That was most excellent for Natalya; it would give her more freedom in blasting the kidnappers to steaming bits.

"It seems two Echo Ops moled themselves into the Blacksnake ranks and dropped a shoe into their gears. Can you pick them up and haul them to the rest of the train? They don't want to miss out on the action. Request of Bulwark, with his compliments and thanks."

Nasrat. "Beink taxi for Echo spies is not what I agreed to when beink signed up for this 'conspiracy.'"

"Of course not. The advantage is that Bull is going to have the back door open for you and a gun and ammo waiting."

"Have both already, needing neither anyways." She mulled it over for a moment; time was wasting, and the train was only getting closer to the station. "Fine, fine, I will be there. Tell them to back away from open doors; don't want to scare any of the little heroes or be squishing one when I land." Natalya flipped in the air and twisted, turning towards the end of the train. She flew in a wide arc, decreasing in altitude until she was almost level with the tracks. Her HUD from Overwatch was keeping her updated on her speed, elevation, and other vital information; a marker in her vision indicated where her two Echo charges were. Increasing speed, she accelerated towards the open door at the back of the rear car, cutting off energy for flight when she was twenty feet away. Her momentum carried her forward, and she was able to clear the doorway by five feet, landing heavily on the floor of the train car.

Two people, a slender young woman and an elfin young man, stepped forward to meet her. They wore what looked like generic uniforms, but were oddly covered from head to toe. They wore battle masks under rough scarves and goggles to cover their necks and faces, their hands clad in tough leather. Her HUD immediately identified them as her pickups, by the tactical armor they were wearing under the uniforms, and the arms they were both carrying. "Good," she said, nodding. "You are not beink fat with Amerikanski fasting food. Am beink your taxi, *da*?"

"More like our angel, Commissar ma'am, if you Russkies have angels," said the young man. "Overwatch gave us instructions on running the car. We've got that under control."

"What we are havink is no time for theological discussions. Are both of you ready? Where am I takink you?" She had placed her fists on her hips, impatient already.

"Where else?" the girl said. "To the fighting!"

"*Davay*, then. Come over here so I can grab both of you, under your arms." They moved as fast as her own comrades in the CCCP, she was gratified to see; Bulwark must train his underlings well. A nice change. She wrapped her arms around both of their chests tightly; she was taller than both, so she had to crouch down slightly to do so. "Do not be shrieking like frightened *babushkas* when we fly." Without another word, she kicked off from the edge of the door, dragging the Echo metas with her. Her energy plume erupted below her feet, carrying them up. Both of the metas kept silent, but she felt them both scrabble and grasp onto her arms tightly as they ascended. With the extra weight Natalya wasn't able to turn as quickly or as gracefully; she felt as if she were hauling sacks of grain on a farm. Fortunately her HUD was able to allow for all of that; it even gave her several options for a plotted trajectory depending on how high or fast she wanted to go. Useful thing, this. Victoria was definitely elevated to Hero of the People.

Very shortly they caught up with the rest of the train; flashes of light seemed to erupt from the fourth car, and there was open fighting on top of the first. She swooped down sluggishly, coming to a rest atop the back compartment. "Packages are beink delivered." She released her hold on Scope and Acrobat; it took them a half second to release their grips on her arms and drop down to grab firm holds of the train roof.

"Commissar, much appreciated!" Scope yelled. She nodded to Acrobat. "Let's go!"

"Which fight?" Bruno shouted back. "Outside or in?"

Scope glanced at Rider's crew. "Looks like the outside team have them on the ropes! Let's get inside to Bull! C'mon! Hurry or there won't be any fighting left for us!"

"I like your thinking, girl!" Nat grinned, and motioned to follow them into the train when her inner ear pinged with an incoming message.

"Overwatch to joint command."

"Chyort voz'mi!" Natalya shouted. *"Vedma,* what is it now?"

"Blacksnake units moving openly on Five Points Station. Estimate twenty based on comm chatter and headcount via traffic cams. Not enough Echo in place to hold them off and what there is, is mostly Echo Med."

"Chush' sobach'ya," Saviour swore. *Small arms, mostly healing powers, they will be target practice.* "Was lookink forward to using *Systema* in close quarters. Have not had enough practice." She sighed. "Overwatch, am comink to strafe *svoloch* Blacksnake from air. With luck, will catch them at entrance; will make nice cozy place for Blacksnake to beink turned into paste." She gave Scope and Acrobat a quick salute, turned on her heel, and kicked off of the train car. As she rose, she saw a group of Echo fighting their way atop the car she had dropped Untermensch onto. There was still one Blacksnake left. Unable to resist, she charged her fists, squinted a little to sight, and blasted that last man off the

top, sending him in a graceful arc that was doomed to end in a not-so-graceful *splat* onto the pavement. Mollified, she accelerated up, using her energy to speed into the blue Atlanta sky.

Be leaving some for the rest of us, Georgi, she thought. *Otherwise it is going to be a boring day indeed.*

"Overwatch to joint command. Man down, car one, Untermensch."

Rider was channeling the novelization of *Enter the Dragon* and thanks to his opponents was a little too busy to do more than swear. The writer hadn't been very good, and as a consequence his Jeet Kune Do was a *lot* weaker than Bruce Lee's.

"Nechevo," he heard Red Saviour say flatly, which he assumed was a swear word in Russian.

His opponent was not going down anytime soon. In fact, his opponent was clearly a master of some sort of nasty, hard-hitting, mixed martial art. And now he was in trouble, separated from the rest of the team, backed into a corner. And the problem was, he couldn't just pick some other book to channel; he was stuck with this one until it ran out, until the last word from the last page scrolled across his skin.

And then—just as the Blacksnake-in-Reb-clothing closed in for what was clearly going to be the kill—he wasn't in trouble anymore.

Someone rose up from behind the Snake, and with a single chopping blow to the back of his neck, not just broke the man's neck, but damn near decapitated him.

"CCCP, Untermensch!" the man barked, clearly expecting Rider to take him on just out of reflex. Rider stared.

"Aren't you supposed to be dead?" he stammered, oblivious to the fighting behind Untermensch. The commie laughed.

"*Da*, they keep sayink that. *Davay, tovarisch,* let us make borscht of these *sooka.*" And with that, he turned, and Rider just followed behind him, mopping up whatever he left.

"I know how to run the train!" he shouted over the shouts, screams, and sounds of combat.

"Then we need get you to front of car!" Untermensch shouted back, ruthlessly plowing his way ahead. What had been eight men, became five, then three . . . then none. Untermensch made short work of the door; shatterproof glass was evidently not nearly up to blows from a pair of hands that might have looked like flesh, but obviously weren't as frail and fragile a thing as skin and bone.

Unfortunately, when Rider wrenched open the door from the inside, and tried to bring up the control panel, he got . . . nothing. Not a flicker. And the cause was obvious, a scorch mark along the top that must have come from an errant electrical cannon shot. The brains of the train were fried, and as the instruction manual scrolled across his skin, he knew what he had to do.

"Get everybody out of here, Unter," he ordered. "Get into the second car. The only way to slow this train is for me to manually decouple from here, then you guys will be the lead car and you can bring the train in under control."

"Overwatch to Rider. I can feed Georgi what he needs to run the panel." Evidently the Overwatch chick was saying something similar to the Russian; he had one hand to his ear, and was nodding.

"What about you, comrade?" the Russian asked, looking up.

"I'll have to hotwire the brakes and hold the wires in place. That's the only way to get them to work. *Go!* We're running out of time! The rest of you, this guy's your team lead now, do what he says!" Rider didn't even turn to see if the others obeyed him; he was prying open the access panel under the controls, hunting for the manual decoupler. By the time he found it, and peered back along the body-strewn car, the Russian had battered open the door between cars one and two, his men were pushing back the Blacksnake, and the Russian was breaking down the control booth door.

Rider yanked on the decoupler. There was a lurch, then a second lurch as car one, now no longer pulling five other cars, surged forward, accelerating.

Rider pulled loose the pertinent wires and jammed them together, holding them in place despite showers of sparks that landed on his hands, stinging and burning them. He didn't have to look to see the words scrolling across his skin now. As the wheels locked up and screamed, he knew very well that there was too little track between him and the Five Points station to actually stop—not with the engine fighting the brakes. The brakes were going to lose. The best he could manage would be a controlled crash into whatever train was still ahead of them. There *was* a train ahead, the track signals told him that much.

Which would be why *The Ballad of Casey Jones* was what was playing across his hands and face right now.

"Rider, this is Overwatch . . ."

"It's okay, Overwatch. I know you can't do anything. It's okay." He kept the wires jammed together. Every bit of speed he could scrub off would be that much less shrapnel flying around the station. Strangely, he felt very calm as he saw the tunnel to the Underground speeding towards him. "Maybe somebody will write a book about this some day."

"Rider—"

But it was already too late, as the words he saw scrolling across his skin came to a dead stop, leaving only two. From the time he first understood his power, Rider had known this day would come.

There it was. His eyes were fixed on the words, black print on white skin, repeated over and over.

The End.

The last of the Blacksnake mercenaries in the terminal was trying to make a run for the exit; the rest of his team had been decimated by the CCCP and the Echo medical teams that had arrived to secure the area and evacuate it. Saviour stepped out from behind the corner she had been using as cover, grabbing the merc by the front of his clothing. In his panic to escape, he had thrown his weapons to the ground, and was wild-eyed with fear. *Good. Wicked men should fear.* The Commissar lifted him from the ground with one hand while she charged energy in her free hand; the gut punch she delivered on the captive merc sent him flying nearly twenty feet, where he impacted a row of lockers with a wet *thump.* With a self-satisfied nod she keyed her comm.

"Status report, Murdock."

The American came trotting up to her from behind a newsstand further down the tunnel, his rifle at low-ready. "All of the opposition have been taken down, Commissar. Any live ones are in custody, with Echo Med securing them off to the side." He glanced over his shoulder briefly. "They ain't got a lot of work t'do, if y'know what I mean."

"Civilians?"

"All evac'd prior to the tussle breakin' out. We're gettin' the train that's here movin' out shortly. Conductor is a touch shaky at the moment."

She nodded, surveying the scene; casings and bullet holes littered everywhere, with broken tile crunching underfoot wherever she stepped. Saviour was walking with Murdock towards the train when her comm squawked once.

"Overwatch to Red Saviour. Untermensch back up. Car one coming in at speed, I've prodded MARTA but... there's gonna be a crash if you can't clear that last train now. *Cars two through five detached and slowing, Unter has the controls, but there's fighting in them and there'll be a crunch into anything left on the tracks."*

"Clear the train *now,* Murdock." Saviour keyed the comm for her team and the Echo Med team. "Everyone, be gettink to cover! Runaway car comink in hard and fast!"

Everyone scrambled; John was already running at a blur towards the front end of the train in the station, yelling to get the train moving. Natalya was directing everyone and helping to clear some of the injured when the train lurched once, then slowly started rolling forward. There was a low rumble that was growing; she could feel it start at her feet and work its way up into her belly. And a scream of metal on metal. *The train... it's here.*

"*Tvoyu mat'*... everyone be gettink down, NOW!" Natalya launched herself sideways, diving away from the train tracks. She landed and covered her head, chancing to look at the last second. The single car came barreling down the tracks, brakes failing, sparks flying from the undercarriage as the wheels screamed. She felt as much as she heard the impact, it was so loud and jarring; both the single car and the evacuated train rippled with the force of the crash, sending pieces of debris flying through the air. The evacuated train's rear car lurched upward, actually raking the bottom of the ceiling. The lone car was crushed, compacted like an accordion to half its length; smoke was pouring out of it even before its momentum ceased to push the train in front of it.

Everyone in the station was dazed; Natalya could hear yelling and some screaming from further down the tunnel. She picked herself up, coughing from all of the dust and smoke in the air and trying to get her bearings. "Prepare yourselves! Train with *shluha vokzal'naja* is comink, will be here soon! We must be ready to properly welcome them!"

Bulwark's strategy had worked like a charm, up to a point. Frankentrain got a running start and charged first, bowling over Harmony's frontline defense. They scattered like bowling pins and Bull heard shrill cries accompanied by awful crunching sounds as they flew back into metal dividers, supports and seating. Frank might have continued along the length of the car, shrugging off a storm of bullets from hand cannons and blast from energy rifles, but he was interrupted as a tall, wiry man stepped in front of him, took an enormous breath, and expanded his body like a balloon. Frank charged right into him, disappeared momentarily in a comical Frankentrain-shaped depression in the man's elastic midsection, and was hurled back like a pebble from a slingshot. He collided into the seats, ripping them from their reinforced stanchions with great tearing sounds of twisting metal and landed in a jumbled mess of steel. He groaned, but not so much from the pain. He didn't usually feel pain, not when he was moving, but the crash had left him rather dizzy. Frank loved to run, but always in straight lines. Sudden changes of direction always made him want to throw up. He was always good as the engineer or the driver on the straight-run tracks; no one wanted him in the steam-loco's cabin on the switchbacks.

When Frank lurched to his feet, he felt the train spinning around him. He might have been an easy target, but Bull and the rest of his team were on the move. Bull led them in, shimmering in his shield as he shrugged off a barrage of thrown knives and bullets. Closing the distance, he had a vague sense that things were going a little too smoothly, when Harmony and a small group of Blacksnake metas vaulted over the riflemen and entered the fray. For Harmony, at least, they were ready. Bull dropped his shield, and three of his ops took immediate aim and blasted her with concentrated sonic, energy and freezing bursts from their hands. Harmony cursed, ducked under the blasts and rolled back behind her troops. The rest of her melee fighters, however, darted in, and it became painfully apparent that these fighters were specialized in close-quarters combat. They seemed to be everywhere—bouncing off walls, tumbling underneath, scaling the very ceilings, and before Bull could blink he found himself in the midst of a brutal fight that ran half the length of the car.

Bull felt a sudden kick to his midsection, grunted in surprise, and tried to return the blow. His attacker easily dodged the punch, and was already moving on to the next target. The Blacksnake skirmishers appeared to be identically dressed in light armor and hooded face coverings. In fact, they were all the same height and build, and moved in the same eerie manner. Their limbs seemed to possess an enhanced range of articulation, bending at strange angles, orchestrating prescient attacks in all directions. They were constantly on the move, not happy to fight just one Echo meta but all of them, lashing out with quick attacks before moving to a new target. Whatever they were, their tactics were working. Bull's team flailed about helplessly as the skirmishers continued their onslaught, an untouchable dervish that was quickly wearing them down. Unable to build up to a run, Frankentrain was knocked over as one fighter delivered a devastating flying kick to his chest while another rolled to trip him up at the feet. Another drove a series of jabs at Arctic, ending in a wild uppercut that sent her reeling. One by one, the Echo metas were falling.

Bull collected himself and watched their dervish dance through his stunned team. He kept focus on one of them, willed a condensed shield to flare up around his fist, and reared back in anticipation. As the agile scrapper attempted to tumble past him, Bull struck, and delivered a massive blow to the midsection, amplified by his kinetic shield. The fighter, and all his dopplegangers, flew back towards the front of the car, their forms merging into one sprawling figure who groaned and gripped his stomach in pain.

"Fall back!" Harmony shouted, seizing another one of her ops by the arm. Bull actually expected her to drain him on the spot, but evidently he was worth more alive than sucked dry. She gave him a rough shove towards Bulwark, snarling "Finish the damn job!" while the rest of her force retreated to the next car. He was a large, heavily armored man, almost as large as Bull. He hunched over, and began to roar as a portal opened up in his chestplate. Bull watched with alarm as a light began to intensify in the man's chest cavity, realizing what it meant.

"Take him down!" Bull shouted. The artillery units on his team, those that could still stand, unleashed hell on the living cannon, but all for naught. The man stood his ground, letting the barrage of bullets and force blasts ricochet off his armor, and all the while his power source continued to glow ever brighter.

"Nice try," the armored man snarled. Even his head was armored, protected by a series of interlocking metal plates. "I'll bet you could eventually find a weak spot in this armor, but you're out of time, and something tells me I won't have problems getting past yours." He began to scream as his buildup hit a critical point, and he leveled his chest to blast them and the entire back of the train to ashes. He began to laugh maniacally, and stopped with the thunder of a single gunshot. His head snapped back, and when it flopped forward Bulwark saw an oozing crater where the man's left eye used to be. He fell to his knees and sank to the ground, the light in his chest extinguished.

"How's that for a weak spot, dickhead?"

Bull turned around. Scope relaxed, and lowered her smoking gun.

"Nice shot," he said.

"We've kept in shape," Scope shrugged. "Even learned a few things."

"Like what?"

"Like how guns don't solve every problem," she answered. "But sometimes, they make a hell of a persuasive argument."

"*. . . freaking nonintuitive . . . Baromarcú faszfej excuses for engineers, can't have a nice big red button that says 'Emergency Brakes,' oh no . . . Overwatch to Unter! Who'd you leave on the controls?*"

"Busy, Overwatch!" One of the Blacksnake metas had been holding his Echo comrades at bay; he was able to generate a sort of bone armor over his skin, with spikes protruding from his knuckles. He was busy . . . dissuading the Echo metas from advancing, leaving the Blacksnake behind him to take potshots. *To hell with this.* Unter vaulted over a pile of seats that had been ripped from their moorings and used as a makeshift barrier, charging straight for the meta. He could see the Blacksnake merc grinning, his grown armor rattling as he braced himself. Just before they met, both metas reared back and punched; Unter altered the trajectory of his thrown punch slightly. With a crack as loud as a gunshot, their fists met; the bone spikes and armor on the merc's fist shattered and started oozing blood, causing him to scream. Unter shut him up with an uppercut that landed on the tip of the merc's chin, sending him to flip over onto his back, knocked out cold.

"*Ura ura ura!* Push them back!" The rest of the Echo team rallied, running past him to meet the enemy. The Blacksnake weren't prepared for the push, and fought a pitched battle as they retreated to the third car. "Ready, Overwatch. The dogs are running." Unter leaned over the controls and began to follow the instructions that Overwatch had given him.

"*Nechevo. Good job.*" At that moment the train lurched a little and metal began screaming. "*This is Overwatch, all Echo, CCCP. Control of train established. You're coming in hard anyway; there's too much speed to scrub and there's gonna be a controlled crash. I'll give you a five-second warning countdown."*

Unter surveyed the fight; this bunch of Echo now effectively had the Blacksnake sandwiched in car three between themselves and Bulwark's team. He idly felt the back of his head where he had been shot; his hand was covered with blood when he pulled it back. *Not something to repeat in the near future. Strange dreams after I've been shot in the head.*

"Overwatch: all troops! Brace for impact! Five!"

"Team, we are coming in hot! Brace yourselves!" Unter gripped two poles, hoping that his strength wouldn't fail and allow his hold to falter.

"Four! Three! Two! One!"

"Overwatch: Command: open Djinni private, open Pride private," Bella whispered. "Red, did you get all that? When the car hits, I'm going to jump away from Verd and have hysterics. That should get attention on me, and when the second train hits, I'll have a meltdown. That should distract everyone from Pride, and he can jet off to the station. If," she added with only a little sarcasm, "that meets with your approval, my lords and masters."

"Make sure you jump far enough away and even if Khanji reacts, I think I can keep her from disemboweling you," Red replied, with just as much sarcasm.

By this time, Bella was so keyed up she almost didn't have to fake hysterics when the first car smashed into the parked train. She shrieked unintelligibly somewhere around high C, leapt nearly to the edge of the stage, and pointed in the direction of Five Points. Tears were rolling down her face for Paperback Rider; even with the station being underground, the sound of that impact meant nothing short of the most resilient metahumans would have survived it.

When the second impact came, her "meltdown" included a controlled tumble off the stage—something she *hadn't* told Djinni was in the program, but which her own parkour practice had ensured wouldn't even leave much of a bruise, and which would absolutely guarantee that all attention and cameras were riveted on her. As people clustered around her, she moaned dramatically, and feigned confusion until Djinni's *"Okay, he's away and not even Khanji noticed,"* told her it was safe to come tearfully to her feet and babble explanations about flashbacks.

"Verd's pissed off. You stole his show. Heh, now he's looking for Pride. So's Khanji."

Look all you want, monkey boy, she thought, viciously. *And come on down here to see if I'm okay. I'll give you a handshake you'll never wake up from.*

John had almost become a head shorter when the first car crashed; a jagged piece of metal had gone whistling through the air where he had been less than a second before. Natalya had been one of the first people up, yelling orders and trying to prepare the troops for the second train. The Echo Med team were still busy dragging off the wounded and putting the still-living Blacksnake mercs out of reach of the Commissar.

He started to look around for the rest of the squad; Mamona was the first one that he spotted. She was leaned up against an overturned vending machine, dazed and bleeding from a cut on her forehead, courtesy of a Blacksnake knife. John trotted up to her, kneeling down and placing a hand on her shoulder. "Y'all right, comrade? We've got more fight comin' to us." She seemed to focus a little more, wiping some of the blood off of her eyebrow before nodding to him. "Follow me; we gotta police up Bear an' meet with the Commissar."

Pavel wasn't too far away; he was standing in front of a large piece of shattered mirror, grunting and cursing under his breath. It wasn't until he turned at the sound of their approach that John and Mamona saw why.

"This may being slight problem." A foot-long piece of rebar was sticking out of Bear's chest cavity, perilously close to his gyroscopic heart. "Have been trying to extricate Amerikanski steel, but there was a chance of nicking plasma conduits." He shook his head. "Not ideal for anyone in the station that is not wishing to become Tennessee Fried Turkey."

"I think I've got a solution. Hold still." With a grunt, John yanked the rebar out of Pavel's chest, dropping it to the ground with a clatter. "Just 'cause I'm a curious sort, what would've happened if it had hit your heart?"

"Station would be having new skylight."

Mamona gulped hard. "Right. Shall we?"

They ran together to where the Commissar was positioning the Echo personnel; everyone had their weapons out, and those with more flamboyant powers had them charged and ready. John, Pavel, and Mamona fell into place, waiting. The second car came screeching in much like the first, sending a shower of sparks off of the rails; it was clear that it was going significantly slower, however. When it impacted with the rear of the wreckage of the first car it further compacted the ruined cabin, causing everyone to duck and recoil.

"Be vigilant, *tovarischii!* They will being in third car!" The assembled Echo and CCCP recovered and trained their weapons on the third car, collectively holding their breath for what seemed like hours but was in fact only a handful of seconds. Finally, the doors creaked open. Dazed and bloody Blacksnake mercs stumbled out, some clutching weapons and others supporting each other.

John was about to move in when a familiar feeling creeped up his spine. In a second it felt like a cold snake was coiled in his guts. *Something is wrong, something is going to go bad.*

At that moment flashbangs went off, seemingly coming from everywhere and nowhere. John was able to recover just in time to see what looked like nearly two dozen more Blacksnake mercenaries pour in from service entrances and back doors.

Shit! I thought we had the station secured! There wasn't any time left to think; almost as one, everyone started shooting—or closing in for hand-to-hand. It was absolute chaos.

Where had all the Blacksnake come from? The last Bulwark had heard, Vickie was only reporting about twenty moving on the station. This was a lot more than twenty.

"Overwatch to Bulwark. No, I don't know where they came from. Working to locate all of them, but they keep shooting out cameras. Overwatch to Bulwark's teams. DON'T MOVE."

A moment later, the earth heaved up beneath the cement flooring, providing barricades of earth and broken concrete behind which they could take some scant shelter.

"Okay, now you can move." Vickie sounded very weak, and shaky. *"AFK for thirty seconds—sugar, caffeine."*

"Take positions behind those barricades!" Bulwark bellowed. "Fan out! I want Omega Tango maneuvers, people!"

"Davay!" Red Saviour's voice rang out as even more Blacksnake mercs streamed into the station. "Squads Odin and Dva, left and right flank!"

For a moment, the dazed Echo and CCCP metas were completely

caught off guard. Within the space of a few heartbeats, they had witnessed one astonishing thing after another: the crash of the train, the sudden onslaught of Blacksnake forces breaching the station, and the very earth rising up from beneath them to serve as makeshift cover. Bull and Saviour's voices cut through their confusion, snapped them to attention, and with shouts of renewed vigor, they moved into position and opened fire on the advancing Blacksnake troops.

It was relatively easy to tell the Blacksnake that had been on the train; they were stumbling around, dazed and confused, and being pulled out of the wreck of the train by their fresher compatriots. A few of the Echo ops immediately surrounded them, guns trained on their hearts, ordering them on the ground. Already battered and bruised, most did as they were ordered, though a few chose to attack, and were immediately put down with short bursts of gunfire. Bull glanced around at the fallen and captured Blacksnake operatives. Harmony wasn't there.

"Comrade Bulwark!" Saviour shouted. "Numbers are *nyet* in our favor! Best defense being offense!"

Bull nodded. "We're going to have to force a retreat then, to gain some ground until we can secure another choke point!" He glanced around the barricade at the Blacksnake forces, who were returning fire from behind stone columns and debris. He looked back at Saviour speculatively. "You feeling reckless?"

Saviour broke out into peals of laughter, so much so that she couldn't speak for a moment.

"I'll take that as a yes," Bull said, as he ran to her side and brought his shield to life around them. "Go!" he barked. "Let's see how much pain you can dish out!"

Natalya looked at Bull like she could kiss him. Instead, she grinned wolfishly and together they charged around the barricade. Without having to concern herself with taking cover, she was able to concentrate all of her attention on wreaking the greatest amount of devastation possible. Her blasts simply passed through Bull's shield, though the glimmering bubble still reflected the Blacksnake gunfire right back at their foes. Granted, the reflected gunfire wasn't even remotely accurate, but the bullets continued to ricochet off concrete floors, ceilings and occasional metal objects, so what the reflected fire lost in accuracy, it more than made up for in being unpredictable.

As for Red Saviour, her energy blasts were accurate and absolutely devastating. If Blacksnake troops took cover behind something that could move, they found it blasted away from them, or *into* them. If they took cover behind something that couldn't move, they found it being eaten away. And if they didn't take cover... Saviour was making no attempt, whatsoever, at nonlethality.

The Blacksnake troopers were forced into retreating—right up to the point where troops showed up with flamethrowers.

"Borzhe moi!" Three flamethrowers belched fire at them at once, and now they were the ones retreating.

But their retreat caused the flamethrowers to advance, which opened holes in the line.

"Echo. Gaps at your nine. CCCP, gaps at your two. Behind two, troops are reloading. Echo, full mags on your side, watch it and stay in cover." Overwatch was doing her job again. *"Check your HUDS if you've got 'em. CCCP, if Echo Med is secure, get your assets downstairs, we need you."*

These were well-trained troops; no bullet-hosing for them, they might have been carrying full-autos, but they were picking their shots and conserving their ammo with short bursts. There was a lot of lead in the air.

As the flamethrowers continued their determined advance, Bull and Saviour traded places with their shock troops, who dove from nowhere to create general chaos amidst the frontline Blacksnake fighters. Saviour broke off from Bull, raining force blasts into whatever openings she could find, pummeling entire mobs of confused Blacksnake metas.

Bulwark fell back behind the barricades, and gripped his shoulder. He winced. One of the jets of flame had singed him. He was about to launch himself back into the fight, when the barricade came under attack. Dodging gunfire and flying over the top, one of his operatives crouched down beside him, and flashed him a grin. It was Mel Gautier—now once again callsign Reverie.

"Report," Bulwark grunted.

"Those were some ballsy moves there, *cher*," she said. "Gave the rest of us an opening. Our melee specialists have opened it up a little more, spread them out a little, and the rangers are picking off targets from cover."

"Enough to turn this around?" he asked.

Mel peeked around the barricade, and jerked back as more

gunfire ricocheted off the warped concrete. "Tough call, but we definitely gained a bit of ground. I'd say we're fifty-fifty now."

"Not good enough," Bull said, grimly. He appraised her with a grave look. "I'm going to need the group shot. You up for it?" He knew Mel had come a long way since returning to Echo. Her sessions with Bella had apparently worked wonders. So far, her fieldwork had been exemplary, but they had barely tested her limits. His discussions with Bella about her had been blunt, but Bella could only shrug and say she was coming along, she was ready and fit for duty, but that no one would know just how big a job she could handle until she tried it under fire. Was she ready to try something so big?

Mel nudged him playfully with her elbow. "I'm back here, ready and waiting. I've been itching to try something like this for a while now."

Bull nodded in encouragement, but he saw past her swagger and assumed confidence. She was nervous, that much was clear, and her hands shook slightly as she closed her eyes. She clenched her hands into tight fists, and when she opened her eyes they blazed with indigo fire. Bull watched in amazement as the doors of the crashed train were blown out, and *streams* of Echo operatives came rushing out. It was perfect. She had gotten it all, from the sounds of the doors being ripped away, to the battle cries of the fresh combatants as they thundered towards the Blacksnake line, screaming for their blood. They very much looked the part as well. They were, each of them, indistinguishable from their real-life counterparts. Bull saw Yankee Pride leading the charge—his gauntlets, a gift from his father, glowing with yellow energy. Unlike Saviour, his energy all went into punches, and no one wanted to be on the receiving end. Behind him were Corbie, Motu and Matai, Silent Knight, the three remaining Winds, Belladonna Blue and Red Djinni. And behind them, still more, the flower of Echo, dozens of heavily armed combatants in full nanoweave bearing heavy assault weaponry.

They were, none of them, real. It didn't seem to matter, as the Blacksnake metas and troopers took one look at them and screamed for a retreat. As they thundered away, the real Echo and CCCP metas followed, taking full advantage of the illusion, and with a relieved grin Mel turned to Bulwark and began to laugh.

"Laissez les bons temps rouler," she said. "Y'know, I think I would even..."

Her words were cut short, as a sudden shot rang out. Her head flew back and Bull caught her as she fell limply into his arms. An angry cut ran the length of her temple, ending with a bullet lodged right above her ear. Reverie gasped for breath, in shock.

"Somebody help me!" Bull yelled, and an unfamiliar young man clad in nanoweave under an Echo Med scrub top knelt at his side. Quickly, he fished out a compress pad, a roll of bandages and forceps from his satchel. He plucked the extruding bullet from Reverie's head, pressed the compress pad to the wound and immediately began to wrap the bandages around her head.

Bull looked up. Where had the shot come from? Aside from the Blacksnake ops that had been captured, the rest were retreating back up to ground level! He scanned the scene, and saw a silhouette pause briefly at the entrance of a service tunnel.

As Harmony looked back, her eyes locked on Bull's. She shrugged an insincere apology, turned, and was gone.

"You got this?" Bull asked the Echo medic, who continued to work quickly on Mel's head wound. The medic nodded.

"I want you to get her out of here, up to the emergency triage bay they've got set up upstairs. Think you can do that?"

The medic gave him an irritated look. "You're asking if I can do my job?" he snapped back.

"Fair enough," Bull said. "What's your name, son?"

"Jakob," the boy answered.

"Well, Jakob, if she wakes up before I get back, tell her she did a damn good job."

"Yessir," Jakob answered.

Bull laid a gentle hand on Mel's shoulder, stood up, and ran for the service tunnel.

Somehow, Frank found himself without a team. He had been on Team Three, but he'd gotten separated after being a meat shield for them when someone threw a hand grenade. He'd blacked out for a second—just because he was tough, it didn't follow he was entirely immune to concussive force—and when he woke up, he was alone.

Where had all those Blacksnake come from? They certainly hadn't been on the train.

"Frankentrain to Team Three. Frankentrain to Team Three." He waited, wincing at the sounds of gunfire and worse echoing in the station as he instinctively took cover against the side of the fourth car. He didn't want to look at what was left of the first one. Poor Rider.

"Frank, where are you?" Finally an answer.

"Next to the train," he replied.

"Stay there, we'll rendezvous with you when we get clear. If you see anything that isn't us, shoot it. We have Snakes crawling all over us."

That made him think of something. Those remaining cars were presumably full of satchel charges, probably C4, military and paramilitary explosive of choice. This was an asset he would rather Blacksnake didn't get their hands on. *Scope and Acrobat probably just pulled the detonators; stick them back in and you'd have working bombs again. I'd better collect them.*

He got himself back in the second car, which had taken relatively little damage. The guy that Overwatch had put on the controls had managed to get the train slowed enough so all that happened when they came in hot was a little crumple at the front and a couple Snakes with broken necks. He began looking for backpack-type bags that were all alike amid the debris and busted signs and other props. As soon as he found two he looked in one, and sure enough . . . bricks of C4 and canisters. The canisters were probably ball bearings or the like for shrapnel. Scope or Acrobat had pulled out the familiar-looking detonator and the end (the radio receiver? probably) was crushed. *Smart kids. Left it in the bag, so no one would find it rolling around and figure out the satchels had been tampered with.*

"Echo to Frankentrain."

"Go, Colt," he replied, piling the satchels just outside the door.

"Your team is supporting Echo Med. Any action where you are?"

"I can hear it, but nothing close. I'm grabbing the C4 satchels the Snakes left on the train so they don't come back here and try to use it. When you can send me a heavy lifter to come get it, I'd appreciate."

"Overwatch to Echo and Frankentrain. Got a man that can take it in three trips or so. Don't shoot him, he looks like a geriatric junkheap."

A moment later, the aforementioned "geriatric junkheap" did come clanking out of the smoke from the ruins of a Caffeebucks. "*Privyet,* comrade!" the creature saluted jovially. "Am beink *the* famous *Sovietski Medved,* the Russian Bear!"

He didn't look anything like a bear, he looked like some Cold War version of an android designed by drunken engineers, but Frank was happy to see him. He piled the old man's back and arms with the satchels, as the odd fellow happily babbled about exploits of the far past and what he'd done five minutes ago, then just as happily trotted off again, laden like a mule.

Frank emptied out what had been the third and fourth car and his commie pack mule turned up to carry that lot of satchels away as well. But it was as he was just starting the fifth and final car that Overwatch reported him being delayed, so rather than leaving something out in the open that Blacksnake would immediately recognize as (a) theirs and (b) useful, he piled the satchels up at the back end.

He was about halfway through when Overwatch came over the Echo freq. "*Overwatch to Frankentrain!*"

"Go, Overwatch."

"Are you still on the tracks? Big trouble coming up the tunnel!"

He ran to the end of the car and peered through the smoke and glare from the daylight out there. And then he saw it, moving ponderously up the tracks, probably because the extra clearance over the tracks gave it the only clear path to move without hunching over. If it even could hunch over.

Blacksnake's been making toys. Someone in their R and D must have been studying the Krieger power armor, because there were obvious similarities. It *didn't* look as if it was made of the superstrong stuff the Kriegers used; this was more like tank armor, which made it as strong as a tank, but also made it as heavy as a tank. Put that much weight on two legs instead of two treads, and you had to have a lot of motive power to make it move; probably why it was so big. Instead of energy cannon, it had twin M134 miniguns for arms. If it started firing it would be able to mow down pretty much anything like a harvester going through a field of wheat. Echo nanoweave was meant for small-arms fire, not 7.26 x 51mm shells coming at four thousand a minute. The damn thing was nothing more nor less than a killing machine, and could probably even take down any OpThree that wasn't invulnerable.

With a moment of impossible clarity, he *knew* that he was in exactly the right place, at exactly the right time, and he knew exactly what to do.

"Got it covered, Overwatch," he said casually, and began clearing the rest of the satchels up to the end of the train. The thing was so heavy it was lumbering at a pace far slower than a normal man's walk, but he hurried nevertheless, grabbing a couple of discarded Reb bandanas along the way. With his makeshift boiler-plate armor, he looked more like a Reb than Echo. He tied one of the bandanas around his neck, the other around his head. By the time he got the last of the satchels piled up, the mecha was halfway to the train.

Dropped tasers were everywhere. He picked one up, and jammed four of the broken detonators into the nearest block of C4, and waved at the mecha.

It stopped. He got the impression of peering, but that was probably because the operator was using zoom and maybe light-amplifying tech to get a better look at him. He waved again, then pointed to his ear, and made a "negative" sign. Even a moron should take that to mean "Hi, I'm friendly, lost my radio."

Nice thing about Echo. We're all so upright and decent . . . well, except maybe the Djinni . . . nobody ever thinks we would lie.

Then again, with twin miniguns, this thing really didn't have to worry if he was friendly or not. After all, what could he do to it?

He waited patiently for the thing to lumber towards him—hoping that if the operator decided to err on the side of caution, his own armor and the back of the train *might* keep him from getting turned into salsa before he got his chance to take the thing out.

But the operator was, thankfully, convinced of his own invincibility and continued to lumber forward, until at last it was within inches of the back glass, peering down at him. An external speaker squawked to life.

"What unit are you with?" the operator demanded.

"Unit Misfits," Frank said. "And I figured you could use a lift."

And with that, he jammed the taser into the detonators, and hit the switch.

Bella didn't have to feign shock when the explosion rocked the entire plaza. She staggered and looked wildly in the direction of the MARTA station, where a plume of smoke was rising.

"Overwatch to Echo," she heard, both on her Overwatch rig and through her normal comm. *"That was Echo OpOne Frankentrain taking out a Blacksnake mecha the hard way."* The grim tone to Vickie's voice told Bella exactly what "the hard way" meant.

Her gaze whipped over to Verd and Khanji on the platform. She was just in time to catch a fleeting look of satisfaction on Verd's face.

But the explosion, coming on top of the two crashes, had set the crowd swirling in knots of confusion and fear. No one knew where to go, and people were starting to panic. Verd was going for the mic again—presumably to try and calm them down—while Khanji turned away to talk to one of his "special" security detail.

This might be my only chance to—

The thought was cut off as a hand grabbed her elbow and a familiar voice growled into her ear before she could react.

"I told you, darlin', she'll gut you before you can blink. I'm getting you out of here before one of them figures out you just *might* know something."

Bella thought about arguing with the Djinni—but then her private Overwatch freq opened again.

"Soviette to Comrade Blue. Skills are needed here!" Sovie was usually calm and contained, but this sounded desperate.

That settled it. In the choice between saving lives and *maybe* taking down Verd, there was no choice. "Right. Let's go," she said grimly.

As hunts went, it was a simple one. When Harmony had fled, Bulwark had only paused to pick up a rifle off a fallen Blacksnake meta and had followed in hot pursuit, and without a word Scope and Acrobat had joined him. Overwatch had contacted them only long enough to tell them that the security cams had been disabled back there, which left them on their own for finding her. They pounded down the concrete corridor under dim lighting from regularly spaced fluorescent fixtures above them. There was no need for stealth. There really wasn't anywhere to hide, and with her speed Harmony was already well ahead of them. She wasn't one for stamina though, that was something they remembered from their time together. Eventually, she would have to slow down. Or had that been a ruse as well? She had kept so many secrets, she had played them so convincingly, but what choice did they have? They continued to run, their feet echoing off the concrete, but they were otherwise silent. There wasn't any need to talk. They all felt the same, each knew what the rest did, as any battle-seasoned team should. There was no way they would let her escape, not this time.

So when they came to the fork in the tunnel, nothing was discussed. They slowed to a stop, and with a look they parted ways. Bull headed left while Scope and Acrobat took the right, with barely a glance at each other. Just a few pointed words.

"Remember, don't let her close in!" Bull's voice rumbled after them.

"Signal if you find her!" Scope growled back.

"We missed you, boss!" That was Bruno's contribution.

As they ran, Bruno found his thoughts drifting back over the past few days. Their time behind enemy lines had seemed so fruitless. Try as they might, he and Scope had never found a way to ambush Harmony. She was simply never at Blacksnake HQ. Still, they kept getting hints and clues that pointed to her whereabouts. When she finally showed up for this, the big mission, it was too good an opportunity to miss. Taking her out could wait. Foiling the scheme against Echo had to take priority. It was all so crazy. This was *Harmony!* How did that shy, crazy nutjob they had all come to love pull one over on all of them, and on Bulwark of all people, for years? Who was she, really? And just how good did she have to be to . . . ?

The thought snapped him back to the more immediate matters at hand. They were chasing her, blindly, someone who had been good enough to take out an entire squad of Tesla's personal bodyguards and Bulwark with relative ease. He glanced at Scope as they sprinted through the tunnel, his hand outstretched to rein her in, when he felt that warm spot in his chest again. That warmth that always seemed to bloom when he looked at her, when he thought of her, that damn near cooked him alive the one time he had actually touched her. Not that he'd had much choice. When that pit trap had opened in the Goldman Catacombs, he watched his deepest, most desperate crush fall headlong into it. Had he known there were jagged spikes waiting for them at the bottom, he doubted it would have made a difference. He would have jumped in after her anyway. For an eternity, they had simply hung there, bouncing lightly on his zipline, their bodies pressed together as she held onto him for dear life. Every day since, he had relived that moment, every time he closed his eyes.

They were chasing a killer, and a damn good one, alone. No backup, no element of surprise, just the two of them against a cold-blooded monster. It *was* crazy. Could they really beat her? He felt his legs seize up, as the thought of losing Scope tore at his heart.

"Paris, stop a second," he said.

Scope skidded to a halt, and glared at him.

"How many times do I have to say it, Bruno?" she seethed, "Call me that again and I will gut you."

"Sorry, sorry," he panted, holding up one hand. "Never knew anyone to be so touchy about their real name."

"It's not my real name," she insisted. "Hasn't been for a while now."

"Fine, *fine*... *Scope*, stop a second."

"You winded already? You girl..."

"No, no, course not... well okay, yes, yes I am," Bruno admitted. "But it's not just that. What are we doing? We really going to Zerg her, just the two of us? Remember all the stuff we heard about her, in the Blacksnake barracks? She's their go-to assassin, she has been for years. What can we do that'll top her? She's..."

"Remember!" Scope barked, and immediately lowered her voice. "Remember what Bull said. Keep your distance..."

"And if she closes in? She's fast, Scope, faster than..."

"Remember," Scope repeated. "Remember what we heard in the barracks." She gave him a meaningful look, then looked down at herself and back to him. "We got this, Bruno. We..."

She was interrupted by the hard clanking of smoke grenades as they bounced around their feet. Scope shouted in alarm but they were instantly enveloped in an opaque fog. At least their gas masks worked, though Bruno was still able to detect a faint acrid odor to it.

"What is that?" Bruno shouted. "Tear gas?"

"Smell's wrong, and the color's off," Scope snarled.

"Do you like it?" Harmony called out from further up the tunnel. "New Blacksnake tech, patent pending. That cloud's going to persist for a while, so don't bother waiting for it to dissipate. And don't move. You can't see me, but I can see you, and I've got my piece trained on both of you." She paused. "Good to see you guys, by the way. You both look good."

"Save it, you two-faced, murderous bitch!" Scope snarled. "Well? What are you waiting for? You've got the drop on us. Why don't you take it?"

Harmony sighed. "Do you really think I want you dead? Whether you choose to believe it or not, you two were the closest I've had to friends in . . . well, decades, really. You could even say we grew up together, in an odd fashion. When we first met, I thought I'd have my work cut out for me, fitting in. You both were so *hopeless*! Then you improved, faster than anyone would have thought, which meant I could let Echo think I was improving too. And look at you now! I'm impressed! Infiltrating Blacksnake to chase down little old me, I can only guess. Who would have thought shy, bumbling Bruno and Paris, the Queen of Piss 'n' Moan, could pull it off?"

Scope shook her head. "All right, seriously, you guys have to cut out this 'Paris' crap, or I'm . . ."

"Going to gut us," Harmony finished. "Yes, yes. Thing about old and tired threats, Paris, they tend to become . . . well, old and tired. You need a new bit."

"What do you want, Harm?" Bruno asked. He was, for once, not bouncing lightly on the balls of his feet. Instead he stood motionless, but through the haze of smoke Scope just barely made out his fingers lightly tapping on his sidearm, which was bound to his leg.

"Payback," Harmony answered. "On a certain billionaire who seems to want me dead. He really rig that entire train to blow?"

"*Yes,*" Bruno answered in a loud voice, drowning the faint snap from his holster as he unfastened the strap holding his gun.

"I guess that means I owe the two of you as well," Harmony said. "You saved my life, and that doesn't happen too often. Wow, it's great to have pals."

"Hey, that wasn't our first choice!" Scope shouted, following Acrobat's lead and subtly flicking the safeties off her pistols. "We were sort of rushed for time. Believe me, if we could have figured out a way to off you while saving everyone else on that train, we would have."

"Do we really need the bravado?" Harmony asked. "Really, all I want to do is talk."

"You want to *talk?*" Scope scoffed. "Harm, you were infiltrating us for Blacksnake, you lied to us for years, you killed our boss, you put Bull in a coma, and it turns out you're Blacksnake's number one hitman! You just tried to off a train full of Echo Ops and veterans and you just plugged Reverie in the head with a bullet! We left the 'talking' portion of this crazy soap opera a while ago. Can we just fight now?"

"No," Harmony answered. "I'm going to need to say a few things."

"We don't need to hear anything from you!" Scope shouted.

"Oh, it's not to you," Harmony said. "But I think you'll be interested to hear it. It'll also do that 'two birds, one stone' thing. You appreciate that, don't you Scope? Look at me, I'm being efficient!"

"Get to the point, Harm," Acrobat said.

"It'll be quick, promise," Harmony said. "Something that should hurt my former employer, and pay you two back in full. Then we can get back to you trying to take me down." She chuckled, and raised her voice. "You picking this up, Overwatch? Do I have your full attention?"

There was a pause, and then...

"Tell her I'm listening," they heard Vickie say.

"Overwatch is receiving," Acrobat said, loudly. "Say your piece."

"This is Special Operative Talisman of Blacksnake, formerly known as Echo Op Trainee Harmony. On this, the first-year anniversary of the global Invasion, Dominic Verdigris III attempted to assassinate a MARTA train full of Echo veterans and their Echo Op escorts by way of a bombing. His aim was to set up the bombing as a failed kidnapping attempt, using the Atlanta rogue meta group known as the Rebs as scapegoats. Prior to today, my understanding was that this plan had two objectives. First, through combat or the detonation of bombs placed on the MARTA transport, to eliminate key members of Echo meta personnel Verdigris wanted neutralized. Second, to discredit and undermine the remaining Echo personnel currently in upper management roles to facilitate an eventual transfer of power completely into his hands. His desire to have the Echo veterans eliminated in all of his contingency plans suggests to me a third objective, though he never chose to discuss this particular point with me. In light of new evidence, I would also postulate a fourth objective. His decision to plant bombs on every car of the MARTA transport suggests he also wished to terminate myself and my team of Blacksnake operatives. My belief is that he wished to eliminate the last key piece of evidence linking himself to the murder of Alex Tesla—me. I was Alex Tesla's murderer, and I state now for the record that I acted under the sole direction of Dominic Verdigris III."

"Harmony!" Bruno said. "You know this won't mean much unless you turn yourself in and testify! Does this mean you're surrendering to us?"

"Please no," Scope muttered. "Then I can't shoot her."

"Don't be absurd," Harmony said. "Do you really think I'd just chain myself to you? Overwatch, I am now transmitting a URL to the Echo Med freq for secure documents, recordings and files that will provide all the evidence you need to corroborate these accusations. The passkey is One-Five-Delta-Charlie-Tango-Quebec-Two-Foxtrot-Zulu. Please confirm."

There was a long silence.

"Package confirmed, you two," they heard Vickie say over their communicators.

"She's got it," Bruno said. "It's done, Harmony."

"Good," Harmony said simply. "Take him down, with my compliments. Now, if you will excuse me, I'm sure Bull's been listening in all this time and is double-timing it towards us. He promised to break me, you see, and as much as I'd find that entertaining, I think it might be best to save that for another day."

"Harmony!" Scope shouted. "You even think of jackrabbiting and I swear I will mow you down where you stand!"

"More tired threats, Scope?" Harmony sighed. "This should be good. I know you, dear girl. I know how much your eyes are your crutch, as much as your strength. Pray, how are you going to hit what you can't see? Are you going to..."

In answer, Scope leveled her pistols in Harmony's direction, and emptied her magazines. Bruno heard the storm of bullets ricochet off the concrete walls, but a few seemed to find their mark. Harmony screamed. "How...?"

"Can't see you, can't help but hear you," Scope replied smugly. "How's that for a new bit, bitch?"

Bruno heard Harmony swear, and then with a loud *fooomph* he saw a gleam of light, growing larger...

"Scope!" he yelled, but it was too late. He dove to protect Scope with his own body, but it wasn't a grenade that Harmony had fired at them, it was a flare. The small flame punctured the dense smoke, and the very air around them ignited in a tremendous flash of light. Scope began to scream while Bruno rubbed at the stars in his eyes. He was dazed, but the haze of bright stars was already beginning to fade, and he saw that the flash had depleted the smokescreen. It had been so bright though, so bright that Scope must have been...

"Blinded!" Scope yelled. "The bitch blinded me! She..."

Bruno heard the pounding of footsteps, caught a glimpse of a brief struggle, and when his eyes finally began to register shapes, he saw Scope sliding to the ground and Harmony standing over her.

"*Paris!*" Bruno screamed. "You killed her!"

Harmony rolled her eyes. "Of course not. She just cut up my legs to hell. She's no good to me dead." She reached down towards Scope's limp body, and frowned. She looked up at Bruno. "Full body armor. Since when do you two wear full body armor?"

Acrobat ignored the question and instead launched himself at the tunnel wall, rebounded and flew at Harmony, feetfirst. With a surprised yelp, she dodged back and tumbled away, landing in a crouch. Bruno noticed she was noticeably slower. After her sprint to escape and a number of bullets embedded in her legs, she was severely weakened and in obvious need of juicing.

"You stay the hell away from her," Acrobat growled.

"Don't be an idiot, Bruno," Harmony snarled as she stood up. "Why do you think I went for her first? Even blind, she's more a threat to me than you'll ever be, you little mouse of a . . ."

She shrieked, threw down another smoke bomb and retreated as he drew his pistol and began firing. Once again, the fog obscured anything beyond a foot away. Bruno bent down, threw Scope over one shoulder, and fell back as Harmony began to return fire. It was awkward, shielding Scope's chest and head with his body while he backed away, exchanging gunfire with Harmony through the thick smoke. He grunted as one shot grazed his shoulder, and after a moment he felt the sting of a fresh wound. He quickened his backward pace, but slowed as Harmony stopped shooting. From the smoke, he heard the pounding of feet on pavement. Harmony was running away.

"God, I miss Echo nanoweave," he winced.

"Bruno," he heard Scope mutter into his back. "Put me down, you moron."

He knelt down and let Scope come to her feet. Immediately, her legs buckled and he steadied her as she sank to her knees. She was clutching her side.

"Easy, easy," he said. "Don't exert yourself. I think Harm gave you a solid shot to the liver. Can you see yet?"

Scope looked around blankly, and her lips quivered with rage. She shook her head.

"It's getting better. The great black blur is kind of a great gray blur now. I'm going to need a minute, just a minute . . ." She exhaled and gritted her teeth, struggling with indecision. "We don't have a minute. You need to go after her, now."

"Acrobat, you will belay that order!" Bulwark's voice rumbled over their comm units. *"I am almost to your position, I..."*

"No, Bull, you're really not," Vickie interrupted. *"You folks are going to have to move. Just gave a look over Harm's files. They're good, but Bruno is right. To make this stick we need a live body, a living witness, otherwise there'll be claims we manufactured it all. If there is a chance in hell you can capture her, do it."*

"Overwatch, Harmony is not to be underestimated!" Bulwark sounded like he had quickened his pace to a dead run. His breathing sounded labored, his footsteps thundering on concrete.

"I freaking helped bring you back from the other side; you think I don't know that? But I also know Verd, I know what he'll do, I know the politicians he's bought and the people he's got under his thumb. We need a live witness."

"Dammit, Bruno, you will wait for me to..."

Scope reached up and felt about Bruno's head for his comm unit. She turned it off, and then hers. She grabbed Bruno by the front of his flak jacket and brought his face within an inch of her own.

"Listen to me!" she hissed. "Harm's getting away! Go! Remember what you promised me!"

"We finish this today," he said.

"We finish this today," she nodded.

Bruno hesitated, looking down the tunnel where Harmony had fled, and back to Scope. She couldn't see him, but her eyes were wide open. He had always been so taken with how intense they were. While the rest of her shook with anger, her eyes stayed fixed in place. She couldn't see him. She never had, and he suspected now she never would. How could someone who could see with such clarity be so blind to what was right in front of her? It occurred to him that perhaps Harmony was right. Scope's vision was a crutch. And if she couldn't see him one way, then perhaps another approach would have to do.

He released the bottom half of his mask, and then hers, and cupped her face gently with both hands.

"Bruno," she said. "What the hell..."

He kissed her, and felt her scorn melt away to astonishment, and right at the end, he felt her kiss him back.

"Stay here," he breathed, pulling back reluctantly. "God, I've wanted to do that for a really long time. God willing, maybe you'll let me do that again."

Scope just nodded. She had stopped shaking with anger. Instead, she just looked utterly bewildered, even a little lost. Which, given her other possible reactions, Bruno read as positive. Bruno refastened his mask, sprang to his feet, and raced off.

Scope could not have moved, and it had nothing to do with her injuries or her blindness. She felt completely paralyzed, mentally *and* physically stunned. Blind-sided. Never had a word been more appropriate.

Finally, she spoke aloud, though there was no one to hear her. "Well, that just happened."

". . . FBI, CIA, Interpol, you name it. Hell, even Red Saviour has a file on him as thick as your thumb. They have all *got little task forces trying to nail Verd to the wall and have been for years. He* always *gets out of it, Bull! Present evidence and either the judges he bought turn him loose or his lawyers throw enough doubt on it that he gets off."*

"You're telling me that full recorded testimony and corroborating evidence by Tesla's actual murderer won't be sufficient?" Bulwark said, his tone incredulous. He huffed as he continued to run.

"Yes, I am. You keep forgetting, my folks are the section heads for their FBI division, which means they need to think and plan past the arrest. Any good lawyer could present evidence claiming to show we edited it, made it up out of whole cloth, or otherwise tampered with it. And they have, over and over again. That's how he keeps getting off."

"Somehow, I don't see Harmony being the most cooperative of witnesses upon capture. Leaving a statement and jetting is one thing for her, but taking the stand is quite another. We know how good an actor she is, too. She'll say and do anything she wants, and she'll be convincing. If I had an entire squadron, it might be different, but the risk involved here, for something so uncertain . . ."

"It depends on what kind of deal she can get out. I expect it will be a good one. Deal, that is."

"You expect a deal? Really? She fingered Verdigris, but she took full credit for the act herself? How good a deal could she get?"

"I've watched DAs and federal prosecutors deal with Mafia assassins, hitmen of all sorts. I've watched them give them full immunity and put them in the Witness Protection Program when the stakes are high enough—"

"Overwatch, is this really the time for a debate? You just overrode a direct order from their field commander."

"Yes, I did. They've been operating on their own for months, and doing damn well at it."

"And now they've cut communications and Bruno is off to attempt capture of a seasoned killer. You just sent him off to die."

"When are you going to let them grow up? When are you going to stop trying to protect them and let them do the job you've been training them to do? When will you allow them to make the same level of sacrifice you ask of yourself? Isn't that what our job always comes down to in the end? Being willing to sacrifice whatever it takes?"

"This isn't just some job!" he roared, now breathing hard. He came to a stop, panting. "I send soldiers off on missions. I give orders that can be met and executed. I just don't think..."

He paused.

"You don't think he can beat her, do you?"

"No," Bull said finally, and began to run again. "I don't."

Bruno raced down the tunnel, keeping his footsteps light, straining to see or hear anything ahead of him. He should have been terrified. His heart should have been beating hard enough to erupt out of his chest. It was, actually, but not from fright. He was reliving the kiss, again and again, and he could hardly believe that it had happened.

I did it, I kissed her, I can't believe I kissed her, and she kissed back, she did, *I know she did, I felt it...*

As he rounded a corner, the thunder of gunshots brought him crashing back to the present.

Oh, right. Harmony.

He dove under the shots, rolled, and came up shooting. He heard Harmony curse and duck back under cover. Bruno took shelter behind an inset doorway, gulped down a breath of courage, and returned fire.

"Bruno!" Harmony yelled, as she fired a few more rounds at him.

"What?" Acrobat yelled back, as he squeezed off a few more shots of his own.

"This is stupid!"

"Of course it is!" Bruno shouted. "If you stop and think about it, the last few months have been a complete waste of time! We should be working together! Kriegers, remember?"

"I meant *this!*" Harmony said. "Right here, right now, you and me! You know you can't take me, so why are you even trying? You were in the Blacksnake barracks, so you must have heard all about me. You know everything they told you? It's true. Yes, I'm the one Blacksnake would send in to take out OpThrees. I'm the one who got the entire Coredonne clan. I'm the one that took down the head yakuza of the Blood Tigers, and his bodyguards."

"Oh yeah," Bruno agreed. "We heard *all* about you. Talisman, the lady who can suck you dry with a touch. Talisman, she'll always see you coming, but you'll never see her, not before she's got you pinned to the ground. You know what *no one* said about you? Your staying power. You've got none, Harmony. You're spent from running, you've left a trail of blood ever since Scope dumped a load of lead into your legs, and now I'm guessing you're not nearly as fast as you usually are. I'm guessing you're pretty hungry right now, too. But if you want to eat me, guess what . . . ?"

"I'm going to have to fight you," Harmony said. "You're covered up. You both did your homework."

They had been trading volleys of gunfire, each ducking behind their respective corners as the other opened up. This time they both leapt out, each rushing the other, their firearms raised. Triggers were squeezed, but nothing happened, their ammo was spent. And neither of them had magazines left to reload with.

"Been a while since we sparred," Harmony said, and smirked at him. "In a way, I'm happy about this. Do you have any idea how much it sucked, having to always throw fights to you?"

"I'll bet," Bruno said, and dropped his pistol. "Care to make a wager on this one?"

"I don't do sure bets," Harmony replied, also dropping her gun. "There's no sport in it."

"That satisfy the prefight banter portion?" Bruno asked.

"Meh, it'll do," Harm said, and launched herself at him.

Bruno rolled under her kick, but Harmony's follow-up backhand smashed him to the ground. She might have lost a lot of speed, but she was still fast enough, and strong. He flipped over, threw his arms up to block a heavy dropkick, and was rewarded with a howl of pain. Harmony fell back a few steps, and he used her brief retreat to flip up to his feet. She wasn't used to being so drained, or wounded. Why else would she have made such an amateur mistake? He looked down at her legs. Bits of torn flesh were poking out of her leggings. She had willed them to heal, just enough to stop the bleeding, but she wouldn't be trying another kick any time soon. They circled one another, and Bruno caught a flicker of fear on her face. At least, he hoped so.

She's cunning. She's got great acting chops. Don't underestimate her.

He darted in and threw a few tentative jabs. She slapped his hands away contemptuously, but missed the feint as he dropped down and went for the sweep. Harmony cried out as his feet buckled her legs, just behind the knees. She toppled over, and received a solid boot to the temple before he dove away. She was on her feet in an instant, though she seemed a bit unsteady.

She's weak in the legs, she's weak in the legs... she's cunning, she's cunning...

He tried again, leading with soft strikes to her head and chest, which she easily deflected and dodged, and dropped down to drive an elbow at her kneecap. Harmony screamed as he rammed the side of her leg, and he heard something snap. She drove down with both fists and slammed him to the ground. He pushed himself up, grunted as she sent him flying back with an enormous uppercut and went limp as he collided with the tunnel wall. He fell to his knees, massaging the back of his head. He felt a little dizzy, and suppressed the urge to vomit.

"All right, you stupid boy, you want to play?" She hissed at him, and Bruno watched as her features began to distort. Claws erupted from her hands, fangs extended from a mouth that seemed to unhinge. Her skin, which had always seemed to gleam with eternal youth, grew dry and scaly. And her eyes! They seemed to sink back into her head, her pupils dilating until only luminous black beads stared back at him in anger. She drew in a long, raspy breath and exhaled. Slowly, the wounds on her legs began to mend, and with an awful crack her kneecap righted itself. When she finally spoke, it wasn't her usual voice, high-pitched and sublime. It was something dark, sinister and bestial. It was hungry.

"Let's play," she growled, and leapt towards him.

Bruno launched himself straight up, snagged an exposed ceiling rung and pulled himself up. Caught up in the charge, Harmony flew beneath him and braced herself for impact with the wall. She recoiled, spinning in midleap and attempted to propel herself up to claw the dexterous man down from his perch, when her face met with Bruno's feet as he swung down. She flew back, but not before lashing out in a wide arc with her claws, catching him low on the leg and tearing up a sizable portion of his calf muscle. Bruno grunted in pain and landed a bit clumsily on his feet.

Just need to keep her occupied, keep her from rabbiting, until help arrives. Come on, Bull, what's keeping you?

They circled each other warily, both hobbling a little and favoring their good legs.

"Give it up, Bruno," Harmony rasped. "Just walk away. What do you hope to accomplish here? I gave Verdigris to you! There's nothing left here for you, except whatever pitiful price your tired sense of justice and honor demands of you."

"Y'know, Harmony," Bruno said, "you're talking an awful lot for someone who thinks this fight is so one-sided. I think you're stalling."

Harmony grinned, and the sight of her lips curled around those horrific fangs chilled Bruno more than he cared to admit.

"Of course I am, you idiot," she chuckled. "Did you really think your locker room chats with Blacksnake minions would make you privy to all my secrets? You think you know so much about me, but you've barely scratched the surface. And with each second, while you bleed and tire, I'm just getting stronger."

"You're bluffing," he said. "You still need a boost; even you're not that good an actor."

"Not that good an actor?" she said, incredulously. "I had you all fooled for *years*, boy! You have no appreciation for what I endured, just to live amongst you, like some common..."

"So you're method, I get that. You're the Marlon Brando of the meta world, kudos. You think it matters now, Harm? All that work, all the lies, and for what? What did you accomplish here? What are you accomplishing now?"

"Well, right now I'm educating one sad little kid who thinks he's developed a lot more than he has."

"You know what I think?" Bruno said, coming to a stop. "I think you're struggling with yourself. I think you actually made friends here, found people you care about. I think that's why you didn't just take Bull out when you had the chance. I think that's why you hesitated with Scope. I think that's why I'm still standing. You're fighting yourself. You just can't bring yourself to do it. It's not too late, Harmony. You've already set Verdigris up, but good. They'll listen to you if you carry it through. They'll give you a fair shake if you come back and hammer that final nail in his coffin."

He extended a hand and his eyes bore into hers.

"Come back to us, Harmony."

She had stopped moving, and heard him out. Her face was so reptilian now he found it difficult to gauge what she was thinking. She looked down at his hand, and for a moment he thought she would reach for it.

"Bruno!" Bull's shout rang out far behind them, and they heard thunderous footsteps in the distance.

Harmony hissed. "You little, two-faced shit, you were stalling too!"

Bruno grinned, and shrugged. "What can I say? Fast learner."

With a roar, she turned to run, but stopped as he pulled in front of her.

"It's over, Harmony," he said, quietly. "This ends today."

He danced lightly on the balls of his feet, moving from side to side, but his intentions were clear. If she was going to escape, she would have to get through him.

"I say when it ends," she snarled, and lunged at him. She swung wildly, in desperation, hoping to break through his defenses with sweeping rakes and quick shots to the head and stomach. Bruno stayed on the defensive, dodging what blows he could, deflecting those he could not. He neutralized her sudden and reckless desire to flee with cold and detached blocking maneuvers, neatly diverting her fury and forcing her to retreat with rapid counterstrikes and feints.

The footsteps were close now. *Too close,* Harmony thought. She took a step back, and with a final, desperate lunge, she tackled Bruno to the ground. They fell, rolled together, and with a tremendous effort Harmony reared back and smashed his head with her own. Bruno gurgled and went limp. With a cry of victory, Harmony laid her hand upon his masked face to pry off his goggles. She hissed as they stuck fast. The little shit had sealed his gear together! From his goggles to his fitted gas filter, Bruno had left nothing exposed, and Bulwark was almost on her...

She took a breath and reared back with one clawed hand. With a final, desperate surge of strength, she plunged her hand into Bruno's chest, tearing through his body armor. Her claws slipped between his ribs, and she felt the tips puncture his heart. She sighed in relief, and began to gorge herself on his life-force, siphoning his strength greedily. She felt her wounds heal, the pain subside, and as she came to her feet, ready to sprint away at full speed, her legs were ravaged with a storm of bullets.

Her eyes went wide in disbelief. Her legs, which had just finished healing, buckled again as fresh wounds erupted in gouts of blood. She sank to her knees, and stared as Scope hobbled closer, her guns still at the ready.

"Give me a reason, Harmony," Scope muttered, and pressed both muzzles to Harmony's temple.

Harmony didn't answer, and simply closed her eyes.

Scope looked down. Through his thick goggles, Bruno stared back at her. He lay in a growing pool of blood which seeped from his chest. His breathing, shallow and sporadic, slowed and came to a halt. Scope let out a startled sob, and with a scream of loss she squeezed both triggers. Harmony's head snapped back, her body went limp, and collapsed on top of Bruno.

"*Scope!*" Bull shouted as he ran up to them. "We needed her alive! Why did you do that?"

Scope glared at him. She knelt down, dropped her pistols, and gently pushed Harmony off of Bruno. She laid a hand on his neck, found the hidden clasp, and pulled off his entire mask. Softly, she pushed his hair back from his forehead, and closed his eyes.

"She gave me a reason," Scope answered. She shook her head. "Besides, do you really think a couple of bullets to the head would kill her?"

Bull tore his eyes away from Bruno, and watched as Harmony continued to breathe. Her wounds had stopped bleeding too. From her legs and forehead, Scope's bullets were slowly pushed out by healing bone and tissue, and fell with a clatter to the ground. He knelt down, fished the reinforced restraints from his belt, and locked them about her wrists and ankles.

Over the radio there came only a single strangled sob. Then Vickie's voice, hoarse and choked. "*Overwatch to Echo. Man down. Harmony captured. Dispatch security team to grid 4-8-1 with containment suit and full metahuman restraints.*"

Scope leaned down, and held Bruno's still body close to hers. "Hey, Bruno," she whispered. "We did it, geekboy. We got the bad guy."

Her head sagged, and her body shook with silent sobs as her arms tightened around him. When the security and med teams arrived, she didn't notice, not until Bull gently pried her away.

Tears spilled down Vickie's face; her vision blurred and she dashed the back of her hand across her burning eyes to clear them, and kept on typing. Her fault. Bruno was dead, and it was all her fault. Bull was right, she had sent him to die, and she had known he was right at the time, and she had done it anyway. Because the stakes were too high, and she had known that too. But that didn't keep it from being her fault.

Bulwark thought like a soldier and a cop. He assumed that once you had the evidence, everything would be fine. But Vickie thought like the sort of FBI agent her parents were; she *knew* that evidence was never enough when it came to someone as slippery as Dominic Verdigris. There was no substitute for the credible witness in the stand, and no one would be more credible than Harmony—because given the right deal, she'd employ her acting ability to the utmost and no defense attorney would be able to shake her. That was why she had sent Bruno after the rogue assassin. And that was why she would never forgive herself for doing so.

She ignored the tears, because it was the mission that was important, not her, and her part of the mission wasn't over yet. There was still something more she could do. Verd was smart, experienced, savvy, but if she could manage to rattle him... "Grey, grow some hands," she said hoarsely. "You're a better video editor than I am and I'm going to need both of us on the boards."

The familiar sprang up beside her without a word; his paws elongated into raccoon-like hands, and he went to work on the video from the feeds and Harmony's files. Meanwhile Vickie pulled up the hack-file to everything that called itself "the media" that she had kept in reserve for just this sort of occasion; when she was done with her data dump, there would not be a single legitimate place for Dominic Verdigris to hide. And maybe, just maybe, he'd rabbit. Then it would be all over for him; running would be a tacit admission of guilt. She was under no illusions that more than a tenth of his operation would be shut down, of course. He operated inside so many shell companies that he wouldn't lose more than a fraction of his net worth.

But governments would drop their open associations with him like red-hot rocks, his legitimate businesses would be sanctioned or shut down, accounts would be frozen, assets seized, he'd have no one that would openly aid him, and from now on he'd have to operate from the shadows, within his criminal organizations only.

And Echo would be safe.

It wasn't enough, it wasn't *nearly* enough, but at least it was something.

You bought us that much, Bruno. Your friends will be safe again.

Dominic Verdigris had the jarring experience of hearing his own voice coming from the ranks of speakers around the Plaza—speaking words entirely different from those he was mouthing into the microphone.

Shocked, he whirled to stare at the Jumbotron, at video of himself, in his office; a bit fuzzy, taken from what must have been a button cam, but unmistakably him.

"*So, Ms.... Krait?*" The Dom up there raised an eyebrow. "*Helena Krait. A serpent name for a Blacksnake agent... why do I get the impression this isn't your real name?*"

An off-camera voice replied with indifference. "*I hardly think it matters what* nom de guerre *I use, as long as I get the job done.*"

"*You have most assuredly, Ms. Krait,*" he heard himself saying, and watched himself leaning forward. "*Very nice intel from the heart of Echo itself. But I am the new boss, and I want more than that. You were Blacksnake's prime assassin for quite some time as Agent Talisman. I'm reactivating you.*"

"*And I presume you have a target?*"

"*Indeed I do,*" said the Dom in the video, leaning back in his chair. "*I want you to take out Alex Tesla.*"

Dominic felt his mind freeze for a moment. Then he whirled and turned on Khanjar. "Get that off of there! Cancel that feed! Stop it!"

Khanjar had one hand to her ear. "Can't. Whoever is doing this is better than anyone you have, Dom—"

The female voice from the feed was saying something else now. "*This is Special Operative Talisman of Blacksnake, formerly known as Echo Op Trainee Harmony. On this, the first year anniversary of the global Invasion, Dominic Verdigris III attempted to assassinate a MARTA train full of Echo veterans and their Echo Op escorts by way of a bombing...*"

She was spilling it. She was spilling it *all.* And she was supposed to be dead! Why wasn't she dead?

Video of fighting on the MARTA train, in the station, was being played as her damning words thundered across the plaza. Khanjar's hand was at the small of his back, and she was shoving him towards the emergency exit, gesturing to the rest of his special security to follow. "Dom, I don't know who this is, but he's a genius. All of this is going direct feed to every possible news organization, political blog, and interested party across the planet and there is nothing we can do about it!" she hissed urgently as they sprinted for the innocuous vehicles they had held in reserve in case they needed them.

His mind steadied. There had always been the possibility that one day he'd be outed. He hadn't planned on it being of the sheer disastrous *scope* of this, but he'd set up for it. After all, he'd been a criminal before he went legit, and he wouldn't lose more than a fraction of his assets now if he had to shed the legitimate side of his businesses. *Hell with it. Being the billionaire playboy was a waste of time anyway.* "Activate the poison-pill plan," he snarled to Khanjar as she shoved him into the back seat of the getaway car. She nodded, and began issuing radio orders. "All Blacksnake. Pull back, pull out, retreat to safe houses. Operation Cyanide is now activated. Repeat..."

"Overwatch to all. Blacksnake is retreating. Verd is rabbiting. Repeat, Blacksnake is retreating. Verd is escaping."

"Well, that is beink explain why offense changes to defense," Red Saviour muttered to herself, as she watched the Blacksnake ops that had been pinning her down with a hail of fire suddenly begin withdrawing. "All CCCP! At them, my wolves! Capture is secondary!"

From somewhere down the wrecked shopping complex she heard Untermensch scream his signature battle cry. *"Ura ura ura!"*

And from elsewhere, she heard over the link, the plaintive cry of Soviet Bear. *"Retreating? What am I to be doing with all this C4?"*

✧ ✧ ✧

Bella glanced at Soviette, who nodded abruptly. "There will not be any prisoners, comrade, unless you take them," the Russian said. "We can handle healings from here on."

Bella did not hesitate. "Overwatch, is there any chance I can get Verd?"

"Not from where you are. I've already lost him. Bastard had a fleet of identical vehicles in an underground garage, killed all the cams in there and ditched his Echo gear, so I couldn't tell which one he got into. I'm tracking them, but I bet they all get to something I can't track in the next five to fifteen. By the time I get a magical lock on him—if I can—he'll be someplace where I can't get at him. Nearest team to you is Corbie, down one level and on the tracks."

"Roger that. I'm going to try and nail some alive."

"Either that, or you might catch up with the security team; I'd feel better if you locked down Harmony. I don't think she has psi-defense."

Bella hesitated. Of the two . . . Harmony was the more important. "Roger that. Give me the rendezvous point."

If she had anything to say about it, Harmony was never again going to be able to move without throwing up her toenails. Messing up someone's inner ear was trivial for Bella now. *We may need you alive, bitch, but I don't have to make it pleasant for you.*

John Murdock leaned back against a wall, and stared, exhausted, at his comrades. Red Saviour was grinning like a sated tiger. Soviet Bear was whooping it up. Mamona was jumping up and down, and where she'd found the energy, JM had no idea. Overwatch had just passed the word. Those of Blacksnake that were left were neutralized, Harmony was a prisoner, Verdigris had disappeared, and already the FBI and Interpol had him on the "most wanted" list, with the Federal and States' Attorneys General cascading a series of warrants into the system as fast as they could be written up. Yankee Pride had declared himself "Operational CEO of Echo," with not a single dissenting voice.

They had won. They had won.

Vickie felt the tide of guilt roll over her. Bruno was dead, and it was her fault. And yes, so were Rider, and Frank, and far too many others, but Rider and Frank had both known what they were doing, and what the cost was going to be. Bruno—Bruno she had *sent* to his death.

Sobs fought themselves up out of her throat, and she grabbed a wad of Kleenex. There was no expiation for this. Bulwark had been right, and he, and Scope, would probably hate her until the day they died. Nor could she blame them. She hated herself. She hadn't thought it possible to loathe herself more than she had, but it seemed there were no limits to how much she could hate herself.

She heard a knock at her door.

Whoever it was . . . damn it, it couldn't be Bella, she knew where Bella was. Which meant whoever it was, it was someone she didn't want to see. She thumbed the intercom, and brought up the camera.

Bulwark.

"Go away," she said hoarsely. "Busy."

"Let me in, Victrix," Bull said, quietly. "We should talk."

"We both know what you're gonna say. Save time and file the after-action report stating that the loss of Operative Acrobat was my fault." The words came out, harsh, stark, and ringing with truth. "I already have, so that will just confirm it. Now go away. You're no good at blowing smoke up anyone's ass anyway."

"You're right," he answered. "I tend to be straight with people, don't I? So let me in; we should talk."

She thought about it, and blew her nose. "If I don't let you in, you're just gonna stand there all night, aren't you?"

"Stranger things have happened."

Nasrat. Wearily she dragged herself out of her chair, slumped to the door, and threw the locks. *Might as well get this over with.* This was going to be one of the nights she either sat awake until she passed out, or took pills until she passed out. Because, of course, she had Djinni's geas on her and until this was over, or she was dead, there was no other alternative but to keep on with the job.

She opened the door and stepped back. It had been a while since she had seen Bull in person. Intimidated by his sheer size, she shrank into herself, hunching over.

"So, talk, then go away," she said, turning away from him. She dabbed at her eyes. She must have looked a mess. Something else occurred to her. "Yes, I can take the Overwatch stuff out of you, and anyone else you want me to take it out of. Is that why you're here?"

If there's no more Overwatch, does that mean... I'm off the hook to Djinni? No, CCCP is never gonna give it up. Saviour would eviscerate me if I took it away.

Bull stared at her for a moment, stepped inside, and closed the door behind him. He scanned her apartment. It was surprisingly neat, but had the curiously neglected air of a room that hadn't been lived in much for a while. The flat-screen TV, inset into the wall-to-wall bookshelves, had dust on it. So did the coffee table. There were no impressions in the chairs or the couch. It didn't look as if anyone had touched the DVDs or books on the shelves in a long time. The only things that didn't have a thin film of dust on them were the CDs, the controls of the audio system, and a couple of books in a shelf full of romance novels. The Overwatch tech in his eye obligingly zoomed in on them. The author was Victoria Nagy.

"So what would you do then, if you gave up Overwatch?" he asked. "Leave Echo? Go back to romance writing?"

She snorted. "What makes you think I'd give up Overwatch? Bella will still want it, so will Echo Med, and probably Pride and definitely all of CCCP. I'm on the hook until I die in the chair," she added bitterly. "And I'll probably get lots more people killed. And it won't matter even if I am a hundred percent right in what I tell them, because it will still have been my words and my decision that got them killed. Happy now? You don't have to punish me. I'm doing a fine job by myself."

"Happy?" he said. "Is that what you think of me, really? That I'm here to twist the knife? No, Victrix. You asked me if I wanted you to shut down Overwatch, so I'm asking what the point of that would be? I'm asking if that's what you want?"

"What I want is irrelevant. I made a... commitment." She sat down abruptly on the nearest chair. "It's not the sort of commitment I can just ditch."

"I learned an important lesson, not too long ago. What you want is the most relevant thing in your life. And for some, it would seem, in the entire universe." Bull held up a hand. "Don't ask. The reason I'm here is to see how you are, that's all. So before you continue with your tirade on how I'm supposed to report you, to blame you, to demand you shut down Overwatch on my teams, can we start again? Victrix, how are you?"

She felt her eyes burning. "I'm . . . so damn sorry. And sorrier that even if I'd known what was going to happen . . . I wouldn't change the decision. Just some details." Because she could actually think of some things she could have done, maybe. Magic stuff. Maybe pen Harm in with earthworks, or shield Bruno? "No matter what . . . it's on me. 'Cause I'm the one that's got all the info at my fingertips."

Bull considered that, and continued to stroll about her living room, pausing to look at the various pictures she had displayed on her wall. He stopped at one in particular.

"You and your parents?" he asked, pointing to one faded, black and white portrait. "The Feds?"

"Alexander and Moira Nagy, Department 39, FBI Metahuman, aka 'Spook Squad.'" She paused. "That was right after I . . . oh hell, why not, you've seen weirder shit. Someone decided to make me 'daddy's little hostage.' I pinned his hand to the table with a silver fork and barricaded myself in the bathroom until they got home. They took me out for steak and ice cream and a picture."

He bent over to get a closer look. "They look quite proud of you. That is a fetching dress, after all."

Vickie chuckled sadly. "I was six. Precocious little brat. Doing rudimentary magic at four."

"I suppose you always knew what it was you wanted to do, what you were good at, what you were meant for."

". . . there was never a question." She let out her breath in a long, long sigh. "If you've ever talked to any other sort of child prodigy, they'll tell you the same thing. I can't *not* do it."

Bull considered that too. "You got to know Bruno a little, before he and Scope went AWOL, didn't you?"

Tears came again. "I never knew anyone to want it as badly as I did before. I mean, all of it. The responsibility as well as the fun part. Even if he was a lot like a puppy that kept piddling on things and chewing the shoes, sometimes. You could see the heart of a mastiff in there, and you had to forgive him for the wee and . . . well, you know."

Bull nodded. "His greatest fear was that he wasn't up to the job, that he wasn't good enough. He was terrified that, in the end, he didn't matter." Bull shook his head. "You made the right call today, Victrix. It's the mission that's important. Acrobat was the only one who could have delayed Harmony. If he hadn't intercepted her, she'd have been long gone."

"And it doesn't help." She reached blindly for tissues. "And I'm still sorry."

"Of course you are," he said. "That's *who* you are. You presume to take full responsibility for things that aren't yours to take. You did what needed to be done today, and in case you didn't notice, your efforts also saved hundreds if not thousands of lives. We can all claim some of the blame here, if you think about it. What I need you to remember is the mission. In case you haven't noticed, you're a vital part of it. We all have sacrifices to make here, and when the time comes that I make mine, I want you to promise to honor me, to remember me, but *after* the job is done. And don't you *dare* blame yourself or anyone else for it. You did your job today, Victrix, and you did a fine job."

She closed her eyes, and stiffened her spine. "You're right, Operative Bulwark. The mission is what is important. The mission is *all* that is important." She opened her eyes again. "I think you might know a lot more than you're letting on. I *do* know you've seen the 'Ides of March.' We both know what the consequences of failure are." She hoped he had forgiven her, at least a little. She *thought* he had. Unexpectedly, it helped.

"We do," Bull replied. "I think we have an understanding then. I'll let myself out."

He crossed to the door, and as he opened it, Vickie got up. Wordlessly she let him out and closed the door behind him. He walked away at a brisk pace, and as he turned the corner to the stairs, he allowed a brief flash of anger to register on his face.

"That was your call, Victrix, but it would never have been mine," he muttered. He took a breath, and swallowed the pain. She could never know.

It was the mission that mattered.

CHAPTER TWENTY-NINE

Testament

MERCEDES LACKEY

Bella was more tired, and more grief-stricken than she had ever been in her life. And that did not matter. Because now that he was done explaining the background to the revolt, and laying out the original Charter, Yankee Pride was introducing her for the gathering of the Echo vets here in the CCCP HQ, and all of the Echo metas all over the world via closed sat-link.

Why her? She didn't know. Yank had only said, "It has to be you. Spin Doctor said it couldn't be anyone else."

She took a deep breath, drew on all the performance training she'd gotten back when she'd thought she'd get a gig at some big casino show on the Strip as a novelty singer, and walled off all her feelings.

"Brothers and sisters," she said, looking out at the solemn faces. "I don't use those terms lightly. You are all my brothers and sisters in a way that we did not share with Dominic Verdigris—" *that we know of* "—or, rest his soul, Alex Tesla. But the founders of Echo knew this when they wrote the charter, and despite the fact that the CEO of Echo has always been a normal human, they knew that Echo was, and had to be, created *by* metahumans, *for* metahumans. Now is not the time for political correctness, and it *is* the time to look that fact in the face and accept it for what it means."

She paused, marshaling her thoughts.

"We are different. When Echo was founded, that difference was frightening to people. That was why the CEO was a human. That was why Echo never fought things like the Extreme Force Act, and agreed to DCOs. We are different, and humans are programmed at the instinctive level to fear what is different. When Echo was founded, the foundations that were laid down were carefully calculated to allay as much of that fear as possible, while building in protections for us in the form of things we could live with. I know you vets in front of me are well aware of a lot of this; I'll bet you were all privy to, or even part of, some of the debates, even arguments over a lot of it."

Nods, grimaces. A lot of intent looks.

"We are different. There is nothing we can do about it. We can no more change that than any other human can change things like skin or hair or eye color. Like them, we can sometimes disguise it, but we can't change it. What we are defines us, negatively or positively. Right now, it's pretty much positive. But that could change in an instant, and as we forge the future, we need to pick a leader who is very much aware of that. Echo must always be an organization that is run *by* metahumans, to protect us from abuse and exploitation, the sorts of abuse and exploitation Dominic Verdigris had in mind for us. Those who are not meta will always have the upper hand, ultimately. There are a lot more of them than there are of us—and today you got a good look at how those without powers are still capable of turning those of us with powers to chutney."

Nods all across the sea of faces now.

"But if Echo is an organization run *by* metahumans, it must also change to one that is run *for* humans, meta and otherwise. You all know the comic-book mantra about great responsibility, and you can all look to whatever faith you believe in to give you answers about why you have been triggered with a power and others have not. The point is this: *meta* is only part of what we are. Deep down, the important thing is that we are also *human*. Our parents, siblings, relatives, neighbors and friends may not have been granted powers. Our children may not be. We cannot divorce ourselves from the human race and we're all on the spaceship Earth together. The minute we forget that and think that besides being *different*, we are also somehow *superior*, well... we turn into Dominic Verdigris."

Vigorous nods, and some approving smiles.

"And one more thing. The Charter is set up so that the CEO is a lifetime position. As you vets know, for one of us, a lifetime can be very long indeed. The CEO needs to be someone who is flexible, who listens to, acts on—and solicits!—advice. Because things will always be changing; change is the one constant no one can fight. So when you are voting for the new CEO of Echo, please remember that, all of it. And choose the flexible person who not only knows what it is to be *meta,* but to be *human,* and to embrace everything that humankind means. Thank you."

She did not stop to acknowledge the applause. Instead, she stepped quickly down off the podium and to the computer link to cast her vote for Yankee Pride.

Just as Alex Tesla had wanted. He really was the right man for the job.

Under any other circumstances, Bella would have loved to mingle with all the old vets, most of whom were only faces in history books to her. But after today, all she wanted to do was sit in a corner, nursing a drink. She would rather have been in her office, but that wasn't possible, Spin Doctor had made that clear as well.

But it would be a good thing to be able to congratulate Pride... and hand over that burden she'd carried. Echo Med was burden enough—but at least part of the time she felt up to that task.

When the voting was announced as *closed* she really wasn't paying much attention, concentrating on what she was going to say to Pride. So when the wave of people suddenly engulfed her, startling her out of her reverie, wanting to shake her hand, congratulating her, she was caught completely by surprise.

Shocked even.

"Snap out of it, Bells," Vickie said in her ear. *"You're CEO. By a landslide. Act like it."*

What? Were they *insane?*

"Yep. Almost unanimous. All in favor except one vote."

Spin Doctor came up to shake her hand. She felt numb. "It seems that they're rather enamored of your style of management. Something about grit, tenacity, and smarts. Oh, and the little Scotsman says that blue is his favorite color."

They kept coming, wave after wave of them, vets, her own Echo Med, all of them. Shaking her hand, smiling warmly.

Even Djinni.

He came after most of the crowd had thinned out, giving her

some space; he took her hand and moved in close, and she clung to it. "I don't want this!" she whispered to him urgently. "Red, I don't—I can't—"

He squeezed her hand. "Y'know who make the best leaders, darlin'?" he whispered back. "They're not always the smartest, they're not always the most charismatic, they're not always the nicest people around... hell, they're usually assholes."

"Where are you going with this?" she asked. Was he trying to say—

"... but one thing the best leaders usually share in common, they didn't want the damn job in the first place."

Then he was gone, slipping away into the crowd, which gathered around her again.

Bella closed the door of her office behind her, leaned against it, and put her head back, closing her eyes for a moment before slumping behind her desk. She was still listed as being on-duty, and she didn't change that. She didn't want to ruin anyone's "victory" celebration, but this whole day, start to finish, had been nothing like a win.

Bruno was dead. So were too many other people, but Bruno was one of *hers,* one of the Misfits. Someone she'd fussed over, worried about, driven herself crazy over. Someone who'd been awkwardly grateful when Bella had patched him up, had tried to cheer her up, who'd been a lot like that puppy who is always underfoot, and yet was so constantly happy and helpful that you couldn't help but smile at him even when he was in the way. He'd been so triumphant when he and Scope had infiltrated Harmony's own organization and put a spoke in the wheels of her plans. And not half an hour later... he was gone.

And despite Verd running like a scalded cat, this had a far too high probability of turning into a public relations nightmare. With Verd out of reach, people would start looking for someone else to blame, and there was Echo, the big, fat target du jour. Unless they came up with some miracle victory and soon, people were going to start asking if maybe Verd had been right all along... maybe someone like Dominic Verdigris *should* have been in charge of Echo. Maybe the US Military should take it over. Spin Doctor was already at work on heading off the inevitable avalanche. She'd sent him the Twins. And the espresso machine from Verd's office. But what she needed was a miracle. A really decisive victory against the Kriegers. Because it was only a matter of time—maybe by tomorrow morning—before the people out there stopped congratulating her and started asking what she intended to do about the *real* enemy.

She'd tried to give up the job. Pride was making noises about how he wasn't going to "let" her step back and just head up Echo Med. Hell, she didn't even want to head Echo Med, much less the rest of this! It had been one thing when it had just been her taking charge of her friends, but this . . . this was all of Echo, and Pride wanted *her* as CEO? They all did? How in hell was she supposed to be a wartime leader? She'd never wanted to be a leader at all!

Who can I persuade not to go back to Sunny Acres that remembers what it was like in the last go-around? At least she had Saviour, and Unter to count on for advice. Even Bear. He might be insane, but his memory of the last round with the Nazis was just fine as long as you ignored all the stuff about his sexual prowess. But she thought about Acrobat, thought about how many more people were going to die before this was over, and put her head down on the desk, too overwhelmed even to cry. She'd asked Dixie to take Scope out to the vets—the ones that were feeling their own losses. They'd understand, and give the "young soldier" the kind of support she needed right now. But there was no one Bella could turn to for company right now. Everyone else was either hurting too much, or like Saviour, relishing this pyrrhic victory too much to offer sympathy.

Never had she felt so utterly, completely alone, or so crushed by the burden of responsibility that she had never wanted, never asked for. But there was literally no one else to take it off her shoulders, so somehow, she would have to try.

She buried her face in her elbow, wishing with all her heart she could hide from the world and knowing there was no way in hell that was possible.

Vickie watched poor Bella putting her head down on her arms, and felt her throat aching. Bell had turned her Overwatch rig to "private," but she'd forgotten about the security cam in the corner.

She only took up being the leader of the coup because there really wasn't anyone else who could that wasn't also being watched day and night. There was nothing *in our plans that would have led us to think Verd would do what he did today. And now she's been "rewarded" by being slammed with even more responsibility, and heaven help her if she screws up. Meanwhile, the wolves outside the door that are howling for Verd's blood are going to come looking for someone else's if they don't get some meat from somewhere.* Borzhe moi, *what a cluster. And there she is all alone, and too aware that anyone else who might serve as a shoulder is hurting too... or someone she doesn't want to give the wrong signals to.*

Well... there was at least one good thing she might be able to do. "Overwatch: Command: open Bulwark, private," she said, her voice shaking. "Overwatch to Bulwark."

"Operative Victrix—this is—"

She took a deep breath. "This isn't Operative Victrix, Bull. This is Vix. Something... something I want to tell you. Bella's alone in her old office in Echo Med, and I'm the only one who knows she's gone off to hide from everyone shortsighted enough to think we won this one. If you want to keep everything on the pro level with Bella, go hit the bar or deal with how you feel right now on your own." She could almost *hear* him stiffen. But she kept right on going. "If you want to stay just her friend, go to her and give her the same stiff upper lip talk you'd give any friend who was also your superior officer. She'll probably be grateful for it, and it will send her a very clear signal about how you want the future to look between you. Both of those choices are perfectly valid. But there's a third choice too." She took another deep breath. To say that Bulwark was intensely private about his feelings was like saying that Everest might be a little tall. If she were in person... he'd probably walk out before she could get very far. He'd probably be tempted to punch her in the nose—not that he actually *would,* ever, but this would test even his legendary patience. Fortunately, she was literally in his ear and he couldn't shut her off before she finished. "If you want more than that, this is your chance to get that door open in the gentlemanly fashion you prefer. I know her, and I think I kind of know you. You are both dying inside right now. You both need someone to lean on for a while. Go help each other through it, and you'll come out the other side with something pretty damn special. That's it, all I have to say."

There was silence for a moment. "Operative Victrix... I would appreciate it if you would mind your own business," came the dispassionate answer.

"Yes sir, Bulwark. Overwatch out," she replied, and closed the channel, and then shut down the system except for the usual twenty-four–seven monitoring, which she could do from her bed. Because right now she needed a shoulder too. She'd stayed "with" Rider until the last moment, watching him in the train's security cam, solitary witness to his bravery. Frank had heard her frantic call and said he was on it, and she had just left him to deal with the threat alone, assuming he'd be all right.

And Bruno. Bruno. She would never stop seeing him in the back of her mind, and he would haunt her for the rest of her life.

On her watch. Dead because of her. And despite everything she could do, the literal magic, she had not been able to save them.

She shuffled off to her room, and Grey jumped up on the bed before she threw herself down on it. <*Come have a good cry, kitten,*> he said with sympathy, and she buried her face in his fur and did just that, crying for all she wished she could have done.

Bulwark listened to the faint white noise of the closed channel, then set his rig to "private" mode. He looked down the hall. To his right was the way out. Although he wasn't a drinking man, he knew which bar the retired vets would be at tonight, and he knew that he would be welcome and understood among them. Toasts would be made. Stories told. Old pain eased a little in the sharing. New pain, too.

To his left, this corridor would lead him to the cross-corridor that ended at Echo Medical. The offices would be empty, except for one; the injured had all been stabilized, patched, stitched, and otherwise mended and were in their hospital rooms upstairs. The Med staff, the metas, anyway, would be taking a break before getting back to work. For the next few hours, the Echo injured that had survived would be in the hands of the purely human staff, and the metas had gone off-duty, unless they were paged for an emergency.

All but one. One, who was still very much on-duty, and probably would not go home tonight, or for many nights to come.

He hesitated another moment longer, then turned to the left.

CHAPTER THIRTY

Here with Me

MERCEDES LACKEY AND CODY MARTIN

John was still sore all over. The latest Op had been . . . interesting, to say the least. More than anything, he was just glad that it was over. He was looking forward to getting patched up, to checking on the neighborhood, to a cold beer . . . and, of course, Sera.

It still amazed him how things had turned out with the two of them. John, who had spent the last few years on the run and making sure that he had no personal connections, had fallen in love with an angel. He hadn't used the "L" word yet, but he knew it was there. Somewhere deep down, he also knew the truth about Sera. His rational mind wouldn't allow him to admit that to her, either; it'd be an affront to his pride as a devout unbeliever. *The world has gone insane, all right, an' I'm right there with it.*

First things were first; since he had taken more than the usual battering on this mission, he had been ordered to check in with the medbay and get himself looked at. He was starting to feel weak again, too; just another thing to worry about. *This nonsense has been going on too long; time to bite the bullet and have Jadwiga figure out this deal with my energy levels, and why my abilities have been up and down. Can't have another weak moment during an op.*

Not that he was looking forward to it, but oh well . . . that was part of the job, get banged up, get poked and probed. He straightened his back and headed for sickbay.

Jadwiga was doing a good job of keeping the emotion out of her face. All except for her eyes. It helped that she was a beautiful woman, and not the modern, so-skinny-as-to-be-sick, supermodel sort of pretty. She was classically beautiful, and very Russian. The Commissar was a bit of a caricature sometimes with her zeal and heavy-handedness; still there were times when she seemed more "old-fashioned cop" of any nationality than particularly Russian. But the "Soviette" screamed Russian with her every move; even in the maternal, yet slightly stern way she cared for the personnel of the CCCP.

And her eyes said that the news wasn't good. It looked to John like she was about to pronounce sentence on a patient in triage, rather than reporting what he had expected to be a dull and routine summary of his physical.

John didn't stop looking at her while he buttoned up the top of his jump suit. "You're awful quiet, Doc. What's the prognosis?"

"You have been coughing blood. Yes?" She didn't wait for his nod. "This is not something trivial, comrade. *Da* or *nyet?*"

Again, she didn't wait, and she must have seen the assent in his eyes. "This is the sign that things are being too far. You have great damage in your lungs. You do not smoke, you have no tuberculosis, you should not have such damage, and it is new. I then take tissue sample. With primitive equipment as Moscow allows us"—she grimaced—"is looking to me that cells are being in apoptosis. Ischemic damage is resulting; thus the much coughing, dizziness, lack of appetite, disorientation, and bouts of weakness. Is being why your power goes—" She made a little "poofing" motion with her fingers. "I do not know what is being cause this. But is fatal." She took a deep breath. "Without knowing cause, is being no cure. If *is* a cure possible. Is nothing I am studying, and is nothing in conventional medicine can being help."

John felt sick to his stomach. This had been going on for a while, but the symptoms hadn't been anything he couldn't explain away due to the aggressive and often violent nature of his new job. Not willing to give in to the shock and slowly twisting horror in his belly, John seized on the word he hadn't understood as a possible handle... something that would show him a way out of this. "What's... apoptosis?"

"Your cells are being suicide," she said bluntly. "Cells are always being die, *da*, but not like this. Too many, and just... disintegrate, from inside. This is making big damage, and is happening all over you, but most in lungs. No cells, no oxygen; no oxygen…" Her eyes were sad, but there was nothing in them to give him the escape route he wanted out of this.

"So, there's nothin' that can be done 'bout it? We don't have any pills, medicines, or surgeries or anything for this? Apoptosis and ischemia?"

"*Nyet* in conventional medicine. You are metahuman. That is not always being… positive."

He mulled this over for a moment. "Who do we know that's the best with metahumans, then?"

"Echo." She sighed. "And Comrade Bella is being head of Echo Medical *and* Echo CEO. She is *nyet* doctor, but…"

"But I trust her. An' that's enough for me, right now." John stood up from the examination table he was sitting on. He sighed heavily, turning himself to face Soviette. "Jadwiga, I need y'to do me a favor. I need ya to keep this under wraps until I can talk with Bella." He held up his hands quickly to cut off the protest she was already beginning to voice. "I need to be sure. There's still a lot of fight that needs doing, and I don't wanna get pulled off of duty based on 'maybes.'"

Reluctantly she nodded. "Just being remember. Your comrades are being depending on you. You are also not wanting to be weakest link that fails when moment is worst."

More fear. That had already happened, almost, a couple of times. Fighting against Ubermensch, when the Thulian suicide squad attacked the HQ, and during the battle with the Rebs. The next time… the next time would probably be the last time; he was never that lucky, and he'd already been beating the odds just by staying alive as long as he had. "I'll make sure it doesn't come to that. Thank you, comrade."

John sat on the roof of his squat. He wasn't drinking; just thinking. *Never can catch any breaks, can I?*

No matter what he did now, he was screwed. End of the line, with no more hands to play. Discounting Bella being able to come up with something amazing and unheard of, John was going to die. How does a man cope with that knowledge?

He could slink off somewhere, a place without people, and die alone, like a dog. It'd be the simplest and probably least painful thing for him to do. At least physically. He might even be able to stretch out his time by a few months, maybe a year given the far-above-average plumbing his body had acquired.

He wouldn't suffer as much, except for the state of his soul. Or at least what passed for whatever his soul was. Not that long ago, that was what he would have done without a second thought. But . . . now? He'd be abandoning everything again. He'd be deserting the CCCP, his neighborhood, the world. He'd be deserting Sera; that thought was almost unbearable now. Everything was on the brink, and had been for a long time. He was just one warm body . . . but everyone counted in the fight against the Thulians.

Giving up wouldn't do. That itch would still be there. It'd been years since he'd been in action, doing what he was best at: fighting and projecting force in places most folks would never want to go. His cause had almost always been just, and goddammit, *Right.* He had that again, now. It was precious to him, in a way, almost as much as freedom and life itself were. He was alive again.

"That settles it," he said to no one in particular. John looked up at the stars; they were a little more washed out now that electricity was stable in this part of the city. The CCCP and some effort from Echo had seen to that. It was still beautiful, and John felt thankful. *Wonders abound.* "So, I'll fight. Besides, it's always okay to punch a Nazi."

In running the revolt, Bella had learned many things, one of which was how to delegate and get the hell out of the way. Paperwork? Ramona had someone. Detective work? Ramona all the way—she was still healing up, and coming to terms with what had happened to her, but giving her something to get her mind off her new condition was good for her in many ways. She was still head of Echo Med; no one wanted her to step down, but that was a lot easier now with the whole team wired. Public Affairs? Spin Doctor, Pride, and give the media the illusion she was always accessible but so modest she preferred Pride to do the talking. Actually it wasn't modesty. It was terror.

Strat, Command and Control? Bulwark.

And that miracle Echo needed? Two brains in a box in far-off Metis. They promised her they would give her something impressive. She just prayed they weren't blowing smoke up her ass.

So being CEO was not yet the nightmare she feared it could

be. Give it time, maybe... but for right this moment she could breathe a little. A little.

She ran down her mental list of things to do. Check in with Panacea via Vickie. Check in with Bulwark via Vickie. Check in with Nat via Vickie. Check in with Tesla and Marconi via Vickie. It amused her no end that despite Verdigris' considerable genius and immense resources he never had had any idea of exactly how much Vickie could do, nor had he or any of his underlings managed to crack her network. And she had no doubt that, somewhere out there, they were trying. Vickie, raging paranoid that she was, was sure that sooner or later he would finger her for the one that had ruined his game.

But he didn't have any magicians on the payroll either. Until he did, Bella was pretty sure Vickie was safe.

Her comm beeped, with the CCCP sequence. She checked it expecting to see something from Nat.

And frowned seeing the ID. Wasn't JM usually on patrol?

She answered before it went to voice. "Yo, Johnny."

"Bella. Got an hour? I need words."

She was good at reading voices, even his. Something was wrong. Any thought of putting him off went out the window. "Now. Where?"

"Peoples Park," came the reply. That was the combination community garden and playground CCCP had put together in his hood once the crap in a section of the destruction corridor had been cleared away. Well. Eaten. It had kept Chug in meals for several weeks. Chug went there regularly to play with the squirrels, usually under Bella's or Upyr's supervision. No time for that now; she'd have to see if Einhorn could be coaxed into it.

"Five minutes," she replied.

She didn't bother to change out of her civvies; she was less conspicuous in the park that way anyway. Well, as "less conspicuous" as anyone with blue hair and skin could be. She sat down on a bench next to the playgym made with scavenged pipe and waited.

John was good, but Bella's telempathy was better than any sneaking skills taught on the face of the Earth. Still, she didn't hear or see him until he was sitting down next to her. "We have to stop meeting like this," she said laconically. "My husband is beginning to suspect."

"Sorry, comrade. Didn't know that Papa Smurf was that cagey." John did his level best to appear casual and relaxed. He stretched out, hanging his arms over the backrest of the bench. But Bella could still feel the steel-taut tension running through him. He was, by her father's favorite phrase, "Wound tighter than a banjo string." And despite everything going on, JM hadn't been that wound up for . . . quite some time.

Which meant her first impression was right. Something was really, really wrong.

"Much as I know you love me, you don't ask me to a clandestine meeting in the middle of the day because you want to know if I want wheat or rye on my Reuben." She gave him the Look. "Spit it out. Or I'll touch you and find out anyway."

So he told her. Told her what little he knew, anyways. Verbatim for what Jadwiga had said, with the scant amount she'd been able to piece together from the ancient medical gear that Moscow supplied them with. "And that's where I'm at. The doc isn't going to tell anybody until I've met with an expert in the field of metahuman medicine. Namely, you."

She wrestled for a moment with a viper's nest of conflicting emotions. Anger, despair, frustration . . . she wasn't going to help him if she couldn't think clearly. "I'm only a paramedic, Johnny," she said, carefully.

"Yeah, you're a paramedic. A paramedic with first-hand experience in a field that most med school grads won't touch because it's not all that high paid, unless you're with Echo. You're head of Echo Med, so you can sneak me in on the QT so Nat doesn't find out. An' you have your fingers in a lot of pies; places that might be able to figure out exactly what's going on with me. Places that'll figure it out without it getting back to the Commissar immediately." He turned to face her soberly. "I'm still in this fight, Bella. I can't let this take me away from it. D'ya understand?"

Only too well. "All right. Now I know Jadwiga's a psionic healer like me, and I assume she would already have tried that on you so we can eliminate that as a cure right now." She drummed her fingers on her knee, thinking fast, running through her options at Echo Medical. "Are you free right now?" She was a past master at running people through tests. Hell most of the time the problem with running tests was not that the equipment wasn't free, but that the techs to run it weren't, and after the Invasion and being short-handed, she was certified on most of it.

"I'm officially on leave for the rest of the week, due to injuries sustained. I was able to suss out an extra five days from Jadwiga, considerin', as opposed to the two that the Commissar originally ordered." He grinned lopsidedly. "Call it my charmin' personality at work."

"Right. Then you sit there for a little while I send some texts." Through Vickie, of course. She wasn't going to chance any of this going on the Echo net.

She thought her thumbs were going to fall off when she was finished, but within a few more minutes, the answers started to come in. Most of them were appended with "If you can run the—" She sighed. Looked like she was in for a long night.

"First thing, Johnny," she said, eyeballing him for size. "We need to go borrow one of Bulwark's Echo uniforms."

Three days of tests, more tests and in the end, a verdict that the patient was terminal. Now all she had for him was no hope and an armful of bottles to keep him going, keep his energy up and the mounting pain at bay. She wanted to break down and cry, but she was going to save that for when she was alone. She waited on the park bench with the bag at her feet and wondered what he'd done to deserve this.

Then the flash of borrowed memories shared with Sera hit her, and she knew what he'd done to have some bad, bad karma. Because not all of the people he'd turned to smoking ash in the rubble of that Project of his had been guilty of anything other than working for the wrong people. Maybe not even most of them. And a good number of them had been victims, just as he was.

"Frickin' karma," she said bitterly. She didn't know those people. She knew *him*. She didn't want to lose him, not only for herself, but for Sera. Dear god, for Sera...

"Still keepin' my bench warm, Blue?" John had slipped in dead quiet, as always. He was way too good at that for Bella to be completely comfortable with it.

"Beats you setting fire to it." She sighed, felt her throat try to close, and blinked back tears, fiercely. "Here. These will keep you on your feet and fully active for as long as you have left. That's what I've got. That's all I've got." She handed him the bag. No point in making a soft sell.

He shook the bag, then stuffed it into a cargo pocket on his pants. "That's all she wrote? I'm really buying the farm, no *ifs*, *ands*, or *buts*?"

"You're unique."

"My mother said the same thing." He grinned. "She also said I was an incorrigible brat an' a pain in the ass."

She wasn't a real doctor. And every second she wasted trying to be nice was a second he didn't have. "I'm cutting to the chase, Johnny. Your powers are killing you. You can stretch things out longer by not using them, but..."

"But you an' I both know that I won't stop. That I can't stop so long as America, the world, an' my new family have enemies out there. Right? So long as the Thulians are looking to make this a world of ashes."

"Nothing short of a miracle is gonna help you now, and nobody's handing me a halo."

He nodded, sitting there silently for a long time. Children were playing in the park. Swinging on swing sets, wrestling and chasing each other, and just generally being little kids, happy kids. He spotted one pair playing with an action figure, clad in black and red, a CCCP uniform. He vaguely recognized the likeness it held, smiling. He thought it might be Perun. "Then it's settled." John stood up, hooking his thumbs into the belt of his pants.

She held out a hand. "Johnny—look, Echo isn't everything. Maybe Vickie can dig up some magic or—"

He cut her off, without any hardness in his voice. "Echo's the best. An' I know y'already went to Vickie. If she couldn't find it on her first run, it probably isn't there; she's thorough like that." He sighed, then grinned at her as he turned to leave. "You're a good friend, Comrade Kiddo. I'll see ya around."

And then he was gone.

She knew, of course. She had known from the moment that Jadwiga told him. And she realized that if only she had thought about it, she should have known before that. Her heart, and being unable to see his futures, had hidden the truth from her. She grieved for him, for the pain he must endure—for his own fears—but not for *him*. She knew, how not, that death was just a transition. But he . . . he did not.

He needed her. He would find her. This time, in *her* sanctuary, not his, not the Suntrust Tower where she could be seen, but a little stone bench in the quiet shelter of some trees that were as old as the city was, at the edge of a tiny cemetery. People often mistook her, those that could see her, for a statue. He needed her; thus, he would find her.

And he did.

He was surprised to see her when he wandered onto the edge of the cemetery. His surprise passed quickly, and he slowly made his way over to her. The same reserve and practiced calm as he had evidenced for Bella, all of it stretched over a writhing mass of fear and despair. He was scared, and she could feel every nuance of it.

"Evenin', Sera. The folk 'round here started dancing yet?"

She looked at him in puzzlement for a moment, until her mind sorted through all the possible meanings and settled on the most likely for him. "No one has played the proper music," she replied, moving over on the bench in unspoken invitation, and making herself look as human as possible. The strange and bitter irony of this meeting being in a graveyard was not lost on her.

"What's a gal like you doin' in a joint like this, at this hour?"

"It is quiet. I can rest. I am not entirely immaterial. I need not eat, drink or sleep, but I do need rest. I can rest here."

He chuckled; there was darkness behind his mirth. "You an' a lotta other folks. Got time for talking?"

She regarded him, unblinking. "I would make time, even if I had it not, John."

"Yeah, I suppose you could." He rubbed his arms against the cold and sat down next to a headstone in front of her. "Weird how things turn out, isn't it?"

"I hope you are not contemplating destiny, John. There is no such thing. The future is mutable." She bit her lip. "Futures. I see many, many. I have told you; it is what I do."

"Naw, nothing like that. I just meant like the location, and whatnot. Angel in a church graveyard. And me, here, talkin' with ya. Just weird how everything plays out, eventually. Irony is a cast-iron bitch." He steepled his fingers, resting his elbows on his knees. "So, do y'know why I'm here to talk to you?"

She closed her eyes for a moment as his pain washed over her. She already knew the answer to the question she would have asked: *May I heal him?* The answer to that was *It is not permitted.* She did not know why—but that she would obey was the difference between a Sibling and a Fallen. She would obey, because she had trust. But this...this hurt. Hurt that she could not save him this. "Yes. But you must also tell me. There are reasons for this."

"Then I'll just say it. I'm dying. It's because of how my powers work; my 'natural' ones, that is. And there's nothing that anyone knows to do about it." He visibly shook. It was the first time she'd seen him like this; he'd been consumed with anger, regret, purpose, and duty for so long. But this was fear, naked and unadulterated. "I think I'm okay with it. What do you think?"

"I think...you are afraid." A tear formed at the corner of her eye, and fell. "I think...I am sorry for your fear, and grieving with you. And I think...I think this is too much pain for you to bear alone." He remained silent and another tear slid down her cheek. Her voice remained steady; she didn't think he realized she was weeping for him. But she could scarcely believe how little time had passed—and how much had changed—between this meeting and the last. Tears instead of smiles, grief and fear instead of laughter. "What will you do now?"

"That's the question, isn't it?" He sat there, staring at his hands for several long moments. "I figure there's only one thing I can do: keep fighting. People need for me to be there. The CCCP, my neighborhood, everyone. There's nothing that I can do 'bout dying. But I can make my time here count for something. I can make the Thulians *pay* dearly for my life, if that's what it takes to keep them from winning."

His answer was unexpected, and not unexpected. It would not have been out of the question for him to say he was going away somewhere, for him to "crawl off to a lonely place to die." It could have been one of his futures...in fact now that he had said what he had said, she could see it, even as that future closed off; see him wandering somewhere cold and snow-clad, lying down, and never getting up again. There were many of his futures that had ended that way. More of them than she had any notion of. Perhaps if she had known, she would already have given up, because so few led to this moment... and only this moment gave way to the Great Blank spot, on the other side of which was hope.

But he had changed. Changed profoundly. This was merely the signal point of that change.

Tears continued to follow one another; she could not stop them, and did not want to. She had wept for humans before, but this was different. John was—so much to her. Things had progressed between them far, far past the love of mere friends. There was no one she was emotionally closer to, not even Bella. The seraphs had emotions, of course, but they were nothing so immediate. Tentatively, she reached out to him, stopping just short of touching him. "John?" she faltered.

"Yes, Sera?" There was pain in his voice, but he was able to bring himself to look at her.

How did humans bear such pain? "How can I help you?" She faltered again. "It is not permitted me to heal you. I wish that it was. But... you are my... friend. Tell me how I may help you?"

He thought for a moment. "Don't suppose y'could turn time back about a decade, could ya?"

She shook her head, and a tear splashed on her hand. "If I could... The past cannot be changed, only the futures." She paused. "I am only permitted to do small—very, very small—things. Greater things require a miracle, and for a miracle, one must sacrifice something equally miraculous." She sighed. "That is... the only loophole in the Law of Free Will."

And I would sacrifice anything if I knew it would help you.

"S'alright. I wasn't holding out too much hope for turning back the clock." He leaned forward, rubbing the back of his head. She could see past his outer self; see the drugs coursing through his veins, helping to keep him conscious and able. He was *tired*, spent. But he was still continuing forward; he'd set his mind to a course of action, and he would not be deterred.

"I can grant you a little more strength."

"I wouldn't turn ya down for it. There are bad guys that need killing, still." He removed the glove off of his hand, the one with the Ouroboros tattoo, and held it out for her. He'd lost his aversion to contact with her what seemed like so long ago, with their first kiss, along with his unwillingness to look at her for more than a moment.

She touched the back of his hand with a careful finger, and

allowed the strength and Grace to flow from her into him. And if other things came with it... so be it. She would not hide that she cared deeply for him.

He sighed, and some of the color returned to his face. He seemed stronger, less drawn, more substantial. "I suppose I just need ya to keep being there. For the neighborhood, for the CCCP. For me." He looked at her solemnly. "It's gonna get a lot worse before it gets any better, y'know. For everyone."

He had no idea how much worse. She sought for permission, and found it. "There are very, very few futures in which... it does become better, John. Most end in a very bad place. So bad that even the Infinite, which does not interfere, has placed me here to do what I may. So yes. I know."

John shook his head. "I don't need to hear that, Sera. Really an' truly."

She tilted her head to the side in that birdlike way she had. "You are thinking. You know I cannot see your thoughts unless you allow it. What are you thinking?"

He frowned, his brows knitting together. "It's not exactly all that easy to put into words, now that y'ask." He was quiet for several moments, collecting his thoughts. "It's kinda like this, I figure it. From when I was young, my old man had always told me that just 'cause I was *me,* if I put my mind to it, I was a cut above the rest. An' that I had to strive to make sure I made the most of the potential I had, that anybody had. So long as y'put your mind to it, you couldn't be stopped. That's what he thought." John's eyes scanned the ground as he nudged some leaves out of the way with his boot. "That got reinforced big time when I was in the Rangers, then Delta. I literally was one of the best out there, for what I did. Cultivatin' a 'never say die' attitude was a big part of being able to make it and keep up with everyone else. It's as much a part of me as anything, now."

She could not "read" him as she could read others. But she knew him now, perhaps better than anyone else but Bella. Perhaps better than Bella. "There is much you are not saying."

He flashed a smile. "You usin' your voodoo on me, Sera?" There was something different in his voice when he said her name, this time. Something unguarded that was familiar to her, but she couldn't immediately recognize.

"You know I cannot unless you allow it." She regarded him

gravely. "And I will go only so far as you allow without reservation. No . . . this is only . . . knowing you."

"Well, bein' brought up like that, having that indomitable, unstoppable attitude ingrained in me . . . it's makin' all of this really hard. I've been taught that with the proper application of force, you can get through anything. Obstacles are only things I haven't torn through yet, that sorta thing. This is one problem that I have that I can't just will myself through. I'm scared shitless, actually, because even though I know what I'm gonna do, I just don't know if I can."

She ached for him; her heart cried out for him. "No one ever does."

"The worst thing in the world for me is to let my friends down. I can't let myself do that. I need to keep going." There was a lot of pain in his voice, now. He was being extremely open with her; it was different from just allowing her to read his memories. This was willful, open admittance of his worst fears.

She clasped her hands tightly in her lap. "John, if you fear what comes beyond . . . John, do you believe in *me*? Believe, at last, that I am what I am?" At least that fear she could take from him.

He grinned lopsidedly, again. That grin. Such a very characteristic and personal trait that he possessed. "Y'convinced me of that a while ago, Sera. No, it's just I'm afraid of losing. Lettin' people that depend on me down . . . an' losing people."

"No one would ever think that of you," she replied forcefully. "Not that you willfully let them down. This was not something you wanted nor planned. This just . . . happened. And if you fear that others will turn from you . . ." She swallowed. There was a strange and painful lump in her throat that she had never had before. She blinked back more tears. "I will never leave you. I will never desert you. I will . . ." She could not continue, strangely. Words deserted her. She looked up into his eyes, pleading with him to understand. Their gazes met, and she felt a sudden sense of shock. There was something unspoken and momentous there. She went very still, waiting. She did not know for what, she only knew it would change everything, and that it was something only he could say.

John was *looking* directly at her, now. And what he saw was both the "human" form she sometimes adopted around him to put him at his ease, and something he had only glimpsed in the briefest of moments, never for long. The seraphim, a creature all fire and spirit, a slender thing of light with wings of fire and glowing, bottomless eyes full of clear, pure power that looked past the surface of everything and into infinity. And those eyes were riveted on his, reflecting his pain and fear. And in those eyes, he saw a pain that mirrored his own that was all hers.

He spoke slowly, measuring his words and letting them roll around in his mouth. "I'm here for you, too, Angel. For every moment I have left. If you'll have me, Sera."

For a moment, understanding deserted her. If she would have him? What—

And then, with a shock as great as the moment she had immersed herself into this world and become incarnate, she understood. He was offering himself. To her. That was what she had seen, and not recognized until this moment. He loved her, loved her as a human and mortal man, loved her as if she was as human and mortal as he. And she knew how much that cost him, how hard it had been to open himself again, to permit himself to care, and to love. And more. To admit it. Yes, they had been kissing, touching, but until now she had not considered it as anything nearly as deep as what he had just offered. *Eros,* without deeper commitment, at least on his part. Something he had needed, as part of the way to break down the walls between him and the rest of the world. This was so much more. This was all of him, given with the knowledge and fear of possible rejection, to her. Sacrifice on his part, of everything that had kept him apart from another, for so many long years. Now, at the last, he had bid to open himself, rather than close himself away, fighting his own instincts to do so.

"Oh . . . my love . . ." she whispered, still reeling from the impact of it. And that was when she understood, at last, what had been in her own heart. He loved her. And she, she loved him.

The seraphim were the embodiment of the love of the Infinite for all of creation, and reflected back that love to the Infinite. It was a boundless love and yet . . . yet it was to this very human love as the countless memories of taste and touch were to actually tasting, actually touching. The love of the seraphim was more and yet . . . somehow less. It had no immediacy. It was less *real* for that.

She could not breathe for joy. "My dearest, my beloved—"

John didn't speak. Instead, he leaned close, pulling her hand into his hands. He rested his brow on hers, sighing in relief. He was still very tired, but she could see that she had responded in the way that he had hoped.

She was swimming in a sea of very human emotions, experiencing them for the first time directly. There was shock, the most incredible elation, wonder that such a thing could happen to her, such a gift be given for them to share. The question *Is this permitted?* was answered immediately with *Love is always permitted* which only doubled her joy.

And then came grief. This amazing, wondrous *miracle* that had grown between them was a flower that was, all too quickly, going to be cut and wither. His last days would be spent in terrible pain. She and Bella could ease that to some extent, but not altogether, and it would be worse at the end.

But of all things, the worst was this. A soul went to the afterlife it expected and believed in, and John Murdock, for all that he professed belief in *her,* truly expected only oblivion. If he died and sealed himself in a sort of self-created Sheol of nothingness, he would never win free again.

That was unacceptable. For both their sakes she must help him in ways he could not even imagine at this moment. Ways that she could hardly imagine herself.

"I will help you, beloved. In everything." She took the hand he had given her and held it to her wet cheek. "Whatever I have shall be yours." She did not know what else to do, but he did. He took her in his arms, and bent his head; she raised her face to his, and they kissed, and for as long as that kiss lasted, there was nothing else that mattered.

They sat together, embraced and embracing, until long after darkness fell, as her light burned defiance against the shadows.

CHAPTER THIRTY-ONE

Running up that Hill

MERCEDES LACKEY AND CODY MARTIN

Sera looked curiously around John's squat. This was the first time she had been inside his building, but something told her that he was going to be too dispirited to make the climb to the roof tonight. And, truth to tell . . . this was the first time she had felt as if she would be welcome in this, his very private space.

But he had offered her his heart. There was no more private space than a person's heart. How strange, that they had shared a few embraces, kisses that seemed playful, like the first kisses of almost-children, and had actually led to something so deep. *Is this how it always starts with humans? It all seems simple, casual, until somehow one is ambushed by abiding love?*

The walls and floor of the single room had been deeply engrimed with enough built-up dirt and oil that they had been stained the color of dark wood. The old mattress on the floor had definitely seen better days. But as she looked about her curiously, taking in the carefully ordered books, the single, battered lamp, and few Spartan possessions he had managed to accumulate, it began to speak to her.

As she closed her eyes and tried to get a better sense of John from this place that he called "home," she lost track of time and place.

The numerous locks on the door each disengaged and turned at that moment, and John entered. He startled her. A flash of something more than light engulfed her and the squat for a moment. His hand flew to the grip of his pistol; he hadn't expected anyone to be inside his squat, and though he must have felt a flash of something, he had not recognized it. The suspicion immediately faded from his face when he saw it to be Sera, and not some sort of malcontent. And there was something else that shouted for his attention: the squat and everything in it had somehow been scoured down to the bare cement. It was no less shabby, but now it was impossibly clean. How she had managed that, he had no idea. "It cleans, too. You're a wonder, love." He strode in, smiling widely.

Sera could see that he was tired, however, and not just from the exertions of the day. He was pale, and sweating. She held out her hands to him, and felt how drained he was. She did her best to pour strength into him, but it was, ultimately, like pouring water into a container that still had a hole in the bottom of it. "It is a talent I did not know I had until now, beloved," she said, trying to bring a smile to him. "Perhaps I should advertise it?"

"Naw, I've got the bills paid for. Besides, I wanna keep ya all for myself." He shrugged off his bulletproof vest and duty belt, dropping both to the floor. "I'm gonna grab a shower, get all of this patrol dirt offa me. The Commissar has made me her favorite whipping boy, lately."

"Have you told her?" She did not have to say *what.*

John called from the tiny bathroom as the water started for the shower. "Nope. But I'll have to soon enough." It was in his nature to not want to be a burden to others, to be self-reliant. But this was different; this was no fault of his own, and it was much too grave.

Her heart ached for him, even as she wondered at his courage. She settled on the now clean, if still battered couch to wait for him. A conviction was growing in her that it was time, perhaps, to use more than mere words with him. And as she asked, silently, if this too would be permitted, the affirmative answer somehow did not surprise her. Whatever was going on, John Murdock was as important to the Infinite as he was to her, now.

She made herself as human as she could, banished even the thought of clothing, and paced silently into the bathroom. He was just stepping from the crude shower, and had a towel in his hands, and stared at her in dazed astonishment. He opened his mouth to say—something. It did not really matter what. She did not give him the chance.

She went to him, put her arms around him, and pressed herself to him.

"Sera—" he choked.

"Hush," she whispered, and kissed him. The towel dropped to the floor.

It had been a very long time for him; at first, she knew, he had been too concerned with running. Then he had been mourning for his lost love. And at last, when that wound had subsided into an aching scar, he had been concerned with survival, and not just his own, though he wouldn't admit it openly. Any woman he was with could potentially be a hunter, or a victim of his hunters.

But now, no matter what he had consciously decided, his body had its own priorities, and made them urgently known. And there was this: he was dying, and the body, knowing it is dying, instinctively yearns for life and will do nearly anything to perpetuate life.

It was a good thing that the mattress that passed for a bed was only a few steps away.

Despite his urgency, he was a gentle and considerate lover, and again, Sera discovered to her astonishment that the memories of others are nothing compared to the real experience itself. Together they joined in fire and joy, in the nearest thing that mortals could do to becoming one.

They lay beside each other in silence for a time; she had the feeling that he was feeling stunned. She understood that something profound had just happened between them, something far beyond the mere physical act. Something to tie him to this mortal life, perhaps? Something to alter that terrible resignation to his fate?

But why, when there was no hope?

Finally, at last, he spoke. "Well, that's one for the journal."

She blinked. "Journal? What journal?"

He grinned lopsidedly, waving his hand. "Remind me to tell y'later. How was yer day?"

She raised herself on one elbow and regarded him for a moment, then nestled close into his side. His arm closed around her shoulders instinctively, before he even had a chance to think about what they had just done. It felt astonishingly natural. "An encounter with a Blacksnake operative. Some rescues. I told a child a story." She kept herself human; that too felt right.

"Blacksnake, huh? Hope you didn't mess 'em up too much. Commissar would be distraught if her favorite punching bags were put outta business."

She thought about Fei Li, and the strange, intent look the General had gotten when the sword struck her. If she had been human, she would have shivered. “Not . . . that one would notice. But it was unpleasant.” She decided to change the subject, quickly. “There are things I must speak of, beloved.”

He sat up straighter, angling himself so that he could see her face. He could tell by her tone that it was something important. “Shoot, love.”

“You know of the Infinite. Of the great Law of Free Will. You know why I am . . . constrained to do as little as I can. This—” she waved her hand a little at the clean floor and walls. “This is in that nature; it changes nothing for me to do this, such things come as breathing does to you. But . . . beloved . . .” She felt herself starting to weep. “I know you have asked inside yourself why I have not saved your friends, saved you—”

He was already shaking his head. “Sera, I don’t blame you—”

“Blame? Perhaps not, but the question—I have heard it, even when you have not spoken it. And the greater question: why has the Infinite allowed it?” She took a deep breath. “And you listen to my words, but they are only words. You see me, what I am, you believe in me, and yet, you do not believe beyond that.” Anguish threaded her. She blinked, and shook her head to free her eyes of tears. “Do you *want* to believe?”

John bit his lip; she wasn’t used to seeing him conflicted in this manner, nor was he used to seeing her this troubled. “Sera . . . by what y’probably are, there can’t be any proof. I’m an agnostic, in that sense; I take it for granted that the definition of any sorta ‘higher power’ leaves it impossible to prove or disprove.” He shook his head, running a hand through his hair. “I’ve seen the worst of people, and the worst of myself. I know we couldn’t prove or disprove a god, but I don’t believe that one would exist that would let *Evil* exist. It just doesn’t make sense.”

How to *show* him? How to—not *make* him understand, because forcing was the last thing she wanted to do, but *bring* him, by his own will and reason, to understanding? “Evil . . . evil is a choice.” She tried to concentrate on finding the right words.

He smiled, and she could sense that he felt as if he were humoring her. “If we really wanna get into the philosophical implications of Evil and how it disproves an all-loving, all-powerful entity, we could, love. But that’d take a while.”

“Beloved, I have heard all these things before. Mortals have been making these arguments since life began. I am old, old.

I am of the Firstborn." She closed her eyes, trying to think. "Listen. This is no mere story. Before there were such things as Time and Space, the Infinite said 'I Am,' and that is what your scientists recognize as the moment when Time and Space came into being. And immediately after that moment, the Infinite knew there were two courses that could be taken. The Infinite could create and control everything. And there would be no evil, all would be harmonious and beautiful and dead. Stagnation. Nothing would ever change, for why change perfection? Or . . . the Infinite could forever hold itself apart from creation, and make the First Law that of Free Will and Free Choice, and allow the universe to evolve as it would. There would be evil, yes. Terrible things would happen. Those creatures that evolved would sometimes tear themselves and others apart, and there would be pain and death and sorrow. But . . . they would grow. They would *become.* That is what the Infinite chose, as a good parent chooses to stand aside and let his child grow and become. But that is also when the Firstborn were created, who are less, who cannot See all, so that sometimes, sometimes, when an Instrument was needed, when a peril was so great as to threaten even more than just a world, there would be help." Someday, perhaps, she would tell him of the Fallen; it was not the time for that now. "We are, if not mortal, the Finite interacting with the Finite. We have less Free Will than mortals, but that is because we trust more, and because we have more power. With great power comes—"

"—great responsibility?" he quipped.

"The need to do the most with the least," she corrected. "I could level a world. I *must* use only what is absolutely needed, with the least amount of interference. I *must not* ever interfere with the exercise of Free Will, even when the choice is for evil." *As it was for Dominic Verdigris . . .* There had been that moment, that single, telling moment at his party, when he could have taken the path for such good. . . .

He held up a hand, still unconvinced and changing the course of the conversation. "Discounting the problems with Moral Evil, what about Physical Evil? Natural disasters, plagues, and the like? It just doesn't hold water, with the logic that's available to frail 'uns like me, dear."

Unexpectedly, without her even thinking to ask, she heard the Voice within her. *Bring him.*

"Death is so far from being the end of life that Physical Evil does not matter... please, may I show you?" she begged, clutching his hand in both of hers, looking up at him pleadingly. If only he could See... that would bring the understanding. Surely, surely.

John shrugged. "You're certainly welcome to try. I don't know how y'could, dear, but—"

She held his hand tightly. He had given permission. Now, the rest was as easy for her as breathing was for a mortal. She concentrated a moment, gathered him to her, and enveloped them both in the Glory. Time stopped. She gathered all her strength, and made the Leap. In that moment, she brought him to the Heart of All Time.

This, for her, was home. She became Light within the Light, immersed in the sound that was the Song of Creation, the great music that came from her Siblings and constantly changed as creation itself changed. More than immersion, it was completion, and she gave herself up to the pure joy of it. Here she was most truly herself, no longer subject to the laws of the physical, mortal universe.

Beside her was John; stubbornly clinging to what he knew, he looked exactly as the mortal self that had been lying beside her, as he pictured himself. Here where all things were possible, he retained his worldly form as he thought of himself: clothing, expression, and scars. She, of course, was her truest form; a slender creature of pure white light, with a halo of wings that resembled wisping ethereal fire, with only a suggestion of a face in which her golden eyes burned, and only his will imparted to her the sense of femaleness.

Initially, John panicked. He flailed in place, trying to right himself where an "up" didn't exist. He looked bewildered, frightened... and then his face softened. Curiosity overcame his sense of awe and fear. He waited a few heartbeats in a place where time had no meaning. "Sera... love... where on *Earth* are we?"

Not on Earth at all. This is the realm of the Firstborn and the Siblings, the Heart of All Time. The Infinite itself is here, insofar as you could say that it is anywhere. Perhaps it is truer to say that the Infinite is visible and manifest here. Everything is possible here, and all that ever has been is remembered here.

"So, this... this is Heaven?" Still accustomed to speaking, John did so, even though there was no air to breathe as such.

There was a sense of joyous laughter. *There are as many Heavens as there are beings to imagine them. This is beyond those. This is the purest place of being beyond death.*

He looked mortified. "Am I dead, then?"

A "wing" caressed him tenderly. *No, beloved. Rarely, we can bring someone here. You have been granted that gift. Best beloved, this is to prove to you—death is not an ending, and forgiveness is always possible.*

"And... Hell? Does that exist? There's gotta be an opposite for every reward—"

They were joined at that moment by another presence. Not as bright, or as shining as Sera. But it was one that "felt" so familiar to John that he was startled—

"Who are you?" John was still guarded, still suspicious, even here.

Like Sera, the newcomer "spoke" without speaking. *Forgotten me already?* A laugh, like one he knew, but without the pain that had always colored that laugh, as the light took on colors and a shape. *Hell, John, I am crushed.*

"I—" He looked at Sera, upset and confused. "Love, what's going on here? I don't understand."

The newcomer chuckled as her form became as mortal as his. A young woman with freckles, intense brown eyes, shoulder-length brown hair and a firm jaw, wearing fatigue pants and a black T-shirt. Tanned and muscled, she was clearly a fighter, but the huge, guileless grin on her face said that she didn't feel the need to fight here, and the gleam of her eyes was a reflection of the joy that Sera radiated. "It's just more proof for you, lover." Jessica turned in place for him. "See? It's me. All here."

"Jessica... how?" John's facade of toughness cracked, then shattered, and he began to cry; first silently, then with harsh, tight, small sobs that sounded as if they were being torn from him.

When Jessie had been murdered, he hadn't wept; he'd snapped. He hadn't cried for her, properly mourned her loss, in all that time. In all the long years since, he had not cried. Not all the times when he had been a heartbeat from ending it all. Not when he had been sure his parents were dead, killed in the Invasion. Never.

Now he did. Now, finally, the last barrier had broken, and the grief was overwhelming. He mourned for the loss of Jessie, for the loss of everything he had been, for the terrible things he had done, for what he had become.

"How is this possible? You've been—gone," he looked down,

not willing to state that she was dead. "Gone for six years. How are you talking to me?"

"You mean dead? Just the shell, hon. Like old clothes. The shell wasn't me any more than that nasty old uniform they made us wear was." She put both hands around his face, and gazed intently into his eyes. "Sera's right. Everything's possible here. Death doesn't end us; I'm your proof. Remember that poem you used to quote? *Though lovers be lost love shall not; And death shall have no dominion.* Forgiveness is there if you want it, I'm proof of that too."

John's whole body shook with grief and despair. "There's so much I haven't said. So much wrong I've done, Jess. It's too much, all of it. I can't ever make it up. I can't ever make it better again." He hung his head. "I don't deserve forgiveness."

Sera's light throbbed, as a heartbeat throbbed, and the beat was compassion. *This is the Infinite, John. Would you put limits on what the Infinite can do?*

He didn't respond, locked within his own terrible sorrow.

You asked me of Hell. Hell is within you, within all thinking creatures. As they make their own Heavens, they make their own Hells, and if they cannot see past them, if they cannot reach for the forgiveness that is freely offered, and as freely make reparation, they dwell in them. A feeling of sadness too terrible for tears swept over all three of them.

"It was all my fault, though." He looked up through tears to see Jessica beside him, her pose a mirror of Sera's. "It's all my fault. I didn't do it right, I didn't stop things before they went too far. I took out the innocent along with the guilty." He shook his head, still sobbing pitifully. "It's my fault."

"Your fault?" Jessica blazed up with anger, losing her form for a moment. "All *your* fault? What about the people that tortured us, tried to break us, murdered me? Was that your fault too?"

"I didn't do anything. I didn't stop 'em, didn't disagree. All I did was kill 'em." He shook harder, violently. "That's all I am. A killer."

Around them, the light dimmed, and darkness spread from him. The Song turned to one of mourning. Shocks of purple, like permanent lightning, shot through the Heart of All Time, spider-webbing through it. It came to Sera that they resembled his scars; scars of mind and soul as much as of the body.

And so you reject forgiveness? Sera's "voice" trembled with anguish. *You would dwell in your own Hell forever?*

Her despair seemed to flow outward to match his. Sparks of muted bronze floated away from her. Tears?

Only Jessica seemed unchanged. If anything, she burned brighter, yet softer. "You damn well better not reject *my* forgiveness, goof. You didn't kill me. You did your best to protect me, the same as I did my best to protect you. Look at me!" She laughed, spread her arms, and twirled, like a little girl in a playground, spinning off ribbons of brightness, "The things I've seen! The things I can do! It's—more than I dreamed—more than I ever thought was possible!"

"I'm so sorry, Jess. Nothin' happened like it should've." The darkness deepened around him, around all of them. Sera's "tears" burned through the darkness, cutting glowing paths in it.

Jessie threw her arms around him. "Nothing ever does, lover. Listen. Hell, would an angel love you if you weren't worthy to be forgiven? Would I? *Believe.* Believe in me, believe in yourself. Believe this. *I forgive you. And death shall have no dominion.*"

At those words, there was a moment of anticipation, as everything in that place waited on his answer, his acceptance or rejection of what Jessie offered. And then, John's body dissolved in an instant of a too-brilliant burst of flame. A new John in the shape of a man took his place, but one of all fire, brightness and pure flame. The darkness that had engulfed all of them burned away in that flash of light and the Song rang out with joy.

It occurred to John that he appeared exactly as the red-headed teen in New York had, before he had died and been carried away by one of the seraphim.

Sera laughed like the ringing of bells, her wings spreading to cover half the sky. *Beloved! You see! You understand!*

"He always was the most hardheaded sonuvabitch." Jessica embraced him in a way more intimate than he had ever felt before, except with Sera. "Now that you're thinking sense, I have to go." She grinned. "My work here is done. Guess that makes me a big damn hero, huh?"

Will I ever see you again? His fires blazed brightly, flickering in the Light of the Heart.

"Silly. I'm always here, forever—unless I decide to put on another set of clothes and go play with a life again. If you want to see me, you will. If you want to be with me, you will." She embraced him again. "Now you go be happy while you can. Feel again. Live—don't just survive—as much as you can. And hang onto that pigheaded nature of yours. You'll need it on the road ahead." She changed back into her form of light. "And love your angel. Love is the most important thing there is."

And then, she was gone, flashing off in every direction, and none. John took a deep breath, and wondered if there was something he should do, or say—Sera had brought Jessie to him, it seemed. Should he thank her? Or—

One comes. Sera's voice had suddenly changed, sounding as full of awe as his had been. *This... was not expected....*

If he had thought that Sera was "bright," the newcomer was incandescent. It appeared in an instant, as if it had stepped out of some door that was not visible beside them. It had "wings" that seemed to stretch out forever.

First and Fairest, I... we... greet you. Sera didn't exactly "bow," but that was the impression John got. *Beloved, this is one of the First among the Firstborn. He has been called Michael Azir.* The being held him, gravely, in his gaze. John held his place. He felt like he had in New York, upon first being Seen by one of the seraphim; like an insect at the end of a microscope, with a giant looking down. It was unnerving, but he didn't let the slightest ripple of emotion show in his form.

John Murdock. There was a suggestion of a chuckle. *Seducer of the Firstborn. You succeed where even the Fallen have not.*

Couldn't say that I'm all that special enough to warrant it; I'm not the strongest, or the smartest, an' certainly not the fairest. Might be the toughest, but I don't figure that's my best selling point.

The being laughed, then sobered. *More special than you think. There is... will be... something extraordinary permitted to you.*

It was as if the entire Heart of All Time held its breath. The Song didn't falter, but muted, still vibrant, but reserved. The tension and anticipation clung to John's mind.

You know that the Seraphym—your Sera—may not heal you. But— The being bent to him, and Michael Azir's regard took on weight. *She may save you. At a cost. For a miracle to occur, something equally miraculous must be sacrificed. That is the way in which the Law of Free Will can be upheld. You, John Murdock, will not die just yet. If you choose. But the Seraphym must give over her Grace and become mortal. She will no longer See the futures, no longer be able to Leap here, no longer hear the Song.*

That is the cost to her. A pause. *There may be further cost to you, to her. I cannot say. Even I cannot read the futures this course will trace; this is new, unprecedented. Only the Infinite may know, and it is not permitted to me to See it.*

John stayed silent for a moment. *And if I decide that the cost is too great? If I choose to die?*

Then you die. Nothing is simpler. And she must . . . find another path.

What does that mean?

You choose. You accept her gift and live, or do not and die. It is not permitted to me to say further. Nor is it permitted to any other being to sway your decision. You need not choose now, but choose you must. Not choosing will still be a choice. As abruptly as he had appeared, the being vanished. And without a word, Sera wrapped John in her wings, Sang a single note—

And they were back, as they had been on the broken-down mattress in his squat.

John snapped to consciousness first. He saw Sera as he had when she first appeared to him on the outskirts of Atlanta: a beautiful creature, inhuman, and made of fire and light. He realized in that very instant the enormity of what she was willing to give up for him—immortality, power beyond imagining, and her own sense of self and belonging. Not just belonging to a family, a country, even a people; belonging to the greatest *Other* there was. She was willing to give up what best passed for Heaven . . . for him. How could he ask her to do that?

A second later, she was back; changed to her more comfortable, more "human" form of an unbelievably beautiful woman with a silken fall of hair so red it defined the word. But as innocently unclothed as Eve. "You want to know," she said. "You need to know? Would I? Yes. Yes, and yes, and yes again. I would. I can. I will. Because I must. Because I can. Because I love you."

They did not so much embrace as cling to one another.

For a second, John thought he heard a whisper.

Go on, stud. Be happy. The moment was perfect, in their love for one another and in the sadness of the choice that needed to be made. For John, for them both, and for the world.

He felt rejuvenated. Was that as much because of this new "out" as it was being in Sera's arms? Or was it because of being in that—place? Whichever, he couldn't be human, and a man, without having the natural reaction to having a very beautiful naked creature who loved him with all her heart in his arms. And without being blind, she could not have missed that reaction. She laughed soundlessly, and kissed him, and the ancient dance began again. This time he took a lot of care with it, lingering, stretching it out. Not just because he wanted to give her all the pleasure he could, which he did. Because in the back of his mind, his thoughts were in a turmoil.

As wonderful as this new joy was—and was it ever wonderful—he couldn't shake the feeling, the nagging voice at the back of his mind that he had only traded one set of worries for another. This was all happening too fast for him; he was having a difficult time coping with the curveballs that life kept throwing him. Kriegers, he could deal with. Blacksnake, he could deal with. Dying, he had just gotten used to the idea of dealing with. Loving Sera... he was more than happy to deal with *that*. But what of this offer that Michael Azir had given him?

She may save you. At a cost.

John had been resigned to losing everything of himself for a long time; he had done his best to hide it, to mask it with honor and duty, but he might as well have been dead the day he "left" the Program. Now... he had everything to lose, all over again. Friends like Bella and Vic, his neighborhood people, even a kind of family in the CCCP. And now, most of all, Sera. Against all odds, he'd found love again.

But to keep it, he would have to ask the one person he had come to cherish more than anything to give up... everything. Sera kept telling him that he was important to the futures; he trusted her, and now more than ever believed in her and what she professed. What John couldn't believe was that he was nearly important enough to outweigh what Sera could do, even with the constraints placed upon her nearly immeasurable power.

How can I ask her to give up everything she has ever known? Is life that important to me?

Long after Sera had closed her eyes to rest in his arms, John lay awake, thinking and fearing.

CHAPTER THIRTY-TWO

Fire on the Mountain

MERCEDES LACKEY, DENNIS LEE, CODY MARTIN

As fast as I could get parts, plans, and bullying to techs on the ground, there was a copy of Overwatch Mark One Point One (without the magic part) in every Echo comm room. I even sent cases of parts and the plans to Saviour Senior in Moscow, though with that supreme tinkerer, Petrograd, gone in the Invasion, I had no idea if they'd ever be able to implement their own version of Overwatch. One Point One was pure tech, Echo-tech headset, HUD, and pinhole camera mounted in a helmet—because the days of jaunting around helmetless with your hair flying in the wind were over. Unless you were one of the handful of truly invulnerable, a headshot from a Krieger, or even a good sniper, would take you out. The Kriegers had plenty of energy weapons and Blacksnake had plenty of snipers... So helmets for all, thankyouverymuch. That made it trivial to integrate Overwatch into them. Some Echo Ops used the HUDs, some didn't; all the HUDs were external retinal projectors and not everyone liked them. My newly recruited operators couldn't hack security, ATM, and traffic cameras as fast as I could, but most of them were hackers I personally tracked down and recruited, including the totally awesome Captain Hackatron of Texas, and they'd learn. They'd never be me, but they would, gods willing, never have to be me. Some of them would be better, much better, at the hack than me on a pure skill level, because I cheated with magic. Overwatch One Point One was a crippled version of the first, but it was also far less of a kludge: a smoothly integrated, fully tech system with easily replaced parts. Including the operator. And let me say, the Colt brothers turned out to be supernaturally good at being Overwatch Sentinels. So good they even got callsigns: Sentinel Alpha and Sentinel Omega.

Another advantage was that now if anyone talked about Overwatch . . . I was no longer "it." I was now one herring hiding in the shoal.

Yes. I am *that paranoid.*

We did keep one little thing. I was still "Overwatch," or sometimes "Overwatch One." Everyone else was a "Sentinel" in the "Overwatch Network." So the herring still had a red tail. But it was better than being the only prey-fish in an ocean full of sharks.

I rushed this through as fast as Bella could sign the orders. Because when our ass-saving, face-saving, "Yes, Echo is doing all it can to defeat the Kriegers" intel finally came through from Tesla and Marconi, I wanted the Network to be in place.

It was. Not one moment too soon, either.

"Ladies and gentlemen, we have our miracle."

That was how Bella had put it, in a joint meeting of her Advisory Council; even Red Saviour was an unofficial part of it, listening and commenting via Vickie's Overwatch. They had their miracle, something to make it clear to the world that Echo was not weak, not ineffective, and not sitting on its collective hands. Something to prove that not even the loss of Alex Tesla and the machinations of Dominic Verdigris could blunt their edge.

Something to prove that they were more than willing to take the fight to the Thulians. Just in time too; after the all-too-brief honeymoon, the US military *and* the press were starting to make impatient noises.

"We have our miracle. Tesla and Marconi have given us the location of the Krieger North American HQ. It's payback time."

"Testing," said Vickie. John blinked a little, jarred out of the memory. The new implants made it sound as if she was standing right next to him. He'd been using them for some time, but he still had not become used to them.

Not everyone had the implants, of course, just the Infiltration Team and the commanders for the ground teams, along with a select few in other areas. The rest had to make do with earbuds and throat mics and HUDs in their helmets. As ground commander, Red Saviour had both. As a former member of the world's most technologically advanced military, John was always wowed and in favor of more gee-whiz fun things that made his job easier. But he still liked to have at least a rudimentary understanding of the tech, too; this new stuff, particularly anything dealing with magic, gave him the creeps. Results counted, though, so he accepted it. The HUD was particularly weird. Some sort of tiny device that fed information into the optic nerve *inside* his eyes. What he saw, floating between his eyes and the rest of the world, looked just like standard HUD projections, like stuff from the Future Warrior project that was all the rage for a while.

John fidgeted in his control harness. He had been—back when the universe made a modicum of sense—a patient man, and had understood that it was a required trait for being a member of the Special Operations community. Right now, he just wanted to get on with things, take the fight to the enemy and do something that had an impact. *Not like I have all the time in the world to do so, anymore.* He shifted again, trying to brush off his imminent mortality. "Are we still on schedule, Vic?"

"That's a Rog. Countdown is on your HUD. Want some music?" She sounded quite calm as if she didn't know she was talking to a dying man. Or a walking dead man. Maybe that was her way of keeping him sane.

"Naw. Just keep me updated." He glanced at the first team leader, an accomplished Echo meta named Bulwark. John didn't like Bulwark very much, and he was sure that the feeling was more than mutual. Bulwark, while just as professional as John, was a company man. To him, John was probably dubious. John had all the moves and the manners of the military, but an unknown background and on top of that, was part of the CCCP...

Then again, the Echo operative was riding herd on Red Djinni. Compared to the Djinni, John probably looked like a Boy Scout.

He wished, with a profound ache, that Sera was here...but she said she had to stay in Atlanta. She didn't tell him why, and he didn't ask. Maybe it was to keep that rat-bastard Verdigris from trying anything while most of Echo was out here. Verd still had Fei Li. It wouldn't be out of character for him to put a hit on Bella if he thought he could get away with it. Sera had filled him with that strength and energy of hers before he left, and to most people he was passing as his normal self. But he felt fragile, like a thin glass bottle holding white-hot plasma.

Mamona piped up from the back of the cramped crew compartment, sandwiched between Motu and Matai. "What happens if they figure us out?"

"Simple, comrade; they blow us out of the sky." John flashed a wolfish smile over his shoulder.

"They won't figure you out as long as everything works right." That was Vickie. *"And I have contingencies on my contingencies."*

The Death Sphere they were riding in had been recovered several months previously from Lake Michigan, one of the captured Thulian orbs that a mysterious "Doctor Dusk" had brought down undamaged. This "Doctor Dusk" character hadn't been sighted before or since the Invasion; for an unregistered metahuman, he would've had to be something else to take out a Thulian orb all on his lonesome, and without damaging it to boot. Bulwark was the only one that was granted clearance to get minimal training for the craft. John wasn't very happy about that, since he'd still rather have cross-training for the rest of the team. No telling what would happen once they were on-site; having another trained pilot for one of these gizmos might save their hides. But orders were orders and it was too late for it now.

"CCCP is in place. Echo Squad One is in place. Echo Squad Two is moving in. Hammer is online and downrange. Air Support is on-station."

John unhooked himself from his chair. "Equipment check, everyone. Smoke 'em if you got 'em, and get your kit ready. Once everything starts, there's no turning back." John crouch-walked through the cabin, being careful not to step on anyone. The conditions in the Thulian vessel were extremely cramped; they had eight people in a space built for five. He function checked weapons, made sure everyone had extra ammunition, quizzed them on passwords and callsigns, and inspected to see if anyone had any gear improperly secured; noise discipline was going to be tantamount for this mission.

Satisfied that everyone was ready, he took his place next to Bulwark. "We're ready to go, Vic. Just give the command." The Death Sphere was located in one of the western peaks, in relation to the Thulian HQ. It gave a commanding view of the entire valley where the battle was to take place, as well as the whole of the HQ's exterior. Bulwark and John, with the help of Gamayun, had consulted the Commissar personally about their positioning, using terrain maps and satellite pictures to get an accurate idea of the elevation changes.

It was inhospitable country. There was a reason why the Park Service strongly recommended no one go off the trails in the Superstition Mountains, and a reason why the BLM flat-out forbade prospecting. Right now, out there, the temperature was 110 in the shade. *Sure as hell glad I'm gonna be inside for my part of the fight. Hope everybody packed enough* H_2O.

"Echo Squad Two is in place. Echo Squads Three and Four are moving in. Hammer is on-station and holding."

John held his breath. This was it. The seconds ticked off, and time moved by at a crawl.

"Echo Squads Three and Four are in place. Hold for Commissar Red Saviour."

The Commissar's voice made him jump a little. He was used to having a disembodied Vickie in his head. Not so Red Saviour. *"Final check. Being sound off. Giving go or no go."*

"Echo Four, go." "Echo Three, go." "Echo Two, that's a go." "Air Support, we're on-station. Go." Bulwark cleared his throat. "Infil, go." *"Echo One, go, Commissar." "Squad Red, ready."* A new voice, with the clipped tones of a military scientist chimed in. *"Hammer, go."*

Saviour's voice was just as cool. *"All squads, confirmed go status.* Molotok, *you are clear for launch." "Molotok."* That was Russian for "Hammer." Figured for Saviour to say it in Russian.

There was a long pause. John kept his gaze focused on the entrance for the Nazi HQ. If everything went according to plan, the favor that Vickie had somehow called in—or used blackmail to get—from some high-ranking muckety-muck in the Air Force Space Agency would hit the entrance dead on.

Seconds passed. John was beginning to suspect that there was a problem, or that those in charge hadn't understood the Commissar, when the biggest explosion he had ever personally seen erupted a mere two hundred yards away. *Danger goddamned close!* It was two thousand yards to the east of the Thulian HQ, and nearly on top of the death machine he was inside. His teeth rattled inside of his head, and he saw spots. A quick glance over his shoulder confirmed that everyone inside was alive, albeit shook up. More tense waiting. *Here's hopin' that they don't drop the next one right on top of us.*

It happened sooner than John thought it would; to reorient something in parking orbit miles above the Earth, calibrate it so that it could strike a target the size of a Buick... it was math that was beyond John. But the NASA and DARPA eggheads had done it. A solid tungsten rod, half the size of a telephone pole with a baby guidance computer and some stabilizing fins, smashed into the top of the Thulian HQ. John realized a moment later that the first round that had almost hit them was merely a ranging shot, nowhere near the full power of what was coming. It hit the stone facade at orbital velocity; the sheer energy released was on a scale with a tactical nuclear device, or some of the largest conventional bombs ever detonated. Debris and superheated dust exploded outward, forming the iconic Cold War mushroom cloud even though there was nothing nuclear about it. John could see some sort of energy shield rippling in the very belly of the explosion. It was awesome: a testament to the preparations of a generation that feared Soviet dominance of space, a true space-age weapon. It struck him as ironic that it was now being used to serve a coalition force that was partially composed of hard-liners. "That'll get their attention."

"Am being glad was never used as planned," Saviour said dryly over the freq. "Davay, davay! *Echo One, comrades, deploy!"*

The side of the mountain that hid the Thulians had evaporated, exposing the entrance. As if they had heard John, the hangar door split open, orange and malevolent light spilling out through the smoke and dust. Almost immediately, Thulian troopers and death machines began to pour out, like ants from a disturbed nest.

Bulwark spoke up. "We're waiting until the second wave comes. Then we make our move."

"Roger, Infil." That was Vickie. *"I've got Saviour on her own freq now. Fewer voices in your ear, the better. CCCP and Echo One moving in to intercept now. Air Support on the way; they're gonna lay thermite bombs and boost-napalm in Arc Light right behind the first wave."*

It was very easy to be detached when you were hundreds of miles away from a furnace-hot valley that was about to get a lot hotter. Vickie tried not to be too detached. This wasn't a video game.

"Air Support ETA, ninety seconds, Commissar."

The Thulians, despite having their visages hidden behind armor and death machine viewports, looked pissed. They moved with a purpose; their supposedly secret North American headquarters had just been attacked with one of the most powerful weapons in the history of Earth, discounting nukes and OpFour metahumans. They charged ahead in attack columns, with additional SS troops attached to the death machines.

Echo One, comprised of fast-movers and shooters, went out to engage them. She recognized one of the metahumans; Speed Freak, with a passenger. She'd taken note of him for being connected with Johnny, during the fight between the whole of the CCCP and the Rebs on the outskirts of Atlanta. Parker, the meta's Christian name, was speeding ahead of the rest of his squad; a very serious-looking Echo OpTwo with a grenade launcher was riding shotgun with him. "Parker," that was ironic, considering he was doing everything *but* park right now. Equally ironic—that was Bella's last name.

"Back it down, Speed. Echo One, *davay* the hell up and close ranks." She switched to Russian and the CCCP freq. *"Povernite napravo, piat'sot metrov. Begite kak esli bi vi shli pod ognem, potomu cho vi popadete pod obstrel esli vi ne potoropites!"* Nothing like telling them that they would *be* on fire if they didn't move like they were already in flames to get them motivated.

She switched to the Air Tac comm freq. This was like touch-typing now, she could switch freqs and cameras without even thinking about where her fingers should go.

Vickie scooted a stealthed "eye" the last couple feet to where she wanted the strafing run to start, and another to the end and painted the spots with laser dots. "Angel Flight, you are go for primary bombardment. T-Bird, you are go for follow-on bombardment." The Air Force Thunderbirds were not the only aerobatic team that had practiced combat against simulated metahuman targets before the Invasion. The T-Birds had gotten all the press coverage, given they were clearing out Vegas where there were a zillion cameras not counting cell phones. The Blue Angels had been itching to prove they were better than their fellow airmen ever since.

Now they were getting their chance in their six hardened F/A 18 Hornets, followed by the six Thunderbirds in their F16 "Vipers" (as the crews called them) literally coming in at Mach one at least.

The first jet crested the ridge. The Mach one shock wave rippled across the battlefield. It was dwarfed by the inferno the jets laid down. And at Mach one, with the expert pilots of the Angels and Thunderbirds at the stick, not even the Thulians could move in time to track them. They laid down their rockets and incendiary cannon fire, putting a slash of hell across the landscape that cut the first wave off from behind, then climbed vertically in what must have been nearly nine-gee climbs. Sadly, the two "eyes" were the first casualties. Ah well. More where they came from. She had a crateload of them out there, and an awful lot fit into a crate. One of the things that Verd had kindly left behind when he rabbited were the blueprints and manufacturing instructions.

"Angel Flight and T-Birds returning to base for re-arm."

She was already flying more of her "eyes" over the battlefield, looking for trouble spots.

"Copy that. Godspeed and get back here as fast as you can."

"Roger. Save some for us."

All that practice with bigger and bigger teams was paying off. She was in a kind of zen state where it was possible to keep track of everything in all of her monitors. Well, almost all. Infil Team was holding off till the second wave, so she could ignore them for now.

Cut off by the gash of fire across their escape route, the Thulians headed for the logical place for defensive entrenchment until the swath of thermite and boost-napalm burned out. Of course they did. They knew this land, and they knew the best places to dig in.

However, as familiar with the lay of the land as they might be, they were not the only ones smart enough to figure out where the good defensive positions would be.

As Echo One and CCCP raced toward them, the Nazis hit the concealed thermite mines that had been planted there in the predawn hours by some very select Echo metas...

A second swath of fire exploded up on the ridge. Even though she was expecting it, she jumped, her heart racing.

Verdigris stared glumly at the view from his spy cam. It showed a vaguely human-shaped swath of light hovering motionless just above the office that he knew held the new Echo Chief Bella Dawn Parker.

It was the Seraphym—just high enough off the ground to put her out of range of a sneak attack from Fei Li. Not that he thought a sneak attack would succeed. Her presence was just a great big fat warning sign. *No Trespassing, Violators Will Be Ashed.* She knew that, and she knew he knew, and he knew she knew he knew.

Feh.

"I could overcome her." That was Fei Le, who was lounging in one of Verdigris' best chairs, feet up on the desk. "If you doubt I could take her alone, then between us, your bodyguard and I could."

"Bad idea." Verdigris sighed. "First of all . . . you've never seen the Seraphym all-out. I have." He'd been collecting eyewitness accounts and video capture ever since she "visited" him. "She's a Four, General. For all I know, she's a Five. Never mind that delusion that she's an angel; in everything else she's as sane as they come, and she has pretty much held back on what she can do." He thought of the footage he'd seen of her taking on not one Death Sphere, single-handed, but a full dozen of them. It had taken her no time at all. That one hadn't made the news. He'd quietly bought the footage and the rights, so he could study it. He still didn't know why she chose particular incidents to handle, but it was pretty clear that if she decided that she needed to, she was definitely not something to cross. "She wants Belladonna Blue alive and in charge of Echo. You make a move on her or the blue chick, and—" He made a little *piff* motion with his fingers. "You only got away the first time on a frontal attack because for whatever reason, the Seraphym didn't feel like killing you. You wouldn't stand the chance of an ant in a deep fryer."

"I think you underestimate me as well." Fei Li shrugged. "Nevertheless . . . Echo is doing us a favor, weakening our greater enemy, and we should allow them to do so unmolested, I suppose."

Verdigris couldn't help but acknowledge the wisdom in that. But his pride had been stung at the loss of Echo and the public disgrace that he had suffered because of it and the allegations that had been levied against him. Bella Dawn Parker would live . . . for the moment. One thing that Verdigris never did was to forget to whom he owed debts, however.

All in time.

Natalya watched through her old-fashioned binoculars as Echo One ripped through the remaining Nazi troopers. For all the witch's magic, she still couldn't give a good distance view of the battlefield that wasn't through a camera, and you had to have a camera in place exactly where you wanted to look. For some reason, this gave Red Saviour a perverse feeling of satisfaction.

The Echo troops moved fast, and they were well coordinated; the Echo metahuman that was serving as their squad leader had dismounted from the race-car-looking metahuman, firing his grenade launcher at a steady pace. A tactic that worked here that had not worked in city streets was to fire at their feet. The friable soil cratered, and they generally toppled over. That left them vulnerable.

With many assault rifles and multiple-grenade launchers, it was short work to take care of the already weakened Nazis. The odd meta that looked like a child's "transforming" toy, Speed Freak, performed a suicide slide, ripping through two weakened troopers under his metal treads. In cover at the ridge behind the skirmish, Saviour had positioned several two-man rocket teams. Armed with Stinger missiles and AT4 launchers, they fired barrages of rockets at any troublesome Nazis. Her heart warmed at the sight of the carnage that the explosions wrought, with her mind flitting back to the massacre at Saviour's Gate. Each Nazi killed gave her joy. *This is right. This is how true Soviets fight—crush the enemy, and no quarter given.*

One of the metahumans, one that she didn't immediately recognize, fabricated a glowing "chain" of energy; it lazily looped itself around three of the armored troopers, drawing them tight together. Immobile, the Nazis were an easy target for the rocket teams and the rest of Echo One.

When the last Thulian trooper was killed, the squad began to set up defensive positions. They were hasty, and made to be retreated from quickly. *Now, we wait. Now they know we are serious opponents, and the real battle begins.*

She amped up the magnification on her binoculars, shifting her view to the entrance of the Thulian headquarters. The force that exited was much larger, much better organized. Hundreds of troopers, dozens of their floating Death Spheres. "Echo One, being stick to the plan. Disengage after initial contact, being sure to stick to primary retreat vectors. How copying?" There had been opposition to Saviour as the battlefield leader. The US Military had wanted one of their generals. Nat had wanted to point out how poorly the US Military had been doing against the Kriegers, but fortunately, all of Echo had risen up and let it be known that it would be someone who had actually *won* engagements with the enemy, or no one, and the US Military could go against the target without metahuman help.

"Reading you five by five, Red Leader. Can't see for the dust here. What's the vector?"

"Is being your six o'clock and closing." Saviour noted with satisfaction that he didn't waste breath in answering; the Kriegers were rapidly closing within firing range for the missiles and grenades.

"Commencing fire on your mark, Red Leader."

She waited until they were just at the edge. This was meant to sting, not be a serious threat. "Now. Slap faces."

A withering, but short, volley of fire issued from Echo One's position. Several Nazis went down; not enough to force them to take up a defensive posture, but enough to let them know that the good guys were still there. *Let their fascist arrogance take the better of them.* And that it did. The remaining Nazis charged forward, powered legs thrusting against the rough terrain at frightening speed. Echo One immediately disengaged; they didn't bother to move in bounds with cover fire. The Nazis were still out of range to use their energy cannons. As frighteningly powerful as those cannons were, they were not precision weapons. Terror and intimidation was the name of the game of the Thulians; get in close and count on their nigh invulnerable armor to keep them safe as they mowed down nearly defenseless foes. *No longer; we are not sheep, but wolves. And we have very long teeth.*

"All positions, be ready." There was, as Pavel liked to say, going to be a "great Dixie fry."

The screens of the death machine had a selective binocular plate; it was weird and awkward to use, almost to the point of necessitating a third arm, but it worked well enough once you got the hang of it. John and Bulwark watched from the two forward-facing seats. They saw the Thulians rush out to engage Echo One, saw the metahumans pull back into the valley; John noted that Speed Freak was among them. He didn't have time to dwell on it, however. Just as the Thulians had the whole of their initial force in the valley, three flights of fast-movers, super-sonic jets, ripped through the sky and loosed their payloads in the kind of maneuver called an "Arc Light." Huge columns of fire shot out across the ground, incinerating or weakening the Nazi troopers. Fire, extreme or prolonged heat made them vulnerable; they were getting their fair share, and then some.

"All right," Bulwark squared himself in his seat, placing his arms in the piloting sleeves. "That's our cue." The Death Sphere lurched forward, almost stuttering along. Beads of sweat stood out on Bulwark's forehead as he concentrated; he made an adjustment to one of the many pedals located in front of his seat. The steering straightened out, and John almost wouldn't have known they were moving forward if it weren't for the scenery flashing past through the viewport.

"Roger, Infil. You're go, everything's green by the timetable. Take her in."

They'd been over the terrain until they probably could have walked in blindfolded. The route was set. Vickie was only monitoring for this part of the trip to keep them updated on what was going on down with the fight if it was going to impact them, and warn them of anything unexpected. One of her little spy eyes was glued to the top of the Thulian orb, so she didn't have to depend on the orb's optics.

John watched the second wave of Thulians spilling out of the base. There were most certainly *more* of them; death machines, troopers, and those weird mechanical eagles. Part of him wondered how many more were in there. The sphere lurched into the air, wobbling towards the entrance. This wasn't due to Bulwark's piloting; this was to simulate damage, to give them a reason for returning to the base. The sphere lurched drunkenly towards the entrance. This made for a miserable ride inside. When they were close to seven hundred yards away, Vickie cut into the channel again. *"Infil, halt, halt, halt. Angel Flight and T-Bird incoming. Steel Rain."* The death machine grudgingly obeyed the commands. Moments later, John saw the ground vibrate as the Blue Angels, flying low and way too fast and too close, went over their heads. They pulled up, clearing the mountain headquarters by a good margin; a split-second later, dozens of small explosions rocked the massed Thulian forces at the entrance. Thousands of bomblets and mission-specific munitions dropped, turning some—but not damned enough, by John's estimation—of the troopers into twisted metal and smoldering corpses.

"Heads up, broken eagle, three o'clock, on an intersect." There was probably something like radar in this thing, but if so, no one had figured out how to use it. Bulwark halted their forward progress, and a wing-crumpled eagle plowed into the ground ahead of them. *"Put some juice in it, Bull; things are heating up out here, and you're gonna wind up as part of the collateral damage."* Bulwark said nothing in reply, but when the sphere got moving again, it was going a lot quicker. Bulwark bounced it along the ground as part of their ruse, and every bounce made the occupants' teeth rattle.

"Remind me never to let you park my car."

"Thank you, Operative Nagy."

"Keep sharp, people. Hug right." They were at the entrance now, and hugged one side while fresh troops streamed out. No one seemed to notice them.

"They're hailing you. I have it covered. Hug the right. See anything like a set of docking bays? Take the third one."

Moving slower, Bulwark glided in. Clamps settled onto the hull. Bulwark and Djinni inserted their hands into two more pairs of sleeves and waited. A few Thulians dashed towards the sphere, but before they could reach it, Vickie gave the signal.

"They're coming to get you out. Light 'em up."

Moving their hands wildly in the sleeves, as if all the weapons had malfunctioned at once, Bulwark and Djinni hosed down the interior of what must be a hangar. The Thulian screams were so intense they bled over Vickie's freq onto theirs. Gouts of white-hot thermite and nitro-napalm scoured the entire interior hangar. Blasts of orange energy scored the walls, ceiling and floor, blasting docking clamps and equipment into vapor.

"Clear."

John was the first one to unbuckle his safety restraints. "Time to dismount." Matai slapped a square orange panel; what had looked like a seamless section of plating separated, irising to become an exit hatch. It was a long way down to the floor. The two infiltration teams had practiced jumping from the craft until their execution was perfect; it only took a few moments for everyone to land on the floor and take a defensive position for their assigned sector. John pulled two of Vickie's "eyes" out of a belt pouch and tossed them up. They vanished.

Her voice sounded calm and steady. *"Rock and roll, troops."*

✧ ✧ ✧

Bella was glued to the multiple feeds from Vickie's station. She couldn't even imagine how Vic was coordinating it all. She was practically on fire with the need to be there herself... except she couldn't. She was head of Echo, not to be risked. If she'd been there, chances were that Verdigris would have somehow managed to find a way to drop one of the "Hammers" on her head. Or had one of the other weapons reprogrammed to target her. It wasn't as if he didn't have people almost as good at hacking as Vickie—and he had probably set up plenty of backdoors when he was all cozy with the US Military. Or—well, there was a lot he could do, and there was also no way of telling whether or not he still had another mole or ten in their ranks. There was a damned good reason why the Seraphym was hovering just outside her window, and it had nothing to do with providing a little more ambient light in the office.

She knew all this.

It didn't help.

John used hand signals, drawing his team in. Untermensch, Soviet Bear, and Mamona took position behind him. He caught Bulwark doing the same in his peripheral vision. Motu, Matai, Silent Knight, and Red Djinni filed in behind their team leader with practiced precision. John reached down to his belt, flicking a rocker switch on a control unit. His subvocal mics kicked in, allowing him to "talk," if you could call it that, without actually making any sound. His voice came over the comms, but seemed flat in a way. "Team two, moving out."

"Team one, moving."

John's team was tasked with taking out the key areas in the Thulian HQ. The trick was, they had to do it without alerting the entire base that there were intruders doing all sorts of naughty things in their midst. They all crept along, almost perfectly silent, with their rifles trained on their sectors of responsibility. John knew they would have to sacrifice some of their stealth, and soon; the longer they took, the more people would die on the surface. Somewhere just ahead of them, Vickie's "eye" flew, invisible, scouting for them.

With a flick of his head, he keyed over to Vic's frequency, patching it into his team's comms. "We're at the hangar exit into the main base. Which way are we headed, and what's the opposition look like beyond this door?" Talking without saying anything was another of the high-tech things that weirded John out; it didn't discount the obvious tactical advantages, which he may well have killed for when he was still part of a recognized military.

"Clear at the door. Left, left, right, left. After the fourth corner, you hit a main drag and it's full of troopers."

"Number? What's their disposition?"

"I count six positive, with a possible seventh. Can't get the eye past them without a chance they'll pick it up. Static positions. I'll scoot this eye down the other way to make sure you don't get a patrol on your tail." Static positions meant they were either a guard post, or had otherwise been in the same general area for a minute and a half.

"Roger. Moving." He motioned for the team to follow. The floors and the walls of the Thulian HQ seemed to be made of the same slick-looking metal that their trooper armor and death machines were. John felt his disgust for the Nazi material welling up in him, and used the emotional capital. His team transversed the distance quickly, stacking up at the intersection with the main drag. John opened a pouch and pulled out one of his personal magic eyes that Vic had given him, dropping it to the floor. It rolled into the middle, invisible, yet patching in a full view of the hallway into his HUD.

"I believe that is the Welcome Wagon." Vic could see everything that he could see, through his HUD implant and, of course, the magic eyes. *"Nothing coming up on your six o'clock."*

Unfortunately, Vic was right: six Thulians. Three were part of a checkpoint guard position, while the other three looked to be technicians of some sort, working on a sparking panel. *Looks like the kinetic bombardment did a little more damage than we thought. Good.* Every Nazi was armed. John signaled for Mamona to come up to the front; she tapped Bear's shoulder, and the Russian automatically took up a rear-guard position. She looked to John, and he nodded to her. Mamona slung her rifle, bending down to kneel. Her brow screwed up in concentration, and she brought her gloved hands to her chest.

John saw the effect of what she was doing through his magic-eye camera. The closest Thulians, which included all of the technicians and two of the guards, completely froze in place. The last guard began to retch and heave violently, bile and vomit spilling to the floor.

"Go." John was the first around the corner, with Untermensch following close behind. Their rifles barked quietly, suppressed rounds stitching through the Thulians. In less than two seconds, all of the Nazis were dead. "Vic, any chatter?"

"So far internal freqs are full of nothing to concern you." How Vickie was patching into Thulian comm frequencies, he had no idea. Probably more of her magic stuff. *"A lot of general quarters palaver and emergency repairs on their internals, a lot of screaming and dying and attack orders on their externals."*

"Roger. Let the bastards burn. What's Gamayun an' the scopes say 'bout where to head from here?"

"Halt, halt, halt." There was a pause. It was long enough that she was probably talking to someone else. Gamayun, most likely. Gamayun was creating a map as they moved, staying a little ahead of them, using her own curious power of remote viewing. Unfortunately she couldn't "see" anything much further away from her own location than five miles. Needless to say, she was the best protected person on the battlefield today. *"Ahead five hundred yards. Right, right, ahead another five hundred. Down stairs on right. Stairs are clear. Stand by for change."*

The team proceeded. Vic warned them when to slow up, when to take cover to avoid a group of running Thulians, when to charge ahead. It went much faster than if they'd been going in without her near-omniscient Overwatch. It took a lot of energy to travel silently, though; John was feeling it when they reached their first destination: the main armory for the entire Thulian North American HQ. John floated his personal magic eye into the room; he saw rows and rows of evil-looking rifles, pistols, and crates of munitions. They were all housed behind some sort of clear door; it looked thick, and hardy. There were four Thulians in the room, all looking very nervous. The corridor floor here was polished stone, not metal, probably to prevent accidental electrical discharge into the munitions. Perfect for Vickie.

"You have two minutes. Patrol just came through. You'll have to take out the next one. And . . . mark." The HUD lit up with a countdown clock in the upper-right-hand quadrant of each teammate's vision. *"I love my job. When all this is over, you guys are stealth-returning all my overdue DVDs."*

John used a control on his belt to tilt his magic eye up and to the left. "Vic, question. I'm seeing what looks like fire suppression systems in this room. Can ya trigger 'em without alerting the rest of the base?"

"Good question. Watch for the patrol, let me noodle on it a second. Unter? Bare hand on floor please?" The Russian complied; he was the only team member with bare—though impossibly resilient—hands, discounting Bear, whose hands were titanium. It didn't take her very long. *"Some of that shite is unstable as hell. If I give it a bounce, it'll go off with a little fireball and that'll set off the suppression."*

"Keep that in mind. Might save us munitions." John kept his suppressed rifle trained down the hallway, careful not to peek the barrel around the corner.

"Roger. I can bounce on your signal."

"Go for it."

"Roger. Two guards, your ten and your three o'clock. Two guards, Unter's four and nine o'clock." There was another pause. *"And mark."* There was a shudder of the floor, a pop, a loud hissing sound, followed by angry shouts in German. John swung around the corner; his Thulian was right where Vicky had said, at his ten o'clock. Two bursts of suppressed fire from his and Unter's rifles, and all four Nazis were down. Some halon gas hung in the air, but not enough to be dangerous.

"Time to get to work. Bear, Mamona, plant the charges. Unter, take up position on the door; an' don't shoot me. It'd ruin my day." Bear and Mamona ran behind the counter of the armory; the transparent door to the main arsenal slid open after Pavel pressed the hand of one of the Kriegers to its reader-pad. They began to set the explosive charges, while John and Georgi took defensive positions on the door.

"Guys, drag the corpsicles over behind those crates. Can't be seen from the door." Vickie seemed to have eyes everywhere. *"Fewer internal alerts we set off before we blow this pop stand, the better."* Bear did so after he finished setting his last charge.

The last few digits of the countdown began flashing in John's HUD. *"Heads up. Incoming."*

The metallic footsteps of the patrol marked their approach, even over the hum of unfamiliar tech and the faint vibrations of floor, walls and ceiling.

Untermensch slapped his hand onto the weapon barrel of the first Nazi through the door; he jerked it towards the center of the room, and the Thulian followed, still gripping his weapon out of reflex. The rest of the patrol quickly rushed in, confused; they were greeted with a barrage of suppressed rifle fire. Unter unloaded the rest of his magazine into the trooper he had pulled through the doorway. John could see a quiet fury behind Georgi's eyes, carefully controlled. There was a lot of rage built up in the man, left over and allowed to stew since the Great Patriotic War.

With the charges in place, the squad moved out to their next objective. *Gravity generators. Gonna have to be sure to document as much as we can.* He spared another thought for Sera, this one of gratitude. If she hadn't filled him with her own strength, he'd have already collapsed by now. *Gotta make this count... and get home.*

Motu and Matai were providing security on the door, with one of Vix's cams stuck right outside it, scanning for threats. The room had been easy to take; there were only four Nazis in it, after all, and they didn't have power armor in this part of the facility. What had been hard was leaving one of them alive, and relatively unscathed. Bulwark had taken care of that; it's amazing what a well-placed rifle butt will do for a man's ability to stay conscious.

Bulwark stared for a moment at the unconscious Thulian, then at Djinni. His jaw tensed. "Djinni—" he gestured at the body. "This would be your job."

"This is gonna play merry-hell with my radar," he bitched, then set about stripping the unconscious Thulian. Roughing in a face—just taking the face he was wearing and giving it a slightly more Thulian cast—didn't involve having to rip it off, and he didn't see any good reason to do a full copy of the guy in his tighty whities on the floor. While the others scuttled around setting charges, he sat on the floor, staring at one of Magic Girl's wizard-cams, while she fed the image of his own face back to his retinas. Boy, was *that* trippy. The eye slits were longer, the nose was more of a suggestion than a real nose, the nostrils were slits. Damn near no upper lip, and a thin, long lower one. Skin a jaundiced yellow. And Victrix had supplied him with something to replicate the orange-cinnamon smell of the Thulians; he sprayed himself down with her concoction.

He stood up. "Ready for my close-up."

Bulwark gave him a long stare. "That'll do."

When everyone was ready, Djinni lead the way. The team stayed several paces behind him, allowing him to go around corners and into hallways first. This paid off, when Vix warned them *"Infil One, little busy here"* and they went on ahead because the clock was ticking. She was juggling two infiltration teams in an enemy base that was buzzing with activity, as well as helping coordinate comms and intelligence for the ground battle raging above; it was understandable. Red was able to hide his surprise when he rounded a corner and almost bowled over a Thulian. The Nazi spilled what looked like a stack of manuals, cursing loudly in German.

"Entschuldigen mir bitte, Uberlautnet," Red bleated, then groveled. *"Das tut mir sehr leid—"* He bent down as if to pick up the manuals, then shot up like an uncoiled spring, catching the Nazi under the chin with his hardened fist. The Thulian went down like a felled tree. Red knelt down to throw the Nazi over his shoulder, and then behind a stack of crates in a small alcove.

"When did you start learning German?" Motu asked.

"When I needed to."

The team moved faster. They didn't run into any more Thulians along the way, so they actually arrived ahead of schedule. Red placed his back against the wall just outside of the supposed Command and Control room for the entire headquarters. He could hear a lot of movement and talking inside. *Looks like the good guys upstairs are keeping them busy. Since we're not dead, they haven't figured our angle out yet.*

"That's an awful lot of talking going on in there . . . and what I don't like is they don't sound panicked." That was Vix in his ear. *"Lemme boost it."*

Red's German wasn't good enough for him to make out what the rapid-fire conversation was all about. But Vix could.

"Oh, bloody hell." Her voice took on that flat tone that told him they were probably in trouble. *"Listen up, peeps. What they just said was that they aren't worried, that they've only engaged about a twentieth of their force out there and it was the second-stringers at best. And that now that we've made them, they are on schedule to pack up and move the rest to a new base by this time tomorrow. There's several hundred of the bastards outside. You do the math."*

"That doesn't change the mission," Bulwark said firmly. "If anything, this makes it more critical."

"That's a big ten-four. Just wanted you guys to know what's riding on it. Already relayed the intel. RD, gimme an eye, please."

Djinni pulled one of the eyes out of a pouch, and held it in the palm of his hand. The weird little dingus that looked like something out of a steampunk illustration slowly levitated up, then winked out of sight. He waited while she scouted with it.

"They aren't even the least little bit alert. We can do this the easy way," she said. *"Showtime, Djinni."*

Red took a limpet from Motu, and stuck a bandaid on it. The moment the adhesive strip went down, the limpet faded from view. The bandaid happened to have a drop of Vix's own blood on it, which was kind of creepy actually, but gave her spell contact. Funny that she entrusted that packet of bandaids to him...

He walked in, trying to look as if he was there to get something, spotted a warmer full of empty coffeepots, and headed for them. He was in the middle of what could have been any big Command and Control center he'd ever seen: desks, lots of monitors, that skewed Thulian control stuff and odd-shaped keyboards and a few sleeves. And...they drank coffee?

"Frischen Kaffee?" asked one of the men at the nearest desk as Red picked up pots and left the limpet.

Red nodded and replied, *"Jawohl, Mein Herr."*

"Gut. Macht schnell."

Red walked out just as calmly, taking up his position next to the door. Matai handed him his rifle, and he checked the chamber to make sure it had a round in it. Bulwark nodded to him. Retrieving a small control with a nice, shiny red button on it, he said, "Ready?" He waited for the nod. Thought of Amethist. "Ignition." He depressed the button, and a too-loud explosion rocked the hallway. Not wasting precious seconds, Red pocketed the control, bringing his rifle up. The team filed in behind him; the entire control room was full of smoke, with several small fires started where the distraction device had caught combustibles. The Thulians were all on the floor and dazed, some that were the closest to the blast being completely unconscious. The team took them down easily, gunfire and rifle strikes finishing off any resistance.

Once Bulwark was certain the room was clear, he slung his rifle and walked over to what he had been briefed on, specifically: a mainframe computer.

The eye unstealthed. It whizzed over the control areas, then stopped. Some sort of plug popped out of its rear, and it backed into a slot. Vix sighed with satisfaction in his ear. *"Bingo. Come to Momma."*

While he busied himself with that and the two brothers providing security on the door, Red and Silent Knight began to gather up any physical intelligence they could: hard-copy, maps, and manuals, mostly. "Overwatch, go private. How're we doing, Vix?" Red had switched over to a direct line with her.

"It's getting ugly outside. JM's commies are on track so far; I gave them the bad news, so the Reds on Infil Two are trying to plant the rest of their ordinance for the biggest possible boom. Good news: the Nazis never figured on anyone unfriendly getting to this computer station, so there's no firewalls, no ice, and no interference."

"So, what're you waiting for? Labor Day?"

"May Day, bonehead. Hush. I'm downloadin' as fast as the connection'll let me. Silly me, I didn't have you pack a T-1 line." In spite of everything going on, he almost grinned. Put her in her safe spot and damn if she didn't have moxie.

Once the team was done, Bulwark gave them the signal to get ready to move. Bulwark unstrapped his backpack; it was his mission-specific loadout, and one that he was going to particularly enjoy getting rid of. Not because it was heavy, but because of what it would do. He plugged it in place of the eye. "Operative Victrix; be ready to initiate the infestation, once we're safely away. On your word, we'll activate the package."

"Roger. I'm giving them a dose of their own worm, and I think I can get it outside this complex."

"Let's be a nuisance. Double-time, everyone." The team jogged out of the command room, running down the hallways that Vickie told them to. They managed to avoid any Thulians, but that wouldn't last.

"Fly my little virii, fly!" The lights began to flicker almost instantly. The vibration in the floors and walls took on a ragged edge. Then both lights and vibration cut out.

"Murdock, this is Bulwark. Light the match." With that, Bulwark pressed a button on his belt controller.

The lights flickered, then cut out. *"Murdock, this is Bulwark,"* came the voice in his ear. *"Light the match."* There was a muted *whump,* and the floor shook slightly. The HUD flipped over to night-vision mode, triggered, no doubt, by Vickie. The team had IR illuminators on their shoulders, to make up for the lack of any ambient light.

John looked over to Untermensch, the Russian gleaming dully in the green glow of NV. "I've been waiting all day to do this." He flipped the safety cover off of the detonator, and depressed the button. A half-dozen similar explosions shook the entire base. The floor, walls, ceiling all began to damn near *hum* with the vibration of something deep inside of the base going very wrong. The team was in what John thought was the biggest room he had ever seen indoors. It was impossibly big, given the dimensions of the mountain and how deep they were supposed to be. *The boys at Echo are gonna be really interested in tryin' to figure out what this means.*

Situated on a gangwalk, they had something like a hangar or storage area combined with barracks, containing the entire massed Thulian army below them. It appeared that the Thulians weren't very conscious of the importance of interior layout; thousands of trooper suits were lined up, mixed in with the open-air living quarters.

"Ranger isn't gonna like this, Yogi. You gonna steal their pickanick baskets?"

"Somethin' like that, Vic." Emergency lighting came to life, and loud, warbling Klaxons sounded. "That's our cue." The Thulians below had begun to scramble, readying weapons, getting into suits, and generally panicking.

"Why is it that people never, ever look up?"

John slung his rifle over his shoulder, readying himself. "Everyone, stay behind me. Vic, kill the NVGs. We won't need 'em in a second."

The HUD went to standard. Vickie switched to Russian. *"Ja ne mogu perezagruzit' eto! Vi nadeli svoi shlemi? On sobiraetsja sam vse obstrelivat'."* And for Mamona's benefit *"I can't flare-screen with these things. You guys got face shields on? He's gonna do a one-man Arc Light."* The rest of the team exchanged a look, and snapped down their face-shields, forgotten until now. John breathed once, deeply, closing his eyes, trying to relax and focus. Visualized what he needed to do. He was going to try something he had never tried before, and wasn't quite sure what would happen.

He felt the fires, and they came freely. It started along his arms, racing down his hands. He breathed again, and opened his eyes.

And for the first time that he could remember, he *let go.*

The fires rippled outwards from his arms, covering the distance to the closest Nazis in an instant, mushrooming out from the center point that was himself. The entire room, as big as several stadiums, filled with flames in seconds, billowing and animate clouds of fire seeking victims. The firestorm rocketed across the floor; every unsuited Thulian was instantly burned alive, screaming. Explosions rang out; exposed and storaged munitions cooking off. John felt the fire feeding off of him, bleeding him dry. But he had to keep it going, had to take out as many of them as possible, had to make it count.

"Holy CRAP!" Almost as quickly as the fires had erupted, a thin sheet of rock fragments cascaded down from the ceiling, and in a few moments, had melded together to make a shield between the rest of the team and the fires. *"Warn a girl next time!"*

Before John could reply to her, a stabbing pain shot through his chest and his vision flared white from the trauma.

John's fires abruptly gave out, and he coughed up a gout of blood, falling to his knees. Mamona bent down to help him, but he waved her off, snatching his rifle from his back. "Take out the suits, before they figure out what happened." John was pale, sweating and shaking, but he managed to raise his rifle. "Weapons free; take 'em down."

Vickie stared in horrified fascination at the carnage under the walkway. She'd expected something big. What John had unleashed was... epic. Fire and brimstone raining down, apocalypse on a small scale, if a cavern the size of five football fields could be considered small. The backblast alone would have taken down the team if she hadn't shielded them. She could magically "feel" the barrier shake with the impact of the superheated air coming from the firestorm.

This is it. This is going to kill him. It's killing him now. They have to get out.

She dropped her control on the shield; the steaming fragments fell apart, and rained off the walkway. John was the first to open fire, prone on the walkway. The rest of the team soon followed suit, with Bear firing off plasma blasts next to his PPSh. The remaining troopers, their numbers drastically reduced, were cut to ribbons; not a one had time to return fire, and those that were out of range were still busy recovering.

"All right, people, go go go! Otlichno, poshli, poshli, poshli! Ne obiazatel'no atakovat' etix, oni pokoiniki! You don't need to finish this bunch off, they're toast!" When they hesitated, she added, *"What? Zshdesh vodki e ikri? Ja skazala idi! Are you waiting for the caviar and vodka to go with the toast? I said GO!"* Untermensch and Mamona helped John to his feet, after which he shook them off. The team ran for the exit, rifles at the ready.

Just because you're paranoid, that doesn't mean that they are not out to get you. If Vickie had a motto by which she lived her life, that was it.

So besides everything else, she had sensor balls peppered all over the edges of the battlefield, looking for anything . . . weird. And she was not particularly surprised when ten of them went off at once, all in a far corner, where there wasn't supposed to be a hangar door.

Well, it wasn't a hangar door.

It was bigger, much bigger, than a hangar door, even by Thulian standards.

She zoomed in cameras as the enormous sheet of rock slid up.

"Oh no," she whispered. "Oh no. Oh *hell* no."

It was an orb. But it wasn't like any orb that had ever been seen before. There were no tentacle ports, no weapons ports, just a single slit that bisected the entire thing. A slit that began to glow a deep and ominous, sickly yellow-green.

"Overwatch: Command: speed-dial Mom." she snapped, her hands flying over the keys. "Command, speed-dial School."

Just because you're paranoid . . . you need to have contingencies.

"Grey, packets."

<*On it.*> Her familiar sat poised over the boxes of USB packets.

Both phones were answered on the first ring, almost simultaneously. "It's bad."

"Roger," said Moira Nagy crisply, and "We have your back, honey," drawled the head of the De Danaan School for Talented Teens.

"Grey, plug in Mom and Charlotte." The familiar pawed through the boxes, then delicately extracted two. He picked them up one at a time with raccoonlike hands, and plugged them into USB slots on a hub at his own eye level.

"Command: phone, disconnect." She cut the calls off. This was her backup. There was no way she would have enough strength all by herself to even dent a regular orb, much less that thing. And . . . paranoid meant prepared, so she had contacted her old school and her mother to put together—well, call them magical power supplies. Two circles of magicians, one headed by her mother in Washington and one at the end of Hudson Bay in Canada at the school, stood ready to feed her magic power. She was connected by blood to her mother's, and by four years of living and working there to the school's—and most of the teachers there would be in that circle. Thirty seconds had passed and the glow at that slit was increasing as it rose out of the bay.

She panned the cameras, looking for the nearest person she had a packet for. It happened to be someone who was already flat on the field, bleeding into the soil. Good enough. "Grey, I need Gavotte."

Got. Grey plugged in another packet. She flew a stealthed ball over to the thing and set it down on the top and hoped they wouldn't notice. It had been forty-five seconds since the hangar door opened. "Command: open, Hammer Freq, command, Ping Hammer."

She spared a glance for the Angel Flight countdown and cursed. They were too close for an abort, but she warned them anyway. "Angels, Birds, Danger. Big Bad Bogie on the ground."

The response from Space Command came gratifyingly quickly. *"Roger, Overwatch? Got a sitch?"*

She fed her cam to Air Force Space Command just as Angel Flight came over. A *sheet* of energy sliced out of the slit and started angling up to the sky, disintegrating everything on the way as the Thulians tried to target the fighters. She nearly sobbed with relief as they managed to pull straight up and out of range. The response from Space Command was unprintable.

The orb rotated down again; the glow dimmed. Evidently this thing had a warm-up and cool-down. But a turret on the bottom popped out, and something like a dish scanned the field.

There was an Echo meta—Cyber-something; he was a multiple amputee, one of the Echo OpTwos pulled out of the wreckage after the Invasion, that had been fitted with a prototype prosthesis, some kind of powered armor. He was at the very outskirts of the fighting, taking on five troopers by himself. The orb's dish centered on him, and a nearly invisible, sickly-yellow beam shot out from it, connecting with the meta's back. Vickie recognized what had happened almost as soon as the beam connected; selective EMP weapon, the color must just have been ambient bleed-over into the visible. The armor pretty much froze in place; the meta's head jerked around frantically, his body no longer moving at all. He didn't have time to scream, being torn apart by several Thulian energy cannons in the next instant.

She swallowed down her nausea. *Bastards. Focus, girl, focus. More people will die if you don't.* "I'm about to open the ground under them. I want you to hit them and keep hitting them until you run out of rocks." She sent them the exact grid GPS coordinates she was getting from her little probe. She didn't dare paint a laser dot on it; they might notice.

"Roger that."

"Five from my mark, fire for effect. Mark."

Absently she heard the countdown start. She took her hands off her controls and narrowed her concentration. This was going to take everything she had, and then some.

She gathered magical energy to her: from the earth, from her storage crystals, from the two circles, from herself. She muttered under her breath, an archaic Celtic chant she had learned from her mother, while in her mind, ever-changing strings of numbers, formulas, and diagrams glowed. But most of all, it was will, the will of an expertly trained mage, imposing itself on the world. Not just willpower; this was the ability to focus, in the way that a laser piercing a diamond is focused, and to hold that focus for as long as it took to get the job done. The energies gathered until she felt she would burst, trying to hold it all inside of herself. And as the count reached zero, she wrenched at the earth beneath the sphere.

It didn't happen immediately; the earth groaned and shook, for she had never done anything this *big* before. Stationary cameras shook with the rumble of the localized earthquake, and in some places the combat ground to a halt as people fought for footing. Sweat streamed down her face; magic was like telekinesis in a way, it worked best on small things. Big things like this . . . it felt as if she was trying to tear the earth apart with her bare hands—

Now people had noticed the new sphere. The Thulians took heart from its appearance and renewed their already effective attacks, while her freqs hummed with curses in English and Russian and a few other languages. She ignored them all. This *had* to work.

The earth split with a groan and a rumble, in a crevasse big enough to swallow the sphere.

A fraction of a second later, the Hammer came down. Huge clouds of earth and rock shot up into the air from the first two strikes; the aiming system wasn't perfect, and had a harder time with small moving objects. The third, however, hit the orb directly.

It didn't even dent it; a force field flared around it, absorbing the damage.

But *not* all the kinetic energy. The Hammer pounded the sphere into the bottom of her crevasse.

She opened it again, deeper. Just in time for another Hammer.

And again. And again.

Her entire world narrowed to that spot of earth's crust and the orb being pounded into it, buried by the near strikes, pounded deeper by the direct ones. The entire area shook from the impacts; they were only using their intermediate projectiles, comparable to heavy artillery. Dust choked through the battlefield, cutting visibility down; she could still see muzzle flashes and energy cannons, and muted explosions. Sweat soaked her clothing, her hands clenched the arms of her chair and there was a roaring in her ears.

Again. And again.

Each time the Hammer fell, it drove the orb deeper into the earth. Each time she opened the earth further, she felt strength pouring out of her. But she couldn't, daren't, stop now.

She could hardly see, scarcely breathe, when faintly, through the roaring, she heard Space Command say, "*Hammer terminated. It's burned out; we're inoperative. Good luck, Overwatch. Space Command out.*"

Using the very last of her strength, she brought the sides of the half-mile-deep hole crashing inward. Then she passed out.

Bella's jaw dropped, as she watched the feed from the cams. *How the hell is she—*

Somehow, Vickie and Hammer were pounding that mega-orb into the ground like a tent peg. She heard Space Command sign out; there was a last shaking that dropped some of the combatants to their knees, and a huge plume of dirt and dust erupted from the hole.

Before Bella could react, even to call Vickie, she heard a pounding on the bulletproof glass door to the balcony outside her office. She looked up; it was Sera, and she instantly knew that Vickie was down and needed them. She slapped the door control and vaulted over her desk, reaching the door just as it opened, Sera seized her in arms that were a hundred times stronger than they looked (if not more) and shot up into the sky in a plume of fire.

The angel flew like a missile: straight up, and straight down. They landed on the roof of the apartment building, and Bella wrenched open the access door and raced down the stairs four at a time. She already had Vickie's keys in her hand, but the Seraphym, speeding behind her, gestured, and the door flew open just as she got there. So did the door to Vickie's Overwatch room.

Take over for her. I will tend her. That was not Bella's first instinct, but she obeyed the Seraphym without an argument, flinging herself into the chair. Things were already going south for the Infil teams.

Echo One was well behind cover when Natalya gave the order. "Fire, sections one, two, three; fire, fire, fire." The Nazis, being pressed with a large number of missiles and grenades, had taken up the only defensible cover positions from their direction of approach. With the planning that had gone on prior to this operation, the Commissar had seen to it that every spot was properly "accommodating" for the *fashista*. Claymore mines, modern oversized flame fougasses, and antitank mines—all daisy-chained together—went up in fantastic explosions, with waves of flame and shrapnel sweeping through the Nazi ranks.

"Weapons free, all squads. Commence firing!" Even more rockets and grenades streaked towards the troopers and Nazi death machines. The first few waves of troopers were torn to shreds, blown to pieces by the planted explosives or launched munitions. Those from her squads with the capability used their powers from a distance, with varying levels of effectiveness.

The Nazis renewed their ranks; with hundreds of the hulking monsters trudging towards the Echo and CCCP positions, there were plenty of bodies to soak up the punishment.

Saviour had a fleeting recollection of little Fei Li "dancing" among the troopers in Red Square, her sword flashing, reflecting the light from the fires, with an uncanny resemblance to a miniature lightning bolt. Secretly her heart ached, and she wished that her old friend were here beside her; just as quickly as the thoughts had come, she swept them away.

"Commence Lei Gong bombardment," she said, bitterly, reciting the code name she had personally chosen. The Commissar heard the dull *thwump* of mortars being fired. She kept her eyes fixed on the Thulian positions; they had begun firing their energy cannons, destroying at least two of the southern ridge rocket positions. She bit her lip and concentrated, pushing back the anguish at seeing even more comrades dying. *This is war, now. A real war.* The mortars exploded, detonating two dozen meters above the Thulians. Hundreds of thousands of what looked like white, shiny streamers covered the battlefield. The streamers, only as thick as a ribbon, adhered to the troopers and the landscape around them. "Trigger Tian Mu. Mark." As per the plan, they had set up several very, *very* expensive and increasingly rare Echo broadcast energy generators in the valley. They were used, primarily, to power localized defensive shields and some of the weapons that the Commissar had commissioned for this operation. Now, the output for the broadcasters ramped up. This was one of Tesla's gifts, an experimental weapon in short supply. *Let's see how the* fashista *like this.*

The streamers, now affixed seemingly harmlessly to nearly all of the entrenched Thulian troopers, were all high-efficiency conductors, specifically tuned to the frequency of the Echo broadcast generators. Most of the Thulian troopers were cooked in their suits; some even exploded, blown apart by gigavolts of electricity. Dozens of her own soldiers commenced fire; the main part of the Nazi force were still advancing and untouched by their secret "electric mortars," and returned their fire.

There were some patches, however, where the Nazis were being cut down with . . . suspicious ease. Saviour frowned. At the battle in Red Square, they were impermeable to damage until they were heated to the glowing point. Here . . . and there . . . and there—mere rifle fire and rocket fire was taking them down, without the Krieger armor having been made vulnerable prior.

For a moment, she suspected some trickery. Fake suits with nothing in them? But no . . . no, they were writhing and dying there.

She pulled down a visor, ignored until now. "Overwatch," she said in a commanding voice.

"Da, Commissar." It was Gamayun, not Vickie, that answered.

"Am seeing odd patches where *fashista* are taking great damage for no good reason."

"Checking now." There was a mixed babble of Russian with a touch of English as the Gamayun consulted with someone on another channel. Saviour's visor lit up with a battlefield overlay. *"This where you're talking about?"* The patches glowed with red light.

"Da."

"Those places are within five hundred yards of an Echo Broadcast unit. Each one."

Before the Commissar could ponder this revelation, the Thulians made a push. They were moving forward, and taking heavy casualties; but with so many hundreds of them, they could afford to. She made a snap decision. "Molotok, Chug, Soviette, on me! *Davay, davay, davay,* comrades!"

"*Sestra,* is wise for field commander to put own head on chopping block?" Molotok mocked. "Then again, is not much of a wise head up for the chopping!"

"Commissar," Soviette interjected. *"Ja ostanus' v tilu chtobi pozabotit'sja o ranenih. Mi sobrali mnogih.* I'll being hang back, to police wounded." An explosion punctuated her sentence. "We are accumulating many."

"Da, fine! Rest of you, *davay!"* The Commissar broke from cover, leaping over and then kicking off of the large boulder that she'd previously been using for cover. She flew straight for a point where she'd intercept the Thulians; they wouldn't be expecting a charge to counter their own. Saviour shot a powerful blast at the nearest cluster of three Thulians; it exploded the ground in front of them in a marvelous shower of hot gravel and dust. Molotok had bounded nimbly down after her; he speared through the air, tumbling into a group of Thulian troopers. Coming up in a roll, he immediately began to chop, punch, kick, and elbow at them. His superstrong body, his metahuman gift combined with years of unparalleled martial arts expertise, began to cut through and knock down the armored suits. Chug plodded after his comrades, bellowing his rage at the foes that had hurt his friends in Moscow. The rockman inelegantly smashed into the Thulians, hammering them with his fists. The Commissar had to look twice when she saw him literally rip one in half, breaking the suit over his knee and ripping top from bottom. Both halves

spurted blood, sparks, and hydraulic fluid into the desert soil. Confusion played over his craggy face for a moment before he bellowed again and moved on to the next foe.

Of course. We are within five hundred yards of a broadcaster…

Saviour kicked off into the air again, charging her fist with her own dangerous metahuman energy. She caved in a Thulian helmet with a satisfying crunch of crushed metal and bone; the Nazi clunked to the ground like a sack of hammers, utterly dead. The Commissar stole a glance over her shoulder. Soviette dashed from behind a boulder half covered in flaming debris, deftly jumping between metahuman combatants. One of the rocket teams from the ridge was still alive. Jadwiga wove her way through the fighting as if she was merely running an obstacle course, dodging explosions and energy cannon fire, stopping short of a knot of Thulian suits, and then running again to miss being crushed by a Nazi trooper. Saviour stopped, staring, her mouth falling slightly open with disbelief. Sovie reached the barely moving metahuman, hooked her hands under his arms, and began to drag him to cover. It was one of the most amazing displays of bravery that Natalya had ever seen from anyone, let alone from her friend and comrade Soviette.

Not wasting any time to dwell on the miraculous feat, Saviour screamed a hellish battle cry and launched herself at another pair of Nazis, fists charged with more destructive energy.

Movement on the screen caught Verdigris' attention. He glanced at it sharply. The Seraphym was on the balcony outside Belladonna's office.

There was a brief flash of blue beside the fire. Then both of them were gone, shooting straight up like a missile, moving too fast for the camera to track.

He could only stare at the monitor and grit his teeth.

Vix wasn't answering hails on the comms, and that was *very bad,* in the grand scheme of things. Which was saying something, considering Bulwark's team was pinned down at an intersection by two groups of Thulians.

Bulwark shouted, "Grenade out!" Red manipulated his ear drums to close against the blast and pressure, saving him the trouble of having to stuff his hands against his head. A Thulian staggered away from where the grenade had gone off; Red dropped him with a burst from his rifle.

"We need to get out of this cave, and soon! This place is shaking apart!" It was the gravity drives; one of the primary objectives for the CCCP infiltration team was to plant charges in strategic places around the base. Apparently, they'd managed to do the generators right.

"I know! Keep firing! We'll have to punch our way out!"

"Which way's out?" That was Matai. He had a point. Without Vix to guide them—

Red closed his eyes; he had to remember how the corridors had *felt* on the way in . . . what turns they'd made. This wasn't the first time he'd had to retrace blind. It wasn't even the first time he'd had to do it while being shot at.

It was, however, the first time he was having to do it during what felt like an earthquake, with gunfire and explosions going on around him.

That way? Maybe. Probably. Hell, any way was better than staying there. "This way!" he yelled, and made a break for it.

He made it just past the first intersection, when an armored trooper stepped out from around the corner. Between him and the rest. An armored trooper with functional energy cannons.

How the hell did he fit in there? Red wondered, as he stared in petrified fascination at the business end of the cannon. There was a sort of whirlpool of dim fire in the barrel as it ramped up—

Red got body-slammed by the armored trooper as Bull's force field rammed into him, literally kicking him down the corridor.

He actually glanced off the hurtling trooper, getting slammed into the side of the corridor as the unguided "missile" went past.

He was still lying there, trying to get breath back in his lungs, when his comm went live again.

"Infil One, Infil One, do you read?"

That was a voice he knew . . . but not the one he expected. Fortunately Bulwark was able to respond. "Roger, we copy . . . Bella?"

"Vick's down. I don't have her magic, but I have your HUD feeds, I have her map, and I have your position on it. One hundred feet, right, right, right."

Red coughed. "Darlin', yer an angel."

"Angel's next to me. Move your buns, people. I think you have incoming. And that trooper's getting up."

"Motu! We need you, brother!" The two brothers nodded, then leaned forward, touching foreheads together momentarily. Motu threw a grenade towards the direction where they needed to go, rolling into the hallway seconds after the explosion. He dropped his rifle to the ground. Red could swear he saw the rifle warp, bend, and then coil from the floor and up Motu's leg. The Samoan concentrated, and more debris gathered to him; pieces of Thulian weapons and armor, shell casings . . . the entire hallway began to creak. It wasn't from the growing earthquake, signs that the generators were going critical; this was localized. The metal plating buckled around Motu, as if he had his own personal high-gravity field. Lighting panels and electrical conduits ripped free from the walls and ceiling, spraying out tremendous showers of sparks. Entire sections of the plating deformed, rent away from the walls, torn to fit to Motu's body. The brave, beautiful bastard actually *roared,* and looked like a nightmarish scrap heap come to life. The dazed Thulians finally recovered enough sense to try to shoot at him.

Covered with the very materials they'd used to make their base, he was protected from any harm they could do him. But they had no such protection from him. Motu began blindly battering and crushing the Thulians that had taken position behind the team, more plating from the hallway replacing his armor wherever it was damaged. Then again, the corridor was narrow enough that he didn't have to see to hit them. "My brother will cover our retreat! Let's get out of this damned place!"

Red caught Bulwark's eye again, and nodded. Bulwark nodded back.

"That's the turn. Right, right, right. I'm taking you out the way you came in, start praying no walls have caved in."

"Is our ride still there?"

"So far. You better get there before someone jacks it."

John was grateful that Unter had memorized their route; he was too out of it to remember. The hallways all looked the same: scrambling Nazis, electrical fires, and other assorted chaos. *This entire place is going to go up. Hope we didn't do our job too well, an' become toast with it.* John whirled to his left, snapping off a burst of rifle fire at a Thulian that had raised a pistol. The man crumpled, dead before he hit the floor.

"We are getting close, Murdock; there are more Nazis." Unter grunted, pausing to fire several long bursts from his rifle. "Many *fashista.*" The team kept running. John could see his vision going black around the edges; he shook his head to try to dispel it, but to no effect. *This is it. I'm runnin' on empty. Christ, they're gonna have to carry me soon enough.*

"Infil Two, Infil Two, do you read?"

Unter responded. "We read—Victrix? What is happening?"

It was Belladonna Blue's voice.

"Vick's down, I'm on the comm. I have her map with you and your path on it. Right, left, right, then up the stairs on the right again. You're about to meet up with Infil One. Don't strafe each other."

The team came to the intersection, everyone taking a sector and covering it with their rifle. Mamona shouted, "Look!" John heard a lot of gunfire: rifles, same model that his team was carrying. He could also see the glow of Thulian energy weapons being discharged, the ambient light splashing off of the hallway panels. Bulwark's team careened around the corner and into the intersection; several members from both teams leveled rifles at each other, lowering them an instant later when recognition registered, or Bella yelled at them.

John coughed, more blood coming up onto the back of his glove; he wiped it off on his pant leg, nodding to Bulwark. "Good to see y'all are still alive."

"You aren't going to be if we don't get you out of here," Bulwark said grimly, looking at the blood trickling out of the side of John's mouth.

John nodded, shouldering his rifle. He gestured with his off hand. "Blue says that the exit is thataway. Shall we, gents?" Motu was still at the mouth of the corner where Bulwark's team had come from. The Thulian rayguns were firing almost constantly, picking at his armor. The hallway reacted to his powers, tearing itself apart to replenish his protection.

"WILL YOU MOVE YOUR BLOOMIN' ARSES?" Bella shouted. *"This is no time for a tea break!"*

The team responded by running as fast as possible, while allowing Motu's bulky form to provide them with a moving shield. They reached the hangar bay without having to kill too many more Nazis; few of them were willing to put enough effort into fighting, as opposed to saving their own skins. John surveyed the situation in an instant; there were a few officers ineffectually shouting orders, and even fewer people listening to them. Almost all of the base personnel were trying to find a vehicle, or running with a weapon. "So, straight up the middle? Kill anybody in the way?"

"Straight ahead, your ride is parked at your front left of the hangar. Uh, your ten o'clock?"

It seemed as if the entire base bucked sideways like an angry bronc, right then. Everyone hit the floor, their footing taken out from under them, with Motu being the exception. "Base is giving out," John said, hoarsely. "If'n we're goin', now's the time."

"Copy that, Vick's sensor packs are all redlining. You don't have long."

He looked to Mamona and Silent Knight. "Care to give the opposition somethin' to think 'bout?"

Both of the metas nodded. Mamona bent down at the entrance to the hangar, closing her eyes. Silent Knight braced himself, being careful to point his helmet with all of them behind him. Bulwark tapped them both on the shoulder at the same time saying, "Now." Dozens of Nazis doubled over instantly, puking their guts out or going into seizures. Those still in armor vibrated; the Knight was using either a frequency too high to hear, or too low; whichever, maybe both at once, it was rattling anyone in metal to pieces. Sparks flew from the joints as the armor malfunctioned.

"Move it!" John shouted, lurching forward and almost tripping over his own feet. The base was shaking itself apart, the vibrations were so violent now. Explosions sprayed shrapnel and debris everywhere, and those Thulians still able to stand were scrambling frantically. Some of the Nazis noticed the teams running for a Death Sphere. Most didn't care, but a few were well-trained enough to try and shoot at them. Soviet Bear took a plasma blast in his left arm; he spun with the impact, leveling his PPSh at the offending Thulian and unloading the rest of the drum magazine into the man. "That was being made by genius of Soviet science, *kulak!*" His mechanical arm melted to the deck, cut off at the elbow, and he kept running.

Matai took a conventional rifle round through the thigh; he didn't even have time to fully crumple to the ground before Motu had scooped his brother up in a fireman's carry, shielding him with his massive form. John switched his rifle to his off hand, chucking a grenade with the other. The explosion had satisfying effect on a group of Thulians trying to take cover behind a stack of weapons crates.

Djinni's hands grew long claws, and he launched ahead of them, grimly slashing at unarmored troopers.

Luckily, the area immediately around their transportation was clear of threats. Untermensch and Djinni were the first into the Death Sphere. There were two Thulian troopers, their plasma pistols on the floor, at the controls prepping the craft for flight. "Good afternoon, *fashista,*" said Untermensch. "Thank you for preparing our escape for us." The two metahumans leapt for the Thulians, impervious hands and wicked claws removing the opposition before the Nazis had time to reach for their own weapons. The rest of the team scrambled onto the ramp of the Thulian sphere, throwing the Nazi bodies out. Motu hefted his brother into the craft; his armor sloughed off with a clatter. He ducked below a plasma blast, inches above his head, clambering into the hatch just before it closed.

Bulwark plopped down into the pilot's seat, his arms reaching into the control sleeves; he didn't even bother to attach his safety harness. "Bella, time?"

"GO!" Bella screamed. *"It's going crit in there!"*

The Death Sphere lurched forward, no pretense of being damaged. Bulwark gritted his teeth; they clipped several support struts for the hangar, bouncing off of another fleeing orb as they shot out of the hangar. The orb shot forward at incredible speed. John's vision was going out. He felt a cold chill creeping over him, and fought for breath. "Are we clear?" he managed to choke out.

"Yes—CRAP!" A massive shock wave slammed into the orb. John felt weightless for a moment, and everything slowed down. He saw Mamona's face, drawn tight and pale. He could see the blood from Matai's leg seeping through his brother's fingers. Untermensch looked unconcerned, and Pavel looked like he was having the time of his life. Time sped back up, and everyone was thrown forward, crashing into each other. John blacked out.

Natalya panted for breath, the dust and smoke thick in the air clinging to the roof of her dry mouth. *So damned many of the swine.* She collected her strange energies, blasting the head off of a Thulian that had left cover too soon. Since the Nazis had slowly awakened to the fact that they were taking more casualties than they should, they had pulled their numbers back to cover. Their advance was stopped, but the fighting was still brutal. Most of her forward rocket teams were dead—overrun or blasted by Death Spheres. The toll was not as bad as it had been in Red Square, or in Atlanta, but any loss was one too many.

Without the furthest rocket teams, the orbs had been getting closer; one had chanced to try to drop a squad of troopers directly on top of Saviour's team, behind their lines. Luckily, due to the proximity to the Echo broadcaster, they were able to finish the assaulting Nazis before they could do too much damage, collect too many kills. The Commissar called the Blue Angels off of Close-Air Support, retasking them to focus solely on making runs against the orbs. The decision had probably saved the entire valley from getting a thermite bath.

"*Sestra,*" Molotok called, throwing an armed grenade with fastball accuracy. "Might be thinking of doing something about our party guests, *da?*" His question was punctuated by the exploding grenade; a chorus of Thulian energy cannons answered, splitting the air and pulverizing boulders around Molotok's cover. "At least they can't shoot. Being hard when your targets shoot back, *nyet*!"

Enough. She cued the "egghead" channel. "Comrades. Is time for second surprise. Deploy Shi—Xi—Zho—" she stumbled over the designation. Curse these people for naming something after an Aztec god!

"*We jest call it th' TDR, Miz Commissar, ma'am,*" drawled the tech. "*Tesla Death Ray deployed.*"

It really wasn't called the "Tesla Death Ray"; that was just the affectionate name that the techs that set it up and manned it had mentioned. Its technical name was the "Xotol Heavy Armor and Light Armored Infantry Suppression Cannon," one of the space-age wonders garnered from Echo. The camouflaged emplacement was on the military crest of the peak at the Echo and CCCP's back; it gave a commanding view of the entire valley where the fight was still raging, and was one of the only places with flat enough ground to mount it. It took three of the rare and expensive portable Echo broadcasters to power it. Moments after she gave the command, the camouflage netting was stripped away; it was some sort of LED blanket that helped mimic the background. Silly to see up close, but at a distance it was a fairly convincing illusion.

The contraption looked like two oversized pincers on a cannon mount. Natalya spared a glance over her shoulder to watch; it was spitting forks of electricity, and she could feel the hair rising on her arms. "Heads down!" Even with her eyes slammed shut, she could see the terribly bright flash. There was a thunderous popping sound that hurt her ears; it sounded like an angry power line sparking out its vengeance.

The sorceress had worked her unsettling magic, implanting one of the HUD devices in her eye... somehow. It worked. And Victoria's method had not required surgery... but Natalya wondered if she ought to be disturbed that she was coming to accept the intrusion of magic into her life.

Still, one could not deny it was useful. And the wretched thing understood Russian, too. "HUD," she commanded, and the system activated. "Battlefield overlay."

An image within an image played over her HUD. She was watching the entire valley from five hundred feet up. It occurred to her that she could have probably been miles away in the sky, and still have seen the "TDR." It looked like a gigantic, brilliant blue-white bolt of lightning, a strike that would not flash away. It twisted and turned, tearing through the ground and the enemy at the rear of their formation. The beam seemed haphazard; it didn't fire straight, and was constantly writhing. It lashed left and right, and where it struck, Nazi troopers exploded, utterly decimated even where they were not close to the Echo broadcasters. The weapon crew canted the device skyward; the beam shifted, cutting through a formation of two Thulian orbs, and setting fire to a third. *What a person could do with ten of these...*

As suddenly as the murderous barrage had begun, it stopped. The lightning cannon sputtered off with a final thunderous pop; the Commissar could swear that everyone in the valley would probably have some sort of hearing damage.

Saviour swore. Then mentally shrugged. There had never been a guarantee of how long the thing would work. At least it had cut a decent swath in the *fashista* numbers. The advantage didn't last, however. Some of the surviving Thulian orbs had risen high above the battle; their energy cannons lashed out, destroying all of the closest Echo broadcasters. *They're softening up our positions for a push!* Several of the Echo metahumans that used tech powered by the broadcasters found their devices powerless; an energy shield fizzled into nonexistence, a bionic arm froze, a set of flying powered armor dropped out of the air, and so on down the lines.

"Comrades! *Vse ognennie sili na peredovuju!* All fire powers to the front lines!"

They would do this the hard way.

Where was the sorceress? Until now she had been more than adequate at steering the infiltration teams and giving the external force help. She had even coordinated with the Hammer at taking out that new orb at the mouth of the valley. So where was she—

As if on cue, the sorceress' channel crackled to life. But it was not her voice.

"Nat. Vick's passed out cold. Handling Infil from her console, it's all I can do."

Bah. But she infused her voice with confidence she in no way felt. "*Spasibo*, Bella. Infil is first priority. We are handling things out here." All right; she was trained and honed as a battle commander. Time to do things the old-fashioned way.

A new voice came over the comms. *"Commissar, we are, ah . . . in position. There's not much cover here."* It was Zmey, the tinkerer. She had anticipated a potential need to make large numbers of the enemy vulnerable at once, in case their air support was no longer operational. This looked like a necessary time to use her last trump card; three metahumans, Zmey and two Echo OpTwos, hidden safely where the Thulians would pass them without notice.

"Fire on my mark. Full power." She waited until she knew she had no choice. "Mark." There was a momentary pause, and then a huge cloud of flame belched from where Zmey and the others were positioned. The cloud extended over the massed Thulian ranks; it contorted, and then came slamming down. The heat was enough to make a fresh sweat break out over the Commissar; it felt like she was in a kiln on a hot day in Hell. Thulian energy beams shot out, going wildly into the sky or the mountains; switching to her bird's-eye view of the battlefield, she saw that nearly all of the enemy were bathed in flames. The firecloud contracted, dissipating into wisps of flame.

"Strike completed, Commissar—Nasrat!" A Thulian orb climbed over the hiding place for Zmey's squad.

Involuntarily, she gathered her energies and shot at the orb; she might just as well have been lobbing rocks at it. It ignored her in favor of the real threat, shooting twice, not at the squad, but at the face of the mountain beneath them. The entire section collapsed with a roar that swallowed up her own screamed curses. In her ear, Zmey shrieked, the sound cutting short as the thousands of tons of rock and earth crushed him and the two Echo Ops with him.

The firefight intensified; dozens more missiles and rockets slammed into the Thulians. They pushed forward, firing their energy cannons, ignoring their mounting losses. *If we die here, we die fighting. We die killing our murderers.* She threw a grenade, waited for its explosion, and then swept around the side of the boulder she had been using for cover. "*Davay,* comrades! *Za rodinu!* In defense of the Motherland!" It was the old battle cry, first her father's, now hers. He had used it at the Siege of Stalingrad that no one had expected to survive. CCCP knew it well. "Come, my wolves!" she shouted in English over the open comms. "Let us show them our teeth! *Podhodite, volki, pokashem im nashi zubi!*"

The entire world chose that moment to open up. A flash brighter than the lightning cannon lit the sky and washed the color out of everything; Natalya was thankful not to have been staring directly at whatever had done it. The fighting completely stopped as the entire valley began to shake itself to near pieces. The quake became so intense, even the Nazi troopers were taken from their feet; she saw one crushed under a falling piece of mountain.

It took the Commissar a few heartbeats to convince herself that she was still alive, after the shaking had stopped. Standing up, she scanned the battlefield, looking for what had caused the devastation. Some new weapon? Some terror device?

Bella Parker's voice called out over her comm. "*Red Leader, Red Leader. Infil scored. They're out there in one of the grounded orbs, please don't frag them.*"

Some of the Nazi troopers had begun to run. Others were surrendering, climbing out of their suits. All of the orbs had already changed their flight paths, and were climbing high into the sky. Very few of the remaining Thulians were still ready to fight. It was this last group that Red Saviour cared about. "Exterminate the *svinyas,*" she ordered, harshly. The surviving CCCP members growled or cheered raggedly, and waded in.

When he came to, everyone was a jumble of limbs and groans. "If anyone is being dead, take a number and being wait in line," said Untermensch, slightly muffled. "Is correct Soviet way."

Bear piped up. "Reminds me of time I was in harem in Tuscany."

"There are no harems in Tuscany, Old Bear," growled Unter.

"*Shto?*"

John untangled himself from someone's leg. "Can it, you two. Is everyone all right?"

Mamona groaned, shifting so she could sit up. "I think my arm's broken." A pause. "Yeah, definitely broken. Ow, sir."

Bulwark was next. "All of my teeth are loose. Besides that and some scratches, I'm fine."

"That was a helluva A-ticket ride. I wanta get back in line and do it again." Red was completely unscathed. He slapped the orange square that irised the hatch. It was now on the "side" of the orb, and next to John. "Anybody with me?"

The teams fell out of the hatch, those on the outside first helping everyone else out. Mamona and Matai were the toughest to get out, with special care attended to their injuries. Finally, everyone was out of the craft. John could see that there were large scars from the shrapnel of the explosion, with jagged tears in the hull.

"Guys, look." Mamona used her good arm to point back towards the Thulian base. "Just look at that."

A very large portion of the mountain where the Thulian North American Headquarters had occupied had exploded and then imploded, collapsing on itself. A gigantic cloud of dust had formed above where the main base was; plumes of black smoke streamed up from the crater itself where underground fires must still be burning. The nearest thing John had ever seen to it was the destruction caused by the Mt. St. Helen's eruption. Luckily, aside from the blast wave, the destruction was localized; after all, they weren't dead. There were dozens of Thulian Death Spheres streaking into the sky; he thought that a couple were actually on fire.

"*Oh, dear God in heaven.*" Bella sounded exhausted. "*Stand down, Infil. Most of the remaining Thulians are either running or surrendering. CCCP can mop up the rest... I think Echo had better concentrate on holding the Russian wolves off the ones surrendering if we want to collect any intel from prisoners.*"

"We did it," Bulwark said, sounding as if he didn't quite believe it. John nodded, then swayed on his feet. He collapsed to his knees, the world around him spinning and going dark.

CHAPTER THIRTY-THREE

Where There is Light

MERCEDES LACKEY AND CODY MARTIN

I didn't find out about any of this until long after—like most of what went on between Johnny and the Seraphym. I'm just as glad... because what in hell would I have been able to do? This wasn't a hack, and that sort of power...

Let's just say it is way above my pay grade. In the astronomical sense.

Seraphym had left him as long as she could. This was important to him, to his decision. Though it had cut her and flayed her with pain, she refrained from interfering so that he could earn what he needed.

A victory.

She looked up at Bella; linked closely as they were, Bella felt it too. She nodded. Before she had finished, Sera was already gone.

Traveling as fast as thought, she was at his side. She felt the shock, then the awe, of those who saw her, but these things were not important.

He was.

She scooped him up in her arms, wrapped him in her wings, and they were gone.

It was not often that she... well, she supposed that mortals would call what she did "teleportation" although that was not it exactly. It was more that she held still and let the world move... but she didn't do it often. She had, the day of the

Invasion. She did, occasionally, when she almost had to be in two places at once.

But she did so now. She folded herself and him inside time and space and unfolded them in his squat, letting him down on the mattress on the floor, then kneeling beside him and pouring life-force back into him. It was altogether like pouring water into a bucket that had very little bottom left.

John was ragged. His face was covered in ash, dirt, and a horrifying amount of blood. His stealth uniform was similarly covered, and he looked like the walking dead. His complexion was growing more and more pale, and he had stopped sweating; this was not a good sign for someone as sick as he was. John was conscious, if only barely; he was fighting for every moment, soon every breath.

She simply thought things into existence: a cool cloth to clean his face with, a cold glass of water to hold to his lips. When she had done everything she could do to make him physically comfortable, she simply took him in her arms and held him, cradled him, while she waited for some sort of equilibrium to happen. This was the crisis. He couldn't last past dawn. He looked up at her with glazed eyes, tried to speak.

Shh. Just think. I will hear it.

John, holding onto his stubbornness even now, chose to speak aloud. Each word was a struggle, with long pauses in between sentences; his sickness had particularly affected his lungs. "We did all right, didn't we? Got 'em good?"

She brushed damp hair out of his eyes. "You did, beloved. Every... what is it? Every mission goal accomplished. You did not even lose any team members."

He nodded, a small part of him comforted by her assurance. "I'm glad. It won't be enough though. Not just today, alone."

"This is at most a beginning." She knew he would not thank her to be any less than honest. And he knew this, already; this was no attempt on her part to influence his decision. It was, at most, verification. And that was critical. This *had* to be his own decision, with no outside influence from her. That had been made very clear to her.

It had been made clear to her... but it was also a choice. *You, too, have Free Will, Seraphym.* This was new and dangerous ground. In all this time, it had never occurred to her that she had such a thing, could make such a choice. Could make a wrong choice.

Could make the sort of choice that had led to some of her Siblings becoming the Fallen.

But he was at his weakest, and for her to exert that kind of influence . . . that would be wrong. Terribly wrong. If he chose against his own nature to please her . . . then he would not be, or not become, whatever it was he needed to be. Assuming he made the choice for life. And if he did not?

It was tempting to think of this as a test. But the Infinite did not test anyone; circumstances might test and try someone, but these were not tests contrived to weigh and measure them, to see if they passed or failed. The Infinite, which saw all things, which saw the paths that she could not, *would not* force a path. And perhaps John, despite their love, would choose to die. And she would continue here, the Instrument, and try to find a new path. That would be his choice, and she, as Instrument of the Infinite, would honor it. That was the truest, best face of love; that one honored the choices of another. So the Infinite showed its love for its creations, by honoring their choices.

Even, especially, when the choice hurt more than she had believed until now was possible.

Tears slipped down her face. She let them. "I think you will see the sun rise, beloved . . . but not more. It is time for you to choose." The room was slowly falling into darkness; she was the only light in it. It was dusk, here in Atlanta. His eyes were locked with hers, as if he was taking strength just from looking at her, concentrating fiercely, as if her face was the last thing he would ever see.

He was still struggling for breath. "I choose life, and you're cut off from everything you've ever known. Somethin' bigger than I could imagine." He paused, trying desperately to compose himself. "I die . . . an' that's a different sorta loss, isn't it?"

"Yes," she replied, softly, sadly. "I will be alone, without you. I . . . I knew *of* love, but you . . ." She could not articulate what she meant. Not without putting pressure on him. "I love you. And you will go on, somewhere." She thought a moment. "I have never been mortal. While I have knowledge of mortals, of mortality, I do not understand it. Here." She put his hand over her heart. "I know, but I do not feel, except when I live for a moment in the thoughts of a mortal. But that is only an instant, and then it is gone. And I do not have that understanding of how you think. What decisions you might make, in the absence of knowledge of the futures. By myself there might come a time when that knowledge... where the cost of continuing to fight is more than mere mortals are willing to pay. How long does one fight in chains when there is nothing in the future but more chains?" She shook her head slightly. "I am not saying this well."

"Well, if you ain't got freedom, what's the point in livin'? Does that cover it?" He coughed, harsh and rasping, into his hand.

She nodded. "I think, something like that. And I do not think—no, I know that as I am, I cannot tell when that point has come. Nor can I make that decision, not even for one person, much less a world." She sighed. "But I will have to try. I accepted the task to be an Instrument. It is my duty, and it can only be taken from me, I cannot give it up. That is my nature. Without that, I would not be what I am, what you love."

John thought on this. He still had duty. He had his comrades in the CCCP that depended upon him. There were the people of his neighborhood as well. A long time ago, it seemed, he'd also taken an oath to defend his country, from enemies "foreign and domestic." John wasn't quite sure where the Thulians fell in that continuum. Overall, he had a duty to see this conflict through and make sure that *people* made it. Humanity. If nothing else, that there were still free and somewhat happy people to continue on. And, failing that, he still had his own wrongs that, while they couldn't be righted, might be able to be corrected for in the grand equation.

And then there was Sera. He had found happiness, again, in his own way. Happiness with her. It was something he'd been missing for years on end. Years of nothing but disgust, self-loathing, and unrelenting fear and rage. To be with Sera... it was something he wasn't sure he was ready to give up.

"Darlin'?" John suppressed a cough, looking hard into Sera's eyes.

She returned his gaze for a long moment, then brushed her lips across his forehead. "Beloved."

"Let's sleep on it. I figure it'll be a nice sunrise, anyways." And, without any further prompting, John Murdock passed out.

She held him close. She could not tell what he was thinking. She was not sure she wanted to. Tears continued to slip slowly down her face as she wrestled with yet another new emotion:

anguish. It was not only for herself, it was for—well—everything. John was important, she knew only that, and not how or why. And so far, the only paths out of the disaster unfolding had him on them and at the end of them. And oh, she loved him for himself and for that alone, she would have been willing to sacrifice herself to make him live again, but the greater burden, the greater responsibility, was her duty. It was a duty not just to this world alone, but to many. Thousands. The Universe. And she knew, that as she had chosen to trust and not to Fall, if it came to a choice between him and that duty, she'd sacrifice herself and her love for the duty. Even though her heart would shatter over it, and never mend again. Wasn't there a poem that said, "I could not love thee half so much, loved I not honor more"?

Part of that duty . . . part of that duty was upholding Free Will at the cost of her own happiness. Even if it meant groping blindly for another path to safety for the worlds.

Even if it meant her heart was broken for that as well.

In the end, all she could do was to hold him, weep, cling to each moment that passed, because this might be the last that she would have, hope the dawn took forever to arrive and know that it was coming and she could not stop it.

Atlanta seemed still, for once, when John awakened. The sun was cresting over buildings, unobstructed by smoke or dust or the machines of invaders. The sunlight filled the room, illuminating his entire squat. In the center, seeming to catch the light itself, was the Seraphym. She was as still as a statue, in a way no human could manage. Those strange eyes of hers never blinked, never looked away from his. She had probably been like this all night, holding him, watching him, never moving, never tiring. It just drove home to him again, how much she would be losing—how her life would change completely—if he took that gift of life she offered.

John, still sweating coldly, managed to crack a smile. "Mornin'."

"Good morning, beloved," she said, so softly her words could not have traveled to any ears but his. "It is time. Beloved . . . not choosing will be a choice, now."

He coughed fitfully, struggling to breathe. "I was afraid of that." He carefully craned his neck around, peering at the room. "Should we do this on the roof? Wouldn't wanna lose my security deposit."

She shook her head. "I dare not move you."

"Love," he shifted, obviously in pain, in order to stand up. "You might be the Immovable Object, but I'm gonna try to be the Unstoppable Force. Or y'could just help me stand up."

With a sigh of resignation, she helped him stand. But before he could demand to walk to the roof, she folded wings about him and folded space itself, taking them both to the rooftop, facing the rising sun. And she still did not know what his choice would be,

John looked out over the city again. "When y'get down to it... it's not that bad of a town."

"The soul of the city is people, beloved. Where there are good people, the city is as good as it can be."

He nodded. "I suppose... that you're right. I just hope that our people... can make it." He looked into her eyes; there was still the same intensity there, even with him being so close to death. "Sera?"

She freed a hand from supporting him to touch his face. "Whatever befalls... I will be here. I will find a way."

"Just wanted to let you know... that I love ya. And I'm scared." He collapsed into her arms. His thoughts opened to her in those very last moments, and she knew his choice instantly.

Yes, Seraphym. It is permitted. Goodbye, beloved child. Only true death will bring you Home again.

It was not just life-force she poured into him. It was all that she had, all that she was.

In all of space and time, this had never happened before. That one Immortal should give all that she had to save a mortal. This was out of all accounting, and changed... everything.

The few people who happened to be out at this time of the morning were the only physical witnesses to what the news later called a "meteorological phenomena," and attributed it either to some failed Thulian ploy or an Echo experiment.

In actuality, it was, in miniature, a recreation of a moment.

Fiat lux.

"Let there be Light."

A soundless explosion of light blossomed atop that roof. It left no trace of itself, except that when dazzled eyes cleared, there was no trace of John Murdock or the Seraphym.

But those who were attuned to the Infinite, and those who were attuned to magic, felt the Cosmos ring like a giant bell, not just in Atlanta, but all over the world. The reverberations disrupted countless calculations and conjurations, leaving them in new patterns.

For this had never happened before. One that had been mortal was reborn. And one that had been spirit was given flesh, and her powers were divided between them. To have a miracle, something miraculous had been sacrificed, and so the Laws were kept unbroken.

Vickie jumped straight up out of her bed, instantly awake. She had gone from sleeping to on her feet, jarred out of REM sleep by what had felt like about a million volts of electricity hitting her.

Something had happened. Something—huge—

Grey had also been startled awake, every hair on his body standing straight out, a giant puffball of a cat. <*Your workroom! Your workroom!*> he shouted in her head. Just that; it seemed that was all he could manage to articulate. She stumbled out of her bedroom, across the hall, and yanked open the door of her magical workroom, feeling very much as if every hair on *her* body was standing straight up.

As she wrenched the door open, the *light* that had clearly been flooding the room was just starting to fade. At the center of that light, in the center of her Circle of Power, was . . . a body.

A naked body. A female naked body. With scarlet hair and scarlet and gold wings.

She stared, licked her lips, as the body began to move. "S-Seraphym?" she stammered hoarsely.

The head moved, the red hair falling away from her face. A pair of the bluest eyes that Vickie had ever seen stared up at her. The lips parted, and a soft, sad voice said—

"Not . . . anymore."

Pavel—the once great Soviet Bear—was spending his off hours in his usual fashion; in the CCCP break room, watching soap operas and drinking vodka strong enough to degrease an engine. His clumsy mechanical feet were crossed and propped up on a wooden cabbage crate. This particular soap opera was one of his favorites, *One Stoplight To Love,* following the quirky and melodramatic antics of a couple of police officers and their families.

Pavel was about to take a swig from his vodka when he felt something happening. It took him a moment to realize that the plasma chamber revolving in his chest in the place of a heart had sped up by several dozen RPMs. "*Shto?*"

There was a flash of intense flame and a *snap-boom*, scattering paper waste and bottles around the room. When the spots cleared from his eyes, Pavel could see a naked figure sprawled on the carpet in front of him. He then looked to the television. An ancient TV set that had seen the moon landing, the Berlin Wall being torn down, and survived being handled by Chug, sputtered, and then died with a small puff of smoke.

"*Nasrat.*" Pavel pounded the set. It did not spring to life.

"Supposing I will have to be reporting to Commissar, now. Naked man in room, too. Double *nasrat.*"

Bella probably shouldn't have been here, but the Echo debriefing wasn't until noon, so—hell with it. She was, by god, going to sit in on the CCCP one, since she'd taken over for Vick at the tail end of the infil op. And anyway, this way she knew that Saviour would get everything.

Unter finished his debrief right up to the point where Vick passed out. Bella picked it up from there. "... so when I got her conscious, she told me she'd neutralized some sort of super death machine by burying it almost a mile into the ground. I dunno, I'm not inclined to send Echo down there to look for it unless you're in favor, Nat."

Red Saviour shook her head. "Later maybe. Are being have enough on plate. We are having leads?"

"*Da*. But my people and Tesla and Marconi haven't gotten done with what the infil team extracted yet. Cross your fingers... I think we're going to have the location of their HQ when we're done."

Saviour let out a breath that she had clearly been holding in. "Then... *da*. Was worth ten times over, the co—"

Bella felt it. They *all* felt it. It wasn't physical, but whatever it was... it might as well have been. Like a body blow that doesn't hurt. Except that in Bella's case—it did. She doubled over with the anguish of it, of something... vital... taken. And yet, it wasn't something that had been taken from *her*.

"... *borzhe moi* ..."

Bella looked up with tears in her eyes from the crippling *sorrow* to see Red Saviour shaking her head as if someone had just hit her with a two-by-four. "... what?"

She choked down the tears. "I—I don't know but—"

The clomping of heavy feet outside Saviour's briefing room heralded the arrival of Soviet Bear. "Commissar—comrades—" he whuffed. "Television is being broken. Also is naked man on floor. Not my doing, either of these things."

Bella suddenly was sure, instantly sure, that this was what she had felt. Or was at least part of it. Before Bear was halfway done, she was on her feet and pushing past him, headed for the break room, impelled by a growing urgency she couldn't even begin to explain.

The group was walking down the labyrinthine hallways of the CCCP HQ, heading for the medbay. Jadwiga, the Soviette, was leading the way, and explaining while they walked. Vickie was not even sure she should have been there. Except—except that somehow she had gotten all tied up with this. Sera had materialized in *her* workroom, Bella was her dearest friend—the two of them were connected somehow, Vickie's mage-sight clearly showed the bond between them. Jadwiga was going on about trauma, transitory amnesia . . . Vickie wasn't paying much attention to it. Sera—well, Sera wasn't the Seraphym anymore, wings notwithstanding. She reminded Vickie of the description in the fairy tale of the Little Mermaid, how, once she got legs, she walked in pain as every step was taken, as if she walked on the blades of knives. Bella reflected that pain. But how, or why this had happened—Vickie still wasn't sure. Sera hadn't said more than a dozen words so far.

As for what they were going to see, in the CCCP medbay . . . Vickie wasn't sure what that was, either, at this point.

Hope and despair flickered over Sera's face by turns.

". . . so . . . here," Jadwiga said, opening the door to the medbay. "Here is being comrade patient."

The group entered the cramped medbay. Sitting upon a gurney in the center of the room was John Murdock. But at the same time, not. This John didn't have darkness in his eyes. The same quiet intensity, but none of the troubles that had seemed to weigh him down even before he knew of his own impending death. The scars were still there, but they seemed fainter, unimportant now. Not really a part of the man that was sitting in front of them. And he still had his same lopsided grin.

"Howdy, y'all." He regarded the group, still smiling. "Now, who exactly are you people, an' what the hell am I doin' here?"